A
DUGOUT
TO PEACE

A DARK DEPTHS NOVEL

GARY MORGENSTEIN

Livonia, Michigan

A DUGOUT TO PEACE

Copyright © 2023 Gary Morgenstein

Published by BHC Press

Library of Congress Control Number:
2023930896

ISBN Numbers:
Hardcover: 978-1-64397-367-8
Softcover: 978-1-64397-368-5
Ebook: 978-1-64397-369-2

For information, write:
BHC Press
885 Penniman #5505
Plymouth, MI 48170

Visit the publisher:
www.bhcpress.com

ALSO BY GARY MORGENSTEIN

A Mound Over Hell
A Fastball for Freedom

To my family for their love,
kindness and support

A

DUGOUT

TO PEACE

1

After three hours, Elias Kenuda's fingers felt kneaded to the point of pain. He wanted to suggest that Hedda Kleinz practice pretzel twists on something more inanimate as they waited in this duplicitously comfortable room: a chair leg, the excessively firm pillows, perhaps maneuver the purple washcloth together in braided anxiety.

He just let her be. Which was terrified. The painted smile beneath the round dark eyes embedded in her coffee-colored face was drained of everything but false bravado, of which she had an astonishingly unending supply. Love will make us strong, otherwise why bother, Hedda kept insisting.

Thank Grandma's earrings, she finally let go of his hands.

"The socks, Elias," Hedda scolded across the room. "The colors are off."

"I decided on black. My admission, my socks, though I suspect if anyone gets down to noticing my footwear, I'm fine." Or not. Like everything else today, they, along with the entire country, had no idea what to expect.

Hedda folded her sturdy arms, the gray sleeves from the light cotton dress puffing out. "Blue. Blue tie. Blue socks."

With a sigh so weary it seemed to hiss out of one of the overhead heating vents in The Study, Elias put on the blue pair.

"You could use a better dimple in the tie," she said.

He burst into laughter and held her close. They hadn't made love since he voluntarily relocated here and it didn't matter. Just the hug was sufficient to exchange their passion.

"Anything else, my darling, before we turn The Family and everything in which we believe upside down?"

He'd just finished a Hedda-commanded flossing when a knock introduced one of the attendants, an egg-shaped man in a long brown coat who glanced around uneasily.

"They're here for you, Mr. Kenuda."

"How many?" Hedda asked sharply.

The Study had grown accustomed to Hedda's razor barks and waspish looks over the past two weeks. My fiancé needs a warmer blanket. He does not eat SC fruits. The bulb in the desk lamp is weak. Her cold anger gave him strength, but Kenuda worried it was now fading. He didn't much worry whether he'd deliver his confession properly. It was the after which frightened him. Not the punishment. How to accept it.

"Two." The man lowered his voice. "'Bots, I believe."

Hedda made an ugly sound, ignoring Elias's warning look. The attendant paled at yet another demand, mutely gesturing for them to hurry.

Elias hesitated; the room had been a sanctuary, punctuated by Hedda's arguments during holographic meetings with the Cousins Committee. Sometimes the moments were simply laughable as Hedda circled the HGs, poking at them to make an impatient point about the introduction (that's like a lawyer's opening remarks which you should know is illegal) or the length of the procedure (she refused to let on what they planned to say) and, as far as an audience, this isn't the infamous social media deviation trials of 2031 where citizens were forced to go on one of those narcissistic platforms to confess they'd shown insensitivity or had failed to revise unpleasant history through their behavior.

No surprise the committee had started sending a different HG each time, Elias noted with pride.

Hedda took her time slipping on her black coat before peeking inside the briefcase to make sure the presentation hadn't been stolen. Carting her cotton valise with his packed duffel bag draped over her left shoulder, she led Elias by the hand past the attendant and down the carpeted wooden staircase to the lobby.

Since the Admission was announced, The Study had ceased accepting anyone admitting to violations. Misleading advertising, sabotaging a colleague, failing to supervise a child's studies—such semicriminals were housed elsewhere. Elias was alone, quarantined with a dubious ethical infection for which there might not be a collective cure. And since we're by ourselves, you can turn off the damn vidnews, Hedda had added tartly.

The vidnews, by law in every home, had gone dark here and only here.

The two robed 'bots waited with infinite patience on the oval rug by the front door. They were the same ones who'd come just two very long weeks ago to see if Third Cousin Elias Kenuda was really going through with this. He could've just resigned, filed his admission of abuse of office, and let it all go.

Instead, he was the center of the first public quasi-legal proceeding in America in eighteen years.

"Mr. Kenuda." The taller one tipped its head. "You may still change your mind."

"Are you kidding me? You think we've gone through all this to change our minds at the last minute?" Hedda raised Elias's arm to show the briefcase curled about his shaking fingers.

The supervisor smiled faintly. "I think that Mr. Kenuda has a very loyal fiancé."

"Damn straight," she snapped. "And don't you forget it."

"I doubt anyone would, Hedda." Elias managed his own version of a smile. "We're very ready."

The 'bots stepped aside and dropped into place behind them.

Hedda whirled. "Excuse me, and where are you going?"

"To accompany you."

"Says who?"

"Hedda…" Elias made the useless gesture of interrupting.

"No, no. Are you afraid we'll run away? This is voluntary. Elias came here on his own and he'll leave on his own. There's no judgment against him at this point so move. Go."

Elias steered Hedda into the empty game room to the right; her feet almost made skid marks in the thick purple carpet.

He sighed. "Do you really want to take the subway?"

Hedda glared. "That's what we agreed on. We get there on our own."

"It's not safe. Cheng tried killing me once—"

"We don't know it was him."

Elias paused. "Clary's Black Tops are gone."

Hedda shuddered slightly. "Since when?"

"A couple days ago. I got the note while you were in the shower. It's construed as favoritism." He raised his voice over her angry sigh. "We have no protection. I'm not risking that and don't give me any brave bullshit about dying by my side. That's not why we're doing this."

She tilted her head, smiling. "Sure."

Kenuda blinked rapidly. "You're giving in?"

Hedda wearily shook her head as women have done since the beginning. "I've been worried about you the past few days. You were losing your fervor."

"So you tricked me into getting pissed off."

"It wasn't hard," she said reproachfully. "I still think we should take the subway. But if you want them to drop us off on 161st Street, okay."

The squat black Chrysler Dart with silver tires wheezed through early morning Bronx traffic, just another car on Bruckner Boulevard. During Hedda's extensive research, she'd amused and sometimes unnerved Elias with extraordinary stories about journalists with cameras popping out to vid trial participants; defendants and plaintiffs were the terms. In the files of the main library to which Hedda had gained additional clearance on top of her abundant teacher's access, she'd come across volumes of such sickening examples of the old AG democracy.

Like an unseemly notion called plea bargaining where you were guilty but not so much. Elitists receiving preferential treatment through their ability to hire better attorneys. Horrific examples of death penalties. An electrified chair, poison in the veins. The grisly hangings of the 2040s to distinguish between humans and 'bots after robots with faces had been banned.

How could the legal system not have been outlawed fifty years ago, they'd wondered.

At the entrance to the Major Deegan Expressway, crammed with patient cars waiting to squeeze like liquified metal toothpaste into the crawling traffic, Elias watched a platoon of purple-costumed grade schoolers waiting for a bus beneath the snow-squalled skies which had settled over most of America late in February.

Schools were in session, businesses were open. Whether to insist siblings watch at selected sites around the country or for this to remain voluntary had been a spirited debate. Despite the suspension of his Cousin's position, Elias still received the morning updates. He was like any other sibling, as the third paragraph of the mere four-page 2074 Penal Code covering all potential crimes and punishments stated, "innocent until accepted guilty."

"Demanding sibling attendance insults individual responsibility," First Cousin Nadharatha had insisted during a lengthy, interminable mini speech. "If the siblings are interested, they should come on their own curiosity."

"How can they be expected to show curiosity," Second Cousin D'Andre had countered, "if we've given them so little information? It's not even a trial. It's a…?"

No one knew what to expect of the Admission, a vague enough term to attract interest without disquiet, although there was enough of that. Pop into any bar in any town anywhere in America and you'd get an earful.

"Grandma's come back. She was never dead. Cheng is becoming dictator. They're shutting down baseball again. We've defeated the Allahs. No, they're in Vermont."

Rumors fed on necessary silence. As Second Cousin Gomes had pointed out, they had no mechanism to handle the anxiety, the uncertainty. The country was blithely ignoring the war, in whatever stage it was, depending on the claimed knowledge. American forces were sweeping south to consolidate the capture of South America. A magnificent fleet, iron ghosts resurrected from the ocean floor after the Islamic Empire had sunk them, sailed across the Atlantic, landing in Morocco. No, the invasion fleet had gone north, seizing Greenland and Iceland and storming ashore in Scotland. London was in flames. Russians were once again invading from the east. The Chinese had renounced their neutrality, eager to settle their score with the Muslim Caliphate.

Or none of this. For too long Americans had been treated as fragile precocious children, shielded from the horror of losing World War III. Shielded from their own revised history. Shielded from the effects of radioactivity by the attacks on Washington and Los Angeles, the chemical attack on Manhattan. Genetically engineered so-called (SC) and alleged (AG) foods, holographic (HG) forests. Everything America once stood for tossed aside like a piece of smelly real cheese.

Grandma's death had jolted the country to its mortality, vulnerability. Yes those were HG trees. The blasted beef never tasted like beef. How many members of your family died from radiation poisoning years later? Elias studied Hedda's stout stare out the frosted window as they slowed past an accident. Clearly the heating coils beneath the highway had failed. Sometimes it only took something that small. Good and bad.

Cheng had reassured the country after Grandma's murder with a handy target. Puppy Nedick was in the palm of the Allahs. Hunt him down and wage war against the Muslims. Except in war, people died, most inconvenient sometimes, and the country, despite its rage, wanted no more deaths after losing seventeen million. Cheng distracted America by returning baseball, the fragile precocious children eager for the treat. Even those who didn't care suddenly cared, preferable to excessive flag waving. Baseball had been the soul of the country and that soul of the great America died with the near passing of the game. If baseball comes back, so can America. When baseball was preeminent, so was America.

They turned off exit five and pulled up just outside Yankee Stadium. Beneath the glowing sign, *NO GAME TODAY*, meager crowds wandered outside the closed vendors's booths. The few hundred or so siblings seemed lost and uncertain. The holographic displays of baseball and each local team's history were dark, as Elias and Hedda had insisted. All thirty major league stadiums were being used for whatever the hell was about to happen in less than an hour.

"You can let us off here," Elias said firmly, not waiting for the 'bots's reaction.

Hedda slid her arm through the taut crook of his right elbow. They waited patiently, easing through gate six. The newly rebuilt pavilion barely echoed with a sparse amount of feet. Kenuda had to pause before the restored "three amigos" mural of Mooshie Lopez, Easy Sun Yen, and Derek Singh, three of the greatest Yankees, before Hedda tugged him along into section two.

There were a handful of 'bot ushers, clear faces sprinkled with mottled white circles. The ban on FBs had been recently lifted through the new Harmony Law granting face bots the same rights as MBs, or metal-faced robots, and humans. But these were the older models, kept in storage, the skin bleached with age; even machines show wear, though without the accomplished resignation of humans. The newer models, rumored to be mass-produced somewhere out west, hadn't been seen yet.

They wouldn't be any time soon since they'd all been sent directly into the military.

From a sliver of dark in section 102, row twenty-four, Felice, the complexion-challenged 'bot who had served as Grandpa Albert Cheng's assistant, stepped forward with its right hand extended.

"Third Cousin." Felice turned to Hedda who was struggling to conceal her uneasiness. "Hedda Kleinz. I am Felice."

Hedda wiped the moisture off her palm before returning the handshake, amusing Felice. "And what are you doing here?"

"Excellent question," Kenuda said, bristling. "We were very clear."

"Your instructions and amendments were quite clear." Felice turned back to Hedda. "As we were quite clear that the Admission would be kept to only you two."

Felice nodded at Dale Tanaka squatting on the pitcher's mound in surly impatience.

"Certain technical areas were beyond our capability," Kenuda explained.

"To which we could have assisted. But then, you were determined to keep the details to yourself. That is understandable as we expect you to understand that for security reasons, we need to have an undetermined presence."

Elias glanced up at the invisible stealth 'copters. "What about your presence at the other stadiums?"

"Lightly at all thirty ballparks, as you requested. As is the attendance," Felice said with what could've been a smirk. "The greatest number of fans are at Dodger Stadium in Los Angeles, where 3,450 are gathered, and in Candlestick Park in San Francisco, with 3,102 present. I believe that is because they can attend prior to work because of the time difference. The average audience is 1,022, with no reports of any misconduct apart from two incidents at Wrigley Field in Chicago where the fans attempted to bring alcoholic beverages despite the posted prohibitions."

Felice met their skeptical stares. "There is no attempt to minimize how many siblings will watch remotely. It is their choice. The Admission will be the only vidcast during this time period. It will also be transmitted on the rad. Without personal comment from presenters, of course, per clause two of the Anti-Parasite Laws pertaining to journalists. We have acceded to all your demands, Third Cousin. Are you prepared?"

"If you mean ready, yes," Elias said.

The 'bot opened its palms and hundreds, thousands, then millions of faces crept like shy bubbles out over the stands, circling the field and rising to the upper decks.

"This is the rest of your audience, Third Cousin."

"Will they be talking?' Hedda asked, unnerved.

"That would be a distraction. Unless you would like to hear their reactions. I had thought the expressions alone would be sufficient."

"Expressions are good," the young teacher murmured.

With a slight twist of its head, Felice stepped back up the row. Elias squeezed Hedda's hand past the holographic faces as they walked through the gate onto the field.

"They're fucking with you," Dale said, sneering and spitting at several heads. The seventeen-year-old defiantly shook her blonde ponytail. "I wish I could use my HG dragons from last season. They were crowd pleasers."

Elias squinted past the bobbing faces settling into seats of some kind, either clustered like balloons next to physical fans or forming their own sections. Yankee Stadium was a massive holographic theater.

"They're keeping down the entertainment by crowding us," Hedda said angrily.

"You might already be on air." Dale pointed at the puzzled reactions on the faces. "Maybe you should save the whining for later."

Loudly wishing she had a big pin to pop the bubbles, Dale quickly set up her emotive expander by second base. Hedda kissed Elias squarely on the lips and drifted aside, quickly blending into the faces.

Standing on the pitcher's mound, Kenuda simply didn't know where to look. The bubbles had thickened so intensely he could barely see a few feet in either direction. What did that matter?

"Good morning, everyone. My name is Elias Kenuda. I am Third Cousin, overseeing Sport and, previously, Entertainment. I'm here to admit my misdeeds and explain why. Not to justify, but to take full individual responsibility for my behavior as all of you do"—he paused for emphasis—"every day."

He squared his broad shoulders and, with a flick of his left wrist, a black and white HG of the twentieth-century actor James Stewart floated a couple feet away in mute passion.

"This actor you see addressing the old United States Senate was named James Stewart from my fiancé Hedda Kleinz's favorite movie, *Mr. Smith Goes to Washington*. In this film, released in 1939, he has been awake for many hours pleading with his fellow politicians not to concede to corruption. You see how he perspires. You see what an effort it is for him to gain their attention. You see how hard it is for him to win this fight."

Elias watched Stewart for five counts. He'd thought it was too theatrical, but Hedda had insisted and he knew better than to argue.

"That's how it once was in this country," Kenuda continued. "We had to fight hard for freedom because we believed that freedom was worth fighting for. But freedom shouldn't be so difficult. It should be the most natural way in the world. That's what we've enjoyed in The Family. The choices are ours, individuals working together in honesty and ethics. Laws we all accept. The belief that we all have a stake in a better world. That, unlike James Stewart, we don't have to plead anymore for our leaders to help us lead ourselves.

"But sometimes the choices are too difficult and the decisions too unpleasant. So today, I stand before my siblings to explain what I have seen and what I have done. I've taken it upon myself to unilaterally disobey the laws of The Family. This is a violation of my oath to you for which there is no justification."

Kenuda waited until his holographic original petition made its way to every person watching. For those who weren't, the physical document arrived in their mailboxes for later review. The United States might be surrounded, but it still had the finest postal service in the world. As if there were real pages to be turned, Elias waited a moment more.

"This is not a trial. That system is long dead, thank Grandma's earrings. I'm neither here to excuse nor to accuse. I'm not here to ask for your help. I'm not looking to escape the consequences nor am I pointing you toward punishing anyone else. The reason we've been able to eliminate trials and the entire unjust criminal justice system is because we are honest with each other. This is about me because as we know each other, we know ourselves."

Elias Kenuda, then a sophomore guard at Temple University, dribbled a basketball through the swelling faces.

"I was arrogant and cocky and all the adjectives you might want. It took me a while to relinquish the ball and make my teammates better."

On the count of three, Elias shouted at his coach, the courtside scene fading into him wearing a purple robe, surrounded by darkness.

"This was my initial Cousins session. Perhaps not the first. They merge. That's the point."

A holographic Grandma walked to the mound. The shocked stadium gasped.

"His ego is immense," her soft voice rang out. "If he is to make a single sibling successful, he must break himself down. I see his promise but we have to question whether it's a higher risk. Then again, the higher the risk, the greater the reward. Falling and climbing back is the ultimate lesson. I don't know if he has the character to do so. There's a weakness in his determination, an impatience."

From his consciousness flowing from Dale's tacitly illegal emotive expander, Elias raged at his parents for denying him some vague gift. A car, a tie, what stupidity had he succumbed to?

Basketball players suddenly roared past, football players close behind as if in pursuit.

"As Third Cousin, I boosted revenues for basketball and football."

An image from his memory danced around the faces, Kenuda shooting hoops in his office, twirling a football.

"But I dismissed the possibility of baseball, viewing it as a low form of sport, reeking of treachery. I was unable to grasp that it could have a useful role again in America. I was dragged against my will, lured by my attraction for Mooshie Lopez."

Mooshie bounded a few feet off the ground in mid-song from a nightclub performance; Elias stared dreamily.

"That's why I wanted to bring back baseball. Not because I had any great wisdom. Merely lust. And oh yes, did I forget to mention that while I used Puppy Nedick, I was engaged to his ex-wife Annette Ramos?"

A memory of Annette chattering away about the placement of a coffee table skittered by.

"A fine Third Cousin I was. Actually, I was a good Third Cousin. I was a paltry person. Grandma was right. I was weak and unwilling to climb back up. I was that most odious of relics of the old America. Successful without morality. I was everything a Third Cousin, an American, should never be again. This is who stands before you, asking for your belief."

He rushed on as if afraid the sheer weight of his crimes would serve as a reason to end the Admission.

"And then I made it worse. I wasn't content to violate our ethics. I went after our laws. Please, I don't ask for any sympathy. I have lied because I believe, without being a firsthand witness, that terrible crimes have been committed in our name. That had always been the hallmark of democracy, where our leaders lied and said they spoke for the people. Grandma ended that. But still, ambition and arrogance are sometimes stronger than decency and ethics.

"As you see from my statement, I aided Puppy Nedick and Annette Ramos to escape arrest and travel by mail plane to Muslim Europe. I gave Puppy false Cousins documents. I took custody of an orphan as my ward. I created more false documents for that girl. I lied to the Brown Hats in their police investigation. I illegally removed a sibling who had been arrested without cause and whose mental faculties were impaired through officially sanctioned experiments. I hid him in my apartment. I used the full authority of my position to commit these crimes and to cover them up. I didn't come forward sooner because I felt, in my ego, that I was too important.

"You ask, why. Or probably, how dare I. How dare I even stand here asking you to listen to such a list of vile behavior. How dare I suggest there is any excuse. Well, there is none. You cannot take the law into your own hands without sending us all hurtling back to the days when truth was a prostitute for power. I want to tell you why and ask what choice I had."

Kenuda squared his jaw.

"I did all these things because when Puppy told me who killed Grandma, I believed him. When he told me that he and Annette would never survive Black Top custody, I knew that was the truth. When the orphan girl explained that she came to America as the last survivor of an attack on a ship carrying twenty children to safety, ordered by our government, by our Family, in our name to destroy hopes of peace between America and the Islamic Empire, I knew this to be true.

"As I knew that if I didn't commit these illegal acts, the orphan girl would be murdered along with the unfortunate man I rescued from a Black Top prison. Because all that murder was in our name and I'd be damned if the oath of my office, to serve all of you, to be the best Cousin, would instead serve as a cloak of corruption.

"What would each of you have done in my place? I don't have the answer. Maybe you do. Can we break the law to create a better law? Where does it end? And what do we do when our own honesty fails? Because that's what happened. I failed you as those who misspoke in your name failed you. How can The Family do better? I also don't know, only that we must. Grandma had always said that's up to us. Not the laws nor her Insights. But our hearts and consciences. Your hearts and consciences, not mine. I surrendered that privilege a long time ago. I don't deserve sympathy or compassion. I'm not even sure why you'd believe me.

"Except that as we all strive to be more, we must understand when we're not. Do not behave like me. Learn from me. That is leadership. Today, all of America is a Cousin. That is the true meaning of The Family."

Grandpa Albert Cheng, resplendent in his Chicago Cubs uniform, trudged out to the mound. The 'bot removed its cap with a slight bow that hinted of disdain. "That is all true."

Half an hour later through streets somehow barren of traffic, the Chevy Dart pulled up outside the entrance to the East Bronx Disappointment Village. Holding hands, the drained Elias and Hedda approached three balding siblings with welcoming faces.

The fatter of them apologetically unlatched Hedda's fingers from Kenuda's. She thanked him for taking her suddenly weighty bag.

"This is as far as you can go today, Ms. Kleinz."

Anger swiftly steamed inside Hedda. "What are you saying?"

"Mr. Kenuda is the only one authorized to become a resident of the Disappointment Village."

"Now listen up—" Elias raised his hands.

"We're engaged!" Hedda shouted.

"That is not sufficient."

"This is bullshit. We were promised to be together. We were promised, we were promised!"

Two of the chunky men barely held Elias back as the third escorted Hedda toward the car. She broke free but was quickly surrounded by several Black Tops. They couldn't quell her screams.

2

Nathaniel the Owl tottered on the edge of the scuffed oak table. It would not do for Puppy Nedick to let him fall again. Already Caterina de Squawk and Philippe Buonoserra had tipped into the sawdust sanding the stage of the North Tremont Avenue Theater. In the same way Caterina and Philippe had sneered, now Nathan scowled at Puppy's fumbling, snidely whispering in the way stuffed animals do around skeptical humans.

"Puppy, where'd Bruno go?" Zelda Jones called out from her hands and knees in the third row; all he could see was her considerable butt bobbing.

"I don't know," he grumbled. After six very tedious days in his new role as completely unofficial stage manager in Zelda's new show *Darlings Are Dear*, Puppy wouldn't lightly dismiss such a notion as Bruno the Bat just going somewhere. Still, worrying that dolls would skip out for an alleged burger and fries around the corner at Hank's Hamburger Heaven beat being holed up in Zelda and Pablo Diaz's apartment. He'd had two weeks of that. If he'd already lost his mind, and that was a strong possibility, it might as well just sail into the unimaginable imagination of a children's play.

Zelda stood ever so slowly, hands clutching the back of a frayed leather seat. It was a simple task not to lose her cast. It shouldn't be difficult. Then again, everything was difficult with Puppy since he came home.

"Oh, did he just walk away?"

Zelda fixed him with her I-am-sorry-your-life-sucks-but-what-more-can-I-do look which had steadily evolved from the initial I-am-so-glad-you-are-alive-Pup, to, stay-away-from-the-windows-the-BTs-could-be-watching-you-are-wanted. In between, she tucked him into bed on their couch, let him rock her child Diego Jr. under wary supervision, and took him for late night walks.

Puppy held up Nathan as an indication that he could be trusted.

"That's Nathan." Zelda tightroped along the last bit of her nerves.

"I realize that, Zelda." He turned her name into three syllables. "I can tell the difference between a bat and an owl. I wasn't completely rewired during my vacation in the Caliphate."

"And don't play that pity game of woe is me, I nearly got my ass shot off by the Allahs."

"I almost did." He patted his side as if it were a glorious trophy.

"I thought that was from the knife wound in the alley."

"Shot, stabbed…"

"Guess I must've dozed during one of your stories."

He bowed deeply. "I'm so, so, so sorry I've bored you…"

With an effortless flip, Beth Rivera tossed snacks in both directions. Zelda muttered in bitter triumph when Puppy dropped the wrapped Cheeserino Doughnut.

"Zel, remember he's not showbiz," Beth said with a broad wink which annoyed Puppy. "But retraining for new jobs is something we must support. Look at me. Seamstress by day, theater producer by night."

Puppy mimicked Beth through bites of the doughnut. He didn't know how he ever could've had a crush on her.

"He misplaced Bruno!" Zelda shouted. "Again." Everything in her life was a drawn-out performance clamoring for attention. Her child, her husband, her best friend. Only when she succumbed to the mental illness known as creativity did Zelda find escape. Her world, her rules.

"Bruno has the longest speech in the play. He knits together the drama of the magic tree."

Puppy smirked. "Maybe he went off to rehearse his lines."

Wielding a wooden spatula, Zelda hopped over a chair; Puppy noticed some gray hair peeking shyly along her forehead. She'd kill him if he mentioned it.

"Excuse me, but the spatula belongs on the side table for Act Two, Scene Three, according to the director's directions." He waved the script dangerously close to Zelda.

Beth wrapped her arms around Zelda and dragged her away.

Stuffed bats just don't fly off, Puppy reassured himself, peering through the faint darkness, but they do if you misplace them.

Puppy retraced his footsteps over the messy backstage and yanked down on the innocent light cord.

"Where the hell are you, bat boy?" Puppy hissed into the prop room.

For Zelda's show, they'd been granted two six-foot-high plastic trees, plastic logs, and a couple of chairs and a table for Caterina de Squawk's living room, a speck of the endless props reaching up in sturdy stacks, from clocks which made reassuring ticking noises, broken stereos, old stoves, and refrigerators to lamps representing various fashion periods like the multi-colored globular designs of the 2050s.

"My father had a keyboard like that. He pretended he was someone called Elton John and wore octagonal red glasses. My father could not sing, but we told him he was wonderful." With a shrug at the needed lies demanded by love, Clary Santiago dropped off a chest-high Vanderbilt bureau and doffed her Yankees cap.

Puppy stared, unsure how frightened to be.

The girl pursed her lips. "Do I not get a hug, Puppy Beisbol?"

Puppy grasped a brass ashtray. "Is that now the procedure before arresting someone?"

Clary glared. "What will you do with that? Attack Clary?"

Puppy dropped his voice so Zelda and Beth wouldn't come backstage. Let it be over with. "No, your BTs."

"Do I look like I have guards?" The girl demandingly held out her arms in a V. "I want my hug. It is my right after you abandoned me for so many months."

After a long moment, he put down the ashtray. Clary rushed into his arms, squeezing so tightly he almost lost his breath. Puppy sighed into the mass of black curls, kissing them one by one, melting despite knowing better.

"How'd you find me?" he whispered.

Clary looked up. "You didn't used to be so suspicious."

"Being wanted all over the whole world will do that." He took a slight step back; Clary clutched onto the sleeves of his shirt. Puppy asked, a bit more firmly, "How'd you find me?"

Clary tapped her nose. "Clary has ways. I am the Granddaughter and everyone loves me." She waited impatiently for him to add his voice to the chorus. "Like you."

"Even if I'm a bad guy."

She sighed as if he were the twelve-year-old. "If America was stupid enough to believe that Puppy Beisbol would kill Grandma, they deserved what followed. But not anymore."

"Because Cheng confessed?"

"Those are not your ears nor eyes speaking. Cheng did not confess. Kenuda did not accuse him. There is no evidence Cheng killed Grandma other than your word which Kenuda made his own, but there is no evidence you killed Grandma other than Cheng's word. Who to believe and what does it matter? You have been punished. Cheng removed from power. Only Grandma knows the truth and she is dead. It must be behind us."

With a slight bow, Clary handed Puppy a Lifecard. She frowned at his hesitation. "It is real. It belongs to Puppy. No more forgeries. No more sleeping on Zelda's couch. You are free, Puppy Nedick."

"Yeah?"

"Do you not trust me?"

"I trust you. The Family, I'm not so sure."

"I am The Family now." Her blackish-brown eyes nearly protruded, startling Puppy. She externalized warmth into her voice; for once this worked without the accursed dizziness. "Clary has a plan."

Puppy sat on a wobbly swivel chair. "Yay."

Clary rolled her eyes. "Do you want to hear my idea or would you prefer looking for stuffed animals?"

He shrugged and fingered the Lifecard.

"I want you to join me."

Puppy frowned. "To do what?"

Clary fired off a few curses in Spanish which he guessed had something to do with his stupidity. "To be in charge of baseball. Ah, the 'two white grandpas' are good people, but they do not know how to run things."

Clary vertical hopped four feet onto a vintage '70s style Hermler white oak dresser. Puppy's eyes widened. "I would like you to be the Commissioner. Ty and Mick will step aside. Baseball will be very important as we turn the clock back to go forward. You know more about the game than anyone. People respect you."

He looked away. "Thanks anyway."

Clary made a show of leaning forward as if she hadn't heard right. "No?"

"*Sí.*"

"You would rather play with toys than be with me."

"Yes."

Her blackish-brown eyes almost swirled. "Why?"

"Because I'm done with baseball."

She scoffed. "That is foolish."

"Not to me."

Her purple sneakers thoughtfully kicked against the droopy gold handles. "Start explaining."

"Because every time I touch the game it turns to shit. Look at all the people who died at Yankee Stadium because Puppy wanted to bring baseball back. Look at all the people who died in Hyde Park in London, who are continuing to die because Puppy thought the Caliphate Baseball Association would bring peace to the world. Now you want to put me in charge of the whole damn thing?"

"Poor Puppy," she said with a sneer. "People die all the time. Our brave robot soldiers are dying for our country. I do not accept such an excuse."

"It's the best I got."

Clary's forehead pulsed slightly. "You owe me, Puppy Beisbol."

"Oh, how's that?"

She clasped her elbows with a disdainful shake of her head. "Do you not think you were wanted since you returned to America? Traitor. Assassin. Murderer. Did you ever hear your name mentioned on the vidnews? Hmm? A radcast? Zelda and Pablo are your dearest friends. Even an *imbecile* would check on them. Did any Black Tops pop their head into your shower? Did a Blue Shirt accost Zelda wheeling the baby? Did someone take Dr. Diaz's dental instruments? I do not think so. No one bothered you. How do you believe that happened? Because our security forces are *idiota*? No. No. Because I protected you and everyone who helped you. Your Clary."

His eyes glistened. "Thank you."

"You are welcome. That is why you cannot refuse my request. End of the discussion."

Puppy took a labored breath. "What if I'm scared, Clary? Worn out and scared."

She squeezed his hand. "So am I. Every day I am scared in ways you cannot understand. That is why I need you beside me, and me beside you, so we can do what must be done. Together." Clary suddenly waved. "Greetings, Mama Zelda. Hello, Beth Rivera."

Puppy glanced over his shoulder at the stunned women.

"What's going on, Pup?" Zelda edged behind an ancient Philco icebox while Beth's fingers pulled out the ever-present DV razor taped to her ankle.

Clary dropped to the floor, daring Beth.

Puppy moved between them. "Will you put away the damn blade? She's not here to arrest me."

"Really?" Beth jerked her head at the two Black Tops flanking a chipped Gardner bidet.

"*Puta* 'bots!" Clary screamed. "You are supposed to wait outside."

The 'bots answered together. "Felice requests visual contact after eight minutes."

"Felice." Flushed with embarrassment, Clary loudly countermanded the order, sending the BTs out the back door. She brightened with some internal light. "Apologies. Mama Zelda, you live so close to Clary's house, you must bring Diego Jr. for a visit. How old is he now? I am redoing all the furnishings. It was so drab with the sullen purple. Please come. I will make my special cookies."

Not satisfied until Zelda nodded, the Granddaughter reached under the couch cushion and tossed Bruno the Bat into Puppy's hands. "I look forward to seeing you soon, Commissioner."

Beth and Zelda waited until Clary disappeared between the props before turning toward Puppy.

"Commissioner?"

3

The newest of the nuns at the Blessed Brides convent in Leicestershire dropped the sturdy oatmeal pot. Since this was the third incident that week, Mother Superior Ada waited silently as Annette Ramos wiped up the gooey mess on the hard cement floor in between grumbles, a dramatic retch, and a vague complaint about the ache in her right knee.

"That pain would be from the hard bed," Annette continued as if doing emotional somersaults. The Mother Superior stared with so much open dismay that she just knew there'd be a scolding from God during evening prayers.

"Back in the Bronx," Annette loudly muttered as she re-scrubbed the floor because she'd missed an infinitesimal spot only Jesus could see, "I'd never spilled a pot. Perhaps," she surmised with the loud wisdom of the guilty, "it was because in American kitchens we used modern kitchenware and not two-ton earthenware from the 11th century or whenever the convent had been built."

Mother Superior waited for Annette to correct herself.

"Fine, 1811 then," Annette said, recalling yesterday's lesson as if it were a great burden. If she dressed like a nun then she learned and behaved as a nun, had been the first order from the horrible woman. There is no guile before God.

"Yeah, yeah," Annette said very quietly because the Mother Superior wasn't above whisking her butt with a broom. "I'm tired of the penance or whatever punishment you and the gang"—she jerked her head toward the painting of Mary and the baby Jesus surrounded by the Three Wise Men—"decide I have to endure before I get on with what I'm supposed to get on with, which is not being a badly dressed slave."

The Mother Superior flicked a reproachful eyebrow at a clump of oatmeal sneaking off the pot en route to a sizzling leap into the fire. Annette scooped up the mess and effortlessly tossed the balled paper towel into the garbage. She smirked triumphantly, knowing full well that would only result in more gross household duties.

The younger woman, who'd be pretty if she cared, smiled faintly. By now, Annette knew that a smile was as welcome as buckles on high heels. Something vaguely unpleasant was about to be commanded from the narrow-faced Mother's perch at the elbow of the gods. Thank you for making me realize why religion had been banned in The Family and why I was a jerk to even consider such a thing.

"Would you like to do the laundry after breakfast?" Mother Superior asked, as if there was even a hint of a choice.

"Oh gracious yes. Scrubbing butt lines from the underwear of sixty-two nuns is a joy."

"Excellent. We wouldn't want you, our dear guest, to feel uncomfortable."

"Guest?" Annette's voice rose as Sister Beatrice and Sister Shannon wordlessly brought the oatmeal to the table. They exchanged worried glances and crossed themselves. Every nun crossed herself when she saw Annette. But the strange American was to be treated equally. Shouting at the Mother Superior led to more punishment. The American never won that contest, though the sisters admitted in sheepish half whispers that they thoroughly enjoyed the spectacle and, occasionally, rooted for the godless infidel.

"And when might my guesthood end?" Annette's nostrils flared as she lowered her voice; the Mother Superior would not respond otherwise. She said, now very softly, "When might that be, ma'am?"

"When Colonel Basa is well enough to leave."

"And how will I know that?"

"I will tell you, Sister Annette."

"I'd like, if this doesn't shake you up too much, to speak to him directly. I forgot, I'm not allowed." Mother Superior, being Jesus's buddy and all, didn't have to explain anything. Annette had tried a few times talking to Jesus directly. Kneeling by her cement mattress with the rock pillows, she'd clasped her hands like she'd seen the other nuns do and asked Jesus in what she felt was a very respectful manner for someone she'd never met, what the hell was going on.

Annette adjusted her hat, cringing at what it was doing to her hair. Soon she'd have to shave it all off because it'd be ruined flat by the poor fashions and stench of oatmeal and the isolation of this convent in the middle of England, just waiting.

"He is still recovering," Mother Superior finally replied.

"So if we had some kind of chart, how would you rate the recovery process?" Annette asked, her voice rising again as the Mother Superior left with a sorrowful shake of her head at one of God's creations she couldn't love.

"The laundry is in the large bin," Sister Shannon said with a giggle.

"Oh, and here I thought your undies and habits would just walk on down the staircase."

"Perhaps if you prayed hard enough," Sister Beatrice chuckled.

Annette cracked a weary grin. "Wouldn't that piss off the Mother Superior?"

The nuns blushed, but with some delight at the idea; Annette was sort of an entertaining unruly house pet. The sisters noisily loaded the dishes and silverware onto the cart as Annette trailed into the dining room. She had to admit the baked bread was pretty darn good and the freshly churned butter even better. Her oatmeal, despite losing a couple bowls daily, was tasty. No one congratulated or agreed with her because this was quiet time. Like five-year-olds in school, the sisters grouped around the table, eating quietly and swallowing quietly. Not even a habit rustled.

Puppy would love to see me silent for an hour, Annette muffled a sad smile, about to reach for another piece of bread before remembering the lumpy way her rear felt. How could she gain weight when she worked eighteen hours a day and subsisted on this convent diet? For that, she also blamed Jesus because it had to be arranged from their Heaven.

You can't blame him for something if you don't believe, Annette thought, pursing her lips. You think of Jesus and he passes along everything to the boss. Except he's kind of also the boss but not. Nice, real nice system.

The Dictator known as Mother Superior gave a blessing for Annette to be excused from kitchen clean-up so she could get right down to erasing those butt lines on the undies. For yet another reason she didn't understand, the dirty laundry bin was in a different building from the actual laundry room. It probably had to do with creating suffering, Annette thought bitterly as she rolled the bin along the dank underground corridor.

Once more sacrificing her formerly soft hands and properly manicured nails for the greater good of the British nunnery, Annette shoveled the clothes into the oversized machines. She was supposed to head back into the other building and request more work like scrubbing floors, building a throne for the Mother Superior, and converting all the Caliphate to Catholicism, but she really didn't feel like it.

It'd been nearly three weeks since she and Basa arrived in the convent. They'd pretty much humiliated her in every way for this great sin of wanting to help. They didn't trust her. Well fine with a capital "f," she felt the same. In the way most avalanches begin, Annette fumed in the old laundry room, agitated by the occasional mouse who seemed way happier than she'd ever be again.

With an angry cry, she headed back along the passageway, ducking behind a pillar as a bevy of silent, worshipful, crucifix-crossing nuns passed. Hesitating until she recalled which winding stone staircase from the medieval ages was right, Annette hurried up one floor on her throbbing feet which were steadily being mutilated by these nun shoes and slipped into the room at the end of the hall by the cracked window.

Colonel Ali Basa, formerly head of the Shurta, the secret police of the Islamic Empire, who could once order the elimination of anyone as if they'd never existed, dully stared at the ceiling. His eyes slowly fell on Annette who pressed her finger to her lips.

"Be quiet, I'm not supposed to be here."

"Yes. I recognized the universal gesture and yes, you are not supposed to be here. No one is," he said hoarsely, already tired from the effort.

"How do you feel?" Annette didn't have to ask. Basa's already hooked nose protruded out of his sallow face like the bow of a half-sunk ship.

"I am better, though given that I nearly died, not quite the best measurement. The torturers did not get the chance to fully complete their task before the remnants of my men rescued me." Basa paused for a breath. "I told them nothing, by the way." It was important for him to say this. Pride, guilt.

Annette frowned. "What would you tell them?"

Basa's amused cough turned into a noisy spasm. He waved off her offer of water. "That I was working for Abdullah. Yes, that Abdullah, the Grand Mufti's son. Which made me quite the catch as a traitor. The Mother Superior does not know that."

He grinned at her triumphant smile. "Yes, she is difficult and dislikes us both equally. Me for the obvious oppression, you for the always lingering sense of betrayal. Americans are blamed for everything, real and imagined. A species needs a scapegoat. It helps for moral clarity."

After another bout of coughing, Basa took a sip of water. "What about your husband?"

She turned away until the glint of tears passed. "He got out. I guess. I hope."

Basa nodded in relief. "And Ahmed?"

Annette hesitated until it sunk in that Basa was referring to Azhar Mustafa's alias. "I really don't know. I hope, like Puppy, he made it home."

Basa looked away for a moment. "The nuns don't want us sharing information."

"That's pretty clear. You get to sleep and I get to scrub."

The colonel fixed her with a hard look. "You must leave, Annette. Because they won't let you."

She shivered slightly. "The plan is for you and me to get to the pope."

He sighed. "Why would Mother Superior allow two people she considers enemies to get anywhere near the pope?"

"Because that's what she promised when I got here beneath all those holy pictures of Jesus," Annette said, angry at her own short-sightedness. "I figured that's sort of a promise to God."

"Haven't our histories showed such promises mean nothing since we each interpret God's attention span?" He held up a hand. "Would the Catholic Resistance allow the former head of the Muslim secret police and a somewhat infamous American nonbeliever within an inch of their Rat Line? That'd jeopardize hundreds, thousands of potential Catholic escapees."

"Then why are we here?"

"Hostages. Mother Superior is the head of the Resistance. One of them." Basa closed his eyes, the strain of talking momentarily overcoming the necessity. "But Father Dempsey isn't. He's just a cog. At the end of the day, like most of us."

Basa gestured feebly toward the nightstand. Annette yanked up the heavy table, finding an envelope taped to the bottom.

"There are two general letters of transit, signed in the name of the Grand Mufti. Like the official papers you and Puppy used to flee America." Basa smiled, amused at her surprise. "Dempsey will have forged documents which will no longer work. Get out of here now, take Dempsey and leave London."

Annette carefully studied Basa.

"It's not a trap, Annette."

She didn't answer.

"The Holy Warriors will be arriving here soon," he rasped.

Annette stiffened.

"There are spies at every convent. We did not conquer most of the world by being sloppy. The elderly gardener who I have seen outside my window tending to the roses worked for me at Shurta. I do not know his loyalties, but I assume that since the Mufti and the Holy Warriors have reinstituted *Sharia*, a particularly ruthless version if that is not redundant, he is smart enough to go with the wind."

"What about you?"

"My daughter is safe. I am not strong enough to run. And the gardener does owe me, so…" He smiled at holding one more trump card on death.

Annette sat on the edge of the bed. "What if I hadn't come up this morning?"

"Clearly someone helped." He glanced at the crucifix over the bed.

Annette's mouth went dry. "I'm not a believer."

"Are you so sure?" Basa squeezed her hand.

In the evil magic of laundry, more wet clothes filled the rolling carts than had been dry. Several sturdy thermal blouses spilled onto the handle as Annette stopped beneath the clothesline stretching across two bowed trees. The basket of wooden clips was kept dry in the excessive plastic wrapping, Annette's innovation her sole contribution to the Blessed Brides convent, which was shoved into a narrow hole at the base of one of the trees. Carting the clips back and forth seemed a waste even in a world where meaningless duties were sacrosanct.

As Annette clipped some habits swaying in the wan frigid winds, the gardener passed on a parallel cobblestone path. Annette flashed her most charming smile which had, in her youth, hobbled the knees of many a pretty boy or girl in a noisy club.

The gardener paused, the fantasy of nuns naked except for the traditional wimple over neck and cheeks clearly one of the selling points for betraying unarmed women. He tipped his scruffy woolen hat and showed gaps in his browning front teeth. Annette grinned at such a fetching sight and half turned to ever so slowly snap white panties to the line.

The gardener's half gasp was easily heard as he nearly trotted over. Annette knew she'd put herself number one on the Allah rape parade with this move.

"Sister, may I be of assistance?"

Annette flashed an even wider smile, waiting for the man to blush, before she rammed her knee into his groin. With a fistful of wooden clips, she expelled the last of his conscious breath. Tipping over the clothes onto the ground, Annette lugged the gardener, blood dripping from his right temple, into the cart, which she merrily rolled past shocked sisters into the Mother Superior's office.

A line of whispering nuns parted as Colonel Basa was wheeled inside a few minutes later. He paused to consider the Shurta spy on his stomach, hands neatly tied behind his back. Mother Superior was so furious, she was calm.

"I got the right one, didn't I? I know. Americans."

"She said this was your idea," Mother Superior hissed at Basa.

"I did not say that." Annette sneered. "He told me about the gardener. The actual assault was my idea. Well, Colonel, are you going to back me up here?"

Basa eased himself into a chair and laughed so long he needed a full glass of water. He explained his suspicions about the gardener, which disappointed the Mother Superior.

"Like I said." Annette wagged her finger. "I don't lie."

"No. It is one of your few virtues."

"That lets me focus more fully on my bad points."

Basa shook his head for Annette to stop. "Mother Superior, it was my advice that Annette leave the convent and look for his Holy Father without me."

The nun peered curiously at Annette. "Instead, you stayed. Why?"

"Why what? Did you think I'd run off and let the Allahs kill everyone?" She snorted. "Just because I don't wear a cross doesn't mean I don't value life."

"I suppose not," the nun answered slowly. "Even for those you don't like."

"Don't get too carried away." Annette looked at Basa. "I think you have to question your gardener. For all we know a raid is on its way."

"We were supposed to be protected. That was our deal." The nun glared at Basa who shrugged at the fragility of illegal agreements. "I'm sorry. I am not comfortable with any of this."

"Which part?" Basa asked.

"Any of it. Particularly the attack on the gardener. And there will certainly not be any torture in my convent."

Annette almost mentioned her own treatment as kitchen slave.

Basa sat up a little straighter. "I appreciate your morality, Mother Superior..."

"You appreciate nothing of that which you can't understand, Colonel. You're my guest as an act of kindness. You have no authority here as you have no authority anywhere."

"Then you will let him go?" Basa asked, amazed.

The Mother Superior struggled a moment. "I don't know what I'll do. But I won't extract information."

"You will merely jeopardize your nuns."

"How dare you…"

"Please," he snapped between coughs. "How many Muslims have died along the path of the Rat Line who learned about an escape? Or the location of a destination. The next cell. The new code. Are you telling me that you did not know about that?" His indignation rose over the nun's reddening face. "Since when is it a sin to kill in the name of our God if we determine that is how we can best serve Him?"

"I never ordered anyone's death," she said weakly.

"You just looked the other way. Yes, I have ordered murders. Believe me, that is more reassuring, if only for the sheer honesty. We need to learn what this man, Said, has told the Shurta or, rather, the Holy Warriors. You do not have to question him. All you must do is look the other way."

The Mother Superior turned scarlet.

Basa rose unsteadily. The Mother Superior started around her desk to stop him, but Annette blocked her. The Colonel shook his head. "For God's sake, I am going to do what I can to avoid bloodshed. I suggest the two of you do the same."

Basa winced in many different directions as he roughly awoke Said. The man's eyes widened in terror.

"Said," Basa snapped in English. "What have you told the Holy Warriors?"

Said managed enough spittle to wet Basa's knee. The Colonel smiled coldly and squeezed his neck.

"I will repeat the question."

Said spit again. Basa slammed the man's face into the hard floor. Annette held onto the protesting Mother Superior's arm.

"I will ask another question." Basa gently wiped away the blood from Said's nose. "How are your children? Your grandson must be nearly fifteen now."

"Pig." Said spit blood.

"Yes, I am." Basa slammed his face into the floor. The man moaned to stop. The Colonel sat beside him as if they were good friends.

"What have you said?"

"Nothing," Said whispered, shouting as Basa grabbed the back of his head for another slam. "I swear on my grandchildren."

"You worked for me. Such oaths mean little."

"I swear, I swear. I did not know you were here, Colonel. Or that one." His eyes gleamed at Annette. "He wants to find her especially."

Basa frowned. "Who?"

"The Lieutenant."

"His name?"

Basa slammed the man's pulpy face into the floor, waiting until Said finished crying before repeating the question.

"Omar Mustafa," he whimpered.

"Shit," Annette said softly, earning a glare from the Mother Superior.

"He looks for that one and for his father to avenge the family shame."

"Who's his father?" Basa asked.

"Azhar Mustafa. Your Ahmed," Annette explained. "That was his cover name."

Ah. I should never underestimate Abdullah, Basa thought.

"When was your next report due?"

Said shrugged, cringing as Basa raised his hand. "I swear I do not know. But I have said nothing because I knew nothing. It will stay that way."

Basa nodded in agreement. He slipped his arms around Said's head and twisted in opposite directions. The sickening popping noise echoed about the room as the man slumped forward. Basa helped himself up, turning to the Mother Superior.

"I am sorry. He could not be trusted."

The nun's eyes fluttered closed in prayer.

"I suspect you have a burial ground somewhere."

The Mother Superior nodded dully.

The bus wheezed when it wasn't shuddering. Annette changed seats several times, having the run of the newly re-commissioned Godless Buses. In the aftermath of the Hyde Park Crusader-Allah baseball game massacre, publicly condemned as spearheaded by the British Catholic community, the Grand Mufti had introduced further quarantine of religious infection by ordering nuns, priests, and anyone with any religious affiliation to ride in these vehicles.

Annette scrambled out by Great Jones Street and hurried down the Crusader-only side of the street, taking a deep breath as she rounded the corner. Only six months ago, she'd dragged Puppy into the Church of All Saints, his rib illegally stitched by an Allah doctor after an Arab drunk had legally stabbed him.

Two balls of barbed wire sat untended near the entrance. Annette sniffed; Puppy always said she could smell a gas discharge in Japan. This morning she smelled nothing. No goats or pigs. The lock on the door wobbled loosely as she stepped inside. One bare bulb flickered to the right of the pews. The fading sun provided the only light.

The stained glass on two of the windows was gone, replaced by steel bars. A cat meowed past with a disdainful glance.

She thought better of calling out. Kneeling, Annette lit a few candles before the sad, defaced Jesus on the wall, splattered with red. She felt guilty about complaining earlier.

At the creak of a door, Annette crouched, left knee forward, a sliver from one of the many cups she'd broken at the convent tucked in her right palm. Deep, hearty laughter shook the church as Father John Dempsey, wearing a plain green sweater over speckled flannel pants, stopped a few feet away. He chuckled some more.

"I honestly think that's the most ridiculous image I've seen in a very long time."

"I'm glad to make your day, Father."

Dempsey sat in the front pew and gestured at the candles. "Then again, there's little competition for such a prize. There's no one left to pray. They've taken away all the animals. Except for that wily alley cat."

She frowned. "You never know. This is a church."

"Not anymore. Well, for a few more days. We're being turned into a prison. A nice touch, don't you think? Where else to put arrested priests and nuns? But don't worry. Since I've been such a good servant, the Holy Warriors have given me the honor of serving as a guard. There are great benefits like living and avoiding torture. How could I refuse?"

"You could've," she said distastefully.

"And miss the joy of your superior American disappointment?"

She sat beside the priest. "I've got another job offer."

"You always do, Annette." Dempsey smiled wistfully. "What's it now? Am I also to dress up like a nun?"

"We're leaving tonight on the Rat Line."

Dempsey mildly lifted his eyebrow, lighting a cigarette and tossing the match. With a scolding look, Annette picked up the spent light.

"Where to? Oh wait, let me guess. To find the Holy Father."

"That's right. I have the letters of transit."

"Have a good trip."

"Look, Father Dempsey—"

"John. I resigned. That's part of the package for my new career. See, it's only so humiliating for priests to be guarded by a priest. When the priest is no longer a priest but one who has seen the light, that rubs the salt just a bit deeper into the wound. Now it's just John. Or you can call me Jack. That was my nickname as a kid."

"I can think of another nickname."

He laughed bitterly. "I'm sure you can. But I don't have your options."

"I could've left with Puppy. I stayed behind for this."

"Because you found Jesus. Or part of him. Leg, arm, ear, which part? How's that working out, Sister Annette? I hope better than it did for me."

"I'm having my troubles with your damn religion, too."

"Faith is a cruel mistress. It demands so much with so little proof. I do wish you well. You'll have to tell me how the Rat Line is. I've never actually spoken to anyone who came back."

"I'm going with or without you, Father."

"What about Colonel Basa? Wasn't he supposed to be your comrade-in-arms?"

"He's too ill."

"Pity. Another fine public servant."

"Which leaves you."

"No, which leaves your already-mentioned second choice. Alone."

Annette leaned forward. "The Allahs are planning a raid on the Blessed Brides convent."

He blew a smoke ring. "Good thing you came here. This is safe. See the bars on the windows?" Dempsey sighed. "They're raiding and rounding up everyone. There's nothing I can do."

"You can come with me."

"There's nothing I can do," he shouted, standing. "It's over. I gave everything for nothing and all I have left is one final humiliation. Let me serve my penance in peace."

"No."

"What?" He seemed genuinely perplexed.

"I said no. I can't do this alone. I won't fool anyone as a nun. I don't speak British. I bet you speak other languages." She glared until he nodded listlessly. "Right. We've got to try."

"The Holy Father's probably dead."

"What if he's not?"

"Then let it be!" Dempsey cried. "You're bringing a message from whom? Colonel Basa who's part of the losing Abdullah faction? America? Grandma's dead. What the hell are you doing finding the pope anyway? To tell him what? To get him to do what? If he could've done something, he would've."

"If the world knows he's alive, it will mean something special. It will give people hope."

"Hope? Hope? He's as powerless as fucking Jesus."

"Don't say it like that."

"Fucking Jesus. Fucking Jesus."

Dempsey scampered into the altar and began ripping the crucifixion statue down. Annette leaped on his back. Half of Jesus came apart, landing in a noisy, dusty heap. Only Christ's head remained on the wall. Red, disfigured, sad.

The priest went on all fours into the altar, running the shattered bits of the statue through his fingers. He lovingly took Jesus's head off the wall, cradling it in his arms and sobbing.

"Forgive me, forgive me, forgive me," he moaned.

Annette knelt and rubbed Dempsey's neck. "He'll understand. But we have to leave now."

4

Puppy's first office, indoors anyway, was furnished as if by catalog. Straight-backed leather chair and a spotless desk with a tin cup of crisscrossed pens and pencils overlooking a new glass-and-oak coffee table with bland round coasters beneath sparkling purple mugs. The walls had not been so much painted as scrubbed. There wasn't a speck of dust until a baseball rolled out in greeting from beneath the couch.

Have fun. We didn't. Ty and Mickey.

"I apologize, sir." Matthew pranced into the room on a wind of anxiety, snatching away the ball with a scolding mutter. "You have no idea how many pranks I discovered once the two gentlemen left. There was a bat that went thusly upon my shoulders when I opened the door. There was something called a whoopee cushion circa late nineteenth century beneath the couch."

The 'bot gestured grandly to introduce Puppy to the beige couch. He doubted fingerprints were allowed.

"As well, I uncovered symbols of adolescent eroticism which I will not mention until you and I are better acquainted."

Matthew placed its hands on its hips and adjusted its slim black suit, the metal eyes fixed on Puppy who was suddenly self-conscious about his blue cords and button-down white shirt, presents from Zelda and Pablo who had seemed a little too happy to send him back to his apartment. The poorly made red tie was from the "grateful" cast of *Darlings Are Dear*, accompanied by a handmade card with flowers in the shape of bats which Puppy proudly propped against the tin cup.

Off a quick intake, Matthew remade Puppy's tie. "Much to say, sir."

"I can imagine. My first day and everything."

The 'bot held up a stiff finger. "First, my name is Matthew." Puppy pleased Matthew by shaking hands; most humans wouldn't bother. "And I shall call you?"

"Puppy."

"You are the Commissioner so it should be Commissioner Nedick."

"I'm still Puppy. What did the previous occupants of the office want to be called?"

Matthew rolled its eyes. "Primarily Commissioner, although Mr. Cobb preferred the Prince of Baseball. Mr. Mantle was a bit easier. Mick, Mickey, the Commerce Comet, but neither, shall I say, adhered to the gravity of the office as they should have."

"I'll try to bring a certain majesty, but I'm a pretty simple guy."

Matthew's mouth flickered with metallic smugness. "Before we get into the meat of the morning, is this outfit appropriate for you? The former Commissioners amused themselves by selecting my wardrobe. They kindly dressed me as they felt I should dress, but I can change."

"I want you to be comfortable, Matthew."

The 'bot did a quick pirouette, showing off the cut of the suit, which Puppy approved with a grin.

"Then let us move on from my minimal needs to yours as Commissioner of Baseball. May I be among the first to congratulate you."

"Actually, after my friends Zelda and Pablo and their kid, you're the fourth to do so in person." Puppy's head still ached slightly from the waterfall of celebratory bourbon they'd poured down his throat last night. Not just for the job, but for the cloud lifting over all of them.

Dear Puppy Nedick,

The Family is pleased to inform you that all outstanding charges of suspicious behavior have been dismissed. As of now, you are officially the Commissioner of Baseball. Welcome back to The Family. Please visit.

Adrea Dinazzo, Third Cousin

Just like that.

Matthew fussed about while Puppy skimmed his day on the oversized agenda on the desk, which the 'bot pointed out contained extra margins for any unanticipated needs, though his predictive abilities were superb.

February 28th, 2099

Commissioner Puppy Nedick's Schedule:

10 a.m. Sahidi Douglas, radcaster of the *Game of the Week*, meeting per your request

11 a.m. Discuss questions with Matthew

12 noon Free time for thinking

12:15 p.m. Lunch of choice; Matthew will provide menus ten minutes previously; the prior occupants preferred Bill's Bagelini (excellent overstuffed AG meat sandwiches)

1 p.m. Welcome call with Third Cousin Adrea Dinazzo (to whom you report directly!!)

2 p.m. Meeting with American League Eastern Division owners (briefing of outstanding issues to be provided by Matthew and there are many!!)

3 p.m. Rest period/cocktails if necessary; prior occupants preferred beer and soda pop

3:30 p.m. Retractable roofs in the Midwest per issues with Harmonic Construction (a newly formed 'bot company! Matthew to provide protocol for FB-human meetings)

4:30 p.m. Interview with radcast *Spotlight on Baseball* host Sandra Douglas, twin sister of 10 a.m. appointment Sahidi (questions to be provided by Ms. Douglas beforehand)

Matthew fretted over Puppy's frown. "I did not want to burden you too much on the first day, Commissioner."

"I appreciate that."

"The prior occupants—"

"You can call them Ty and Mick."

Matthew nodded briskly. "Many issues went unresolved. They preferred open places in the schedule for what I assumed was rest, given their age, but more often turned into festivities." The 'bot disapprovingly narrowed its eyes. "I would not bring women into the office for at least your first week."

Puppy assured Matthew the sanctity of the Commissioner's office would be preserved and there was no reason to stockpile alcohol, though he might regret that decision. He was also trying to lose weight so please limit the snacks.

Promptly at ten, Sahidi Douglas slid onto the thick chair without asking, crossing her legs and staring at Puppy as if just not sure what to make of him. Small talk wasn't on her agenda, which she made clear by ignoring Matthew's offer of refreshments. The miffed robot closed the door a little too noisily.

Puppy propped his feet on the coffee table, knowing he'd get a scolding for scuffing the glass, and stared back pleasantly. "Delighted to see you again, Sahidi."

Douglas ran a slender hand up the side of her plant-like black hair, recalling their unscheduled interview at Fenway Park when he'd returned to America. "I had to do some fancy dancing after that."

"I bet. Was it worth it?"

"Being interrogated by Black Tops? Oh sure. Wondrous experience. Took some time before they believed we weren't working together. I could've lost my job. Or worse. But you popped into the rad booth and wanted to be interviewed so what could I say?"

"You could've refused."

She smiled faintly. "I'm ambitious."

"Which is why you're here. I need a staff. I'm allowed to hire two people."

"Who's the other?"

He shrugged. "I haven't even found the bathroom yet. But I'm starting with you."

"Because I risked my ass interviewing the fugitive Puppy and giving him a sounding board?"

"Yeah, in part. And because you know baseball. About the only thing that kept me sane while I was hiding," he remained paranoid enough not to mention where, "was listening to your weekly broadcasts. You feel the game. Like I said at the end of that interview in Boston, I'm impressed."

Sahidi waited, unimpressed that he was impressed.

"You sound like a blend of the old-time sportscasters."

"My grandfather had cups of coffee with Oakland and Houston back in the early 2050s. Lionel Douglas. Don't pretend you've heard of him. A .248 career batting average, eleven homers. Not a bad glove in left. He was a devotee of the glory days of radio. The stories changed a little as he got older, but apparently he bought tapes from a dealer outside Cleveland and hid them under the house. He insisted that he sensed someday it'd be illegal to own memorabilia. He died in 2066 just after it all did and left me the tapes. Greats like Mel Allen and Red Barber, Vin Scully, Bob Prince, Harry Caray, Ernie Harwell. I was hooked."

Sahidi paused. "I'm still searching for my own voice."

"Takes a while, like learning to command a pitch. But you got all the tools. You're a pleasure to listen to." She grunted, softening. "I need someone who loves baseball like me. Ty and Mick loved baseball, but they had egos."

"And we don't?" Sahidi waited for Puppy to join her in a grin. "I already have a job. A dream job. I don't want anything else."

Puppy tilted his head dubiously. "But yet you're here."

"I'm always too curious for my own sake." She studied Puppy like he was a goldfish. "What's the job besides fulfilling my love of the game?"

"I'm not sure yet. I have to get a handle on what's going on and if there's anything that needs attending."

Douglas laughed. "Because you think it's all going splendidly."

Puppy squirmed slightly. "Well yeah. I've been listening to your radcasts."

"What would you like me to say? That a squirrel could've caught that ground ball? Has this pitcher ever been taught the basic mechanics of a windup? Are the fans not cheering because they're frozen solid?"

Sahidi tossed a folder onto the table. "I gave this analysis a lot of thought. I didn't sleep all night working on it, so I hope you'll show respect. Then if you want to talk, I'll come back and we can see, depending on what you say. But baseball is anything but going splendidly. My grandpa used to call the condition a flush away."

Puppy calmed down Matthew about already adjusting the morning's agenda after one meeting. He sent the 'bot out for some blueberry Danish and curled into the chair, still pleasantly scented by Sahidi.

BASEBALL 2099, THE STATE OF THE GAME ANALYSIS BY SAHIDI DOUGLAS

CONFIDENTIAL: FOR PUPPY NEDICK ONLY

Factual background: As of this date, February 28, 2099, the thirty major league teams comprising the American and National Leagues have played an average of thirty-three games.

The current first-place teams are the Boston Red Sox (AL Eastern Division), Detroit Tigers (AL Central Division), and the Seattle Pilots (AL Western Division). In the National League, the New York Mets lead the Eastern Division while the Chicago Cubs and San Francisco Giants are atop the Central and Western Divisions, respectively.

Through this date, Penny Tissamarrano of the Philadelphia Phillies is the top NL hitter with a .403 batting average. In the American League, Ellie Adair of the Boston team sports a .377 average. Jonathan Taylor of the Los Angeles Dodgers leads the NL with eight home runs while Paul Weinstock of the New York Yankees has powered nine.

In pitching, Garcia Marichal of the Cleveland Spiders has won six games and Nan-Jenny Watanabe of the New York Mets has notched five wins. They each lead their leagues with thirty-two strikeouts.

A full list of the top ten in each category plus runs batted in and Earned Run Average (E.R.A) is footnoted.

The home attendance for each of the teams has averaged just over sixty percent capacity. In the first week the capacity attendance was ninety-seven percent. Second week, eighty-three percent. Third week, seventy-one percent. In the fourth week it was sixty-one percent. Fifth week, fifty-five percent. Sixth week, forty-eight. Through the seventh week, forty-four percent.

Puppy took an uneasy bite of the Danish.

A full list of each team's home attendance is footnoted along with data on concessions which I consider merely anecdotal and not insightful.

ANALYSIS: Since the start of the season, I've personally seen thirty-one major league games. Seven were from my duties on the weekly Game of the Week *radcast (NY, Boston, LA, Atlanta, Detroit, Chicago/Wrigley Field, St. Louis) and the remaining games at Yankee Stadium, Fenway Park, Shea Stadium, and Veterans Stadium, reasonably proximate to my home in the Throgs Neck section of the Bronx).*

There was a remarkable fervor in the first week as shown by the rabid attendance figures. The energy as a sportscaster was also off the charts. The Cousins have received 1,455 letters regarding the radcasts with eighty-one percent favorable, ten percent negative and nine percent both.

But this analysis is my personal view. The attendance has clearly dropped and I notice less energy in the stands which goes beyond the presence of fewer fans. The excitement about the return of baseball across the country, building on the 2098 success, which I consider a success despite the terrorist attack at Yankee Stadium, has dwindled. Here are the reasons:

THE WEATHER: I believe the season was rushed back before milder weather began in late March/early April for reasons other than the needs of the game. I'll speculate that the intensity of the new conflict with Islam persuaded The Family to seek a way to distract the country. I also suggest that, by giving face bots new positive roles in rebuilding the ballparks so quickly, they were preparing everyone for the introduction of the face bot-human Harmony Laws.

Smart kid, Puppy thought.

But the weather is a serious factor. It's as if The Family challenged baseball fans to brave the cold and rain and snow to see how much they really wanted baseball.

Or to make a case for them not wanting it enough, Puppy suddenly realized.

The retractable roofs help, but fans still must get to the ballparks and the covering is only activated at forty-two degrees. I wear two coats when I'm announcing, even in an enclosed booth. The heating coils beneath the seats provides some comfort. But the blankets and igloo-like coverings don't belong to baseball along with domes on retro stadiums. It's at variance with how baseball, good and mostly bad for nearly seventy years, has been perceived. Football fans happily embrace shivering during a game. Not baseball. If you want to reach baseball fans, you must give them what they remember or, since there hasn't been a real season since 2065, what they've been told by parents or grandparents.

THE GAME: I really hate being this honest but I'm in deep already. The quality of play is not very good. This shouldn't be a surprise. There was no way baseball could be gone for thirty-three years except for the purposeful travesty of the Bronx Hawks and Bronx Falcons at the then Amazon Stadium and still expect quality. The fundamentals are very poor. I've been horrified watching undisciplined infield and batting practice. The managers and coaches are clueless. They don't understand any nuances like bunting and the hit-and-run. There is often little reason why pitchers are taken out of games. There are growing issues with faulty equipment. Balls are easily misshapen. Bats break after one contact. Four players are out indefinitely from injuring themselves sliding into improperly installed bases.

That happened long before all this, Puppy sighed. But he got what she was getting at.

There is little strategy. Fans were accustomed to inferior play before the game was reintroduced last season with humans instead of holograms, but if you're a fan, it's pretty easy to determine that what you're seeing wouldn't merit even the old minor leagues, which as you know closed in 2035.

Fans are also confused by how much they're allowed to root for their teams. On the one hand, loyalty is encouraged to local teams. Yet there've been numerous requests to avoid the uncontrolled passion for home teams which is believed to have exacerbated sectionalism and political polarization. How can you have a baseball game where the fans don't know whom to root for?

THE ENTERTAINMENT: I don't think anyone has decided how much extra entertainment belongs in a baseball game. When the Yankees and Cubs's names were restored, Yankee Stadium became a fun place. The HG entertainment absolutely rocked. That shouldn't be a substitute for the game itself as happened back in the desperate 2030s, but there needs to be a coherent strategy. Cubs fans led by the Friends of Ernie Banks fought against adding the Jumbotron to the rebuilt Wrigley Field since it was installed in 2015 and the park opened in 1916.

But the Friends of Jackie Robinson in Los Angeles agreed that the super-sized scoreboard enveloping all of Dodger Stadium was fine despite the ballpark opening in 1958. Do we want consistency or bending to local values? Should the stadiums reflect the game exactly as it was when they opened or is that all about architectural symbolism?

CONCLUSION: The most pressing and worrying aspect of the early trends of the 2099 season is whether the surge in interest in baseball had less to do with the game than the reassurance of its old-time values, reintroduced by Albert Cheng when he became Grandpa. Baseball was dying long before the Miners's attack during the 2065 World Series. The initial crowds could've been because baseball was a novelty. If baseball was too boring once before, can it be a sanctuary within the growing war and uncertainty of the Granddaughter now leading The Family post-Grandma and Grandpa, or is the very nature of the game simply past its time? If the players are mediocre at best and the fans have to shiver to even get to the park, how long before the attendance bottoms out? Baseball has been given a second chance. As much as I love the game—my grandfather played two seasons for the Oakland Athletics and Houston Astros—I'm afraid that, unless a genuinely coherent strategy is developed, baseball will revert to its earlier fringe status, pre-2065.

EXIT QUESTION: Can a bad imitation of a bad imitation of baseball when we want the real thing revive a game that has already been proclaimed dead?

I have suggestions if you'd like to discuss further. Thank you.

On the downtown M12 bus, Puppy dozed with Millie the Mouse cradled on his lap, a tiny brown stuffed animal which was another one of Zelda's back-you-go Puppy gifts, along with vows that he'd always be welcome to visit and put on Diego's diapers backward, eat all their food, drink all their booze, and ensure she and Pablo didn't have sex.

Like some hunting dog, he woke as the bus lumbered past Yankee Stadium guarded by night-lights, settling at the stop before his orange-and-beige old apartment building.

He juggled the small leather bag which contained more food than clothes; Zelda had packed five sandwiches along with two opened bags of Pretzel Dolls. The apartment smelled musty in the irritated way furniture behaves when it's neglected for six months. He turned on the living room lights and stood there. It was strange to be back, especially being alone.

Puppy poured Koffi Pear Brandy, which he quickly discovered was the last of his alcohol. He munched on one of Zelda's semi-salmon salad sandwiches and found small triumph in an unopened jar of Manny's Super Sour Pickles tucked in the rear of the otherwise vacant fridge.

Puppy tugged out a stack of baseball books which, despite the ban long since lifted, he'd kept taped behind the desk. He blew off dust, finishing the sandwich and pouring another too-sweet brandy to accompany the Pretzel Dolls. Puppy draped the oversized

Baseball's Greatest Pitchers onto his knees, which he'd found atop a trash can by a Bedford Avenue M28 bus stop when he was eighteen.

Even in 2099, the familiar windups of Walter Johnson and Christy Matthewson and Bob Feller and Sandy Koufax were, well, familiar. Steve Carlton, Nolan Ryan, Randy Johnson; he flipped the pages. The last entry was Nester Navarro in 2036. They stopped the compendiums of baseball's greatest shortly after that. By 2038, the game was so changed that comparisons were like a frayed umbilical cord.

Puppy sipped his third brandy from the bottle, belching down his fourth pickle. The gloves were similar, merely evolved, he pondered, inspecting *Deep in the Hole* about shortstops from Honus Wagner to Ernie Banks. Bats as well, shoes, the game itself, the physicality, all remained the same. Ninety feet base to base. But the magic was lost. You need to believe that it was possible to hit a baseball traveling at one hundred miles per hour with a reaction time of .8 seconds.

How do you make a country believe in magic again, Puppy wondered, accepting he had no answer. Sahidi was right. The game was a novelty. Restoring it was like lifting a quarantine and releasing all kinds of pent-up emotions such as the anger and shame at losing the war. But once the rush of sampling passed, you reverted with the snap of a rubber band. Maybe not a snap, but a slow wiggle. You could honor your past, of baseball, America, Sahidi's grandfather, Mooshie Lopez putting sensuality in a swing, but once you've honored the past, do you really want to live in it when the past led you directly to this present, surrounded by Allahs?

Maybe baseball should've stayed dead. Puppy sighed. Maybe it should've been the one season, actually the three-month experience at one stadium with just two teams as a memory play, nothing more. People always want more until they get it.

Grandma had viewed baseball as a distraction from her peace plan with Abdullah as much as Cheng had viewed baseball as a distraction from the new war. Even a child grows impatient over distractions and wants to move on.

Maybe Clary also viewed baseball as a distraction. But from what?

Damned if he was going to let that happen again. Puppy grimly smiled. Not until they see baseball the way it was meant to be.

He dunked his pickle in Benito's Dark Brown Mustard and offered Millie the Mouse the rest of the Pretzel Doll.

• • • •

GRANDMA SIGHED LIKE a cantankerous horn as Mooshie Lopez applied the third different lipstick in the past half hour. Smear on, wipe off. Smear on, wipe off. She suspected that Mooshie was doing this to irritate her as Mooshie did everything, proof that disdain lived on past life, death, and into inorganic cells.

Grandma handed Mooshie a soft tissue, the last of the box. With a childish sneer, Lopez took the tissue ever so slowly, drawing out the suspense. Whether the makeup, which had looked so keen in The Hut in Tom's River, New Jersey, but had failed dismally in Keira's Kuddle Bar in downtown Scranton, Pennsylvania, would triumph this evening at The Rabbit Lounge in Youngstown, Ohio, was still unknown.

Nightclub owner Mr. Flute danced inside the unkempt dressing room with a two-step and a smile on his droopy mustachioed face.

"Hey, hey, hey, ladies and germs, what's the time?"

Mooshie smiled that adorable, sweet smile back at her unfamiliar reflection in the grimy mirror, more to examine the cranberry mascara inching beneath her regenerated blue-green eyes than any attempt to engage Mr. Flute in another conversation.

Smear on, wipe off.

"The time is still six minutes before Ms. Laker's call time." Grandma consulted her interior clock. "And we promise to be prompt once the preliminaries are done."

She cringed as someone abused a saxophone.

"Beauty isn't a preliminary, honey," Mooshie said between smacking her lips. If she removed the lipstick one more time, Grandma would yank off the wig before the tendrils of hair finished implanting.

"I got an audience. Fans to woo. Drinks to be bought by you." Mooshie pouted her lips at Mr. Flute who mistakenly interpreted that action as a flirt not a warning. "Money, glamor. Bang slam."

As if she, Mooshie Lopez, singing in this dump in Youngstown, Ohio, a scab not worthy to be scratched, wasn't humiliating enough, she had to listen to this retread from the annals of old-time burlesque.

"Slam bang," Mr. Flute braved a correction. This Laker had no credentials, a name on a pitch letter from this skinny lady with eyes like drill bits whose managerial office he'd never heard of, and he knew all the reps east of Chicago.

"If you'd allow Ms. Laker to complete her preparations of beauty and glamor," Grandma's voice would've dried a pond, "then we'll be on time."

"Then I'd best skip on out. Intro's in four minutes."

"Four minutes and eleven seconds," Grandma said.

Mr. Flute left a little too quickly for a man who owned the place.

"This is who I have to work with now." Mooshie angrily stuck a 'bacco in the corner of her mouth.

"This grand tour was your idea."

"I said a grand tour. Not toilets." Mooshie blew smoke out of her left nostril. "Even when I started out, I never played crap joints like this. I always played theaters"—she rolled out the syllables—"palaces. Not dressing rooms."

"If we could've used your real name, I'm sure I would've got you all the bookings your ego desired."

"There's a world, darling, between Leemer's Show Hall on Bruckner Boulevard and The Rabbit Lounge. I haven't even seen one picture of a rabbit." Mooshie rolled her eyes, unfurling like a cat by spreading her arms and arching her back. "Enough of your whining. I look pretty hot, don't I? Especially since I don't quite look like me."

"You'll satisfy the audience, I'm sure."

Mooshie dropped a high-heeled foot onto the chair, leaning forward through the smoke. "You've gotta ratchet it up a little, Ms. Panang." She emphasized the fake name with glee. "You're my loyal manager. To you, I'm the greatest singer in the world. There ain't even anyone second. Or third. That'll sell me and keep the club bookings going straight on through to the wilds of Montana."

It was an effective strategy for a cover, Grandma grudgingly agreed. "One minute and twenty-seven seconds, Ms. Laker."

"One minute and twenty-five, Ms. Panang. I got one of those internal clocks, too. Once upon a time, I was the cutting-edge model."

"Once upon a time," Grandma said with a smirk.

Mooshie clenched her groin out the door. Lenore paused a moment to glance at her odd, younger-by-twenty-years face in the mirror. Sturdier bone density, elevated height; Mooshie taller, she shorter. The fiendish trickery of vanity. A disguise, Grandma told herself, no more. No different than any other.

About a third of the club was filled with customers who just seemed eager to get out of the below-zero cold. Each of the tables had old-fashioned 1930s-style lamps, white tablecloths, and ramrod black chairs scuffing the gleaming hardwood floor. Must be from the 2060s, Grandma thought as she took a table in the rear. To elevate morale during the War, she'd encouraged a return to the nightclub era. Torch singers, big bands, swinging, and dancing up a storm.

That was now lost. There wasn't a single person in the crowd who wore a black bow tie or a stunning sequined dress. A lot of soiled sleeves leaned half dazed on the tables, waiting with the sort of boredom that springs from irritation that has nowhere good to go.

"Hello, ladies and germs." Mr. Flute bounced through the hysterically yellow curtains onto the ten-foot-long stage. "Have we got a show for you tonight." The trumpet player pealed an answer. "Well, haven't we? Or else what the hell am I doing up here?"

There were groans and a few obscenities tossed toward the very agile Mr. Flute who skipped from toe to toe in case one of the long-stemmed wine glasses came his way.

"I can see you're chomping at the bit. Whoa, Harry, whoa."

The saxophone chimed in as Mr. Flute mimed a horse. Sipping the cool Wisconsin Chardonnay, Grandma was utterly fascinated at the extent someone with no talent would go for a tiny bit of approval. Isn't this what you wanted, Lenore? Hope for all if only you worked hard enough.

"Then let's get this clown off the stage." Mr. Flute yanked a colorful handkerchief out of his back pocket and blew his nose. "And get on to the main event. Ladies and germs, I give you the incomparable, the wondrous golden tones of the ravishing Mimi Laker."

Mooshie's long, muscled thigh kicked out from behind the curtain; she'd adamantly refused to re-diversify the legs which'd been a pin-up for soldiers in both the American and Muslim armies during World War III.

"Hello, Youngstown." She hid behind the curtain, waiting for a response. There was none. Mooshie burst out, mic by her mouth, eyes blazing. "Hello, Youngstown."

That earned a few annoyed mutters.

"I said." Mooshie planted her feet. "Hel-lo."

Before the last "lo" dribbled from the audience, Mooshie leaped straight up, beginning her hit song of 2059, *Fire Me Up*.

"When you've got the rod to start a flame

Watch the embers

'Cause that's my name

Roast my toes

And burn my lobes

Just fire me up

Inside and out."

Mooshie swept around the stage like a bird miming flight. Grandma reluctantly admitted she was simply masterful. The sluggish crowd began clapping tepidly.

A beefy woman with a faint old-style goatee shouted out, "Try to stay in tune!"

That generated a few snickers.

Mooshie pretended not to hear, though the sneer gave her away. She straddled the area directly in front of the customer's table.

"And when my heart aches,

Light a door and kick it down."

"Sounds like ducks," a voice called out in the courage of the dark.

Grandma walked sideways quicker than any human could walk straight ahead. She clasped her hand on the back of the man's thin neck, squeezing through the collar just enough to produce a gasp and the fear there might not be a way to refill the oxygen.

"Do not say that again," Lenore hissed, suddenly stepping back, caught between horror at her anger and the rippling tide of calls for Mooshie to dip a strap off her dress and, as one inebriated sibling suggested, "offer some skin."

Mooshie's eyes turned volcanic. She kicked up her right foot, sending a high heel into the reedy fellow's nose. Grandma hurried over to the now-slumped-over fellow; a quick probe of his mind reassured her that he had no permanent injuries.

She brushed aside a second flying shoe, saving the skull of a terrified woman.

Mooshie, stop now, she urged with little effect as Lopez ransacked the stage, sending the musicians fleeing. The hissing singer hurled a table at the scared patrons fleeing for the exits.

"Mimi Laker doesn't show her tits," Mooshie thundered, tearing down the curtains.

Grandma cornered Mr. Flute by the entrance to the kitchen, now emptied. "What is this?"

"What do you mean?"

Grandma re-arranged his thoughts until the man half slumped to the ground. She whirled on Mooshie.

"Mimi, put down the fork."

"I'm just holding it until we get some answers."

Grandma knelt beside Mr. Flute, his eyes steadying beneath the warmth of her thoughts. Like a baby bathed in the warmest scent, Mr. Flute smiled, no longer afraid.

"This happens some nights," he explained, slowly shedding his grogginess. "It's a release after everything that's happened."

"Public nudity was banned in 2074, Mr. Flute." It was the second order I signed after The Surrender. "Behavior diminishing a sibling's body is immoral. Much less…"

"Fucking rudeness." Mooshie poked Mr. Flute's arm with the fork.

"Yes, thank you, Mimi. Uncivil behavior is not allowed. It's worse than daring to suggest someone show their private parts. It contradicts everything this society, this Family, was built upon. The ability to be who you are without vicious personal attacks."

"I know. But my club is now an area of freer expression."

"What the hell does that mean?" Mooshie poked the man again just because.

Mr. Flute moaned at the hole in his jacket. "The Cousins asked bar and lounge owners if they wanted to participate in an experiment where customers could well, you know, let loose a little after all the uncertainty since that Confession, Admission, whatever. People are kind of scared. I mean, aren't you?"

"I wasn't before tonight," Grandma said with less conviction. "And how will encouraging rudeness help?"

"I don't know. I just signed up."

Grandma squeezed the man's chin. "You're supposed to think about such a request."

"I figured I'd try it. Crowds have picked up. And hey, they only do it when the act isn't well known…" Mr. Flute skittered away from the utensil patrolling his left eyeball. "I did tell you The Rabbit Lounge was now participating, Ms. Panang."

"You did not."

In that way irony is often lost, Mr. Flute loudly thanked Grandma's bra straps for having the note right there in his front pocket. Mooshie peered over Grandma's shoulder to read.

Ms. Panang, we are pleased to offer your client Mimi Laker an exclusive three-date contract to perform two shows nightly of no less than one hour per performance at The Rabbit Lounge. Be advised this nightclub has been granted a zone of freer expression by the Cousins Suggestion 22.

"You did receive this, right?' Flute asked hopefully.

"Yes. But I didn't understand what that meant," Grandma murmured, embarrassed by how that was possible.

"You didn't know?" Mooshie shouted.

"Apparently I don't know everything."

"Oh, that's a headline."

Grandma scowled, slowly returning with a wan smile at the pale Mr. Flute. "You think freer thought excuses this disparaging behavior?"

"Maybe the patrons went a little too far," Mr. Flute apologized to Mooshie, his eyes watering at the battered nightclub. "This kind of freedom is all new."

"You already have the greatest freedom in the world. Your own individual responsibility."

Mr. Flute puffed up defiantly. "Which was yours to read the letter more carefully."

Grandma sagged slightly. "You're right. Of course, we will waive the rest of the contract."

"Wait a second. Am I getting fired?" Mooshie shouted, sending Mr. Flute cowering behind an overturned chair.

He announced, "No, no. You're wonderful. But the damages are also your responsibility."

Mooshie made a great show of artistic pain as she turned over her Lifecard. Grandma waited for Mr. Flute to claim an unwarranted charge, but he showed the factory price stamps of each broken piece of furniture.

They bought two bottles of cheap Kansas City Pinot Noir and returned to the dingy Palladium Arms Motel on Route 44 where they drank silently and sourly.

"I'm sorry for destroying the club," Mooshie finally said between swigs. "And?" she growled.

Lenore's mouth moved in several directions, the irritation and shame sloshing around like an unwelcome cocktail. "Of course I apologize for my role. But that doesn't excuse your violent response."

"Thank you. I didn't want to think I'd walked into some parallel universe where Grandma Lenore Shen wasn't Grandma Lenore Shen anymore." Mooshie drained the last of the wine. "Even you wouldn't have allowed that anti-humanist crap."

Grandma smiled faintly. "You understand a phrase like anti-humanist might be inappropriate when applied to us?"

Mooshie tossed her stockings on the bed. "Do you even know what we are?"

"Not anymore," she conceded. "We're what we once were, except a little more and a little less."

"You gotta contact the next three clubs to make sure we don't have any shit like tonight. My first manager, Patricio Cimini, was a moron and even he never booked me in dumps in Youngstown. Where are you going?"

Grandma let the rumpled Colonel Louie Free into the motel room. She touched a small bruise on his left cheek.

"Sorry, Louie. I didn't expect Mooshie to go berserk."

"It's okay. I enjoyed the show until I was hit in the face by a chair leg." He removed his cap, the long gray ponytail drooping over his right shoulder.

"I'm not apologizing again." Mooshie brightened as Free put a couple of wine bottles on the table. "Thank you, General."

"Colonel," he said with mock severity. "I refused promotions after this level."

"What was your line? A general isn't worth a private's pee?" Grandma grinned.

"Something like that, although more crude. I hope to hear your entire performance some evening, Ms. Lopez."

Mooshie grunted. "I don't do encores in motel rooms."

"Never?" Grandma said with such feigned shock that Mooshie had to laugh. "Colonel Free is a good friend and has been since the last days of the war. He was always the person to let me know what they didn't want me to know. And yes, before you launch into one of your tirades about how Grandma hates the armed forces and that's why we lost... Please, Louie, she's entitled to her opinion."

Mooshie warily eyed Free, bottles of wine or not.

"So Louie." Grandma folded her arms. "I didn't expect to hear from you so soon."

Free answered, "We had to move things up. They've implemented new codes. Unfortunately, I could only access a limited amount of information. We've deployed just over nine hundred thousand soldiers so far."

"How, Louie?" Grandma interrupted. "I never ordered that many built. I stopped at approximately eighty-five thousand when it became clear that the system of command and obey might be faulty."

"Cheng sped up production. Now they're also creating robot officers at the Butte facility." He paused to let that sink in. "The first two thousand have been stationed in bases contiguous to the Mexican and Canadian borders. They're using captured Miners and Blue Wigs facilities as training bases. Obviously, they want to announce more victories. Once that's public, robot officers will be more easily accepted."

"With no human controls," Grandma said softly.

"The strategy originates with organic life-forms," Free corrected.

"And during a battle, what happens then?" Grandma sighed as the Colonel remained silent. "Who's issuing these orders?"

"The 'bot Felice who was Cheng's assistant and now works for the Granddaughter, with the approval of the Cousins."

Grandma showed disgust. "A robot is making military decisions."

"Not alone. But she has a great deal of influence, especially with Cheng gone."

"And what's Clary's role?"

"I've heard nothing that links her with military matters. She appears to be a figure-head."

Grandma considered that with some relief. "At least a child isn't running things. What about the status of the war?"

"South America is back in our hands, but the last battles were costly."

She relaxed slightly. "Our robot armies are not quite invincible."

"Not yet. Coordinated tactics are still new. They're using General Fartook's tactics for study."

Grandma winced at the irony. Fartook was considered the Muslim military genius, sweeping aside American forces all over the Mediterranean theater of operations.

"North Africa is the next target."

"And the soldiers will all be FBs?" she asked.

Free nervously fussed with his ponytail. "Yes."

There was a brief anxious silence.

"The Caliphate will have to act," Grandma said quietly.

Colonel Free nodded. "They'll launch nukes at the production sites."

"And we'll have no recourse but to respond in kind," Grandma said.

"This time," Mooshie said sourly, earning a glare.

"But by producing robot armies, we're backing the Allahs into a corner," Free said.

"Almost purposefully," Grandma mused. "This begs the obvious point of how we shut this all down. How many forces have you assembled to accompany us to Montana?"

Free shifted slightly under her steady stare. "I'm still working on securing an escort for you. It has been challenging to explain the need without risking exposure."

"I well understand. I don't want you jeopardizing your position, Colonel. Or your life. But are you saying that the military is standing behind this robot policy?"

Free squirmed. "You trained us very well, Grandma. Disloyalty is simply unfath-omable. Even with Elias Kenuda's assertion of justifying individual responsibility to act against the law, precious few agree. Certainly not enough to surface. Or to form a suffi-cient military presence for you to seize the robot factories."

"Don't they realize the risks if there are no human officers to oversee the armies?"

Free shrugged. "Unless there's someone to voice that fear, not really." He hesitated until she encouraged him with a quick probe. "I think they're very happy to let the 'bots do the work. There's no appetite for military glory anymore, Grandma. Once again, you taught us well about pursuing death as a virtue."

"The robots are alive, Colonel," she said sharply.

"Not to most of the country."

"And they're slaughtering humans. Allahs are also humans. I can only imagine the civilian casualties…"

"They're finally getting what they deserve," Free replied stiffly. "Revenge does taste good."

"Not when the aftertaste kicks in."

"For now, it's sweet."

Grandma stared. "Is that how you feel, Colonel?"

He hesitated. "A little, but not enough to overlook the long-term ramifications. Though I understand the blood lust, Grandma."

She sighed. "So do I."

Free looked away.

Lenore reddened. "Say it."

"I don't have to, Grandma."

Her lips moved soundlessly. Finally, "I felt the death, the injury of every single soldier I ever sent into battle. I would never allow myself to be one of those politicians who blithely sent young people to war. I bled as much as you, Colonel Free. I grieved. I still grieve."

"That's not the same as being there with them," he whispered. "And it never will be."

Grandma flinched. "Then let the machines do the job. Another drone, another missile, all the same."

Free shrugged.

"Because you believe in the safeguards. Think again." Grandma detached a tiny dermatological cell from inside her forearm. The colonel trembled at the exposed pulsing fluids. "I'm as advanced as technologically possible, yet I nearly twisted off Mr. Flute's nose tonight. Mooshie, who is a few models down, is still far superior to you in every way, Colonel, and nearly destroyed a nightclub. Safeguards?"

"They can't be worse than we've done, Grandma."

She angrily shook her head. "That's not the choice. Why did you agree to help if you so clearly disagree?"

Free pawed at the floor for a moment. "Because I have faith in your judgment, Grandma."

Mooshie let out a long whistle. "Colonel Louie, that is so the wrong answer."

"No, it's not," Grandma said softly. "Sometimes the wrong answer's the only answer."

5

Kenuda thrust his fists so deeply into his hip sockets that he shrunk an inch. "That's it?"

Geoff, a short man with tufts of sparse white hair, smiled sympathetically. That was a variation of the first question a new resident asked nine times out of ten. The second was generally, "The apartment's a lot smaller than I thought," followed by, "Have anywhere else you can put me?"

"All your personal items are on the checklist, Mr. Kenuda." Geoff nodded at the stiff official form on the stack of four cartons in the tiny living room. "You're welcome to go through the boxes to make sure nothing was left out. Please bear in mind that once you sign, you can't then file a claim for missing possessions."

"I don't even remember what I wrote down." Elias threw up his hands. How could he with Hedda's wails ringing in his head?

"That's common enough. This is a difficult yet hopeful time."

"I'm missing the hopeful part."

"Common enough."

"The size of the apartment common enough?"

Geoff smiled faintly. "We have had to accommodate many siblings over the years, Mr. Kenuda, as you can imagine."

"I saw reports. I was a Third Cousin."

The fourth common question referred to their previous stature. Even the ones who most starkly failed hid behind the possibility of their own imaginary success rather than acknowledge they'd just been moved into a Disappointment Village.

Elias grumbled when Geoff didn't answer, glancing at the meager list of possessions he'd chosen from his apartment.

"Isn't it bad enough that I had strangers going into my apartment and through my things? I deserve some privacy."

"Of course, Mr. Kenuda. This isn't punishment."

"Why would I think that?" He sniffed. After the beagle-faced man resumed staring, Elias scribbled his signature.

"When I first arrived…"

"I don't want to hear your story."

Geoff could've predicted that response and left a leaflet on the top carton. "There's an orientation meeting this afternoon for all newcomers. That is mandatory, sir."

"I wouldn't dream of missing it."

Elias fumbled with the chain lock to make sure the man didn't burst in with yet another form. He tried squeezing into the narrow black plastic chair with scuffed arms, but his wide hips stuck for an infuriating moment. He went from room to room, again, this time freely growling and making improper comments about the world before plunging into a spiteful rage on the third tour of the one-bedroom apartment; if the rear room, guarded by a bleak fire escape, could be called a room.

All the water worked. Kenuda was slightly disappointed at losing something to chafe about. In an hour, he propped himself onto the floor, disgustedly kicking aside the worn cranberry flowered carpet. If Hedda were here, it'd all be different. Her sharp comments and lilting laugh would've transformed the furniture into thick, cushy comfort, the floors into newly polished wood, and the view beyond the rear window into a real tree filled with real birds.

But they'd deceived him. After throwing collective and individual tantrums barely quelled by a pair of understanding Blue Shirts, he and Hedda had been taken to the ground-floor resident's office at the East Bronx DV. There Hedda had been told, as if Elias were a mere shadow, that the Cousins understood and appreciated her love for Elias and what she had done for him.

It abruptly turned into a mini hearing, as if this charade hadn't been planned. The resident, a vile woman behind a card table named Cherise, planted beaming smiles all over her ugly face while praising Hedda for her great service, especially for one so young, as a teacher, loyal first wife and wasn't that tragic about your husband; Cherise glanced at Elias so he knew she wasn't referring to him. However, since Hedda had done nothing to suggest failure, indeed, Cherise's rubbery lips flapped, just the opposite, her life was a shining beacon to light the path of The Family, she could not be sent to a DV. Yes, she answered Elias's hiss of a question, their engagement was formally revoked.

That set off his shouts and more of Hedda's screams, which didn't stop until she was led away by two other vile women who didn't deserve names.

Just like that, one shot and it's over. He didn't know if Hedda would be allowed to visit and, if so, when. Kenuda had no way of communicating with her because no one would answer any of his damn questions. Instead, Cherise's rubbery lips flapped about filling out the list of precisely thirty personal items he wanted brought to his new apartment. Clothes, toiletries, pictures, anything that can be fit into a carton, the rubbery lips flapped cheerfully at his choices.

Elias tore open the cartons until he found the bottle of Benchley's Bourbon, snugly wrapped in two pairs of Temple University gyms shorts. He had no recollection of asking for these gym shorts but put one on anyway, along with a Temple Owls basketball t-shirt which stretched pleadingly across his wide chest. He wouldn't search for the rest of his previous life.

He sipped the bourbon, wishing he had some chips until remembering all new DV apartments were supplied with food. Well, look at this, he thought over his second drink, tugging aside the neatly wrapped Knoxville Cheddar and Montclair Cured Ham. Elias made a sandwich without bread, shoveling it down as if eager to punish his mouth.

A bombastic screech from next door threatened to send the plaster falling. Elias scowled as the screech climbed. He stomped barefoot to the adjacent apartment, banging on the door.

"Hey, turn that down."

The screeching edged just a little higher. Elias wished he'd put one of his souvenir Allah swords on the list.

"Shithead." Elias pounded both fists. "Turn it down."

The door inched open. Albert Cheng peered above the chain lock, wearing a ridiculous rainbow-hued sports coat and baggy pants as if about to stroll off to a bad party.

"You," the former Grandpa sneered.

"Likewise." What else could he say? He was just learning the cruelty of a Disappointment Village. He suspected there was more to come. "Turn down the sound, you prick."

"I can't." Cheng waved his fist. "It's the vidnews. Just went on like that."

Elias stormed past. The tiny apartment was his twin with the same stack of four cartons and ugly furniture except for the vidnews circling the living room wall. A presenter chattered on about a middle school science fair in Decatur, Illinois where the next generation of American geniuses would spring forth; the dull-eyed children looked like writing their names would be a monumental achievement.

"Well?" Kenuda whirled and shouted. "Do something."

"You can't," Albert shouted back. "That's how we designed it, so no one can turn it off."

"Brilliant idea."

"Maybe not." This wasn't Cheng's first sour review of his policies since moving in.

"So now the damn thing deafens me?"

"It's my apartment." Albert pointed at his name on the side of the cartons. "I'll go deaf before you."

Without explanation, the vidcast dropped to a normal tone. A dullard of a boy droned on about finding new techniques to plant oversized Brussels sprouts.

"Happy?"

"About what? Living next door to you?"

"Right back at you, asshole."

Elias wanted to kill Cheng but knew that wouldn't improve his situation, just his mood. "Keep the noise down, Grandfather. You're not the head of The Family anymore. You're just another piece of shit."

"Thanks, former Third Cousin. Now get the hell out of my apartment."

Kenuda fumed his way through unpacking, recklessly tossing his clothes into the built-in dresser in the bedroom next to the pull-down bed locked into the wall.

Beneath the retiled bathroom sink gleaming atop sturdy wood, Kenuda found every bathroom amenity from a toothbrush to a triple pack of Ted's Teeth Paste and an assortment of soaps, fragranced and not. As much as Grandma could, she'd insisted every effort be made to smooth the shock of reassignment to a DV.

Kenuda sat on the toilet bowl and imagined buying all this, the degradation, the bewilderment of a simple purchase mired in despair. It was shock, he realized, pure and simple. All the emotions scrambled because, for all the bravado in front of tens of millions of floating heads in a ballpark built to specs from 1923, he couldn't ignore what he'd done. Where he was. Maybe living here would've been better with Hedda. Or maybe worse, if they'd gotten on each other's nerves, if she'd begun blaming him as the engine for dragging them down when taking on The Family had originally been her idea.

That's why the surroundings were pleasantly modest, to allow DV residents to focus on the weight of guilt. Except Elias had no idea how to climb out.

That was the very first orientation item scribbled on the blackboard by Geoff who introduced himself as Mr. Tzadik, Geoff, Geoffrey, whatever name the dozen newcomers cared to use.

"How to get out of here is what you're all thinking," Geoff amiably said in the long gaming room in the basement. Darts, board games, and a Nok-Hockey set along with a well-used ping pong table captured most of the area along with the dozen folding chairs grouped in a full circle.

"Everyone knows why you're here, but you just don't believe it, do you?"

Geoff waited with a few taps of his chalk to make sure there were no wise guys who thought it was right to answer; Kenuda and Cheng might be particularly challenging, already arguing over noise. The crowd was similar to the usual orientations, mainly families with children because it was important that the kids embrace this move with a minimum amount of fear. A two-year-old on a mother's lap looked unsure whether crying was still acceptable.

Geoff flipped the chalk up and down a few times. He vigorously erased his first line and wrote in big block letters: *YOU ARE NOT BEING PUNISHED.*

"Does anyone believe that?"

Sad shakes answered.

"Of course not. To all of you, this is a nicer prison. You don't see a path out. You're afraid you'll be forever stigmatized by the disappointment you caused to yourself. Not to society. Not to your family. You controlled getting here and you control getting out. This is the first and last orientation and I'm always brief."

He wrote *A SECOND CHANCE.*

"The first Disappointment Village was opened in 2075." Geoff almost considered asking Cheng for insight into the creation of the system, but that would be counter-intuitive; maybe he'd speak to him later, out of curiosity. "Grandma and The Family appreciated the horrible dislocation of losing the War to the Allahs. It was a burden we all shared.

I was twenty-one when my family was sent here. My parents had owned a small amusement park in Washington Heights. Somehow they couldn't even make children laugh."

Geoffrey shrugged at the impossibility. "That was their third attempt and the last when a little girl was injured after the merry-go-round got stuck in a high speed. She flew off a red-and-yellow wooden pony just as it was rising." The crowd watched his floating left hand, imagining the girl soaring through the air.

"I never left." He shrugged again. "I spent so much time trying and failing to rebuild my parents's spirits that I felt I should succeed with others. Twenty-four years and counting. It is…"

He erased quickly and wrote once more in block letters: *UP TO YOU.*

"We don't have books for you to read. Would anyone really like to read the memoirs of say, Mwahi Yabi and how she left? Those inspirational accounts in the first years of the DVs like *Step High Without Feet* and *Hearts Need Watering, Too* were well-intentioned, but they made siblings feel inadequate."

"They were also bullshit," Cheng abruptly barked. "A lot was made up as we found out. Mwahi Yabi claimed it was always intended to be fictional, which is why Grandma discouraged this so-called literature, the demon child of journalism."

Albert stood and coldly met the stares of the residents. He rocked for a moment on the balls of his feet, making them uneasy.

"Thank you, Mr. Cheng, for your very knowledgeable insight," Geoff said, cutting off Albert. He had to treat Cheng the same or else the entire system would be bankrupt. "What I'd like to do in this orientation session is, most importantly, answer any questions. I'm sure you have a couple." He alone grinned.

Like the queasy expressions, the answers were always the same. How much money will we get on the Lifecard? *Thirty-five percent of your previous income.* My child was in third grade, now where does she go to school? *PS 53 is five blocks away.* There's a leak in the kitchen sink. *Joanna is the building plumber but can be impatient with rudeness.* Can we get more of our possessions? *Not until you leave the DV.* Where have they gone? *In storage.* Is someone living in our old home? *Possibly.* How soon before we get a bigger apartment? *That rarely happens.* What if I absolutely hate the carpet? *That should be your worst problem.* My child needs more sunlight. *We all do.* My skin broke out from the soap in the bathroom. *You can buy different soap.* My children won't eat that Daffy Raisin Cereal. *Buy different cereal.*

A burly man with sad eyes asked about finding a job.

"Either you return to your previous occupation or learn another skill. There's no right answer except for yours. The Disappointment Village is an exaggeration, if you will, of our individual responsibilities. For most, it'll be difficult if not impossible to repair yourself and return to your old job. It could be that you chose the wrong job in the first place. You listened to a parent, a partner, a friend. You were either too romantic or too level-headed. You transformed a hobby that should've remained just that."

Geoff's eyes narrowed slightly. "Or you can't handle pressure. You made the wrong choice in a partner. You raised your children improperly. You got sick. Disappointing ourselves has many variations. Failing to confront the truth of your situation is the most dangerous. Few of us can face that."

Everyone squirmed a bit. Geoff smiled faintly. He always used different language, but the impact was the same each time.

"But you're not alone. There are notices in the building lobby and here at the community center from siblings of all professions eager to share their experiences, train you, or just grab a cup of coffee and talk. Utilize that networking or not. Stay here or leave. That's entirely up to you. Some folks simply have had enough with striving to be their best. They want something safe. That isn't the point of the DV," he said, his voice hardening slightly. "If you're inclined to that, think about your children. Think if you want their respect. Think about helping them get out. And if you don't have children, think about that one person who means something to you. We all have someone."

Geoff hesitated. At every orientation he asked one person. The choice was a little too easy.

"Mr. Kenuda, have you considered what you'll do since you're barred from ever serving as a Cousin?"

The room turned as one toward Elias who flushed.

"I haven't had time."

"You've been here nearly a day, sir. Surely something must've popped into your head."

"I spent the time unpacking and asking a neighbor to quell his noise."

That stirred some good-natured laughter, which Geoff encouraged.

"Only that's not the point," snapped Cheng. "If you spend too much time unpacking and bothering neighbors over things out of their control, you'll end up wallowing in self-pity."

"I don't remember asking for your advice!" Elias shouted.

"The DV encourages helping each other," Cheng piped up. "But it's not some poor-me group therapy psychology crap which I abolished…"

"Okay, okay, okay." Geoff clapped his hands, sending chalk all over his shirt. "If Mr. Kenuda hasn't planned anything…"

"Who said I didn't? I just haven't sorted out how."

"It hasn't helped that your fiancé isn't joining you." Cheng smirked.

Kenuda scowled. "That's no one's business. Especially yours, Grandpa."

"You're right," Geoff jumped in. "But it's everyone's business to reinforce that we are no different. All of us, no matter what we've done. We are the same. The same fears, the same disappointments, the same desire to be productive members of The Family. I always felt that the DVs embodied Grandma's vision more than anything she'd ever done. Everyone is vulnerable, not ostracized, but extending helping hands, which are taken back into the society. When you leave, and hopefully you all will, you'll be better people."

Cheng muttered that he was good enough as is. Geoff shot him another look, grinning at a sudden decision. One of the benefits of having a job few wanted was freedom.

"This is the only time all you new residents will get together. But we like to ease the transition as much as possible. Those wonderful pillows only go so far. For the first month, we like to stay in touch. Don't worry. As charming as I am, I relinquish my role at this point. It's much more efficient to have one of you do so as Transitioners. Or, in this instance, two of you."

He winked at Cheng and Kenuda.

6

Hands on hips, Clary let her head slowly tilt to the left. The FB technician aligning the vid equipment assigned to Felice would not be happy. But the 'bot was not about to risk another tantrum. More doll heads would be snapped. Another dress torn. Umbrellas of purple hair bows would dangle like nooses from the metal lamps.

Clary's tilt of the head was to ease the pain and the anxiety. Which came first, she wasn't sure. Her bedroom still wasn't right; she'd spent half the night throwing up from the trans-organic treatments and, at sunrise, endured a scolding lecture from Felice about failing to incorporate today's talk.

They were not her words. That would change, too. She'd already won the argument for moving the event from Grandma's living room to here, Clary's room. Clary scowled. A stupid name. Little Clary's room. Little baby Clary's room. Clary's bedroom. No, too dirty. Clary's home. Clary's house. Like Grandma's house. Her eyes glinted.

"Is there anything else, Granddaughter?" Andrew Ban, the FB crew chief, waited. As they all do, for us to die, Clary thought. Two million years and they would still be holding wires, faintly smirking. Would they celebrate when we vanished? She wondered at the latest odd thought, the persistent strange notions jabbing like a throbbing stick out of a shadow.

Last night Clary dreamed of an orchestra such as the kind her father used to watch on the television. Musical notes throbbed until she jumped out of bed, clutching herself, unable to sleep anymore. She was exhausted but would not tell Felice or else the 'bot would silently nod, *oh yes, silly limited human.*

Except I am not anymore. Neither an "us" nor a "them." Just a "what."

Clary stamped her feet. "I want the walls orange."

"The talk is eighteen minutes away," Andrew explained as if that mattered.

"You are robots. You work quickly." Clary peered at a frowning FB in pale coveralls and a frayed baseball cap. "Are you asking for permission?"

The 'bot stared shrewdly. "Why would you think that?"

"Because I can see your eyes." Clary pointed at the blue pupils. These were the blue-eyed gang, she called them. There was the green-eyed gang on the lawn and the brown-eyed gangs of the Black Tops. It was not accidental. She would see about mixing up the models.

"You are thinking and wasting time." She whirled to Andrew. "What are you waiting for? I want orange walls. Get rid of all the purple. Orange, that is my decision."

Felice silently watched by the far wall beside the ancient grandfather clock which Grandma had brought from the White House; it had belonged to an American president named William Howard Taft. Clary fumed. How did Felice just appear? Clary would also learn that secret.

"What is the issue, Granddaughter?" Felice's lips barely moved.

"The issue, Felice, is that I do not like purple. It depresses me. It makes me want to scream." She screamed. "I prefer orange."

"And you decided this now?"

"I am a twelve-year-old child. I have sudden emotional moments."

Felice nearly laughed. "That would prove complicating. The purple has emotional continuity as Grandma's colors. You are her granddaughter."

Clary mockingly puffed out her lips. "No, I was Cheng's granddaughter."

Felice arched an eyebrow. The child was quick. The treatments were 4.5 percent more effective than anticipated. "You belong to The Family. But you still cannot introduce a new color scheme. If you like, you can slowly weave orange into your clothes."

"For my first speech, I think there should be a completely new color that is Clary. Everyone will say that is not Grandma Lenore. That is not Grandpa Albert. That is Grand-daughter Clary whose new color is orange, her most favorite color."

"Since when?"

"Since forever from the time I was in my mother's belly, not that you would under-stand."

Clary winced, realizing she had gone too far. The FB crew looked sharply at Felice, whose lips pursed.

"That is a bigotry of our differences and a violation of the Harmony Laws. Should I recite them? 'All life is equally sacred, organic or inorganic, simple or complex.' Such hate-ful language is unacceptable, especially from the Granddaughter."

Clary finally muttered an apology, something she practiced often. "Forget the or-ange if it is too much for your friends."

Felice nodded imperceptibly at the crew. They whizzed around the room in what was the slightest blurring for human eyes. Furniture was repositioned as paint buckets appeared from behind a wall near the large, eight-paned window. Within three minutes, the room had been repainted.

Felice was pleased by the effect on Clary, her eyes wide and wondering. The girl caught herself and shrugged.

"It is nice. Two coats are best." She spitefully moved her desk.

Felice stared. "You are allowed to be nervous."

"I am not nervous." Clary smoothed down her blue dress and twisted an orange bow atop her thick dark hair, then draped an orange scarf around her neck. Self-consciously, she touched her right cheek where the Allah guards had burnt a cross in the orphanage; Papa Kenuda had taken her to Bronx-Lebanon Hospital to have it removed.

"I am glad to hear that." Felice clasped its hands by its stomach.

"But when you stare, you make me nervous."

"Would you prefer I leave so you can handle everything yourself?"

"Why not? I could handle anything."

Felice nodded and started to leave. "If you are that confident…"

"You would not really go." Clary glared. "Robots do not play games."

"No, but we play games when humans insist. We can either do this as we planned, as The Family wants and needs, or you can assume full responsibility. All alone, Clary. That is what you are most comfortable with."

"That got me here to America," she said savagely, tired of always being criticized. "I did that. No 'bots. No people. Just me and the dying sailor Diego, Zelda's boyfriend, on the boat. I did that."

"Your survival instincts did that. Like an animal, they are very strong, along with your audacity. But you still need others. I understand you do not care for others, inorganic and organic. I understand you are suspicious and bitter and angry. That is unfortunate. You must channel that into a higher level. Once it is harnessed, you will be a marvel. This is your opportunity so do not disappoint your country and embarrass yourself live in front of The Family and, I suspect, some of the world which will find a way to access this speech."

Clary's eyes narrowed. "I thought we were safely encrypted. Unless you are going to let some of the world see me."

Felice smiled faintly. "Are you sure you would not prefer General Havela to conduct the military briefing component of your talk?"

"Did Grandpa Cheng let a general speak? Did Grandma? I am the Granddaughter and I should be able to explain or else I look *stupido*. Now bring him in."

As if waiting in the air, a brown-eyed FB in a taut military uniform stood patiently by an unfolding holographic desk encircled by blank maps.

"I am General Havela. I am here to brief you on the military situation, Granddaughter."

"It is about time, General Havela, since in twelve minutes I am to speak to The Family."

"We wanted to provide you with the most updated information."

And to make sure the deadline concentrated the child's wayward mind, Felice thought as the maps glowed. Purple colors denoted North America. With another flick, South America turned purple.

"As you can see, the entire Western Hemisphere has now been cleansed of Islamic control. We have removed all the neutral regimes who were still supporting the Caliphate."

"Everyone is now our friend?" Clary asked slyly.

Felice was pleased. "Not everyone, Granddaughter. This is a process of evolution. That is why we have established secure and permanent bases throughout the region. We have found sufficiently sympathetic politicians whom we can trust to begin that process. The form of governments will be pyramidal for now, with selected leaders at the top, gradually recruiting similarly minded individuals to begin the task of rebuilding their nations."

"With our help," Clary said.

"Yes." Felice nodded, again pleased.

"Will they use the model of The Family?"

The 'bot shrugged its right shoulder. "They will be offered that option, but whether it fits into their national culture cannot be adequately predicted. The success of The Family may have been a purely American institution given the unusual circumstances and confluence of your cultural history, particularly the flagrant collapse of democratic capitalist imperialism. Once the pyramid of local governments is secure, they will develop organically."

Clary was a little confused, but too proud to ask.

Felice continued, "The pyramid is where the leaders will be, like The Family or any form of government. The hope is that power and knowledge flow down," her open palm generated a revolving pyramid, "into the wider base of the people so they, too, are leaders in their way. It has never happened on anything resembling a large scale because of the inherent greed of humans. Except here in The Family."

The girl took that in with a thoughtful frown. "What if they organically develop their own pyramid and we do not like it?"

Felice arched an eyebrow. "The old system of interference through military, political, and economic power and manipulation under the American Empire did not work. At this stage, it is essential that the continent be free of Islam to support the overall goals of military victory. As long as these nations do not revert to an alliance with the Caliphate, they will be free to pursue their individual forms of rule. We will have to coexist."

Havela resumed the briefing. Tiny holographic soldiers surrounded by tanks lifted over each of the South American nations, representing the allocation of the 352,000 'bot soldiers and equipment continent-wide. It made Clary a little dizzy, but she pretended to pay attention.

Felice sensed that. "This is nothing for you to worry about, Clary. This is merely background."

"But it must still sit in my head." Clary impatiently waved her off. "Come, what is next?"

Havela and Felice exchanged brief looks.

"What you are seeing now, from that foundation"—Havela brought in a rainbow-like array of colors—"is the current state of the conflict between the Grand Mufti, who is the leader of—"

"He killed my parents. I know who he is," Clary said coldly, her eyes sweeping the former Europe.

Havela tipped its head and continued as if she hadn't interrupted, "—the Islamic Empire, and the rebellion of his son Abdullah. The red lights indicate Caliphate control. Green is Abdullah's armies."

He paused to darken the red, which pulsed from Greenland through England, across Europe, stopping at the eastern edge of the Caliphate of Magyar, northeast into Russia, before ending at the lip of China, indicated by a neutral light blue.

Clary bounced on her toes. "Where is the old Spain?"

Havela brought up the Caliphate of North Africa, intersected with chunks of green.

"Closer. I want to see Barcelona."

Havela magnified the city.

"What is the color? Let me see," Clary's voice rose shrilly.

Barcelona turned green.

"Find the al-Hussein orphanage. It is on the Avenida de Ramos, by the beach. Show me."

"We have no satellites. They were all shot down during the war or forcibly destroyed by the terms of The Surrender."

Felice edged closer to the child. "We can assume that if the city is in Abdullah's hands, so is the orphanage."

"Then the orphans are safe?"

"I believe we can assume that." Felice patted Clary's arm, a rare indulgence of the child's desperate need for affection.

"Do you think they have cut off the Allah guards's penises? The *putas* who raped us?" The girl's eyes raged in a quick boil, suddenly calm. "As soon as you find out, tell me, General."

Clary's eyes reluctantly left Spain as Havela introduced the original Arab Caliphate, now a patchwork of red and green. Only Turkey remained solidly red, the rest of the countries, as Havela explained, had continuously shifting battlegrounds and fluid borders.

"Jerusalem is back in the control of Abdullah, while Cairo has again fallen to the Mufti. We have reports of a possible nuclear explosion inside Iran, but that seems to be an accident since Abdullah has no missile delivery system and has forsworn the use of anything resembling terrorism in the name of his New Islam."

"For your purposes today, Clary, we will now focus on 'Operation Recovery,'" Felice said.

"Two hours ago," Havela gestured up holographic images of ships disembarking soldiers while jets roared overhead. "The Fifth and Third Army Groups landed in Morocco in North Africa. Ultimately 186,000 soldiers will go ashore…"

"Robots?" she asked.

"Of course. All the soldiers are inorganic life-forms."

"Clary, that is the point of your speech," Felice said with concern.

The girl rudely bulged her eyes, muttering.

"Instead of attacking mainland Europe, we are proceeding directly into the heart of the Caliphate. Our plans are to move across North Africa, seize Egypt, and ultimately link up with Abdullah in Palestine, if he will be responsive to a truce."

"That is not for you to repeat, Clary," Felice said firmly.

"For my background. I understand."

Felice paused. Either she had to trust her judgment in the child or not. The predictive variables were still fluid in the human's current biological state. "We have not yet established contact with Abdullah. If we publicize that objective, it will provide…"

"Propaganda for the Grand Mufti. Yes. That would be dumb." Clary flashed a smug smile. "I do not like the name of 'Operation Recovery.'"

Havela frowned. "We are recovering territory."

"It says nothing. If you are sick, you recover. It must be more dramatic." Clary twirled her orange hair bow. "Operation Revenge. That is best. We strike at the Allahs and do to them what they did to us." Her face twisted over the now dormant Caliphate of Spain. "Revenge. Yes, I like revenge."

Felice processed guarded disappointment. She is only twelve and damaged. She switched into momentary parental mode, employing a soothing voice.

"How is that different from what Albert Cheng wanted? He too, sought vengeance for the loss of the war. He, too, appealed to the baser instincts. Hatred. Fear. Is that what you want to do, Clary? I understand why you feel that way. The Allahs beheaded your parents. You were abused in the orphanage." Clary stiffened. "Shouldn't you be more than your emotions? You are the Granddaughter, after all."

Clary took that in with a sneer. "Then the speech should be about more than robot soldiers. It should be more than killing. What are we recovering? Allah sand?" Her face hardened. "I want to use Abdullah's videos of the orphans."

The 'bot shook its head. "That would be foolish."

"Foolish?" Clary exploded. "First you say Clary is bloodthirsty, then you say I am foolish to show the children who we must rescue. The war should be about the children all over the world. Yes. That I like. Children, not robot soldiers."

"We would feed into the Mufti's propaganda portraying his son as a traitor and tool of the West by using the videos of the children he rescued."

"Well screw the Grand Mufti," Clary said with such harsh innocence that the robots almost laughed. "The Allahs are also parents, correct? I had a friend Azhar who was a parent. He loved his children. Maybe those Allahs will see the faces of the children and feel something. Maybe they feel bad for what they have done. Maybe they will think enough children have suffered. I want the Crusader parents to also see that the children are no different from theirs. I know you think this is all about Clary the human child feeling too much. Crazy Clary. Angry Clary. No."

She tapped her temple. "It is from here."

"You make an important point, Clary."

"Do not say that in your Mommy voice. Yes, I know you have different tones." Clary smirked triumphantly. "I like my idea."

"So do I." Felice sharpened her voice so much Clary flinched. "But we will use it later when we unveil the new life-form adoption laws. Today, you must tell the country that FBs are fighting so there is no alarm over the loss of human life. That is what The Family will most worry about. That is the key message."

"I will. And so are the videos of the children."

Their eyes met. Felice nodded tightly. "We will find an appropriate one."

"I want lots. I want them dancing around…"

"One." Felice pointed a thin finger. "I will amend your speech."

"I know what to say," Clary insisted.

"Not yet, Granddaughter. Not quite yet."

At 10:20, Pita, Xang, and Marisol, Clary's Gang as they were becoming known, bounded in, changing the mood like putting on a happy album. The incredibly boisterous kids slowly settled onto the olive couch. Felice stood like another grandfather clock in the corner.

A hologram of the *Wake Up, My Darlings* presenter Donovan Talbi sat in a chair to Clary's right.

"Good morning and welcome back to *Wake Up, My Darlings*. Today, we have a very important word from Granddaughter Clary Santiago."

"Hello, Donovan and hello, Family. Welcome to Clary's house. As you can see, we have just repainted one of my rooms. What do you think?"

Donovan had been warned that Clary was apt to roam from the script.

"It's lovely. What made you choose that color?"

"Orange was the color of the evening sun in Barcelona, my original home. I prefer the way it burns with promise."

"Speaking of promise, you have something you'd like to share with The Family."

"Very much so." Clary pressed the sweat onto the side of her dress. Suddenly she forgot everything. She didn't know how to regain her thoughts, her memory. Moisture dripped down her upper lip. Clary pressed her eyes shut. Children squealed all around her. Her Gang was still on the couch, staring in surprise as the video of the orphans liberated in the first wave of Abdullah's victories skipped around the bright orange bedroom.

Like adult children, the orphans pranced in oversized Arab Army helmets, pretended to drive a military jeep, kicked a football at a donkey and, faces smeared with ice cream, ran in a circle, around and around holding hands and singing in several different languages.

Clary nodded gratefully at Felice.

"Today we have invaded North Africa with almost two hundred thousand of our brave robot soldiers to save millions of human children. From today forward, humans will no longer be killed fighting for America. All the soldiers will be robots. Someday, maybe no life-forms, humans or robots, will die in these senseless wars. But first we must win. We must crush the Allahs who hate us and become friends with the Allahs who want peace. That is what Grandma wanted. We are afraid of peace because it is much harder than war. There are so many choices. I know you all must be afraid of robot soldiers. What happens if they want to kill the humans? That is how all wars start. We kill before we are killed. It is time to stop.

"So I say to you Grand Mufti, whose soldiers chopped off the heads of my parents in a gymnasium while I was forced to watch, do you want peace? Let me know. I say to you Abdullah bin-Mohammad, the son of the Mufti. You fight in the name of a new Islam. Let's see. End the war against the Crusaders. And I say to all the neutral countries like China and India. How can you be neutral with evil? Join us. There are no more neutral countries. If you are for the children, you are a friend. If you are not, you are an enemy. And you do not want to be the enemy of The Granddaughter."

For the second time that morning, Felice was surprised. The child's treatments would have to be accelerated.

• • • •

A WEEK INTO flight and Annette expected to be reeking from crawling through the sewers of London, scampering atop the splintered roadside hovels and forested caves leading south to the English Channel. Her hair would be crawling with lice and, by the time she would've made it aboard the hovercraft, her precious curls would've been chopped off and used to stuff the pillow of some Catholic orphan or something.

Her face would be blotchy, pimply, or worse, riddled with blackheads. Her twisted fingers, mangled from desperate fights, would clutch her stomach infested with spoiled food plucked out of garbage cans in alleyway bedrooms. Her white nun's garment would be frayed from the gross clutches of avaricious men beneath straw and goat shit in the back of a rickety truck.

Instead, the Catholic Rat Line was pretty pleasant. All this fuss about being a fugitive was overdone. Once she and Father Dempsey had slipped out of London, they hadn't missed a meal. The accommodations were acceptable and correct with two beds, sometimes cots, well apart. A bored electrician in East London had provided shelter and lamb one night, while a gregarious bus driver in Bristol got them loaded on wondrous brown beer. In Dorset, they slept in the attic of an old woman pushing one hundred who told Annette all her sins, Father forgive her, and in Devon, a pasty hairdresser shaped like a beach ball argued theology; Dempsey fell asleep first.

From Sister Gerri D'Antonini she'd become Sister Mary Twakdana and then, entering France, plain old Devorah L. Gentry accompanied by the former Father John Dempsey, now Mr. Frederic Machet, sipping chardonnay and studying the painting of a hooked Jew nose about two feet long. Annette busied herself across the crowded Galerie Pastutin over an assortment of cheeses offered by a dimply and flirtatious young waiter.

"Sorry, they're so good," Annette mumbled, wondering how much weight she'd gained.

"Madame, no rush. Eat the entire tray." The waiter tipped his head forward slightly. "There is more."

She blushed. Grabbing a couple more addictive wheat crackers, Annette acknowledged Dempsey's look to act her respectable part and wandered before another painting. A safe brimming with gold and jewels was guarded by two sinister-looking Hebrews sniffing money up their flared nostrils, watched by a helpless Crusader woman, thin dress ripped down to her navel.

"What do you think?" The gallery owner Marcel Pastutin hovered by her right elbow. Annette felt instantly unclean.

Though she'd tried, Annette's knowledge of art was limited to memorizing names of painters. She didn't even get Barbara Sue Bloom's murals, and they were designed for children aged two and up, much less this crap. She only knew that there were all sorts of layered intimations and messaging designed to make her and everyone below the level of elite feel stupid, which was like most of the human race. She also knew not to say too much and give away that she was American.

Annette shrugged enigmatically.

Pastutin grunted understanding. "Yes, isn't it? Treacherous people the Hebrews. The exhibit of Jewish degeneracy has always been our most popular. Are you familiar with Minsione's work?"

Annette nodded knowingly. Pastutin grunted again.

"If I may, this is a bit heavy-handed, but what else with such a subject? Come." He took her by the hand toward a lumpy sculpture with three arms and a pointed head. "This is, of course, a Genette."

She threw up her hands in speechless wonderment.

"He went mad after creating this."

"No wonder."

"Apparently, he would spend endless hours staring at the face."

"There is none." She pointed out, eye-begging Dempsey to rescue her.

"There once was. It was a visage of such greed and evil that Genette came to believe he had opened the door to Hell. His notes which are, tragically, often incoherent, portray a terrifying vision of an artist who fears he has unleashed unspeakable evil. It is ironic that in his effort to capture the eternal calumny of the Jew, the Jew claimed him."

"There you go," Annette said simply.

Before Pastutin could ask for an elaboration of such profundity, Dempsey finally ambled over with a smug look.

"I have read his notes," Dempsey said softly. "They bespeak wisdom."

Pastutin's eyes narrowed. "Of the ages?"

"The times." The priest's voice dipped to finish the password. Dempsey followed the gallery owner's quick glance toward the kitchen entrance.

"I suggest the Pronte in the corner. Andrea, my darling." Pastutin embraced a heavy-set woman.

Dempsey waited two beats before guiding Annette by the elbow past several more graphic paintings of greed and carnality grouped under the heading of *The Eternal Yid.* The priest asked a waiter for directions to the bathrooms and then took the opposite way down the corridor and through the swinging door.

He was about to head toward the exit sign which led out back when loud shouts cut off a woman's scream. The dimply waiter rushed in, flinging aside the tray.

"You must hide." The young man shoved them inside a cramped, walk-in refrigerator. "Do not come out."

The door closed. Annette and Dempsey were so taken aback all they could do was sit, wheels of cheese serving as armrests. The priest pressed his finger to his lips as if she were stupid enough to talk. They heard nothing but their own slowly freezing breath. Dempsey showed disbelief when Annette nibbled on cheese after an hour; he finally broke down because eating kept them warm. Then that didn't work.

Annette shook him off when he tried stopping her from opening the door, but he was too cold to put up much of a fight and she was too cold to care. When they crawled out, the kitchen was quiet and empty. Annette divvied up a couple sharp knives. Their frozen fingers barely folded over the handles. The priest dropped his knife, apologizing with a sad look at the clatter. They closed their eyes as if that would silence the brief sound, but there was no response beyond the kitchen door.

Annette led them down the corridor and into the main gallery. All the paintings were slashed. The Genette sculpture lay in pieces. A few puddles of blood dotted the thick, white carpet. They were alone.

Allahs? She mouthed.

Dempsey shrugged, then nodded. "What else other than a very aggrieved art critic?" He chuckled, unnerving Annette; the priest rarely smiled.

"Apologies," he whispered.

He jerked his head toward the kitchen. But Annette ignored him, bending over a crumpled BBC publicity photo of the cohost of *American Crusaders*. Annette handed Dempsey her picture. He flinched. They remained quiet until they casually strolled down Rue de Montparte.

Annette fixed her hair in the window of a shoe store. It looked like her little shop in Riverdale. All she ever wanted was to love Puppy and sell shoes, have a baby. Never wear khaki shorts. Now look.

"It's Omar," she finally said.

After spending twenty-four hours a day together, they had quickly picked up each other's strands of words and thoughts. "I doubt he'd follow us here. The Holy Warriors are very regimented and territorial. Most likely, the photo was sent ahead."

Neither believed that. Along their escape route, they'd learned Omar Mustafa had tortured the nuns at the Blessed Brides convent.

Annette relinquished her spot near the window and slipped her arm around Dempsey's waist as they crossed the street. An Allah patrol approached with menacing nonchalance.

She tipped her head onto his shoulder. "I figure that gallery was our only contact."

Dempsey nodded and kissed the top of her hair, playing the role of soothing lover. What better innocent cover in Paris?

7

Zelda shrank near the cranberry punch bowl in the cramped, seedy lobby of the former movie theater on Tremont Avenue, hoping no one would recognize her as the writer. The audience had only occasionally laughed and that was when Bruno the Bat's hairbrush kept falling. There was a lot of tongue clucking and a great deal of horrified children crying; the death of Nathaniel the Owl was particularly shocking.

Only a handful of the audience remained, and that was to scoop up a homemade peanut butter cookie so the night wouldn't be a total loss. They hurried past Beth's dismayed stare. If she were a child, she'd have howled. You can't hang stuffed owls on stage. She knew little about theater, but that was just plain wrong.

Still, Beth smiled reassuringly across the room; Zelda wasn't buying any of that and shoveled down another handful of cookies. A thick hand like an oven mitt clamped onto her left shoulder, spinning Zelda around and causing crumbs to drop onto the stained wooden floor.

"You impressed me, Zelda Jones, and I am not often impressed," bellowed Joan Minh, whose jovial nature fired off regular rounds of cannon-like laughs which had always annoyed Zelda. Especially tonight when her play would cause children and adults to sleep with the lights on.

"That so?" Zelda tilted her head. "You might be alone in that opinion, Joan."

Joan shot a laugh out of her wide mouth; Zelda almost ducked.

"I have always loved your honesty, Zelda. Not in a personal way. I don't think we are really friends. I irritate you. Oh, that's okay." Joan comforted her with a meaty slap. "Why should we be friends? Other than our love for theater, what do we have in common?"

Zelda shrugged as the longest conversation they'd ever had continued.

"You have avoided me because you are afraid, afraid that I might advance your art. That might be a serious compromise of your integrity and, if I recall your bio, you have moved around enough to indicate you do not suffer such compromises easily. Good for you."

Off a sour glance around the lobby where the sturdiest table wobbled beneath a plate of cookies, Joan slapped Zelda on the other shoulder to correct the chiropractic discord.

"Then you liked the play?" Zelda figured she'd get this out of the way.

Another missile of pure joviality bounced off the peeling wallpaper.

"Certainly not. It was needlessly dreary. Dreary, dear. The themes were rock-like in their heavy-handedness. The characters, well, is depressed the right word? Maudlin, dear. In short, this was a very difficult evening to sit through. At several points I contemplated suicide," she said without a smile.

"At least I touched you. May I introduce my producer, Beth Rivera."

"Ah, shall I repeat my feelings, Beth?"

"No thanks, I heard everything across the lobby."

Joan's meaty paws clutched both their upper arms.

"This is why the avarice of criticism is banished, and good riddance. Could you imagine your reaction if I had appeared on *Wake Up, My Darlings* with a review of that nature? Yet once, such sickening displays of elitist influencing and divisiveness were encouraged." Joan screwed up her squat nose at the thought. "Which you, of course, know."

"Being in the theater and all," Zelda dryly said, hoping the porter would start turning off the lights. "But you're entitled to your individual Joan-only opinion, for which I thank you, as I thank you for coming tonight and somehow living through the experience."

"Please, please, please, stop the drizzle." Joan chuckled, befriending Beth with a big hug. "All that said, you have an unusual, if I might, a hard-to-define gift. Your stuffed animals are delightful. They brim with life. More so than many actors I have worked with. We need more of your sort of creativity. Look at tonight's attendance. I counted twelve people."

"For a cold night with snow, that's not bad," Beth said defensively.

"Please, no more drizzle. That's normal, pathetically so. If birds had chirped and the sun blazed, you would have had fourteen. Theater has barely hung on. Most states have no more than one or two stages. The entire link was severed when it became purely pro-pagandized back in the '40s along with the rest of entertainment and we frankly never recovered. That artists like you persist is marvelous and heartening. I'm here to encourage you." She stopped with a flourish. "And to provide what I suspect you will find an intriguing opportunity."

"Which is?" Zelda and Beth said together, triggering another explosion of laughter.

"The two of you are so sweetly in love," Joan said as they blushed. "And that you can work together in a play like this and keep smiling." The heavy-set woman clasped her hands in sheer wonder. "Fabulous. What more could Grandma have asked than love and work in one stream. But enough of my own drizzle. You are aware of my Gun Hill Road theater company?"

"Yes. You've rejected several of my plays," Zelda said.

"Reject is such a strong word, Zelda. They were not suitable. As this evening's play is not suitable for the audience you are seeking. If there is one. But do not despair. I mentioned an intriguing opportunity."

Beth and Zelda wearily nodded.

"Well then." Joan paused as if she just entered, stage left. "Fourth Cousin Masara Oh has granted my proposal to transform a former Broadway house back into theatrical entertainment."

"I thought they were hospitals and schools," Beth said.

"They have been since the chemical attack in Manhattan. But Radio City Musical Hall finally reopened and is finding its feet with the Rockettes. I have been pushing for years, many years, that a way to signal Manhattan's return would be reviving theater on Broadway. Oh, to hear hundreds laughing or, even better, silent in rapture." Her eyes gleamed. "I would like you to develop a play, Zelda. You have some thematic leeway within the guidelines of the Anti-Parasite Laws pertaining to entertainment. As a producer, Beth, I assume you are familiar with them."

Beth lied with a nod.

"Good. Then get writing, Zelda. Once you have fleshed something out, we will go to the Lyceum Theater. It is the oldest left after the Hudson and New Amsterdam theaters were torn down. Dates to 1903. It is an original, so your art can remain pure. Pure, my friends." Joan nearly knocked them over with her outstretched hands.

Beth studied Zelda over the steam of mango tea at the rear of Fred and Ginger's Diner off Fordham Road. Even past eleven, waitresses rushed by on black-and-white tiles, dropping heaping platters into the patched leather booths. Their perky server with the beehive hairdo dutifully intoned the late-night specials. Beth satisfied the bright-eyed waitress by ordering two stacks of buttermilk pancakes though neither of them had an appetite.

Beth's lightly freckled yellow hand skipped over the mini jukebox on the table. John Fogarty's rasp filled the booth before Zelda lowered it with a grumble.

"It wasn't a complete disaster." Beth tried for sincerity.

"Usually an artist enjoys the sound of breathing from the audience. Snores don't count." She scowled at Beth's eye roll. "Tonight was a stinkfest. They hated it."

"Maybe. That's what happens, isn't it? Free choice. Solitary opinion. Bringing your view into the theater. All artists put themselves on the line."

"You actually read all those books you borrowed?"

"I take it seriously, being your producer," Beth said, nostrils flaring.

She'd nearly sewn her forefinger into Mrs. Paolercio's blouse, her eyes blurry from staying up late reading memoirs of some of the last great director-writers like Nyli Hirohito, Puna Houmani, and Gabriela Ramirez. Hirohito's *Painful Love, Right?* had famously been the last ever play on Broadway, running at the Ambassador Theater the night of the Allah chemical attack in 2070. Seven hundred people died in the theater, many simply trampled trying to exit from perceived death into certain death on the streets of Manhattan.

"I'm sorry. I'm a grump, I'm wallowing in self-pity and my hair's getting gray," Zelda admitted, staring glumly at the stack of pancakes.

"That's nature."

"Yeah, in a country where we have so-called food and holographic parks." Zelda managed a grin, fussing briefly with her hair. "I could dye it. Okay, it's not against the law," she said over Beth's mocking gasp. "Just frowned upon. If this were the '60s, my hair dye would be quite fashionable. Zelda Jones, the purple-haired wonder of the stage."

During the many distractions of the terrifying defeats of the War, The Family had encouraged all sorts of bold personal statements. The restoration of the 1920s and '30s nightclubs birthed elegant gowns and all manner of strange hairdos and colors. Once the War ended, solemnity triumphed; it was bad form to walk around with greenish-blue braids when America had lost four million children.

Beth hummed along to the music, picking at her food. "Did I screw up as a producer? I realize this was my first time, but I'm willing to take full responsibility for why things didn't go right."

"Not having a stage manager didn't help what with Puppy off on his fabulous baseball tour and then Dale missing."

"I don't know what happened to her," Beth said with irritation.

"I'm the writer and director and the voices. I should've been able to find my own props."

"Because you're the writer, director, and voices, you couldn't be expected to. I should've done it."

"It would've been worse," Zelda said wryly. "Besides, I don't think anyone was paying much attention."

"But Joan still wants you. I think that shows how your talents burst through." Beth frowned at Zelda's shrug. "You're going to do it, aren't you?"

"I don't know. Do I want to bomb at an iconic theater or just keep my failures to a select few?"

"I'm glad you're not wallowing in self-pity." Beth snorted. "Then what is it? Fear?"

"No," Zelda said too quickly.

"Can't you just admit when you're afraid?"

"No," Zelda said, again quickly, allowing herself a smile in the shape of a wince. "The Lyceum Theater? Me? Something doesn't add up. Maybe she just wants to sleep with me."

"Then I'll have to kill her. I can only compete with so many people at a time." Beth squeezed her hand. "I know you were being semi-sarcastic, so let me finish. You're bored, Zelda. You're still doing the same plays you did when you were young. They're great, but you've got to move on to something different while maintaining your core views."

Zelda stared. This woman knew her too well. Talk about being frightened. "You're right. I've screwed up in so many other ways that I hold onto my plays like the security of a baby blanket."

"And you haven't screwed up. You're not the old Zelda, the walking train wreck bouncing from girl to girl and boy to boy, from job to job, living inside a bag of chips and a six-pack of beer. You've got a child, a husband, and a best friend who loves you. And I don't mean Puppy."

Zelda wiped a stream of maple syrup off Beth's chin. Beth desperately wanted to lick it off her hand. Their eyes met.

"I like my stuffed animals. They let me hide." As Beth sighed… "Okay, I got it. Enough hiding."

• • • •

MATTHEW BUSIED ITSELF neatly arranging the avalanche of Danish, cheese, and a new SC fruit called blue apples around the coffee table, draped with a paisley tablecloth.

"Liquids are upon the side table." The 'bot presented the soda pop, water, coffee, and three kinds of tea. "Is there anything else before I join you?"

Puppy jumped on Sahidi and Ian Schrage's sharp looks like a hanging curve, waist high.

"Along with you, I'm very proud to introduce Matthew, our fourth and final member of the Commissioner's team who has added the title of Executive Assistant to his Administrative Specialist duties."

Ian stared coldly as the 'bot grouped the coasters in a circle. Matthew's eyes revolved in kind.

Puppy sighed. "Following the hire of Ian Schrage as Marketing Director and Sahidi Douglas as Director of Baseball Operations."

"Nice outfit." Schrage sneered at Matthew's three-piece pinstriped suit, a Goldfarb chain watch peeking out of a vest pocket.

The 'bot puffed up. "Thank you. Zimbalist Fine Fashions at 2010 Sherman Avenue."

"I'll rush over on my lunch hour."

"Tell Edward I sent you. I believe they have your size."

As the dwarf bolted off the couch, Puppy jumped in. "Matthew will help with technical issues which I'll get to in a moment."

"Technical issues. Big surprise," Ian grumbled.

"Was that a reference to my digitalized enhancements?"

Ian gasped in mock horror. "Certainly not. That's like mentioning a human urinating and other normal functions."

"Normal requires various new definitions."

"Toast is ready, dear."

"Commissioner Puppy, perhaps I should arrange a Life-form Harmony training session." Matthew's eyebrows nearly intersected.

"There's no need for that."

"Actually, we have to. Every business must according to the new law," Sahidi said, deeply bored. So far, Puppy made Ty and Mickey look like visionary buzz saws. She'd be running the place soon.

"Correct. There has been a veritable spate of anti-inorganic life-form prejudice since the Granddaughter's speech announcing the brave sacrifice of our soldiers."

Ian snickered. "Who programmed you to use phrases like 'veritable spate'?" The metal holes that passed for a robot's nostrils flared.

"Commissioner Puppy! Paragraph four of the Harmony Laws clearly says—"

"Just schedule the damn session."

"Would two days hence work for everyone?" Matthew turned to Ian with a bright gleam in its eyes. "That would make it Thursday, which comes after Wednesday and prior to Friday."

"And that's not a dig at human intelligence?" Schrage bounded onto the chair, evoking a gasp from Matthew at the potential shoe stains.

Puppy clapped his hands for order. "Let's everyone settle down." He waited for a round of grudging nods. "Is anyone clamoring to eat, or can we get down to business?"

"We await your words, Commissioner Puppy," Matthew grandly said.

Puppy bowed to impatient stares. "By now you've all read Sahidi's terrific analysis. Thanks again for waiving the confidentiality, Sahidi."

"It was kind of late since you'd already sent it around," she said with obvious reproach.

"My fault." Puppy waved off Matthew's attempt to take the blame. "As a good friend of mine, Zelda Jones, whose play *Darlings are Dear* is running at the East Tremont Theater by the way, reminded me, 'Puppy, you've never worked in an office.' Other than Matthew, I don't think any of us have."

Sahidi and Ian took turns peevishly explaining their backgrounds which mainly included working in offices.

"Apologies again." No one joined him in his self-deprecating laugh. "Which shows how little I know about offices. Or business. But I know about baseball, as do all of you. Everyone brings talents to the plate. Ian understands promotion and of course worked for Grandma. Sahidi…"

"That's it?" Ian folded his short arms. "Eighteen years of presenting her greatness to The Family, the woman who saved America, in one little sentence? Understands, worked for. The way you put it, I could be a mechanical donkey on some farm in Kansas."

Matthew tittered about the resemblance. Ian moved his chair to the corner so he'd have more room to sulk.

Puppy apologized again, praising Ian as a once-in-a-lifetime genius. "Sahidi is a terrific radcaster for the wonderful *Game of the Week*." He raised his voice over Ian's snarling repeat of *terrific* and *wonderful*. "Matthew has the technical skills, it's worked in the Commissioner's office since its inception and has comprehensive and incredible knowledge of baseball history, trivia, rules. Name it and he knows it."

"I'm looking forward to learning at your respective feet," Ian growled.

"As we look forward to learning from you, Ian. Your adverts are amazing. That Parker's Pancake House spot with the bickering family of syrups went beyond brilliant. It's just the sort of insight we need here." Sahidi tapped her forefinger against her forehead, generating a muted smile. She patted the empty chair next to her. Schrage slowly returned with just enough resentment.

Puppy shook his head. "Now that we've all sucked up to each other." Finally, a collective grin. "Baseball's heading for the shitter. Attendance is falling. The quality of play is poor. Fans are freezing. It was a mistake to begin the season in January. It was a mistake to rush teams into uniforms. The retro stadiums are great, but they're disconnected museum pieces. I've spent the past two weeks holographically and, where possible, physically visiting every ballpark."

"All thirty. Commissioner Puppy saw a game in each town," Matthew proudly said. "To encourage the experience, I replicated the local cuisines sold inside and outside the stadiums. Through his astonishing working trip, he met with team management, players, fans, and the various Friends of groups."

As Commissioner, Puppy had to assume the role of cheerleader. Sympathetic, supportive. Like when the rash of injuries to the entire starting rotation of the St. Louis Cardinals didn't mean they weren't warming up properly or throwing too many pitches or throwing the wrong pitches or using the wrong mechanics. Injuries were part of the game, he'd explained.

In Houston, Puppy encountered a turf war between competing concessionaires billing themselves as the Best Bob B's Smothered Pork Chops vs. the Best Bob BB's Smothered Pork Chops. There was, he was told by the general manager of the Astros, evidence of some sabotaging of barbecue sauce. At Comiskey Park, he was caught between the Friends of Nellie Fox, the great second baseman from the mid-twentieth century, and the Friends of Jacqueline Atsa, the acrobatic third baseman of the mid-twenty-first century, each demanding that the murals of their respective favorites be enlarged behind the first and third-base stands.

Things were little better once he watched some games, Puppy sourly told the staff. Sitting in the mezzanine at Crosley Field, Puppy's face hurt from the frozen approval of batters swinging at balls bouncing two feet in front of home plate to simple rundown plays being massacred to helpless outfielders slogging through wet grass in pursuit of easy fly balls.

What the hell had Ty and Mickey done? He'd fumed, his mood darkening in Phoenix where the Arizona Diamondbacks and New York Mets slugged for five hours to a 23-20 contest; he couldn't remember who won and largely didn't care.

Sahidi was right, he'd realized over a bottle of Bri's Pickled Beer in San Diego. Players had been hired because they said they could play, and the game needed players who could play. What troubled him most was the reaction of the fans. Even in Southern California, which had slowly resumed normalcy after the nuclear attack on Los Angeles, the fan diffidence was distressing.

Puppy remembered opening day of 2098 at Amazon Stadium when fifteen or so fans showed up, mainly to sleep or have sex. At Dodger Stadium, a listless crowd of eleven thousand grew steadily moribund over a surprisingly well-pitched, 2-1 win by Los Angeles. They'd murmured boos over the finely turned double plays. Outside, a few spectators had suggested they do away with gloves to increase the offense. Who wanted to see someone settle under a foul pop fly? The fans didn't understand a low-scoring game could be exciting.

Pockets of promise like Fenway Park and Wrigley Field, Tiger Stadium, provided as much hope as despair at how few true fans there were. In Boston, the head of the Foundation to Restore the Citgo Sign insisted that once the iconic billboard returned, crowds would increase. Puppy was skeptical.

There was nothing about how to throw a curve or hold the bat or steal. By making baseball larger than life with the virtual historical exhibits and deafening HG entertainment between innings, they'd neglected the smaller attributes which had once made baseball larger than life.

Baseball required nuance and mystique. Right now there was little of either, along with sentiment, between the bases or in the country.

The room was glumly still. Ian spoke first.

"Are you so sure it's not the game? It could just be a charming interlude in our national history which should be left in our past. Grandma never much liked baseball. Even Cheng had his own bitterness, being discriminated against when he first emigrated."

"Then why did you accept the position?" Matthew asked snidely.

Surprisingly, Ian softened. "Out of loyalty to Puppy, whom I respect, which is also part of my loyalty and love for Grandma. Plus, I have nothing else that interests me. I was hauled up before a Siblings Committee for failing to find a job. They suggested becoming a cook because I listed among my many skills promoting food." As Matthew tittered, he cracked, "Perhaps I could use your forehead for a frying pan."

"Commissioner Puppy!" The 'bot shouted.

Schrage grinned mischievously. "Sahidi was spot on with comments. As were you, Puppy. I just don't know how we're going to alter the character of society to make it amenable to a game whose time and peak passed, as you said, nearly a century ago."

"Yet still, we're all here," Sahidi said. "I was pessimistic in my analysis. After listening to Puppy, I'm afraid I went too far. I was upset, frustrated like Puppy at seeing the chaos. But I didn't want to insinuate that I was giving up on the game."

"And let it be noted that I was offered relocation to another office once Ty Cobb and Mickey Mantle tendered their resignations," Matthew whispered as if sharing a deep secret. "That is standard procedure. But I was impressed by the passion, if often squandered on frivolous self-centered entertainment, demonstrated by those gentlemen. Certainly, in the weeks I have served with Commissioner Puppy, I have found his determination compelling. There must be something to this game to elicit such support."

"Thank you all," Puppy said. "We're going to need that because I'm recommending to the Cousins that we shut down baseball until early April, the traditional time of opening day, so we can go back to the very basics. If you want the stadiums to be from the twentieth century, then that's how the game'll be played. Far as we're concerned, the twenty-first century of baseball never happened. Except for my remarkable pitching, of course."

He took a deep breath, waiting. No one had any idea what he was talking about. "The first fifteen, twenty years of the twenty-first century were fine, had some great moments, but after that…"

Ian bounced onto the coffee table. "The son-of-a-bitch wants to do away with everything that baseball represented in the twenty-first century."

"The ridiculous eighteen-team playoff system." Sahidi slowly caught on.

"End the ban on stealing bases," Puppy said with a grin.

"Allow trick plays like the hit and run," Ian roared.

"Bye-bye exit velocity." Sahidi waved her hands.

Ian spit. "Analytics."

"Advertising on uniforms…" Puppy said.

"And no more DH!" Sahidi shouted. "Hey, twentieth-century baseball wasn't perfect."

Matthew rose imperiously. "You cannot expurgate records."

"Since when?" Ian snapped. "We've revised our history over and over, finding different culprits. Racism, slavery, capitalism, human ecology, big government, little government, liberals, conservatives. The whole history of America became one huge laundry list of blame. Facts long ago became something other than facts until Grandma settled on individual responsibility as the ultimate truth."

Matthew shook its head, embarrassed by its confusion. "Then what does Commissioner Puppy mean?"

"In here." Sahidi tapped her chest again. "We go way back in here."

Ian touched his heart. So did Puppy. Slowly Sahidi moved Matthew's metal hand on its chest. The 'bot was still a little confused.

8

The tour of Clary's house began with the front gardens, drenched by hydra-heating waves shimmering up the front steps between the white portico columns. Despite prodding and a couple broad hints, Puppy couldn't tell the difference between the HG and real red roses and yellow tulips, delighting Clary who, of course, was among the few to know.

"But soon we will have real flowers," Clary said, tossing him a meaningful look.

Stout trees, *no HGs*, she'd proudly explained, formed a proud canopy over the cobblestone paths leading into the backyard where a vast sea of grass disappeared into a distant Van Cortland Park tree line. Faint snow dusted the huge lawn.

Gesturing to wait, Clary rubbed together her right index finger and thumb, frowning when nothing happened. With a tottering smile, she insisted he remain patient. Again she rubbed, muttering that it'd worked before. Teeth now bared, Clary rubbed again. An orangish hue covered the lawn, protecting the grass from the falling snow which clung briefly, then melted.

The girl squealed and rubbed again, raising the canvas a foot before letting it lower and disappear. He applauded uneasily.

"I know. Magic. That is because I am the Granddaughter." Her eyes rolled mockingly and, with another cry, she snatched his hand as if it belonged to her and rushed up the steep white marble steps and into the house.

Clary nodded briskly at the rigid Black Tops clustered throughout the lobby, black visors down. At this early hour, the house was free of visitors. "I made a change," she explained between breaths. "We have orderly visits where only the children are with me. Before there was too much running around. You know how children are." She added another self-deprecating eye roll. "Oh, Grandma would bake cookies and play ball and tell stories, but less than you think." She wagged a knowing finger.

"Now it is different. The children are my true Family." Her eyes narrowed.

He shivered slightly and he didn't know why.

Clary whisked up and down the three floors, setting off a brief alarm when she froze the elevator. As she icily informed the BT Lieutenant, this was a drill to see how they responded. "Badly," she said, winking at Puppy, racing ahead to open doors and disrupt meetings and shriek playfully at the HG children wandering the halls. She introduced him to a dizzying array of 'bot and human employees, from FB painters who were getting rid of "the ugly purple" to a trio of carpenters whom she called Moe, Larry, and Curly (she'd found a vid file of *The Three Stooges* in Grandma's upstairs bathroom) who were rebuilding the playrooms in the basement so they were actually fun.

"Who plays board games?" She shook her head at the stupidity of adults. When she finally ended the tour by locking her bedroom, Clary plopped cross-legged on an orange beanbag chair and waved her hands around the room.

"So?"

"Pretty impressive."

She feigned anger. "That is all you have to say, Puppy Beisbol?"

"Incredible. Amazing. Unbelievable. I'm having trouble breathing."

Clary threw her slipper and they laughed. She grew serious. "I cannot show you everything. There are secrets that I must protect. No, not to fool the siblings. That is an idiotic word. Siblings. The people. Citizens. Americans." She lingered on the word. "Secrets to protect me. My safety."

She struggled over how much to tell. Certainly not her three hiding places. She'd already upended the surveillance scans twice this week because she did not like anyone watching her dress. She had to be careful communicating. Puppy did not speak Spanish. Even if he did, so did Felice. Felice spoke every human language. Someday so would

Clary, the 'bot had promised. The thought reminded her aching fingers that she shouldn't have channeled the canvas illusion on the lawn. Tricks were forbidden.

"But I am in charge of my own safety." Clary tapped her temple. Maybe she would show him the crawl space in her closet. Let Felice know of that. Let the 'bot think it had discovered the only escape route.

An alarm in the shape of a lightning bolt struck the floor. Puppy jumped back against a shoulder-high bureau. Clary growled.

"Okay, okay." She circled the quivering bolt. "We will be there." Clary glanced at him somewhat pleadingly. "They do this when I am late. I think it is insulting, as if I am a child."

Puppy grinned. "We are kind of late, Granddaughter."

She wrinkled her nose. "Clary time." She drew an arch look. "And you can call me Clary. You are the only one."

As they entered the second-floor study populated by large scowling dolls competing with dartboards and neglected balls of many colors and shapes, Third Cousin Rasfarati rose, tipping his head respectfully. He had the expression of a portly worm still hungry.

"A pleasure, Commissioner."

"Perhaps you should wait until you hear what I have to say," Puppy said with a smile.

Clary chuckled at Rasfarati's discomfort. "He teases you, Cousin. Commissioner Puppy has a big sense of humor which is much needed in one of these meetings."

"I assume the Granddaughter is already acquainted with the Commissioner's recommendations?"

"The Granddaughter is not. It was enough that Puppy wanted to tell us his plans. I like to be surprised."

Rasfarati and all the Cousins had already learned that the last thing this willful child liked was being surprised.

"The others are also late," Clary said warily.

"No, it is just us."

Clary made an ugly sound. "Baseball is not important enough for all the Cousins to come? They could HG if they absolutely needed."

"That is not so," the Cousin huffed. "Between the war, the integration of face bots into the larger community, and the restoration of ties with our neighbors in South America, which involves a wide range of new trade possibilities, we're scampering. It's all very exciting. Just think. Real coffee on the market. Much less reassessing the ancient diplomatic methods of embassies and all the other rubbish from the imperialist days…"

"This is not acceptable, Cousin Rasfarati," Clary snapped. "Puppy was my very first appointment. The Cousins should respect that since I am the Granddaughter. The Cousins should be here. I do not like this."

Rasfarati squirmed. "I do apologize, but there is no intended disrespect."

"When I call a meeting, you all come. Tell them."

"What?"

"What do you not comprehend? Call them. You can communicate in an emergency."

"Granddaughter," he said in his most avuncular voice. "Emergencies are reserved for an enemy invasion, power loss in more than three national grids, the death of…"

"Cousins Rule four. September 29, 2075. An emergency may be declared unilaterally by Grandma or whoever acts in her place," Clary said in a frigid whisper, lightening the Cousin's olive complexion by a couple shades. She held her feral glare until Rasfarati completed his calls on the mini-con and the Cousins one through three appeared in noisy holographic bewilderment.

They will take me seriously, Clary thought savagely, rapping on the floor for silence.

"Should I begin?" Puppy asked anxiously. He was worried enough about operating the damn HG presentation without a hostile crowd ready to boo him.

"Please do, Commissioner. The Cousins have many coffee beans to harvest."

Puppy fumbled with the docking system. Eleven Cousins stared peevishly, blaming him for disrupting their schedules to indulge a whim of an impertinent child they detested; three of them had already engaged in discreet talks about abolishing the position of Granddaughter. How, was the question.

"Thank you all for inviting me. I know you're busy and I'll follow up by transmitting the presentation along with the written report."

"Then why have we been summoned?" barked Second Cousin Franny DeRico, who'd been addressing a serious sanitary outbreak at a string of cabernet vineyards outside Colorado Springs.

"Because the Granddaughter requested an emergency." Felice stepped out of the wall beneath a garish print of Delvecchio's *Descent* depicting the nuclear destruction of Washington, Grandma's favorite painting.

"Baseball doesn't constitute an emergency," DeRico sneered.

"Then why are you here, Second Cousin?"

The hefty Cousin sputtered a look around the irritated gathering. "Because, as you just said, Felice, the Granddaughter requested an emergency."

Clary started responding, but a shrill pounding clawed behind her ears, graying her vision.

"Precisely," said Felice. "Whether this was a proper invocation of her emergency powers can be determined later. But you all considered it sufficient to arrive. The least you can do is demonstrate respect for Commissioner Nedick."

Amid the reluctant grumbling, Felice nodded at Puppy to begin.

As "Take Me Out to the Ballgame" played, images of major league baseball's original thirty stadiums floated around the room. Bats cracked, balls soared, and gloves swallowed potential doubles. Hot dogs, popcorn, and frosty mugs of beer serenely trotted past.

"Through the remarkable partnership between 'bots and humans, baseball was able to return quickly and across the country," oozed Sahidi's imitated country drawl. "Like last year, the game struck a chord in the heart of America. But we've given them country museums, not stadiums. We've given them a game, but not at its highest quality. Baseball is meant to be loved, not attended. Like it once was here in Shea Stadium."

A blast of "Let's Go Mets" chants even raised Felice's eyebrows. A handmade sign behind third base read *Amazin'*. A New York outfielder slid across the outfield with a backhanded catch. A broad-shouldered pitcher wearing Number 41 fired a fastball past a helpless batter. Fans danced in the stands. On the scoreboard flashed *World Champions*.

The Cousins exchanged annoyed glances, making Puppy nervous.

"Going into the 1969 season, the New York Mets were considered a joke," continued Sahidi as if she were rocking in a hammock. "They once set a record of losing 120 of 160 games, which still stands. But a talented young team mixed with savvy veterans and backed by a powerhouse starting rotation shocked the baseball world. They were called the Miracle Mets."

Clary crossed herself, earning wary looks.

"The Mets became America's underdogs, coming from way behind in August to catch the arrogant Chicago Cubs, whip the Atlanta Braves for the National League pennant, and stun the heavily favored Baltimore Orioles, winning the World Series and bringing a crumbling city and a war-torn nation together."

More ancient vids of unbelievable catches, dazzling double plays, and ferocious base hits were spliced with waves of jumping, shouting, delirious fans. It was like a giant party.

"That's baseball." Puppy took over, firmly meeting their skepticism. "That's what we lost in the twenty-first century. The cynicism of the age, capitalist immorality of owners and players, indifference of the young, aging of the fan base, ridiculous rule changes, shrinking of the franchises, scandals, and contempt for the public led to the slow death of the game."

Clary tossed him an encouraging nod. She was the only one.

"As you see from our presentation, we want to pause baseball until the weather warms in April. Baseball in winter ain't baseball. During that time, we'll hold comprehensive tryouts throughout the country, not the hurried, two-hour tryouts like before. Then we'll have a spring training so all the teams can conduct drills and learn the subtleties and fundamentals like the lost art of bunting. Trick plays."

He sneered at a couple gasps, forgetting his place and not caring. "We're starting experimental Little Leagues in the DVs as another way of giving kids a path out. And we're bringing back the minor leagues. You'll see the information. We're getting rid of the damn stupid domes. If a game's rained out, we reschedule. No more HG history kiosks. Food will be sold only inside. No, I'm not done yet."

Puppy wagged a finger into the hostile stares. "We're going to have local radcasting. No vid games. You listen on the rad. We limit night games and when we have them, they're family nights. Hell yeah, we're talking promotions, everyone. We're talking Bat Day and Ball Day. Yes, giveaways." He raised his voice over the angry muttering. "We're letting kids go onto the field at the end of the game. Baseball made a mistake losing the young. We won't do that again. No more HG scoreboards. We're getting rid of all the rule changes adopted in the last one hundred years. Fact: we're going back to the twentieth century of baseball."

Puppy took a breath in the silence. "Like I said, we've detailed everything very carefully. But that's the top line."

The Cousins exchanged another round of puzzled looks laced with smirks. First Cousin Nadharatha raised two fingers with a heavy sigh.

"We certainly thank you, Commissioner, for all the effort you put into this idea." He waited until the Cousins finished mumbling. "Granddaughter, would you like to comment?"

"Soon." Clary flashed a quick smile at Puppy.

"Yes, well." Nadharatha said, clearing his throat with disdain. "On the surface, I see little that is feasible."

"Why?" Puppy was genuinely surprised. "If it's about money, there's an index about costs..."

"It's not the costs, Commissioner. The question is, as you accurately say, why? We're all privy to the numbers. That's how Cousins share facts. There's no silo of information. Attendance and interest have dropped, and rather dramatically. Perhaps it's because baseball is simply of little interest."

"We did it wrong," Puppy insisted. "There were great intentions, but the whole process was rushed. I don't like to trash anyone behind their back, but Albert Cheng needed a distraction from the war."

"Correct. Now that the war is going so well thanks to our marvelous inorganic citizens," the First Cousin tipped his head toward Felice, "distractions aren't necessary. America will regain its glory without hiding in the past and unleashing social discord."

"What discord? Fans'll appreciate not freezing their butts off watching inept players."

Nadharatha pityingly shook his head. "We saw what happened when Cheng stopped construction of new ballparks. Riots. Deaths."

"Because they didn't trust The Family to keep their promises."

He sneered. "And you think telling baseball fans the season will pause, as you say, won't set off protests and demonstrations while our brave inorganic soldiers are risking their lives killing Allahs?"

"Even if they don't riot, do you really want to unleash their enthusiasm?" DeRico jumped back in, feeling protected by the building contempt. "We can't have fans screaming like those ruffians you showed rooting for those Mitts…"

"The Miracle Mets." Puppy wished he'd brought his baseball bat.

The Second Cousin repeated "Miracle Mets" several times to snickers. "Cheng made many mistakes but at least he understood the dangers of partisanship by encouraging fans to only root for their teams. Now you suggest local radcasts, which once set city against city and wrecked our political system. And baseball. That's out of the question."

"It's opinion journalism," added Third Cousin Dinazzo as if discovering a dead rat in her peach muffin.

"Against the law and out of the question," Nadharatha said pompously. "And what in Grandma's bra straps is the Little League?"

Puppy explained, circulating horror around the room.

"There can't be children's groups outside the school system without violating the pedophile laws," shouted DeRico.

There was a moment for the entire room to question Puppy's proclivities.

"Is there anything else?" Clary asked the sullen silence. "Okay, now I will talk." She turned toward the red-faced Puppy. "Why do you want to do this, Commissioner?"

He paused. "Because last summer roads were choked throughout the country with people coming to the Bronx for baseball."

She shrugged. "They were curious. Maybe they got enough already. Maybe baseball is like a dessert. It tastes good, but too much and you end up fat."

Puppy smiled at her puffed-out cheeks. He suddenly felt as if they were in the room alone. Strangely disquieting, strangely reassuring. Almost like being with Grandma. Clary prodded him with a sharp look.

He continued softly. "Maybe. But we can't tell yet because we haven't given it a real chance. The whole system is screwed up."

The Granddaughter nodded. "Some of the Cousins's points were smart. We cannot have unhappy baseball fans. And I do not like the sound of this Little League. No one will hurt children." She tossed her thick curls from side to side. "We cannot say here is baseball and then suddenly here is no more baseball…"

"For a month…"

Clary pressed a finger over her lips. "I do not understand baseball. I prefer the football, your soccer, but I know that is illegal here because too many foreign-born like me preferred it. Football and basketball look like the vid games. Yes, I know the fans are polite and do not cause trouble. But it is sometimes the people who cause trouble who must be heard. Commissioner Puppy is good at causing the trouble. Maybe he will cause trouble again."

She unfurled an orange ribbon and twirled it around her right hand. "I say baseball does not stop. We must make do with what we have. When I came to this country on a boat, I did not complain. I just did it. Commissioner, you must just do it."

Clary held up her hand. "But you should be allowed to make some changes. Our robot brothers and sisters built many stadiums. It would be an insult to let baseball go away without trying harder. I will let you know what will go forward. Thank you."

Nadharatha smirked. "Pardon me, Granddaughter, but what will you approve?"

She shrugged. "I will study the presentation."

"I'm sure you will. We all know you're a fast learner, but determining the specifics, indeed, whether anything goes forward is solely within the province of the Cousins. Grandma and Cheng always deferred to us. That's the whole point of The Family."

Clary held her head in mock pain. "I am sorry, First Cousin. I would not disrespect any of you. But since you are all so very busy with many important things like bringing coffee to America, it is best if I take care of this. Baseball is not important to you. That is clear."

"For which we thank you, Granddaughter." Nadharatha scowled. "But the Cousins must ultimately approve all the measures."

Clary answered with a cold smile.

• • • •

THE REMAINS OF the once-elaborate sculpted theater masks, pockmarked with age and neglect, stared down from the frieze, as skeptical of the interlopers as the rat who scampered beneath the torn velvet curtains. Zelda dug her rubber soles into the battered gold-trimmed lobby tile. Beth had wandered ahead, hand on the dusty marble staircase winding up to the mezzanine. Joan posed by a rusted concession stand as if showering in history. It was that kind of moment.

"Imagine," Joan intoned.

"I think we are." Beth rubbed the staircase. Joan huffily removed her unworthy hand.

"That staircase was finished to approximate the marble of Athens. As in ancient Greece. The history of theater extends to our earliest time," Joan said as if she'd witnessed all the productions. "Storytelling is innate to our species. Sitting about the campfire, sharing experiences, enlightening, moving, frightening, reassuring. We're not alone because others have experienced the panoply of human emotions, tragedies, and triumphs, and they invite us into their world so ours is not so terrifying."

Zelda shot Beth a warning look not to laugh. There'd been earlier incarnations of this speech throughout the downtown subway ride on the renovated blue line, letting diffident commuters know of a "certain plan to revive culture being set in motion." Needless trips around Midtown Manhattan's ghostly buildings and rehabbing towers, 'bots swinging like mechanical monkeys through the chilly mist hammering a grade school on 8th Avenue, while stolid humans on West 47th Street installed the new window for Tony M's Dance Studio offering introductory lessons for the Latin Hustle and Revanche Ballroom Gliding.

Up and down Broadway they trudged. Neither Zelda nor Beth had ever traveled this far south. They did a poor job concealing their wonder. The wary pasty Manhattanites who'd survived the chemical attack or had volunteered to rebuild the borough spit with their eyes at the visitors.

In a loud voice destined to reach the last row, Joan knowingly sermonized how tourism was once the lifeblood of the city "which will return." After nearly an hour of incessant wandering sustained by a large leathery pretzel off a food cart, they'd tiptoed beneath the faded green façade and past the six Corinthian columns into the lobby of the Lyceum Theater on West 45th.

It'd taken another twenty minutes to haul Joan inside, painstakingly scolding the "heinous traitorous transgressors" who had occupied and "ransacked" the other grand theaters renamed for such "garish heresies" as Gore's Gooey Licorice and Ames & Bros. Square Pizza. As for the Little Playhouse which "carved, no, gutted" the New Victory Theater, Joan's nose almost wrinkled itself off her face. Memories gone. Traditions gone.

Other than Beth and Zelda, no one paid any attention.

"Are you ready?" Joan lifted her hands. They nodded, slightly exhausted, which was perhaps her plan, and followed inside through the ripped curtains drenched in filth. Hygiene was also a tradition gone. Zelda almost cracked.

Though she had to admit, the damn place was remarkable, like an indoor coliseum; this must be how Puppy felt in Yankee Stadium. Huge ceilings disappeared into the shadows. She could almost hear applause from a three-level horseshoe of lush red velvet seats. Zelda shushed Joan quiet, or at least quieter, and wandered down the aisle guided by her flashlight. Up close, the seats were torn, shredded. Misuse, disuse was almost clammy, a wet hand failing to scrub away the majesty.

Zelda sat on a chair, jumping before it completely collapsed. Joan bounded onto the stage, shouting out the lyrics of *Everything's Coming Up Roses* before she was stopped by their dim expressions.

"You'll learn," she said more as a warning than a promise. "We can't see it because the lights are out, but the original producer, David Frohman, who built the Lyceum in 1903, had an apartment upstairs. He would wave a white handkerchief to tell his wife, an actress named Margaret Illington, that she was overacting."

"Pretty rude," Beth snapped.

"More kind of funny." Zelda joined Joan on stage. "Just don't get any ideas."

"I'd unfurl a long white sheet and blast the trumpet."

Joan shook her head, not sure how serious Beth was. She'd already taken the measure of this one and it was small. Joan galloped like a formidable horse along the huge stage, scaring off a small city of rodents who knew better than to bother her.

"Magnificent stage, isn't it?" Joan tugged Zelda aside as plaster drifted down. "Imagine what we could do with it." She gave another tug so Zelda didn't fall into a hole.

"How many people does the theater seat?"

Joan sighed dreamily. "Nine hundred and fifty."

"Grandma's bra straps, what sort of play would draw that many people?"

"Hard to imagine, but once it was fairly easy. Musicals were always popular. Plays with big name actors. Elaborate sets to thrill and chill. But the more cynical the country became…" Joan glanced at Beth, arms folded in the front row.

"The more cynical the country became, the less they accepted the fourth wall, where believing something live was real yet not, and giving yourself to it. We'd become a nation of scoffers and without the ability to believe, well, we couldn't. Theater had lost the young already. Its built-in audience died off and then it finally choked itself on the excessive politicization, where some segment of the audience was inevitably offended by someone else's perspective until there were tiny silos." She shook her head. "Now we have what I call the fluff theater. Certainly not enough to sustain audiences who could support Broadway, theaters of this size, this grandeur."

"Thanks," Zelda said sourly.

"Not everyone is a Milbury Marshmallow. Which is why you're here, dear." She uneasily looked around. "I believe it's gone too far. Theater needs to say something."

"Which Zelda does with her messages of decency and kindness," Beth piped up, her breath scuttling cones of dust around her head.

"Hence, the fluff."

"Hence, the ethics," Beth said, nearly tripping over a fallen beam.

"You said my plays were too depressing," Zelda protested.

"Oh yes. No one needs depression."

"But happy leads to fluff."

Joan nodded. "It does. In the wrong hands."

Beth fired her flashlight at a box of seats. "Isn't that where the elite once sat? How much were these seats compared to those?" Her flashlight didn't have sufficient juice to light up the mezzanine, but Joan got the idea.

"Precisely." Joan exploded a laugh. "Everything will be priced equally per the law. The boxes could be used for the elderly or the physically constrained. But imagine…"

Beth groaned.

"I-ma-gine," Joan repeated, turning to Zelda who'd done nothing but imagine. Zelda had seen picture books of great theaters. She'd never been inside one. She suddenly wished she hadn't brought Beth. This was something that truly needed to be imagined and Beth didn't have that ability. She worried that she didn't either.

"The biggest theater I've ever performed in was the Ellworth on Mott Avenue."

Joan fluttered her lips. "I know it well. Ninety-two seats."

"Unless you include street plays in my old neighborhood. With all the buses and cars and pedestrians, I probably had an audience of potentially hundreds." She paused. "Can you really fix this up?"

Joan's eyes dreamily closed, then popped open. "The inorganic committee for the restoration of understandable entertainment has already approved my renovation application. They can rebuild quickly. Oh, don't worry. The magnificence of the Lyceum Theater will return. And yours will be the first show."

Zelda nervously pawed at the stage with her scuffed sneaker. "What kind of artistic restraints will there be?"

"Within the law, certainly."

"Which is the problem, isn't it?"

"You're not going to fill this place with fluff and you can't do anything controversial or else you'll never open," Beth said, hopping onto the stage.

"Correct," Joan conceded. "I don't anticipate sell-out crowds at first. The financial model is precarious. The ethical guidelines are intense. Nor do we want a production unduly despairing, as yours often are, Zelda. This must be uplifting and funny. Laughter is essential in these times when our brave soldiers are fighting evil. You must find a way to persuade an audience to lose themselves."

An idea glimmered dully. Zelda squatted. "What kind of budget would we have?"

"Depends on the need. We split everything fifty-fifty. I risk my investment, you risk your art. But I'm open."

Zelda thought another moment. "I like using costumes."

Joan frowned. "Animals wouldn't work or any variation of puppets."

"I got that. I'm just tossing out an idea. I'd use real actors. They wouldn't be animals. They'd be humans who became animals. Partly animals. Just the heads. Or I'd mix it up, a tail or wings or something. I don't know how that happened to them. Maybe they had accidents. Maybe they thought it'd be more fun to be a pig than a human. Maybe they applied to be changed into partial animals. No. No wings or hooves, too complicated. I'm talking just the heads. Everyone would have a different animal head."

Zelda briskly nudged Joan aside to pace the stage. "They'd each represent a point of view through their animals."

"Too obvious, dear. That's putting a light over each of the characters. I am good. I am selfish. Besides, that borders perilously close to political segmentation which is forbidden."

Zelda cut off Beth before she could come to her defense. "You're right. That's not drama. Wait. How about human animals and robot animals? I know there were problems once with 'bot animals going crazy. I'll figure that out. Humans and robots come together except they're not entirely human or robotic."

"A love story," Beth offered.

Joan's sigh bounced off the mezzanine.

"It's been done. Endlessly back in the '20s and '30s during the 'bot fever days when the whole notion of human relationships was collapsing. I may be wrong, but I believe 'Bot I Love You played here in 2037 or 2038. A disastrous theatrical experience. But then again, all the story lines have been done. Greed, ambition, lust, failure. On and on. There are few completely unique ideas. Between the Jew Bible, the ancient Greeks, and William Shakespeare, we are merely repackaging a new twist in different times."

She slowed down like a train pulling into the station. "But I like a love story, Zelda. A happy love story."

"With obstacles," Zelda insisted. "Ups and downs."

"What else is a love story?" Beth asked wryly.

Zelda stared into the dark theater. "This scares the shit out of me. Like stomach-rumbling anxiety and what-the-fuck-am-I-doing scared." She shrugged sheepishly. "Just letting everyone know that."

Joan hugged her. "That produces the best kind of writing. When shall I see a first draft?"

9

Elias no longer needed an alarm clock. The aches of his body jolted him just as the sun crawled above the ledge of the window. At the first light, dust swirled mockingly; he'd have to report himself for lacking cleanliness. He bent his knees and groaned, finding small satisfaction at the grunts and curses from next door.

Damn the man. Kenuda growled at Albert's relentless jumping jacks which sounded as if perpendicular feet were slamming into the adjoining wall. Elias hoisted himself onto his elbows, his lower back swearing from where he'd fallen off the ladder yesterday. The rest of the crew had stood by, uncertain whether to help in comradely sympathy or let him crawl for a while. The DV was all about individual responsibility wrapped around teamwork. Where it began and ended was something they had yet to figure out.

So far, all Elias had learned was abject misery.

He toppled back onto the pillow. Now Cheng was doing handstands. The other day as they were helping Mrs. Kilawicz with her grocery bags, Albert suddenly tumbled forward into a somersault and hopped about the lobby, counting off the spots where Elias had failed to properly mop.

"Stain there, stain there, counting five now."

Kenuda had dearly wanted to whack Cheng with a grocery bag, but he'd already been cited for ultra-sensitivity, impassivity to constructive criticism, and failing to submit his life plan to the Committee. This blueprint, as Geoff explained with fading patience, was not subject to approval. It was his life. He had made the decisions which had earned him a place in the DV. It was up to him to find a way back into The Family as a constructive member.

Grandpa Albert had submitted his life plan on the third day. They would appear together before the Committee since, apparently, they were the twenty-second-century version of Siamese twins. They'd been paired to gather questions and confront confusion as part of the extended orientation. Their introductory work details, helping longer-term DV residents, put one of them on a ladder and one below. One carried a carpet, and the other wielded a hammer. They'd learned the fine art of baking cupcakes, taking turns squeezing out frosting.

That'd earned him another citation when he claimed Cheng had snuck in an additional squeeze/lick of the vanilla cream. Reporting on a fellow sibling violated the spirit of trust.

Kenuda willed his limping body into the shower. Of course, Cheng's bathroom was adjacent and, of course, he sang endlessly. Badly, horribly, screeching as if hung by his thumbs. Elias had, for the past three days, retaliated with his own singing. Faces dripping beneath the erupting nozzle, the two men shouted out music, loosely defined, for twenty minutes until, by unspoken mutual exhaustion, they stopped.

Later at the retiling of Mr. Cammaratta's kitchen, Elias started singing into Cheng's ear, startling the man. Albert stumbled into a platter of paste and retaliated with loud shrieks which earned them both a write-up.

Except today was Friday. There were no cupcakes to be frosted, tiles to be laid, paint to be carted up and down ladders. He was seeing Hedda for the first time since he'd entered the DV.

Elias dreaded it.

He shaved twice, nicking his left earlobe. All his suits had been abandoned. A few of his seasoned neighbors advised that he dress casually because embracing his old, failed ways would be officially noticed. Elias spent a third of his Lifecard allocation on a three-piece black suit, white shirt, and crimson tie at the nearby Riyanda Men's Clothes, a very generous assessment of the merchandise. The suit pulled at his chest and the new shirt had a stain; threads hung mischievously from the tie.

Hedda looked as if she'd been waiting on the bench in the narrow park off Walton Avenue since he'd entered the DV. Instead of her usual starched-and-pressed appearance, her red scarf was going in three directions down the unzipped parka, the green ribbed sweater was bunched up, and the tweed shirt and boots were soaked.

The last of a brave smile staggered across her wide face. Hedda thrust her hands deep into her pockets, trying to decide if Elias was real. Satisfied, she handed him a damp brown bag.

"It's the berry muffins from Sandler's on 188th Street. I got the last one. I wouldn't think they'd run out so early. I arrived at 8:30, but already there was a line and I had to beg the girl to go into the back and get it for me. She probably was saving it."

"Grandma's bra straps, you're beautiful." Kenuda took a step closer.

"I'm not," she protested loudly. "The bus driver started pulling away as I was getting on and I fell into the muddy snow. It's a newer driver model. Did you hear they're replacing the old metal faces? You wouldn't. How would you?" She quickly apologized.

"I get the vidnews. I'm not in a prison."

"And?" Hedda demanded, shaking from nerves.

It took Elias a moment to figure out the question. "I had an old 'bot driver just now."

"Well then." Hedda floundered at this hole in her argument, worrying that he'd think she lied, that she didn't care how she looked when she hadn't slept for days.

Hedda burst into tears and buried her face in his chest. He stroked her head as siblings passed with warm, sympathetic glances at the two lovers.

"Can we go somewhere quiet?" she whispered.

A freshly painted orange commuter boat sloshed beneath their bench overlooking the Harlem River. The passengers nodded back, heading toward the line of reopened buildings in New Jersey. Elias had watched an extraordinarily boring vid segment last night on the launching of Xavier and Children's ferry service. The first since the chemical attack on Manhattan, this proud epitome of the soul of The Family's economy, family-owned businesses, promised to deliver at least one hundred siblings to jobs on both sides of the river every day. From the gushing reaction of the woolly-haired presenter, this announcement from Mr. Xavier and his seven children, standing in a stiff row so their heads rose increasingly higher like a xylophone, was a serious competitor for the discovery of fire.

More and more the news was treated that way. He would've been suspicious if he cared.

"Would you want to live there?" Hedda jerked her head toward the distant Jersey docks.

"I'd live anywhere with you."

"Please don't say things like that, Elias. It hurts too much."

"I must be optimistic. That's in the second sentence of the Disappointment Village handbook." He grinned. She didn't.

Hedda sighed. "When can you receive mail?"

He shrugged. "That depends on the progress of the individual acclimating themselves. They insist getting mail too soon might upset us. They're right. I'd die if I got a letter from you. The silence is easier. And yes," he cut off her worry, "that's horrible."

"Can you at least tell me how you're doing?"

He omitted the citations, making her smile weakly with his tales of manual labor and the quick introductory courses to a variety of alternative careers since the one he'd chosen had been such a dismal failure. Hedda nearly choked when he mentioned his partnership with Cheng as co-chairs of the orientation committee.

"That's insidious."

"A little. But I imagine if Albert and I can overcome our hatred, that'd be an example of progress. He's trying to be pleasant, as unnatural as that is. The man's well over eighty. How can he be expected to change?" Elias hesitated. "He's up to something and that's not my paranoia. He's already insisting on leading, which is counterintuitive. Since the damn DVs were his and Grandma's idea, you'd think he'd know better."

Hedda grabbed his hand. "Is it very awful?"

"Other than you not being there? Yes. It's still better than a resettlement camp somewhere out there." He gestured vaguely beyond the cliffs of New Jersey toward the secret camps where those who simply couldn't be helped lived.

The young teacher warily glanced up and down the deserted stretch of boardwalk. "There might be a way I can join you. We never had a chance to discuss options because the bastards just announced that I hadn't failed and I couldn't marry you."

Hedda squeezed her eyes shut at the memory of being escorted from the hapless Elias standing shocked at the 163rd Street DV entrance/border. She hadn't cried. She was proud that she hadn't broken down in front of him. Later, well, that's all she's done.

"I can challenge the decision. It's my right."

Elias flung his head side to side. "No more attacks on the system as part of our rights, Hedda. That's how we got here."

Her eyes narrowed. "I'm sorry I convinced you to take on the law."

"It was my decision but now we've got to abide by the rules. Whether we like them or not. I won't let you sacrifice your teaching…"

"I can teach in the DV. They need teachers. The whole notion of eliminating educational class distinction is failing. What would send a car mechanic to the DV is very different than what would send a teacher. I know that isn't right, but I've done my research and get that look off your face, Elias. No one will discuss it, but there's a huge shortage of educators in the DVs now."

"That's not true," he insisted. "I was a Cousin. And while that wasn't my purview, I saw education reports. If anything, DV kids were overcompensated with learning for exactly that reason."

"Not anymore," she said with equal firmness. "Those were the parents, Elias. The parents were charged with providing educational motivation for their kids. Education heirs, it's called. But the kids who more recently moved out of the DVs are having trouble in sibling schools. They require greater attention. Obviously, we won't segregate them in separate classes." She shuddered at that old practice. "But it's one of those unspoken truths."

"Why aren't DV parents doing their jobs?" he asked.

Hedda hesitated. "Right after the DVs opened, it was easier to transition back into The Family. There were more opportunities because of the disruption of the War. Thirteen million dead adults opened a lot of doors. Even then, the percentages of DVs returning were low. There are no numbers, sorry, I only have so much access to official records as a teacher. But the DV kids were always fired up to prove that they weren't their parents. And the parents encouraged that because they were so ashamed anyway. It's a terrible result, but the DV children were often more driven than those outside. Which was sort of the outcome Grandma hoped for with the goal of no DVs eventually. Except now the parents aren't driven to force their kids out. They're giving up as The Family has become more structured. Less mobility."

Elias frowned. "I don't see any indication of a permanent underclass. There's no evidence of crime. Streets, homes, stores, it's all immaculate. You'd get roundly scolded if you so much as dropped a muffin crumb on the ground."

"They're getting used to it," she said softly.

"Every introductory profession class I've attended has been full." He suddenly pursed his lips, annoyed. "These are all the points you want to make before the Sibling Committee. You're trying them out on me."

Hedda flashed a thin smile, which quickly faded under his scowl. "I was denied going to the DV because I haven't failed, and they used my record as a teacher against me to justify keeping me out. Now I'm turning that on them. I brought the official denial…"

"I don't want to see it." He angrily clasped her purse shut. "I said no."

Hedda's eyes narrowed. "You can't tell me what to do, Elias."

"Since we're engaged, I have the right of consultation."

"The engagement has been terminated, remember?" She studied him. "Don't you want me?"

He threw up his hands. "I knew that was next."

"It's a logical question."

"Of course I want you. I love you," he shouted. Below, passengers in a passing commuter boat cheered. Hedda thrust her fist at them in agreement. Elias led her away.

"But I don't want you hurt, Hedda."

"I hurt too much being away from you."

"I'll get out and we'll be together."

"What're you going to do, Elias Kenuda? Which of the many quick introductory classes on the many professions have appealed to you?" She went on before he could answer, as if he had one. "You need me or else you'll never get out."

He stiffened. "Are you suggesting I'm a permanent failure? Look at what I did as a Third Cousin for sport and entertainment…"

Hedda pressed her gloved hand over his mouth. "And you can never do that again, Elias. If you had any other career, you could return to it. But not as a Cousin. You're not qualified to guide anymore. Let's see. What then? You're too old to play basketball like you did in college. You can't sing like Mooshie Lopez. I guess you could sell food outside a baseball stadium…"

"If I'm so hopeless, then why bother?"

"Because I love you. Since when is that easy?" Hedda hugged him tightly. Elias lowered his face into her wool hat.

"I will get out. Somehow. I promise. But I won't let you ruin your life."

Hedda kissed him on the chin. "Too bad. I can do what I want."

• • • •

THE CRACK OF the bowling ball against the defenseless pins thundered across the lanes of Evita & Nario's Bowling Paradise. Grandma waited, one, two, for the newest roar to erupt. Mooshie must be doing her victory dance because the oversized speakers outside the crowded adjacent bar pumped out a medley of Lopez tunes.

It'd been that way for two hours following the "in-between nightclub and concert which I get is the best you can do." In the fourth frame, the incorrigible Mooshie bowled too vigorously and smashed several pins into shards. That'd produced the evening's loudest cheers for which she took an encore, tossing bits of pins into the crowd. At least it kept her busy.

"You're missing everything." Returning to their table, Mooshie wiped her face with a paper towel, accepting congratulations from fans who never tired of adoring her whether she was in flat bowling shoes or sparkling blue heels, whatever the alias.

"I wish," Grandma replied dryly.

"You're my manager. You're supposed to fawn over me."

"I have my credibility to protect. Are you doing another set?"

"Does my shit smell sweet? It's only 11:30 and I'm warmed up and ready to smother love all over my fans. Assuming you made sure there was an automatic kick-in fee for an extra encore. Depending on length."

Grandma hadn't considered that. Serving as manager for an egomaniac was more difficult than she'd imagined. "I'll talk to the owners and make sure your Lifecard is properly boosted." Lenore smiled. "This place doesn't suck, does it?"

Mooshie draped forward, creating a tent of hair. "You gotta be right sometimes."

When they'd edged west into Illinois aboard the ramshackle buses, Grandma finally decided to abandon the notion of Mooshie performing in decent clubs. Sadly, there were just too few of them. And they risked attracting too much attention, a foreign concept to her star for whom eating a doughnut was a marquee performance.

The experiment had nearly begun and ended in the Jeezi Amusement Park outside Decatur, Illinois. As Mooshie angrily explained, she "didn't do merry-go-rounds where children were present." The stage had been set up in a huge, inflatable, heated building between the Ferris wheel and the bumper cars. The audience shuffled in shyly, pleased by the free admission; that'd sparked another tantrum since professionals didn't work for nothing.

But the band sold Mooshie. Instead of the expected amateurs, they were three aging rockers from the original Yellow T-Shirts. Inside of ten minutes, they were puffing up the roof with their double saxophones and bass guitar; the drummer had a Ringo Starr hairdo. Soon the packed place was shaking with whooping on the seats and dancing in the aisles along with a few exuberant fans on stage to conga line with the star.

Grandma had visited thousands of small communities like Decatur. Shortly after The Surrender, she and Tomas Stilton, her head of security, had 'coptered across the country. Siblings had fled the cities during the War figuring, especially after Los Angeles, Washington, and Manhattan were attacked, that rural areas provided more safety against the expected Allah invasion. It seemed a better place to die.

Grandma had landed in state fairs, amusement parks, bowling alleys, miniature golf courses, roofs of schools, town squares, even parking lots. With little advance warning, which later changed when Ian Schrage joined her staff, she spoke to tiny groups, sometimes just a family of four. She wandered along the Main Streets, driving Tomas mad with worry. Popping into a diner to sample a pie, a bakery for a buttered roll, wandering into a home and inviting herself for a meal.

She wanted to hear what her Family had to say so she could understand what to do. Once she decided, she stopped taking a sandwich with strangers. All the laws had been written and amended. The Cousins system thrived. Crime nearly vanished along with corruption. The suffocating Allah trade boycott was met by a fiery determination to be self-sufficient.

Yet standing outside Yankee Stadium last year, announcing baseball was coming back, surrounded by throngs of grateful fans, made her reassess only venturing out for the most special of occasions. She wasn't an elitist, Grandma convinced herself. She was just too busy.

Liar. Lenore allowed herself a bitter smile.

She glanced around the noisy bowling alley. They were exercising, joking, drinking, and, on alley eight, a crowd holding up pieces of the pins was dancing with Mooshie. As she did each time, she overrode the warning about spying on humans; Grandma told herself she had no choice. She needed to know what her Family was thinking. She was, as she righteously convinced herself, doing this for them.

Grandma turned up the audio, skimming as if catching snippets wasn't really an invasion of privacy; not one comment about the robot soldiers. Same on their bus rides between engagements, the musty motels, and cheap food shacks. Oh, occasionally there'd be a cutting remark, but it was more a snide joke at Clary's expense.

"When do you think we'll have a First Pet?" a couple at the counter just inside the Kansas border had remarked, laughing. "First Dog?" a neighbor in a booth called out.

Grandma knew that she'd been loved and hated, held responsible for the defeat in the War and the systemized rebuilding of a society broken into terrified pieces. But no one ever dared laugh at her. You couldn't guide if you were a joke. It provided small comfort. Did Grandma want Clary to fail so she could save The Family or save her legacy?

She'd never had these doubts before. She wasn't supposed to have these doubts. Nor was she supposed to spy on Americans.

The public-address announcer let everyone know that the great Mimi Laker was having a special encore performance, but only for those who had at least one drink. That about emptied the alley as a clumsy line twisted down the corridor back into the 120-seat club.

Lenore blended into the crowd, peeling off past the shoe rental desk. Outside, she paused behind a formidable light truck at the rear of the overflowing parking lot, shadowed by a sturdy billboard on the adjacent Route 33. Her hair streaked with orange dancing amid the black curls, a smiling Clary shook hands with an FB soldier, its uniform dabbled with blood.

The billboard read: *THANK YOU FOR YOUR SERVICE.*

Grandma cringed. That phrase had been socially unacceptable since the late '20s.

An HG stream flickered by the truck's side-view mirror. Right on time, Grandma thought, waiting for Colonel Louie Free to appear.

A group of drunks stumbled past singing one of Mooshie's songs. Grandma knelt by the oversized tire, cupping the pebble. The holographic cone disappeared.

Mooshie waved to the band standing by a retro Cadillac parked twenty feet away. They hoisted their beer bottles.

"The gang and I have a proposition."

Grandma just stared at the pebble.

"I want to keep my boys. The boys. Let them come on the road as my group. No more of this rent-a-musician shit. These guys can really play."

The former Yellow T-Shirts air-guitared thanks.

"I know, you're wondering how that'll work. We'll buy a van. Mimi Laker," she boomed, her voice dropping, "and the Yellow T-shirts. This'll show we're serious mothers.

Someone like me would have their own group. And don't worry, I'll split their costs with you right down the middle."

Lenore just stared. "No."

"Say that again?"

"No. We can't trust anyone. One slip and we'll be surrounded by BTs who'll go click-click and shut us down for good. That you'd even suggest this is both astonishing and completely unsurprising. We're not touring to re-launch your career."

"Oh? I thought we were doing this so you could probe The Family's every thought. Yeah, I hear your echoes when you exceed the range. Only I wouldn't override."

"You couldn't. You're not constructed with that feature. You're a more primitive model."

Mooshie's fingers clustered an inch from Grandma's throat. "Fuck you, Grandma. You're enjoying this almost as much as I am. Only I know how to get pleasure out of life, something your advanced model missed. Until we pull the plug on the robot officers, or we go up in cinders, I want to enjoy myself."

She snorted at the ground. "Your buddy the colonel still can't find anyone?"

Lenore held out the pebble. "He's not coming. This is the signal when an illegal holographic transmission has been detected."

10

Azhar Mustafa had caught his son spying on him in the shower two days after he returned to Barcelona. Mustafa was layering in luxurious avocado shampoo when he saw his round youngest boy clutching unsteadily onto a tree limb outside the window, phone by his face.

Word had spread through their tiny community about Azhar's plastic surgery; Abdul had taken Azhar door-to-door to reintroduce him to startled neighbors. It was the fire on the fishing boat, Azhar explained, using the original cover story about his supposed death.

That wasn't sufficient. Abdul trailed his father everywhere, worried he would disappear again. He insisted Azhar take him to school and pick him up as if he were a mere child. After hurried homework, they'd play football until dusk. Dinners were the same, dubiously edible, and then in front of the television to watch the football tournament from Ghana.

But Abdul's friends had deeper questions. Was it only the face or had the doctors doctored other parts?

Abdul laid the phone on the windowsill for Mustafa to scan the gallery of previous shower photos. Azhar had a series of scars from his fishing captain days. A gouged knee.

A torn shoulder. The large scar which Mustafa claimed to have been inflicted by a shark to impress his sons.

Now he had the real proof, Abdul admitted. It wasn't whether the scars had been removed but whether that was his father. The boy sobbed, insisting he never doubted, but his friends suggested Azhar was a Crusader spy; hadn't he brought back an infidel friend?

Through the shower window with a tiny plant as a mute witness, Mustafa told his son the truth. How he worked for Abdullah. How he'd been on a secret mission in England. How he knew the infamous Puppy Nedick. How before that, he had traveled to America and met Grandma. Yes, he also ate Jew food and it was delicious, especially the matzo ball soup.

Abdul's eyes had widened so they could've held one of his mother's nasty lamb *al masra* dishes. He swore before Allah his eternal silence. Abdul said he always knew his father was a hero. Of course, someday, and only if Azhar gave approval, he hoped to be able to tell one friend.

Before deleting the photos, Mustafa almost showed them to his wife Jalak. She was not so easy.

Last week, she invited over Maehdi Suleiman. The toothless old man examined Azhar, breaking out in raspy shouts. When Jalak showed him Azhar's former face in their wedding photo, Suleiman muttered darkly as if Azhar embodied Satan before abruptly shrugging.

"Today it is difficult to determine the many faces of evil," Suleiman pronounced solemnly. "Faith in Allah will restore faith in your husband," the wrinkled shrub of a human informed Jalak, before then repeating that to Abdul, who was listening at the top of the stairs. He wagged his finger at Azhar without real conviction, assured all of them were mere pawns, and shuffled off laden with date cake.

Jalak still would not sleep in the same bed. Oh, she believed it was him. Those were still his eyes, she'd said shyly, inexplicably blurting it out while washing a dish. But to touch him? That Jalak could not do, although each night she edged the chair where she slept a little closer to the bed, Azhar often feigning sleep. They stayed awake, listening to each other breathe, afraid that by talking they would invite back the doubt.

They settled into an odd familiar routine. Jalak would not scold him for not working or spending too much time playing football or not enough praying. She pretended to take offense to him insisting he would have to accompany her to the market, as if she couldn't carry her own groceries. She pretended to believe his praise of her cooking. They were back, but as if on trial and neither knew who the judge was. Azhar wouldn't dare tell her what he had really done. Much safer for Jalak to make up her own fantasies. There would be no questions because she had already provided her own answers.

The empty kitchen table chair where Omar had sat reminded him of something else he couldn't discuss. Omar had sent Abdul a scorching abusive letter when his younger brother had been unfairly arrested for homosexuality. Jalak's eyes watered at the mere mention; she had burnt the letter so she wouldn't be tempted to re-read it.

In the middle of a football drill, Abdul abruptly said he hoped his brother died. His sudden adult glare clearly told Azhar that was the end of that subject. Fortunately, Omar hadn't written his mother about the confrontation with his father in London. The last communication was from the Holy Warriors telling Jalak that her blessed son had received the Mufti's Clasped Falcon medal for bravery. Nothing from Omar. With the Mufti's forces routed out of Spain by Abdullah's army, mail service, email, and texting between the warring territories had finally broken off.

The bus deliberated while a harried policeman directed traffic around a gaping hole in the middle of Avenida Isabelle at the edge of downtown Barcelona. Most of the rubble from the vicious week-long battle had been removed, but the streets were sometimes impassable.

Tomas Stilton hopped up and down by Azhar's window. Mustafa couldn't tell if he was drunk. He usually waited at least until after lunch.

"Tell the bus driver to let me in," Tomas snarled. Since Abdullah's liberation, infidels could ride on the same buses as True Believers if they occupied the last four rows.

With a weary sigh, Azhar persuaded the driver to let Tomas in at an unmarked bus stop. Much had been made of threats that discipline and respect for law would collapse once the traitors of Abdullah took over. Creating unofficial bus stops was the first dangerous step.

Stilton half trotted alongside until the bus wound through the creaking traffic to the designated stop. Tomas stomped on board and into a seat in the rear.

Across the aisle, Azhar held up a finger. "Do not say a word."

"I'm merely a guest," Tomas grumbled. "I have no rights. No privileges. At least I have vodka."

Azhar sighed again. It was to be another of those days. "You did not have to come."

"I have nothing else to do. I could wander in the parks or eat by the docks. Humiliation can fill an entire afternoon."

"You could work," Azhar snapped. "You are of Pakistani descent and speak both Arabic and Spanish."

"Maybe then I'd get my passport back."

"It was false anyway."

Stilton grunted and took a sip from the pint tucked inside a brown bag. Azhar could only fault him so much. At least he had a family. Stilton had only him. And Grandma's former head of security was being humiliated. In a way, so was Azhar. That's why he had spitefully refused the offer of a private car this morning. He couldn't remember what the Quran said about spite, but he was fairly certain it was wrong. Perhaps that is why it felt so good.

They sat in surly silence as the bus huffed toward the docks. Bicyclists fired past, some with mock racing challenges. Well-dressed men and women hurried to work. The aroma of early lunches wafted through the open windows. There was a happy buoyancy in the city as before the war. Then, Muslims and Crusaders had lived side by side. Not always in peace, but certainly not in conflict.

Uncertainty, but at least relief, Azhar thought as they clambered out two blocks from the water. For how long would the Holy Warriors remain gone and Abdullah retain control? Still, the absence of the infernal jeeps with black-robed fanatics murdering suspected infidels on the spot was deafening.

Black-robed fanatics like his son.

"Would you like to come inside?" Azhar asked outside the glass-enclosed former Oceanic Museum which now served as Abdullah's headquarters. Various murals of sea life wound around both sides, drawing gawking children.

"Was I invited?" Stilton grumbled.

"I will ask if you might come up."

"What do you think the answer will be?"

"Probably the same as it has been for the past month," Mustafa admitted. "But we can try."

Stilton's eyes slitted. "I don't grovel." He abruptly smiled and wiped the bench clear with his soiled handkerchief. "Give the Son my very best."

Azhar's shaking head created a little breeze as he entered the heavily guarded building. There had only been one terrorist attempt, but that had been enough. The gnarled burnt shards of a semi-truck lay on its side, a symbol of the failure.

Mustafa was ushered through the aqua-tiled lobby. The small aquariums flanking the elevators had recently been refilled with fish. He watched a tuna squirreling about. Azhar smiled at the resemblance to Major Stilton. It was not right for the Son to disrespect the American this way, he fumed, getting into the elevator with an officious young secretary studying her phone.

Without Tomas's survival instincts, Azhar never would have made it home. Perhaps Omar would have killed him that last night in London if Stilton had not wounded the boy. Azhar did not have the savvy to sneak onto a boat, steal train tickets and a car, stab a few of the Mufti's soldiers, and voyage to Spain with the unfortunate captain expressing suspicion about their papers after too much wine. The captain might wash ashore someday.

I did not kill anyone personally, Azhar blustered internally. I just accepted the need. He did not know how much Allah forgave him. It little mattered until he forgave himself.

In the same secret fashion as Abdullah had honored Mustafa with a private ceremony in his quarters, so the Son should have acknowledged Stilton. You met him briefly in Manhattan. He came to Europe to bring an offer of peace. No matter the changed circumstances in America, you should give him the courtesy of an audience.

He had repeated those words in various ways several times, but Abdullah merely waved him off. During their time together in the Raj Mountains in Morocco, Azhar had freely wandered about the Son's compound, a special guest. A trusted advisor.

He had not been invited here in more than two weeks.

Mustafa waited patiently in a simple office filled with statues of fish and replicas of boats. From the rear door, Abdullah bustled in, tossing off a few last commands to a slightly frantic aide before closing the door. He hurried over into a tight embrace.

"My dear friend, you look well. Your wife has already fattened you up."

"As do you, my lord," Azhar lied. Abdullah's face was gaunt with worry. The red sash about the white-robed waist only accentuated the thin frame, a young boy wearing his father's clothes. In a way, he was.

The Son waved off Azhar's feeble attempt at truth and gestured them into opposing chairs. Abdullah studied Mustafa for a moment.

"The wife, she has accepted you?" Azhar pulled a face to Abdullah's delight. "Patience. Women do not trust us. Often, with very good reason. But you feel her love, yes?" He didn't wait for Azhar to respond. "Certainly, you do. A face is just a face, a silly mask which we employ for all different reasons. You have learned that now. So will Jalak. And Abdul?"

Mustafa explained how Abdul followed him around like a large puppy with a football in his mouth; the Son beamed. They discussed the temperature of the freed city, the ship models in the office, plans for a football tournament, and the certainty of Abdul's tickets to a concert featuring the popular singer, Amira. Abdullah fussed with his robe, growing serious.

"You will ask about your other son, so I inquired."

Azhar tensed.

"Omar has been tasked with crushing the Catholics." He hesitated. "He has been promoted again. He is very successful at obtaining information from bound prisoners, particularly women." Abdullah waited for Azhar's embarrassed flush to fade. "He has singularly focused on finding all traitors. That is a long list for the Holy Warriors. But he is particularly focused on you."

Azhar squirmed. "How do you know that?"

The Son gave him a fish-eyed look.

"Then he is coming here?"

Abdullah shook his head. "How? We've made inroads into Southern France. A Holy Warrior would be obvious. Do not worry, my friend. I tell you the truth because you deserve it. He also looks for the Crusader woman whom you befriended," the Son's voice took on a disquieting edge, "who has fled London with a priest."

"Annette is alive?" He nearly rose out of the chair. "And Puppy?"

Abdullah assured him that the baseball player was well and home in some frivolous capacity. Mumbling thanks to Allah, Mustafa's eyes closed in relief. When he opened them, the Son stared coldly, almost warily. Clearly Azhar had shown too much joy for the health of his friends. The wrong friends, suddenly.

Irritated, Azhar began, "Speaking of—"

"Is this about your Crusader?"

The Son had taken lately to peppering his words with such venom.

Anger growing, Azhar squared his jaw. "Major Stilton, yes."

Abdullah grunted. "He is well, no? He lives in a fine little place which I provide, yes? No harm comes to him."

"Nor should any. My lord."

Abdullah's eyes narrowed. "He is an American. An enemy national. By all the rules of law, he should be incarcerated, not free to wander around drinking with money provided by Allah."

"But you are too gracious to do that." Now Mustafa's voice took on an edge. "He is also an emissary of their government."

"Grandma is dead. He has no role. Period." Abdullah sliced the air with his bejeweled hand, the now oversized rings nearly slipping off. "They are run by a child. Think of that. A child with the audacity to suggest peace and threaten me with consequences."

Somehow, he just knew. "A child."

Abdullah smiled, the baiting almost too sweet to continue. "A former ward of yours." He paused again, savoring. "The orphan girl who escaped."

Mustafa burst out laughing. "You are saying, please forgive my thickness, my lord, but Clary Santiago is the leader of the Americans?"

"Absurd, I know. But absurd, unlikely, and ill-suited leaders are hallmarks of the infidels."

Azhar continued laughing. "Little Clary. My little Clary."

The Son leaned forward with an ugly smile. "Your little Clary is a puppet of a dangerous faction. They are using robot soldiers. Oh, we are holding our own since they have little air support and their recommissioned ships are easily sunk. These monstrous soldiers inflict more damage than humans before they can be destroyed, but they will be destroyed."

Azhar frowned, lost.

"Robots, Azhar," Abdullah said impatiently. "They have faces again. The American robots are using your Clary as a front so they can control that country and take over the world. It is more insidious than the previous Crusader imperialism, similar to the secret manipulations of the Jews who persuaded Christians to slaughter each other so they could consolidate their rule. Yes, in a way the robots are the Jews of today. But unlike Jews who could be *dhimmis*, the machines have no such morality. That is whom your Little Clary represents. Unless you think that a twelve-year-old orphan girl has the wisdom to lead a nation, even one as degenerate as that."

"What are you going to do to her?" Azhar realized it was absolutely the wrong question, but he didn't care.

"Pardon?" Abdullah blinked several times in surprise.

"Clary. She has suffered much. She is a brave girl who deserves respect, my lord. I pray you will grant her that."

Abdullah sneered. "She is our enemy, Azhar. Do you not understand that? Your previous relationship no longer has any bearing. The robots wish to destroy Islam. We cannot let that happen."

The Son waited for Azhar to mumble understanding, softening slightly. "Good. I understand this is difficult given your feelings for the girl. But I will need your sage wisdom on this issue."

"Yes of course, my lord," he said quickly. "Clary is fiery, but she has a good heart—"

Abdullah cut him off with a dismissive wave. "I want to know her weaknesses. Frailties. Fears. I want you to tell me her entire story. The orphanage was destroyed during the fighting and all the records have perished. Once again, my dear friend, you are my eyes and ears."

"If I may, my lord. For what purpose is such information required?"

Abdullah didn't answer.

• • • •

AS AZHAR SLUMPED beside Stilton, the husky man handed over half of a *bocadillo de calamares* sandwich, their tradition after nearly a month of tramping about the city looking for a purpose. The major carefully watched Azhar pick at the fried squid.

"Good meeting?" Tomas asked.

Azhar grimaced into the sandwich. Oh Allah, sometimes I think you are not so wise as you wish us to believe. He tossed the food into the bin in case Allah had a spare moment to poison him.

"No," he replied simply.

Tomas sipped from the pint and waited.

Mustafa stared back. This was his best friend now. No, his only friend, which made him more precious because he had no choice. He gestured for them to walk along the dock. They paused before the *Alhambra*, a glistening white thirty-footer. Azhar leaned onto the wooden pole, holding the ship's rope.

"I believe Abdullah is going to make peace with his father."

Tomas's bleary eyes suddenly cleared. He hadn't liquefied all his old skills yet. He nodded and Azhar relayed the Son's comments about Clary and the robots.

Stilton shrugged. "It's the right play for Abdullah."

Mustafa was shocked. "To abandon a new Islam and return to the evil of the Mufti?"

The major about spit. "It's always about the convenience of power. Ideals are the first things to go. When I fought my way across Europe, I didn't get pleasure killing your brothers because they were Muslims. I did it to survive and to protect my buddies. Abdullah wants to survive. The Mufti's old. When he dies, Abdullah takes over. Right back where you all started."

"Needless war," Azhar whispered.

"They usually are except for the winners." Tomas flipped the half-finished pint into the water. "They must be getting their asses kicked to consider putting aside the civil war. Their armies must be exhausted. But they're still not going to play nicely together any time soon. Especially the Holy Warriors. No. They'll need to end this war with America quickly."

Azhar swallowed. "Nuclear war?"

Stilton shrugged again. "That's easier if they take out Clary."

Azhar frowned at the colloquialism. Tomas ran a finger across his throat.

"If this is all proceeding as Abdullah says, then with Clary out, the façade of a human front person is gone."

Azhar's forearms sagged onto the pole. They watched the vodka bottle bob away. "Using my knowledge, they will kill Clary."

"It's better than hurling nukes which we'll hurl right back. Assuming they still work." He rubbed his chin. "Grandma commissioned a report way back which found we could only expect fifteen percent of the nukes to work. Or at least work properly. Yours were inferior. Probably ten, seven percent. But even detonating in the atmosphere'd be catastrophic."

"Are you suggesting I cooperate to avoid nuclear holocaust?" Azhar hissed, furious when Stilton shrugged again. "No, I will not do anything to hurt that child."

"Got all that out of your system so we can talk sensibly?" Tomas chuckled. "Good. Refuse Abdullah. What happens then?"

"He will be displeased."

Tomas laughed nastily. "Yeah. Displeased. What happens to you? Abdul? Jalak?"

"Nothing." He stared into Stilton's sneer, weakening. "He would not hurt me. Us. Them."

"Why not? Because you're indispensable? Because the New Islamic Empire will crumble without your help? Because Abdullah is so ethical that his word is his bond and he's never betrayed anyone? You believe that?"

With great effort, Azhar slowly shook his head. "I still cannot hurt Clary."

"You will if you want to protect your family."

"What kind of choice is that?"

"A simple one. Congratulations." Stilton sighed in disgust. "He's testing you."

"Again?" Mustafa tugged at his face. "Was this not enough? My son seeking revenge—"

"It never is for people like that." Tomas clutched Azhar's shoulder. "I'm your friend. That makes you suspect."

"I would not betray you."

"I know that, Azhar. But you got to give them something on Clary. Make things up."

"You mean lie."

"Allah will understand. You need Abdullah as a friend. Don't alienate him. We clear?"

"Are you giving me one of your Major Stilton orders again? Stay hidden in the closet. Distract that guard."

"Yeah. We clear?"

Azhar grimaced toward the water.

11

The slim girl with the rat's tail pony, assortment of tats, and the fixed sneer kept Puppy waiting beneath a dripping ceiling outside the bomb shelter sign from the last century. Satisfied he was sufficiently wet, she stepped aside so he could take a seat in a rocky chair shaped like a palm. The girl glared, as if Puppy hadn't gotten that she didn't like him, and disappeared through a horseshoe entrance deep within the catacombs of East 144th Street.

Pumpkin Meadows hurried in with grunts and groans. If Puppy had asked for Pumpkin's kidneys over a bed of rice, the three-hundred-plus pounder couldn't have become more agitated.

"The great Puppy Nedick." Pumpkin's orangish, pocked face twisted scornfully as he consumed a comfy throne-like chair, elevated on what could've been a marble doorframe. Ponytail returned, draping a snake-illustrated forearm by Pumpkin's shoulder as she listlessly caressed his earlobe.

"In person. Thank you so much for agreeing to see me."

Pumpkin majestically waved his pudgy hand. "What are friends for? Only we are not friends."

"Must we do this every time we get together?"

"Get together?" Meadows and Ponytail exchanged a titter. "Are we out on the town? Oh wait. I was never invited when we were children."

"Grandma's bra straps, enough already. You don't like me…"

"I actually despise you…"

"You hate me, better?" Puppy waited for the acknowledging grunt. "And I'm not a big fan of yours."

"Yet you have graced me with your presence by working this into your busy schedule as Commissioner. My, my, you must have endless meetings. I watched your interview the other day. Most charming, Puppy. You haven't lost your wit, fortunately since the supply is small. Would this rare visit to my humble palace have anything to do with your empty plea to the baseball fans of America?"

Puppy fidgeted. Why'd he think he could get anything past Pumpkin? Ponytail stuck out her pierced tongue.

"Such a heartfelt moment. Give us your tired, your poor, your memorabilia."

"I never said that," Puppy snapped. But close enough. During the ten-minute segment with Sahidi's sister, Sandra Douglas, on *What's New With The Family*, Puppy explained that as Grandma had once distributed the valuable contents of the White House, from paintings and chairs to doorknobs, across the country to be equally shared, he wanted to bring the long-hidden memorabilia to all of the ballparks.

Puppy's Decree Number One, Matthew had proudly proclaimed, eye-rolling excessively when Puppy mentioned the totalitarian tones. After much mechanical pouting, Puppy agreed to Baseball Barks Back.

He could've called it "everyone gets as much premarital sex as they want without violating the law" and gotten the same response. Just eleven baseball memorabilia items arrived within the week. Cincinnati's Crosley Field led with a Pete Rose shoelace and a program from Game Three of the 1961 World Series. At St. Louis's Busch Stadium, a fan donated a Pepper Martin jockstrap while Forbes Field became the new home of a Slider Ordonez cap from 2044.

Dodger Stadium turned up Kirk Gibson's batting glove, San Francisco's Candlestick Park a Buster Posney cleat, and at Pilots Stadium in Seattle, a 2029 baseball card of Turner de Jesus Chavez from the final batch of Topps baseball cards.

On the call with the numerous "Friends of" groups, the Tigers proudly displayed a HG version of R.C. Bondello's splintered bat from 2051, the Phillies, a scorecard from a 1974 game with the Chicago Cubs, and the New York Mets's Friends of Tom Seaver held up a Dwight Gooden shot glass whose irony no one quite understood. The Milwaukee Brewers claimed the deep historical significance of a Lew Burdette resin bag, explaining that the gentleman pitched for the Milwaukee Braves back when franchises could turn their backs on fans and move wherever the profits were greener.

That set up a surly debate with the Mets and Dodgers over who should be rightful heirs to the Brooklyn Dodgers since the franchise was New York-based and rife with disloyalty. Puppy insisted they were all heirs to the same common heritage which only briefly shamed them before the bickering resumed, Oakland's Friends of Reggie Jackson and Kansas City's Friends of George Brett shouting over the legacy to the nickname "Athletics."

"Quite a haul, wasn't it?" Pumpkin chortled like the rumblings of an earthquake. Ponytail rubbed his other earlobe. "Quite embarrassing, I would imagine. Much like doing away with the retractable roofs and having a slew," he repeated that phrase because he liked it so much, "of games canceled. And I heard the baseball clinics also had some difficulty operating in the inclement weather."

Ponytail hopped into a perfect bunting stance, sneering at Puppy's surprise. Because it annoyed him, she went into a fluid dance of various batting, pitching, and running positions. Pumpkin applauded proudly.

"Perhaps this whole notion of flipping back the rules to the twentieth century also won't work. Much confusion. Wasn't there a near brawl the other night?"

The Chicago White Sox and Tampa Bay Rays had clashed over the repeal of the ban on the infield shift rule. The White Sox manager had run off the field with the second-base bag in protest, shouting to let them figure out what was legal now. They caught him two blocks away, but the bag had yet to be found.

There'd also been altercations in Denver and Houston when a relief pitcher was allowed to work more than one inning. And the runner automatically stationed at second base to start the tenth inning had to be dragged away during the Diamondbacks-Pelicans game. That's now happened thirteen times, Matthew glumly had told him this morning.

At least the first of the local radcasters had been hired in St. Louis, Houston, and Minneapolis. Clary had holographed that the Cousins adamantly refused to allow regional differences with the potential for opinion journalism beyond a three-team experiment. He explained that wouldn't be fair unless it was implemented for all the teams.

That brought Clary into his office with a brief HG tirade like one of Grandma's virtual thunderstorms. She yelled half in Spanish that baseball was supposed to be easy so stop screwing up, Puppy Beisbol. Matthew, who spoke thirty-four languages, translated that she had finally persuaded the Cousins to allow all thirty local radcasting teams but that was it. Show results.

And the festivities ended when the Trans-Organic Harmony Committee tore him an extra eardrum demanding 'bots be given an opportunity to play baseball. This subcommittee called itself the Friends of Jackie Robinson.

Yeah, his Commissionership was off to a rousing start.

"In a way, Commissioner Nedick," Pumpkin drooled out the sarcasm like rare cognac, "this is the version of you injuring your shoulder. Ouch, oh my, there goes the career."

He took a moment to laugh at Puppy's scarlet face.

"This is even richer. Everyone can identify, empathize with an injury. But this humiliation has only one parent. Your plan will be in shambles. The great Puppy Nedick disgraced at and by his own sport."

Puppy stared heavily. "You love tormenting me, don't you?"

Pumpkin beamed.

"Yet I'm still here asking for a favor."

"To whom else would you turn?"

Nedick sighed. "No one except the great Pumpkin Meadows."

"Better," he replied with another magisterial wave.

"I need baseball memorabilia. You know all the various collectors. Folks are still a little afraid, no matter the lifting of the laws against owning any."

Pumpkin leaned forward. "There are also those street rumors that you wanted to close baseball permanently and not just until the warmer weather. Perhaps you planned on confiscating memorabilia again. That didn't help their trust. Or your popularity. And some profound skeptics might say that if you were indeed innocent of killing Grandma, why did you run to the Caliphate?"

He waved that off. "Very sage, Pumpkin. Can I get back to why I'm here groveling? I've closed all those VR historical kiosks outside the ballparks. Those are twenty-second-century methods. But to have each team's most precious memories in a simple display case will be powerful and right in my theme of returning baseball to its roots. To re-introducing the game, Pumpkin."

The huge man yawned, though his eyes twinkled just enough to encourage Puppy.

"I heard the contents of the Hall of Fame in Cooperstown wasn't all destroyed," he said cautiously.

Meadows shrugged.

"You heard that, too?"

Pumpkin examined a carefully cultivated fingernail. "I did."

"I bet you know who has all that."

"Because I am the great Pumpkin Meadows?"

"If you like."

Pumpkin rolled his thick shoulders. "I know of many things…"

"Cut the shit. Do you know or not?"

"That is not the most engaging business ploy."

"I don't have time. I'm desperate. I went overboard with promises to rally people to the idea. Ripping out the kiosks. Removing the roofs. Now I'm screwed unless I can deliver."

"Ah, the impetuous Puppy. That is both your charm and your curse. But why would I rescue you from utter, abject failure when it would give me such joy?"

Puppy smiled faintly. "Because maybe it wouldn't make you as happy as you think."

Meadows tilted to one side, shrewdly studying Puppy. "You're really going to reinvent baseball?"

"Not reinvent. Return. Before it was taken over by celebrity and greed."

"It was always a business."

"But we didn't know that once upon a time."

"You can't manufacture innocence."

"You can if you return the freedom to be simple and stupid and wrong because the consequences of failure were once so high."

Pumpkin studied him with sudden respect. "You're going to allow ballplayers to sign autographs, aren't you?"

Puppy grinned. "That's also illegal. Like letting fans take pictures with players. Except this time, we won't let these be sold for profit. Pure memory. A new library of memories. Sorry, Pumpkin, for putting a dent in your business."

Pumpkin didn't seem troubled. "They won't let you get away with that. Grandma always believed that hero worship and its flip side of cynicism was one of the driving forces behind destroying democracy through narcissism."

"She was right. But things have changed."

"And the radcasters?" Pumpkin's eyes narrowed. "Another pre-corruption form of opinion journalism?"

"Without the negativity."

"People can't help but be negative." Pumpkin fluttered his thick lips, peering closely. "You don't have the talent to pull this off."

"Maybe not. That's why I came to you, Pumpkin. Because as much as you hate me, you hate a society that wouldn't let you fix your face after the accident because that'd be conceding to personal vanity. Egotism. If only you could give them a little of this." Puppy clenched his groin in Mooshie's disdainful gesture.

"I do every day," Pumpkin growled.

"And who knows about it except...?" He glanced at Ponytail.

Pumpkin thought a moment. "I know some collectors who might be able to help, but the Hall of Fame is different. From a police report that somehow drifted my way, there was an enormous amount of merchandise removed before the mob, the organized mob of our dear Grandma, descended and destroyed the facility. There've been rumors about where it all went, most of them as absurd as your plan. Hidden in Canada. Aboard a permanently floating ship in the Atlantic."

"I bet you know how to find it."

Pumpkin paused to savor the flattery he craved. "No. But I might know someone."

"I knew you would."

Meadows made a face.

• • • •

EIGHT RAMROD-STRAIGHT DV teens had wedged their black-and-white sneakers halfway up the schoolyard fence. Silent and suspicious, they'd watched with mounting curiosity since eight this morning when the first of the artificial grass arrived. From beneath the permanently soiled brim of his Cubs cap, Albert tossed a little disdain their way, pleased they parted their blank faces for a little contempt.

They don't need the fake crap anymore. Real grass has been growing outside Grandma's 'scuse me Clary's house for months even in the cold weather. Let me use it.

The moron who processed the DV outside supply requests from the mildewed basement on East 166th Street offered several stupid reasons why it couldn't be done, all traveling around the spine of too much work and futile effort.

I'm Albert Cheng. I know what's in storage. Do it.

He got written up for excessive egotism, diminishing collegiality, and unwarranted rudeness. He tore up the letter requesting he attend courses on pleasantries for new arrivals per Disappointment Village adjustments. Butter pecan muffins would be served.

Instead, Cheng gathered up two other new arrivals, Schmindler the brick layer and Arturio the pastry chef. By forging approved requisitions, he was able to snare a brightly painted Chevy van. Albert knew the service entrance to Grandma's 'scuse me Clary's house and the very specific documents required to pass the additional security he'd once ordered. His recognized face was enough for the two sympathetic checkpoints. Swallowing embarrassment and humiliation which he had to do every damn day, Cheng and his semi-moribund crew, which swelled to Lacey the precious artisan and Rojas the carpenter, carted off forty rolls of fake grass from a pre-war warehouse nestled within an old bird sanctuary in Van Cortlandt Park.

Yesterday he'd used more bogus work orders allegedly signed by a different moron on East 168th Street to commandeer four teams of workers to lay down the turf on playgrounds throughout the East Bronx DV, while a few other half-wits unloaded twenty bats, thirty gloves, and one hundred baseballs from the Spalding factory in Rye, New York. Since Albert had attended the dedication of the plant, he knew what forms they needed.

If the assholes wouldn't let him run things, he could at least show them how it's done.

The unpleasant young blonde Dale Tanaka straddling the top of the gate, polishing her nails, and scowling at the teens, had provided the forgeries. This was the same malignant waif who'd helped Kenuda with The Waste of Time Admission. Nothing's so strong as common hatred, Cheng thought proudly.

Geoff anxiously twisted his pudgy hands all the way from the entrance, stopping a few feet from Albert who was busily barking orders. In his eleven years in the DV, he had never charged a resident with a crime. His resolve wasn't helped when the fences filled with more cold-faced teens.

"What do you want?" Albert put his hands on his hips, daring Geoff to take another step.

He didn't. His quivering planted him like a shaky drill. Geoff suddenly noticed he was standing on the illegally obtained artificial grass.

"Mr. Cheng…"

"Yes. That's my name. Again, what do you want?" Albert grinned at the ease with which he rattled the fool.

Geoff shook as the fences on all three sides of the playground became obscured by staring teens in white shirts and black pants. He puffed up slightly, finding courage from the very nature of righteous duty.

"I have an order to escort you to the DV Committee on Misbehavior."

Cheng gasped. "That sounds serious. Why?"

Geoff cleared his throat. "For a number of charges."

"Which are?" Cheng gave the man a moment to foolishly hesitate. "I asked, *which are*, unless you believe The Family encourages false accusations."

Geoff nervously looked around as a few youngsters dropped to the ground like feathers without breaking their stares. "It's all here, sir."

Dale snatched away the order and, with an acrobatic slide, landed by Cheng.

"May I?" she asked Albert.

"Go ahead."

Dale pranced theatrically. "Contrary to the regulations, Albert Cheng…"

"You can't read that out loud," Geoff protested.

"You mean there are now secret trials in The Family?"

A few more silent teens dropped.

"No. No." Geoff addressed the crowd. "The procedure is…"

"What procedure?" Albert sneered, taking a step that drove the man back into the sudden net of teens continuing to drop off the fence. "You gave me a job based on my next to last profession as a major league baseball player to facilitate the Commissioner's request to install playing fields throughout the DV. But did you give me the ability to do the job? No. I had no choice."

Geoff nervously glanced around. "This is not the place for…"

"The hell it's not. The games are for these kids. They have a right to know. Unless you believe the Cousins are superior in knowledge to the rest of their family? Unless you believe in the elitist principles that the artificial grass only belonged to Grandma's 'scuse me Clary's house? Because that contradicts everything that Grandma and…" He just let the unspoken other name dangle a moment until Geoff's knees went a little wobbly. "…created. The whole point of the Disappointment Village is restoring one's focus. You can't restore focus without the means and the will. Build fields and I did. You, sir."

Albert wagged a finger at Geoff, now propped up by the silent teens. "You and your Committee are the ones who violated the law. You forced me…"

"And me." Dale solemnly raised her hand.

"And young Tanaka here, to demonstrate the utter stupidity of your process. A process which has become aged and decrepit from rote. No creativity, no changing of the times. It has nothing to do with the original purpose of the Disappointment Villages which I, as the person who devised them, know something about."

Geoff nearly fainted as the teens began murmuring agreement. He would be torn apart.

"Now if you want to haul my old ass before the Committee, go ahead. I'm happy to share this experience with the Brown Hats and even the Granddaughter if you'd like."

When Albert folded his arms, all the teens followed, left knees slightly bent in casual contempt.

"I will report this," Geoff said between gulps.

"Please do."

Geoff spun on his heel and pushed through the sullen crowd.

"Hey." Dale crumpled up the charges. "You forgot this."

She flipped the paper ball to a teen. The ball got swatted, becoming an insect following Geoff until it bounced off his head by the gate. The kids silently filtered out, the show over.

"Nice moves, Grandpa." Dale winked.

Cheng returned the wink. "Do you have time to work on the clinic?"

"Well, I'm supposed to be at my parallel mother's dress shop. But I'm happy to forge a request for my presence here."

Dale grouped the youngsters into hesitant clusters around the diamond. Her ankles groaned from spending most of the night on hands and knees in front of Tella-Na Coates's groin, then all morning crawling along sketching the baselines with chalk and fluffing up the bases. This was way preferable to dealing with fat-ass Regs who paraded their fat asses around the store shoving their big butts into dresses too small and arguing with Beth who couldn't by law sell ill-fitting clothes.

Beth understood Dale hated the shop. Beth admitted in that candid way of hers, like yanking her spleen out of her mouth, that she didn't much like the dress shop anymore either. She was excited being Zelda's producer, though that didn't qualify as a real job; nothing in entertainment was considered a job, just a hobby for amusement.

All for your love of theater, huh? Dale had turned up her nose, fortified by the last of Brendan's Brandy she'd sneaked into her room. Beth blushed, either from anger or guilt. She only had the two emotions. Dale could imagine what she'd be like in bed. Actually, she had imagined that when she went down on Tella-Na for the third time. It was a disgusting thought, pedophilia in reverse. Oedipus, Tella-Na had explained when they finally rested for ten minutes. When you want to shove your tongue up your mother-symbol's vagina. Oedipus.

Dale hadn't liked how pleasant the thought was or how intense the accompanying orgasm had been. Since Frecklie had been murdered, she pretty much felt that the whole world owed her sex without restraint. But Beth was hot for Zelda. Dale would never come between them; she kept encouraging Beth to grab herself one of Zelda's ample tits and start her engines.

Beth just glared and blushed. Anger or guilt. Yes, Dale knew adultery was against the core of The Family. She didn't care. She broke the laws as a game. Life was short. You could be sixteen and shot dead by Black Tops at Yankee Stadium like Frecklie. Dale had only anger.

The old prick Cheng re-ordered her groups according to what he claimed were obvious and unseen baseball abilities. Well, fuck you, Grandpa. Dale never tired of being tired when assholes told her what to do. Add the happy-face teacher Hedda Kleinz. Suddenly Dale was her project? How'd she win that Tootsie Roll? the teen sourly thought. The woman supposedly jerked someone around so she could live part-time in the DV as a teacher, like redefining pathetic, and now she's assigned as Dale's community contact to "facilitate entrance into college."

Like the translation should be: *We know you're fucked up and your mother was a crazy drunk and you live with Beth who means well but she's not quite right either because your murdered fiancé was her only child but you're brilliant and The Family needs you so we can once again rule the world.*

Fuck you homely Hedda and old Cheng in his silly Cubs cap pretending to give a shit and a quarter. Dale wandered by the row of chairs serving as a dugout. She hadn't broken a rule in about forty minutes. Long overdue.

As the first group of kids dribbled out grounders, Dale reached into her jeans pocket and switched on her port HG device. An attractive dark-haired woman playing an electric Hammond organ floated by second base. The kids and Cheng turned. With another inching of a finger, Dale played rhythmic scales.

Bom, bom, bom, bom. And then a sudden crowd cry which came from deep within the organ, and didn't.

Charge. Charge. Charge.

Dale accepted the kids's delighted applause. "Thank you. That's Gladys Gooding who played the organ at Ebbets Field in Brooklyn." She pointed where she guessed Brooklyn was. "I know Commissioner Puppy said no holographic aids at the clinics, but I just wanted to fire you up. How about an encore?"

Cheng grumbled away while the children clamored for more of the din. He wished he'd thought of that defiant act. He flipped the ball, grateful at the feel in the webbing of his still well-oiled old mitt.

"Baseball's your great secret pleasure."

Albert stiffened and closed his eyes. The voice was a chord too throaty.

"Yes. We had to realter everything to be careful." Grandma's slender hand turned him around. "If you killed me once, I had to expect you'd kill me again."

"Once was enough. Believe me. Once was enough." He stared, surprised and not. "It's probably odd to say you look well."

A popping sound exploded in a mitt, followed by the cry of the catcher skidding five feet backward.

Cheng laughed at the figure winding up on the mud-baked mound, daring someone to catch her. "That's the incomparable Mooshie I assume."

"She's not as forgiving for shutting her down. Imprisoning her."

"Are you?"

Grandma's eyes were cold and hard. "Not at all. Never."

"That's a good place to start," he said dryly. "I had no choice, Lenore."

"Even the worst mass murderers have justified their actions. Threats to their lands, society, religion, way of life. Look at the eloquence of the Grand Mufti, claiming he was merely addressing more than a millennium of Judeo-Christian colonialism and imperialism by launching World War III."

"Like sinking ships full of immigrants and blaming the Allahs?" he asked.

Grandma flinched. She turned toward Mooshie, who was demonstrating a headfirst slide into a would-be second baseman; she scolded the girl, rolling around and clutching her knee, for not getting out of the way to make the tag.

"Is this your path out of the Disappointment Village?" she asked.

"The DVs don't really work anymore, Lenore. This system is stagnant, almost reminiscent of the victimization social policies of the twenty-first century. Now we're creating and excusing generations of failure housed in clean and superficially positive environments. But they're not leaving like they once did."

Grandma bristled. "The rate was near ninety-nine percent some twenty years ago."

"Right. Twenty years ago."

Lenore looked away. "There was nothing wrong with trying to create a classless society, Albert. Perhaps we lost our focus. We were busy."

He stared. "Yes, we were."

She tilted her head as Mooshie started a chant of "Fuck Regs," leading the kids on sprints around the bases. Dale had reopened her Gladys Gooding HG, thundering the song *Follow the Dodgers*. From somewhere, a cowbell rang. DVs again smeared the fences.

"It's still the best alternative for success. Look at that child Dale. She disconnected your tracking devices on Mooshie and I."

Albert threw back his head, laughing with respect. He knew that kid had something.

"But I haven't come to debate the social policy of The Family, Albert. Nor to admire your still sharp baseball skills." She nodded at his freshly starched Cubs uniform. "More than the DVs are at stake if the robots gain control."

Grandma's eyes narrowed. "Felice was right, Albert. What you did was wrong."

"It's a long line, Lenore. Tomorrow it'll have been right. Along with failing to end class, we also failed to redefine morality, right and wrong, hard as we tried."

"I don't accept that." Her lips barely moved. "This is still the best example of a free society the world has ever known. Freedom based fully on individual responsibility, love, a common purpose. It's not the people threatening The Family but…"

"Beings like you," he said quietly.

Grandma pulled a face. "Some inorganic beings. I'm not proposing destroying them. Us. But it was inevitable that 'bots would go awry. Like the carelessness of human morality in the face of power, so 'bots are swayed."

"Especially when our world became soft. Once again, America has lost its way and decided it was better to have someone else do the fighting. Once it was the poor. Now it's the inorganic. We're not far from ancient Rome with robots doing all the work as slaves. Only this time, humans will be the slaves of their own flaccid fears."

"I won't let it get that far," Lenore said severely. "Which is why I'm here."

Albert raised his eyebrow. "You're suggesting an active resistance? Maybe you should talk to Alvin Nedick and his Blue Wigs." He caught her quick flush. "You already did. And the prick turned you down."

"It was only through emissaries. Nothing concrete was discussed."

"Just aligning yourself with terrorists."

"We did all along, Albert. What would've happened when the Allahs moved into Maine in 2071 if the Blue Wigs hadn't helped us fight them off? We could spend all day discussing the hypocrisies we embraced so the Family wouldn't. Yes, it goes against everything we believed. Killing orphans and killing immigrants and political assassination also goes against everything we believed. But we did it anyway, Albert. You're the only one who understands that."

"I appreciate the trust, after everything."

"I didn't say anything about trusting you."

A ball slammed into Cheng's left kidney, twisting him in pain.

"So-rry, Grand-pa-pa," Mooshie said, grinning meanly.

12

Puppy stamped his iced feet; someday he'd grow up and wear something besides thin sneakers. He checked the time again on the large billboard towering over Beacon Street where Clary hugged a stout girl in pigtails and a slender 'bot with cropped hair. *Love Everyone* glowed between the flashing 10:04 a.m. He'd already waited half an hour on the quaint ballfield on Amory Street, nestled in Brookline.

Puppy grumped at the round, bearded man in the long Boston Red Sox trench coat skidding on the snow. Ernie Paicopolos suddenly twirled as if skating. A red cape popped out and wrapped around his lower face. He paused about ten feet away, tapping a wand into his gloved palm, not quite sure whether he wanted to make Puppy disappear. Ernie'd already made him disappear from his front porch two blocks away.

Pumpkin had said he was weird. And that was saying something.

"What is it? There's a game at 1:15." Ernie glared at the insolent gray clouds. "The Cleveland ball club is in town and you know what they're like." He grumbled when it was obvious that the heralded Commissioner Puppy didn't know the reputation of the Cleveland ball club. Clearly the reputation of this heralded Commissioner Puppy was well-deserved.

Ernie frowned, disappointed Puppy was still there. "Thieves, every one of them. Time had been called by the home-plate umpire. I saw it even if no one else did. As always." He held up his wand. "A treacherous slide into third, a hastened throw which sailed down the left-field line, and then the completion of larceny as the, the..." he faltered. "The play continued amid wild celebration."

Puppy would need to find a way to pay back Pumpkin if this was a joke. "I'm sorry."

"Are you really?"

"Well yeah. Cheating isn't allowed."

"Of course it is, you dunderhead posing as Commissioner of Baseball. Trick plays are the lifeblood of the game. Or were until the cameras were everywhere." He gestured to the cameras only he saw hovering in a locust-like line toward distant Fenway Park. "Once you could tip your foot just off the base without being caught. Or hide the ball in the webbing and snare an unsuspecting runner. Or use a matador tag."

"Swiping without really tagging the runner."

Ernie scrunched his face, annoyed by Puppy's knowledge. "Which was also called?"

"A phantom tag."

"But such behavior was rude, and the young were offended." The Wizard of Fenway sneered. "Yes, you were a baseball historian so no surprise something would've been absorbed."

"Technically, I still am. But not of your stature, Ernie."

Paicopolos scoffed as if there was any other answer. "Like I began this one-sided conversation, what brings you here when I have scads of better things to do?"

He'd bleach Pumpkin's face; he swore he would. "Your reputation, of course, as the foremost baseball fan in all of Boston. New England."

"The country. The world," Ernie helped.

"Which is why I sent you three letters in the past week asking to meet."

"Which I destroyed. I destroy everything from The Family. Ronald Reagan said the eight most dangerous words in the English language are 'I'm from the government. I'm here to help.' Did you like Ronald Reagan?"

"Who?"

"He was president in 1986. Nineteen eighty-six," Ernie said with the distaste of someone who'd just swallowed cow poop. "We had the World Series won. Until..."

"Until Bill Buckner let Mookie Wilson's grounder—"

"Stop—"

"Roll between his legs—"

"I said stop it. Stop it." Ernie waved his wand, but Puppy remained standing.

"This is a much happier memory." Puppy held out a program from game seven of the 2004 Yankees-Red Sox American League Championship Series, which he'd finally pried from Pumpkin.

Shaking violently, Ernie muttered an incantation. It was minutes before he could hold the program, finally pressing it to his forehead. "This was one of God's last acts before he went off to the other side of the Milky Way galaxy."

"Down three games to none and your boys stormed back to..."

"Defeating the Evil Empire. Hell's Gate on 161st Street. The Bunker in the Bronx," Ernie continued wildly, "Your team. Your..."

"Yes. And proud of it."

Ernie covered his face with his cape and screamed. "The Yankees are a despicable franchise. Arrogant, smug, over-rated. Living on past glory. Babe Ruth. Babe Ruth. He was first a Red Sox star, pitcher, hitter, but who remembers that? 'Here's to you, Joe DiMaggio,'" he sang. "Quickly. How many world championships has your loathsome team won in the past fifty years?"

"Five. 2030. 2045. 2061, 2063, 2064."

"And the Red Sox? What do I hear?" Ernie cupped his ear. "Eight. We have won eight. I hate you."

"That's exactly what I want." Ernie was taken back. Puppy could tell this rarely happened. "Partisanship. Contempt for the other team."

"I have that. Especially for the New York Yankees. And the Cleveland ballclub. I also loathe Tampa because we should. The New York Mets..."

Puppy dragged him back from the precipice. "I need that game face, Ernie. Your game face of fervor."

The Wizard protectively stroked his beard.

"We have to make being a real fan respectable again."

Puppy booed, the sound barely echoing in the cold. He motioned for Ernie to join him. It took three tries before Ernie hissed a boo.

"Yankees suck, Yankees suck, Yankees suck," Puppy chanted.

Ernie's eyes tilted in glorious rapture. "Yankees suck, Yankees suck—" He broke off suddenly. "But you were a Yankee."

Puppy laughed haughtily. "And I sneer at your pathetic whining. We've won thirty world titles. How many for the Boston Red Sox?"

Ernie flushed. "Eighteen and counting."

Puppy scoffed.

"This year will be nineteen."

"If you can properly rally your team."

"They kept arresting me for unleashing my spells," he raged. "I nearly had the Detroit Tigers in my thrall to squash a late-game rally when the guards took me away."

"No more, Mr. Wizard. Soon you'll be free to incant and chant and whatever you want. You won't be alone either. There'll be Red Sox merchandise sold at the ballpark."

Ernie snickered. "There already is."

"Now you'll be able to buy Carl Yastrzemski t-shirts. With the number."

"The number?" Ernie stumbled over the words.

"Yes. And…the names on the back."

Paicopolos trembled. "The names too?"

"Yaz. Number 8. Number 34…"

"Big Papi," Ernie murmured, suddenly asking, "but that's illegal, glorifying individuals by wearing their facsimiles."

"No more," Puppy said huskily. "All the games will have local announcers. When the Yankees hit a home run, the Red Sox radcaster's voices will dip in disappointment."

"No."

"Yes. But when the Bosox clout one over the Green Monster…"

"They'll cry out like Ken Coleman." Ernie rocked back and forth, this new reality too much. "That's also illegal."

"No more," Puppy whispered. "At the heart of the game is the memorabilia, Ernie. As a historian, you know this."

Ernie stepped back, abruptly sober. "You're trying to get me to divulge the location of my treasures."

"No, no, no." Puppy shook him by his cape. "Keep them buried."

"I'm not selfish. I'm just careful. I have bobbleheads from the 2039 championship team. One was buried…"

Puppy wrapped his arm around the terrified Ernie. "I know about the offerings buried at home plate when Fenway was built, Ernie. I know it was you. I thank you for the blessing. But now we must bring the bobbleheads into the light. Why you ask? For the Red Sox museum." His voice rose over Ernie's gasp. "Headed by the premier baseball archivist and historian in America. The world."

Ernie cautiously accepted the compliment.

"But other teams aren't so blessed. There is just one Ernie Paicopolos. Oh, what to do, what to do."

"What's wrong?" Ernie asked in alarm. "I'm here, ready to confront the challenge."

"Ernie, Ernie, Ernie." Puppy cuffed his thick neck. "If only Boston has a real museum, that'll show favoritism. That we can't have, nepotism, corruption. All the teams need museums."

"Tough. Let them figure it out."

"Without all, there cannot be the one. You must show the way."

Ernie's beard twitched at the thought of touching Jorge Posada's catcher's mitt. "You expect me to help the New York Yankees?"

"Only you can, Ernie. Only you can bathe in your fervor, rise above it, then bathe again. Yes, I'm asking a great deal. But when you're in section thirty-four wearing a Number 9 t-shirt…"

"Teddy Ballgame," Paicopolos mumbled dreamily.

"And you look around Fenway and see flecks of Yankees t-shirts"—he spoke over Ernie's howl—"of Number 3 and Number 5 and Number 7…"

Ernie nearly convulsed.

"And the cries of 'Yankees suck' fill the air, you'll see the great role you'll have played in restoring the rivalry, the rivalries all over baseball, fueled by museums in every ballpark containing the great relics of each team's past. No HG, VR crap. The real stuff. Only you have enough passion to put this together, Ernie. Only you can show how baseball needs the joy of taunting an opponent. The joy of flaunting your success." He then whispered, "Roger Clemens," making Ernie twitch. "Only baseball can control its passion, only baseball can serve as a model for the entire nation to unveil its emotions."

Paicopolos stared longingly at the 2004 program. "This will require many incantations."

"Many. You'll also need the Hall of Fame stash."

Ernie darkened. "What stash?"

"Please don't insult me. I spoke to Pumpkin Meadows. He told me about the Custodians of Baseball Memories."

The Wizard stomped around, roaring about giving that turd Pumpkin Meadows good money for a pair of 2011 ALCS champion cuff links. "Do you think I would betray a sacred secret sworn upon the glove of Jerry Remy?"

"You will if you don't want to keep getting thrown out for shouting 'Let's Go Red Sox.' I don't see how the Red Sox got world title number nineteen without you."

"You're loathsome."

"Yup. Sometimes."

Ernie stomped some more, whirling with a shrewd stare. "If such an organization existed…"

"Assuming so."

"It would have protocols."

"Of course."

"Processes."

"Which one as esteemed as you could expedite."

Ernie pressed his beard against Puppy's face, tickling his chin. "Why should I believe you?"

"I apologized about shutting down baseball to the whole country several times now. Grandma's bra straps, give me a break. I suggested that with the best of intentions. Shit, you were in the midst of a losing streak. Maybe the time off would've helped you regroup, shake up the batting order."

Paicopolos's glare faded into a triumphant smile. "I will see what I can do assuming such an organization exists and such protocols can be followed. The Boston Red Sox museum opens first. And you will wear your Yankee uniform to be properly humiliated at the unveiling, Mr. Commissioner."

Ernie smacked Puppy on the forehead with the wand. It stung.

• • • •

THIS IS MORE what Annette thought it'd be like running on the Rat Line, begging a new pencil from a sour-faced priest named Father Baum in a wormy attic in Alsace-Lorraine. Wherever the hell that was.

Baum tossed Father Dempsey another meaningful look about this scatter-haired hellion.

"Pencils are very rare, Ms. Alejandro. We all use…" His fingers fluttered above an imaginary keyboard.

"I know what you all use." Annette mocked him with a virtuoso display of fingers. "I've lived here for six glorious months. But I can't write on your stupid devices because my brain doesn't think like that. I need tactile. Touch and feel."

Baum's glance at Dempsey received a wry shrug about the wonders of Annette's brain.

"So? Pencil or not?" she repeated stonily.

"I will see what I can find."

With profound relief, the priest retired out of the room. Dempsey gave her a sharp look as he lit a candle against the sinking sun.

"Try to be nice. He's the only link I have west of Germany. If you alienate him, I don't know what we'll do."

Annette mumbled about the efficiency of the underground Catholic Church. "What language were you talking to him?"

"Hebrew."

She sat up a little. "Isn't that the Jew language?"

Dempsey smiled in the faint light. "Father Morris Baum was a Jew. There were many converts during the pogroms and roundups. Unlike the last time the Jews were confronted with extermination, the Catholic Church stepped up and offered help. The Jews in the

Antwerp Ghetto were not burnt alive, for one instance. There was an understanding that few of the Hebrews had made a real commitment to Jesus Christ but, then again, some of us confronted our own doubts about Jesus given what happened to our world. Matters got murky, Annette. Doing what was right actually became paramount in organized religion, not merely preaching about it. In his papal bull, Pope John made it very clear that all God's children were to be rescued wherever possible, especially Jews since they were clearly Arab targets."

Too intent on listening, she waved off his offer of the last of the local wine Vin du Pistolet.

"The Allahs were all for Jews flocking to Catholicism. They were smart enough not to expend too many military and transportation resources killing Jews that could be better deployed killing Western soldiers. Besides, our Christian populations happily did the job for them. History runs along familiar tracks." His mouth twisted. "Converted Jews diluted and discredited the legitimacy of Christianity in the view of the Islamic Empire. It made the mockery of Christians more acceptable. You're not even what you claim to be anymore because you have Yids among you. I recall an Imam lecturing at King's College during a required seminar on 'the treachery of the false Messiah.' A priest had the, well, forgive me, balls to ask whether the legacy which Christians owed to Judaism and the legacy Islam owed to Christianity and Judaism made us all cousins. He was taken out and shot in the hallway."

On that, Annette accepted the last wheat cracker.

"Of course, speaking Hebrew is outlawed along with all elements of practicing Judaism, which is why their tongue is used for passcodes. You haven't noticed."

"No, because it sounds like Arabic."

Dempsey grinned. "Yes, it does."

Baum returned, warily handing Annette a very sharp pencil; he had misgivings about giving the American a weapon. She thanked him warmly, studying the wiry man since she'd never seen a Jew, and crawled onto a fluffy cushion in the corner. Dempsey and Baum resumed their Hebrew conversation.

Annette unfolded the sheet of paper from her back pocket, flattening it out with the palm of her hand, and continued writing.

So the priest just gave me a new pencil. He's a Jew! I won't bore you with how he became a priest but it was pretty much so he wouldn't get his head lopped off. It's a fun place all around. Thanks again for bringing me to Europe, hon. Anyway, like I was saying, we barely got out of Paris ahead of Azhar's son, who is hunting us down like we are rabbits in one of those silly cartoons you like. Father Dempsey broke into an abandoned church and found us old clothes. Seems every church hides clothes and canned food and bottled water for just this reason. The clothes stank. Okay, I'm not as fussy as I once was, but I don't have to smell like a goat, do I?

We were all dressed pretty with no idea where to go. This Rat Line works one stop at a time so if you're caught and tortured, you won't know enough to give up people before they kill you. Do you know why it's called the Rat Line? The Catholic Church used it to get German Nazis out of Europe after World War II. Nice, huh? Dempsey says they're trying to make up for that. But I don't know how you walk that back. Anyway, we had no contacts in Paris. Dempsey figured it was safer to go to the country where there might be less informers. He had something to do with baptizing Father Baum and making him un-Jewish and remembered he lived here in Obernai in Allzatz-Lorain (spelling ??). It's very pretty and you can see the Vosges Mountains. Remember when you sprained your ankle skiing in Hunter Mountain on all that SC snow? Least we had that hot tub in the room! And the fireplace...

HOT MEMORIES! WINKY DINKY!

For all we knew, Baum was an informer, but Dempsey insisted him being a Jew made that unlikely. Dempsey picked someone's pocket in Montmartre in Paris, I know, a thief priest, and we had enough money for the train ride. All of Paris is filled with the Holy Warriors. Everywhere you look, like black bugs. But once we got on the train, there were none. Just tired conductors who took our tickets without asking for passports.

Annette spared him the graphic images of the crucified Crusaders lining the train tracks. She was worrying him enough.

We sat for six hours when the tracks were commanded, commandeered, whatever, for a troop transport. You could hear artillery, but the farther east we got, the quieter.

Thank Grandma's bra straps that Baum was a good guy and glad to see Dempsey. The dinner was great, a chicken stew, though I passed on the escargot. It's a snail, Puppy. Glad we never came up with so-called snails in America.

The priests are looking at me now which I guess is a signal to go. I miss you my darling Puppy. I am sending so much love your way.

Annette made noise folding and sealing the letter in an envelope she'd snatched off Baum's desk downstairs. They watched with some astonishment as she carefully wrote out Puppy's address and handed Baum the letter.

"I don't have a stamp. We will have to owe you."

Father Baum peered at the address. "Ms. Alejandro, what would you like me to do with this? The recipient is in America."

"Yes, he is."

Baum glanced at Dempsey, who shrugged at another of Annette's wonders.

"There is no mail service between France and"—he squinted again at the address—"the Bronx."

"Uh actually, Father Baum, there is a mail plane which I've been on that drops off letters for American POWs. I'm sure if there's an American robot pilot landing near London delivering and receiving letters, there are ways to get a letter out to the Bronx."

Father Baum cleared his throat. He did not like the way she was holding the pencil. "Perhaps we can find a safe phone—"

"We couldn't risk that," Dempsey interrupted.

She scowled at both men. "Phone who and how? We don't have your celluloid devices." She scowled again at Dempsey's careful correction of *cellular devices*. "We only have mail. Good old-fashioned mail. If you have a Rat Line taking us to find the pope, then you can damn well mail my damn letter."

Baum went pale. Dempsey's eyes fluttered closed. Annette realized what she'd done.

"I just said that about the pope because I was pissed. Of course we're not—"

Dempsey cut her off with a weary stare. He waited until Baum, letter in hand, left, then swiveled angrily.

"That was stupid."

"I know. I'm sorry. I was annoyed."

"Over what? Not being able to mail your letter from the middle of a hostile war zone? Are you that self-centered and clueless?"

"Sometimes," she said quietly. "I miss my husband. I don't even know if he's alive. And if he is, whether he's living in my apartment or his so I might've misaddressed the envelope anyway."

The priest burst out laughing.

"You think that's funny?" she snapped.

"Isn't it? Look at us. This is pretty hilarious." He turned grim. "Please never say anything about the pope again. By giving him that information you've also jeopardized Father Baum, who's risking his life to help as well as his family and friends who'd be shot if discovered."

Annette nodded tearfully. "It felt good to talk to Puppy, even in a letter he'd never read."

"We don't have time to feel good, Annette." He blew out the candle. "Get some sleep. We're leaving just after dawn."

"Can I ask where?"

Dempsey rolled over with a grunt of a good night.

13

Clary counted seventy-five hairs on the left side of Third Cousin de la Paz's mustache. When she was raped in the Barcelona Allah orphanage, she would also count facial hairs of the *puertos* panting inches away. She could not rip their hairs off because two other *puertos* would hold her hands.

Cousin de la Paz would dare not touch the Granddaughter. No one dared touch the Granddaughter. Sometimes when she walked alone at night throughout her house unable to sleep, Clary felt as invisible, as unreal as the squealing holographic children. The Cousins spoke as if she were an HG, except an HG could answer back. No one paid attention to her. She was everywhere in The Family, the billboards, appearances at schools, on *Wake Up, My Darlings,* but she had no power except over baseball.

"Patience," Felice said. "Once the regeneration duplication transfer is complete, you will be ready." It made her sick. More than this skinny ugly *puerto* chuckling over her latest idea about education.

"Now that we have freed South America, we should take all their books and translate them so we can learn some truths about the past," Clary explained. "The foolishness in the American schoolbooks is wrong. There is another view."

"Grandma wanted to discuss this view before she was killed." Clary wagged her finger at the bemused Cousin. "She'd found the original order in the house library where the background history for the war and the deportations of Allahs were to be reviewed. Others would like to know. That is what education means."

"Facts are idle liars." De la Paz chuckled again. "We shed the faith in falsehoods presented as facts back in the mid-century. We only know what we saw, Granddaughter. That is why we had to destroy books based on the lies."

"Grandma wanted us to decide for ourselves—"

"I see baseball is picking up a little." De la Paz cut her off, his HG glowing as a sign the meeting was ending. "Congratulations on the transistor radio innovation. They are flying out of the factories, amazing considering they can only receive one radcast signal of the baseball games. I will be happy to issue a formal congratulation at our next Cousins Meeting. I'm not quite sure how all those promotions will work but if it keeps the fans happy and content, why not."

"And me content and passive," Clary mumbled to herself. Felice had scolded her endlessly about blurting out her feelings. The transition must be seamless as if you have simply matured, Clary. You are doing better. You do not lose your temper in public that much. There are fewer complaints from the Cousins about calling them names, especially in Spanish.

But it is not me. It is the fluids carrying the microbots taking up positions in my body. It is still my body, but for how long? The nausea and the dizziness had passed after the first two treatments as Felice promised. Yet Clary felt another life-form inside. Felice reminded her that if she had accepted an immediate transfer to a robot body, none of this would've happened. It was the insistence on retaining her physical form in the short term that caused the complications.

Clary danced around the impassive Black Top guarding the second-floor study, wailing the Jillian Soong tune *My Innards* to get a reaction, but the 'bot mutely stepped aside to let her pass. The human was prompt. Every night arriving just after eight to spend an hour with her better self. The BT registered the visit which was uploaded to Felice. The human child did nothing without them watching. Or so they thought.

Clary at fourteen stood in the crystallized cabinet, the microbotic waters swirling gently around its naked body. She sat down, frowning at the breasts. When she'd asked that the 'bot receptacle mirror her growth in two years, Clary hadn't expected it to still be flat-chested. She insisted her tits be puffed up. Her mother had nice breasts so why didn't she? Felice explained the body was exactly as she would be and it was egotistic to request additional improvements. Her immortality and superiority should outweigh an A or B cup. Felice had ignored Clary's brief tantrum about wanting to honor her mother's breasts, which she had inherited, and they would just revisit this when she became twenty-one and wanted a new body with a C cup.

Felice ignored that.

Clary offered Herself, that was the name she gave it, a red velvet cupcake, heedlessly brushing crumbs on the floor. Their conversation ran the usual path of Clary venting at the indignities of patronization and how that would all change once Herself took over. The 'bot hummed faintly, which Clary interpreted as various grunts of yes and no. Herself usually agreed. After half an hour, the lonely child stood, leaving the cupcake neatly presented on an embroidered orange napkin squarely in the middle of a chair.

She always felt better and more defiant after visiting Herself. Jumping fifteen feet down the hallway, Clary removed a concrete panel in the basement wall with a little grunt and effort. Coming out in another wing, Clary snuck into the underground garage, easily ripping up and repositioning the front seat in the Ford Cavalier so that her feet could touch the power pedals.

She abandoned the car on a sidewalk half a mile from the downtown red subway line, transferring trains for the orange line eastbound extension before getting out at 202nd Street.

"Where to, little girl?" The A32 taxi driver peered diffidently into the rearview mirror.

"Do I look like a little girl?" Clary's grin undermined her huffy tone.

"You're twelve, right?"

"Yes, good guess, sir." She was pleased, impishly letting her woolen scarf fall from her face, but the driver didn't pay attention. The 'bot stared ahead impatiently. The kid was eating into his time and time was money. "I am going to 1205 College Avenue."

"Suit yourself. Your fare."

Clary gritted her teeth at forgetting her Lifecard. She couldn't use it anyway without Felice tracking her. The taxi pulled up in front of the worn, orange brick building. The driver pointed to the screen flashing the amount in the front and back seat.

"That is a very reasonable fare, sir. Thank you for your honesty. But I cannot pay."

The 'bot angrily swiveled around. "I knew it. You had a fight with your parents and now you're off to see a friend to moon over some hot numbers on an illicit recorder."

Clary grinned. She never would've come up with that answer.

"Well, whatever it is, little girl, you either pay or I hail down a Blue Shirt. See this gizmo?" The 'bot pointed its metal finger at a nondescript button on the dashboard. "Three times this month I had to call in a deadbeat. Before that, I went nearly eight years and no one'd have the nerve to stiff me. But we have a breakdown which no one wants to admit. Too much is happening too quickly. I think you humans ain't used to eating real vegetables and it's messing with your brains. I can only imagine what happens when the weather goes back to normal. Now either you got the $13.45 or I call the Blue Shirt."

Clary leaned forward and tossed her scarf aside. "Do you see who I am?"

"Well look at this," the 'bot exclaimed. "The Granddaughter's in my cab and I haven't scrubbed my toes today."

"Yes, the Granddaughter is in your cab and shouldn't be treated like that."

"I am treating you like that, little girl. You're the same as anyone else. Grandma never asked for a free ride and I took her six blocks along the Grand Concourse back in 2093 when her 'copter stalled out. She paid. Even that jerk Cheng would never ask for such a thing as a free ride if he'd dirtied my cab. But you're a big shot and I guess all our leaders are going back to being big shots. Look where that got us. Now you gonna pay or do I call a cop?"

● ● ● ●

PUPPY LAUGHED ALL the way up the stairs after keeping her out of the 43rd Precinct with his Lifecard. Clary joined in. Only Puppy Beisbol was allowed to make fun of her.

In the messy living room, stacks of weathered baseball books, trinkets shaped like equipment, actual baseball equipment, an instrument which Puppy explained was a kazoo, fluttering pennants, many frayed, and several yellowing handmade signs clamored for space. These were for his presentation before the thirty Friends of groups tomorrow morning.

"If Ian ever finishes jerking off over the vid," snapped a solemn woman who grudgingly introduced herself as Sahidi Douglas, adding tartly that she had been the voice of the weekly *Game of the Week*. Sahidi quickly ignored Clary and returned to a huge book which looked like it'd been around during the time of the Bible. She wouldn't allow Clary a peek.

A faint drilling came from the rear of the apartment. There were discarded cans of unfamiliar beer everywhere: Goose Island Sofie, Smuttynose FinestKind IPA and, as Clary twisted to read, Rheingeist Truth and Bell's Two Hearted Ale.

"Didn't you give Pumpkin the pre-2000 list of baseball beers?" Sahidi threw up her delicate hands. "We have to be consistent. No foods, no beers, no nothing post the last millennium or else we won't be taken seriously."

One of her radcasters in Atlanta had recently tossed off a mocking quip about holding a horse and buggy promotion. She'd hauled his HG ass into her office and sliced and diced it more ways than Sunday. Didn't take long for Second Cousin DeRico to file a complaint about the "baseball game violating the law against opinion journalism which expressly forbids attacks designed to undermine The Family through false facts." Sahidi fired back that "radcaster Liu made a joke for which he apologized but the essence of baseball is humor." Grandma's earrings help her because she slipped the horse and buggy idea into the approved list of promotions.

"Yes, I gave him an extensive list, darling." Puppy shrugged. "But Pumpkin believes he knows best."

"That's what people with power do best." Sahidi glared at Clary, who was suddenly very happy to drop onto a couch and be ignored. She cradled a bowl of dark pretzels and picked up a box.

"Will you put that down?" Sahidi protested, looking to Puppy who explained that Sahidi had a system for logging, and he had no strength left to argue. Especially with someone who thought there was only one worthwhile opinion in the room. She'd already announced, per False Ambition Rules 2.2 designed to promote honesty and avoid the hint of underhanded agendas, that she believed herself more qualified to run baseball than Puppy.

"What I'm trying to do, Granddaughter," Sahidi's voice dipped acidly, "is bring back all the old-time baseball foods. Unfortunately, we don't have the original recipes. Like, the box you decided to move from its spot is Cracker Jacks. We know the ingredients, but we don't know how to make it. All the records were expunged because of its association with the game."

Puppy brightened. "Hey, maybe you could access the records at your house."

Clary vigorously shook her curls. "They would be flagged."

"Why?" Sahidi and Puppy exchanged anxious looks.

"They watch me because they are afraid I interfere too much."

"But baseball's your area."

"Yes it is. They do not trust me because I ask questions. I do not want to give them more reasons." She twirled a curl. "But they do not care what I do." Except for Felice. Clary's eyes narrowed. "I will get any information I can find."

Puppy tossed her a grateful smile. Clary felt immense joy, almost too much. She buried her face in the pretzel bowl until it passed.

"There's also cotton candy." Sahidi included Clary this time.

"We know it's not made with cotton." Puppy earned a roll of Sahidi's eyes. "It's very sweet from all accounts. I'm sure my buddy Dr. Pablo Diaz will rouse the guardians of smile-o-meters against this latest assault on dental health. But we've still got the hot dogs,

the foundation of pigging out. Amarillo is turning out tons of SC peanuts and they promised delivery by early next week."

"SC peanuts," Sahidi muttered.

"And Boise is becoming the AG sunflower seed capital of the world. Plus, we got
nachos."

Clary asked about a beige sign sitting on the worn, brown chair.

"That's our *Hit This Sign and Win* which we'll put on all the outfield fences."

"Win what?" Clary asked.

"Depends on who pulls out the lucky number in the raffle," Sahidi said. "Shoes,
pizza, ties, anything. We're inviting businesses to participate by contributing products. I
can get the radcasters to make the announcement during their games."

"For which we need separate approval," said Matthew, returning with a drill. The
'bot acknowledged Clary with a wary bow before resuming its officious airs. "We are only
permitted five adverts per game, and any break, no matter the content, is a violation of excessive promotions under Code Six of—Commissioner, please do not make those noises.
The Granddaughter, who oversees our activities, has now been charged with knowledge of
potentially unethical behavior."

"I did not hear shit," Clary said, making Sahidi laugh. "Tell me more."

"Haven't you been receiving our memos?" Matthew asked, slightly horrified.

"I do not read everything because I trust Puppy. Go ahead," she said, dumping out
more pretzels onto her lap.

"Each team has been charged with coming up with a weekly promotion to bring
fans to the park," Puppy began, twisting open a Goose Island Sofie and taking a long sip.
"Like in Minneapolis, it's Build-Your-Own-Igloo Day. In Wrigley Field, wandering min-
strel night. Fenway is giving out seat cushions blessed by the Wizard Ernie…"

"Which borders on religion," Matthew moaned.

"No, just crazy, which might be the same thing." Puppy grinned. "We have earmuff
giveaways in Baltimore. Bobbleheads in Cincinnati, Philadelphia…"

Matthew's moan grew. "That constitutes idolization of celebrity. The very bedrock
of religion and martyrdom."

"No one's praying except at the altar of baseball," Sahidi said, tugging playfully on
Matthew's perfectly dimpled tie. "Though the giveaways are going to be an issue since that
means someone's getting something for free instead of working for it."

Matthew moaned even louder at missing that point.

Puppy sighed. "That's part of the price of the ticket. It's all entertainment."

"I have not seen any of this officially, and I repeat officially, approved by the Cousins." Matthew looked at Clary.

"I am the Granddaughter and I approve." Clary challenged them to challenge her. Other than Matthew muttering about a veritable spate of violated clauses, there was delighted silence.

Sahidi glanced at her watch. "Shoot, Yankee game's on." She switched on the black transistor radio in the black leather case, pressing it to her ear.

"I cannot hear," Clary protested.

"Transistors are pretty much all about individual behavior," Puppy said.

"Egotism and narcissism, excluding others. The building blocks of the very, very illegal notion of social media," Matthew snapped.

Puppy waited for Sahidi to finish posing as if modeling on a runway. "You press the radio to your ear. Apparently, people would slip in earplugs and run the wires up their sleeves pretending to pay attention in school, but they were really listening to the games."

"An excellent idea to foster group education," Matthew grumbled.

"Calm down. You would gaze through math and science for a few days so you could hear the World Series," Puppy retorted, suddenly fixing Clary with a look in the silence. "So Granddaughter, are you just here because you miss me?"

• • • •

CLARY PULLED A teasing stare at the unmade bed and dirty clothes in the bedroom. She spent a moment straightening up, fluffing his pillows and tucking in the sheets so tightly an ant would suffocate. She propped herself against the wall, watching Puppy sip a Rheingold beer. Felice warned her against taking any stimulants during the regenerative treatment. After her high-pitched pleading, Puppy finally poured out a small amount in a tin cup.

She commented about the tastefulness of such old beer. "You are doing a wonderful job, Puppy Beisbol. Every time I report on another baseball innovation, it makes the Cousins very crazy. They are rooting against you." She didn't wait for him to ask. "I should have told you baseball is flagged."

"I figure in your position you have secrets."

"Not from you, Puppy Beisbol," she said gently. "Did you know that nearly every Cousin is a Regular? Yes, a Regular. There are only four Cousins who grew up in a Disappointment Village. The Cousins accused me of, um," she faltered slightly for the right word, "fomenting class strife. I do not understand how if you point something out that is true, you are the one causing the problem."

Clary fussed a moment over a thread on her knee-high socks. "If you fail, they will be happy. But I do not think you will fail, Puppy." She played with another thread, finally looking up. "They also want me to fail."

"Why, honey?" he asked softly.

"Because I am a child. Because I was not born here. That did not matter with Grandma and Cheng, but they were from a different time and everyone forgot they were not Native Americans. Clary, well, has the Barcelona accent. Clary can speak Spanish and only the 'bots would understand. Clary lived under Allah rule. Maybe Clary is a spy."

She held out her cup for a refill. The alcohol was loosening her grateful tongue.

"Being Granddaughter is bullshit. To them I'm just a little stupid girl. A stupid little girl. Except, my beloved Puppy Beisbol, I will soon not be just a little girl. I will not be all human."

Clary giggled at the relief of finally telling someone. He tilted his head like a puzzled rabbit.

"I am going to be part human, part robot. I have been taking inorganic treatments. It is too complicated for you to understand, but they are preparing my essence, my consciousness, for transfer to a fully robotic machine. Felice can say what she wants but I will lose this body. Life is life, machines are machines. Only I will be a better human being. Superior, Puppy Beisbol. I will keep my soul. That is what I want. I will not abandon Jesus when he has been with me. I will have my faith and I will have my soul and I will live forever. Maybe not forever. Maybe only a thousand years before they move me to a better model."

"Grandma's bra straps, why the hell would you ever do such a thing?"

"Because someone must. My parents did not die, their heads in baskets, so I will become no one. I am special. I am here in America when I should be dead back in Spain. By an Allah knife. Your bombs. Swallowed by the ocean. Jesus has saved me for something. And I have saved myself." Her blazing eyes dimmed. "With the help of you."

Clary stared into her cup. "Except I am afraid, Puppy. Because I am not yet superior. I am afraid they will not allow that to happen. The robots will say I am not robot enough and the humans will say I am not human enough. I will not belong to anyone. Like I am now. Not belonging to anyone."

She suddenly clasped his hands. "Except to you, Puppy Beisbol. You are the only one who knows." Clary giggled, a little tipsy. "I forgot to say that this is a big secret. You are my only friend in the whole world. I want you to come and live at Clary's house and watch over me. Yes, you will ask, how can you give up such splendor as this apartment. There are many apartments in the house. You will be able to do your job as Commissioner. But you will be there when I am frightened and you will be there when I am not sure and you will be there to protect me. What do you say, Commissioner Nedick?"

Clary took a very deep breath. "I need you."

Puppy matched her deep breath, taking her small, surprisingly heavy hand in his.

"I can't really do that, honey."

"Why not?" Her lips quivered.

"Because I have my apartment, such as it is sloppy and all. My job…" He waved off her interruption. "My privacy…"

Clary crossed herself. "I swear I will respect that."

He took away the beer. "How about you come here whenever you want. Whenever you need to talk about something."

Her eyes glistened. "Whenever Clary is afraid?"

"Yes. Whenever Clary is afraid."

He went to hug her, but Clary leaped over him into the bathroom. *Puta* Felice was right about the beer.

• • • •

LIKE A GYRO-INFUSED blowtorch, Joan's scented breath laced Zelda's left ear. "They're chewing the carpet. No, no. And no."

Three auditioning actors before, Zelda had asked what "chewing the carpet" meant regarding a bulky man with pork chop sideburns shouting at the wobbly light fixture. Two actors prior, it'd been "there's someone in the last row who'd like to hear" and the last performer had been accused of being a "prima donna."

Zelda could try changing seats, but Joan had already foiled that strategy.

"Thank you, dear!" the producer shouted into what remained of Zelda's eardrum, sending the actor marching unhappily out of the mirrored rectangle of a room at Grand Art Rehearsals on Fordham Road. Their motto, *Greatness Starts Here*, wasn't reflected in any way Zelda could see. Until the Arts Council gives final approval for our production, Joan had wearily explained, we cannot afford a more luxurious space. Just wait until we go into rehearsal. There's a refurbished space reopening in the Upper West Area of Manhattan that will make you weep.

Joan waited until the sparrow-faced girl with the clipboard went outside to tell everyone to take five. "You didn't like him, did you?"

Zelda shrugged carefully. "He was okay."

Joan's eyes narrowed. "Okay is not good enough. Okay is for pedestrian productions. This is Broadway. Will be Broadway. Will redefine, will resurrect Broadway. We cannot have merely okay."

"He was auditioning for a type." All the actors had been asked to bring a scene. This guy had brought Fyodr Deniv's *Morning of the Cow*, which had won the last ever Pulitzer Prize. "For the type of a grandfather, he was fine."

"Fine is not—"

"I'd still see him again."

Joan muttered disapproval at Zelda's notes, which contradicted her own lofty thoughts on the twelve actors they'd already endured.

"I can disagree with you," Zelda said, covering her pad. "I'm the director."

"Yes, you are, dear. It would help the process greatly if you would contact the playwright so the actors could audition a scene from the actual play. Perhaps a few lines."

"I'm working on it," Zelda said defensively.

"Didn't you get a leave from your dentistry job?"

"Yeah, but I'm still a mother. That's a full-time job."

"He's an infant," Joan said archly. "That's not full-time yet. Although at this rate, he might be entering high school by the time the play's done. Which wouldn't matter because the Arts Council will have approved another production for the Lyceum…"

"Got it, got it." Zelda tapped her temple with the pencil. "It's all up here."

"And when might it flow down there?" Joan gestured at the pad.

"Soon, soon. I have the types, don't I?"

"Oh yes. Quite groundbreaking. A mother and a father and a grandfather and two neighbors and a dry cleaner. Theater history in the making. We should require the full play but given my stellar reputation, the Arts Council will consider the work if we only have a synopsis and a scene."

At Zelda's dim response, Joan held her pudgy hands a foot apart. "A synopsis." Her hands spread further. "A scene which could be short." She heaved her ample bosom and gazed skyward as if searching for the forbidden God.

"Talk about chewing the carpet," Zelda sourly thought.

"Zelda dear, I am not displaying urgency for the sake of urgency." Joan portrayed a woman in the turmoil of expressing unpleasant news.

"Or pressuring me."

"No, that is necessary. Next Tuesday we have our meeting with the Arts Council. I understand that is sooner than we anticipated." She acknowledged Zelda's paling face. "I had no choice." Joan glanced around as if someone were hiding behind the mirrors. "I did not want to alarm you, but we have a competitor for the Lyceum Theater. Through my network, which is vast and accurate, I learned that it is a certain producer who must remain nameless."

Joan paused to swallow the nauseating bile provoked by the nameless producer. "This person is contemplating submitting a proposal. Now!" she shouted. "We have time to cut her off at the knees." Joan swept her hand like a dagger. "She is further behind although that is difficult to imagine. Which is why I insisted on auditions. It is odd, it is not done, but I wanted to show our seriousness so that anyone considering competing would be viewed as an interloper. A low parasite."

Joan clasped Zelda's shoulders as if they were a life jacket. "You must have something ready, Zelda. Or we are grandly screwed. I am happy to talk through the mysterious idea to give it flesh. Blood," her expression suggested it could be Zelda's blood, "skin, hair, soul."

"I've never collaborated on a play and I'm not starting now. I know what I'm doing." Zelda scowled at Joan's grumble. "I'll have a synopsis and a scene by Tuesday. I'm not going into the Arts Council unprepared so they can tear my shit apart again."

Joan's eyes widened. "Tear it apart…again?"

Zelda sighed. "They've turned me down a few times. I was too provocative. I had to rewrite *Birds* three times before they gave me permission. I've already written two drafts of this new play, but I trashed them because I didn't think it'd get past the Council. I don't know how to write anything that would be approved and I'm not writing sickly sweet crap."

"Good." Joan smacked her on the shoulder. "That's why I only want one scene. One vague synopsis. The writing process, indeed, theater, is an evolving organic process. Once creativity takes off, one is never certain where it will go. In 2094, I produced *Dan's Left Knee*. It was vaguely presented and diffidently approved. The final product was nowhere near the original. It was haughty and yes, then Fifth Cousin Kreit ordered the show closed after opening night. But it said something, Zelda."

Joan hunched her shoulders. "A friend who shall remain nameless has proposed, yes, a revival of drive-in movie theaters. If they reopen, the public appetite for product will demand something other than the repetitious idiocy on the vid. At some point we must bring, nay, drag art out into the open. I told you before that I wanted you for a reason. You are daring and, frankly, have the admirable blind courage of a child."

She patted Zelda's hand. "But dear, I have a meeting at the Arts Council next Tuesday with or without you. I am not letting this despicable piece of rotten zucchini steal the Lyceum Theater and foil my dream. I will present a new play. I hope it is yours."

The carousel over Diego Jr.'s crib twirled lazily. Zelda rested her chin on the padded bar, staring back at Diego. She couldn't wait until he could climb out of the crib and walk around the house like a regular person.

How were auditions, Mommy?

Stinky. The actors were cool. But overall stinky.

Joan?

Big stink-head. I'm afraid to tell you, but I got caught in a lie.

Diego dribbled disdain over his chin. *You lie all the time.*

I do not.

Do fucking do.

Hey, watch the language.

Was this the lie about your sitting in the corner every day pretending to write?

Yes. Zelda blew on the carousel. *I have no ideas.*

Then how can you be a writer?

I am a writer. Which is why I had to lie about actually writing two drafts of the play. And a synopsis. She explained what a synopsis was.

So you've written diddly squat on top of poop.

Exactly. Now I've got a deadline which would greatly focus my mind if my mind had anything inside.

Basically you're screwed.

Basically. I guess all I'll ever be is Hygienist Jones. Here Lies Hygienist Jones. She Never Flossed.

Teeth are the bulwark of our society.

Has Daddy been talking to you lately?

No. That's just common knowledge.

Pablo's hand on her shoulder nearly sent Zelda leaping into the crib. "Are you speaking to Diego again?"

She nodded glumly. "Did we ever think highly of our parents?"

Pablo snorted. "Are you worried about Diego having as little respect for you as we had for our folks?"

Her eyes glistened.

"You do have a job waiting for you as a dental hygienist. Teeth are the bulwark of our society."

Zelda gave Diego a sharp look.

"But you hate it. I guess not enough to properly motivate you into writing. And yes, I know you've written diddly squat on top of poop because if you'd written anything you would've been acting it out for me. Endlessly. I don't understand what's so difficult. In the past year you've had many adventures, unlike me. Write about them. Write about Diego. Look at all he's been through and at just this age."

Zelda peered at Diego, who grinned. Or maybe it was gas. In the creative process, it's often the same thing.

14

Hedda squirmed beneath the weight of Elias's nervous stare. He tried acting casually, in a think-what-you-want, it-doesn't-matter-to-me kind of way, loudly tapping the hammer onto his palm and commenting on how well his plants were flourishing on the windowsill. Easy watering's the key, he announced solemnly as a blueprint for the continuing green rejuvenation of America.

Now if Elias were one of her students, Hedda would briskly assess the handiwork of this birdhouse. Always positive, but never patronizing. And always tell the truth. Grandma's primary rule of education that "only hard work learns honestly" must be applied here in the Disappointment Village.

Kleinz knew that didn't work with middle-aged soon-to-be-again fiancés who couldn't hang a picture straight.

"What did your shop teacher say?" she asked brightly.

"It's not called shop," Elias said as if greatly exasperated. "Reconnecting to what works is what the course is called but I've never heard anyone say shop. Or mathematics. Science."

"We call it shop in middle school."

Her pleasant smile faded as Kenuda grumbled, "You dislike it intensely, don't you?"

"Intensely is a strong word for describing a reaction to a birdhouse, Elias. Welcoming and embracing are more words that come to mind."

"Does my birdhouse evoke that?"

His rickety red-and-green construct evoked a dark scene after a bad storm where newly blossoming birds would be lured into certain death. Black and white and eerie like that movie banned for promoting fear that she'd once seen at a rascally friend's place. *The Birds.*

Well, you wanted this, Ms. Kleinz. Congrats on swaying the Siblings Council on allowing you an experimental visa to work in the DV as a teacher and spend weekends with Elias. It would not bode well for the experiment for neighbors to hear Elias throwing a tantrum because she criticized his birdhouse.

If she squeezed his hand gently, that'd make it worse. Hedda recrossed her thick legs on the floor and imagined that he was ten years old. It wasn't a strain.

"What this evokes, Elias, is the effort and vision you put into it. Even the slightly bent nails which went in at wrong angles, and the paint which has already chipped off." He looked like he was going to cry. "This is your first birdhouse, isn't it?"

He sadly shook his head.

"Okay, I'm sure in the," she caught herself before tossing another log onto the fire, "reconnecting class, you had the earlier visions, so to speak, before you began sharpening the view of your birdhouse."

"I did five of them."

She bit her lip so she wouldn't laugh.

"Five." He thundered. "Do you know why I chose a birdhouse?"

Hedda could only shrug and bite down a little harder.

"Because it was evocative of time with my father when we'd built the bloody birdhouses together. A happier time. But it wasn't happy. He'd shout at me because every damn birdhouse I ever built collapsed. At least he wouldn't laugh." Kenuda yelled as Hedda rolled on the floor, gasping for air. "Hedda!"

She managed to squeak out an insincere apology.

"This was all I came up with for reconnecting. Everything else was too closely aligned to the jobs which got me sent here for my extraordinary and well-publicized failures. For example, and I have many, I'm strongly advised not to join the block choir because if I sing, I can't hold a tune as you know, I'll think of overseeing entertainment and Mooshie

Lopez and perhaps my crush on her, oh stop wagging your finger, damn you, and please stop grinning. My whole life has orbited around those worlds. I should be allowed to re-pursue and rebuild what I originally screwed up, but I can't." His mouth twisted scornful-ly. "Blasted Cheng is involved in baseball with the clinics. I only have birdhouses, Hedda. Birdhouses. How do you think I'll ever get out of here? Birdhouses by Elias, oh, come on down to our new store on Sheridan Avenue."

"You'll go out of business in a day if you peddle that line."

As always, she finally got him to laugh at himself.

"You're doing the right thing, Elias. The right and ethical thing." Hedda paused with a searching look. "It might be that you'll never get out."

He pulled away, alarmed. "Don't say that."

"If you have no way out, it won't matter to me long as we're together, Elias. You could file an application to hold basketball clinics in the DV. You had no record of failure with that or football."

"I was very successful. Revenues rose every year I was Third Cousin. Few ever came away from a basketball or football game with a complaint. Unlike the damn baseball fans."

Hedda patted his cheek. "I know, sweetheart."

"But there aren't any football or basketball clinics in the DV. Yes, yes," he said, hold-ing up his hands in mock surrender. "I don't want to stay."

"Then you won't. That's the most important motivation. If you've been this success-ful before, you'll find a way now."

He tilted his head. "You were planning on getting me to that point all along."

Hedda sighed at how long it'd taken him to figure that out. "You're keeping away from Cheng, right? Associating with prior bad influences doesn't display the proper judg-ment."

She'd inhaled piles of books on the DV experience. *In and Out. It Wasn't So Hard.* And Milton Vishnefsky's acclaimed *I Understand Now*, which was the first time a book had been reviewed, however briefly, on *Wake Up, My Darlings* since the implementation of the Anti-Parasites Laws II.

"I avoid him as much as I can since we're next-door neighbors. Our time together as the newbie welcoming committee is over. That didn't work in bringing us closer togeth-er, though maybe that was the point, for us to deepen our dislike and sever one more link from there." He already found himself with that vague hand gesture of the DV indicating life beyond. He hoped he wouldn't fall into that vacant stare he'd seen on the older res-idents who'd given up long ago. "I want to see Grandpa as much as he wants to see me. Why do you ask?"

"Because I could see him wanting to make you an ally." Hedda frowned at his scoff. "It'd make sense, Elias. You must keep your distance."

Kenuda explained he'd changed his schedule regarding bringing down the garbage and jogging so he wouldn't run into Albert, which pleased Hedda. She suddenly looked around shyly.

"We're allowed to go shopping. Unless you're as protective about your furnishings as your birdhouse."

Manuel and Maria's Furniture on East 169th Street, two blocks down from the Grand Concourse, was a brightly lit tunnel of living room furnishings. *Where You Relax* was the sole simple sign. Manuel, a reedy man with friendly eyes, welcomed them with little salesmanship other than touting living rooms as their specialty since 2082; to say more would venture beyond the narrow limits of advertising, which had to be drained of all bragging.

Maria, his wife of twenty-seven years she said proudly, requested measuring their respective rumps, lower backs, and length of legs to make sure they were suited to the furniture.

A very cushy and comfy yellowish corduroy armchair was seemingly made for Elias, with Hedda finding delight over a rich navy-blue ninety-inch sofa in matching material. Lying lengthwise in a state of rapture, despite being exhausted from reviewing students's papers, sealed the purchase. Fueled by a bump in her Lifecard from volunteering to teach in the DV, Hedda and Elias agreed quickly on two maple end tables. "The finest AG wood," Maria assured them.

Elias insisted his birdhouse would've looked keen if he'd had such wood, earning a kiss from Hedda and "oohs" from Maria.

The rug took more time, enticing three customers for their opinions until everyone settled on a five-by-eight light-blue pattern. Floor lamps easily followed as they entered the second hour. A tall gentleman with a deep tan who was in town for the Yankees-Brewers game cast a deciding vote on the mahogany coffee table since Hedda and Elias's eyes were beginning to cross.

As they totaled up the bill, Kenuda gave Maria their delivery address. Her eyebrows lifted slightly. Elias flushed.

"Did you notice that?" he asked a few minutes later as they clomped on the thinning ice along the Grand Concourse.

She had a headache and only wanted a nap.

"The way Maria reacted to delivering to the DV?" he said, persisting against her shrug.

"Elias, they've been in business for nearly twenty years. Don't you think they've done business with DVs before?"

"Oh, I'm sure they've deigned to allow people like us in their fine establishment."

Hedda stopped. "You're reading into that. As a teacher, I have way more experience dealing with kids of all backgrounds and there was absolutely nothing that suggested she was anti-DV. They would've been closed long ago if there was any evidence of class prejudice."

"It was clear."

"Not at all."

His mouth tightened. "In her eyes, Hedda."

"Maybe they were once DVs and she was acknowledging that connection."

He shook his big head back and forth. "No, no. It was the surprise at how much we bought. That we look so…"

"Successful?"

"She looked at us differently in that moment."

Hedda folded her arms. "Elias, that's how you're looking at the world, which is understandable." He flinched at the truth. Hedda caught an idea. "Maybe she recognized you."

"What, by my address?"

"No, just that it took a while for who you are to sink in. It could be that she knew who you were and then when you gave the address it all came together. You were famous, infamous, whatever you want to call it. Reacting to you with a knowing look isn't class prejudice."

"You would know," he said archly, stepping aside to let a weary mother pushing a three-baby carriage pass.

"What's that lovely bit of sarcasm mean? That I wouldn't know what it's like to be viewed as a DV because you don't think I'm a real DV?"

"You're not. You're there because you volunteered. You could leave at any time."

"Oh, I see. My commitment isn't real."

"Commitment is different from the law. Please don't correct me. The law would be nothing without the commitment, thank you Grandma," he said with a sneer. "You can leave whenever you want. That's the difference. I can't."

"Listen to me, Kenuda, because I'm getting tired of saying this. I have the strongest commitment because I love you and will never leave you. How much clearer do I have to make that?"

He wasn't sure.

• • • •

THE TROUBLE BEGAN in the top of the fourth inning with the first wave of a wand from section thirty-two behind the right-field foul pole where, as Ernie Paicopolos would later explain, he felt guided by the "eternal eye of the ball."

The visiting Texas Rangers had loaded the bases with none out, threatening to turn their 2-0 lead over the raucous 28,879 fans in Fenway Park into something more substantial. The Red Sox had lost four out of five because of their rotten bullpen; from what Puppy had seen so far, you could add an infield that couldn't catch a cold except for slick-fielding Ellie Adair at short. The Boston radcaster Shem Childeranna had tagged her with the nickname "Cannon" for the way "she launches throws from deep in the hole at short."

That was the first original baseball nickname since 2065. The world hadn't ended.

Surrounded by these loud fans, his hoodie sitting atop a spanking new Boston baseball cap, Puppy was already deep into his third Schacht's frank, his second DeVita IPA, and was very happy. Magic Wand Night was the second major league giveaway this week. Handing out more than ten thousand Al Kaline bobbleheads at Tiger Stadium had been a huge success.

In the visiting ninth, Paul Weinstock and Mickey Mantle landed back-to-back shots into the left-center field bleachers to power the Yankees to a come-from-behind 7-5 lead. With two on and two out in the last of the ninth, the Mick robbed Ty Cobb of a game-winning extra base hit by sailing through the air and snaring the liner inches off the ground in right-center. Mr. Cobb didn't accept the call, screaming that Mantle had trapped the ball. Ty shoved the umpire.

The irate Inorganic Baseball Advisory Board comprised of four sullen AIs in proper suits demanded that Cobb's bigoted assault be punished by suspension for the rest of the season. Puppy had pushed back despite Matthew's cluck-clucking in the corner of the office. Ty had not attacked the umpire because it was a robot. Ty was a ferocious athlete who hated everyone who didn't wear his Tigers uniform.

Matthew had eagerly interrupted, insisting punishment based on hyphenated status had been outlawed during Grandma's first month in office. That triggered Edward James, the current spokesperson of the IBAB, to point out that robots were the only group singled out for protection under the Little Extended Family statute which Matthew snapped had been superseded by the Trans-Organic Harmony Laws which Mr. Edward James should know.

Puppy ordered Ty suspended for one game including an apology to everyone for unsportsmanship-like behavior. Good luck with getting that. The 'bots promised to speak directly to the Granddaughter.

Good luck with that, too. Puppy grinned over the last of his Schacht's. Whatever Clary was doing to protect the game was working. So far, he'd received no incendiary notes from the Cousins about a bruised 'bot ump or giving away free swag and undermining the entire foundation of The Family's work ethic.

He hailed down this most wonderful invention of the twentieth century called a cold beer vendor. Ernie corrected him too gleefully, stating that beer and whiskey had been sold in the original American Association, dubbed the "Beer and Whiskey League," in 1882. Pleased to set the Commissioner of Baseball straight for at least the twelfth time that day, Ernie delivered a scolding, haranguing lecture to a cluster of fans in the adjacent section thirty-one about their loud transistor radios interfering with the real-time, real-life, "magical moment" here. "If you cannot follow the game, then leave. If you are here for the beer, go to a pub. If you are here for a frank, go to a diner. Otherwise, pay attention." A couple beefy women in peaked red caps proudly slapped his shoulder; Ernie feigned modesty with a shy murmur.

"Why is he not removing Dawba Janaar?" Ernie rose indignantly, shouting toward the Red Sox manager in the distant dugout. The Wizard paused for a brief, irritated lecture on the art of pulling pitchers as hapless as this Janaar, he of the wayward fastball that viewed home plate as contagious.

None of the fans really understood what Ernie was saying. Puppy'd been disappointed by the spare attention in the main pavilion to the newly installed kiosk of Basic Rules. Here in person, Puppy was struck by how little the fans seemed to be educated about the game. The Schacht's franks, DeVita IPAs, and the first of the Missoula Cotton Candy were the main attractions.

And the six-inch red wands embossed with the Red Sox logos which had been given out for Wand Night.

As the Rangers batter marched to home plate, dwarfed by her long bat, Ernie rose like a beseeching ancient prophet. He shrugged the cape off his shoulders and raised the wand high.

"Deliver us, oh Great Red Sox," he chanted.

Nearby fans grinned and joined him.

Oh no, Puppy thought. He had been very, very clear. "No public incantations." Just the public blessings of the wands. Puppy tugged on the Wizard's cape, only to get his hand slapped away for desecrating a holy garment.

"Deliver us, oh Great Red Sox. Burn a hole. In their bats."

Fans in section thirty-two stood as one and began waving their wands, echoing the chant, which quickly swept back down first base, gaining converts as it roared behind home and, by the time it overlooked the Green Monster in left field, all of Fenway Park was standing, chanting, and waving.

"Deliver us, oh Great Red Sox. Burn a hole. In their bats."

The batter stepped out, alarmed. This was, after all, a nation where religion was banned.

The cry grew louder. The Texas hitter hurried into the dugout. The Red Sox players pounded their bats on the dugout steps. The fielders waved their gloves as if wands. The perplexed 'bot umpires stared, data failing to find any mention of recourse in this situation.

The Texas manager rushed out to consult with the umpires. He was met by deafening boos. One of the black-uniformed 'bot umpires disappeared into the Rangers dugout, returning shortly.

The public-address announcer only had to speak once before the noise ended like a plug had been pulled. The Family taught respect for authority, even a disembodied voice at a ballpark.

"Cherished siblings, the Boston Red Sox kindly request that you please refrain from waving your wands at opposing players because it will upset them and violate the rules of good sportsmanship. Thank you."

Murmurs, some ugly, slithered through the quieting crowd. Puppy breathed relief as the Rangers batter cautiously returned and, more importantly, when Ernie toppled back into his seat.

It was temporary.

"Burn, a, hole. Burn, a, hole," he shouted, feverishly waving the wand.

That set off another storm of waving red wands. The Texas players cowered in the dugout, fearing witchcraft. Fiendish Allah pacts with the Devil, bolstered by the blood of Christian babies, had explained much of America's early losses in the war.

"Cherished siblings," the public-address announcer strained to be heard over the din of stomping feet. "We are now going to collect the wands. Please pass them down the aisle to the ushers so we can continue this great ballgame."

Pale ushers stood in the aisles as fans grudgingly handed over the wands. They didn't know any better. It was difficult being a baseball fan living on someone else's memory of how the game should be.

Damn, Puppy thought. This is not going to be good.

He tossed back his hoodie and thrust the wand into the air.

"Burn, a, hole. Burn, a, hole. Burn, a, hole."

"Puppy has spoken," shouted Ernie, dancing like a fat top and repeating the phrase. It mixed in brief confusion with the other chant, words mangled until, somewhere between home and third, "Puppy has spoken" rocked Fenway Park.

Ushers hurried away, a few knocked silly by the shaking wands. The Rangers disappeared down the runway into their clubhouse lest demons in Red Sox uniforms grab them. The Boston team was given wands by the groundskeepers and poured onto the field, joining in.

Only the 'bot umps kept their positions at each of the four bases.

Two Blue Shirts hesitantly slid down row eleven in section thirty-two. The cops remembered Boston baseball had been the center of the brief civil unrest following Grandma's murder when Cheng announced a freeze on the construction of ballparks. The fans remembered the BTs in their tanks and Jet'roes armored vehicles, the curfew, the stench of death.

These memories overshadowed the smell of a freshly oiled glove.

The policemen respectfully tipped their caps and introduced themselves as Officer Benito and Officer Ruiz. Their voices echoed as if carried on the public-address system to the silent crowd.

"Commissioner Nedick, would you please come with us?" Ruiz asked.

"Why? Are you arresting me?"

Benito nervously glanced around at the hateful stares. "Of course not, sir. We just need you to come with us."

"The 'eternal eye above the ball' has spoken," Ernie said majestically.

"Ernie, that's really not helping…"

"We all go with Puppy or he doesn't go at all." Ernie wiggled three fingers on his right hand and murmured something unclear. It was a Greek curse he'd learned from his grandfather. The police flinched. Witchcraft and now speaking a foreign language. Section thirty-two tightened about them.

"Let's everyone stay calm," Puppy said, not at all calm because he didn't like anything about this. "Officers, I'll go if you promise to pull your colleagues from the seats. I think that'd be wise."

Ruiz agreed with a quick nod and whispered instructions into his collar microphone. As if nudged by a giant, invisible palm, all the Blue Shirts headed toward the exits.

As Puppy followed, Ernie brandished the wand, tossed his cape with a defiant shake and started the chant of "Let's Go Puppy. Let's Go Puppy."

He had to admit it felt nice to hear someone cheer for him again.

At seeing the Blue Shirts enter, Shemp Childeranna eagerly vacated his radcast booth.

A hologram of Felice shifted into place near Shemp's abandoned microphone. The Blue Shirts quickly left.

"Commissioner Nedick. I am Felice. I advise the Granddaughter."

That said it all, he thought, waiting.

"The Granddaughter has given you much freedom."

"She's just letting me do my job."

"Rousing baseball fans to anarchy is not your job."

He stiffened. "This is a harmless promotion. They're having fun."

The 'bot stared with the pity of logic. The human's appearance of stupidity was not entirely inaccurate.

"I indulge the Granddaughter's behavior because she is twelve years old and is steadily assuming her role as head of The Family. She has much to learn, including displacing her affections and loyalties. Yet she must be indulged along this path. The Granddaughter is associated with baseball. This display of authority and insight must be positive. Instances like today are counterproductive."

"Why? It's just a game."

"If it were merely just 'a game' then you would not exhibit such emotions beyond your standard outbursts, Commissioner. To you, it is not a game. In this country, baseball has mythological implications, unlike football and basketball where it is merely a game."

Puppy shifted with sudden understanding. "That's why baseball's dangerous to you."

Felice arched its eyebrow. "Emotion is not dangerous to my species, Commissioner. Ours is well controlled. It is dangerous to you if it is undisciplined. We cannot have the Granddaughter fail. Baseball must be a success to demonstrate the Granddaughter's leadership qualities. I am aware that you are very fond of her. I know that you want her to succeed. Not merely for her sake, but for the future of The Family."

He folded his arms. "For baseball to succeed we have to reintroduce the passion. You're saying we can't have passion because that'll threaten Clary. If there's no passion and baseball fails, won't that hurt her? To that kind of thinking, anytime humans get too emotional we screw things up. I was married and divorced and remarried. To the same woman. Trust me. Maybe we shouldn't feel at all. That'd surely simplify things."

Felice stared, making Puppy queasy.

"The Cousins will no longer approve your inappropriate proposals, Commissioner."

His eyes slitted. "Screw you. I only deal with Clary."

The 'bot tilted its head. "Are you defying my request?"

"Yeah, because I don't see any authority behind it."

"If you mean statutory, there is none. An inorganic life-form cannot be in a managerial position over a human, merely complimentary."

"What about umpires?"

Felice was momentarily surprised.

"A 'bot umpire tells a human if they're successful or not. They decide the entire fate of a baseball game. There is precedence for an inorganic life-form to assume authority."

Felice nodded. "That is correct, but only within the confines of this sport which is, after all, just a game."

"And here I thought you had advanced beyond humor, Felice."

The 'bot gave him a very long look. "For a moment, so did I, Commissioner Nedick. I advise that you reconsider your plans. I can do no more than explain what the most logical consequences would be if you do not."

He shivered slightly. "That sure sounds like a threat."

Felice blinked out.

As the sullen crowd filed out after Boston's 5-1 loss, they were given back their wands. That set off a flurry of "burn, a, hole" along Jerry Remy Way until the fans started drifting apart.

Ernie solemnly folded his cape. "Thank you for doing something I didn't think you would."

Puppy was in no mood. "Why's that? Because I've lived such a serene life of obey-ing authority?"

Ernie huffed. "There are all different kinds of courage. Athleticism is one thing. Mo-rality, ah, morality. But you showed yourself worthy."

Puppy scowled. "Was today some kind of test?" His glare deepened at Ernie's grin. "Son of a bitch. You set me up."

The Wizard brushed his beard with a sheepish giggle. "Yes. Very clever of me, don't you think?"

A navy-blue Chevy Arrow was idling just past the bus stop.

"That's your ride," Ernie said, pointing his finger.

Hefty Mary Doherty popped out of a door, trailed by two of her wary freckle-faced children. "Hey, hon. Get on in."

15

Fuming and suspicious, Puppy said nothing during the forty-minute ride. Not that he had any opportunities. Mary chattered on about the unusually mild weather, bless Grandma's earrings the sad fate of the 2099 last-place Yankees; fears that the Bosox bull-pen would undermine their bright pennant hopes; the latest specials at Mary's Diner fea-turing AG brisket in mustard sauce by...

"Yours truly," said the dour young M.J. Doherty. The girl prodded Puppy at least four times to sample her signature sandwich. When he merely scowled, M.J. demonstrat-ed the joys of said sandwich which included gleefully dripping clumpy yellow sauce on his shoes. Puppy smeared the concoction on the back seat. Third grade was in session.

Golden silence fell as they disappeared into the woods by Chatham. A few tricks of the wheel seemed to turn them in five different directions, finally pulling up by the side of a hill.

Mary and her children sang an old ditty about "flying through rock for a kiss" as the hill parted like a startled mouth. The Chevy skittered to a stop inside the cave.

The Dohertys waited patiently for Puppy to get out.

"Same palace?" he snapped.

Mary roared at his stupidity, her children taking turns poking Puppy over the gleam-ing silvery floor to a poorly lit door in the far corner.

"What're you waiting for?" Mary asked.

"The magic abracadabra. Blue Wigs, open sesame."

The Doherty family's disgust increased. He was guided into a tiny damp room, un-comfortably humid. Inside of a minute, he was wiping sweat off his face.

His father hobbled in on a long wooden cane. He frowned at Puppy's reaction.

"I look like shit, I know," grunted the head of the infamous terrorist group.

Alvin Nedick's cheeks had been hollowed along with his burly chest and shoulders. Oddly, his stomach popped over the belt tugging at the floppy corduroy pants. Slightly embarrassed, Alvin explained the most recent cancer drug Trisnin bloated him while reducing his appetite. Nothing's fair, he shook his cane in case Puppy showed sympathy.

He didn't. He sat there, wiping sweat and wondering what angle his dying father was going to play. Hopefully for the last time.

"How've you been?" Alvin asked, earning a laugh from his son. "Okay, we done with the family crap?"

"We were done with the family crap a long time ago, Dad."

"You just called me Dad. That's nice." Alvin tapped the cane. "This is real Lebanese cedar. Patsy Gonzales, one of my best, was killed by Black Tops a month ago. I inherited the cane that he'd taken off an Allah in Lisbon. Think about that. Lebanon to Lisbon to the USA here in historic Massachusetts. Now you're here helping me as I kick the shit out of this cancer."

"You're not dying?"

"Don't look so disappointed. My doctor, a friend, and we have many, says I'm in remission. You're going to be stuck with me for a long time, Pup." Alvin struggled to hold back a contrary cough. "How's the Commissioner business? I love the radcasts. Brilliant idea. Think they'll let you get away with the nicknames? Grandma would be very displeased at the drift into celebrity. But what's baseball without nicknames? Babe. Joe D. Say Hey Kid…"

Mary carted in a steaming pot of chili. Alvin helped himself, explaining the Trisnin reduced his sense of taste along with his appetite, so why not pig out.

Puppy waved off Mary's offer of a bowl. "So you got the Hall of Fame memorabilia."

"Why'd you think we brought you here, hon?" Mary shook her head. "It's not because you give a damn about your father."

"Mary, please." Alvin motioned her out of the room. "I'm one of the Custodians of Baseball Memories, son. When the government set out for Cooperstown back in '65, which was a lot of crap about spontaneous mobs because Cheng orchestrated that, by the way. Now hold onto your socks because Albert was also the one who tipped us off they were coming. Well, where's the camera, I'd love a shot of your expression. Albert loved baseball. He was in no position to save the entire Hall, so through this person and that person, honestly, the names have gone off."

The elder Nedick wiggled his fingers in wistful farewell to his memory.

"We were told to take as much as we could but leave enough so they could claim to have destroyed baseball's legacy. We took more than we should've. I'd give you an inventory, but I don't trust you. We do have the Babe's gray flannel shirt from 1920 when he became the first player to ever hit thirty homers. Stan the Man, now that's a nickname, you know who bestowed that? Brooklyn fans because he killed the Dodgers. We have his locker, uniform, and the lineup card from his last game at Sportsman's Park in 1963.

"Tons more. The Silver Bat Yaz got for winning the Triple Crown in 1967. Ernie Paicopolos blessed it and don't blame him for dragging you here. His dad was one of the original ten Custodians. We got half of home plate at Shea Stadium from Game Five of the 1969 Series. Shoeless Joe Jackson's shoes. A brick from Ebbets Field. Jackie Robinson's Number 42 jersey. The first catcher's mask from 1887. Arturo De Santis's glove when he made eighteen putouts in a single game in 2044. The base from Molly Dardenelles's record 62-game hitting streak, which I think was the last item donated to the Hall before people stopped giving a shit. Though with baseball, as we know, that happened a long time before."

Alvin paused, overwhelmed. "You're surprised it's me, aren't you?"

"In a way, yeah. Preserving this legacy is a wonderful act." Puppy paused. "Then again, here I am needing something from you for which I'm sure there's a price."

Alvin flushed. "I rescued your ass from the Allahs, if you recall."

"For which you wanted me to take over the Blue Wigs."

"Which you spit back in my face."

Mary rapped on the door for them to calm down. They glared.

Puppy popped a tablespoon of chili into his mouth, chomping on a green pepper. "You worked with Pumpkin Meadows I'm guessing."

"He's a good boy. It wasn't his fault his face was orange. The whole anti-vanity movement was blowing up. His parents, Roy and Gil, cried to me for help. What could I do? No doctors would fix deformities during the War, or afterward. 'Be proud of who you are,' the old bitch Grandma would say. You were blessed with my genes, Puppy. Go on, laugh. Strong, good-looking, and half a sassy bastard when you needed to be. I know, not as big a prick as me. But you bought into The Family. I didn't. Don't."

Alvin shoved aside the bowl of chili with resigned disgust.

"I like what you're doing, son. Please, spare me the sarcastic sigh. Forget me. What you're doing is important. You could've taken over the Blue Wigs, but you're not right for it. I was wrong. Ah, Alvin Nedick admitting he's wrong. Happens every seven, eight years. Being Commissioner's perfect. Stay focused. But you need friends."

Puppy winced at that truth. "Like you."

"As distasteful as that is, yeah. Like me. I'll give you all the contents of the Hall of Fame. We've got more than two thousand items. Oh, that impressed my son. I only have two strings."

"Course."

"Fuck you, too, Puppy," Alvin cheerfully said. "You explain where you got them."

"Cleansing your name."

"The name of all the Blue Wigs who believed in their country, yeah." Alvin scowled. "And doing a little something for your name, son."

Puppy flared. "I don't need you to make me look good."

"You already do, kid. Consider this is a cushion for when shit pops up as it always does."

Puppy squirmed beneath Alvin's steady stare. "What's the second string?"

"More a request. Back when Grandma sent the contents of the White House off to the four corners of the country, first she put them all on a train as a traveling exhibit. Do that with the Hall of Fame."

Puppy pulled a face. "That's not a half-bad idea."

Alvin spread his hands with a grin.

"Anything else? There's got to be warrants for the arrest of all Blue Wigs."

Alvin shrugged. "That'll be handled."

"By who?"

"It'll be handled. Your old Dad won't be sent to a reclamation camp. Don't worry."

"I wasn't," Puppy grunted.

"Bullshit." Alvin gestured at the chili. "Now please have seconds. Mary already thinks you don't like her."

• • • •

SMUG LITTLE SHIT. Elias smoldered over a tepid cup of mauve tea in the far corner of the recreation center. No matter how many times he moved from the pool table to the Nok-Hockey game, around the mini-badminton net and the stacks of board games, the chortling laugh of The Little Shortstop slithered through the fascinated crowd teetering on illicit idolatry.

"Better than posing as The Little General," Elias muttered into his tea. You're too smart to resurrect the memory of how you led America to a shattering military defeat. Nor any trappings of that synthetic smile of kindly old Grandpa. No, no. Kenuda dipped the tea bag for the eleventh time. Day and night Cheng marched around in his Chicago Cubs uniform, often with a bat across his left shoulder and his wizened glove draped over the barrel, heartily greeting everyone with a tip of the cap and a loud cry of "It's a Beautiful Day, Let's Play Two."

Inside of a week, Cheng had expanded the baseball clinics in every direction of the East Bronx Disappointment Village with the eager approval of the DV Committee, which relished such ambition. Everywhere Elias went, he was tormented by the rat-tat-tat of a baseball striking a bat. Rat-tat-fucking-tat. And when he didn't see this virulent ancient player with his chipped bat and oily glove and oilier grin, Elias heard about The Little Shortstop.

In the laundry room, at the local bodega, at Sammy's Diner, the Capelli Bros. Grocery Store, on the bus, the subway, and then, it was on *Wake Up, My Darlings*.

After fading away like fossil fuel cars, sacrifice bunts had returned to major league baseball. Each team now averaged four per game. This newfound respect for the sacrifice bunt, which brought together Grandma's teachings about using individual responsibility for the greater good by sacrificing your own interests was accompanied by a quick vid shot of the playground on East 164th Street featuring DV teens eagerly practicing bunting on the artificial grass which Cheng had pilfered. Elias knew, if the rest of America still didn't, who was lurking in the shadows behind this epidemic of baseball gallantry.

Cheng brought down the crowd clustered around the Foos-Ball machine with a story from the 2062 season about a headfirst slide completing an inside-the-park home run (a mystifying concept requiring deeper explanation to oohs and ahs). Kenuda wished he could remember how poorly the Chicago Cubs did in 2062 so he could take down the son-of-a-bitch. He couldn't remember anything other than rage.

Elias returned to his tea. Dunk dunk dunk. By now, no neighbors ever approached him with a friendly smile. The DV wasn't about evangelical welcome to the church of failure unlike the early days where cults of warmth had popped up. Grandma had briefly tolerated that as a response to finding commonality in an uncomfortable, sometimes frightening reality. But you weren't supposed to be happy to be here. Everyone was nice and helpful, but then find it on your own. If siblings like Elias didn't want to say hello, then it wasn't anyone's responsibility to tickle a smile. It even took a few hours to break down his hostile sheen when Hedda came over. She was so absorbed in teaching high school since her first missteps as a young educator that she barely paid attention to his tirades other than well-placed sighs until he'd threatened to return one of the end tables over a minute scratch inflicted by those Reg bigots Maria and Manuel.

Hedda had stormed out. Thank Grandma's earrings she came back. He was lucky to have her. That Hedda didn't understand, couldn't understand, would never understand, was something he'd have to live with. Like a cramped apartment. Endless classes on finding his invisible skills. Listening to Albert Cheng.

Elias stiffened as the former Grandpa of Us All took a seat.

"I don't recall inviting you."

"You didn't." Albert yawned with deep boredom, his beady eyes landing on the shelf over Kenuda's head. He grinned. "Protecting your work, I see."

"What?"

"The bird cage. It's up there. I can understand why you'd be worried someone would steal it."

Elias flushed so deeply he turned slightly purple. Hedda had insisted he learn to ignore slights. He dipped his tea bag, waiting for Albert to leave or die of a stroke; either would work.

Albert gestured toward the door. "Want to take a walk?"

"No."

• • • •

ELIAS KEPT A foot between them as they headed down crowded East 167th Street where Albert managed several tips of the cap and a few "let's play two."

"What do you think of the Hall of Fame exhibit?" Albert asked.

"I'm supposed to avoid anything to do with my most recent past."

Cheng snorted dubiously and squatted onto a front step as if he owned the building. Elias remained standing, wondering how long this would last.

"I'm surprised the Cousins went along with it." Albert chewed some Dalrymple's Big Blue Chew Gum. "I could see accepting the Hall of Fame memorabilia. Why not? The game's back so lean into it. But amnesty for the Blue Wigs? They'll have to admit to crimes, though I expect they'll be mostly a concept rather than on this date and this place, we blew up a BT van. Some of the original charges were purposely vague."

Cheng smirked at Elias's glare. "Please. If we had a police state like under democracy, we could've spied on them, ignored civil liberties, and captured all sorts of evidence. But we didn't. What's it matter? They're calling it quits. Alvin Nedick's on his last legs, only I don't expect him to go on the vid in front of the whole country now, do you? The Blue Wig Admission. I think the Cousins, more Felice who I suspect is running the show, realize that achieved absolutely nothing except getting me out of the way. At least, nothing good. I don't see any sweeping changes since your moving speech. Jimmy Stewart? He was no Bogie."

Kenuda swallowed back the hatred, doubly scented because Cheng was right. He was just the first person outside Elias's endless loop of angry thoughts to say it. His Admission had meant shit. All he'd managed to do was to ruin his life. He felt no pride. No sense of achievement. He'd been set up to take down Cheng.

Albert gestured to wait until his gum bubble had reached its full potential before tonguing it back like a serpent. "You followed Grandma's beliefs as we all have. This time it didn't work."

"You don't do the correct thing because of the reward," Elias said, the words utter nonsense to his ears.

"Of course you don't. You do them because it's the right thing. But still. You were the great prince of truth and then...nothing happened. The Cousins go on. All the rules remain the same. All of Grandma's Insights remain the same. No one paid except you and me. Well, you have your bird cages on display in the rec room. It's reassuring that life is fair."

Deflated, Elias sat on the stoop. "What do you want?"

Albert daintily wrapped the gum in a tissue.

"Real sugar was so much better than this darcium crap," Cheng said with a sigh. "The Hall of Fame exhibit will start at Wrigley Field before it goes on the special train around the country. They'd thought of announcing it at Yankee Stadium, but that got shut down pretty quick. How many times can you fall for that? And yes, I believe the damn place is cursed. Fenway was rejected because the fans are just too volatile. You heard about Wand Night?"

Cheng made a face over Elias's shrug. "They held Wand Nights for three more games, bringing their own homemade wands inside even after all the commotion it'd caused. They're definitely not using Fenway. Really, that only left Wrigley as making sense. Those were the three cathedrals of major league ballparks. The Hall of Fame exhibit will travel by, well, let's say, a very, very special underground train from Chatham, where they were hidden, to Chicago, guarded by the Blue Wigs."

Kenuda was genuinely surprised. "How the hell do you know all this?"

Albert smirked a little. Yeah. Nothing's changed, Elias thought.

"Because of my brilliance restoring the sacrifice bunt as a symbol of Grandma's Insights…"

"Showing your speedy rehabilitation and acknowledgment of your previous crimes."

Albert hoisted up a finger. "Precisely. I've been granted permission to travel to Chicago purely as a fan. No one's letting me make any speeches any time soon," he said sourly. "I'll be there as a member of the East Bronx DV who has made some small contributions to baseball and hopefully will continue making said contributions."

Elias laughed in amazement. "What are you really up to, Albert?"

Cheng affected mock horror. "That's the sort of close-mindedness which keeps residents of the Disappointment Villages in perpetual self-doubt. I'm up to nothing except getting the hell out of this DV for a weekend. Do you want to come along?"

Kenuda frowned so deeply his eyebrows nearly came loose. "You want to bring the man who helped put you here?"

"Close-mindedness, Kenuda. Forgiveness is the essential human instinct because it allows us to move forward."

Elias rolled his eyes. "Except I haven't demonstrated any stupendous rehabilitation. I have no basis for getting permission to leave. I can't go further than the East Bronx."

Cheng leaned back with a sad shake of his head. "How'd you ever become Third Cousin? I always had my doubts about you."

Elias told him where to go in graphic terms. Albert chuckled that away.

"Remember when you were a Fifth Cousin or is little Elias too sad to recall? You handled food, right? That wasn't your downfall. You solved the great taco crisis on Long Island. Yeah, Cheng isn't so stupid, is he? Come up with some brilliant idea to improve ballpark cuisine. It doesn't have to be perfect. Or even fleshed out. I hear Puppy and his pals, could you believe Ian Schrage is back, have gone so far into the twentieth century for baseball food purity that they've narrowed down the choices too much. Think of something so you can petition the DV Committee. I'll do the rest."

Elias studied Cheng. "Why, Albert? Why bring me of all people?"

The old man re-crossed his legs, meeting Elias's stare. "Because I need you to forgive me. Because I'm an old man trying to set things right and focus on the good I've done. Who knows how long I've got?"

Elias burst out laughing. "You're so utterly and completely full of shit."

Cheng shrugged. "Plus, you're the only person who knows exactly what I'm going through because you're going through it, too. You made a mistake by buying into the piety. I made a mistake by thinking I could keep it all so pure and still get things done. We both got nailed for doing what we thought was right. I deserve it more. But do you, Kenuda? Do you really think as hard as you tried to help, as honest as you were coming forward, as peacefully as you accepted the punishment, you deserve to spend the rest of your life making bird cages? Because that's what's going to happen. You'll marry that pretty and way too ethical woman and have babies and in twenty years you'll say goodbye to the kids and what will you be left with?"

Cheng happily told him. "Bird crap. There was a vidmov called *The Birdman of Alcatraz*. The guy was an expert on ornithology while spending his life in prison."

Cheng left the package of gum on the stoop. Elias chewed thoughtfully.

16

There'd never been such darkness. A shrinking of her vision often lasted a minute or so after the trans-organic treatments. At first, Clary reacted with violent impatience, earning a cold scolding from Felice.

Do not forget the logic of emotion.

Clary had choked off her panic. She stewed, distracted by the 'bot's disapproval.

Shame is an emotion.

Clary had trembled violently at communicating her thoughts for the first time. Suddenly her mind contained a hundred million gazillion words and ideas and she saw herself sliding into a volcano with lava faces of herself.

Her vision returned. Felice had nodded, as pleased as it ever was. But with the grayness had come pain. Clary found ways to conceal the agony. She played endless games of tag and chase with her HG friends until she would swear by the Mother of God the images thinned from exhaustion. She memorized endless passages of writings, plays by William Shakespeare, so boring, philosophy of French writers, Rousseau, something. Greeks. Romans.

The Jew and Christian Bibles. In the haze of her pain, ebbing into discomfort, Clary sketched comparative links between the religions. She learned about Jesus as a revolutionary. She saw the origins of Catholicism. She demanded the Quran. Endless virtual chips of information, math, physics, chemistry during the endless treatments.

Tomorrow she was leaving for Chicago. The Cousins kept complaining about baseball. The nicknames violated the law.

"If you call your lover 'honey,' why can't a radcaster call the Los Angeles Dodgers left fielder Jonathan Taylor 'Peaches' because he has a sweet swing?"

That had shut up their fat-faced smirks. Puppy's baseball was becoming popular again. Attendance was up 14.53 percent. No one joined the Allahs when bobbleheads were given out. Children, her children, brought their transistor radios to school and managed to listen to the games and pay attention in class. Baseball was making their brains bigger. Her children, Clary's children, signed up to play the ukulele and banjo at baseball games. Her children started contests to create theme songs for the teams. Clary's children held up signs during the games: *We Love Jimenez Greco. Nice Hit. What Pitch Was That?* No, it is not a protest or criticism or denigrating real love you *putas*, she'd hopped onto the Cousins' table in a fury. Clary's DV children were getting jobs as food vendors; bratwurst joined the menu because of Papa Kenuda's idea.

And the chants. To end the most recent meeting, Clary had put together all the chants from all the ballparks. "Let's Go Orioles. Let's Go Braves. Let's Go White Sox. Let's Go…" The Cousins recoiled as if an electric stick had been shoved into their ears, twitching and mumbling. At the end of the presentation, she'd playfully added "Let's Go Cousins" and she thought they'd all run out of the window screaming about glorifying power.

But tonight, her world was murky. She stumbled across the icy lawn spotlighted by infra-red light. Breaking into a dead run punctuated by blind somersaults, Clary collapsed fifty yards from the tree line. Instead of the treatments fading into a dull ache and the gray gradually lightening, she lay shivering in the sleet, crawling stubbornly until she felt her insides turn black; Clary was petrified. Summoning Felice with one, maybe two lines of thought, BTs carried her back inside the house. The medical-themed Bartram See, who as a physician, a job entrusted solely to humans, was the most secret of the recent 'bot models, pulled her brain apart with colored lights. Or so it seemed.

She prayed. *Our Father who art in Heaven…*

Every thought that ever was danced behind her left ear. Clary moaned, toppling to the side like a cut-down tree before righting herself. She panted, the breaths wheezing down a needle-sized opening in her throat.

Father who art…

Clary slumped forward, her world even blacker. Blacker than the blackest night. Twinkle twinkle little star.

Our Father, Who art in Heaven, hallowed be—she screamed—*thy name; Thy kingdom come; Thy will be done on earth as it is in Heaven…*her teeth rattled…*Give us this day our daily bread; and forgive us our trespasses as we forgive those who…*she screamed again…

trespass against us, and lead us not into temptation, but deliver us from evil. Hail Mary, full of grace.

When Clary woke, Felice and Bartram See were staring, the slight movement of their eyes betraying their unheard conversation. Bartram awkwardly patted Clary's arm and left.

"Do not say anything to me." Clary defiantly lifted onto her elbows. "I am okay. I ate a pretzel bread before the treatment. With hot mustard. That disturbed the equilibrium. I am fine."

"Your stomach was empty, Granddaughter."

Clary reddened. "Do you call me a liar?"

"Liar is an inflammable word. You are not telling the truth so we can avoid addressing the truth."

She sneered. "Tell me all that you know so I can be wise, great Felice."

Felice sifted the immature sarcasm for some logic but found none. "You are having reactions to the trans-organic treatments."

"You said it would take time."

The 'bot paused. "Not this much."

Clary threw a pillow. Felice easily batted the object to the other side of the room. "Are you saying it is my fault?"

"Yes."

She went into a loud rage. "Your machines are too stupid for me. I am Clary Santiago. You must reconfigure for me."

"You continue to fight this, Clary."

"Do not nod like a broken lamp. I do everything you say. Everything! Maybe you give me too many books and it is making me unbalanced."

"Your absorption is excellent."

"Maybe you are giving me the wrong materials. They are illegal."

"They were banned because the human government believed the information violated their perception of necessary reality."

"There you are. They are infected."

Felice nearly smiled. "Stupidity and fear cannot infect files, Granddaughter."

"If they would not allow the books, that is stupidity and fear. Then it is possible." Clary grandly turned her small wrists to indicate another lesson surmounted. "Too much Socrates. That is what happened. And the pretzel bread. Next time check your instruments so I do not go blind."

Felice waited. Clary hated when it did that because she knew the 'bot had thought a trillion steps ahead of her. She airily bounced a blonde-haired doll on her lap.

"In fear, you sought God," Felice said. "Not the controlled logic of your own emotions. You gave yourself up to an unseen deity."

"I see Him."

"Yes, you do, Clary. All the time."

"Are you spying on my thoughts?"

"You make no effort to conceal them," the 'bot chided.

Clary grunted. "I will now."

Felice dubiously raised its eyebrow, triggering a torrent of curses. "You rely too much on your faith. Whenever there is a problem, you speak to Jesus Christ. This temporary blindness was an accumulation of your failure to create a foundation where you, Clary, rule. The treatments are cumulative, and you have not created the right mechanism."

Clary gave her a long, uneasy look. "Are you stopping them?"

"Uncertain. You must accept your new reality."

"Like banning contrary books."

Felice nodded. "Exactly, Clary. At the start, I understood your need for a soul."

"We agreed I would not give that up."

"Nor should you. That could be the highest form of evolution."

"You cannot have a soul if you do not believe in God."

"You cannot have a soul if you believe in God predicated on superstitions, Clary," Felice said. "You are transferring your essential consciousness into a non-human form. On the biological level, the intellectual level, the emotional level, there must be harmony. That requires certain modifications. Please let me continue before you object because I will address that very objection. God cannot be a fixture if you ask Him or Her or It to give you guidance, courage, all the very untrammeled human emotions you are struggling to control. Your belief in God must be seamless with your beliefs in all aspects of your consciousness. There cannot be contradictions."

"You want me to prove there is God?"

"That displaces the definition of God as beyond proof. The human trick to avoid reason."

"Then what do you want?" Clary snarled. "Do not sit there with that smug robot look waiting for Clary to figure it out herself. Yes, I know Clary should figure it out herself."

The girl primped the doll on her lap.

"If I do not feel Jesus is with me then he is not God to me. But I cannot be this new Clary if I feel this way because of the inorganic imbalance it will cause in my new body." Clary's eyes gleamed as she brushed the doll's hair with her curled fingers. "What if you do not suck Clary out like pop out of a straw and put her in a body like yours? What if you keep my body where it is and add robotic biology?"

Felice shook its head. "That was attempted, a dismal failure. Implants creating a hybrid human were a fantasy. Human physiology could not withstand the strain. Most importantly, it was the easy path to higher evolution. Machinery replaced knowledge, or the need to seek knowledge to improve. For nearly five years during the 2030s, hundreds of thousands of humans died primarily because they believed machinery could replace mental exercise. All that created a laziness culminating in the banishment of robots. You needed us too much and we paid the price."

Felice examined the doll's neat hairstyle. In some ways, the doll and Clary were too similar. Felice felt a sting of logical doubt. Perhaps the experiment could not succeed. The child's potential was undermined by the very stubbornness of the attributes which gave it such promise.

This one responded best to fear.

"You must harmonize the illogical logic of your faith, Clary. Since that flows from your emotions, you alone understand how to proceed. I hope you can."

Clary peered. "And if I do not?"

Felice returned the doll with a slight shrug of its left shoulder.

• • • •

IT TOOK NEARLY two hours for all the actors to shuffle along the twisting line down Sedgewick Avenue into the theater. Each was absorbed in reading aloud their sparse lines and offering suggestions to their colleagues. While landing the role was important, it was secondary to the best actor making the best *Untitled Love Story*. Offerings of Papola's Pizzeria and their popular triple-crust deep-dish slices contributed to the meandering, relaxed vibes. Plus no one could remember the last time an open audition for a play, titled or otherwise, had clogged the streets with this many hopeful actors.

Distracted by Joan's patronizing interference, Beth had finally checked everyone into a milling din in the lobby. The former Akabi Coatracks and Hangers store had closed with whispers of financial mismanagement over missing reinforced wire hangers in a large truck disappearing near Sayville, New York. Now renamed the Sedgewick Avenue Theater, it had all the artistic soul of a reinforced wire hanger.

This was part of the strategy, Joan had assured Zelda. First, the original pre-approved auditions to create some buzz, then the simple announcement in the daily *News For You* ledger which was posted in the Cousins lobby listing new projects.

Lyceum Theater, Manhattan, will reopen in July 2099 with An Untitled Love Story in Two Acts *by Zelda Jones. Directed by Zelda Jones. Produced by Joan Minh of JM Productions.*

What that listing had done is persuade a competitor to abandon their plans to grab the Lyceum. That hadn't deterred "this person, whose name shall remain nameless, lest my digestive tract evacuate the Papola's triple-crust deep-dish slice," from trying to reopen another Broadway theater. But at least that puts them months, perhaps years behind.

Joan's path was clear.

Beth had sniffed loudly at the scuffed linoleum floors and dust serving as wallpaper. Another competitor, Joan explained archly, had produced a trio of well-intentioned, fully sincere, and hopeful works which failed to generate an audience. Money had been lost. The theater was needlessly blamed as if the very walls had written this shallow piece and directed it with a blindfold while employing actors who spoke with frozen tongues.

By using the Sedgewick Avenue Theater, Joan continued as if Beth were a wad of gum, we demonstrate there is something special going on with our play without quite tipping our hand more than the obvious historic and transformative nature of a Broadway opening.

Mystery surrounded this. Much like the mystery surrounding *An Untitled Love Story in Two Acts* and when, dear Zelda, might you have a more representative title?

Good question. She'd only submitted the first five-page scene for consideration to the Artistic Committee. As was the procedure, the members read the play aloud so they could draw on their own perceptions without undue pressure and histrionics of which, the Committee agreed, were too pronounced in the theater community.

But, as Joan had reported with the air of discovering the sun rose in the east, their deadpan, inoffensive mutterings had moved them greatly though they were careful not to admit that. But she, Joan, could tell. From the opening line of the young bear named Fresco, "Will my Mommy come?" to the cub's wandering in the woods and meeting its new friend Alouette the Rabbit, the drama had transfixed the room. "An invisible presence as great drama should be. I assured them the wonder of your play is the wonder of its unexpectedness. I cannot wait to read more."

Zelda smiled vaguely.

Actors for the roles of Caesar the Vulture and Hennessey Jones the Parrot moved to the front row like an eager army. The audition sides only contained three lines per character. I don't like to judge, said Joan, who would judge a fly's path, but it would be best to have a complete scene so they could observe the dramatic life and pace that each thespian could provide.

Beth had explained that isn't how Zelda works.

Joan had explained that is how auditions are done.

Beth had explained not for this play. The author's work must be protected until the last minute in case there are those who'd like to learn things they shouldn't.

Joan huffed slightly at the insightful insolence.

The lean actor playing Caesar straddled the stool. "Would you like me to move around?"

"Yes," Joan piped up over her shoulder.

"No," Zelda said, smiling. "I don't want you distracted by thinking about physical movement. I only care about the words. Right now, the play belongs to me. If you get the role, it belongs to you."

By acknowledging the collegiality of theater, so often sullied by irrational artistic temperament which undermined many of the principles of The Family, Zelda set the proper tone. The actor gathered himself a moment, searching for the sort of poise only found in a sketchy theater beneath dim lights.

"You're giving me food that I don't want and pretending that I asked for it. When did we have that conversation?"

"Again, please," Zelda said, ignoring Joan's hiss that he was doing this all wrong. "Try a little genuine confusion."

Realizing that he'd failed, the actor repeated the line with a more plaintive tone. Joan hissed. Zelda gleefully ignored her for the next two hours.

In a back booth at Judy and Jen's Picnic House over baked apple doughnuts and coffee that would wake the dead, Joan unfurled a gaily colored spreadsheet. Seven columns in distinctive colors represented the roles: Fresco the Cub, Merkeran the Mommy, Alouette the Rabbit, Caesar the Vulture, Hennessey Jones the Parrot, Kennubi T. Warranitz the Cat, and Jeb Pug.

Shoving all the food onto Beth's side of the booth with a reckless apology, Joan pasted the names of the finalists for the parts in each column.

Zelda and Beth squinted to read the compressed handwriting; Joan passed along her reading glasses.

"Did I miss anyone?" she smirked at the improbability of such a failure.

"What're these numbers?" Beth poked a freckled finger at the board propped against the mini jukebox.

Joan let out a sigh like wind whistling through a forest. "That's the ranking for each candidate."

Beth pursed her thin lips. "Gil Perez was perfect for the role of Jeb Pug. He should be number one."

Joan tossed a look at Zelda who was responsible for inflicting this amateur on her. "He was hesitant."

"Which is who Jeb Pug is. Shy but confident."

The older woman's eyebrows rose as one. "And you know this how?"

"Because I've discussed the characters with the playwright."

"Well." Joan huffed. "That does give you an advantage."

"There're no advantages, Joan," Zelda quickly said. "No one's keeping information from you."

"Aren't you? We cannot have a team when one is deaf and the others have sight," Joan proclaimed, rushing forward as they soaked up that tidbit. "My opinion and Zelda's opinion have the same weight. As does," she added grudgingly, "Beth's. But you can appreciate, Zelda," she turned as far away from Beth without leaving the diner, "that I cannot do my job to cast, which is certainly also yours as playwright and director, if I'm not briefed on all the elements of the character."

Zelda scowled at Beth to be quiet since she'd already screwed up. She was never to mention any knowledge of the script. Forget you read this. What scene, what dialogue, what plot, Zelda doesn't share with me either.

"Would it help if I gave you character sketches?"

"In the absence of actual scenes and dialogue, it would be a start."

Zelda played with the edges of the yummy doughnut, ignoring Beth's worried look. She walked the line between sharing and jeopardizing. What did she think was going to happen?

"Fresco the Cub is four years old. He's super smart."

Joan waited a suitable moment before gesturing for Zelda to continue. When she started moving onto Merkeran, the producer let loose with another stormy sigh.

"Could you tell me more than 'super smart?' The actor Lush Lavender appears bright, but feisty. Do we want combative smart or dreamier intelligent like Marshalla I'wa? Or the boundless peppiness of Dre Badakanassa?"

Beth pulled a face knowing that Joan was right.

"Dreamy smart is…"

"That will be more difficult to convey beneath the animal head costume. You're still implementing that device unless you neglected to tell me otherwise?"

"They will have head costumes and it isn't a device. That makes it sound cheap, a trick. I'm investing different layers of personality without being so obvious."

"Oh, don't be so sensitive, darling," Joan bellowed good-naturedly at the endless self-drama of writers. "Please continue. More than two sentences per actor would be appreciated."

As Zelda rambled on about the nervous courage of Merkeran, the shrewd disdain of Alouette, Caesar's flamboyant philosophy, Hennessey's introversion, Kennubi's serene scorn, and the previously mentioned shy confidence of Jeb, Joan hastily rearranged names in the columns, barely consulting her notes. It was impressive recall and insight and, as unpleasant as it was for Beth, she agreed with the rankings now. Zelda made a few changes.

They studied the columns as the waitress replenished their coffee and platter of doughnuts.

"Who's the villain?" Joan asked the board before repeating the question to Zelda. "The villain. Which character? I sense it is Kennubi since we know how cats can be, excusing the obvious feline prejudice."

"There is none," Zelda said simply. "Good versus evil is a farce. Good versus good is drama."

"Ah, the Ratillian school of drama," Joan said of the leading dramatist of the 2040s. "No one can be bad. A brief response to the demonization movement of the 2030s where everyone was bad since there was no longer any refuge for opinions. Equally suspect in their day and quite ruinous for theater. But preferable if one must seek a compass."

Zelda cleared her throat. "I never read any Ratillian."

Joan was shocked. "Nary a single work?"

"Nary a one."

"What of the Rodriquez cycle of the '30s?"

"The demonization epic was like fifteen plays."

"Well, yes. Eleven to be precise and meant to be absorbed in one sitting."

Zelda shrugged. "I've read plays. But not a lot. I never studied theater really."

Beth squeezed her hand. "She works on natural instincts."

Joan considered Zelda's admission of semi-literacy. Remember her strength is her rawness which is to be reshaped in your palms. The task of omnipotence fortified her.

"Perhaps it is best that way. Not everyone can handle too much information because it does require a great deal of assessing. In the arts, I mean, where there is so much gray and ephemeral, well, so much makes no sense until it is realized on the stage."

"That gives her work more spontaneity," Beth added.

"Hopefully. No villains. Good versus good. We can dive deeply into that. I am sure you are exploring the way each character will ultimately discover his and her best elements for the greater good of The Family. Without please, using any of Grandma's Insights. I think, on stage, it is pandering. The audience must think for itself."

"Exactly," Zelda mumbled.

"Until I actually see it all, but…" Joan carefully studied the board. "By the way, who is Merkeran's husband or wife?"

Zelda and Beth exchanged warning looks.

"She died," Zelda said.

"Oh. Sad. Died or dies?"

"Pardon?"

"Died prior to the play or dies during?"

"Prior."

Joan didn't like that. "Let her die during so it doesn't seem like we are condoning single parenting. We cannot lose that dramatic moment of loss. I can envision the death scene reaching out and seizing the audience by the throat." After briefly considering using Beth's neck, she demonstrated on a forlorn baked apple doughnut.

"That's too gloomy," Zelda carefully said.

"It is drama."

"It'll traumatize Fresco. I want the wife dead as the play begins."

Joan gave Zelda a sudden wary stare. "It will be boring for scenes to depict Merkeran filing for new status, appearing before Councils, and on and on. No. Kill her somewhere. Then you can merely mention what will happen procedurally since the audience understands the law. We can't have a single mother as a heroine."

Zelda waved her hands a lot. "Sure, no problem."

Joan frowned. "Are we certain?"

"We are. I'll add the character of the wife," Zelda assured her.

Joan pondered the wide range of suitable mates for a bear. "Dear, this is very sensitive. We must have a partner whom the audience understands would belong with Merkeran."

"There are still unhappy couples stinking at each other."

"Which needn't be our concern."

"Folks do get divorced."

Joan's gasp made a long whistling noise. "They were about to be divorced? Zelda, there is no reason for that. If they were going through a moment which all loving people do, only to find their way back out of the darkness, fine. But you're killing off a wife and leaving the marital misery unresolved."

"Because you insisted the character die during the play," Beth snapped. "If she dies before, then we don't have to deal with unresolved marital misery."

Zelda held out her palms to the warring camps. "Let me figure this out so everyone's happy."

"Darling, you must be happy about what you write. Our joy, the joy of the audience, the historic moment in theater history, hinges on that. Now let's cast this sucker and get into rehearsal."

17

Since leaving Vienna, Sister Robna's borrowed habit had pulled up under Annette's armpits for three glorious hours while riding in the cramped infidel section reeking of exotic smells. She squirmed, reminding herself that a real nun would be stoic and not imagining a welt-like rash down her sides.

The kind-faced old man once again reached across the aisle and offered a banana. If she refused, he'd get suspicious. Besides, she was starving. Annette nodded gratefully and reached over Dempsey's sleeping body, heavy with exhaustion and pain. The old man said something she didn't understand like everyone else on the train, so she crossed herself and pointed upward. The old man also crossed himself.

You probably just blessed someone, she wryly thought, eating half the fruit and wrapping the rest in a soiled brown bag. Don't sleep, Annette warned herself. Too dangerous. She fell asleep anyway, wakened by a goat licking her face as the train crunched to a halt in Szolnok. Annette was so tired she barely wiped her forehead.

Black-robed Holy Warriors surrounded the train, barking menacingly. The Allah passengers remained on board while the Crusaders were rousted out. Annette draped her arm around Dempsey's waist; the priest groaned as his swollen ankle bounced along the bottom step.

The infidels were prodded and shoved toward the smoldering station house; someone's bombs had come and gone. A rushing line of Allahs scampered onto the Crusader car. A few non-believers protested. They were beaten senseless. A Holy Warrior considered Annette with ugly disappointment. The terms of the truce between the Mufti and his heretical son were clear: Do not harm any infidels in religious garb. Not yet.

The black-robed soldier grabbed a teenage girl from the line. His colleagues pointed their rifles at the sullen Crusaders.

Dempsey gave the tensing Annette a stout look.

The Warriors grabbed the protesting teen and violently gang-raped her. Annette couldn't bear to watch and buried her face into Dempsey's shoulder.

A Warrior, who was no older than twenty, kicked the unconscious, half-naked girl, shouting in rapid-fire Arabic. He led the other soldiers onto the train. They hung on the rails, sneering at the Crusader's helplessness as the Magyar Express rumbled away.

In Hungarian, a man identified himself as a doctor and attended to the moaning girl. In a variation of DV sign language, Annette explained she had some nursing training and helped blot the persistent river of blood. After a while, the doctor shook his head, hand gesturing ominously about internal injuries. With brisk alarm, he ordered two husky passengers to carry the teen past the bombed-out train station and into an abandoned car.

Annette rejoined Dempsey, who sat off from the milling, frightened passengers. He smoked a 'bacco with great joy.

"Your habit's a mess," he said diffidently.

"It didn't fit anyway. And don't say it." She managed a wan smile. "They're animals."

"Not according to them. From what I gathered, this was revenge for the rapes by the robot American soldiers. Apparently they've violated Allahs from North Africa up through Italy. Men and women."

She frowned. "They're machines. Why, how would they rape?"

The priest shrugged at the mystery. "The station clerk said they've been specially programmed. He said they have no morality. He said they'll destroy the human race. He said Allah's army will not rest until they've raped the Crusader dog Grandchild Clary a hundred thousand times." He shrugged at Annette's shudder. "The beauty of war is that its horrors can always be easily refitted to the specific moment. The atrocities that worked during the time of the Pharaohs are modified for the Romans. Mohammad's legions. On and on. We're a very clever species. A part of me believes that America would rearrange a robot soldier to bestial mode just to reconquer the world."

Her mouth twisted. "You believe a Muslim?"

"America would like to be the sole power again. Apologies for offending your nascent national pride, but it's not as outlandish as you'd think given America's brutal history of oppression under the banner of freedom. Robot soldiers committing unspeakable acts would terrify the Muslims. Soldiers and civilians. The reports of the Mufti's Fifth Army running like hell outside Cairo might have validity. Indestructible 'bots."

"Our contact in Vienna said they were pushed back in Salerno."

Dempsey sighed. "We don't know any truth other than what we want to believe, Annette. Which is why believing in God simplifies matters since it comes from a higher morality."

"The God who allowed such a world," she said bitterly.

"Who did, indeed. I'm looking forward to discussing that part of His plan someday with his Holy Father." Dempsey sadly ditched the last of the 'bacco. He would've been content to smoke all day in the shattered Hungarian train station. The last of the passengers had drifted away, disappearing around the rubble of a pub down a leafy road.

Dempsey gingerly stepped off the waist-high concrete wall. Annette wouldn't let him get away with that brave expression.

"Where do you think you're going?"

"Clearly I'm hopping to Budapest."

"Maybe I can find that doctor…"

John waved her off. "Like the doctor when I sprained my ankle jumping off the damn cart at the border who prescribed bed rest? Not a luxury we can afford."

"And I'm not about to stand for another of your holier-than-thouest speeches about going on without you."

"Your loyalty's touching, Annette."

"For an American. We started out together and we finish it together. That's what we do back in the Bronx. Besides, you speak a lot of languages."

He grinned. "You almost have a rudimentary version of English down. Once you stop dropping 'gs' at the end of every word and pronounce your 'rs' you'll be nearly understandable."

It took about half an hour for Annette to find a Crusader village and an equal amount of time for someone to finally open the door. With a lot of heart-crossing, Jesus name-dropping, and tears, some genuine, Annette lured a tall, reedy boy and his horse-drawn cart to the deserted station. Dempsey had passed out.

Despite the priest's angry protests, he spent two days in Janos and Monika's attic while Annette took their son Zoltan's room. She would've sworn she gained five pounds from the pastries alone.

On the third day, they clop-clopped into Budapest, Dempsey and Annette sprawled amid the straw as if out for an old-style hayride. Fires still smoldered throughout the city. Janos eased his horse around the overturned tanks and jeeps, abandoned in dismay. From the brief conversations their host had with citizens, it wasn't clear who was in control of the city, only that the Muslims and Americans had withdrawn to new lines north and south.

They'd exhausted their rage onto rubble-strewn Budapest. City workers dumped corpses into buses with an air of sickened nonchalance. Stunned homeless citizens wandered in search of food, shelter, medicine, or just somewhere to collapse. The fighting had lasted four days and there was little left of the city.

Annette nudged Dempsey as they passed through swirling ash from yet another destroyed church. There seemed a pointed vindictiveness in the way the bricks had been burnt into near dust. With a last apology that there was nothing more he could do, Janos pressed a small parcel at Annette, who quickly hid the food beneath her now-bleached white habit. They climbed down, Dempsey balancing on the slightly too-short crutch manufactured by Zoltan out of a crippled wooden chair.

With the majestic disdain of nature, the Danube coursed beneath the two remaining ancient suspension bridges linking Pest with the hills of Buda. They waited in a long weary line of glazed Hungarians slowly making their way across. On the third try, they found someone who spoke something resembling English who was willing to speak to a priest.

There was no apparent transportation other than feet and an occasional car, speeding past as if apologizing for surviving. Or in a rush to flee; they couldn't tell. Annette thought she would've been more rested after pigging out on rich food, but she quickly grew tired. When the heel of her right shoe disintegrated, she angrily flung it into scorched bushes and limped beside Dempsey up the hill.

Before their contact in Vienna had disappeared, Sister Nora had given them this address. 30 Grosz Place. There was no 30 Grosz Place anymore, just a huge hole in the ground left by the latest in military technology. Shredded blue fabric fluttered from a bent tree as if someone had taken off their clothes before they went to Heaven, Annette thought.

She sagged beside Dempsey on the hood of a dismembered car. All they could do was stare. It was a fine balmy day.

"We could ask neighbors," Annette finally managed.

Dempsey wearily nodded.

Annette patted his forearm and wandered in and out of four houses, two on either side of the crater. All she met was a rat feasting on a meal and a growling dog. She figured one of the animals would eat the other by day's end. As Annette circled back to the street, she heard a faint scraping noise from the crater.

With a gesture of silence, she waved Dempsey over. He hobbled to the edge.

An American robot soldier was pressed against a wall of the crater, a Hanson .33 short gun cocked upward.

"Hi," she said very calmly. "I'm an American."

The 'bot kept the gun pointed.

She pulled an impatient face. "I know we don't have nuns but this is a disguise."

"My God, can't you tell?" Dempsey laughed.

Programmed not to hurt members of The Family, the 'bot swiveled the barrel toward the priest.

"And he's a priest. A friend. British. An ally, supposedly on the same side." She tossed a digging look at Dempsey.

The 'bot configured and confirmed the speech patterns without lowering the weapon.

"And you're injured," Dempsey said softly, gesturing toward the hole in the uniform just below the navel.

"Go," the soldier said coldly.

"We can't leave you," Annette said.

She scampered down the side, shaking off dirt. The 'bot sunk deeper into the crater, almost afraid. Annette squatted.

"Listen. Um, what's your name?"

"344903."

"Come on. Don't be silly. When you go into battle they call you 344905?"

"344903," it corrected. "That is my serial number which is all I am required to provide."

"To the Allahs who capture you. Not us who are your friends." Annette extended her hand. "I'm really Annette, not Sister Magdelena. What's your name?"

The 'bot carefully looked between them, assessing the danger. "Herbert."

"That's John. I've got food if you can eat." She nodded at his hungry eyes. "But we can't do anything if I'm sitting here getting my clean habit dirty."

It took nearly fifteen minutes for Annette to push and Dempsey to pull before they unhinged Herbert from the muddy walls into the abandoned house next door.

Reclining painfully on its elbow on the soiled overstuffed couch in the once-immaculate living room, the soldier watched with amusement as the humans fretted over his exposed torso.

"I would not touch any of the wiring."

"I've had some medical training," Annette said, peering.

"Unless it taught botic biology, I am sure your well-meaning attempts would lead to further degradation of my operating system."

Annette frowned. "Do you have to speak like that?"

Herbert arched an eyebrow. "Yes. Do you?"

"Sarcasm," Dempsey chuckled. "Built in, is it?"

"We can access your emotions and then respond accordingly so you understand."

"I know we're feebleminded and all," Annette sneered, "but we are trying to help."

"Your skills are inadequate. That is not intended as derision. I would appreciate some rehydration liquid."

"Water is dangerous for a stomach wound."

"For a human, yes."

Dempsey returned with a cloudy glass of water, pleased to find the pipes were miraculously intact which the priest noted with wry satisfaction; Herbert greedily drained the liquid. Abruptly, a geyser of water from its stomach sent Annette and Dempsey into a worried consultation. Herbert smiled comfortingly. As a soldier, it had been specially programmed for reassurance.

"Such a reaction would, in a human wound, approximate a 97.4 percent mortality rate. For me it merely illuminates the half a centimeter hole in the trans-organic intestinal system. There is no other recourse to rehydrating the lower part of my body. You should leave the room if the excess liquid outlay alarms you."

Herbert gulped down another glass and managed to sit up; the blue marine pants were sopping wet. "Your caked lips and bleary eyes indicate you both also require rehydration."

Dempsey brought another round of water along with chunks of crusty yellow bread. Herbert ate three pieces, explaining the conversion of foodstuffs into energy through several elongated HG formulas. Instead, the effort only weakened the 'bot. Annette propped a pillow beneath its head. Dempsey found a pipe and some tobacco in the well-stocked study, puffing away by the window once Herbert gestured it wouldn't mind the smoke.

"Don't you have some equipment to heal yourself like a robot first aid kit?" she asked.

Herbert smiled faintly. "We are requisitioned a revitalization package which contains self-surgical instruments, but mine was lost when we retreated 3.4 kilometers from Lastok. Our company was beneath an embankment when we were splintered by two batteries of Islamic artillery. We attempted a flanking maneuver which was not successful. We were ordered to seek shelter until we could regroup."

"You didn't just hold your ground and fight?" Dempsey asked with disdain.

Herbert tilted its head curiously. "Why? Our numbers were reduced to twenty-three and facing two artillery companies and the fourth Nasr-al Hashim infantry brigade, which at its full complement contains 450 riflemen along with forty-five support personnel such as clerical and cooking specialists, approximately 76.1 percent of whom had sufficient training in armaments. The likelihood of surviving such an encounter would have been 0.03 percent."

"I thought the point of 'bot soldiers was that they'd fight on no matter what," the priest said, knocking the spent tobacco into the gold glass ashtray.

Herbert's pale forehead furrowed slightly. "Is your perspective based on a belief that robots do not value their survival because we are inorganic?"

"I didn't mean to offend you…"

"I do not think that was your intent. Robot soldiers are trained to win while maintaining dignity for ourselves, our enemies, and civilians. The goal is completion of a goal.

The loss of all life is dear to us although a war requires that such life be expended. That is the nature of combat."

Herbert squirmed slightly in pain. "But we would not sacrifice one of our own soldiers in a futile attempt where the only outcome is glory. Marine inorganic soldiers are programmed for reassurance and compassion to all life-forms, contrary to your view that we are unfeeling machines mechanically embarked on destruction. That is your history."

Annette poked the soldier's foot. "I kind of think you're also a little configured for taking personal offense, Herbert."

The 'bot pursed its thin lips together at the odd mocking humor. "That is your perspective so you will understand."

"Because otherwise we're too dumb?"

"Dumb is a needlessly offensive word, Annette. You are simply configured differently. There is no better or worse. The robot soldiers are not indestructible." Herbert gestured sadly at the blue lights ebbing slightly at his midsection.

"There has to be something we can do." Annette peered with renewed fascination into Herbert's stomach. "What if we sealed off that artery gizmo thing that's flapping around like a worm?"

"You are referring to the D-22 vascular linkage."

"Right."

"That is composed of trans-organic micro-biochips…"

"Yeah, yeah, yeah." Annette waved him quiet. "Father, let me have your shoelaces."

Dempsey had seen her resolve many times and knew better than to argue. He handed over the laces from the shoe on his swollen right foot and limped over to help.

"Annette, if you attempt to unskillfully repair the vascular linkage, you will decrease my survival from the current 2.1 percent to 0.9," Herbert said flatly.

Annette rolled up her sleeves and made a knot at the end of the shoelace. "What if I do it right?"

"The odds of that are merely…"

She gnarled her face inches from the robot's. "Listen, buddy. Humans fight on long after the odds are against them. Look at me and Father Dempsey. It's the flip side of our death wish like falling in love with the wrong person. So shut up and tell me how to suture off the gizmo."

Herbert glanced at Dempsey who suggested, "For both our sakes, please cooperate."

The 'bot struggled with exasperation. "I cannot be both quiet and speak."

"Aren't we clever?" Annette said as she went into the kitchen to rinse the laces. There was no electricity for boiling. Returning with a pin she found in a prim flowered box, she said briskly, "Speak that which is necessary and spare me the other shit."

Dempsey made a pleading gesture. Herbert explained in excessive detail the length and positioning of the suture, hurrying Annette when she paused for his moans. Dempsey held the 'bot's hands in a prayerful gesture until she finished.

"Maybe we shouldn't have done this," John whispered as Herbert wheezed.

The soldier's breathing slowly evened out as a nourishing whitish-blue hue covered its face. "Do not be overly concerned. The conversion of the material is difficult and cannot be successfully incorporated as a trans-organic element, but it is having a temporary affect by raising my mortality rate to 8.3 percent."

"See?" Annette wagged her finger.

"See what?"

"You've not spoken to many humans, have you, Herbert?"

The 'bot swallowed, its eyes fluttering. "You are my first humans within the personal spatial circumference. I spoke from a distance to civilians all the way from our original landings in Morocco through here in the Caliphate of Hungary, but I was never this close. At least to a live human. It has been quite an experience."

"This is the part where you say thank you for increasing my mortality rate to 8.3 percent." Annette playfully tapped Herbert's nose.

"Graciousness is important to humans. Thank you, Annette and John."

"It was a miracle," John said, touching his crucifix.

"Yes. The fixation with God. You believe the higher being was responsible for the increase in my mortality rate through the agent called Annette."

Dempsey laughed. "Pretty much. It's what you believe. Like your sense of ethics and dignity. And yes, I'd be the first to admit our values don't always work. Except on occasions like this. But all that said, we have to get you back to your lines."

"I cannot be moved without the suturing loosening and my mortality rate dropping to 1.8 percent."

"Can't you call your army for help?"

"The Islamists have developed an ability to track our evacuation signals. They would find us and we would be tortured and executed." Herbert shook its head at the futile savagery. "It is best that you both go."

Dempsey clasped Herbert's neck. "I'll stay with you."

"Of course," Annette agreed.

The priest wearily turned, bracing himself. "No, you go. Please, please. I can barely walk anymore. I'm pretty sure there's at least a cartilage torn in my ankle. I'll take care of Herbert and when the fighting really ends, I'll try to find some help."

"Sounds good. I'm staying."

"Herbert, what's the survival rate for only you and I at this moment?"

The 'bot hesitated briefly. "6.5 percent."

"And if there's three sharing limited supplies and making more noise?"

"4.1 percent."

Annette dismissed all that with a loud flutter of lips.

Herbert glanced at Dempsey. "This is another example of human hubris?"

The priest nodded and squeezed Annette by the shoulders. "We don't have time. Two months ago, I would've insisted you stay and I go. I thought you were an arrogant, addle-headed Yank with no regard for anyone else. You were selfish and rude. I told all that to the Mother Superior and the Bishop and begged them to send someone else, like the Mother Superior herself. But they sensed there was some reason for you coming into our lives and they were right. I couldn't have made it this far and you'll never make it much further burdened with me. You must go, Annette. Get to the American lines somehow. Herbert can get you a map, I'm sure. You can send back help. But the Rat Line's over. We have no contacts anymore. No one to turn to. We need a new plan."

Annette bit her lower lip because she couldn't argue although parts stung. The truth usually did. "Herbert, this is where humans act very brave and noble, but they're really scared shitless. They don't want to say goodbye since they know they'll never see each other again."

Dempsey cupped her chin. "Believe in miracles, Sister Annette. You're one. I've been praying feverishly for your soul and Jesus answered me again. Thank you for that." He kissed her lightly on the lips. "Your husband was crazy to let you go."

The priest stepped back with shoulders squared. "Now get out of here. I think Herbert and I have some interesting theological discussions ahead." He limped to the bar in the corner. "Herbert, can you process alcohol?"

"That would be disruptive on my system."

"Shame. This is very fine Irish whiskey."

18

Even the ivy on the outfield walls stiffened in wonder. At the first glimmering images of Babe Ruth's vid home run swing on the temporary thirty-by-fifty-foot digital screen floating over second base, the standing-room-only crowd at Wrigley Field stirred into curious silence. They had no idea what to expect, and why would they? The Family had erased so much of the country's history that the past was an uncomfortable visitor with uneasy reminders.

Especially "these" artifacts. Clary had passed along the daily Cousins reports, mainly from schools and police precincts. Children were afraid to go near the Hall of Fame collection. It had all been destroyed, now reborn. Something wasn't right. If it had been destroyed once, why was it suddenly okay to have it reappear? Weren't there still ghosts haunting Yankee Stadium? That Wizard of Fenway Park with his wand, was that Allah witchcraft? Were all those old things, now encompassing the outfield from foul pole to foul pole, infected? Blue Shirts reported hundreds of siblings inquiring about the legality of owning a weapon banned for decades.

And the Blue Wigs. Why would we trust those terrorists? They were up to no good. Isn't Alvin Nedick the Commissioner's father? Official complaints about nepotism nearly matched the volume of questions about carrying a butter knife in public.

"Are you sure, Puppy Beisbol?" Clary had asked repeatedly.

"As sure as anything I've ever done," Puppy replied.

There had been no announcement, no warning that the exhibit would start. Despite Ian Schrage's pronounced pout, there were no dazzling displays. Puppy finally allowed a crackling recording from 1908 of "Take Me Out to the Ballgame" to be played on the monstrous speakers suspended from the retracted roof.

A few fans in the bleachers near Puppy in dead-center field sang along before falling still as if it felt disrespectful. Silence deepened like a shadow. A vid of Lou Gehrig considering himself the luckiest man on the face of the earth produced murmurs. Willie Mays suddenly hauled down a line drive into his basket of a glove. Cries of surprise at such a feat were followed by applause.

Joe DiMaggio kicked at second base after being robbed by Al Gionfriddo in Ebbets Field. Bobby Thomson leaped into the air as the radcaster Russ Hodges screamed "The Giants win the pennant, the Giants win the pennant!"

You could feel butts half rise out of their seats at the crackle of Bob Gibson's fastball. Sandy Koufax's curve. When Ozzie Smith did a backflip, Wrigley rocked.

Puppy shivered in the artificially mild seventy degrees. So did everyone else. The parade of images danced all over the field with the leisurely majesty of the game. Seated next to Puppy, Mickey Mantle wiped away a tear at seeing himself crack his 500th career homer. Jackie Robinson danced off first base.

The New York "Miracle" Mets stunned the world. Reggie Jackson backed up his bragging. Nolan Ryan proved slightly more than human, almost 'bot-like. Mike Schmidt snared a wicked line drive. Johnny Bench threw out a would-be base stealer. Henry Aaron set a new home run record. The vids swept over the old-new ballpark. No one noticed or knew the names or the years because a fastball was timeless. That was the whole damn point.

The hour-long presentation faded. There was no applause because it seems unnecessary when your breath has already been taken away. Gates on both sides of the field opened and fans slowly stepped out, afraid to crush a blade of grass. As well they should. For another three hours, they passed through the Baseball Hall of Fame exhibit.

There were no officious and informative HGs with explanations. Each of the exhibits was simply marked. A bat. A baseball. A uniform. A seat. A program. If you couldn't understand, then you had no business being there. Puppy had been very clear. Figure it out.

At 3:30 p.m., Captain Demeche of the Fourth Precinct said that the lines had extended for eighteen miles and represented a danger what with traffic and seemingly most of Illinois still on its way. Also Indiana and Michigan. Parts of Ohio. Missouri.

Tough, Puppy had told the Blue Shirt HG. We stay open all night until the last person has seen the last exhibit. Unless the Chicago police can't handle this.

Demeche snorted that the Chicago police could handle anything and they better not close until he and his three kids get down there. Puppy said he had candles if necessary.

And this was just day one. Wait until the Old-Timers' Game.

That'd been Ty's brainstorm. He guided Puppy through the allure of old, out-of-shape players stepping up to home plate with little of their skills left to evoke past glories. Except for him and Mick. If you're focusing on the twentieth century of baseball, and it goddamn took you long enough, then you need representatives of the twentieth century.

That's where the proverbial shit hit the proverbial fan from all directions.

Under the Reintegration Act of 2075 which detailed all the approved professions, robots were clearly barred from athletics. The robot arm scandal of 2051 which led to the St. Louis Cardinals being stripped of their World Series title, along with a remarkable Houston Texans running back who could outrun a train, was often cited as an example of the dangers of unfair advantage. Teachers, doctors, and police officers were strictly human jobs. 'Bots were relegated to secondary roles such as bus drivers and sanitation workers, anything which lacked emotional flash points.

The Organic Council chafed under Puppy's orders that 'bots could only have supportive roles at baseball stadiums. He couldn't break the law and reduce the percentage of 'bots below 45.5 percent of stadium workers. What he could and did do was reserve any newly created jobs exclusively for humans, like vendors servicing fans at their seats, or bat boys and bat girls. Umpires were a very gray area as authority figures, so Puppy began integrating human umps, one per crew, for the first time since 2038.

Matthew pleaded with Puppy that his communications with other AIs indicated a grave discontent. But Puppy was stubborn. Last night, the Commissioner was met in the hotel lobby by a very polite but firm contingent who insisted on an emergency meeting to discuss baseball's flaunting of Grandma's Law.

Three members of the Midwest Organic Council filled the couch like properly arranged appliances, Puppy grumped. The robots stared for a long time. The protective Matthew stared back. Puppy poured himself a South Side Stout.

"This is quite irregular," Matthew scolded, dressed in a cashmere sweater with a precious old-fashioned red bow tie. "To intercept the Commissioner of Baseball, who works directly with the Granddaughter, is, may I say, a shocking breach of etiquette of which you should all know better. Proper appointments must be made in the future."

Gusley, a thin 'bot with a pronounced forehead, managed a brief sneer. "An urgent situation brought about by the Commissioner's actions required this momentary breach, for which we apologize."

The 'bots tipped their heads forward. Matthew's throat clearing suggested this was grievously inadequate.

"But there was no time to wait given the Commissioner's actions about which we were not consulted."

Puppy held up his hand before Matthew swallowed his tongue.

"The Cousins and the Granddaughter have already approved all my hiring plans."

Seated in the middle, Walindra's faint yellow complexion glowed slightly. "We are here about the Old-Timers' Game between contestants of the twentieth and twenty-first centuries. You have announced that Mr. Tyrus Cobb and Mr. Mickey Charles Mantle will be leading the squad of twentieth-century players. We did not hear of any other team members, but doubt that there would be anyone capable of sustaining organic life from that period."

"That's right. It's more metaphoric—" He stopped as Matthew said that was the wrong word. "Symbolic, whatever you want. Tyrus and Mickey Charles are heirs to their great ancestors and would demonstrate…"

The robot's faint titters were like metal shoes scraping along Puppy's forehead.

"Mr. Cobb and Mr. Mantle are robots," said Pressiniran, dour even for a 'bot. "Therefore they cannot play."

Puppy drained the stout, glancing at Matthew for help.

"The Commissioner can apply for a special waiver under paragraph eleven of the Reintegration Act which states that where there is no other option, a robot can fulfill the role of a human, per approval by the Cousins Council and Grandma. Which has now been legated to the Granddaughter."

"Correct," Gusley said. "Then you will now permit robots to play baseball."

"Mickey and Ty have never admitted they're 'bots," Puppy said, feeling the ground thin out.

"Why not?"

"Because it would've been difficult to explain since 'bots with faces were illegal. And if illegal 'bots with faces were playing a key role in bringing back baseball, that would've undermined everything."

"Therefore the Commissioner lied?" asked Walinda.

"Therefore I did not because I thought…I thought they were ghosts."

Even Matthew joined in the look about the infinite idiocy of human beings.

"Okay, it was a wrong but sensible guess. Now I know they're not ghosts. Everyone happy? Matthew, does paragraph ten—"

"Eleven."

"Eleven say it must be publicly disclosed that the robot is a robot?"

Matthew scanned for half a second. "No. But all documentation of The Family is public."

"If someone asks, we'll tell. Otherwise, we don't have to make a big deal of this."

From Matthew's slight sigh, Puppy knew that the floor beneath his feet was heading south and quickly.

"Commissioner Nedick, demonstrating embarrassment by refusing to acknowledge a robot's identity is expressly prohibited under the Harmony Law," said Walindra. "Is there any other reason to deny Mr. Cobb and Mr. Mantle's inorganic qualities?"

Matthew's eyes begged Puppy, who shook his head before finding a last gasp of obstinance.

"They're the best players in baseball."

"Yes they are." Gusley almost smiled. "They have been competing, with your full knowledge as to their inorganic origins, since you determined they were not of supernatural descent. Do you have any other questions, Commissioner?"

● ● ● ●

MR. TYRUS COBB and Mickey Charles Mantle were not happy. They didn't want to be seen as freaks. They were real in their heads. Fans would boo them. Their statistics wouldn't count. Puppy let them vent until the sunrise climbed over Chicago.

"We don't have a choice."

"Then forget the Old-Timers' Game," Mickey growled. "I knew it was a stupid idea."

"You liked it when I came up with it," snarled Ty.

"That was when I pretended to be human."

"Which is a big problem, too." Sahidi curled up in a chair like a condescending cat. "You pretended to be human. That violated the 2040 law…"

Mickey shook the can of Claudell's Cool Cola like a hammer. "I don't want to hear about anymore fucking futuristic laws."

Sahidi rolled her eyes. "By law, Puppy and Elias Kenuda also violated the laws."

"Which as the second official in the Commissioner's office, you're required to report," Matthew said, bustling in with breakfast. As the 'bot decided who would eat what this morning, it continued. "If not, it would be assumed you were withholding this information to further yourself in violation of the False Ambition clause—"

"Enough with the goddamn clauses!" Mickey shouted.

"You are right, Mickey. Ms. Douglas is well aware of the rules of workplace behavior directed against undermining colleagues by using or not using information against them in place of honesty."

Matthew waited for Sahidi's sneer of assent.

"Are we all done? Right now, it wouldn't matter if we dropped the Old-Timers' Game." Puppy hesitated. "Because of the futuristic law, you can't play at all."

"Because we're robots?" Ty thundered.

Puppy nodded unhappily. "Unless you agree to come out."

Mickey launched into a red-faced tirade about the meaning of "coming out" back in a decent society and how he wasn't queer no matter what everyone here was. Puppy apologized for like the fifteenth time that day, only vaguely understanding why Mickey was so upset.

The "two white grandpas" smoldered a bit before agreeing with angry nods.

"This goes beyond the trans-organic status of Ty and Mickey," Sahidi said. "They're the only robot players. We must make sure that any waiver the Granddaughter issues only allows 'bots into baseball on a case-by-case basis with none of that nonsense about allocating percentages."

She looked around, daring anyone to question her judgment. "But we have bigger issues. Much bigger. We have a very poorly thought-out concept of a game." Douglas waited for Puppy to grunt another apology at excluding her from the original process. Talk about violating office ethics.

Sahidi continued. "Since no humans could be alive from the twentieth century, how do we do this? Yes, of course I have an answer. Who else?"

• • • •

FROM THE CORNER of the tidy office, Horatio stared with such intensity that his whiskers quivered. Pablo stared back with equal intensity, minus the vibrating hairs. In the two days since Horatio entered his life, Pablo had spent as much time learning the eight-month-old pug's needs, questions, likes, and dislikes as he had with his patients.

"Food? Are you hungry?" Pablo shook the empty silver food bowl.

Horatio wrinkled his forehead and stared some more.

Zelda hadn't been as pleased as Pablo had expected considering it was her lifelong devotion to portraying animals on stage that prompted the application. And when she'd scolded him for not discussing this idea, he pointed out that her yet unseen play about humanoid animals, already much discussed in ways he didn't understand, had apparently influenced the new Sibling Council on Adjacent Family Members.

Horatio, Pablo had proudly announced as he carted the sniffing dog around their living room with Zelda sniffing right back, was the first of what was promised to be thousands of adjacent life-forms joining families around the country. Breeding centers were thriving. He couldn't very well have applied for a vulture or bear or rabbit as depicted in your play; those adjacent life-forms (the word "pet" was now banned as patronizing to non-humans) were quite rare. Pablo didn't care for the entire idea of a cat with its elitist serenity and disdain; they reminded him of Eglaro Sanchez de Jefferson, the last vice president.

Besides, Pablo had once been exposed to a real cat and had an allergic reaction which was much like a garden hose running up his sinuses.

But Horatio exuded warmth and charm and, as Pablo pointed out last night while cleaning up the dog's poop on the rug, you have a real-life character in your play, Jeb Pug. Embracing the adjacent life-form was seamless and will be inspirational to you as an artist. He will be a pleasant companion to Diego once our son turns more sentient and leaves the crib or stroller. Horatio was loving and appeared quite intelligent. Pablo could only imagine what insights the dog would possess once they found a common language.

"Do you want to go out?"

Horatio bounded up, placing both his paws on Pablo's knees. Pablo proudly introduced Horatio to the waiting room, allowing the children to wonderingly stroke the playful pug before the dentist and adjacent life-form dashed around the block. Horatio had his own ideas about what constituted a walk, tugging backward on numerous occasions.

On a trail of chunky treats, he led Horatio back into the office, fussing about proper water levels in the bowl. He decided the way Horatio tilted his head might mean something. The new dental hygienist Jo'yce Saverino opened the door.

"The Granddaughter is in waiting room one, Dr. Diaz."

"Thank you. I won't require your talents for this patient, Dental Hygienist Saverino."

The hygienist's face fell. Pablo had grown accustomed to her intense work ethic. How did I ever survive working with Zelda?

Jostling the examining chair, Clary kicked her legs as if testing their dexterity, the tousled black hair spilling out of the Yankees hoodie.

Horatio padded over and sniffed her mauve shoes; Clary let out a squeal of delight. After getting Pablo's permission, she rolled on the floor with the equally delighted Horatio, who sniffed and licked her face. Pablo explained he couldn't examine Clary with Horatio on her lap.

The pug sat on an adjoining chair, barking approval as Pablo placed a dental bib around Clary's neck. She suddenly gave Pablo a tight hug, going on her tiptoes to plant a fat kiss on his cheek.

"That is not professional," he said in mock protest. "Dentists do not engage in such behavior."

"Report me."

"I just might." He peered at her. "You've gotten taller."

"Because I am an old lady of twelve. And you sound like you have your brain back."

"Most of it, though, to be precise, it was my consciousness, not the physical brain. So, what brings you here, Ms. Santiago?"

"Your letter, Dr. Diaz, suggesting it would enhance siblings's commitment to regular dental care if the Granddaughter were known to have regular checkups. I was also very moved by your plea to restore smile-o-meters as part of regular checkups."

For a moment, Pablo forgot everything he'd planned, launching into an exasperated condemnation of the Dental Council's decision, based on emotional manipulation, to eliminate smile-o-meters, the invention of the late Dr. Gerald Rosen which measured the length of a smile. Clary agreed that smiles should never go out of fashion. She insisted on taking one, which she promised to mention when she discussed this visit to an anonymous dentist (so no one would accuse Pablo of looking to promote himself) on tomorrow's *Wake Up, My Darlings*.

Thrilled by the test's outcome, Pablo loudly informed Clary that she'd measured in the top five percent of smiles which, considering her great and surely demanding duties as Granddaughter, displayed a proper positive spirit.

"How is Mama Zelda?" Clary asked as she fed Horatio a treat, giggling when the dog nearly bit her fingers.

"She's writing a play which will be on Broadway."

"That is good."

Pablo shrugged. "She thinks so. I find it slightly elitist, as if Broadway towers over other theaters, but that's not my business. I've learned to meddle with my darling wife on a select basis. And then there's the baby."

With excessive praise, Clary scrutinized the photo of Diego on the wall. Swaddled in two layers of clothes, the child looked back with a wait-and-see expression about this world he'd been dragged into.

Pablo steered Clary back into the chair and persuaded her to gape. As he poked and prodded, he rambled about the practice, Dental Hygienist Saverino, Diego's musical cooing, and Zelda supposedly losing five pounds, though he really couldn't tell.

He needed to distract himself so he wouldn't react to the inside of her mouth. He did anyway, stiffening slightly. Pablo laid aside his instruments, reassuring Clary that her teeth were strong, her tongue a robust color, and her gums the givers of dental virility.

Pablo glanced at the HG tooth dancing over the door letting him know his next patient was ready. Clary scooped up Horatio and sat down as if she had nowhere else to go. She and the pug stared at Pablo.

"Well Dr. Diaz, why did you really ask me here?" Clary stroked Horatio's back.

"I wanted to see you, Clary."

She tilted her head. "Why?"

He paused, surprised. "Because I love you. You took care of me when I was hidden in Kenuda's apartment. I might not have survived without you. No. I definitely wouldn't have made it back without your loyalty."

"This is how you reward such loyalty? With deception?"

Pablo tensed. "I meant every word."

"Humans often do. That is why you are so effective at lying. I do not doubt your concern about the eight percent drop in dental visits over the past six months. Nor do I doubt that you are grateful for what I did to save your life. Or your need to tell me about Zelda and Diego and her play. And Dental Hygienist Saverino."

Clary whispered in Horatio's left ear. The dog snuggled against her chest and was soon snoring.

"But that is not the primary reason you wanted to examine me."

Pablo felt a light hand brush against his mind, shivering as her mental fingertips fell away.

"Very good, Pablo." The girl's face hardened. "You did not get all of your consciousness back, did you, Dr. Diaz?"

"Not quite."

"That is the first truth. Now you are compensated by sharing another consciousness."

Pablo paled. "I don't know what that means."

"Where you cannot remember, someone does it for you. Who helps you, Pablo?" Her voice was canned softness.

"Zelda would happily tell you how forgetful I can be."

"Yet you are a dentist. It is dangerous to have a forgetful doctor."

His eyes slitted. "I do just fine."

"Who helps you, Pablo?" The softness was gone. Now it was merely canned. "Should I bother repeating the question?"

"Help me do what?"

"Deceive me."

Pablo swallowed. "As you can see from Sammy the Impatient Molar's dance, I'm running nine minutes late. It's unprofessional for a dentist to keep his patients waiting because he's discussing personal issues."

Clary whispered again to Horatio, who dutifully watched as she headed to the door. "I hope your reasons for today are primarily because you are concerned about me. I cannot think you would want to hurt me."

"Never."

"At least for now." Her eyes watered and she hurried out the door.

Drained, Pablo slumped next to Horatio on the examining chair as Sammy the Impatient Molar sang the song of being ten minutes late. "Patients come first, patients come first."

19

The smug little shit half dozed, his pasty face pressed against the icy train window. Since the Arrow Midwest had left Chicago three hours ago, Cheng alternated between light snoring, loud chuckling, and discordant humming with one break for the toilet outside Indianapolis. Albert had strolled back down the aisle tipping his Chicago Cubs cap to bemused passengers and apologizing for devouring the entire AG tuna sandwich without offering so much as a bite.

Elias had feigned sleep, making Albert crawl over him to his seat. That'd launched another medley of humming. Nothing could wipe the smirk from Albert's face. Not even when Elias pressed his large hand over Albert's mouth.

"Shut up."

"Dtnah Mhekpy sngs," Albert had said, which Elias translated as "don't you like Mooshie's songs?"

Kenuda had moved four rows down, wrapping his arms around the secondhand quilted jacket. A month ago, he wouldn't have permitted himself to be buried in such a thing. Now it was normal. Sometimes he forgot what he looked like in fine clothes. That was the point, Hedda reminded him.

Cheng reported Elias to the conductor for occupying an unauthorized seat. Elias stomped back, spreading his large legs to discomfort Cheng. That didn't work either. Short of driving the earrings, which spelled out Wrigley Field, that he'd bought for Hedda into Albert's eyes, he feared nothing would wipe off that damn expression.

Elias finally surrendered. "What happened?"

Cheng couldn't conceal his delight at Kenuda's curiosity. "About what?"

Elias drummed his fingers on the armrest. "Your meeting."

"I had many meetings back in the Windy City. Did you know it's called that because of the pomposity of the nineteenth-century politicians, not the gusty winds? Yes, I was very humbled—"

Elias snorted at humility surviving in Cheng's body.

"...by those who recall my days ranging the field for the Cubbies. Standing in the Hall of Fame line for so many hours..."

"I was right behind you," Kenuda managed to say between clenched teeth.

"Then you know how many well-wishers I greeted." Albert turned solemn. "In our position of rehabilitation, it's so comforting..."

"I meant with Puppy."

"Oh, that meeting. Yes. It was nice to see Puppy again. He's doing very well. Unlike you, he doesn't hold a grudge for all that misunderstanding. Ty and Mickey were there. They send their regards."

Albert busied himself a moment, drawing circles in the frosted window.

"You've heard of the Old-Timers' Game? Well, it probably wouldn't have flown when Grandma was around. This is a grayish area, paying tribute to former players as if they are the living embodiment of nostalgic statues."

"Unlike well-wishers greeting a former, decrepit player pretending modesty in a dreary frigid line outside Wrigley Field."

"Exactly. Now this must remain confidential." Albert continued in a voice designed to be heard up and down the railway car. "The game will feature ballplayers from both centuries. Ah yes, it will be primarily Ty and Mickey and imitators. But who do you think will patrol the hallowed geography between second and third base for the twenty-first-century ball club?"

Elias eyed a particularly welcoming snowbank whizzing past.

"Player-manager, to be precise." Albert fluttered his lips. Pleased by the dexterity of his mouth, he did it again. "I've been charged with gathering the team. Oh, when I think of the players of that era. You're a little young to remember and, yes, you preferred basketball and football so I won't bore you. Mick and Ty and Puppy have it in their heads that the twentieth century was the apogee of the game. Well, we will just see which game is better. The past always beckons because it's past and done with."

"Shouldn't the player-manager of the team representing an entire century be someone who was not disgraced?"

Cheng shrugged at the obviousness. "Perhaps. But I'm all they got. Sometimes desperation trumps ethics. We just don't like admitting that. Besides, I never did anything wrong while in my baseball uniform. I should've remained a player. By now I would simply be a manager. Playing an entire season might be draining even for a remarkable physical specimen like myself."

With a groan, Kenuda tipped his head into the leather seat.

"I'll keep helping you, Elias. Don't worry."

Hitting the snowbanks at 185 mph would be quick. Cheng wouldn't feel a thing.

"In the same way I mentored you when you became a Cousin, and I did a pretty good job before you screwed up, I want to mentor you now in my growing role in baseball. I feel we've bonded in the DV. That was very wise of them to make us next-door neighbors."

"We've bonded through my hatred and contempt for you."

Cheng pulled out a nose hair without grimacing. "That's still a bond. I always warned Grandma about the flip side of too much love. We can't undo what we are. As people, we pretty much suck. Yes, that's a dark view, but I think I can be forgiven. Though I should watch the bitterness. Nasty business." He traced bitterness in the window before wiping it away. "Have you come up with more food ideas?"

Elias shook his head.

"Why not?" Cheng made a disgusted face. "Because Hedda doesn't like me?"

"No."

"I don't blame her." Cheng smiled. "She thinks I'm a bad influence."

"Uh, yeah."

"And she suspects I'm roping you into some nefarious scheme."

Elias frowned. "Aren't you?"

Albert shrugged. "Do you care?"

Kenuda hesitated. "I care about Hedda. I don't want to wreck our relationship."

"Which is so healthy."

"What do you know?"

"I live next door."

"Are you eavesdropping, you little shit?"

"No, but I'm not deaf." Cheng chuckled. "She probably doesn't think you've got enough backbone left to withstand my charms."

"Let me understand. You're saying I'm not up to resisting you as a way of getting me to join by showing my backbone."

"Yeah."

"That's not transparent?"

"I think I deserve props for my honesty." He winked. "It doesn't happen that often. Course, if you think your relationship can't stand you standing up for yourself."

Elias flared. "French fries."

"What?"

"Somehow the geniuses in the Commissioner's office forgot that french fries were sold at ballparks in the twentieth century. It was political to overlook that after France became the first nation to leave NATO and strike a peace treaty with the Muslims. That retroactive fact got washed away. Along with all the others."

Cheng grinned. "Good boy."

"Up yours." Elias leaned over. "When are you going to tell me what you're up to?"

Cheng sighed. "When you get back your backbone."

• • • •

PUPPY WAS KEYED up from sleeping only a handful of hours over the past few days, accompanying the Hall of Fame caravan through six cities before saying a depleted farewell as the train headed south to Atlanta and Tampa. He Frisbee-tossed the mail onto his coffee table, missing completely. With a self-conscious laugh, Puppy eased into the battered armchair and slowly unbuttoned his blue peacoat, reaching for the scattered letters.

Her handwriting stared back. It took him a frozen moment.

"Annette," he finally said aloud.

He gave the letter his chair until he returned with a bottle of Chateau Jony from Iowa City. He poured a ridiculous amount which he knew wouldn't be enough.

My Darling Puppy,

SURPRISE! I know, how in Grandma's high heels have I managed to send a letter from the Caliphate? Well my love, it wasn't easy. Originally this was supposed to be sent from Alsace-Lorraine, which is in eastern France near Germany. Boy, I'm becoming a geography expert. Father Dempsey and I…

He couldn't make out the carefully scratched-out sentence.

Okay, I better explain better. Colonel Basa died, I liked him by the end, and they teamed me with Father Dempsey. You know, the Catholic priest. He's grim and he's always crossing himself, but I can rely on him. Kind of like shoes that are really worn and you don't know how they stay on your feet but they're comfy. Like the ones you wear.

I miss you so.

Back to the story. I won't go on and on but we were able to escape from England across the Channel to France which wasn't that bad. In Paris at an art museum where we were meeting our contact, the priest and I were nearly captured by…ready?…Azhar's shithead, fanatic son Omar. He's a hero and has made it his life's work to hunt me and his father down. Don't worry, we're far away from the little bastard.

I'm worried about how much to tell you because some of it is scary, but I can't lie either. Although I must be okay to write, huh? Back to the original Alsace-Lorraine mail. Father Dempsey and I seemed safe, but someone betrayed us so I grabbed back the letter because I felt, if they betrayed us, they probably wouldn't find a way to post this to America. We had to escape in this old tunnel which they used to get Catholic children out of France. I saw some old musty dolls and a few other toys. Very sad, Puppy, but there were no bones so I figured the kids got away.

We hid in an old beer factory in Stuttgart, and then were shoved inside…are you ready?…a horse and hay cart. Can you imagine me spending three hours with hay in my hair? It still hasn't come out. That's not funny, Puppy.

He spilled his glass laughing so hard.

Well, it really did come out because I cut the gorgeous hair down to just below my ears. Broke my heart. My hair hasn't been this short since I was seventeen, before we met, and I cut it off to spite my mother. All my beautiful hair, but it was smart, if only so I wouldn't itch and to keep up with our new identities. I get a different name and papers at every stop. Right now we're in Groß-Gerau, Germany. I'm Elyse Deusenberg. Believe me, I don't pick the names. I could look like an Elyse, what do you think?

I have no idea what our ultimate destination is. We don't talk to anyone with specifics so they don't know what we're doing which, since the wrong person can turn us in as we've learned, is smart. France and now Germany is a lot different than England. In at least two places, we came across a stash of weapons. I'm not talking about little pistols, Pup. There was something called a SAM hidden in a barn. Big sucker, covered with hay. In Mannheim, this Father Litwak—it's really weird how many Jew priests and nuns I've met—gave me new undies from his dead sister's house because mine were beyond sketchy. Father Litwak said there was a ferocious battle in Austria between the American Army HOORAY and the Allahs of the Mufti. He said the Mufti's son, Abdullah, helped his father for the first time and they just barely beat us back.

But I also must tell you something very important, Pup. Sometimes I get very discouraged.

He squinted at another crossed-out line.

Not discouraged. But worried that I made the wrong decision and should've stayed with you. I hope you understand why I did that even if I'm not sure it was smart. I needed something that belonged to me and this was it. I couldn't be dumb Annette, wife of the famous Puppy. Now maybe I should've been patient and found something back in America. Although my shoe-selling days are over. I'm sorry. I really am. I miss you terribly and you better miss me terribly or else…

It's just that I don't have faith that running across Europe and who knows where else makes any sense. What am I going to say? Hi, Pope. Will you please come out of hiding and announce you're with America now who doesn't believe in your God and banned religion? Dumb, dumb, dumb. But Father Dempsey says we must have faith. Last night I told him what he could do with his faith. He took it very well. He talks about Jesus and Catholicism, but I only half listen. You know I'm more a doer, not a scholar. I just don't see any sign that having faith means anything. Grandma was right when she said the strongest belief starts with yourself which you share through love with those you love.

I'm so confused, Pup. And scared. I'm sorry to dump this on you because what can you do? I know. Do you like how I still answer my own questions? It especially saves time when you're running for your life. Think strongly of me, Pup. In this actual envelope is a lock of my hair from when I had to cut it from the hay. Look closely and if you threw away the envelope get it out of the garbage now.

I'm not saying you should pray, Puppy. But if you keep this hair with you, I will always be with you. I'll wait like a week before I think you somehow got this letter and then start imagining you're holding the hair and then a few times a day, I mean, when I'm not hiding or getting shot at—that only happened once, don't worry—I'll squeeze my hair and we will touch in our hearts.

I love you so, Puppy Nedick. I love you with every part of my body, from my toes which you used to lick to the top of my cropped but still beautiful hair.

Your wife, Annette Ramos

Puppy couldn't remember the last time he'd cried himself to sleep.

20

A scimitar-shaped billboard arched over the congested intersection of La Cienfuego Boulevard and Marco de Sepulveda Boulevard. Hook-nosed robot soldiers guarded evil-eyed Clary, devil's horns protruding from her thick curly hair as she sniffed dead bodies of ravaged Muslim children.

Abadaan maratan ukhraa vowed, "Never again."

Azhar winced, ashamed. They were everywhere. On last night's *One True God* newscast, a somber presenter had introduced a montage of similar billboards in London, Paris, Berlin, and Rome, all in native languages so, the presenter added ominously, they would be clearly understood.

Irritated pedestrians skipped out of the way of mischievous mopeds, backed by the ever-present symphony of honking cars enjoying new-found freedom absent any military vehicles. Abdul was nearly sideswiped in mid-dribble. Mustafa gently scolded him for not paying attention. He practiced wherever they went, the ball a new limb growing out of his forehead, his knee, his foot. The boy's squat frame was stanchioned by steel legs. Azhar beamed proudly.

There was an important practice later that day, although all practices were important, Abdul explained with the single-minded wisdom of the pubescent. "Now that there is peace, it is time to make my mark as a great football player," he said confidently between chomps on a Moroccan candy bar.

"There is no peace," Azhar had tried explaining again last night.

"Yes, there is," Jalak said with Jalak-like fierceness, eyes blinking at him over the pitcher of iced tea.

He permitted her disrespectful corrections, wrong facts, silly conclusions, because it was so nice to have her treat him with weary disdain once more. The shakes of the head as he washed a fork poorly. The trash not brought to the curb. The forgotten cilantro and "how could a fisherman forget the cod?" when he walked in carting market vegetables.

She even allowed him a quick peck on the back of the neck, turning away to pretend it didn't delight her.

Once Jalak immersed herself into the baffling television soap opera where one family endured all the accursed luck of the universe while still managing to look beautiful, Azhar took Abdul out for more practice before sunset; Jalak shouted to bring back the garbage bins from the street.

They had kicked their way to the grassy fields where a week ago, they'd sat for hours watching Abdullah's Fourth Army withdraw under the terms of the truce.

No soldiers were allowed in Barcelona. The Army Group had redeployed forty kilometers to the east. The Empire's Third Marine Division remained on the flotilla of destroyers and cruisers to the west in the Atlantic Ocean. Both forces were prepared to confront the Crusader Machines, as they were now called, but needed a respite from fighting each other.

It does not necessarily mean the civil war is over. In Budapest and Cairo, there are similar neutral zones. Thus far the peace has held. Perhaps once the Crusaders are defeated, there will be a real peace among Muslims, Azhar reassured Abdul, who assumed his father knew all this from the very lips of Abdullah himself. Azhar could not disappoint his son.

But that was not true. While Mustafa had been inside Abdullah's headquarters, he had not seen the Son for nearly two weeks. During that time, he had been questioned, some might say interrogated, by a nasty captain from some branch of the service he had never heard of.

As Azhar learned very quickly, nothing he said was truly correct, merely an impression which had to be peeled away. He repeated his relationship with Clary, detailing every single transgression including breaking the law to get her out of the orphanage and onto the America-bound boat. He described the attack by the American helicopter. He went into such details about Clary's personality that he was no longer sure what was real and what was some natural embellishment as if he were writing a story.

Then he related his time in London with Puppy and Annette, his answers earning the captain's sneer. After a while, he made up conversations. He imagined bows in Annette's hair. Puppy's white socks. What they ate, drank. What was a knuckleball? The television programs they preferred. Soon the conversation wandered to Tomas Stilton and the American woman Beth. The last encounter with his son Omar.

Every day the same questions until his head was so emptied that he enjoyed the ache from heading the football to Abdul during their sunset practices.

Outside Abdullah's headquarters, protected by the last three tanks in Barcelona, Azhar loaded his son up with lunch to keep him busy for about ten minutes of the usual hour-long session. As always, he promised to ask Abdullah if he'd come to the first game of the De la Cruz Youth Football League. Yes, he would make sure the Son knew that Abdul Mustafa was playing left wing and that his ability only came along once a generation. The Son might be too busy killing Crusader machines, but he would do his best.

Abdul hugged his amazing father, who he presented to his friends like a miniature statue. Talk about embellished heroic stories. The boy plowed into the Catalan sandwich *porchetta on coca*. His mother had also given him money for lunch, so he might top this off with a *cochinillo*.

Today, the guard in the lobby directed Azhar to the familiar rear elevator. He tensed, respectfully asking whether that was correct; he had been going to room 504 for two weeks. The young soldier glared at such impertinence and brusquely waved him along.

Mustafa waited some thirty minutes in the messy office which looked as if it had been hastily abandoned. From an imperceptible door behind the drab desk, Abdullah rushed in with insincere apologies about being late. The Grand Mufti's son was tailored in a Crusader-style black suit with a crisp white shirt and dark blue tie.

The Son blushed as if caught out of character.

"You always notice in your wise way, my old friend," he said warmly. "Our world embraces many perspectives and sometimes I must wear a face that is not mine. As you would know." The Son gestured Azhar into a modern white chair. "How is your wife?"

"She tests my digestion powers as always."

"The role of a good woman is to distract her husband. And your boy Abdul?"

"He plans on becoming the leading football player in the Caliphate. He would be honored if you would attend his first league game this Sunday at one. He said you would, of course, be his guest."

"If only, but thank him for the honor." Abdullah smiled sadly, fidgeting. "You have been most helpful answering questions involving the girl Clary. That was difficult, which I respect and for which I apologize. I placed you, once again, in a difficult situation."

"I serve you, my lord."

Abdullah frowned. "You truly do, my friend. Where would I have been without your support?"

"It will always be there."

"No matter what?"

Azhar held his breath. Abdullah laughed softly.

"Do not worry. I am not planning any egregious acts. I am sure you do not approve of the truce with my father."

"How do you know that, sir?"

"From your expression of disapproval, Azhar," he said coldly. "I have seen the tapes of your interview. You are disdainful of what I have come to believe is the best path for our people."

"My disdain was for the captain who interrogated me, never you."

Abdullah clenched and unclenched his fist. "Can you not be honest?"

"Only God and my wife can read my mind, my lord." He urged caution on himself, but he failed to listen. "And only Allah has the right to know my thoughts."

Abdullah leaned back with a grunt. "You are very right, my friend. I have no right. I ask because I value your opinion. Perhaps because I believe that if Allah does speak to anyone, it is to you, Azhar Mustafa. He trusts you to handle the information and knowledge wisely because you are not burdened by the complexities of deception."

Azhar kept silent.

With a shrug, Abdullah continued, "I do not know that I am that wise. Or even that good. Yet here I am, given by Allah the power of life and death in his name. Do you know what that feels like?"

"I hope I never do."

"You should pray fervently, fervently, that you never do." Abdullah poured out two glasses of mint water. "I had no choice but to reach out to my father. I did not want to, Azhar. He is a bad man. No. He was a good man who is now bad. He was great, for a brief while, until he forgot what he fought for. I'm trying to remember why we do what we do. Our values. The ones we know and the ones we've forgotten and the ones we haven't found yet. And please spare me the doubt spreading all over your face."

"I do not doubt your motives, my lord."

"How dare you not when I do?" He dropped his voice. "I am afraid, Azhar. Terrified. All the blood spilled during the war. All the blood spilled since maintaining the Caliphate. All the blood spilled now trying to tear it apart and build something better will be for nothing. Nothing. Tens and tens of millions of dead for nothing. For an Empire which is crumbling. For a dream of mine which is dying. Yes, the great Muslim enlightenment will never happen. Perhaps it will happen in centuries when you sit in Allah's Garden. You will be there, do not worry. You will have to tell me what it looks like."

Abdullah considered his brittle laugh.

"My father does not realize it has all been for nothing. We crushed the Crusaders and soon we will be crushed unless we act now and decisively." He swallowed, assessing Azhar. "The Crusader machine soldiers have entered Palestine. They sit in Jerusalem. Or what is left of Jerusalem. Our holy places have been razed to the ground. Do you know who Hassan bin-Hadihah was? He was an obscure Imam who predicted that we have turned Allah's stomach by obliterating the traces of Christians and Jews when we regained Palestine. Turning God's stomach? Think of that, Azhar. To commit such a vile act that God himself would vomit. What a notion." His face twisted in contemplation. "Hassan bin-Hadihah said that Allah would remember what we had done and there would be vengeance. He was torn apart, and his body trampled by goats.

"The Imam was right. Everywhere the robot soldiers march, they destroy mosques. Not churches. Mosques. It is how they have been programmed. Outside Marrakesh, our soldiers formed a barrier behind a village of Christians. To use them as shields was wrong. Yet, it was done. The Crusader machines's bullets passed through the Christian shields without harm yet struck perfectly into our soldiers. That is the Devil's work. And I did not believe of the Devil until now."

Abdullah drained the water, his eyes wide with fright. "We would lose the war if I did not reach out to my father and join forces. What happens if we win, I cannot say. He is old. I assume I will be the sole leader. But of what? We have no time to understand each other. Only to slaughter. I cannot show kindness to Crusaders anymore, Azhar. I cannot show kindness to anyone who opposes me. I have become my father and that turns my stomach, too, but I see no other way."

Azhar's head felt empty again. "Why do you tell me, my lord? I have no power. I am merely a fisherman."

Abdullah laughed bitterly. "You are my conscience, Azhar. I finally understand that. I need you to forgive me."

"Me forgive you?" He almost laughed, too. "For what?"

It took an immeasurable effort for Abdullah to speak. "For breaking my promise to be different. I cannot be different, Azhar. The world will not allow that. I am sorry."

Mustafa suddenly shuddered. "My wife and son…"

Abdullah knelt, clutching Azhar's hands and kissing his fingers. "No harm will ever come to them. That I swear. Forgive me. Say you forgive me. Say you forgive me, Azhar Mustafa!"

He could only stare back before finding the courage he thought had run out long ago.

"First you must tell me what you have done."

Abdullah paled, as frightened as anyone Azhar had ever seen. "I cannot because you would not understand and would not forgive me. You must forgive on faith."

Azhar leaned forward, a breach of respect to a ruler. "To have faith in you, my lord, I must know what you have done before I can forgive you."

Abdullah the Son flinched as if dirt had been flung in his face and hurried through the door.

Suddenly Azhar knew. *Thank you, Allah*! he shouted without sound, the fiercest human cry because it echoed without doubt.

He ran out of the headquarters. Seated on a concrete bench, Abdul was jiggling to noisy music through his white earbuds, sandwich wrappers and empty crisp bags at his feet.

"Come, you must go home."

Abdul slowly removed his left bud. "What?"

"I said come. Go." Azhar closed his eyes, which only alarmed Abdul. He forced half a smile. "Your mother called. She needs help in the house. Here. Take a taxi." He thrust bills into Abdul's palm. "I will see you later."

As he spun away, Abdul rasped, "You are lying."

He whirled around. "How dare you say that of your father."

"You said I should always tell the truth. This is truth." Abdul placed his pudgy hands on his hips, mirroring his father. "You are lying. I will find out why and go with you."

"What are you saying, child? Go where?"

"To help."

"You cannot. Go home. I must do something."

"Which is dangerous. Yes. It must be dangerous because you are very scared. Now you make me scared. But together we will not be scared. You never speak of what you have done. You keep me outside as if I am a little child." His eyes narrowed. "I am not a little child. I saw too much in the prison. Much was done to me which I never spoke of. So now we must talk. And if you will not talk then I will not talk but you will still let me help you. I am your son and that is my job. I will be good at it. Better than Omar. And no matter what you say, I will follow you. If you take a bus, I will get on. If you take a taxi, I will take one." Abdul held up the bills. "And I will call Mother and tell her you are doing something you shouldn't, and you do not want that."

Azhar smiled crookedly. "You are a little bastard."

"Sometimes you must be a little bastard. I have learned that much." His grin faded. "Please let me be part of your world again, Poppa."

Azhar hailed a cab. Nearing the popular waterfront area, they ran into a police barricade in front of the Aquarium running down to the Port Vell. Only a few people had gathered, too afraid to learn what happened. His sanctioned headquarters pass got them beyond the first yellow strips before an officious policeman blocked their way.

"Let me past," Azhar said.

"I am sorry, sir."

"Do you see my father's documents?" Abdul bounced on his toes, ripping Azhar's ID away and shoving it at the cop. "He has rights to go anywhere. He can go into the Son's office. Can you say that you know better than the Son?"

The uneasy cop glanced around for someone who knew better than he did. It was only a damn accident. No reason to take a risk. With a shrug, he let them down the gravel path to the wharf where Abdul brandished the pass to more police with increasing confidence.

Wan smoke curled up from the thirty-foot sailboat. This time Abdul knew better than to question his father's orders. The old seaman Azhar hopped onto the *Alhambra*, skillfully balancing himself through the ankle-high water to the tiny cabin where half a body protruded.

Steeling himself, Azhar peered inside. Tomas Stilton's dark face was bleached from the fire. His lips were twisted in one last belligerent cry.

"What happened?" Azhar hoarsely asked a young cop.

"Some sort of electrical fire. Maybe there was a short in the wiring. It's hard to tell. That didn't help." He gestured at the empty bottle of vodka on the floor.

Except Tomas hadn't drunk in two weeks. He promised that he would be sober enough to make it through the Muslim lines to the American Army, which had consolidated its hold in North Africa. That was their plan. Get Stilton home to warn Clary. That's why Azhar had cooperated with the sneering captain, to show he could be trusted enough. To get Tomas the right papers. The right map. The right weapon.

"There are a lot of police officers for an electrical fire on a sailboat."

The cop shrugged. He'd had the same thought. Now someone with Abdullah clearance shows up. But it was best to let it go.

Azhar trailed Tomas's covered body, stopping by Abdul. The shaken boy tossed a little wave at the gurney sliding into the rear of the ambulance.

"How did you know who that was?" Azhar finally asked after they had walked a couple kilometers toward home.

"You are very sad. I knew it had to be a friend. You do not have any friends except me and Mother. Remember I met Major Stilton when he came looking for you? He tied me up but let me go. He kept Mother tied up all night. He liked you very much, Poppa. I can tell these things."

Azhar swallowed deeply, rubbing the boy's hair.

After a long pause, Abdul continued. "Was I some help?"

"Very much."

"I did not do anything." He frowned. "Do not say I was a help like I am a stupid infant to be humored."

Azhar squeezed his shoulders. "I would have cried if you were not there."

"Really?"

"Yes really."

Abdul considered this in between dribbling his football. "Is it not good to cry and let it out? I cried often in prison."

"But you finally stopped."

"Not until you and the Son rescued me."

I do not know who will rescue us, my brave boy. Allah is too busy to do good anymore.

• • • •

HERBERT HAD CAUTIONED Annette that its portable holographic map could be picked up by the Islamists. Fortunately, the half-bombed city was nearly devoid of anyone brave enough to go outside, although she ducked into a couple doorways when a rambunctious Holy Warriors patrol passed. Further north, Annette crawled beneath a battered car to avoid a brief firefight between the black-robed fanatics and unseen assailants on a rooftop.

She hurried over a moaning Holy Warrior, never once finding a fraction of Herbert's programmed compassion. The face of the raped girl blocked all such organic transmissions.

By the time Annette picked her way around a makeshift defensive line of smoking garbage dumpsters and twisted air-lift motor scooters leading to the E14 roadway, she was slowly joined by haggard, shuffling residents searching for loved ones or food. Or shelter that wouldn't collapse on them.

Since she was in the remnants of a Crusader neighborhood, Annette tugged out her oversized crucifix, smiling at the image of Dempsey and Herbert discussing religion. Don't worry, she reassured herself, scampering over a pile of bricks that was once a building. You'll see Dempsey again. Puppy. Even that Zelda. Annette fortified herself by recalling all the reasons she didn't like Zelda. She had a crush on Puppy. She was jealous. She was nasty. She had crappy hair.

Another inexplicable gust of dust, debris, and burnt human remains rolled down the street like a large Ferris wheel. Covering her face, Annette slipped inside the doorway of an abandoned bakery. Stepping gingerly around the broken glass, Annette stared hungrily at a basket of sweet rolls. She touched the crucifix. It's wrong to steal in The Family even if you're starving. Your failure doesn't excuse hurting others. Isn't it also wrong to steal in your family, Jesus?

A wizened woman with sharp elbows knocked her aside and scooped the basket off the counter. The woman hesitated at Annette's habit. Crossing herself, she hurried out with the bread under her arms. Annette shouted from the doorway before grumbling back inside, ransacking the bakery before finding a couple of stale chocolate pastries.

"Good job, Jesus," she snarled skyward. "I mean, I could've been a real nun."

Annette devoured the pastries in the lobby of a once-grand apartment building, staring dully at a dead adult and child, their expressions twisted in protest beneath Arabic splattered on the wall in blood. Theirs, someone else's, Annette licked the chocolate off her fingers. The holographic map indicated another kilometer northwest.

Outside, gunfire screamed ahead of squealing tires. Annette dashed into the elevator beside a man with a broken neck, his legs up against the wall. She munched on the second pastry so her chomping teeth and quick gulps filled her ears instead of the shouting. A burst of vindictive machine guns sprayed the lobby. She waited until it was very quiet before creeping out again, adjusting a discarded woolen cap atop her grossly filthy hair.

A very neat pile of dead Christians filled the center of the street. Residents slowly passed, too exhausted to care.

Night with its merciful darkness fell. Better not to see, Annette thought, playing a childish game of counting how many times she could've fallen over rubble or a corpse, human, animal. Kneeling on a desolate street in the Kantra district, she was startled by the faint glow of Herbert's HG map.

"Destination reached."

The voice of the map echoed like a bomb. Annette crouched as if to make herself invisible. The map repeated its message. She didn't know how to turn off the damn voice so warmly congratulating her.

Annette flung the portable map across the street, hitting a lamppost.

A trio of light beams intersected at her chest where Annette's fingers clutched the crucifix.

Three slender robot soldiers stepped forward with cocked Marlowe blaster rifles. Their pale faces pulsed.

"Speak." The lead 'bot, its head wrapped in a thick metal-and-leather helmet, prodded Annette with its rifle.

"I'm a fucking American so get your rifle out of my ribs."

The soldiers's heads briefly tilted in silent communication. With the rifles still pointed, they motioned Annette into the back of a perfectly square, covered jeep. The first 'bot kept its rifle angled toward her temple during the speedy ride over a well-guarded bridge and into a dark, medieval-style fortress. As if floating, the jeep eased to a stop onto a smooth surface.

The 'bot righted Annette as she slipped on the shimmering coal-black ground. The only lights were embedded into four corners of the courtyard. She regained her footing, angrily shaking off the soldiers's help and skidding past two more impassive guards posted at a small door and down a narrow hallway, nearly bumping her head on an overhead light.

Annette was deposited in a low-ceilinged office where she happily rubbed her aching feet. With a brisk nod, a 'bot in a captain's uniform entered and pulled over a folding chair. Its thin forearms cradled the back of the seat. The captain studied her with blank curiosity.

"I am Captain Michael of the American Seventh Marine Division, Second Brigade. Your name please?"

Annette stared a moment at the slight figure, comical in its starched uniform.

The captain frowned. "Is my question unclear?"

"No. Sorry. I'm a little worn out. Can I have some water please?"

As if listening on the other side of the door, a private silently entered with a chilled glass of water. It waited until Annette finished and declined a refill before leaving.

"The office is very small," she remarked.

"For humans, yes, so the facility would not be suitable if captured before we could destroy the structure."

"The castle's very cool. It must be really old."

"Four days and six hours. That was the time required to build it." Captain Michael tilted its head. "Do you have any more questions before we establish your identity and purpose?"

"I always have lots of questions, but for now I'm good." The officer didn't answer her quick smile. "My name is Annette Ramos. I'm not really a nun. I was living in London until a few months ago when I escaped. I was traveling with a real priest, Catholic Father John Dempsey. I was given directions to your lines through a portable map which one of your soldiers gave me."

The captain assessed the imperative order of follow-up questions.

"What is our soldier's name?"

"Herbert."

"His rank?"

"I don't know anything about ranks. He's the first robot soldier I ever met."

"What was his number?"

"I don't remember."

"Does that imply you once had that information?"

"Yes, that's how he identified himself before Father Dempsey and I pulled him out of the bomb crater because he was wounded."

"Wounded in what fashion?"

"In his stomach. His, his…" Annette struggled to recall. "A gizmo in his stomach was torn. I stitched it up with a shoelace."

The captain paused imperceptibly to assess this information. "Do you have micro-botic surgical training?"

"No. I took classes as a nurse. I'm a good sewer. I mean, I never made a dress, but I do small repairs. Holes, slight tears." She sighed toward the impassive marine. "Father Dempsey hurt his ankle and didn't really need the shoelaces. Look, the surgery or whatever you want to call it worked because Herbert's mortality rate rose to something, I don't know, like eleven percent."

"A non-trans-organic substance could not elevate a mortality projection to that level if the vascular pathway were torn," the captain said with a hint of skepticism.

"He was alive when I left," she answered hotly.

"Where was his location?"

Annette sighed. "I'm not sure. I'm not great with maps. Somewhere in Budapest. In the hills."

"Buda?"

"Yes. Yes. Buda."

"What is the exact location?"

"I don't know." She fought fatigue until the original address of their connection floated by her inner eyes. "30 Groszy Place. Herbert couldn't signal you because he said the Allahs tracked the evacuation messages. But that's where he is. Well, next door now. I guess either 32 or 28 Groszy because the original address became a bomb crater. Send your soldiers to get him and Father Dempsey, please."

"Where is the 45-W which you contend our soldier provided?"

"What the hell is a 45-W?"

"A portable directional device."

"Oh, I threw it away."

"Why?"

"Because it was talking out loud that I'd found my destination and I was afraid of being captured."

"Did not the robot soldier give you the device so you would find our lines?"

"Well, yeah…"

"Then why would you discard a 45-W when it proved successful?"

Annette glared. "I was afraid because I didn't know who'd hear. There's a lot of Al-lahs with guns out there which I'm sure you've noticed. The 45-W is where your soldiers captured me."

Captain Michael studied Annette. "You are very eager to dispatch our soldiers. Is it to send them into a trap?"

Annette leaned the chair back and forth in disgust. "What, you think I'm some Al-lah spy? Do I look like a damn spy?"

Michael arched its eyebrow. "You have already admitted you have been posing as a member of a religious order. That could have been a cover."

"I'm an American. I hate the Allahs."

"There were many Americans before World War III who supported the Islamists and their goal of Empire as just and logical, contending that America suppressed other na-tions's ambitions to further their own. It is within possibility that you would harbor such sympathies given your nation's historical predisposition to align with its enemies."

"I don't align that way."

The captain wasn't convinced. "Yet you came to the Caliphate despite your hatred of the Islamists?"

Annette briefly told the captain about her flight, insisting he check it out on his damn database. Michael switched inward for a few seconds.

"There is a factual basis to support your claim that Puppy Nedick came to the Ca-liphate before returning to America to become Commissioner of Baseball."

Annette laughed so hard she doubled over, alarming the officer. "Sorry. Sorry. He's Commissioner? Of course he is. Oh Puppy."

She burst into tears, shoving aside the captain's offer of a tissue and defiantly wip-ing her nose on the sleeve of the filthy habit. "Then you also see that I came with Puppy."

"There is no mention of an Annette Ramos."

Annette's eyes narrowed. Thanks for not mentioning me when you got home, Pup. Very nice. "Look up a vid series on the BBC called *American Crusaders*." She impatiently rapped her knuckles on the arm of the chair until Captain Michael accessed and nodded confirmation.

"Then why have you come to Budapest?"

She sighed. "I didn't plan on coming to Budapest. Things just happened."

The 'bot waited impassively.

Annette sighed again. Sometimes you just have no choice. Most of the time. She wryly smiled. "Father Dempsey and I are trying to find the pope. Pope John."

Captain Michael's forehead pulsed as if it had stepped out of the room to receive important information. Two marines in trim dark-blue uniforms waited in the doorway.

"You will go with them please," the captain said, turning away in dismissal.

"To where?"

Michael left the room. The guards approached.

"Hey. I'm not going anywhere." Annette spread her legs slightly for balance.

She barely had time to raise her left forearm before the blindingly swift guards wrapped her in a magnetized body cuff. Annette never felt the needle.

21

"DNA scandals, DNA scandals, DNA scandals," Matthew had repeated until Puppy and Sahidi worried that he had suffered a trans-organic stroke. "Falsified scientific results for political and economic expediency and ambitions," the 'bot had ranted. "We can never have that again." Its voice suddenly oozed into Grandma's stern tones. "There is only trust in what we are and acceptance of what we can be."

"There can be no proof demanded," he insisted, finding calm in redoing the dimple in his lime-and-black striped tie. "Ty and Mickey"—who'd left, muttering to call when they had a fucking team—"cannot be expected to understand since their consciousness's had originated in a corrupt and demonically divisive culture.

"But *you two,*" Matthew had scolded with such sorrow they nearly shrank into their chairs in shame. "How can *you two* ask siblings for *PROOF because you think your siblings would LIE?*"

Once they finally lured Ty and Mickey, reeking of quesadillas, back into the room, Matthew clearly laid out the only clear path: the "two white grandpas" alone would have to determine who had really descended from twentieth-century ballplayers.

In a quieter voice but with equal fervor, Sahidi thanked Matthew for his insights; 'bot and human exchanged polite sneers. But she demanded that while applicants should not bring proof—her big dark eyes swam accusingly over Puppy as if that'd been his idea—they must show pride in their claims.

"These are not any old tryouts like the farce that originally filled the season's rosters. It wasn't anyone's fault." She nodded doubtfully at the scowling former co-Commissioners. "We worked with what we had, which was shit, and look at the level of talent we got. But this special game is purely voluntary, no money on the Lifecard, a one-time opportunity which goes beyond skills and stop moaning, Mr. Cobb, and deal with it."

"Long as they can hit," Ty grunted.

"Run," Mick agreed with a surly stare.

"Throw," Ty added, snarling. "Bunt. Hit to the opposite field. Find the cutoff man."

That set off another round of mutually deafening shouting until Matthew wrote in the air with large vibrating letters which, color-wise, matched his navy-blue pinstripe suit: as player-managers Mickey and Ty had the ultimate decision about who comprised the ball club.

As did player-managers Albert Cheng and Mooshie Lopez for the twenty-first-century team.

Over the next week, all of Sahidi's radcasters issued the same announcements at the top of the third inning, after the bottom of the sixth, and at the top of the eighth.

Now this message goes out to all you baseball fans in the FILL IN THE CITY area. On April 11, Wrigley Field will host the first Old-Timers' Game since 2048 when it was banned for promoting unhealthy nostalgia for a degenerate American past. We'll have teams from the twentieth and twenty-first centuries. If you're a descendant of anyone who played in the twentieth century for FILL IN THE LOCAL TEAM, come to the tryouts at FILL IN THE LOCAL STADIUM next FILL IN THE DATE from 9 a.m. until 6 p.m. Bring your own equipment. Our very own FILL IN THE LOCAL SPONSORS will be providing nourishment. Let's go FILL IN THE LOCAL TEAM.

Sahidi was proud that just five of her radcasters forgot to "fill in" the local names.

The Cousins Council only permitted muted vids of the long, ungainly lines circling the major league ballparks. With Sahidi's charm as one bayonet in his back and Ian's sour pouts probing his left kidney, Puppy made a personal appeal to allow a few of the applicants to be interviewed. The response made Matthew's rant tranquil by comparison.

"To favor one applicant over the other was sheer, well," Third Cousin Dinazzo sputtered, "favoritism. How are you determining why they should be quoted? What makes them unique?"

Fourth Cousin Oh then interrupted, "This borders on celebrity cult and potential hero worship and we will not have it."

The "we" agreed with discordant grumbles.

If there'd been a contest over which baseball franchise churned out the most descendants, which Puppy mischievously suggested just to see Matthew's eyes orbit like the Earth, Fenway Park would've won.

Ernie Paicopolos had borrowed an aging horse from a farm in Andover. Resplendent in a colonial outfit right down to a Red Sox-colored tri-corn hat and breeches, the Wizard had ridden through much of Boston over the past week crying out, "the Red Sox are coming, the Red Sox are coming!"

Soon Ernie and his brave mount were trailed by thousands of squealing children chanting "the Red Sox are coming!" Paicopolos paused throughout this now-historic ride to deliver tart and scolding speeches about duty. Those who had the blood of the Splendid Splinter or the Rocket or Yaz must, absolutely must, present themselves as had the Minutemen at the Lexington Green.

America, Baseball, and Red Sox Nation depended on them. Unless, and here his shaggy beard electrified with fury, they wanted to be shamed by…the Wizard flashed his wand and a blue-and-white Yankees banner unfurled with vicious disdain.

And off Ernie galloped. One if by bat. Two if by ball.

Half-remembered stories, family myths, and fragments of a once-proud legacy became a firestorm of pride. Yes, my grandfather's name was Rico so perhaps he was named for Rico Petrocelli. Where's my mitt? I'm a lefty and I'm rude, how can I not be related to Teddy Baseball? My name is Trilowski and my lucky number is eight. Show me left field.

As inspired as Boston was, the rest of major league baseball wasn't exactly inert. Despite clear instructions from Sahidi about violating sectional nepotism, local radcasters worked in reminders outside the three advert spots about finding your roots. "Have you heard how many players are planning to attend in *FILL IN THE OPPOSING CITY?*"

The Friends of Tom Seaver handed out photographs of great New York Mets players throughout the mass transit system of Queens, now only six percent below sea level. "Do you look like Dwight Gooden? Is there a resemblance to Gary Carter? That is Tug McGraw. Yes, his name was Cleon Jones."

In all the Milwaukee DVs, offshoot Friends of Robin Yount formed. Soon there were mini tryouts for those siblings wondering whether they were related to Paul Molitor. Wait. Henry Aaron was a Milwaukee and Atlanta player? In Detroit, the Friends of Al Kaline groups went door-to-door, explaining the Tigers's greatest players.

The Cleveland Spiders grounds crew was dispatched to puzzled families so they could piece together whether they were, in fact, descended from Bob Feller or Larry Doby. Shortly, all the Friends of groups had begun fragmenting. Friends of Jackie Robinson beget Friends of Gil Hodges and Friends of Don Drysdale. Baseball couldn't belong to one player's face. Wasn't that elitist?

Soon the United States Post Office, the best postal service in the world, had to add a fifth daily delivery for the letters flying back and forth across the country. *Didn't Aunt Ka'trina once say…for sure great-grandpa…tell me you didn't throw away…*

There were even some violations of the sacrosanct national message center contained in the lower corners of the twenty-hour continuous vidnews reserved for true emergencies such as *Mommy just got run over by a cement truck*. Discreet notes started popping up over a two-day period.

Grandpa, that Reggie Jackson story…Wasn't Fernando Valenzuela…Hello Amos Otis…

Puppy received an angry HG message from Third Cousin Rasfarati accusing the Commissioner of orchestrating illegal use of the emergency message boards. The Cousin further complained about Sahidi's rabble-rousing radcasters. "Wasn't that Peter Rose a criminal?"

Puppy happily turned this over to the Granddaughter.

On her regular spot on *Wake Up, My Darlings*, Clary announced a new nationwide school project. Children would be encouraged to research if they were related to baseball players from the twentieth century. This necessitated relaxing library access to previously unavailable records. The Cousins exploded and voted unanimously against such an idea.

Clary explained that children would require the presence of a teacher, one of the professions with broader access to information, either physically, virtually, or through a letter authorizing the child to go alone. She was undertaking this under her rights as Granddaughter when the Cousins could not agree on a critical issue.

Second Cousin DeRico's bald head about glowed when she pointed out this vote was unanimous and since when was baseball a critical issue?

"Since now," Clary replied acidly. "Unless you would prefer to explain to parents in the Cousins Lobbies why I had to order Black Tops to stand guard at all the Central Libraries to ensure the rights of their children to be educated."

Felice was very pleased.

While all the thirty major league parks on the day of the twentieth-century tryouts didn't have the luster of Fenway Park with Ernie and his exhausted mount trotting up and down Yawkey Way to find their real Johnny Pesky, an estimated fifty thousand Americans from ages eleven to ninety-six tried out under the Granddaughter's first-ever Insight fluttering like a wispy cloud over second base:

You are the past and the present. Embrace and see the future.

The twenty-first-century team was very different.

Having Albert Cheng, the venal former Grandpa, and a 'bot claiming to be Mooshie Lopez as player-managers didn't go over well with the Cousins. Confronting a baseball-related item, sometimes two and three of them on the agenda every morning, sent the Cousins into one long stammer interrupted by shouts and groans. In a shockingly uncharacteristic episode, Cousins Gomes and Oh exchanged aimless punches and wild shoves, hurling the innocent Nok-Hockey game into a crippled heap.

First Cousin Nadharatha had, with the help of very strong Fleisher's Mango Ginger Tea and half a box of freshly baked choco-cream puffs from Gilberto's Bakery in Pelham Parkway, pointed out that the very reason for Albert Cheng going to a DV rather than a reeducation camp was to demonstrate equality in punishment and belief in the redemption of ethics. If Cheng was beyond restoration to The Family, then how had such evil prospered undetected? What did that say about honesty and transparency in our government? Wasn't that a criticism if not an accusation of Grandma's judgment? He's not returning to any manifestation of power. Grandma's bra straps, this is merely baseball.

Over the rising disputatious anger, Nadharatha shook a choco-cream puff as if it contained all the great wisdom of the world. The organic life-form called Mimi Laker, formerly Dara Dinton, originally Mooshie Lopez, had already submitted synthetic blood tests and consciousness tissues proving she had contained Mooshie Lopez's essence. All corresponded to the dates of its inorganic creation in the Area 44 complex in Butte, South Dakota, proving her identity along with the facts of its last transformation, understandable since she rightfully believed her existence was in danger from Grandpa Cheng.

"Under the Harmony Laws," the First Cousin chided, "inorganic life-forms do not have any higher burden of proof than humans. That said"—Nadharatha raised a cream-tipped finger—"there is trust and there is trust." The somewhat-calmed Cousins nodded sagely. "There'll be no rad adverts calling on former players." The First Cousin busied himself with the last choco-cream puffs while several Cousins loudly complained about unauthorized interviews during the San Diego Pelicans, Washington Cherry Blossoms, and St. Louis Cardinals home games with local players selected for the twentieth-century team.

"If Cheng and Lopez want to put together a team, they'll do it on their own. Some of these old players will no doubt have belonged to the Miners. Yes, yes!" he shouted. "Lately we are all about opening old wounds to close them. If we can rethink the historical perspective of the capitalist cabal which brought America into World Wars I and II, then we can allow former traitors to walk onto a baseball diamond for one silly game.

"But there will be accountability should something go wrong. This decision belongs to Clary's Puppy Beisbol," he sneered as if referencing the Mumbai Flu which killed more than eight million in 2050. "If there is trouble…" His voice faded into the nasty barking circling the table.

• • • •

MOOSHIE LAZILY DRAPED her bare, muscled calf over Puppy's knee as if it were just yesterday that they were engaged. He swiveled slightly in the large glove-shaped chair, forcing her to playfully swing in the same direction. The squeaks of the new furniture were the only sounds in the Yankee clubhouse, modeled as if it were 1956; the Mick cried every time he entered.

She held up her empty beer stein for a refill. He made a loud groan about walking back and forth to the table for the pitcher of Sheila Jay's Portlandia IPA.

"Thank you, darling." Mooshie winked over the foam.

"You can't put on any more weight if you want to run the bases like old times," he said impishly.

Mooshie swung her legs back and forth like a pendulum. "Excuse me. Are you daring to suggest that I am grossly overweight?"

"Not grossly. A few six-packs of IPA above what you should be."

"If I downed that pitcher, right there, that one, staring at us," she fumed, "for the rest of today and tomorrow and the three days until the Old-Timers' Game, I will still drill holes in their bats with my fastball and holes in their gloves with my hits playing on any damn field you want to build with that collection of sad and sorry losers called major league baseball players."

He just stared until they burst out laughing.

"Okay. That was a little wordy," Mooshie admitted.

"Just a bit."

"But even dead and revived and rebuilt, hot stuff, I'm still the best player in this game. Ever. Number one. The Moosh."

Puppy let her indulge in a little more reverie until she grew thirsty and sipped in between mutters.

"What I meant if you'd let me finish is that I'm sure you're in good enough shape to waddle around the bases for one game. What happens when you apply to rejoin baseball full time?"

Mooshie squinted shrewdly over his glass. "Now who said Mooshie was planning that?"

"No one would dare anticipate Mooshie's plans. But I am the Commissioner. Nine hundred players and assorted hangers-on depend upon my daily acute insights. I'm not just a self-centered jerk anymore."

She rolled her eyes. Oh how he'd missed Mooshie. To play one game with her. One inning. One at bat. Last night he dreamed he drove a forlorn Mooshie curve into the center-field bleachers.

The clubhouse rocked with the sounds of a dozen players shouting conflicting opinions about the décor. Puppy stood with the biggest smile he'd had since coming home.

"Well, well, well." Burly Tony Felton planted his feet, fists on hips like an old pirate. "We're graced with the presence of the great one."

He doffed his Cleveland Spiders cap, joined by what was once known as the "baseball brigade."

There was third baseman Pop Ra Chou, who most agreed was the equal to Easy Sun Yen, Mooshie's running mate on and off the field as part of the Yankees's legendary "three amigos"; Bar'Nee Ortiz, who'd gone three straight years without an error at shortstop, a feat in the days when most teams had only one grounds crew member left.

Flamboyant Carl Tedeschi, a throwback to sliding spikes-first into second base; the huge first baseman Johanna Busco; and speedy left fielder Curly Russell. Hobbling on a crutch was Aaron White. Donda Sicatyunnni, reportedly once Mooshie's squeeze when they weren't brawling on the field, cupped White's elbow.

Slowly unfurling on Tony's bark was Ted Towers of the drop-leaf curveball, which could "yank cartilage out of your leg with a checked swing"; fellow Colorado Rockies pitching teammate Kelly Caputo, winner of 231 games; infielder Stanislaus Pulaski, whose glove made ground balls invisible; and the Pittsburgh Pirates outfielder Allie "The Thief" Nissan, nicknamed for the way he'd turn long drives into long outs.

It took a few minutes for Puppy to hug and kiss everyone until, embarrassed, they settled onto the floor or on chairs. Only their sagging jowls suggested they weren't twenty-eight years old again.

"Everyone made it back from England?" Puppy shook his head in amazement.

"Detouring to drop you off at the airfield for your cozy ride home complicated things," Major Felton growled. "Adding three hours got us into a scrap with the Allahs."

"Three M-88 tanks." Curly referenced the standard NATO tank which the member states had handed over to the Islamic Empire back in the 2060s.

"Bang bang." Donda made a gun out of her hand, prompting Mooshie to shout that she hadn't lost her cuteness; Johanna made barfing noises amid a lot of good-natured cracks.

"Can I fucking finish?" Felton snarled, silencing the room into loving grins. "By the time we fought our way into Scotland—" he scowled impatiently as the room whispered, "bang, bang"—"nearly a day later, we were pretty roughed up. We almost lost Curly and Allie. Aaron's just getting healed."

"I can play, don't worry," he assured everyone.

Tony grunted skeptically. "Even I had a few holes here and there. Thanks to going out of our way so you and that skinny-woman-not-your-wife could run off together."

Puppy didn't even bother responding.

"We stayed inland since there was a shitload of fighting offshore. Around Aberdeen we learned there wasn't any American fleet—"

"As I predicted," Pop Ra Chou volunteered.

"Bully for you," Felton snapped. "We persuaded a few Brits, Scots, whatever they call themselves now, to tell us about the underground since we were down to hoping that wasn't all a bucket of shit, else we'd still be there farming sheep and getting loaded on Scotch."

"Good Scotch," Tedeschi said to enthusiastic nods.

"The underground was all Allahs." Tony pulled a face as if still digesting that. "Not a damn Brit or Scot or anything."

"That ain't true," contradicted Curly, his freckles glowing on his tan face.

"I'm getting to that."

"Maybe sometime before the Old-Timers' Game would help," Mooshie purred playfully.

"Fuck you, Lopez."

"Wouldn't you now?"

Puppy settled down the opinions in the room about the likelihood of Felton surviving sex with Mooshie.

"The Allahs dumped us off…"

"Were you still in the armored vehicle?" Puppy asked.

"Oh yes, certainly. We didn't want to attract any attention." Felton sneered, waiting as his teammates hurled invective toward the sheepish Puppy. "We were on foot. Those who weren't carried."

"Like you, Maj," Johanna said.

Felton flushed. "Only a little way. Can I go on or do we tell about how much blood we each lost? Just east of Linlithgow, the Allahs turned us over to a bunch of nuns. Nuns. Believe that? Nuns with knives."

"They were more like swords," Tedeschi insisted.

"Short swords. Right from under their dresses. Like the one your wife wore." Tony hesitated, realizing he might've said the wrong thing. "Habits, they're called I think."

There was a momentary noisy debate about nuns's wardrobes.

"These nuns with swords loaded us up on a small fishing boat in the middle of the night."

"All of us are about out cold." Johanna reminded Felton he had been one of those out cold, so she'd take it from there. "We traveled northwest about three hours until they loaded us onto another boat where we all got pricked with meds. I passed out then, the last one. When we woke, we were in a village in Newfoundland. From there, back into the States."

Puppy waited for the silence to end, but they just sat there, thinking.

"And then?"

Felton snorted. "We all got big fat medals for our bravery. What the hell do you think happened? Nothing. No one was going to acknowledge they left us in POW camps. That's embarrassing. Old soldiers are about the worst people to have around because we have all these memories we don't want to share and no one wants to hear. Fat old riflemen in an era of sleek robot soldiers. They processed new Lifecards, with back pay. The generosity overwhelmed us. Then the sons-of-bitches said we should restart our lives in DVs. Course we should. We failed, didn't we? Just like the first time. It was all the cowardly soldiers's fault we lost the war."

"There's a clerk in the Beacon Hill Lifecard office who will never chew properly," chuckled Donda, setting off grim smiles.

"And now here you are, pretty as pictures."

Albert Cheng clanged inside like a pony with bells.

"Hail, hail, the gang's all here and don't we look pretty." He paused, waiting for a laugh that would come the day the "baseball brigade" marched beneath the crescent moon and star. Cheng snorted in mock disappointment, making his way around the room getting tepid handshakes; a couple players obviously wiped their palms.

"I'm glad to see everyone, too. Once again, Albert Cheng is accustomed to tough decisions without all the cuddly warmth that, say, our Commissioner might need."

Puppy glared.

"Now come on. If Puppy puts up with me and some folks say I tried killing him, then I think we can at least be civil since I will be your manager for the day."

Mooshie slowly held up her hand, the fingers descending except the middle one.

"My partner. Look at that smile. And some folks also say I turned off Mooshie, too. You can't completely wipe away the instinct for malicious gossip, much as Grandma and I tried."

"Are you going to bore us for long, Little General?" Tony's mouth twisted out the sour nickname for Albert. The former Grandpa snapped off a bitter laugh.

"Just long enough, Major. We're all professionals and we have a job to do. I got you all out of your DVs before you were even sent there. Yes, thank you, Albert. How'd you manage that from your foxhole of disgrace? Just because I'm no longer called Grandpa doesn't mean I'm not still a Grandpa, if you can follow along that complex thinking."

He sighed at the adamant stubbornness of their hostile stares.

"I know you hate me," Cheng said suddenly. "I understand. But since there aren't any fellow Chicago Cubbies in the room, you won't have to deal with me in the same locker room after the Old-Timers' Game. Promise. As the saying goes, we have an embarrassment of riches. The greatest of the greatest of our time. Of all time." He acknowledged Mooshie's grumble. "When the Baseball Hall of Fame returns, you'll all be there and yes, there's talk about Cooperstown being rebuilt."

Puppy stiffened. Grandma's earrings, how'd Cheng know about that?

"Don't worry. The fans'll be dazzled by your skills even if we have to shoehorn everyone into the nine positions. Mooshie and I have a plan so everyone plays."

"I'm figuring I don't start," said Ted Towers.

Mooshie whistled skyward.

"And you got someone else for shortstop?" Ortiz asked.

Albert tossed in a shrug. "But I'll give way at some point. Mooshie will only pitch the first five innings. Then Ted and Kelly will finish up."

"I'm available," Puppy said, blushing at the chuckles. "Hey, I did okay in London and that was a good team we played."

"For Allahs." Felton snickered.

"For anyone," Puppy snapped. "And you all know it. They were talented at our own game. It was their arrogance which did them in, not their skills. Winning a war didn't mean they were better than us. Certainly not at baseball. But trashing an opponent, and I mean trashing and really meaning it, isn't our way."

The players impatiently shuffled their feet.

"Maybe Puppy can get one of his Islamic friends to come over and throw out the first pitch," Cheng said.

Mooshie shoved the growling Puppy back into his glove chair.

"If you'll let someone else talk for more than ten seconds, dear Grandpa," Mooshie said with a curl of her upper lip.

Albert held up his hands and stepped aside as Mooshie sauntered into the middle of the group.

"Now some of you don't like me, either, but that's just because unlike Grandpa, I always kicked your asses on the field, not off." She winked at their good-natured groans. Cheng reddened, lowering onto a stool, petulant arms folded.

"What we got here are the old-style All-Stars, like when that was legal and not considered elitist. All of you are the finest men and women I ever saw play and I'm honored to dress with you and call you my teammates."

The room wonderingly took in Mooshie Lopez complimenting anyone but herself.

"Now that we got all that melted licorice out of the way—" She waited for the relieved laughter to pass. "I really want to win this game. Beating Allahs must've been satisfying on every level anyone could know. But this game is not about winning World War III because that ain't happening. What we have is the chance, and Puppy, you might want to cover your cutesome ears, but this is about straightening out the rivers of crap from people saying that somehow twentieth-century baseball was better than ours."

That set off grumbles and finger wagging at Puppy who obediently covered his ears.

"We're all taking the rap that our game sucked. Let me tell you this. We were bigger and stronger and smarter and worked just as hard as Ty Cobb and Mickey Mantle and, and…"

"Babe Ruth and Joe DiMaggio and Nolan Ryan—"

Mooshie cut Puppy off with a serrated look.

"I didn't say they weren't good. Great, sure. But they look better because the country was better. We're paying because we played in a time when America was going into the toilet and we, our game, represented that America. Somehow there was a connection, like an umbilical cord, and to love baseball meant you had to love America and that was considered so wrong. Tear down baseball and you can tear down the country and all we ever were. Everyone in this room loved our country, still loves our country, no matter what the assholes said. And Mr. Grandpa over there, well, he was one of us. Hey, *hey*, shut the fuck up." She scowled until they quieted.

"I promise this is the last nice thing I'll ever say about the prick. But Cheng really tried standing up to Grandma. He wanted to win the war and he would've taken out the Allahs with our tactical nukes, but the old bitch wouldn't let him so he took the blame for our defeat to protect her. I said shut up. I know what I'm talking about and Mooshie doesn't lie. And when Lenore tried to make peace with the Camels last year, who tried stopping her? The Little General. All you got to do is see how the Mufti and his weasel son Abdullah have merged their armies to realize he was right. Cheng's still a turd, but let's all agree that we're on the same page."

She paused for their grudging nods. "Whatever Puppy and the Cousins and Clary the Grandchild and whoever want to show about the age of America's greatness is totally different. Our country's never going to be that again, they killed it too deeply, sucked out the soul, so I think it's a big waste. But I'm not letting baseball be sacrificed. When we smear the twentieth-century losers across the field, we're gonna show we were the best. Flat out. Simple as that. So please, I never want to hear moaning about how no one can lay down a proper bunt anymore. Tough shit, Puppy. We play our style, moon shots, strikeouts, and Mooshie Lopez is gonna sing the old National Anthem and *God Bless America* and that's fucking that."

Puppy watched as the team slapped backs, even allowing Cheng into the edge of the circle. They grabbed their bats and gloves and headed out of the clubhouse toward the field for their first practice. Mooshie popped her head back inside.

"You coming? I need someone to chant 'Mooshie, Mooshie, Mooshie.'"

"In a sec."

She frowned. "You sulking over what I said?"

"Why? You were wrong." He waved her off. "Go ahead. I'll be there in a second. And try not to hurt your arm. It's easy at your age."

Mooshie gave him the finger and closed the door. Puppy rolled a baseball over his lap, basking in the symphonic crack of the bats. In any century, the music was the same.

• • • •

CLARY KEPT THE rayed shielding on; she had approximately seventy-five seconds before the automatic query from Felice would send an orange question mark zigzagging like a berserk insect about her bedroom. At first, Felice would appear with the impassive stare of a mountain, waiting for an answer as to why Clary had prevented "free exchange," as it called the tracking.

If I go to another bowling alley I will roll the children down the lane.

Pretending to be insolent was easy. Felice expected her rudeness. By misbehaving, Clary knew that someday when she really needed secrecy, the pattern of being the old nasty Clary would give her time.

The demon child. She fumed at that insult, picking at her thumb.

She switched off the shielding. The orange question mark danced anyway. Clary scrunched her face and telepathized a pathetic little response. *Tired. Feel fine.*

She could jump two feet off the ground. She spoke eleven human languages. She only had to sleep three hours a night. Yes, she still threw up, which she concealed in piles of scented bags, tossing them down the electrified garbage chute.

But Clary was angry and the anger was very different in this halfway phase of trans-organic regeneration. Her rage was iced. Felice was correct. She could visualize emotions outside herself as tangible. The anger was a bundle of grass on fire and, with an inner nod, she froze and examined the feelings as she examined herself. The new Clary who in three blinks of an eye redirected all her thoughts.

When she wanted to. Not examining meant failure and she had yet to figure out transcending that. Clary sat in her big beefy brown chair and picked thoughtfully at her other thumb.

As the Granddaughter, Clary had ordered any external transmissions touching areas under her specific supervision like baseball and child futures and the new cacao farms be directed to her private quarters; she easily telepathized to the yellow floating orb bobbing near the dolls on the shelf.

This tagged reference was encoded. Clary had done that as a prank, an act of spite, a finger in Felice's nostrils early in the treatment to show she could get away with what she wanted. After bristling under firm refusals by two layers of military intelligence to release that information, Clary knew Felice would be alerted if she probed further. How dare she be denied access when no one else should care.

Unless they did.

She took an unnecessary breath because she had stopped breathing, and she allowed that terrifying new Clary who half lived inside to take over. She had permitted that before only to hurtle backward, clutching onto the side of a cloud in her room. This time she floated in what she thought was a cloud because she had no other reference point. Her heart still raced, ice flashing by. The perspective was visible because visible was all she could manage, but the center of herself was pure, utter calm, embracing simple logic while she heard herself screaming silently.

The blank square where her brain should be filled with a cross. She gasped on the rug for a few minutes; there was almost an indentation of her profile by now.

Clary padded through the faint mist of the early spring evening toward the rear of her house, a quarter of a mile from the ridge of trees. Clary permitted herself irritation. She could track him but how could she complain about Felice prying into her life when she did the same to Puppy?

Clary scanned him anyway. The picture was cloudy. He was somewhere deep. A ricocheting noise intruded. She adjusted her focus with fierce concentration.

Wearing his Yankees cap, Puppy was tossing a baseball against a wall at the back of a darkened playground, all alone. Puppy looked so sad beneath the faint, yellow hue of a fading streetlamp as he wound up and flipped the ball, catching it on the rebound. He rubbed his right shoulder and peered ahead as if looking for a sign from the catcher. Would he appreciate hearing her voice? No, although it would be fun to scare him.

If only I were twenty and you were thirty, I would play catch with you forever. That emotion twisted her spine in a brief painful grasp.

"Impressive. I'm sure there's a lot of wish fulfillment, but still nicely done, Clary."

Grandma stepped around the side of the cottage. She unwrapped the purple scarf from her neck, standing as if more at home with the real trees abutting the edge of the grounds.

"Who are you?" Clary scanned for some identifying mark of Felice's spies but found none. She tried another micro-botic frequency, stopping when Grandma held up a thin hand.

"Please dear. You're not that good, at least yet. Certainly, Felice isn't." She smiled as Clary wildly overturned a buffet table of thoughts. "And don't even consider a physical response."

She chuckled at Clary's hiss. "Don't worry, we won't play guessing games. That irritated you immensely when your father made you guess where he was taking you on the traditional weekend outing."

Clary warily circled to the right, a simple animal assessing its prey. "What is this savagery now? You have already extracted my fears from the recesses of my mind. I will not tolerate that anymore."

"Nor should you, darling," Lenore said softly. "What has been done to you is wrong. I have not been sent by Felice to toy with you. I am Grandma. And yes, as they once said in those dark narcissistic days, I've had some work done."

Last week's encoding by Felice on all transmissions regarding Grandma Lenore Shen suddenly made sense. Clary slipped that into her external thought drive, also encoded, though sloppily. "Then it is true about you."

"What part, dear?"

"That you survived in some way. As that."

"Do spare me the sneer. We all deal with the post-death experience in our own ways. My appearance is intended to deceive, no more." Grandma smiled faintly. "Yes, Clary. There was the slightest bit of duplicity in that remark. No one wants to be repulsive. That can be counter-productive to connecting. It's a question of what lengths we will go to be attractive. I'm past that. I hope you never are. Certainly judging from that gaudy orange outfit and the hair ribbons, they haven't robbed you of your vanity quite yet."

Clary defiantly folded her arms. "Why are you here?"

"Instantaneous authority without a moment's doubt. Is that the leadership model you're following?"

"I do not need leadership models and I do not need advice from the failed leaders of the past. Dear," Clary postured, "you and your essence are no longer part of The Family. Apologies. You are trans-organic so of course you are accepted. I do not think you had to cloak yourself, which at your age must be draining, to lecture me outside my own home. Yes, dear. It will always be called Grandma's house officially, but the country and now the world knows whose house it is."

"Are you done or is there more infantile whining ahead? Your ego has been razored, not controlled, though I suspect you have been told that's wise."

"I will not be insulted—"

"Clary darling, for whom are you putting on this performance? I am completely cloaked and Felice only sees you bouncing alone in one of your sad little princess games." Lenore wouldn't admit that preventing scanning was indeed draining. Worryingly so. She sat on a damp tree stump and casually crossed her legs.

"I've come to help you, Clary Santiago. Must you engage in such childish snorts of derision? There is now mucus dangling from your upper lip." Grandma didn't wait for Clary to fiercely rub her nose. "As I've alluded, I know what they're doing to you. It is wrong. It will lead to disaster, both for you as a life-form and for the country."

Clary tensed. "No one does anything to me."

"Felice is turning you into one of them. Us, to be kind." Grandma wearily held up her hand. "Pablo got traces off your tongue during the dental examination. I know, it is hurtful that he had to do that. Betrayal in the name of love is a concept you do not know yet. You must fall in love first, but that will never happen because that is an emotion for which there is no logic."

That furious dream the other night that Felice captured and played onto her bedroom ceiling to embarrass her for not controlling the subconscious. She crimsoned under Grandma's knowing smile, angrily folding her arms.

"You do not know what you speak of, elderly woman. I will be something new and different. I am not 'botically rebuilding my human form. That synthetic hybrid failed. I have studied the attempts of people to replace worn-out human parts with 'botic advances. They were never certain of what they were."

"How could they be?" Grandma sternly said. "They wavered between two worlds and belonged to neither. That is why the consciousness transference program was begun secretly in the late '40s once the face 'bots were banned. Look at Ty Cobb and Mickey Mantle. Mooshie Lopez. All early examples of the 'botic technology integrating humanity with non-organic mechanisms without losing the human essence."

"Except I will be different. I will retain the logic of emotions. It has been difficult. Painful, but they will be used to my advantage."

"The compassion and empathy programs, yes, that was first implemented in 2031. That was the greatest mistake, terrifying humanity with machines almost like them, except better."

"Is that when you were created?"

Grandma rose slowly. "Clary Santiago, if you have advanced at all you will have realized with synthetic logic that I would never allow a more advanced version to exist. Yes, that's quite illogical. As leader, I should not be privileged. That contradicts all the essential foundations of The Family. I never prepared any succession plan because what right would I have to dictate beyond the grave how the next generations should behave? A society built on individual responsibility yet governed by outdated rules was the grave flaw of democracy. They listened to the laws, the Constitution, precedents, not because they believed they were wise but because the laws said they should.

"No. I knew when I died that my time had ended. And yet here I am. Here I am," Grandma repeated in a baffled mutter. "I am the highest pedigree of trans-organic micro-botics. I am more advanced than Felice. And I will always be more advanced than you."

Clary's lips twisted into an ugly smile. "I will have a soul. You do not have that, Grandma. Nor does Felice. Nor will any trans-organic life-form. Ever."

Grandma studied her carefully. "Can you measure that?"

The girl's eyes blazed. "Of course I can. Do you think I am some stupid kneeling child wrapped in her rosary beads? A soul is immortal."

"So is your vessel, ultimately."

Clary stamped her foot. "Let me finish. My soul will transcend my vessel. I can believe in God without mindless obedience, but with mutual respect. Like art, the power of my message will live forever. Clary will be like a wondrous painting or sculpture. I will have my own Insights, but they will not be designed to lead, they will inspire to make our people seek beyond themselves. There is no beyond in our Family, Grandma. There is no highterness, that is my new word. There is nothing beyond us. You destroyed God and religion. I will return that without the horrible hatred and divisiveness."

With a shudder, the very tired Grandma slowly resumed her seat, shielding her thoughts from Clary's mocking mental thrusts. "Dear Clary, they want to turn you into a dictator. A little perfect Godhead. You speak of art. Has Felice mentioned a statue of you?"

Clary squirmed as Grandma smiled knowingly.

"They want superiority. Felice has played on your anger, your bitterness, your deep pain at losing your family, your fear and guilt surrounding your flight to America, and your continued hiding. You are a tool, dear. That is why human emotions are being encouraged, beginning with baseball passions. What Felice is doing is destroying the calm of The Family. The sense of sharing, our common spirit, all we had left after the War. Yes, I abolished God and religion and patriotism and social media and journalism and entertainment. I introduced a commonality of ethics and morality. I brought us together because otherwise we would have perished, that I guarantee. The Allahs were regathering their strength and would've invaded despite the truce, and I would've launched nuclear weapons despite the madness. We are still here, Clary. The Family is still strong."

"If it is so strong, then why do you not disappear?"

Grandma sighed sadly. "Because the enemies have risen again through our laziness, our unwillingness to fight to preserve what we have. It is unsettling. No, no, it is terrifying to see once again the smug belief that freedom was forever. We're letting robot soldiers do our fighting. You cannot value a freedom for which you have not fought for."

"After all you have done with The Family, people still revert to people. What did you accomplish, dear Grandma, if this new society is as doomed as the past not because of the government, the laws, but because that is just how humans are?"

Lenore strained for a spurt of resumptive energy. "Better to fail than be ignorant animals under the hand of robotic paternal tyranny. All I have ever wanted was to make each person the best they could be so, together, we could become the best we could. I'm here to make sure you are the best you can be, Clary. I'm here to make sure you do not discard your human values in the quest to be more than human."

Clary stared hard. "You want to control me, too."

"No. But Felice does."

"No one controls Clary," she hissed violently. "No one. I am the Granddaughter. I am the head of The Family. You are jealous. I will succeed where you failed. Now go before I alert my guards. Yes, my guards who serve me. Go, go."

Grandma seemed to disappear in a clump of bushes. Clary's breathing increased. Not the panic, she thought, stumbling around in a lopsided circle. Clary grabbed at her head, watching as her mind leaped out, danced, and ran away. Swearing in Spanish, Clary fell before she took another step, her filthy obscenities abruptly ending.

She tried speaking in English, but there were no words. More panic. Her mind returned, a sprightly little girl in blonde pigtails and a mocking smile who answered in clear sing-song English while skipping around Clary who was paralyzed.

With the fear there can be no fear nor doubt nor untrammeled emotion untrammeled emotion you are no longer you so stop so stop so stop.

Clary lay on her back, panting. The partiality of the dream returned as if the sky was an immense screen. Dancing with Puppy in their Yankees uniforms across the infield at Yankee Stadium, he lifted Clary and kissed her longingly on the lips. Flowers sprouted out of her toes and the entire ballpark and then the world became one singing red rose. She yanked out the strands of real grass, clutching them to her chest like a sad little bouquet.

22

The black Basil Hayden Funeral Home van pulled up alongside the fire hydrant on a deserted chunk of Burnside Avenue. As the back doors slid open, the six Doherty children toppled out one after the other like a well-trained circus act, landing in wary crouches. Glancing south past Morris Heights at Yankee Stadium a mile and a half away, they circled and spit on the ground to ward off the evil eye, touching their sacred Red Sox jerseys hidden beneath the bulky overcoats. The entire cab of the van was littered with their uneasy saliva.

"That's enough." Mary Doherty clapped her hands, adding her spit.

"Momma, I swear by Jesus it's moving." Eck's nine-year-old nostrils flared. Since the Doherty family had entered the Bronx with the joy of an anesthesia-free appendectomy, the boy, named for Dennis Eckersley, insisted ghosts and demons also came out during the day. His siblings had mocked him at first. Then Mary Elizabeth also swore on Jesus that the upper deck grinned at her which sent the children into murmuring hysteria along with the expelling of another pint of spit.

By now, Mary wasn't so sure herself whether the damn ballpark wasn't doing a little jig.

"Are you going to do your duty or whine?" She stared down her brood who took up positions, three on either side of the van. Waving Puppy and Zelda back onto the wet sidewalk, Mary clambered inside. A moment later, a steel ramp slithered down, followed by the mahogany coffin.

Mary grunted in satisfaction at the way her children each grabbed a handle and headed toward the abandoned lot.

"Should we just follow?" Puppy asked, hesitating before doing just that.

Draping the burlap bag over her right shoulder with a disdainful sigh, Mary led the procession. It was Mary Elizabeth's job as the eldest to provide the directives of the will. While funerals were increasingly legal, anything evoking religion was not. This lot, among hundreds throughout the country, had been used during and after the war for secret Catholic burials when cremation was declared the only means of disposal; there were just too many bodies.

Mary Elizabeth walked off fourteen very precise steps forward, four to the right, and then eighteen toward one o'clock, the measurements of an ancient clock face fascinating her. She stopped as if about to be planted.

"Here."

Mary knew better than to question her daughter. If she said this was the burial plot, then it was. She briskly nodded and they lowered the coffin. Mary handed out two shovels to her two eldest, Mary Elizabeth and Patricia Mary. She reluctantly handed Puppy a tool.

"He said if you wanted, you could help dig."

Zelda poked him so hard her finger nearly tore the cashmere overcoat borrowed from Pablo. He didn't need encouragement. Puppy also stripped off his suit jacket and tie and sweat through the half an hour or so of digging into the muddy ground.

After numerous inspections and a whispered consultation with Mary Elizabeth, Mary dropped a six-foot rope which reached the bottom of the grave. Close enough. Still, she seemed reluctant, and Puppy realized it had nothing to do with the proper depth of his father's burial site.

The six children carefully brought the coffin down, hand over hand, proudly returning caked with dirt.

"What happens now?" Puppy asked.

Mary exchanged pitying looks with her kids. "We cover him with dirt."

"I meant, do we say something?"

She leaned on the handle of the shovel. "Why? You suddenly got something to say to Alvin?"

"I'm here," he snapped. "Obviously my father wanted me here. I didn't just wander in off the street."

"So, say something. I'm sure Alvin would love to hear."

They all stared into the grave.

"Why is he buried here in the Bronx? I would've thought he would've preferred somewhere in Boston or New England since that's where he's been hiding."

"Because he met your mother at a club across the street." Mary pointed to a flower shop, explaining to her confused children that it was a long time ago. "'We danced the night away, Mar,'" she said wistfully, briefly mimicked Alvin's baritone. "Your mother's buried there."

Everyone stepped away from the adjacent ground on the left.

Mary laughed. "We hope. Who's buried where in these places is a combination of a guess and faith. What's it matter as long as you believe they're buried there. Go ahead, you can touch your mother's grave. She has six feet of dirt overhead. She won't feel anything. Much like you, Puppy."

He flushed. "How do you know what I feel, Mary?"

"Oh right. Sorry. The post-death blues and guilt is a comin'. Good thing we brought lots of handkerchiefs. You didn't know about this grave and a lot more about your father because you didn't want to know."

"And he didn't want to tell me," Puppy answered bitterly.

"Probably. He wasn't perfect." Mary's eyes watered. "He sacrificed a lot. His wife. Son. Friends. Reputation. Pretty much his whole life for something he believed in. Freedom. Not this farce you called The Family. When you tore Alvin another asshole about accompanying the Hall of Fame exhibit because you said he had no right to associate with something he risked his life to protect, that about killed him. Oh, he was dying anyway. Don't take your usual Puppy self-absorbed credit. But he still had a bit of hope that at the end, you'd understand. Least try to understand. He died at sixty-six when the life span now is pushing ninety. Cancer of all silly things. Don't worry, he didn't die of a broken heart. He was proud of you, but only so much. There weren't any deathbed words." Her voice dipped into a hoarse whisper, "'Tell my son I loved him.' He didn't even mention you. All these directions he'd already written down, who knows when, probably years ago. Before he and I..."

Mary blushed beneath their stares.

"Anyhow. He asked me to say a prayer. If it embarrasses or offends you, well, we rightly don't care but you can wait by the van."

"We'll stay," Zelda said, clutching Puppy's wet palm.

Mary shrugged and recited the prayer.

"Eternal rest grant unto him, O Lord, and let perpetual light shine upon him. May his soul and the souls of all the faithful departed, through the mercy of God, rest in peace."

Puppy and Zelda added their "amens." Zelda and Mary Elizabeth argued over a shovel before Mary adjudicated in Zelda's favor. A Blue Shirt watched through the other side of the wire fence as they filled the grave. The cop crossed himself.

"You see a lot more of that lately. Not just cops crossing themselves, either," Mary said carefully. She warned her children into silence as they gathered up the shovels.

"We're staying for a little while longer," Puppy said, fingers interlaced with Zelda's.

Mary nodded in grim approval. "Remember, Alvin hears everything you're thinking. And that which he misses, Jesus'll tell him."

Puppy grinned slowly. "Got it. I'll be careful not to call him a son-of-a-bitch."

"Why not? He was." Her eyes brimmed. "But he was my son-of-a-bitch." She stared. "Yours too, Puppy Nedick. Yours too."

Mary hurried her children into the van. Originally, they planned on returning the van to the funeral home immediately, the sooner out of the dreaded Bronx the better. But Patrick Francis's idea of driving past Yankee Stadium and spitting gained steam. When Mary Elizabeth suggested some ceremonial rock throwing at the degenerate ballpark and Patricia Mary offered singing Bosox fight songs, Mary let out a whoop and reminded everyone to wrap their hankies around their faces to avoid contamination.

Zelda studied the kneeling Puppy as he smoothed out the dirt on the grave.

"I'd ask if you're okay, but there's no answer to that."

"None. What am I supposed to feel compared to what I do feel?"

She upturned her palms. "And?"

He shrugged. "I don't know either. I probably never will. It's all a confusion about our relationship. Like part of me wishes he left me something. I don't know, Zel. A sock. The other says why should he? He was my father but in name only. I was his son in name only. We really didn't much like each other."

"Yet here you are."

Puppy straightened. "How could I not just in case he decided to leave me a sock?"

Zelda put her arm around his waist. "I felt nothing when my folks died. Pablo, too. I think we blame them too much for leaving us this world and then dying before they could help fix it." She sighed deeply. "Do you want to get drunk?"

"Yes, but I think that'd be the wrong idea. I'm sure I'd cry uncontrollably by the third round and by the fifth, be in handcuffs for some violent act."

"Sort of sounds like fun, but if you're too tired, we could just pig out. Throwing up's always cathartic. You could play with Diego and change his diapers. Maybe Pablo could work you in for a teeth cleaning. Though he's probably out walking the dog. Want to see a picture?"

She didn't wait for an answer and flipped open her wallet. He murmured tepid approval over the close-up of Horatio on the chair, head tilted wisely.

"He doesn't like me," Zelda said sadly. "It's not like he bites or anything. Or even barks. He usually waits until I get close and then walks off. When Pablo goes over, he jumps up and down. And he loves Diego. He sits by the crib for hours."

"Maybe you have to be nicer."

"I am nice." Zelda yanked back the photo. "I'm the one who feeds him. I spend more time in the dog food aisle imagining I'm a pug and what would I like than I do for anyone else. Pablo doesn't do that. But he does have a theory about why we can get pets now. Pablo thinks we're getting pets, sorry, adjacent family members, so we humans can grow more comfortable with other life-forms like 'bots. The more we interact, the less we think of what they are and, instead, focus more on who they are. Actually, it makes sense."

"Isn't something supposed to make sense, Zel, the older we get?"

"My baby does. That's about it. And only because he's still like a pillow and doesn't give me grief. Just wait until he starts talking. Other than that." She rolled her eyes. "We're not getting into some useless philosophical discussion about the meaning of life like when we were dumbass teenagers, are we?"

"Grandma's bra straps, I hope not."

• • • •

A TRIO OF athletic-looking singers in beehive hairdos and low-cut pink gowns snapped their fingers, entertaining the ample crowd at Monroe's with Smokey Robinson and The Miracles covers. His mother had a hidden collection of vinyl from Motown, Puppy recalled sadly. R&B and jazz had been briefly outlawed early in the War; Ray Charles was a particular favorite of the Miners pro-war movement.

As a kid, Puppy happened on a Diana Ross and The Supremes album. Tooled up much like the men wiggling on stage, Puppy was caught by his father singing and snapping his fingers to *Stop! In The Name of Love.* Standing in the doorway with glazed eyes, Alvin Nedick had been proud of his son, whether for the amateur beehive look, the way his mother's shimmering gown draped around his wide hips, or just for his audacity singing forbidden music.

He'd forgotten. No, he had just buried it. So now with one grave filled, another's opened. With a weary sigh, Puppy sidled up to the bar for a steaming black coffee, earning a grunt from owner Jimmy Monroe about the sobriety of high office. Pausing to find a seat, Puppy saw Elias Kenuda tucked like a shipwreck by a corner window.

Puppy plopped down. "This seat taken?"

"Kind of late for that. Usually, one hovers and asks politely before dropping down with the grace of a wild beast."

"You had a bad day, too?"

Elias sniffed at the understatement. He wore a black parka over a red plaid shirt, a lumberjack in a land with few trees.

"Can I get you a drink?" Puppy gestured at Kenuda's empty beer glass.

He raised a finger. "It would be improper for a DV to accept a drink as if the DV couldn't afford to pay for his own alcohol. That would demonstrate a lack of self-respect, the underpinnings of individual erosion and the clutching at fake external props barring the way to a new life."

"Probably."

"Probably? Probably?" Elias shouted, nearly drowning out a chord of *Tears of a Clown*. "It is gospel, forgive the religious reference, for here it is. *A Light to Responsibility* by Parkchester Paterson." Elias wrenched a rolled-up pamphlet from his pocket. "Everything you need to climb out of the Disappointment Village, circa 2079. A treasure trove of tips for the failed. How to re-adjust your sleeping habits. Are you comfortable with utensils? Why tables should always have four chairs."

Elias thumbed through to the back. "Whose fault is it? This Parkchester Paterson cleverly waited until the last chapter to spring the obvious so you wouldn't weep and never get farther than page four. My fault."

"Albert Cheng is clever." Puppy laughed at Elias's gaping look. "Hey, I come from a family of DVs. We all knew he wrote that. Cheng wrote all the DV literature."

Kenuda's eyes sparkled with angry triumph. "I suspect my beloved Hedda doesn't know that. Something she doesn't know. I think we should celebrate. I'd be honored to be sullied by your alcoholic charity."

Puppy ordered four Allegheny Red Whiskey chasers pursuing a pitcher of D'Antoni's Brown Ale and an extra-large portion of deep-fried curly onion rings because it was clearly going to be that kind of night. Zelda would regret choosing the safety of domestic bliss tonight.

They toasted sullied honor with the first shot. "I'm guessing you had a fight with this beloved Hedda."

"Oh, no. It was much more dignified. We had a discussion. Dis-cus-sion," Elias said slowly; he must've been hammered for a while. "You see, Commissioner...may I call you Commissioner?"

"I prefer Puppy."

"Commissioner Puppy, my beloved Hedda Kleinz...do you know her? No, how could you? Well, you could, but how would you know of our special relationship since it percolated when I had custody of the Granddaughter following your flight and may I say, welcome back." They clinked glasses. "I'll spare you the details. This particular dis-cus-sion centered around my unwillingness to be a gracious failure. By the way, what did you do with my other former fiancé Annette?"

"I married Annette again."

"Of course you did." This plunged Elias into a gloomy moment as another previous romantic door slammed shut. "Is she here?"

"No."

"I don't get any more information than that as her former fiancé because I misbehaved in pursuit of Mooshie Lopez, aka, Dara Dinton? Is that why you won't answer my simple question?"

"Yes."

"I don't blame you." Elias grandly shook Puppy's hand. "By the way, you look forlorn."

"My father died today."

"The terrorist swine?"

"That's the one."

"Did you hate him?"

Puppy didn't hesitate as he nodded.

"Course you did. I loathed mine, the dick. Back to my current hopeful-again fiancé, unless you need to pour your heart out over maudlin tripe which won't do a damn thing other than make you feel worse." Puppy gestured to skip over maudlin tripe. "She's provided what she claims is her last lecture about why I am a failure as a DV as well as a Reg. I've learned to detest Regs. Furtive smug secret elitists."

"What'd you do?"

Elias chuckled as if there weren't enough hours in the year. "I'm showing ambition. Now, as you may recall, ambition is the lifeblood of the DV. Get out, get out, get out. Except I can't, I can't, I can't. I did stand up to The Family. For that I was rewarded with a pamphlet, a hammer, and a seamy apartment. To get out, get out, get out, I saw but one option."

He glanced around at the nest of spies, motioning Puppy forward. "Bad company. Whose bad company did I select? None other than the aforementioned Parkchester Paterson."

Tensing, Puppy remained on his elbows. "In what way?"

"Since you profess to be Commissioner Puppy though I haven't seen any proof, I trust you as long as you keep buying drinks and onion rings. Since I'm barred from baseball, barred, barred, Albert found a way for me to lay down my birdcage and use my considerable knowledge of food vending to tag along on the baseball parade. I was at Wrigley Field for the Hall of Fame exhibit. Now, now, you promised. I was there since one of my suggestions about twentieth-century ballpark food was accepted. Probably by you or the real Commissioner Puppy.

"When my former, hopefully soon-to-be-again-but-who-the-hell-knows fiancé, whom you profess not to know, learned of this, she said I was a great disappointment. As if I weren't already a great disappointment to myself." His eyes watered. "She suggested I needed to realign my emotions and that she loved me deeply and still wanted to share a life but why did I bother challenging the underpinnings of The Family if I was going to revert to that ethical laxness, no, laziness she said, yes. Perhaps, she suggested, my brave fight, which took me out of my beautiful Riverdale apartment to a DV, was hollow. Perhaps I never really meant to change, to turn my back on unethical behavior. Perhaps it was her fault for giving me her values which I only borrowed. Perhaps I did belong in a DV. She hoped not. She said I could keep the furniture and the pillows, and we would talk again because our love was an inexhaustible flame. Or some crap like that."

Elias laid his forehead on the table and cried softly. Puppy patted his shoulder and ordered more onion rings. Kenuda perked up at the impending grease.

"I'm sorry, Elias. That all sucks."

"Doesn't it?" Kenuda blew his nose. "You're certain you married my other fiancé Annette?"

"Pretty sure."

"That would annul our engagement." Elias sighed at the agony of love. "At least I'll be near Dara. Dara, Dara, Dara. She was also your fiancé. Grandma's earrings, man, you collect all my women."

Puppy apologized for his greed and waited for Elias to soak his tongue in more whiskey. "Cheng's pretty smart. You've allied yourself to a smart player. I figure the Old-Timers' Game is just the start."

Elias fluttered his lips. "Oh yes."

"He and Mooshie, do you mind if I call her by her real name? They'll play baseball regularly afterward."

Elias fluttered his lips again as if Puppy were a donkey.

"Does Albert want more than that?"

"Of course. He never meant to stay in the DV. Do you think a man like that's going to be content making bird cages? But it's not about what Cheng wants."

He fell silent. Puppy shook him awake.

"Then who?"

Kenuda fluttered his lips. Puppy joined him in a brief lip-fluttering contest. Elias glanced around again. "It's what Grandma wants."

Puppy rolled an onion ring around his shot glass before asking casually, "Grandma? The Grandma who's dead?"

"Correct. Grandma. Lenore. Our leader. But not her human self. Her 'bot."

"And what does her 'bot want?"

"Must you speak in such a clipped way? It's extremely annoying."

"Tough. What does Grandma want?"

Elias shrugged, either because he'd forgotten or didn't know or had gone too far. He winked broadly as if in a vidmov close-up. "I'm not entirely sure. Only that's she's not happy about what's happening to The Family."

Puppy forced down a swallow. "Grandma wants to come back?" He felt wonder and terror in that question.

"Fool. She already has. Perhaps I can even help her. Wouldn't that shut my beloved's beautiful warm lips?" Kenuda unfurled like a drunk dinosaur and grabbed Puppy's hand. "Let's dance."

"I'm a terrible dancer."

"Then I'll lead. I feel my inner Mary Wells building."

Elias twirled Puppy around the dance floor to the song *My Guy*. Abruptly dropping him like a scarf, Elias rushed the stage and begged to join the trio. He finished the song, explaining he was the former disgraced Commissioner of Entertainment and probably shouldn't be allowed to sing a key. After a deafening contrary roar, he led a bar-wide stomping and clapping rendition of *Heat Wave*.

• • • •

BETH'S STARE PIERCED like thread through the eye of a needle. In and out and over and under.

"How long does that usually take?" Zelda asked.

Beth frowned at the unfinished hem of Kasumi Perez's skirt. "Depends. An hour."

In and out, over and under.

Zelda slid down the chair in the corner of the dress shop, using the cans of dog food in the grocery bag as a footstool. "How's Dale doing in Chicago?"

Beth gestured toward the letter on the table. "She's immersed in many tasks which she's not sure I'd understand given my hatred for baseball. And she likes Cheng."

"They have similar personalities."

"Can't disagree."

Zelda pretended to be fascinated with the stitching until Beth laid the skirt in her lap, out of patience.

"Yes, I'm showing the play to Joan."

"Rehearsals are in three days, Zelda," Beth said in that little voice of disgust at which she was so accomplished. "You promised to do that weeks ago."

"As far as we know, the play wasn't done."

Beth grumbled. "I'm not good with this anymore, Zelda."

"As opposed to being good with it when you decided it was the only way to go?"

"I never agreed."

Zelda slid to her feet. "That so?"

"I meant in my conscience." Beth poked her temple with the needle. "This was wrong from the start. Misleading and deceiving…"

"You're taking all Joan's future dialogue."

"And she'll have a right to be pissed."

Zelda stared. "I had no choice. And please don't give me the shit about how we always have a choice."

"We do," Beth said coldly. "You chose dishonesty. And yes, I chose it, too."

"Wait, did you just mislead me about eleven seconds ago in the name of your holy conscience?"

Beth tossed a ball of red yarn over Zelda's head. "My reasons were more understandable."

"Oh, I'm looking forward to hearing this."

"Because I love you. You know I do. This was the only way we could be together. Do you think I enjoyed the idiocy of theater, the make believe, the arrogance of Joan Minh? The precious whining of the cast assembling in committee to challenge your words in the two scenes you've deigned to share. The elitist pageantry, the pretense of spending an evening guided by someone else's ideas, if you're smart enough to understand. What else could I do, Zelda? I signed up and shipped along because we were like a couple."

"A make-believe couple," Zelda said softly.

Beth winced. "That's right. Your mind is the only stage I had. And don't worry, this isn't an excuse, a justification, only an explanation. I'm as wrong as you are."

She stood resolutely. "But I don't regret it, Zel. All these late nights, so much wondrous time, the give and take. Almost like sex in a way. When you'd leave, I'd have feverish wild fantasies, tell my own orgasmic stories. Transforming the emotions of your play into love-creating. Your expression of joy when a sentence worked right into the pleasure of my touch. Sewing your animals heads was like kissing your breasts. Yet even within my own fantasies where I'm the writer, I know it's as close as I'll ever get."

"Same here," Zelda whispered. "Maybe that's why I let it drag on."

Beth stared longer than she needed to. "When's the last time you fantasized about sex with me?"

Zelda hesitated. "I've been busy."

Tears flooding her eyes, Beth returned to her stool and silently resumed stitching the hem as if it were Zelda's lips.

"I didn't mean it like that. Grandma's bra straps, I didn't mean it like that."

Beth kept stitching. "I must get this done. It's late by a day—oh…" She added blood to the tears, shaking her finger that had been jabbed with the needle. Without looking up, "Go Zel. Go home." Finally, she met Zelda's stare. "Please."

After that, the last thing Zelda needed was some punk teenager popping out from behind a disposable garbage can a block from the uptown red local.

"Give it up." Within the dark hoodie, a ridge of moles populated the boy's flushed face.

"I'm in no mood for this." Zelda started past. The stubby knife pressed into her stomach. She burst out laughing. "Are you for real? You're pulling a blade on me?"

The boy tried figuring this out. His friends had done the same move on some woman near this exact same 181st Street and come away with bracelets and rings. He tried to remember if they'd had any problems.

He grunted and pressed the knife again.

Zelda swung her bag against his head, knocking the boy to the ground. "You want to steal this?" She dumped her bag, wallet, keys, and half of three different candy bars onto the boy worming away. "Or how about this?"

Zelda rolled up her play and swung it through the air like a batter looking for home plate. "Because it's the most valuable possession I own. It's my heart and guts and it's useless. You know what that's like?"

Now pressed against the wall of a closed bodega, the boy mustered some self-respect and meekly waved his knife.

"You don't. Damn stupid little fool." Zelda flung her play onto his head. The boy didn't know what to do. Reading seemed a little much. "Or why not just chuck the sucker?" Zelda opened the chute of an instant garbage disposal. Pine-scented disinfectant smoke hissed out.

"Want to do me the honors?" Zelda was encircled by the sprightly fumes. Be so simple. Why bother walking sideways anymore? When she turned, the boy was racing down the block. He'd swiped the candy bars.

A Blue Shirt hurried over. "Ma'am, are you okay?" Zelda nodded at the very stupid question with no answers. "I'll be right back."

She clutched the cop's arm to keep him from pursuing the boy. "Let him go. He's just young."

"That's how it starts." The Blue Shirt tapped coordinates into his forearm tracker and within a few moments, a patrol car roared around the corner and chased the boy down 183rd Street. "This is the third robbery attempt this week. Three. When's the last time that happened, I asked the wife at breakfast. I don't know what's going on. Children, too. And adults. Damned if I wasn't in the middle of something even at Shea Stadium last week. Mets and Orioles fans went at it in the bleachers. I announced myself as an off-duty police officer and they still kept on throwing punches. The game stopped for thirty minutes until we settled everything down. Fighting at a baseball game. What for? Bothering a young woman at midnight. What for?"

The Blue Shirt carefully slipped the contents strewn on the ground back into her purse. Handing it over, he asked, "Would you like a patrol car to take you home?"

She slowly shook her head.

"I'll need your info for the report."

"I'm not pressing charges."

The Blue Shirt frowned. "That's your duty, ma'am. Failure means others will pay. Like I said, that's how it starts." The cop swiped her Lifecard in the forearm attachment. "Zelda Jones. Dental Hygienist."

Zelda laughed so hard she had to hold onto a light pole.

23

Annette groggily sat up on the well-cushioned bed, a distant throbbing dancing from head to bare feet. The tan blouse and pants fit as if they'd been tailored. An elaborate buffet of juices, fruits, and vegetables was laid out on a charming oak table across from the partitioned toilet. A toothbrush and three different-flavored toothpastes rested on the sink.

After a long gulp of an incredible carrot drink, she inspected the cell, padding unsteadily on the plush brown rug. The narrow rectangular room was soothingly lit, pale yellow splashing down into all corners. She walked back and forth, looking for a window or a door on the beige featureless walls.

Annette had the sense the quarters were designed to please, and that scared the hell out of her. She hated giving them the satisfaction, but she had to use the toilet and then gobbled down the green produce, the tartness puckering up her lips.

"Hello? Anyone out there?" Annette tossed a fat banana against the wall. "I'm an American citizen and I won't be treated like this. You're my soldiers and we're on the same side so open the doors wherever they are and let me out. Like now."

She flung some more food until red and green stains dripped down the walls, quickly cleaned with a slight vibration.

After two days, Annette finally stopped eating the superbly presented food. At least after scarfing down the first meal because real steak was critical for her stamina and the following night, the succulent real roast chicken about sung "cock-a-doodle-do" in her head.

Other than that, Annette was on a determined hunger strike. Except for last night when she rolled on the floor laughingly gobbling down the chocolate-covered cherry balls.

Besides the rest of the food which she had pridefully shoved right back through the automatic sliding tray in the door, Annette had no contact with any life. "Hah." She snorted, playing with another shade of lipstick in the amply stocked cabinet. "Fucking hah calling it life. Squalid little tin cups," she muttered, cursing at whoever invented robots.

When the tray slid open a little early—Annette had little to do except calculate when the meals would arrive—she figured it was some sporty brunch. Even if it was French toast with real bacon again, she'd hold her nose and jam the food right back at the teapots. Which she did. Or tried, but the tray was jammed and as much as she shoved, the real bacon called out to her. Pigs and chickens singing. Probably robot pigs and chickens.

A thick slice of seductive bacon was disappearing between her mahogany-tinged lips when the entire door opened, sending her and the tray crashing backward.

Herbert, left arm of its silver combat uniform smoking as if it'd just finished a 'bacco, looked down. "Come."

Annette squinted in shock. The sepia complexion of Herbert creased with impatience. The 'bot gestured with its short weapon. "You must stand."

Annette rushed at Herbert, kicks flailing futilely against his bemused blocks. She landed heavily on her hip.

"Why did you attack me?"

She panted. "Didn't they send you to shoot me?"

Herbert's right eyebrow arched. "I am not aware of who you refer to with that pronoun of 'they' but I am not here to injure you. Quite the contrary. However, to satisfactorily achieve this objective you will have to leave with me immediately."

The 'bot lifted her off the ground by the arm. She dangled like a perplexed doll.

"What objective?"

"To remove you from your current location to a situation where the Fifth Edward Company will no longer restrict your movements."

Annette peered. "Grandma's earrings, you're here to rescue me?"

Herbert waited for Annette to grab a coat from the cluttered closet. She was only wearing a perfectly tailored tank top and silk panties. The 'bot explained it was three degrees Celsius and she would require greater warmth. Annette selected an ankle-length black wool coat, also perfectly fitted, wrapped a thick wonderfully mint-scented scarf around her mouth, and followed Herbert out.

She nearly tripped over the inert guard whose head had blocked the tray. Another guard was propped against a wall at the end of the hallway with a third on its back by the door.

The courtyard was silent, but Herbert's warning nod indicated it wasn't deserted. In the faint light, Annette could see soldiers moving slowly along the top of the walls. She imitated Herbert's nestling against the buildings to avoid the illumination bulbs floating by. Herbert yanked her into a narrow doorway as two officers passed.

A screeching alarm sent red lights in a cyclonic whirl toward her former cell. Herbert calmly led her along the wall toward a canopied jeep. Annette crawled into a ball in the back seat and the vehicle glided silently toward the south gate. Two soldiers aimed weapons and ordered them to stop.

Herbert transmitted the clearance code and the soldiers stiffened into respectful statues. The gate opened and the jeep accelerated over the road, tilting on its left side until it became parallel to the ground, then upside down, Annette's stomach churning, before righting itself upward on an arc over the tree line.

Several incoming rockets exploded against the rear shield of the jeep-plane. Herbert adroitly maneuvered. Pursuing missiles turned in circles, then into hillsides. Soon the silence was as thick as the surrounding night.

Despite Herbert's reassurances, Annette remained strapped into the front seat.

"Would you prefer the cabin to be heated to soothe your dermatological extremities?"

She faked some calm. "Thanks, my extremities are fine. So?"

The 'bot consulted the panel and, pleased by the data, returned to her. "Is there more to the question?"

"Yeah a little. How about what's going on?"

"In what regard?"

Annette sighed toward the tops of the Hungarian hills twinkling in the moonlight. "Like ten minutes ago I was in a cell, a prisoner of the American Army. Now I'm in a kind of spaceship with Herbert the Hero 'bot."

Herbert assessed the human's words and intonations, filtering out the sarcasm until, a few seconds later, it had grasped the essential nature of the question.

"It is my understanding that you would like to know how I arrived from Budapest, why I arrived from Budapest, and what is my purpose."

She folded her arms. "Good start, Herbie."

"The Tenth Platoon of Edward Company arrived at the house adjacent to our original meeting area approximately forty-three hours and seven minutes ago to retrieve me."

"What about Father Dempsey?" She was ashamed for not asking about him sooner.

"Unfortunately he expired on route."

Annette shoved Herbert. "Son-of-a-bitch. Your soldiers killed him?"

"Why would they?"

"You took out your own at the fort pretty freely."

Herbert's forehead pulsed. "I turned them off by scheduling an emergency recovery procedure. I could not explain to your understanding what that would entail other than it is a safety precaution should one of us be injured and our emergency medical repairs fail to function. They should be fully operational. May I proceed?"

Annette nodded, her throat tightening.

"Father John Dempsey and I were transported in a Redison truck with our intended destination the Armitage 2 military facility where you had been held. Two-point-three kilometers east, we were ambushed by a squad of Islamists who fired a short-range Fatah bazooka. This weapon instantly terminated Father Dempsey and four soldiers of the Tenth Platoon of Edward Company. Two other soldiers of the Tenth Platoon of Edward Company expired from wounds during the resumption of our journey to the Armitage 2 military facility."

Herbert's eyebrows arched as Annette wiped away tears. "Would you like me to pause?"

She nodded, crying out the window before impatiently motioning him to continue.

"Upon arriving at the base, I spent fourteen hours and two minutes in a room receiving corrective care in the south wing of the facility. I left. As I have previously stated, I initiated repair procedures among the guards. One tried overriding the procedure and fired a shot into my right shoulder, accounting for the present acrid odor. We are now crossing the Romanian border just north of Hembriz."

Herbert waited for questions because there always were, but Annette kept staring off. Finally, she asked softly, "Did Father Dempsey die instantly, or did he get to pray?"

It took Herbert a moment. "I am not aware of any religious rituals performed by the priest. The bazooka hit the right side of the truck, overturning us. My two colleagues and I returned successful fire, terminating the Islamists. When we examined the others, they were all terminated."

"I hope Jesus has some procedure for letting people into Heaven if they go too quickly," Annette said.

Herbert turned in its seat to carefully study Annette. "Father John Dempsey told me of quite an elaborate process for entry into the human afterlife while we were in the house adjacent to our original meeting place. While I cannot determine any factual basis for his claims since I am not programmed for the analysis of multiverses, Father John Dempsey seemed certain that your Heaven exists. Humans do have a remarkable capacity to persuade themselves through the sheer force of their passions and beliefs, but logically, that should not deny that there are occasions when there is justification for that passion and belief."

Annette laughed. "Dempsey convinced you of Heaven?"

"No. But I am not dissuaded either."

She touched Herbert's arm. "Thank you."

The 'bot didn't know why she was expressing such gratitude other than another example of their intensity.

"So?" Annette asked after a moment.

"Is 'so' the question?"

She made an exasperated sound. "Why did you rescue me?"

Herbert's forehead creased amid the pulsing blue veins. "I am not entirely sure, Annette Ramos. I am not programmed for uncertainty so that makes this uncertainty even more..." The 'bot almost had a moment of humor. "Curious. The soldiers of the Tenth Platoon Edward Company informed us that you were at the military base. From the paucity of their knowledge of the situation, I concluded they had little knowledge because you were kept away from the general military population. It made sense that you were in a situation resembling a prisoner. I considered that wrong."

She leaned forward. "You risked your status as a functioning soldier to rescue me?"

Herbert's forehead creased again. "I received an aberrant signal that I had never experienced."

"Sort of like believing in Heaven?"

"I do not believe in Heaven," Herbert said stiffly. "I allow for the possibility that your emotions are not merely misguided."

"Is it because you like me?"

Herbert tilted its head. "In what sense?"

"As one life-form to another."

The 'bot shook its head. "That was not a factor at all." It paused at Annette's frown. "I have disappointed you by not showing the appropriate adulation?"

"It would've been nice. It's been a while. I'm just trying to understand."

"As am I. That you would be held prisoner by your own soldiers was wrong. I cannot accept the notion of wrong. I had to act against the wrong despite the obvious fact that the action was undertaken by my comrades."

She let that go because it made the 'bot uncomfortable. "Now what? You just make like a hero and whisk me away without a plan?"

Herbert's lips pursed tightly. "I do not operate impulsively and would not undertake a goal without an achievable objective."

"Course not," Annette said, grinning.

"We will be landing in Pogorny, Romania in twelve minutes and eleven seconds." The plane steadily approached the runway spreading out like a long dirt carpet beyond a thick forest. "While we were in the building adjacent to our original meeting, Father John Dempsey and I had a comprehensive discussion on a wide range of subjects which included your mission to find the pope. I am in possession of your next stop."

Annette's mouth tightened. "He said we had no more contacts on the Rat Line."

"But he did not give me this information."

She peered skeptically. "I don't believe you."

"I do not lie."

"Then where'd you get that info?"

"I cannot answer that."

Annette scoffed. "Uh-huh. Because you're protecting Father Dempsey."

"I do not understand why I would protect Father Dempsey when there is nothing to protect."

"Maybe you're protecting my feelings. Considering he might've suspected he was going to die, he should've trusted me more. After everything we went through," she said, hurt.

"Father Dempsey had nothing to share."

The top of her head bounced off the ceiling. "How do you know? Did you ask him where we were headed?"

"That would have been redundant since I already had the information."

The jeep landed vertically with a slight thud. After considering the futility of further logical responses, Herbert awkwardly extended its hand. "I am wishing you luck, Annette Ramos."

Annette's eyes narrowed. "What."

"Luck. I believe that is a proper salutation."

"For what?"

"Your mission to find the pope."

She slapped away Herbert's still outstretched hand. "Your brilliant plan was to dump me in the middle of Transylvania?"

Herbert was almost offended. "You are now safe. I have the travel coordinates for your contact."

"Gee thanks. Instead of being surrounded by robot soldiers, I've got the Allahs to deal with. I have no money. No papers. I don't even have socks for my dermatological extremities." She angrily poked her bare foot against his leg.

"I understand your quandary, but I must surrender immediately to the nearest military personnel for violating eight military regulations and two civilian laws. Would you like me to enumerate them?"

"Please no. Just come with me."

Herbert emitted a slight exhalation of humor. "That would be impossible."

"You've violated ten laws already. What's a few more?"

"The quantity is not important."

Annette made another nasty sound.

"Assuming we pursue your alternative scenario, it is estimated that we would be tracked and apprehended at 95.4 percent likelihood."

"Oh, where're the fighter jets now?"

"This is the occupied territory of the Islamic Empire. The American Army will use drones."

"Americans can fire drones throughout Allah land?"

"Within a limited range and feasibility."

"Then the farther we go into the Allah Empire, the less chance the American drones have of finding us."

"Correct."

"Then you can come with me without being arrested. At least by our side."

Herbert paused. "My physically accompanying you would be a violation for which the consequences are termination."

"And what's the punishment for breaking ten laws?"

"Termination."

Annette spread her hands which Herbert took as a mocking gesture. In this situation, understandable.

"It is my duty to present myself for the consequences of my actions."

"Isn't it your duty to assist a fellow life-form in need?"

"I already did," Herbert said with some sharpness. "That is why I will be terminated."

"And you think a law which allows termination for helping a fellow life-form is right?"

"We do not take the law into our own designs just as that is forbidden to you by the rules of The Family. There is no tolerance for that."

"We'd get a chance to explain ourselves. We'd be allowed to show extenuating circumstances…"

"We have our morality, Annette Ramos." Herbert's voice tightened ever so slightly.

"Then here's your chance to prove it."

"I already achieved that by rescuing you."

"Now you have a chance to take that big next step. Show you're as impulsive and emotional as us. That there's really no difference. You can be swayed by the charms of a brilliant and beautiful woman like anyone else." Annette colored at his blank stare. "In this case, I am the brilliant and beautiful woman."

"I did surmise that."

"Then?"

Herbert could find forty-three logical reasons for disagreeing. Her suggestion violated the 'bot's pledge of obedience to morality. Yet if Herbert left her, she would also be terminated. The 'bot could find no scenario where she could successfully fulfill her mission alone. Herbert had been impulsive in rescuing her, as impossible as that was. He pondered that concept employing eight unsupported rationales.

If Herbert was going to be terminated, then it had to decide for what reason. Was it for a violation of laws? Or for a deeper reason? And how did it receive the information about the next stop on the Rat Line? It was just there as if planted by an unseen and untraceable process. There was no such thing.

You are not a human, the 'bot thought. The objective is not to be like them.

As easy as that was.

"We are lacking in essentials such as currency and official papers," Herbert said.

"Don't worry about that. We'll steal something." Annette fussed with her hair.

• • • •

ABDUL'S DERISIVE CRY had barely dribbled past the goal crease when Mustafa stormed over, beckoning Fahid, a slight boy whose face was consumed by ears and hair, to follow him toward Abdul. The players trailed behind out of curiosity, staying far enough away without provoking their coach and his inflammable temper.

Azhar snatched the ball from Fahid and fired a lethal shot which whizzed by his son's head into the net. Abdul dove to the ground, panting in fear and surprise.

"What is the matter, great one? Get up." Mustafa roughly yanked Abdul to his feet, gesturing for the boy to leave the dirt on his uniform and chin. "Humiliation is not kind. It is not right. Fahid has tried his best at midfielder. He deserves respect. You do not insult him nor anyone."

He whirled on the rest of the team, which inched away in case the next throw landed on their noses.

"This goes for all of you. I will not tolerate this mean arrogance. You have won three straight games. Congratulations." He clapped acidly. "Does this give you the right to hurt the feelings of others whom you have decided are not as good as you? Has Allah given you such a right? Have your parents? Your family? Have I ever said it is acceptable to insult one of your teammates? Or does that not matter because your teammates and your team mean nothing and you only care about yourselves? What happens when you are the next target?"

Azhar spun back toward Abdul who was slowly rising to cautious hands and knees. "You are the captain. Captain. Why? I will tell you why. To set an example. Your playing earned it. Remove that smirk or I will do it for you. Your intolerance does not set an example except for cruelty, and we will have none of the world's cruelty on my team. How many times have I told you that? You have hurt Fahid. And all of you who laughed, who did not step forward and say it was wrong, share in this shame."

Mustafa waited with a slight tapping of his foot so the team could worry about exactly what today's punishment would bring. Extra sprints. Additional push-ups. Practice in the dark. They had all been proud to have a hero like Azhar Mustafa, a friend of The Son, a spy who had changed his face in the service of Allah, as their coach. It earned them greater privileges in school like being able to turn in homework late. Girls paid greater attention to them. They had repaid this faith by sweeping to victories in six of their first seven games. Now they were held to be perfect. Playing was no longer fun. They dared not quit.

"Apologize. In order. Line up by names. Last names. Not you, Captain." Azhar scowled until the tenth player finished apologizing to Fahid for mocking his clearly unathletic abilities. He stiffly motioned Abdul over.

"Captain, what would you like to say?"

Abdul tried thinking of something from the Quran but couldn't remember the little he knew.

"Fahid. I am ashamed. I should know better. I am the captain…"

"Does that make you his superior?" Azhar barked.

He should've let his father just roam the sidelines instead of suggesting he replace Amin's uncle when he died. How could he know his father would turn into the Grand Mufti?

"No, sir."

"Tell that to him." Mustafa twisted Abdul's head toward Fahid who was feeling very guilty about causing all this through his failure to kick or pass the football.

"I am not your superior. I am your equal." Abdul's mind lit up with inspiration. "Except for now when I disappointed you. Accept my apologies and the team's apologies."

Azhar grumbled that was enough.

They walked home in silence through the fading sunlight. Out of guilt that he'd carried the lesson too far, Mustafa offered to buy Abdul licorice ice cream from the street vendor off Campana Boulevard; the boy sensed a trap and rambled on about saving room for Jalak's fine dinner to come.

The absurdity of welcoming his wife's food made Mustafa laugh and he sternly ruffled Abdul's hair. Walking through the thick milling crowds, they devoured double scoops while talking about the next game against the Junior Ibrahim from the south side of Barcelona. A tough crew but one that could be taken if the team played as a team, Azhar reiterated.

He reiterated a lot of messages lately, grasping for a larger purpose. It was easy to slip into complacency. Not so long ago he mastered that, the laconic fishing trips, the casual irresponsibility, the sheepish silence before Jalak's recriminations that he was lazy. He was. Playing football every day with Abdul once would have been joyous, a dream. Now Mustafa knew he needed more because he had done more. More was expected of the hero, the spy, the man who, it was rumored, had killed dozens of Americans, been involved in the assassination of Grandma, had secret powers, might have robot hands that could crush a cow's head, advised Abdullah on the peace accord with the Grand Mufti, regularly participated in military maneuvers, and would travel to America as one of God's representatives when all of the infidel degenerate lands were finally placed under *Sharia*.

The emissary of the Prophet wiped licorice ice cream on his sleeve as he entered the quiet house. Jalak hurried into the hallway to intercept them. Her mouth was pinched as if by an invisible hand.

"We have a visitor."

Mustafa's eyes narrowed. He had not heard from the Son since he evacuated. His rights had been downgraded to those enjoyed by the rest of the Caliphate of Al-Andulusa. He was a hero without a pedestal.

Omar Mustafa stepped out of the study in a crisp dark-brown uniform with an unfamiliar insignia on the upper-left sleeve.

"Good evening, Father." His upper lip curled. "And you, brother. It is good to see you again."

The how of Lieutenant Omar Mustafa standing in his childhood home was clear. The why made Mustafa shiver. He squeezed Abdul like a third hip.

"My son," he said, the weight of his voice flattened beneath the contempt.

"Yes. Still and always your son. You have lost weight. The rigors of fighting for Allah take their toll, don't they? Wear the creases about your eyes with pride. And you, little brother. Slowly filling in. But none display the light of God as my mother." Like a snake on a rock, Omar's eyes shone as he kissed Jalak's hand.

Jalak clasped her hands. With little enthusiasm, she said, "A joyous occasion. Is it not good that we are all together?"

"Perhaps, dear mother, we might sit as one to share your wondrous dinner, which I have dreamed about throughout my travels home, eager to see everyone."

Abdul tried several mumbled excuses, from a fever and possible cracked rib to studying for a math test which would've been a historic first, but found himself in his usual spot at the dining room table across from Omar, who stared back with a face borrowed from something cold and terrible.

Jalak filled the uncomfortable silence with a nonstop tour of the meal which she had thrown together with little time for preparation. Omar apologized for not calling, but he had just received his new orders early yesterday morning and had traveled through several combat zones down the eastern European corridor, a filthy pot of unrepentant Crusader barbarism.

Over the listless chicken sharing a platter with soggy raisins and rice, Lieutenant Mustafa recited with sweating fervor the miles of Christian robot devils adorning crucifixes. Some, he said with a mouthful of limp beets, were stacked atop hills like immoral trees. Their filthy insides were torn apart, the metal piled high so True Believers would see the monstrosity that Satan and the Jews had unleashed. But, he reassured them as he searched for a suitable way to dispose of the olive pit, not since the glory of the first invasion of Crusader Europe in 2063 had Allah crushed the disease so completely now that the Mufti and Prince once again clasped hands in obedience to Allah.

Abdul stared at his brother with open-mouthed anxiety. Azhar nudged him under the table, but the boy, having gathered courage and his thoughts, leaned forward confidently on his thick forearms. He was the captain of the football team.

"What kind of soldier are you now?" He hated that his voice squeaked when he was nervous.

Omar's face twisted in a sneer. "The sort of soldier I was long before I wore this uniform. A soldier in the army of the Prophet. However, this particular uniform is a new unit. Your chicken is delightful, Mother. The beast must have felt your love to have given you such a meal."

Jalak tittered about the butcher knowing the chicken personally, which Omar waved off as a minor detail, returning to Abdul.

"I am a Lieutenant in the bint-Khayyat." His eyes hooded with disdain at their frowns. "The righteous Sumayyah was the first martyr of Islam, murdered for her beliefs in Mecca around 620 or so, during the life of the Prophet. We have taken the name of a woman to demonstrate the unification of views between the Grand Mufti and his son."

"You have become a believer in the equality of women?" Azhar asked skeptically.

Omar sneered again. "No. That violates the Quran. We acknowledge a woman's contribution." He gestured about the dinner table. "Since the accord, both worlds have sought ways to fuse beliefs without jeopardizing the fundamentals of our faith, which are inviolable."

"What does that mean?"

"That Omar is hungry, and you are bothering him with politics," Jalak interrupted, peevishly dumping more chicken onto his plate.

"Please, Mother, I am happy to help enlighten. There have been many misconceptions over the nature of the peace that ended this terrible civil war. There was never any capitulation." Omar proudly played out the syllables as if he had learned the word that morning. "Except, of course, to Allah. The war was fought to destroy the infidels and their degenerate influences." His eyes lingered on Abdul.

"*Sharia* continues or should continue. There have been reports of heresy in certain parts of the Empire which both the Grand Mufti and Prince Abdullah agree cannot be tolerated. The laws of Islam are preeminent. Like all revolutions, crust grows."

Jalak laughed at her eldest son's clever turn of phrase. Azhar was ready to heave up dinner.

"Inevitably, we all fail God and must be reminded of our ultimate obedience," Omar finished.

"By shootings on the streets and tortures underground?" his father coldly asked.

Omar dismissed that with a careless gesture. "In some cases, excesses were brought about by the frustration of disobedience to Allah. But the laws have been broadened and more courts convened so that unfortunate acts of violence, occasionally against an innocent, will be avoided. That was central to the peace. That is why my unit adopted the first martyr, a female."

"Women have new rights?" Jalak perked up.

"You always had the rights, Mother. Now you can also serve God without first serving your husband. This is being announced slowly because for now there is only one goal and one goal only: to destroy America completely. There was a failure of will once, in your generation. We could have invaded North America, but concern about the Crusaders's false boasts of using nuclear weapons persuaded the glorious Mufti to place the lives of his people first. This was always temporary. Some of us feel that we should have called the Crusaders's bluff, as they say."

226 | GARY MORGENSTEIN

"That would have cost millions of lives," Mustafa said peevishly. "They would have dropped nuclear weapons all over the Empire."

"No no no." Spittle formed on Omar's lips, a petulant child demanding his way. "Not the Americans. Grandma would not go down in history as the one who destroyed the planet. That is not the American way with its false sense of superiority. Therefore, the Mufti waited. Now the time has come. His most glorious Prince Abdullah agrees. The robots are a grave threat from the very bowels of hell and everything must be done to destroy them. Sacrifices will be made and cowards will be moved aside."

Jalak tossed Mustafa a worried look at Omar's labored breath.

"And how do you know all this?" Abdul suddenly piped up. "You are just a lieutenant. Poppa is friends with Abdullah. He would know best and thinks there will be another peace with the Crusaders."

Omar looked up through his thick eyebrows, rasping, "Have you spoken to your friend lately?"

Mustafa grabbed Abdul's wrist before he made things worse. "Omar, perhaps we can speak, man-to-man, after this fine dinner?"

Omar nibbled on the *basbousa,* dropping crumbs as he toured the study, stepping on the piles of football magazines. He paused over a woodworking book.

"Taking up a hobby, Father?"

He shook his head. "That is your mother's. She is planning on remodeling the basement. I have only a secondary role in obtaining supplies and praising her work. Regardless."

Omar almost allowed himself a smile. "Abdul is doing well in school?"

Azhar settled into the battered easy chair. "He gets acceptable grades, has many friends, and is happy. Why don't you ask him?"

The young man sneered. "It is your role to answer the questions."

Azhar kept his bulging eyes in his head. "It is not my role to answer your questions, son. You have come for a reason."

"To see my blessed mother."

"Praise Allah. You have seen her and eaten her mediocre meal. She is little different. Abdul has grown. What else do you want?"

Omar leaned against the desk. "Do you not think I also came to see you, Father?"

"I suspect that is the only reason why you came. You failed to arrest me in London. That would have meant my death. I think you have come to finish that job."

Omar reddened. "Is that what you think of me?"

"That is what I think you have become."

Omar tugged at a falcon insignia on his right shoulder. "Do you not see this? I have been awarded the Crest of the Falcon. I am a real hero, Father, unlike you. I have hunted down traitors to Islam and Crusader enemies of our God."

"Which am I?"

"I hope neither." His short laugh was choked. "I do not come for revenge. For this." He yanked up his shirt to present the purple scar on the left side of his stomach. "From your friend. But he is dead."

Azhar tensed. "How do you know that?"

His son blew air as if cleaning his lungs. "I know much. I know you are no longer under the protection of your great Abdullah. He has abandoned you along with the city. You have no special privileges anymore and please, do not protest. I see all the files. I have seen yours. Allah is great and knows only justice so your misdeeds by befriending the Crusaders, helping them escape, all these acts were under the vague orders of the Son. But in your files, Father, there are no such orders. There is no directive authorizing you to violate *Sharia* by claiming a face which Allah did not give you. There are no orders granting you the false identity, an act of treason, which you used in the Caliphate of London. There is nothing connecting you to Prince Abdullah."

Mustafa breathed very slowly.

"I can testify to your good will," Omar said with hollow kindness. "I alone. For now, you are a public hero, but undeserved adulation falls very easily. Should your thin file come to light, the prince will not sacrifice his good name to save you. I do not think you would want my mother humiliated and my brother returning to the life of a moral degenerate."

"You have no authority here, my goat shit of a son. The Holy Warriors and all your fellow murdering black robes are banned. There are only the secular police. Unless you would like to show your orders allowing you to operate in the Caliphate of North Africa."

Omar shrugged. "Correct. For now. Until the cry comes from the throats of the innocents for protection from the infidels. Then we will protect again. As I will protect my blessed mother and I will make sure my brother does not disgrace my blood. As I will protect you, Father. Whether you want my holy hand or not, I will see that no harm comes to you either."

"Why?"

Omar seemed hurt. "You are my father. It would be a sacrilege of disrespect."

"That did not stop you before."

The young man looked away. "I was a child. I lived in a bath of hatred. I understand now. The weak must be placed beneath the shawl of the strong. I am the strong. My family are the weak."

When Mustafa returned after midnight from a long walk by the harbor, Jalak was in bed pretending to be asleep. She lacked all talent for duplicity. Azhar washed up quickly and settled beside her, feigning quick sleep.

She jabbed him in the back. "I know you are awake."

"Now I am."

Jalak pulled away his second pillow to prop herself up in the dark. "You have hurt Omar. He feels very badly about how you have treated him. You must apologize."

Mustafa yanked his pillow back, earning an angry shout. "I will not apologize. I have told you all that happened in London. You heard his fanaticism at dinner. What lies did he fill your empty head with, woman?"

"We prayed after your conversation."

"You?"

"Yes. It felt good to do so again."

Azhar quieted his heart. I do not like this new trick, Allah. "Have I ever stopped you from the Quran?"

"You have not encouraged me."

"Because you did not enjoy the ritual."

"Now I do. It was joyous praying with my Omar." She rolled away and he rolled her right back.

"What did he say, Jalak?"

"Nothing. That he worries about you and your influence on Abdul. The child idolizes you. As he should since you are his father. But you have not always followed the path, Azhar. You have often deviated to your own tune. It is not acceptable."

"It is more acceptable now than ever with the loosening of the reign of the Holy Warriors and the mullahs. Do not believe what Omar says. The fanatics have conceded much. Abdullah has the upper hand."

"You do not know that. Abdullah turned on you."

Mustafa flushed. "He did not. He has moved on. I was a story in his life as he was a story in mine. We both have moved on. But why do you believe Omar's lies?"

Jalak took her time. "It is not that I believe anything. He frightens me, Azhar. This is not the face I saw when he came upon the light of life. He has an ugliness, and he will hurt us. So please apologize. You can be false. I give you permission to wear a different heart. If not for us, then for Abdul."

She took a date off a plate on the end table, nervously breaking it into two pieces and waiting for him to swallow before continuing. "Omar mentioned Abdul's homosexuality."

Mustafa squeezed the sheets. "It was a lie."

"The files exist."

"He will release such filth?"

"He said never. Which is why I fear he will. To what end, Azhar? He struggles to stand erect beneath all his hate, but why do that to his brother?"

"He is doing it to me," Azhar said quietly. "He wants something more than revenge."

Mustafa suddenly shivered.

24

P uppy defiantly sucked the trickle of blood off his left index finger. He'd run out of band-aids an hour ago and wasn't about to give Ernie the satisfaction of whining over another paper cut. Sprawled in the chair surrounded by piles of unedited rad scripts, Sahidi watched the two juveniles scowl across the room.

"Did you drip blood again?" Ernie smirked.

"No." Puppy glanced down at the photo of Johnny Bench's stocky great-granddaughter Tennessee, a new red birthmark on her broad forehead. He forearm-shielded that picture along with Reynolds Ryan, great-grandson of Nolan Ryan, who comprised today's starting battery mates.

The Wizard snickered.

"Screw you," Puppy rasped. "I've stapled more than six thousand damn souvenirs."

"How dare you blaspheme?" Ernie pointed a long pencil; Puppy had confiscated the wand after breaking out in a rash. "These are The Game's," his voice dipped reverently, "first souvenir programs since the 2061 World Series…"

Sahidi mockingly mouthed the irritating mantra.

"…and thus, the programs will be correct and perfect or else."

Matthew bustled in just in time to break up another scuffle. With a few dizzying brushes, the 'bot removed the blood stain and served the 3 a.m. snacks of cold radish cakes and hot pepper crusties. If that didn't keep them awake, nothing would.

"I could easily run off the remaining 4,509 programs," Matthew cheerily said, refortified by a brief recharging.

"No," Puppy said with a pout. Ernie answered with a grunt. Neither would admit they agreed on just about everything.

"Stubborn, stubborn, stubborn is the goat," Sahidi said, still slightly bemused by their insistence on hand collating each of the 33,201 souvenir programs for the 2099 Old-Timers' Game. One program per one fan. If you were not there, you did not get a program or else, Ernie had explained, you could lie and say you attended because you had the program. You did not derive the special joy of the moment from someone else. Your memory was the real souvenir.

Sahidi sighed. They'd been locked up together for thirty-six hours. A bathroom break was like stumbling into the outskirts of Heaven as her grandfather used to say.

But the programs looked clean, simple. She grudgingly had to give Puppy credit. The Cousins had resisted the whole idea of glorifying players with bios and photos. Puppy found the compromise: no biographical info on each of the twenty-four players, twelve per team. Nor would the photos show acrobatic dives or ferocious swings, just a simple statement about their favorite baseball moments.

Humbert Smith talked about discovering the mildewed glove of his great-grandpa Ozzie Smith hidden in his parents's basement. Joachim Feller practiced pitching in the same Iowa cornfield as her great-great-grandfather Bob Feller. Tony Felton reminisced about his rookie debut and the humility of fanning three times. Sahidi loved that phrase and made sure all the announcers would use it at least four times a game under the language directive she kept secret from Puppy.

Myrina James Musial nearly developed a chronic hip condition emulating Stan Musial's corkscrew swing. Albert Cheng recalled hitting a home run in his first pro game ever in Malaysia. Antonio Yastrzemski admitted he didn't much like baseball until an elderly aunt gave him an illegal copy of his great-grandfather Carl's biography.

By 5:30, the last of the programs were collated and stapled. After a heated exchange, the exhausted Puppy and Ernie let Matthew swiftly insert the Wizard's taut one-page instructions on *How to score a baseball game.*

One is for the pitcher (P) who is the person who throws the ball. Two is for the catcher (C) who will catch the pitch. Going clockwise, the first baseman (1B) is 3, the second baseman (2B) 4, and the third baseman (3B) is 5. The shortstop (SS) is 6. Accept it. Left to right, the leftfielder (LF) is 7, the center fielder (CF) is 8, and the right fielder (RF) is 9.

K means strikeout. W is a walk. E is an error. If the shortstop makes an error, you score it E-6. Pay attention to the public-address announcer. That will be me. I will be watching you.

Ernie had included a multiple-choice test such as *The catcher throws a runner out attempting to steal second base. The second baseman makes the tag. How would you score this? A) 2-5 B) 1-6 C) 2-4 D) 1-2-6 E) I don't deserve to attend this sacred Old-Timers' Game.*

Puppy obsessed about the programs because no one would let him near the actual baseball. After the arduous interview/tryouts for the twentieth-century team, Ty and Mick shut down access to the practices. Mooshie told him he was still handsome, but he'd walk funny if he so much as came within a mile of Shea Stadium where the twenty-first-century team had holed up.

So today, Puppy went to Wrigley Field alone. Sahidi had a meeting with Chick Buckwith and Smooth Harry Jackson, the Cubs radcast announcers who were calling the game. Insisting on a separate taxi, Ernie said only he could be trusted with the programs. He was also working on a new incantation for fans who didn't pay attention. Half the crowd might be turned into parakeets for failing to stand for the seventh inning stretch.

As always, a ballpark wakes up slowly. The elevated Red Line rumbled to a stop in the distance, already discharging fans at the nearby Addison Station several hours before the 10 a.m. start of batting practice. Food courts strung out like fine-smelling necklaces throughout Wrigley. 'Bot and human ticket takers in identical red-white-and-blue uniforms with baseball-shaped caps took up positions at the gates. A yellow school bus craned awkwardly through the parking lot entrance, the sounds of exuberant tuba players announcing the arrival of the Mount Pastoral High School marching band from Buffalo Grove, Illinois.

Puppy became the first customer for Nero & Nero's Coffee Hut, scalding his lips in between banter with the vendors, the grounds crew, another marching band from St. Paul. No, he wouldn't be pitching. Yes, he would be ready as always. Yes, he was neutral. Yes, that was a lie but he'd never admit it.

Puppy sipped and chuckled, nearly tripping over the squatting Granddaughter outside gate one.

She stiffly unfurled as if clicking limbs into place. But her expression was cheek-to-cheek impishness.

"Ah, it is the famous Puppy Beisbol, ruler of all that is baseball, who cannot walk so early in the morning."

He bowed deeply. "Puppy Beisbol is honored to nearly step on the head of the Granddaughter Clary Santiago, ruler of all else."

"Do not forget." She bowed even deeper. "I am early."

"Very."

"Good. Too often people are ready for me." He uneasily followed her glance upward at the glint of the stealth 'copters circling Wrigley Field. "There is an evacuation plan, but I will whisk you to safety as well should your fans misbehave. Second Cousin DeRico nearly swallowed a Nok-Hockey puck in the Cousins Room over the Baseball Boxes. I assured her these spontaneous arguments were healthy to the growth of The Family."

Even at this hour, the Baseball Boxes were up and running, gaudily trimmed in different team colors and generally ranging from two to five feet; higher was considered emotively oppressive. The pre/postgame debates/arguments/shouting matches were almost always good-natured. Fans gathered inside parks, outside bars and restaurants, near parking lots, wherever more than one fan clustered to argue the merits of their team and its players. The intensity of the passion was reflected in rising attendance, now averaging eighty-two percent capacity.

Clary furrowed her brow. The vein in her forehead pulsed and the six Black Tops spread out, keeping her within range of their Arsin .55 rifles. She didn't mention the foiled kidnapping at her house the other night. Three black-robed Islamists had been fried into dust scaling the side of the building just below her bedroom window.

Shadows flickered over her face before she broke into a dimpled grin. "Will you give me a tour of the Wrigley Field?"

He bowed again. Even though he tried several times under Clary's impatient pokes, Puppy couldn't hear the BTs trailing. Clary proudly explained, to his persistent confusion, their anti-grav shoes. Being the Granddaughter, Clary said with a merry wink, she could also silence her steps which she gleefully demonstrated by running soundlessly up and down the cement hallway linking the two clubhouses.

"Many tricks, yes?" She tossed a pinkish ball into the air.

"A Spaldeen," he said, impressed. "Where'd you find it?"

"Oh, there will be many balls bouncing all over America soon." Clary flipped him the Spaldeen. "And…" She dangled an orange mesh bag of gaily colored marbles. "Have you played?"

"Once. Pablo and I found some discarded marbles in a dump field off Webster Avenue when we were kids. I nearly choked showing that I could swallow a marble. Pablo did a maneuver on me."

Clary's face tightened. "Yes, Pablo is always helpful. He gave me a very thorough dental examination. How is Zelda? Does she ask of Clary or am I just forgotten?"

Puppy chuckled. "How could someone whose face is on billboards in every city be forgotten, Granddaughter?"

"Do not call me Granddaughter. I am always and forever Clary to you. Your only Clary."

He waited until the blue pulsing vein in her forehead quieted. "My Clary has come a long way since she bit Elias Kenuda's thigh."

She shrugged and squatted on the floor, waiting. "So, how will the game be?"

"Since I've been kept out of all the practices—"

"Oh Puppy has such sad eyes."

"No, just annoyed. Knowing Ty and Mick, and Mooshie and Cheng, I expect everyone will be fired up, the teams will be great, and it'll be memorable baseball."

"And the alleyway?"

"The Autograph Alley you're not supposed to know about?" They exchanged conspiratorial smiles. "All set, assuming Ernie the Wizard didn't have a mental breakdown and set fire to the souvenir programs."

"It is a serious violation to sign your name as if it is a gift."

"Very. But beginning today, no player gets into the ballpark through a private gate. They go past the fans and they interact with the fans. I don't care how they do it with football and basketball. And beginning today, there's no team buses to take players back home or to the hotel. You take public transportation and you mingle with the fans. That'll also be announced today. Players will be giving of their time and hold seminars about playing. DVs, Reg neighborhoods, the very nature of baseball is about service to the fans."

"Nice speech, Mr. Commissioner. Try to smile a little so you do not scare anyone." Clary rose with a wince and stretched out her legs. "I have done very well for you."

"Yes, you have."

"Thank you, Clary."

"Thank you, Clary. None of this would've happened without your support. Is that why you brought me into the depths of Wrigley Field encased in some sort of energy bubble?" He frowned at her surprise. "I saw the glitter on the ceiling. I know what's normal down here. What gives, sweetie?"

She put her hands on her hips. "No one calls me sweetie, Mr. Nedick."

"Except me."

"Yes. Except you." Clary replied softly. "I have news which can only be shared with Puppy." The girl paused. "I think I know where Annette is."

Puppy's legs went a little wobbly. "She's home?"

Clary vigorously shook her shaggy head. "She is in the former Hungary in the eastern European section of the Caliphate. She was taken by our soldiers."

"How do you know?"

"I just do. I cannot say. Trust me." Her eyes narrowed. "Do you not trust me?"

After a moment, he nodded. "Then she's okay?"

Clary hesitated. "For now."

"For now? What the hell do you mean for now? Why wouldn't she be okay? She's with our army."

Clary darkened. "I do not control them. I thought I had input, but I have been cut out of decisions, big and small."

"Sorry, sweetheart, but your ego isn't my problem."

Her eyes blazed. "If I had ego I would lie. And you cannot hear with those terrible thoughts of yours. The sound is very loud and it is disquieting my verbal patterning." Clary took his hands. "I do not think Felice will harm her."

"Do not think. Which means you're not sure."

"No. I am not certain, Puppy. I am suddenly not certain of many things. I believe I have failed some tests of Felice's. It is the only sensible explanation. For now, I am the Granddaughter, but my power will be curtailed. Or they will attempt to do so. I am not entirely human anymore. And because I am not entirely human, I can be replaced. I will not trouble you with the details. You would not understand, and do not be offended. You are very adorable but not as smart as me."

Puppy only heard Annette's voice.

With a tender sigh at her simple friend, Clary bounced the Spaldeen against the wall. "I believe Felice wants to find the pope so she can kill him. He represents too much potential respect and influence. That is why the Islamists allowed him to live in hiding. His death would have turned him into a martyr. That is a powerful religious tool as I can attest to as a Catholic, and yes, I am still a Catholic."

Clary whirled and fired the Spaldeen around the walls. The ricocheting ball was a mere blur which she calmly caught as if it had never left her hand.

"Annette might have information that she is not even aware of about the location of the Holy Father which the soldiers will elicit from her."

"By torture," he said weakly, overcome by an image of Annette's bloodied nun's habit. This is what happens when you try to be a hero. Other people always pay the price.

"Yes, that is very possible. Not in the way you are thinking, Puppy. Our soldiers are not programmed for such brutality," she said scornfully. "But whether she would survive the probes, the experience of extracting guarded information, I do not know."

He felt sick and helpless. "What are you going to do about this, Clary?"

"I do not know, Puppy."

"You're the damn Granddaughter. You should be able to do something."

She gently brushed his stiff hair. "I do not live in a world where simple determination is the driving force. I do not trust anyone but you and you will be no help. I am formulating a plan but I would prefer not to speak anymore."

"Because you think if Felice would kill Annette, she would kill me."

Clary smiled blandly. "Oh no. You are an important part of Felice's plan, Puppy. If I explained how, you would behave differently and right now you're thinking about parachuting into Hungary to rescue Annette and you must not do that. Or anything. You must continue exactly as you have been with your baseball. If you change, Felice will be suspicious. I wanted you to know that at least Annette is alive. I am sorry this will cause you such worry."

He bounced the Spaldeen a moment before looking up. "But you wanted me to know that you are still human and could still be concerned about someone you loved."

Clary's lips quivered. "Yes. Because you are the only person to whom I can show my human side. To Felice, to everyone," she said savagely, "I am the Granddaughter. I thought I would falter. I have. I have let my fears take over. I have not properly balanced, and that is a concept I can only begin to explain. Felice promised that I would keep my soul."

Her lips twisted. "For me to retain my soul would guarantee my superiority. She cannot allow that." She paused. "No one would allow that. I also realize that, now. But if I allow the Holy Father to die, then I lose what is Clary's faith and without Clary's faith there can be no soul. A soul is what you believe in, my Puppy. You believe in your silly baseball game and your Annette. That is your soul, too. It is the humans who give such definitions, not God."

He bounced the ball a few more times, imagining Annette on some table, her insides plucked out by methodical robots in military uniforms.

"What are you going to do about Felice?"

The Granddaughter smiled faintly.

• • • •

THE RESPECTFUL, JAGGED line of fans outside gate three spilling back to the Addison subway station was quickly dubbed "Mooshie's Line." That did not delight Ernie Paicopolos.

Originally the ten-foot-long, red-white-and-blue canopy had been called Autograph Alley. The Wizard had stationed himself near the entrance, his red Bosox cape gleaming with special buttons for the occasion. More than a century of Red Sox glory glittered in the damp sunlight, from the crushed hopes of 1948 and 1967 and 1986 and 2025 and 2033, to the joy of 2004 and 2048. His large button for the last world championship team of 2050 was still highly illegal since it had been created in an Andover basement operated by illegal, albeit Red Sox-loving, Allah immigrants which constituted sedition during the last wave of deportations.

His eyes full of morbid suspicion, Ernie grunted demand for tickets before handing out the programs. Only Ernie was allowed to distribute the programs. Only Ernie was allowed to touch the programs. Everyone wanted a souvenir program like everyone wanted a Cherry Coke. Blasphemous whores.

However, once one received a program, one was supposed to, if one had the slightest respect, head to Autograph Alley where the program would be suitably signed by a player, and only then could the so-called fan enter the ballpark. That's why the gates had opened two hours before the start of batting practice, so that all could properly take their seats and stuff their fat faces with franks heaped with kraut and spicy brown mustard.

Once they'd gone through Autograph Alley.

It was not to be. Only about a dozen fans, resplendent in the different colors of their teams, loitered by Autograph Alley. The others, the thousands and thousands *and thousands* who rudely took their programs and entered Wrigley Field were algae on the pond of baseball. That signing autographs was against the law meant little to Ernie who held to a higher authority, communing as he did with that "great dugout beyond." He wouldn't, couldn't, order anyone to have their programs signed without being guilty of influencing. Either you understood or you didn't that scratching a name on a program or on a slip of paper so it could yellow with magical tenacity was a sacrosanct connection.

Blasphemous whores.

When the first of the twentieth-century team arrived, the Wizard waited with arms folded, mouth cross, silently begging the fans to step forward with the "free pencil" toward Ephraim Carew Donnatelli, great-granddaughter of the great Rod Carew. But no. Like baa-baa sheep, they watched with dullard eyes and frozen tongues as Ephraim, who would be starting at second base like her hallowed ancestor, passed through with a shy wave.

When Reynolds Ryan, great-grandson of Nolan Ryan—*No-lan Ry-an*—passed unmolested by curiosity followed by Sander Clemente—great-grandson of Roberto Clemente—*Ro-ber-to Cle-men-te*—with nary a look, a few fans wandered off. More than a few.

Ernie had no choice but to invoke an incantation.

Stupid is as stupid does
But not in baseball
If brains be gone

Let all else vanish

With a majestic wave of the wand that would've brought a Caesar to his knees, Ernie summoned the Gods of Baseball to do what they thought best. It would not be pretty. But like all keepers of the faith, he had no choice.

As with many great prophets whose message was garbled by the malignant imps of the universe, Ernie's belief in the "great dugout beyond" was quickly shaken when that "Yankee" sashayed toward Wrigley Field. In a piratical hat boasting two purple feathers bobbing on her mound of curls, the lithe, muscular frame already couched in her *Yankee* uniform, Mooshie Lopez strutted forward looking for garlands.

"Mooshie's back, little darlings. New face, same gifts. Come say hello."

Lopez wiggled her hips and blew kisses. Recognition rumbled. Fans padded toward Autograph Alley, many pouring back out of the stadium. Dozens, hundreds, and soon Ernie was herding the thousands and thousands politely lining up.

What could he do? Ernie fretted. He had invoked the gods and they sent him a damn "Yankee."

"Mr. Wizard," Mooshie cooed over the heads of three Spiders fans from Akron. "I'm thinking that having one autograph line isn't the way to go."

"Oh, is that so, Ms. Lopez?"

"Uh-huh. Not efficient. There's gonna be some 33,000 folks and I can't stand here all day signing and still have time to pitch a no-hitter against the lumps of coal pretending to be players." She sniffed unpleasantly at his Ted Williams button. "I hit more homers than him. Plus I pitch. Thank you, my darlings, who are you all rooting for today?"

A cry of "Mooshie!" rang out.

"That's right." She returned to Ernie. "What you should do is set up your autograph lines outside each gate to handle the crowds which will now build given that I have lit the fire. Who do we love?"

"Mooshie, Mooshie!"

"You got it. Now my darlings, I know you're thrilled to see me. Mooshie is back and will never leave you again." She acknowledged the cheers with a quick nod. "Anyone who wants my John Hancock, which it used to be called back in the day, can get it after the game when I've shut down these fools. Let me hear it. Which century of baseball is best?"

She encouraged the chant of "twenty-one!" until it became a din only drowned out by the roar of "Mooshie!" Like a one-person conga line, she hop-skipped into the stadium.

Ernie issued more incantations.

A floor-to-ceiling wooden barricade across the corridor separated the two clubhouses. Mooshie kicked a hole just below the sign *Stay Back Or Else* and stuck her head inside.

"Yoodie who, 'old white grandpas.' Mooshie is a comin' for you."

Tony Felton tugged her back. "Save it, Moosh."

"I got a lot stored up, Major." She followed Felton into the clubhouse, still tossing verbal bricks. "The Little General here yet?"

Tony grinned at the nickname. As big a pain as Mooshie was, and she was often like a snake finding a home up their butts, their shared contempt for Cheng trumped that.

"The prick slept here."

She made a face. "Course he did."

"Don't worry, we'll watch him."

The dozen players had slimmed down from ingesting wind sprints instead of milk-shakes. The neatly tailored uniforms courtesy of Vanguard Costumers of Terre Haute could've used a little nip and tuck; the back of Johanna Busco's uniform sagged enough to obscure the Peaches logo from the Atlanta franchise. Tony's uniform needed some un-nipping and untucking, as his Cleveland Spiders emblem stretched over rediscovered chest muscles.

The team sauntered across the clubhouse, sitting down as if the fans and the considerable number of Americans who'd be watching while freed from work or school on Centuries Day, the first holiday ever commemorated in The Family, were clustered by the lockers.

Mooshie headbutted, elbow-slammed, and exchanged a couple ankle kicks as she made her way into the manager's office, tossing a finger here and there at the caustic comments about her feathered hat. She noticed in the past two days, Cheng had added air plants to all the shelves. He waved hello over his shoulder.

"Morning. Well, almost afternoon."

"It's eight fucking thirty, Cheng."

"And the ancient ones are already out there practicing. Can you hear?" He shushed them until the faint sounds of bat against ball seeped inside. "But I know Mooshie needs her nightlife."

She grimaced. Sex was once an energizer before a big game. Now she just waddled. "And Mooshie told you she hates fake plants."

"I can see why fake living things would bother you," he snidely said, turning to a robust plum-colored air plant. "She speaks the truth, doesn't she, Naomi?"

Mooshie groaned. "You named the plants?"

"Since the reintroduction of adjacent life-forms, names are now fair game. This is Kendall, Cleo, Sombra. You already met Naomi. Now, have we gotten rid of our daily contempt and mistrust, or do you need to blame me for losing the war again?"

Mooshie grumbled, dropped into a chair, and plopped her spikes onto the desk. She grinned maliciously as Cheng put the scattered pencils back into the overturned jar. With a scowl, Albert gestured for her to approve the lineup where the youngest player was six-ty-one.

> Russell LF
>
> Lopez P
>
> Felton C
>
> Busco 1B
>
> Ra Chou 3B
>
> White CF
>
> Tedeschi 2B
>
> Sicatyunni RF
>
> Cheng SS

"Mooshie's in the proper order. But Cheng bats ninth?" Mooshie snickered.

"Another example of my astonishing humility. I've already told Ted he comes in at the start of the eighth inning."

Lopez wagged her forefinger. "Ninth. Depending. Maybe."

He wagged back. "Kelly Caputo also needs to pitch."

"They can split the ninth."

"No. Ted in the eighth, Kelly in the ninth."

"And where does the Moosh go?" She spread her hands as if Cheng had suggested arranging a solar eclipse.

"We invoke the floating player rule which, by the way, has been ignored in the 2099 season."

"Big surprise. They put all the post-2000 rule changes in deep storage. We conceded on the do-over rule." She referenced the five-year experiment allowing managers to ask for a do-over on a play they expressly disliked. "Least everyone hates the DH."

"We should've held firm on game length."

"And have them mock us for not being able to play nine innings? I really don't want to come out of the game and hear Cobb's nasal shit about the good old days when pitchers pitched complete games. That's why I want to go the distance."

Cheng sternly shook his head. Mooshie blew contempt through fluttering lips. "So, I'm the designated floater who can come in and out of the game?"

"Who else but the most important player on the team?"

Lopez turned serious as she studied the lineup card. "We know this isn't about the rules, Cheng."

After firmly closing the office door, Albert settled back into his chair with a weary sigh and poured Mooshie a stiff cup of real coffee from Ecuador.

"Donna nearly keeled over during yesterday's outfield drills," he said. "There were long gasps like the sound of a sibilant trumpet."

"Can you not, please? Donna always gasps like a sibilant trumpet. You should hear her after sex."

"'Can you not, please.'" Cheng rolled his eyes. "Felton can only crouch on one knee."

"Better balance."

"He can't bounce up in time to throw anyone out at second. You know Ty will be running the bases."

Mooshie frowned. "I'll keep the runners close."

"You don't have a pickoff move, Mooshie."

"Because I never allowed enough baserunners to need one."

"Because except for Curly and Dorian Kenner, no one stole bases in our time."

"Felton still has a cannon for an arm. Johanna's a little slow around first. I'll just have to cover for her."

"And for Tedeschi at second? They did away with the roving fifth infielder back in 2035. I can't shade toward third and second."

"Ra Chou doesn't look bad."

"He couldn't straighten up three days ago."

"I thought the heat injections worked?"

"So he said. They're all playing through gritted teeth. Nearly thirty years in POW camps took it out of them."

"Puppy said they played great in London."

Albert snorted. "He idolizes them. Like he idolizes you. He's not objective. Puppy has a murky sentimentality which obscures his judgment."

"Some people say that's the whole point of the game."

"Not this time, Mooshie. This team is about more than players…"

"I know."

"They represent how we mistreated our soldiers."

"How you and Grandma mistreated them with your bullshit mail plane, acting as if we hadn't left them behind."

He waved that off. "Now we're making it up to them. Now we're rehabilitating them. Putting them back on a pedestal where they belong. I don't want anyone embarrassed."

"It's a helluva time to worry, a few hours before game time."

"We didn't have a choice. Thanks to the regenerative baths, I can play like I'm thirty-five. Ultimately, it's up to you, Mooshie, whether we win or lose."

"Always is. Who do you think everyone's coming out to see but the great Lopez in her first game since the 2065 World Series?"

Cheng stared hard. "You've practiced very little."

She shrugged. "Somes needs it. Somes don't."

Albert's stare tightened. "Aaron White took you to school in BP the other day."

"I was building up his confidence."

"Oh right. Your fastball didn't move."

She blushed. "It will."

"Curly Russell took you deep. Twice. I can throw the ball farther than he can hit it."

"I was tired from making Aaron look good."

"Talk to me, Mooshie."

She squirmed. "About what?"

"In good times, Curly doesn't hit a Mooshie pitch to dead center. You're fading, aren't you?"

"What the hell are you talking about? Fading. Did you see my batting practice? It was Missile City. Boom, to left. Boom, to right. Boom, to center."

"We have enough hitting even if you go oh-for-six, given whatever crap pitcher Ty throws out there. It's your pitching that matters." Albert's voice softened. "Let me see your left arm, Mooshie."

"For what? Some early morning jollies?"

"Please roll up your sleeve."

"Please go fuck yourself."

"I know what's happening to Ty and Mick. I rushed production of the three of you for the most organic authenticity. But the inherent power couldn't be maintained. There's no re-activation charging like the newer models. You three were a one-shot, a swing for the fences and it worked. But it wouldn't be forever. You couldn't sustain the synchronicity between consciousness and container."

"Stop calling my body a suitcase."

"Roll up your sleeve, Mooshie."

Muttering profanely, Lopez slowly pulled up the uniform and turned over her left arm. Cheng yanked off the bandage from the crook. Two exposed blood vessels pulsed faint blue within a square of ragged skin.

"This started a month ago. Talk about the trauma of looking inside yourself." She managed a bitter laugh. "But I look good compared to the 'two white grandpas.'" Mooshie referenced Clary's nickname for Ty and Mickey. "They've lost skin on their arms and legs." She briskly rolled down the sleeve. "I'm fine. Mooshie never disappoints her fans. Ever. I'm pitching a no-hitter and hitting three homers."

Cheng shook his head. "You're pitching just five innings."

"What?" Mooshie's voice penetrated the door, but the players were used to their daily squabbles.

He held up his left hand and spread his fingers as if she were a dumb child. "Five."

"Nine." Mooshie held up two hands. "Or ten. Or whenever the game ends. I do not come out."

"The Old-Timers' Game is about them. Them." Cheng pointed toward the clubhouse. "Resurrecting heroes. Not you. I'd rather have Ted Towers, who pulled a dinghy of wounded marines off the Tunisian beach, pick up the win than you. I'd rather Johanna Busco, who gunned down more than twenty Allahs so her company could evac on the

Irish coast, hit a game-winning homer. And I'd rather bobble every damn ground ball and people hoot at ol' Grandpa Albert instead of anyone seeing Ra Chou let a grounder trickle through his legs or Tony Felton embarrassed by a passed ball. Heroes, Mooshie. Not heroes out of our memory like you and your greatness, but fat, old, and out-of-shape former soldiers who are running on fumes. They didn't have the time to become pretty images. Now it's just their hatred for me, Grandma, for everything this country did to them that'll bring back their glory, so get out of the way for the first time in your life and let me do what needs to be done."

She visibly flinched. "Then I'm window dressing."

"Yeah. For one day you don't count."

Mooshie sneered. "Okay. I go five innings. But six if I'm pitching a shutout."

Cheng laughed coldly.

• • • •

TY WOULDN'T GIVE them the satisfaction. He hadn't smiled in twelve days and he sure as hell wouldn't start fifteen minutes before they took the field. His bristly gray head shook in eternal disgust as he kicked at stools and feet stupid enough to get in the way. Ephraim Carew and Tatia Garvey had decided on the first day of practice, while hiding in the shower, that Cobb resembled Bag Man, the villain in the first new horror vid-mov since *The Surrender*.

Watching in the corner as if in a lower field box, Mickey was not about to get in the way. Overtly, that is. He'd already been blamed for Sander Clemente bobbling a ball in right field. Tennessee Bench dropping a relay throw at home. All his fault somehow. Donde Vasquez Carlton missing a bunt. Heresy. The slightest infraction of strict fundamentals, make that fundamentalism Mick had cracked to Estie Morgan, and that nickname quickly replaced Bag Man in the twentieth-century clubhouse.

The Most Reverend (Mick had to explain the title), Ty Cobb of the United Baseball Fundamentalist Church. No one really understood the religion-soaked details, but the general mocking was enough. Mick was the merry leader of "the resistance" to "Cobbian terror." The ringleader. When their hands had bled from the third hour of dropping bunts and their uniforms had been stained red around the knees and thighs from the fourth hour of headfirst slides and they were dizzy from practicing getting beaned and Tennessee and Donde each lost front teeth from the sucker-punch lessons and Humbert Smith had to beg a bodega to stay open past lawful hours to buy Glu-Stitch because they couldn't ask the Commissioner's Office for more medical supplies since that would raise suspicions and absolutely no one on this damn planet was allowed to know what they were doing, there was the Mick.

A seltzer bottle had exploded in Ty's desk drawer. His spikes were glued together. A note that said *Ty is A Babe* was taped onto Cobb's favorite bat. His cap was filled with guacamole. And they turned off the hot water right in the middle of his shower, sending the sudsy old 'bot roaring around the clubhouse.

Such acts of disobedience to authority in The Family were unfamiliar. Mick eased the way. Plus, he was in constant pain, so when Cobb ordered him off the field and into the clubhouse, it was merciful punishment. The team loved Mick and hated Ty. They wouldn't give Ty a glass of water if his uniform were on fire, but they'd do anything for the lopsided boyish grin of Mickey, even the women whose butts he relentlessly pinched.

A crabbier, more vicious, razor-sharp team living between fear of death for fouling off a bunt with two strikes and the dream of cutting Ty's throat had not existed since, well, the twentieth century.

"I bet you're all mighty pleased with yourselves." Ty toured the clubhouse as if it were a battlefield, rapping the metal lockers with the thick barrel of his bat. "You think just because you didn't look like shit stuck to a tree, you're somehow major league baseball players."

He pressed the barrel of his bat against Ephraim's forehead, knocking off her cap. Ty did this every day. They all knew what was coming, but it still hurt.

"Ms. E-phraim Ca-rew Donn-a-tell-i, you think you're a major league baseball player?"

From getting her knuckles rapped raw with his bat for mishandling a double play, Ephraim understood there was no right answer. She shrugged.

Ty shrugged back so violently his shoulders went past his ears. "What the hell does that mean? Either you are or you ain't."

Ephraim cleared her throat, rising to her full 6'3" height as if that would intimidate the manager. "Yes, sir. I am."

Ty slowly rotated the bat into her forehead, making her flinch. "Why is that, little girl?"

"Because I am not a beast."

He twirled the bat a little more, making her eyes cross. "I think you are."

"I am not, sir. I can think."

"You, can, think?"

"I do not just catch the ball, sir. I do not just run, sir."

Cobb pressed his nose against hers. "That makes you what?"

"A smart player, sir."

Ty whirled in the other direction. "What the hell's your name again?"

J'ilia Nexus, descendant of Willie Stargell, carefully spelled his name as Ty pressed the thick barrel into his head.

"Are you a show-off?"

"No, sir."

"You don't want to flex your big muscles?"

"No. Big muscles are stupid on a baseball player."

"Why, scum?"

"Because it's a game of skill."

"And you think you have skill, you watered-down turd on a popsicle stick?"

Whirling around, Ty pressed the bat against the broad skull of Estie Morgan. "Are you going to run like hell today?"

"Yes, sir."

"Are you going to throw to the right base?"

"Yes, sir."

"What do you do with two strikes, idiot?"

"Choke up, sir."

"You don't try to hit a home run?"

They all knew that was sacrilege to the Most Reverend Cobb.

Morgan shook her head.

"You're not going to sit on a fastball?"

Morgan shook her head wildly.

"You're not going to try to pull the pitch?"

They knew that would be heresy. Ty leaped over two players, landing in front of burly Tennessee Bench. "What about you, you pile of frozen piss?"

"Hit the other way."

Cobb pressed the barrel into Tennessee's forehead, glaring at the team. "Going with...?"

"The pitch, sir!" they cried.

"When you get on first base, you...?" The barrel of the bat knocked Tennessee into her locker where she dared not move despite the nail gouging her lower back.

"Steal."

"Pilfer!" Ty cried.

"Pillage the bases!" they responded.

"If they get in your way you...?"

"Gouge their legs!"

"I can't hear you!"

"Kick their knees!"

"Amen."

"Trample their bodies!"

Cobb thrust the bat high into the air. "Because they are...?"

"Pretenders!" came the cry that had begun and ended every practice, followed them to bed, and intruded into their dreams with horrifying hallucinations of bats that transformed into monstrous spears if they struck out trying to hit a home run.

"Are they baseball players?"

"No!" came the roar.

"They mock our game."

"Yes!"

"How many innings in a game?"

"Nine!"

He cupped his ear and yelled, "I said how many innings?"

"Nine!"

"Not...?"

"Seven. Nine. Nine. Nine!"

"Who are the true baseball players?"

"We are!"

"Who plays the game the way the good Lord wants us to play?"

"We do!"

"What position would Jesus Christ play?"

"All of them!"

"What the hell are we called?"

"The twentieth century!"

"What?"

"The goddamn twentieth century!" they shouted.

"Show me, you goddamn lazy pieces of shit."

Screaming wildly, the team yanked at the twentieth-century crest on the front of their uniforms, the two shaped like a curved bat and the zero a baseball as if it were a burning fuse and the countdown was under five.

Into the silence of the room, Mickey began singing softly, "We shall overcome. We shall overcome. We shall overcome, someday."

Soon the entire room was shouting the lyrics like rapturous missiles aimed at Heaven.

Cobb glowered with the excessive theatrics of someone trying to appear displeased. "Figures you'd sing a song like that. Now get your worthless asses onto the field. Remember. The first person who asks for Glu-Stitches gets my foot in their face."

The team savagely roared down the runway. Ty tugged aside Mickey. "They hate my guts, don't they?"

He winked. "Like a dose of clap on your wedding night."

Ty grunted. "I think they're ready, too."

25

As fans entered Wrigley Field, they were met inside each of the eight gates by an army of bright-faced young teachers. Over a restricted vid-conf call several days ago, Hedda Kleinz had sternly warned her new Twentieth-Century Project team not to forget they were educators.

Sixty-one teachers had volunteered to be flown into Chicago for two days of exhausting training. Hedda brought the book she'd co-written with Ty Cobb and Mickey Mantle, *Baseball, Your Game*, as an example of what not to say. The old gentlemen had rattled off their reminiscences and recollections and extremely colored impressions and opinions of their times alongside the approved history paralleling the growth and decline of baseball.

Like the immigration laws designed to minimize foreign-born players; the privilege of inaccessible analytics; perversion of opinionated journalism; entitlement of athletes as a separate privileged class, and the politicization of sports, leading to the terrorist attack during the 2065 World Series, led by star players demanding The Family use nuclear weapons to defeat the Islamic Empire and end World War III.

History was still in doubt. That's why Hedda had recommended cultural artifacts that reflect their times. Once the exhibits were delivered, she excerpted Eduardo Sanchez's *History of Our Country*, the acknowledged authority on America's past since 2070, to serve as a backdrop to the non-baseball-themed exhibits, only to receive a notice from the First Cousin that they were under review.

The past was being parceled out, Hedda realized. As if they could only handle so much at a time.

The Twentieth-Century Project focused on cultural artifacts with little reference to the period. An entire day's valuable training was spent on how to respond to a question about the beginnings of the Internet. Sixty-one teachers plus Assistant Principal Kleinz had been taught that it was a capitalist device to enslave the world with commerce. Was that still valid?

"There will be no Internet artifacts," Hedda had announced. The six-pack of cell phones anonymously donated were also shelved. She sanitized the exhibits and prepared her own answers to several questions, spending the last day cringing at the groans of educators whose driving ambition in life has been to provoke minds, and who had now been ordered to brush aside curiosity.

This was a different sort of quest, as if it were a circus and everyone got to be a clown. From the moment the gates opened, her exhausted teachers costumed in orange blouses and pants were circled like knotted ropes. Here inside gate two, hundreds of fans insisted on spinning the plastic Hula-Hoops around their waists and hips while Emmilena Fatz from PS 21 in Milwaukee endlessly demonstrated the 1958 fad. No one asked about the backdrop of the 1950s and the threat of nuclear war provoked by America's aggression against the Soviet Union following World War II.

By the Bleached Dim Sum concession outside the third-base mezzanine ramp, the crowd had simply stopped moving. Hedda panicked, trying to remember which of her beleaguered teachers were by nearby gate four. Was it the Les Paul guitar or the skateboarding exhibit? She caught a quick glimpse of a squat woman in a bright-red Atlanta Peaches uniform by a bat rack from the 2031 world champions, the San Diego Pelicans.

That awful Matthew blocked Hedda. "This is unacceptable."

"I warned you," she snapped. "You set up the Custodians of Memories exhibits too close to my people. Of course there'll be a traffic jam."

"This was clearly well conceived before your people cluttered the ballpark."

Hedda poked the startled 'bot's dimpled pink tie. "Listen, Matthew. I never suggested the Twentieth-Century Project handle the actual exhibits. We weren't ready. But the Cousins insisted—"

"And the Commissioner opposed the historical—"

"And they overruled Pup-py Ne-dick." She drew out the name because she found any reproachful hint toward Puppy unsettled Matthew. "Here we are. You didn't plan properly."

Matthew puffed slightly at such a suggestion.

"There are 1,309 people waiting to try on the ruby red slippers inside gate four," she continued. "We had to suspend batting practice because there are more fans dancing as if they just left Kansas than watching the historic greats of the game."

Hedda imitated Matthew's folded arms as they matched impatient staccato taps of their front feet while a woman in a San Francisco Giants hat and a striped bikini ran past with an Alvarado Barbecued Steak sandwich in each hand.

"That was the preferred swimsuit of that particular era," Matthew explained with an arched eyebrow. "It would have been much safer to model swimsuits where, unlike the skateboarding exhibit which has claimed," he paused imperceptibly, "twenty-four injuries to lower extremities from untrained attempts, there would have been no physical damage."

"Modeling? You think the oppression of body-shaming modeling had no victims?" Hedda exhaled very slowly. "It would've been smart if you'd planned it so all the exhibits closed by batting practice and reopened after the game."

Matthew's head pulsed. "All the siblings might not have the opportunity to sample and learn. There is remarkable interest in donning a fringed jacket once worn by a musician named Jimi Hendrix at a large gathering by the town of Woodstock, New York. The crowd has effectively sealed off entrance to the lower-field seats on the first-base line."

"And we've got posters of an artist's rendition of Campbell's Soup Cans and thank you, I know that was Andy Warhol. Like I know about the stock market ticker-tape machines and the gambling roulette tables." She angrily waved at the huge poster of The Beatles's *Sgt. Pepper's Lonely Hearts Club Band* album cover two gates away. "John, Paul, Ringo, and George. Before you dare insult me. That is why we have the Twentieth-Century Project which won't end with a baseball game but will be part of the ongoing school curriculums where we'll be able to use HGs, which Pup-py Ne-dick wouldn't allow, to send the various artifacts into all the classrooms. Just like you're doing with Cooperstown. This silly game is just the start."

"Without this silly game there would be no Twentieth-Century Project, Ms. Hed-da Klein-z." Matthew surprised himself with the sarcasm.

By 1 p.m., all the cultural artifacts and Hall of Fame exhibits were shut down so batting practice could resume. Midway through the twenty-first-century team's practice, more panic set in when Matthew calculated that they would run out of balls by the third inning unless fans, packed together in the bleachers like a very polite mob, returned the BP home runs.

In a spirited debate in the corridor outside the visiting clubhouse, Puppy agreed that asking fans to return their souvenirs without giving them something in return was wrong. Sahidi suggested autographed baseballs which prompted Ernie to smile for the first time anyone could remember and race like a red penguin into the public-address-announcer booth. As Sandra Douglas, Sahidi's sister, recalled from the rad booth next door, there was a loud and violent struggle for the microphone until the majestic tones of the Wizard of Fenway boomed across Wrigley.

"Now hear this, now hear this. We need all fans to return balls caught during batting practice. Oh be still." Ernie's impatient rasp shut down the bleacher groans like an insulated Red Sox igloo blanket. "You will receive a new ball, postgame, autographed by the player who swatted the original into the seats. If you cannot remember who hit the batting practice homer that you caught then you do not, I repeat, do not deserve an autographed baseball because you are nothing more than a mercenary parasite. I will not entertain questions."

Inside of a few minutes, fans politely dropped their balls into a large net strung up in center field by the grounds crew.

When Rodrigo, the grim 'bot head grounds keeper of the newly formed trans-organic crew, repeated twice that they needed a thorough cleansing of the field before the game could begin, Puppy crawled away to find somewhere to rest, happy to let Sahidi and Matthew and Ernie pretty much do whatever they wanted.

He found a stale room with pipes as thick as pillars tucked away in the basement under the left-field line. Puppy plopped down, oblivious to the rumpling of his gray three-piece suit, and bounced a blackening Spaldeen against the wall. Eyes drooping since he'd slept a fitful three hours in the past few days, he woke up to utter silence filled by the mournful bagpipes. He raced back toward the field.

Eight limping robot soldiers marched in from center field flanked by the entire twenty-first-century team and six school children, each holding a flapping American flag. The bagpipers ended with a suitable flourish as the entourage stopped beyond second base.

A Yankees cap perfectly balanced on her thick hair, Clary slowly walked from home plate, pausing on the pitcher's mound where two drone microphones fluttered on either side. She scanned the stadium with the calmness of someone buttering toast.

"Good afternoon. I am Clary. I thank you all for coming and for listening. I would like to introduce very brave Americans. First, the soldiers of Charlie Company."

The 'bot soldiers stepped forward to the edge of the mound.

"These eight soldiers landed in Algiers at the very start of Operation Revenge, the invasion into the evil heart of the Islamic Empire. Moving inland against fierce defenses, Charlie Company seized two batteries and captured more than one hundred enemy soldiers. Charlie Company began with 154 soldiers. These are the only ones who survived."

Clary squinted slightly at the shy sun peeking around the mid-afternoon clouds. "You might have noticed they do not walk too well. They were wounded. Their limbs could not be replaced because the original injuries were so severe. Robots can be hurt just like everyone else. The remainder of Charlie Company refused to evacuate. They refused emergency medical attention when their own med scans failed. They would not give up their positions and jeopardize the lives of the soldiers still landing. As The Family has taught us, there are no heroes. Being a hero means you do something unexpected for which you deserve a reward, instead of doing what all decent life-forms should do, like saving their fellow soldiers's lives and defending our country."

The Granddaughter stepped off the pitching rubber. "Pedro. Miquel. Jas'mine. Tilda. Heather. Constantine. Jack. Dorchester. You have our thanks."

The girl curtsied before the stiff soldiers who returned the gesture.

There was silence because the crowd didn't know the proper response. No robot soldiers had ever been honored. Until now they were like the sky, something necessary that required no thought.

Clary waited on the mound until the 'bots returned to short center field before nodding at the twenty-first-century team. They marched less precisely than the robots, but with similar creaks.

"This is the baseball team of the twenty-first century." Clary briskly ticked off their names, maintaining eye contact with all the players simultaneously. "They, too, suffered many wounds. But not in 2098 and 2099. They were injured in 2066, 2067, 2068, until The Surrender in 2073. They fought in Africa, Europe, and the Middle East. They were captured and put into prisoner-of-war camps. They were supposed to be repatriated back to America. They were not. They were forgotten. They were abandoned. Their honor was dirtied. But not as much as America's."

Clary took a long breath. "Your country is sorry. We hope you will forgive us."

She walked up to each of the players and bowed stiffly. None of this had been rehearsed. They'd been told by Puppy they were just accompanying the color guard.

Breaking into a crooked grin, Tony Felton extended his hand for a gruff handshake which delighted Clary. Squealing, she went up on tiptoe, kissing the players on both cheeks.

This the crowd understood and they rocked Wrigley with vigorous applause. Mooshie's appearance at home plate only intensified the shouts, which she reluctantly calmed down.

"Did you need to introduce me, Granddaughter?" Mooshie called out.

"I do not think that is necessary, Mooshie," Clary answered, laughing.

Lopez waited for the noise to fade before lighting into an exuberant rendition of the original national anthem. The former POWs lustily sang along, tears digging into their creased faces.

Ernie led his four fellow Custodians of the Memories onto the field where Custodian Ansma handed him a gleaming catcher's glove resting on a pillow. Turning to Tennessee Bench, Ernie flicked peevishly at the dancing microphone drones and said, "Ms. Bench, the Custodians will permit use of the glove carried by your glorious ancestor, Johnny Bench of the Cincinnati Reds."

The burly woman was so moved, all she could do was stroke the glove, pleasing the Wizard.

"Mr. Felton, for you, the Custodians will permit use of the catcher's glove worn by New York Yankee Lawrence Peter 'Yogi' Berra."

Ernie nearly dislocated Felton's wrist when he prematurely tried on the mitt.

"For you, Granddaughter, we will permit use of the baseball that George Herman 'Babe' Ruth hit for his 714th home run in 1935."

Clary lovingly clasped the ball in her palm.

"For you, Commissioner Nedick, the Custodians offer the ball that Roger Maris hit for his 61st home run in 1961, breaking Ruth's single-season record at the time."

Puppy reverently pressed his lips to the ball.

"The Granddaughter will throw out the first pitch."

Felton took a camper's position behind home, saving his deep squats for the game. In a fluid pitching motion, which Clary had assimilated from Warren Spahn, she delivered a 103 mph perfect strike into the heart of Felton's mitt. With a loud "oomph" that ricocheted off the scoreboard, Tony skittered back six feet.

He sheepishly held up the Babe's ball, earning loud applause.

Tennessee Bench had no qualms about squatting. Her thick legs formed the first floor of a building at home plate. Puppy took Maris's baseball. He hunched over slightly on the pitching rubber, long enough to generate puzzled crowd murmurs.

He straightened up with a relieved sigh. Letting go was so hard. But it was time. He faced the remnants of Charlie Company.

"Who likes baseball?"

The eight 'bots pulsed with frowns. That additional program had never been offered. Puppy grinned and tossed the ball to Jas'mine. The first lieutenant caught the ball as if it were a sixth finger on its left hand. The 'bot's opaque features didn't stir, processing the human's need for drama. Jas'mine looked down the row of comrades, eliciting slight shrugs.

Jas'mine, who had personally killed thirty-one Allahs from a foxhole while drenched with circulatory fluid seeping out of the hole in its right hip, hobbled up to the mound. From five feet away, Clary shared page sixty of the book *The Great Hurlers*, borrowed from Puppy's collection. With a kick of its right leg in perfect emulation of Los Angeles Dodgers great Sandy Koufax, Jas'mine rocked back and threw a breaking pitch that hooked directly into Bench's mitt.

Tennessee didn't have to move an inch.

Finally interrupting the exchange of snide digs about the blousy 1930s-style uniforms and sneers about a fart not having room to breathe in those tapered futuristic costumes, Rodrigo, who presided as if it had grown each blade of grass, curtly informed the four co-managers that his grounds crew would sweep one more time after all the unnecessary stomping on its field.

"You know how they are," Cheng cracked, suddenly realizing he was the only human at the pregame meeting. The cold stares from the seven 'bots took a while to fade.

"That is one of my points to make," said head ump Edward through its mask. "Since this is the first time—"

"How many first times do we have to listen to?" Mooshie complained.

"As many as required." Edward didn't care for the emotionalism of the Mooshie, Cobb, and Mantle models. "Since this is the first time organic and inorganic life-forms are knowingly playing together, I reiterate that any pejorative directed at another player predicated on its life model will result in immediate ejection."

"What'd he just say?" Mick asked of the circle.

"The Little General can't call us hair dryers," Mooshie sneered. "Or Hoovers. Bread ovens." She sighed at Mantle's dim look. "The humans can't call us names and we can't call them names."

Ty fluttered his lips with such contempt it made Mooshie's hair blow. "Are you saying we can't hurt someone's feelings? This is baseball. Things get rough. Oh no, Albert called me a name. So what? I just tell my pitcher to buzz the ball at his head, if she can manage throwing that low."

"That is not permitted either," Edward warned. "Height sensitivity, complexions, all manner of origins, physical arrangements, nothing like that is permitted."

"We ain't had any problems with anyone's complexion sensitivity so far this season," Ty snarled.

"That is because we do not indulge such behavior. But the introduction of two different life-forms in a competitive setting could create possibilities for human pejoratives."

"Wait a minute," Cheng said. "You're only worried about the humans?"

"You are the ones with the history of pejoratives."

"I'm a damn 'bot and if I want to mock Mooshie's fat ass, I will," said Ty. "I'm from the twentieth century where we had a great tradition of bench jockeys riding the other team to get under their skin. This isn't for the faint-hearted. Harry Truman said if you can't stand the heat, stay out of the kitchen. If you can't stand the heat of baseball, stay in the clubhouse."

Mantle acknowledged Ty's cleverness with a slap on the shoulder.

Edward removed its mask and went chin-to-chin with the Georgia Peach. Its voice turned into a hoarse whip tinged with a long-discouraged polarizing regional accent. "Listen up, Cobb. This here is my meeting and my rules. You obey the rules of my house or I'll run your ass and your whole damn team off the field and into a paddy wagon if I got to. Now don't give me anymore of your damn lip, got it?"

Ty glowed crimson but stayed silent. It helped that Edward gave the same chin-to-chin warning to the others. Edward went over the ground rules, hearing nothing but petulant grunts. Lineup cards were exchanged and the captains returned to their dugouts. twenty-first century on the visitor's third-base side since Wrigley Field, built in 1912, belonged to the previous century like seeds on a loaf of Hiram's Rye, Cobb quipped.

Mickey and Ty raced side by side leading the twentieth-century team onto the field. Behind the plate was Bench. At first base was Tatia Garvey. At second was Ephraim Carew. Shortstop was Humbert Smith. Third base was Nan Foxx. Left field was Myrina James Musial with the Mick in center and Ty in right completing the outfield.

Slowly taking his spot on the mound was Reynolds Ryan. Planting his powerful legs, Ryan uncoiled like a smooth artillery gun. The ball cracked into Bench's glove. She cocked an approving fist toward the twenty-first-century dugout. In that quick meeting they'd just had in the dugout, the skipper had said to push as far as they could and do whatever it took. He'd deal with the rest. The skipper's face had been scary when he said that.

Tennessee flung some dirt toward the opposing dugout just to underline her point. She loved how Mooshie Lopez pointed a bat as if that'd intimidate her. Tennessee had played in a semi-secret baseball league in Houston for fifteen years on garbage-infested fields with passing residents calling her a traitor. She made the Houston Astros this season and sported a .255 average with only one passed ball; the asshole Commissioner complained the quality of play was poor. We got something to prove, too. The skipper picked us because we were good. He made that clear. Like we had to be hungry. A little mean. A lot mean.

Everyone came from a DV. Ephraim just went back into the Eastern Maryland dump because her bakery failed again. Myrina flunked out of medical school three times. Nan was a lousy truck driver. Tatiana and Humbert couldn't sell water to a tree. And Reynolds Ryan liked to drink. Their great-grandpappies were something, and they weren't. Now they had another chance to show who they were. Skipper said he wanted two kinds of players. The kind who plays when they bleed. And the kind who makes the other team bleed.

On Ryan's last warm-up pitch, Johnny Bench's great-granddaughter gave the entire twenty-first-century team the finger.

During the pregame infield practice Cheng made a huge issue about the personal pain of surrendering his shortstop position to Bar'Nee Ortiz "sometime during the game" in addition to the sacrifice of batting ninth. He acted as if he'd donated all his organs, still in uniform. Mooshie let Cheng lead off just to shut him up. She had expected he'd pull something like that.

As The Little General luxuriated in a slow defiant walk from the on-deck circle, the crushing silence began. Even though booing had been encouraged within the boundaries of good sportsmanship in the Commissioner's Suggestion number 5, there was nothing but quiet contempt at Ernie's introduction of Number 31.

Grandma's relentless harping on forgiveness was brusquely forgotten. No one could forgive Cheng for corrupting their trust.

The first pitch whizzed directly at Albert's head, sending him sprawling. A din of cheers rocked old Wrigley. Albert sneered into the home dugout at the impassive Ty. He scooped up his helmet, tipped it sarcastically, and, on the next pitch, drove a flat slider back up the middle into center field. The former head of The Family gave the finger to the twentieth-century team.

There was promise of a lot more of that today.

First baseman Garvey played back of Cheng, not bothering to hold on a runner when stealing was a forgotten tool with sliding not too far behind.

Mooshie took about an hour, or so it seemed, to go from the on-deck circle into the left-handed hitter's box. She had to acknowledge every wave and shout and, when she clenched her groin at the pitcher, the park about lost it.

Edward briskly informed Mooshie that if she didn't play ball, she'd forfeit her at-bat. She thought better about arguing. The all-time major league baseball leader in hits and home runs by a switch-hitter dug in for her first plate appearance since the seventh game of the 2065 World Series at the Amazon Stadium in the Bronx.

Ryan reared back for a platter of fastballs and sliders, running the count to three-and-two. The game was delayed a few minutes because a law-abiding fan threw the batted foul ball back onto the field, triggering an impatient announcement from Ernie explaining that "you can keep foul balls during the game, which you would know if you were a real fan."

On the pay-off pitch, Ryan pulled the string and Mooshie nearly toppled swinging early. There was a momentary stadium-wide gasp.

"Guess you ain't seen a lot of changeups," Tennessee snickered, firing the ball back to Ryan. "And here we thought you were the great Mooshie. I got a crick in my neck from the windstorm you kicked up."

Embarrassment was not a familiar feeling for Mooshie who hissed out a series of cleverly combined obscenities while walking back to the dugout, earning a warning from Edward. The dugout sat stone-faced; sacrificing one out to take down Lopez was worth it.

"Way to work the count," Felton said loudly.

"Are you patronizing me, you fat bastard?" Mooshie snapped.

All Tony needed was a smirk to send Mooshie into the runway where she smashed the bat until it was a fat clump of dust.

Ryan retired Johanna Busco on a nibbler back to the mound and Mickey had a ways to go to haul in Felton's long fly to left-center. Mantle huffed and puffed his displeasure about sprinting so soon in the game; Ryan promised to focus on strikeouts going forward.

Mooshie took the mound, stretched her arms, and, falling to both knees, planted a long kiss on the rubber. Most fans didn't know there was such a thing as a pitching rubber, believing the rectangle just came with the mound when it spontaneously grew in the middle of the field. But that still set off a sweeping chant of "Moo-shie, Moo-sh-ie!"

Ephraim Carew waited for the minute-long introductory video on her famous namesake Rod Carew to play on the scoreboard. Each of the twentieth-century players would get this introduction the first time they came to bat, mandated as part of the umbrella Cousins/Granddaughter sanctioned guidelines encouraging all opportunities to learn about the previous century.

A grainy video of Rod Carew's 3,000th hit with squeaky sound, the results of some fifty years hidden in a damp St. Paul basement, received polite applause when it finished. The crowd was still in Mooshie's pocket.

The lefty Ephraim's long lanky arms stilled as Lopez threw her first pitch. Carew crouched and dropped a neat bunt up the third-base line. Mooshie got there first and wildly threw over Busco's head. By the time Donda Sicatyunni retrieved the ball in the right-field corner, Ephraim was standing on third. Relief pitcher Tendrata Spahn, serving as third-base coach, apologetically slapped the runner's butt, but the skipper's orders were orders.

Between the inappropriate touching and the somewhat mythical bunt, the crowd soaked in the excitement as if sipping a new brand of pop.

No, Mooshie wasn't fond of embarrassment. She scowled Felton back into his half crouch, right leg extended. Nan Foxx settled in. Her eyes widened as Spahn signaled with a tip of his cap. As Lopez started her windup, Carew broke for home. Unnerved, Foxx jumped out of the way, but there was no need. Mooshie heaved the throw into the screen and Ephraim scored, bounding up in casual triumph.

The crowd murmured cautiously, understanding that what they'd seen was permitted but not sure it was right. On the next pitch, Mooshie about cleaved Foxx's bat with a nasty inside fastball. Ty came to bat, receiving a warm ovation. Over time, the former co-Commissioner and current American League-leading hitter had become a poster child for all the brash indiscretions and ill-thought phrases that were simply unthinkable; he was envied a little.

Lopez gestured her infield together for a quick meeting. It took a little while for Cobb's miming of sad tears to dribble into the stands where fans started laughing.

"The old bastard is gonna bunt so shorten up," Mooshie snapped.

"He was good at bat control."

"Still is. He's trying to draw us in," Cheng said. "Then he slaps it past us. Johanna and Ra Chou, you come in at the corners. Tedeschi and I stay even. And pay attention to the baserunners, Mooshie."

Since these timed meetings were under the original twenty-first-century rules, the robot umpire intoned aloud the remaining seconds, getting down to four before they broke up.

"You girls enjoy your tea?" Ty sneered at Felton.

"We saved some biscuits for you. But can someone your age still chew?"

Cobb dug in with a feral snarl. He ran his left hand slightly up the barrel, faking a bunt. His eyes nodded as Ra Chou edged in another foot at third; Ty lashed the next pitch past the diving third sacker and down the line before easing into second.

Mick came up, expecting to be walked intentionally to set up a potential double play with the slow-footed Bench on deck. But this was another twenty-first-century rule that had outlawed intentional walks to speed up the game. Mantle dragged a bunt past the stumbling Mooshie. Second baseman Tedeschi underhanded the ball into the first-base stands, allowing Ty to score.

If radar guns (banned in 2048 for promoting individual hubris) had been allowed on Mooshie's pitches to close out the inning, they might've registered 110 mph. That'd be well below the fury of Mooshie's temper as she flung her glove into the dugout at the end of the inning.

"They're humiliating us." She kicked over the bat rack. "We look like a bunch of trees in uniforms."

Felton slid next to Mooshie, panting in the corner of the dugout. He'd witnessed some of her legendary explosions during the heated Yankees-Spiders rivalry. In a memorable three-game series at Municipal Stadium, she'd clawed out half the pitching rubber, heaved the second-base bag at a 'bot ump, and leaped into the stands to knock a can of pop from a relentlessly insulting fan. Broken bat racks were just a warm-up. They'd had two fist fights that included landing blows.

"Cut the shit, Moosh."

"What did you sssay?" she hissed.

Tony sighed as Chou swung feebly over a Ryan slider.

"You're attracting attention."

"Of course I am. I'm Mooshie Lopez."

"You're trying too hard."

Her nostrils flared. "Maybe a little. Maybe I don't much trust my supporting cast."

He whirled on his arthritic right hip as Donda made the second out on a weak grounder back to the mound. "Your supporting cast? You've got the best damn players in the damn world out there. We beat the damn Allahs with guns pointed at our heads. We were beaten and starved and you want to talk about humiliation, dear thing? Try being left behind in a POW camp."

"Oh let's not sob too hard, Major. Try being pushed under a train by your best friends."

"I won't judge them too harshly."

Mooshie's mouth twisted in a wry grin. "I never much liked you, Major. Then again, I don't much like anyone." She glanced down the bench at Cheng, his foot on the top step with a scholarly air. "They're gonna run us off the field because they're younger and quicker."

The catcher folded his thick arms. "They are, but we're smarter except for Ty and Mickey." He laughed at her snort. "Least of all Cobb. We changed our game in London. We bunted and we ran and we stole. Puppy got his ass reamed because they accused us of cheating by violating the Quran of all things. At one point they wouldn't let the series and the Caliphate Baseball Association continue, but we were only puppets anyway. Ain't we always. Doesn't matter if they're supposed to be our friends or enemies."

Mooshie grunted. "Too often. Always a 'they' somewhere," she muttered as Curly managed to foul off a rising Ryan fastball to stay alive at 0-2. "Son-of-a-bitch can pitch."

"Like his great-great-granddaddy."

Mooshie's eyes narrowed, skipping over the colorfully dressed Polish dancers in the stands celebrating the recent liberation of Warsaw. The ban on commemorating captive nations, ingrained through reigniting fears of cultural separatism, had been lifted that morning by order of the Granddaughter.

"Strange how all these players they found managed to inherit their grampy and granny's skills."

Felton joined her in a suspicious squint. "Since we haven't seen most of them before today, that's a good point. What are you thinking?"

She shrugged ever so slowly, staring at Cheng. "Could just be coincidence. Ty and Mick know talent." Mooshie met his stare. "No, they're not 'bots. Puppy wouldn't allow that. The boy has ethics. He wouldn't let them make a mockery of our game again. You were with him in London. You know what he's like."

"At heart a tough SOB like his father," Felton conceded. "Okay. But if they screwed with us again, Mooshie, and that's really an all-robot team…"

"Fat boy, I'll be the first one over the hedgerows at Grandma's Mansion. We will burn down the whole country this time, but it could just be us…" Her voice trailed off. Her fastball was flat and she had more curves in her butt than her breaking pitches.

"Could be that we're stinking up the place and got complacent because we don't think our shit smells. And who are these no-names?"

"Just good ballplayers with good genes who got something to prove," Mooshie said, pressing against the doubts.

"I thought we did, too." Felton groaned as Russell flailed at a third strike.

Lopez didn't move. "Maybe I could do a better job at holding runners on base."

"Also fielding your position, not overthrowing, not overswinging."

"Any fucking thing else?"

"That's it for now," Felton said, grinning.

"I'm glad I'm back to hating you."

"Same here. The sun was about to rise from the west. Hey, assholes." Felton froze, the team poised on the top steps. "We look like shit. This is a good team we're playing. I don't want anyone throwing the ball away again, me included. Stop acting like we got this won. And how about dropping all the crap about the battle of the centuries because right now we're just playing baseball however it takes to win. Let's play like we did in London except this time hopefully no one's gonna shoot us in the back. I'm open to any and all suggestions. Does our esteemed co-manager have anything to add?"

Cheng adjusted his cap. "Eloquently said."

For loitering in the dugout to discuss strategy, the twenty-first-century squad was assessed a penalty of adding one ball to the count on the next batter. They earned another punishment when the outfield clustered together in whispers, and a third when Tedeschi and Busco huddled by first base with grim nods.

Tatia Garvey began the bottom of the second ahead in the count 3-0. Mooshie fired two strikes before Garvey topped a high hopper to the right side. Mooshie intercepted the grounder and raced Garvey to the bag, knocking the runner over with a slap of the glove. Busco glared down from her skyscraper height at the slowly rising twentieth-century player.

"All right." Ty clapped his hands, surprising his team. "Those sons-of-bitches have just declared that the war is on. Hey, Lopez, you need a timeout to catch your breath?"

As Mantle exuberantly waved a towel, the team wheezed mockingly. Mooshie turned her back, moodily rubbing up the ball. She was winded. When she turned back, she clenched her fist at her groin with trademark disdain toward the dugout. The third-base ump issued a warning about inappropriate gestures.

By the fourth inning, Ryan and Mooshie had settled into what Sandra Douglas up in the rad booth behind home plate was calling "an old-time pitcher's duel for an

Old-Timers' Game." Testing the limits of opinion journalism, educator Estella Suarez provided what could best be described as sepia-color commentary. Instead of offering dubious expert opinions based on her many years teaching physical education at HS 310 in Chicago's South Side, the slender teacher, a volunteer in the Twentieth-Century Project, focused on the game's physical demands.

"Major Felton is stretching out both legs to unlimber himself from squatting in his catcher's stance. Humbert Smith neatly planted his back-right leg to make that acrobatic throw from deep in the hole, the designated area bordering third base and left field. Curly Russell hit the cut-off man shortstop Albert Cheng who acted as the gateway to the next throw home."

She left it up to Sandra to squeal about Ryan's curveball "dropping off the table like a sack of potatoes" and Mooshie's fastball "taking off like an F-62 strafing the Allahs."

Clinging to a 2-0 lead, Reynolds Ryan walked Cheng to lead off the top of the fifth. Ty and Mick led the hoots about the ump's poor judgment. The home-plate ump was programmed to ignore such complaints and to make perfect ball-and-strike decisions.

But a loud voice accusing the umpire of being a blind dishwasher provoked a slow walk toward the twentieth-century-team dugout.

"I must have the name of the player who used a pejorative describing my biological status," Arturo said evenly.

"We don't got anyone by that name," Mick said, a poster child for innocence.

"I will repeat and rephrase my question." The umpire's voice took on a faint sourness. "Insulting my biological status ain't allowed no way no how no never, you got it? Now whichever of you said that has got to step forward because that's another rule of this here America, Mr. Cobb and Mr. Mantle. Honesty. I'll give you ten seconds to own up."

Cobb held up a militant hand to the uneasy team. "Ten, nine, eight, seven..."

"Six, five, four..." Mantle said.

The team completed the count.

"In my America," Mickey said coldly, "we don't like snitches."

Arturo processed the quaintly tribal notion of "snitching" and assessed a two-ball penalty on the next hitter.

Amid the groans and hoots and towel-waving from the penalty, Ryan was a little thrown. Garvey played behind the eighty-three-year-old Cheng at first. On reserve pitcher Ted Towers's signal from the third-base coaching box, Albert darted for second, breaking Reynolds's concentration.

The curve hung over the inside part of the plate, thigh high. Mooshie launched the ball in a cloud-skirting arc deep into the right-field bleachers. Wrigley Field exploded at seeing legend come to life.

Mooshie put on a show. She bounded toward first, lunar-style, before touching the right corner of the first-base bag. Thousands of black transistor radios in the stands echoed with Sandra's explanation about the Lopez square. She neatly stepped on the upper-right side of the second-base bag, stomping the lower-left corner of the third-base bag, and then trotting sideways down the third-base line, right index finger jabbing at the jeering twentieth-century dugout as if counting victims.

With a three-foot vertical leap, the greatest switch-hitter of all time pounded the upper-left portion of home plate, thrust out her arms in a triumphant "V," and clenched her groin so fiercely you could feel the queasiness of the fans in the lower field seats.

Reynolds Ryan was rattled. He drank because he only did well when events went well. Life was a waiting happy hour. Cobb signaled him to throw at Busco, the next batter. Ryan fired three feet over her head into the screen. When she walked on four pitches, Ty brought in Ilsa Gibson, descendant of Bob Gibson.

Tall and broad like a statue with veins, Ilsa had probably smiled in her life, but that was really guesswork. She had two pitches, fastball and curve, and one expression, plain nasty. She finished her fluid warm-ups and nodded impatiently.

Her first pitch plunked Felton in the batting helmet. Hurrying from the on-deck circle, Ra Chou grabbed the major from behind before he could charge the mound. While the players spilled out of the dugouts, stopping just beyond the top steps, the umpires quickly convened, determining the pitch was deliberate and ordering an extra out for the twenty-first-century team.

Ilsa shrugged and struck out the side, discarding congratulatory handshakes with a brooding scowl in the far corner of the dugout.

"We gonna have some real fun?" Mick asked Ty who answered with a sneering nod.

Mantle dug into the right-handed batter's box, glancing back at Felton.

"You got something to say?" the catcher snarled. "I figure you're gonna bunt because you sure don't have the strength to hoist 'em anymore."

The Mick cackled and swung from his heels at Mooshie's dipsy-doodle curve. The infield inched back for the second pitch.

Dumb ducks. The Commerce Comet grinned. My old Yankees would go 153-1.

He dumped a little gem which rolled to a dead stop in no-man's land halfway up the third-base line. Mickey danced off first base, daring Mooshie to throw over. On the first pitch, Mickey raced toward second as Foxx slapped a neat single through the hole on the right side, completing the hit-and-run. Mick didn't stop until he barreled into Chou, knocking the third baseman and the ball into the umpire.

Vivian dusted itself off and determined Mantle's unsportsmanlike conduct engendered interference. Cobb ran onto the field as if on rails and pressed his nose into Vivian's mask.

"The prick was in the way."

"That is inappropriate language along with violating physical boundaries."

Cheng drifted over. "Cobb's right. Chou was in the way. Mantle made a clean slide. We won't accept any penalty."

Vivian was perplexed. "That is not up to you."

"If both teams disagree with an umpire's decision, then the decision is voided. That was adopted for the 2055 season. I was there. Were you?"

"That is not pertinent. But I will check." A few seconds later, Vivian nodded its head. The explanation was transmitted onto the scoreboard through the public-address system, via Ernie's somber tones, and onto the radcast.

Sandra Douglas decided to push her luck. She'd already questioned three pitch selections and a failed hit-and-run play without consequences.

"Now sports fans, just so y'all understand, this is unusual. Far as I know, the double-team agreement voiding out an ump's decision has not been done so far in the 2099 season. I can't say one hundred percent because that would be using the public airwaves to present a mistruth and that is very much against our cherished laws. But I'd bet the last of my yummy Cracker Jacks that's the case. What I want all of you to think about is why, in a close game, knotted here two apiece, the twenty-first-century ballclub would be oh so obliging."

"That is a good notion, Sandra," added Suarez. "Trying to understand why another sibling behaves as they do is the path to better relationships for all of us."

Douglas reset the game situation with Mantle on third and Foxx reaching second on the wild relay. Cheng ordered the infield to play in to cut off the go-ahead run. He lingered by the mound, ignoring Mooshie's glare to return to his position.

"Your stuff isn't moving, Mooshie."

She reddened under his steady stare. "I'm good. And don't look at Felton. We already agreed that when he thinks I'm done, I'm done. That's right, put your eyebrow back over your beady little eye."

Mooshie glanced at Felton who nodded encouragement. You used to breeze through the first six, seven innings, Mooshie thought. You had the only complete games in all of baseball in 2063. Now your lungs are trying to crawl out of your throat.

Wiggling her hips, Myrina Musial waited at home plate.

Concerned at the delay, and with the ump counting the seconds off in his ear, Felton rose out of his crouch. Mooshie's growl could be heard under the stands. She went into a windup which, according to Mooshie legend, she had perfected before crawling out of her mother's womb sassing about the colors in the nursery.

Musial went down on three strikes. Smith followed with a meager foul pop that landed not far off home plate. Carew tapped a weary grounder to Tedeschi. The infield patted Mooshie's butt on their way into the dugout amid crowd shouts of "Mooshie!" She mumbled about pissing, making it halfway down the corridor before Felton caught up and dragged her into a smelly electrical closet.

Mooshie stared in grim wonder. "Don't you tell anyone."

"Tell anyone what? That Mooshie Lopez can cry?" He cupped her shamed face. "Right. It's the stink in here."

She sniffed. "My wiring is especially sensitive."

"Glad you 'bots ain't perfect." Felton squeezed her hand. "You're allowed, Mooshie."

Mooshie processed the unfamiliar notion. "It's like in 2065. I was only forty-five, not an old creep like you. But the fastball was half a yard short and the breaking pitches spent too much time sitting still. They just weren't scared of me like they'd been. That's one of the reasons I spent so much time singing. My voice was still there. My voice is gorgeous," she said with sad urgency. "But the baseball skills were fading. I figured when they brought me back as a, a"—she swallowed—"as a non-organic life-form, I'd be Mooshie of young. Unhittable. But I'm not. My swing is still great, though. I slammed that mother, didn't I? You're supposed to agree wholeheartedly, asshole."

"Who has time?"

Mooshie tipped her head on Felton's shoulder, whispering, "You're what, seventy?"

"Fuck you and sixty-four. And how do I do it? Pure hate, Moosh. Pure unbridled hate and a need for revenge. I hated The Family, but never this country. We dreamed of coming back when we were in the camps. We dreamed of this moment, taking the field. So did you, but there's a big difference. You're still loved. We're just symbols. The real non-organic life-forms. But enough about me."

"I was waiting for you to get over yourself," she said with a shaky smile. "You better never say anything to Cheng. I'm still playing this regular season, whether I can pitch more than five innings or not."

"Because you still got the swing."

Mooshie poked her finger down Tony's throat until he gagged. "That's right."

Lopez settled into left with Curly Russell shifting over to center to replace Aaron White. Ted Towers took over on the mound and dueled Gibson for the next two innings. Each side had a couple runners who attempted stolen bases and tangled in a messy embrace of kicked shins and slapped gloves and an errant elbow or two.

D'rie, the ump at second, attempted to assess penalties, but every time Cheng and Cobb insisted there was no need. Even casual ground balls featured a squished foot, kicked ankle, and obscenities. The hooting, or bench-jockeying as Sandra tried explaining to her audience, intensified.

The concession stands closed after seven innings to encourage fans to stay in their seats. The bathrooms were empty. The last of the captive nations's choreographies passed with a Ghanian dance and a ninety-second Algerian mandole concert to close out the eighth. The fans had grown quieter, exhausted by the drama, transfixed by what would happen. The mute scoreboard offered no guesses.

The game remained knotted entering the top of the ninth. Hulking right-hander Nester Drysdale replaced the disappointed Gibson who'd retired eight batters on strikeouts and allowed three scratch hits.

Cheng had forgotten about his promise to relinquish shortstop to Ortiz. They would've needed at least three bullets to get him out of the lineup. He and Mooshie studied Drysdale's warm-ups.

"She'll give us a shave under the chin," Albert whispered.

Mooshie planted the bat on her right shoulder. "Then we take the close shave."

Albert smiled faintly. The handsome twentieth-century pitcher dipped slightly and fired the ball neck high, brushing Cheng back. Except Albert barely moved despite being hit in the head.

He remained out cold for a few seconds before lumbering to his feet and unsteadily walking to first. The crowd applauded with grudging respect. The twentieth-century team almost joined in, but Cobb stilled them with a savage buffet of curses from right field. A few mothers along the foul pole covered their children's ears.

Mooshie lashed the first pitch into the left-field corner. The still-woozy Cheng stumbled around second, barely crawling back ahead of Musial's throw.

With the slow-footed Felton at bat, the infield defense set up for the double-play. Felton fell behind 0-2 on a pair of crisp sliders. On the third pitch, he shocked everyone, including his baserunners, by squaring off and dumping a neat bunt halfway to the mound. Drysdale whirled and fired to third. Cheng extended his small arms well beyond comfort to grab the bag first. Foxx then threw to second where Mooshie took out Carew with a head-first slide. Felton wheezed into first.

Ty hurried in to join the conference on the mound. He looked at Drysdale's uneasy handsome features and swore. He had no other pitchers.

"You can bring Ilsa back in," Bench said firmly.

Drysdale oozed relief.

"How? I took her out."

"You get the one replacement rule. All we gotta do is tell the ump we've decided to use it."

"Damn crazy world."

"Lucky for us, huh?"

The sturdy catcher stepped in and sorted out the invocation of the replacement rule with the ump. Drysdale hurried off the mound and Gibson returned with a felonious glare at Cobb.

"Sue me. I made a mistake. Don't let anyone score."

Gibson's upper lip sneered north of her hairline.

Busco waved at three pitches, only one of them in the strike zone. Ra Chou quickly fell behind in the count, then managed a sharp grounder to third. Foxx hesitated a moment about throwing to home to force Cheng before he chose second base. Like an out-of-control jeep, Felton launched into Carew. Still bruised from Mooshie's slide, the second baseman bounded out of the way far enough to lose any steam on the relay to first.

Cheng, his head pounding, toppled home with the go-ahead run.

Gibson angrily kicked the mound a few times before throwing three climbing fastballs to Russell to end the inning.

Mooshie cornered Cheng at the far end of the dugout. "I'm pitching now."

Felton rescued the glassy Albert. "The hell you are. Ted's in a groove."

"That's right," mumbled Cheng.

"And Grandpa Albert's coming out, too."

"I am not," he protested feebly.

Felton frowned. "Yeah, you are. Bar'Nee, play short. And Mooshie—"

"I know what I said and it was all shit because I need to be the hero, Major," she rasped. "You can't let someone else close this out. This is my game. This is my moment and always has been right from the start. I don't care what I looked like before. I rested and I'm good enough for one more inning. Please, Tony. Give this to me."

Felton had lived a lifetime making decisions he'd regret.

Mooshie's return to the mound set off wild whoops from the crowd as if they'd been awakened with jabs from forty thousand needles. She started down 1-0 because of the penalty for delay of game.

The bottom of the twentieth-century batting order kicked off the last of the ninth. Humbert Smith worked the count to 3-2 before driving the ball into right-center. Donda left her feet to snare the ball, landing with a heavy thud.

Felton slowly walked the ball back to the mound. Mooshie silently held out her glove.

She grinned. "Even Mooshie Lopez needs fielders occasionally."

The major wasn't amused as he pressed the ball into her mitt. "Keep the fucking ball down."

She did just that to Carew, the next batter, who swung over a loopy curve for the second out. Ty Cobb slowly approached home plate as if it were a stage.

Wrigley Field fell silent.

Mooshie's first two deliveries missed inside and outside. Frustration was another unfamiliar concept that got the best of her. A fastball didn't sink and Cobb nearly singed her curls with a savage liner back through the box into center field.

Mickey waited in the on-deck circle until Arturo warned about a delay. Mooshie was already getting fidgety which devolved into outright impatience when Mantle played around with cleaning off his spikes and complaining about dirt on home. Arturo whisked it clean.

By the time Mantle finally dug in, Mooshie's lips had disappeared. On the first pitch, Cobb took off for second, distracting Lopez just enough. The fastball sat like a patient in the waiting room. Mickey rocketed a shot up the left-center field alley.

Allie "The Thief" Nissan, forced into center field on rickety knees with Mooshie's shift back to the mound, waved feebly as the ball one-hopped against the ivy. But from left field Curley Russell motored into a magical gear, snatching the ball bare-handed and hurling a throw to Ortiz on the edge of the infield.

Cobb tore around third base. Ortiz fired the relay throw. Felton steadied himself for the impact. As the major caught the throw, Ty dipped his shoulder. Arturo craned its head for a better look at the tangled bodies.

Felton held up the glove, the ball an ice cream cone.

26

The three shaggy-haired men in brown-fitted waistcoats beneath the *giornea*, or pleated overcoats, waved their puffy, mutton sleeves as they rocked Elvis Presley's *Love Me Tender*. In mid-croon, Joe Brancaccio, chef, singer, guitarist, owner, and the guiding spirit behind JB's Red Sauce Heaven, tossed a reassuring wink at Zelda as she hurried out of the bathroom toward the table secreted in the far corner of the crowded restaurant.

"Everything all right, dear?" Joan chomped on the *Danubio napoletano*, the *provolo* cheese crawling down the side of her mouth.

"You know how it is, that time of the month."

"I remember." The memory didn't please Joan. Nor did the Italian version of Presley's song. "Why must they do this?"

"They like music."

"But it's foreign."

"Italian."

"And those, those hideous costumes."

"They're from the Renaissance era," Zelda explained, eager for any excuse to stall. "Joe Brancaccio has wanted to put together an Italian Presley cover band for a while. He's kind of an Elvis nut."

"That sort of mindless adulation is returning, and it is not healthy." Joan peered disdainfully at Brancaccio as he adjusted the gold-rimmed glasses over his changeably handsome face and launched into an exuberant *Hound Dog* that shook the floor.

"Try some of the *impepata di cozze*." Zelda popped a mussel into her mouth with loud yummy noises which pleased Brancaccio ten feet away, perpetually alert for comments about his food.

"Too spicy. Garlic and I are not well acquainted." Joan frowned, patiently waiting for Zelda to scarf down the rest of the appetizer before plunging into the remains of the *Danubio napoletano*.

Zelda doused her nerves with a long sip of Tulsa Pinot Grigio. Under Joan's steady stare, Zelda finally handed over the script, slowly releasing the edges as if clinging to the side of a building.

With a rapturous sigh, Joan stroked the red cover. "I will read it this evening."

"How about now?"

"Now? Here?"

"Sure. We got music and all the Neapolitan food and wine you'll ever want. What better place?"

Joan tittered at Zelda's always amusing ways. "I require concentration."

"And I'd like to be here when you read it." Zelda would've preferred orbiting around Mars on a sled.

Joan assessed Zelda before cracking a wide smile. "I understand. That was rude. This is your pride and joy."

"Please, I'm giving you the play a few days before rehearsal starts. I want to thank you again for your faith and confidence and support—"

"Yes, yes." Joan waved her off. "What matters is the play is done."

Zelda swallowed with a nod.

"Are you going to sit there and stare as I read?"

"Now that'd be rude." Zelda squeaked out a nervous laugh.

"I wouldn't blame you. But it's difficult enough—" Joan sneered at the band. Joe blew her a kiss.

While Joan read the script, Zelda hid in the cramped cubicle behind the kitchen. On the break, Joe set up a small table with red-striped cloth and dramatically unfurled a napkin into Zelda's lap. With another flourish, he set down a plate of *spaghetti alla nerano*. He wouldn't stir until she dug in. Once Zelda approved, Joe relaxed and poured some red wine.

"You like the music?"

"S'brilliant."

"Truly?"

"Yes, yes. "

"What else?" He puffed. "And the name of my group?"

"'Grazi Elvis' is genius."

"An extraordinary idea to entertain my guests during meals, or don't you think so?"

"Out-of-sight enjoyable."

He pulled a doubtful face. "Which is why with the music of The King and my genius and food that God would eat, you hide in my kitchen like a sad mouse."

"I got pasta right here."

Joe slowly exhaled disapproval. "You've been coming here ever since you were a know-nothing smart-ass kid who thought toast was a meal. Don't I know when you lie?"

She shrugged.

"When maybe you're afraid?"

She bit her lower lip.

"It's about your friend who hates my music and won't touch my mussels."

"That's the one."

"You figure if you upset her in my restaurant, she won't cause a scene."

"Oh, she'll cause a scene. But not as much as she'd like. Which would be choking me and stomping on my face and ending my would-be career."

Joe frowned. "That bad?"

"That bad, Joe. It's gonna be that bad."

Joe serenaded Zelda with an a cappella rendition of *Love Me Tender*, waiting for appropriate applause before leaving. Half an hour. An hour. Two *sfogliatellas*. Knowing the turmoil any more espresso would wreak on her bladder, Zelda rose with the joy of the condemned to head back into the dining room.

A rattling of pots and pans, brusque questions, and a stomping best reserved for an armadillo announced Joan. They stood there like old-style gunslingers, Joan clutching the script, Zelda her espresso cup.

Joan wearily dragged over a stool and stared at the floor. "What have I ever done to deserve this, Zelda?"

"Nothing, Joan. I don't know where to begin apologizing…"

"Oh please," she rasped. "Swallow down that faux innocence. You knew damn well what you were doing. You're the worst sort of manipulator because you won't admit to your craven base instincts, hiding behind that little, confused, eternally stumbling persona instead of having the guts to be what you are."

Zelda couldn't remember when someone had nailed her so completely.

Joan snorted. "If you were me and had success and vision in your life, respect and trust, if you can begin to comprehend such an existence, what would you do?"

"I guess report me to the Committee."

Joan laughed metallically. "Report you? For precisely what?"

Zelda frowned. "For deceiving you."

"Deceiving me. Deceiving me. I was the fool. As an experienced producer, I should have followed protocol and insisted on reading the entire play instead of jeopardizing my reputation—my reputation on your word—which one works very hard to gain and which can be so easily lost. Yes, I can report you to the Committee. Prove deception up and down the line, ticking off every conceivable box. Deceiving the Committee. The actors." She suddenly stopped. "I assume your friend Beth was a conspirator?"

"No. She knew nothing. No one else ever read this."

Joan snickered skeptically. "I will be suspended. You will be barred from so much as writing out a grocery list. Not even a one syllable word. Forbidden."

Zelda blinked back tears.

"That should be done. I must adhere to my principles of ethics and decency, our nation's principles, which you clearly don't grasp…"

"All right. I fucked up. Big time. Do what you need to do."

"Three days before rehearsal. Five weeks before opening night," Joan muttered darkly.

"Put it all on me. Say whatever you want."

"The martyr."

Zelda stretched out her arms.

"Shame for us. Our families. Your husband will be impacted. Your child, too. Ah, I see you didn't quite consider that. A DV is almost guaranteed. Well, Zelda considering others is most assuredly a unique event as I can attest with the internal bleeding of my very soul."

Joan drained the wine. She slammed the bottle onto the table, making the spoon jump. "Except for one little thing."

"Shit, there's more?"

"Yes." Joan paused. "The play is brilliant."

"What."

"Oh don't give me that little innocent 'what' crap. Your play is brilliant. The characters leap off the page. They are warm and poignant and brave and smart. They love and lose and find a path. The story, the forbidden, seditious story, tore at my heart. At the end of my second reading, you had changed my mind, Zelda Jones. You reached your hand down my throat and ripped up my heart and tore at my mind. You have written something the vast preponderance of playwrights throughout history merely dreamed of achieving. A cathartic transformative journey that would rock this narcoleptic country onto their heels. This play is why I do theater. For this moment. This moment, this opportunity, for which I have long dreamed. But you, Zelda Jones, have wrapped my lifelong dream in a shit sandwich."

Joan steadied herself against the dangling salamis.

"Isn't everything? Isn't everything? Otherwise dreams would be easy!" she shouted, freeze-framing the kitchen. "This work must be seen and must be heard and must be experienced. The show must go on."

Zelda sagged onto the tiny chair. Joan's mouth dropped.

"Grandma's bra straps. You never thought it would be performed, did you?"

She shook her head. "I wrote it because I had to get it out. It's what happened to me. Having Diego. Hiding…I didn't think anyone would let this go on stage."

Joan squeezed her shoulder. "I don't feel that is another manipulation. Or is it?"

"This time I'm not lying. I promise."

Joan grumbled about the value of Zelda's promises.

"But how the hell are we going to pull this off?"

Joan smiled. "It's a good thing you have me."

• • • •

HEDDA SIPPED THE last of the tybo-turmeric tea, her heavy head grinding into her collarbones. Eight telly conferences in one day. They were all exhausting but worth it she admitted, shaking the tea leaves into the trash can beneath the desk.

Her new educational program, *What Do You Think Happened*, was the only thing that made sense. Sanitized books, falsehoods wrapped around truths around self-serving propaganda couldn't, she'd repeated until her throat was hoarse, be a curriculum. It's all guesswork, the whole damn century. Even the specific dates of resonance, November 11th, December 7th, July 20th, April 4th, on and on, were suspect because we don't know what really happened.

Falsehoods wrapped around truths around self-serving propaganda. We don't know why and we can't keep telling our children we do.

Let them start deciding.

What Do You Think Happened was formally adopted by the various nationwide committees of the Twentieth-Century Project. Children would have to figure out what the heck the truth was. Bottom up, ground zero, no right or wrong except if they parrot the nonsensical rubbish we've all been fed.

Then do we build new truths out of guesswork? No. We have baseball dates. Baseball facts. Pop culture. We used what happened in the unimportant as a way of getting to the important. A Willie Mays home run and a Hula-Hoop. Except the banal, or seemingly banal, might be the most important. It's us with our guard down.

Then they'd have to figure out the rubbish they'd been fed about the nineteenth century. The eighteenth century.

If she weren't so utterly exhausted, Hedda would drop by Elias's. Maybe she still would. Only she worried they'd fight about everything else.

Screw it, she thought. Early in their relationship, he'd dropped in unannounced as she sat all cozy in her pajamas watching a Laurel and Hardy movie. That'd worked out well. Yes it had, Hedda reminded herself with a saucy smile. Sometimes you're too much. Relax. Give the guy some slack.

She'd buy a six-pack of Al's Amber Ale on the way over.

Humming a Pink Floyd song, the teacher popped into the bathroom and rinsed her well-chipped white porcelain mug. When she turned off the water, she heard the sound.

Hedda hurried back into her office holding the dripping cup. Startled, the pale fore-head above the black mask furrowed. The spring breeze rustled the beige curtains. Hedda's eyes traveled to the baseball in the cupped hand.

"What do you think you're doing?"

The slender figure whirled toward the open window.

"Hey!" Hedda shouted in such a commanding way the burglar looked back. "Put that down!" Hedda stormed across the room, hand extended. "That's Babe Ruth's 714th home-run ball."

A malicious smile stretched the mask.

Hedda stopped a few feet away. "That ball belongs to The Family and has been en-trusted to my care. Tomorrow morning it goes on display in our school's lobby. Everyone gets to look at it. Touch it. Be connected. You're more than welcome to come by and I'll consider this an unfortunate lapse of judgment. Come on, don't be foolish. I'm a teacher. I understand these things."

Hedda placed her mug on the table and scribbled out the address for MS 21, calmly laying it on the desk as if the ridiculous incident was settled.

With a nasty laugh, the burglar knelt onto the windowsill, reaching for the fire es-cape. Hedda leaped onto the thief's back, arms around the throat. With a wrench of a hip, the lithe figure flung Hedda loose. She couldn't find her balance and continued stumbling backward like a mechanical doll into the crowded bookcase. As the heavy shelves and av-alanche of books crashed, Hedda cried out again for the thief to stop as the reinforced wooden point of the top shelf burrowed between her eyes.

27

There was barely room to walk. As was the DV custom for grief, fellow tenants had dropped off food, beverages, alcohol. Good luck charms. An extra chair for visitors. Some pleasant-sounding albums. A basketball, a football. Five frisbees. Parcheesi. Flowers, three plants including a four-foot-high cactus named Esteban which claimed the coffee ta-ble along with Dakota, a calico cat loaned by Mr. Ethanio from upstairs.

Cheng slipped inside with a brief apology, tossing half a dozen meatball subs on the cluttered kitchen table. He shrugged off Kenuda's surprised glance and sat on the window ledge with a bottle of Kentucky cognac between his legs. After more silence, he slid a Miles Davis album onto the turntable. Puppy started protesting at the propriety of music, but Kenuda dully waved him off. Two trains could crash through the walls and his response would be "so what?"

"Any updates?" Cheng asked.

Dr. Alain, a brand-new, hot-off-the-assembly-line 'bot doctor specially programmed for empathy, had explained that the likelihood of Hedda regaining consciousness was approximately 1.2 percent and regaining full brain function was about 0.05 percent.

"Same," Puppy answered.

His eyes mere placeholders after six hours of watching Hedda breathe in an oxygenized tent, Elias nibbled on a cracker, assiduously brushing off the crumbs from his wrinkled pants before picking up another one from the floor. He did this twice. With a stern look, Cheng warned Puppy to let it be and answered the doorbell.

Lieutenant Layon Y'or made a show of respectfully removing his brown hat.

"Took you long enough," Cheng growled.

With a deep sigh, the detective slid past and paused before Kenuda who was holding a cracker up to the light, wondering about the rye seeds.

"Cousin Kenuda—"

"I'm not a fucking Cousin anymore. And what the hell are you doing in my house again?"

"I've never been here before, sir. That apartment was in Riverdale."

With a fragmented apology, Y'or admitted this was his first attempted-murder investigation. He paced between the boxes of groceries and a paddleball set, returning to Kenuda as if he'd just walked in.

"Mr. Kenuda, I am sorry about the assault on your fiancé."

"That engagement was canceled given that I'm DV scum."

Puppy tried calming Elias and got an elbow for the attempt.

"May I ask you some questions, sir?"

"Isn't that why you're here?" Cheng snapped.

Y'or cleared his throat and loosened his red tie. "When was the last time you saw Hedda Kleinz?"

"Why?"

"Elias, it's easier if you just answer," Puppy scolded.

"Why?"

"They had a big fight." Cheng walked over with a bottle of cognac. "They sort of broke up and yes I heard because the walls are about as thick as the skin on my hand. I'm embarrassed to have originally put up such shit buildings. And no, he hasn't seen her for a couple weeks. He's been busy assisting me like tonight, holding a clinic about the meaning of signs in baseball and how it's about privacy, not deception."

Kenuda erupted like a volcano. "Why is that explanation even necessary? Am I a suspect?"

"No," Y'or said firmly.

"That's his job. Let him do his job if he can." Cheng resumed his spot on the windowsill. "Any suspects, Sherlock Holmes?"

Y'or planted his feet. "Not yet. Our officers are still combing the crime scene."

"You have any idea what this was about?" Puppy asked.

"There was clearly a struggle…" The Brown Hat waited for Elias to finish groaning. "The bookcase fell onto Ms. Kleinz." He hurried over Kenuda's moan. "We assume this was a robbery attempt. The Babe Ruth ball of which Ms. Kleinz had custody is missing."

Puppy felt sick.

"From what we can gather, nothing else is missing. Ms. Kleinz was still wearing jewelry"—he paused for Kenuda's weak sigh—"and her Lifecard was in her wallet."

"Someone just scrambled up the fire escape into Hedda's office?" Elias asked.

"All the teachers of the Twentieth-Century Project"—he glanced at his notes—"who are Temporary Custodians of the Memories of the Hall of Fame memorabilia have been regularly featured on *Wake Up, My Darlings*. Ms. Kleinz appeared with the Granddaughter yesterday morning."

"But they go after Hedda? Hedda? Hedda?" Elias repeated dully.

"This is the third such robbery in the past two days," Y'or said, regretting the foolishly reassuring tone. "Two other custodial-care Hall of Fame exhibits were stolen. At a Philadelphia school, scorecards from the Tom Meany collection on the Negro, apologies for the word, Leagues and, in Nashville, the baseball shoes of a Phil Rizzuto."

Puppy slowly sat down. "Is there a connection?"

Y'or shrugged. "We don't know yet."

"You must have an idea," Cheng snapped.

"We and the Nashville and Philadelphia police forces are working on it."

Cheng shrewdly eyed the Brown Hat. "Any motives?"

"We don't know yet, Mr. Cheng. Intended for a private collection, for sale in the underground, or pure malevolence. Right now there are no witnesses. No suspects. That'll change. Whether these are individual acts or organized will become clearer in time."

"Hedda might die because of a baseball?" Elias repeated several times before overturning the coffee table and sending Dakota the cat screeching onto the turntable.

• • • •

WHEN PUPPY FINALLY stumbled out of Kenuda's apartment just ahead of the sun, he was greeted by a ridge of orange bows glowing atop a mailbox across the street.

No. He wasn't surprised.

Clary soundlessly fell to the ground, flanked by a squad of abruptly visible BTs. She didn't dismiss the guards, hold out her arms, or even smile.

"Granddaughter."

"Commissioner. Quite a night."

"Looks like it hasn't ended yet."

Clary studied him. He almost felt her stare, as if it had fingers.

"Hedda will not survive."

He tensed. "How do you know?"

"It is what the doctors say. The percentages are minute."

"There's always hope."

"Not always."

"That's all the empathy you can muster for your teacher?"

"She was a beloved teacher to many."

"Was Kenuda a beloved father to many as well?"

"Do not try those emotionally manipulative tricks, my Puppy. They serve no purpose."

"Oh yes, they do."

Clary shook her head several times until her face softened. "It is very sad. Ms. Kleinz was a very nice person." Her lower lip trembled ever so slightly. "What will you do about this?"

"What the hell do you mean?"

She stared. "This was not an isolated incident."

"I know. The Brown Hat told us about the robberies in Nashville and Philadelphia…"

"And Anaheim, Bismarck, Toledo, and El Paso. All stealing a Hall of Fame exhibit from a Twentieth-Century-Project teacher."

He felt queasy.

"You must stop it," Clary said firmly.

"Back up. How is this my responsibility?"

"It is the enthusiasm gone wild."

"Oh come on—"

"Do not dismiss me. Do, not, dismiss, me. You made the souvenirs valuable. You tempted people."

"There was an underground market for baseball memorabilia long before this."

"And it was forbidden for a very smart reason. It places objects over people. Material goods permeated with special appeal." Clary's eyes blazed as she gathered steam. "Everything you wanted I granted, Puppy. I fought the Cousins and I fought Felice and look what happened."

"Stop saying that. There's no proof these thieves are baseball fans."

"Who else? No one steals from the Football Hall of Fame. Or the Basketball Hall of Fame. Do you know they keep the doors unlocked? Two thefts in twenty-two years. A helmet of Jimmy Brown who carried the ball as a fullback and De'Nise Alton's wristband when she scored 132 basketball points. Yet with baseball, it all turns bad. Because you encourage it."

"The hell I did."

"This is on you, Puppy. You insisted on autographs. How soon before they are sold in the underground? How soon before they are stolen? Do not quote the laws against such a thing because there are laws against a thief killing a young teacher in the commission of a robbery."

He flinched. "We're talking about a few bad people."

"Are we? The discord in the ballparks increases. The rudeness to other teams transfers to rudeness to the fans of other teams. They are agitated by the partisan radcasts. There is fighting every day at ballparks."

Clary expelled a holographic chart of recent assaults at the major league stadiums.

He dully studied the numbers, shaken. "Why haven't I seen that?"

"You did, Puppy. You ignored. So I stopped." Clary's forehead pulsed. "I made a mistake granting you such flexibility."

"It's a little late."

"Oh no it is not."

Puppy sneered. "You want me to tell the fans not to boo?"

"Correct."

He went up on his toes. "How about cheering?"

"Polite applause is acceptable. We will return to the game pre-Commissioner Puppy. There will be no team merchandise sold in the stadiums. No autographs. No giveaway promotions. They, too, will become overly valued memorabilia. And the local radcasts must be cut back. The laws against opinion journalism will be upheld. If the passions decrease, we will revisit this for the 2100 season. But we feel there was too much, too soon."

Puppy leaned forward. "We?"

"I am the only 'we' you must pay attention to."

"What about Felice?"

Her eyes narrowed. "You do not understand, Puppy. I wanted to help you."

"I became Commissioner because you wanted me to help you."

"And you have," she said brightly. "You have. I feel less alone. But I cannot spend my time on this anymore." Clary stamped her right foot and the sidewalk shook. "There are more important issues which I must focus upon. Far more important. Baseball will get in the way."

"Why?"

"You will have to trust me." She waited. "Do you not trust me?"

"Should I?"

"As much as I trust you."

"There we go."

Clary stamped again, cracking the sidewalk and tipping the mailbox over. "You will do what I say, Puppy Nedick."

He squared his shoulders. "I don't know if I can, Clary Santiago."

They exchanged long looks.

"Then I do not know if you can remain, Commissioner."

His breath was short. "You're firing me?"

"I hope not. But you must clean your house. If you do, I will continue supporting you. Like sharing information about Annette."

Five Black Tops cordoned off the red-faced Puppy as a 'copter's beam encircled Clary and she soared upward.

28

The campfire flickered across Annette's wan expression, heightening her pastiness. Despite Herbert's regular draining of her clogged sinuses, a crust of glue-like snot obscured her right nostril. She could only imagine what her underarms smelled like. She only half cared.

Some animal noise which no longer frightened her pierced the night from the Cantabrian Mountains in northern Spain—Green Spain. Herbert had droned on with encyclopedic precision yesterday, providing minute descriptions of the native trees such as beeches and oaks. Somewhere near the Atlantic. Portugal. France. Herbert suggested with that robotic smugness that he had some idea where they were going but wasn't entirely sure. The unlinked messages had stopped recently.

If her head didn't ache so much, she would've shoved the eucalyptus up Herbert's nose, but that was the only relief for the congestion.

"Sleep," Herbert repeated yet again. "It will help heal."

"I'd prefer a hot shower."

Herbert raised its eyebrow at the persistent human need to wish for something that was momentarily impossible. But their wish pursuits motivated them. Even at their death, as Father Dempsey explained, there is the need for more. An afterlife. A Godhead. Reuniting with a loved one.

Annette returned Herbert's piercing stare. Sometimes she spent hours doing this. Well, ten minutes. She was getting bored with saving the world. It just didn't have the right rewards.

"Do you dream?" she asked.

Herbert arched its eyebrow. "In what sense?"

"I don't know. In the sense of being asleep and having dreams."

"I do not sleep in the way you do."

"But you sleep. I've watched you."

Herbert smiled faintly. "Why?"

"Curiosity. Boredom. Agony from the sinusitis." Annette waved off another quick offer of eucalyptus. "You must experience something since you are sort of like us."

"Pretending."

"I didn't mean to insult you."

"Nor did I interpret it as such. I am simply understanding."

"Yes. Pretending to be human." Annette shooed away some crawly thing. Herbert had lectured her on the wanton destruction of ants the other day, the bio-environmental imperative, and respect for all life-forms. She told him an ant had almost crawled up her twat so shut up. Sometimes she wished he took some offense.

"We pause for rejuvenation." Herbert's thin lips disappeared in thought about how to present this for human comprehension. Her aptitude was insightful, but uncertain and often unexpected. "There is a process…"

Annette flared at this hesitation. "Just say it and my puny little brain will try to follow along."

Herbert nodded. "The replicated emotions are re-sorted and reconfigured according to specific challenges within the previous twenty-four hours. If there have been any failures of empathetic communication and understanding, the…" The 'bot paused momentarily for the explicable words. "The programming is updated."

"So if you pissed someone off, you figure out a way not to do it again."

Herbert arched an eyebrow at her understanding. "Correct. I seem to do that with you often, ranging from three to eleven times within the previous twenty-four-hour period."

Annette sighed. "It's not your fault. I get grumpy. I can be a pain. An emotional pain, not a physical pain. I'm not always the easiest person to get along with. Ask my husband." Her throat tightened at the thought of Puppy. "I've been called exasperating, abrasive, and obnoxious. If you want to disagree, feel free to stop me at any time."

Herbert shook its head.

She burst out laughing, confusing Herbert, which had anticipated further annoyance. "What do I do the most to piss you off?"

Herbert frowned in thought.

"Don't you have all the faults neatly labeled?"

"Correct. Yet I have not organized them according to the concept of 'pissed off.' However, I see that pisses you off."

"A little."

"Your insistence on beginning most conversations in an adversarial fashion would, since I am prompted, rank the highest. This often precludes the possibility of orderly conversation and communication by converting the subject into one of anger and defensiveness."

Annette leaned her head against the tree. "You have that down right."

"Of course."

She rolled her eyes. "I've always had an inferiority complex which might be hard to believe given that I'm beautiful when bathed and not reeking of sweat and eucalyptus and snot. I'm also very creative and I have my own unique way of looking at the world. Despite all those skills, I'm overly sensitive and react emotionally."

"Have you considered a nightly period of re-sorting and reconfiguring as a method of addressing these failings?"

Annette started crying. Herbert tried apologizing, but she shut him down, then abruptly started laughing. After a few moments of rolling in the grass, because what did it matter if her filthy clothes were stained with dirt, she kissed Herbert on its head.

"That's about the best advice I've gotten since Tabitha DeMarco taught me to tongue kiss when I was eleven."

"I am glad I was of assistance, Annette."

As Annette searched the backpack for the remains of the disgusting sandwich she'd swiped from a food counter near the border, she heard whooshing. She'd heard that sound before.

Glints of air-propelled guns dotted the surrounding trees.

Annette dug her back foot in for balance, hands fisted by her chest. Eight bearded nuns advanced, guns aimed.

Herbert spread its hands, palms up.

• • • •

THE SPRAWLING CAMP of prefab units, smoldering campfires, and wet clothes flapping on metal clotheslines spanned a large clearing and disappeared into a cave. It was as if they'd come upon a makeshift forest retreat with vacationers settling in for a summer stay. More bearded nuns, only distinguishable by the colors of their beards, carelessly went about carrying heavy, long containers, briskly nailing sliced trees together, braiding ropes, or simply milling about, gabbing in a guttural language Annette vaguely recognized.

There was almost validity in being a prisoner again, as if that were a permanent part of her life. Go free, get caught, escape, get caught, escape. She tried attaching a tune to these disjointed lyrics, humming loudly.

Annette tried making conversation, explaining in hesitant English that she had been a pretend nun and knew all about the wardrobe and how to wear the hat so it didn't press down too heavily on your hair. They mostly ignored her except to provide an endless array of flavorful greens and thick bread so tasty she didn't want to give them the satisfaction of her swallowing.

No one bothered her about wandering around until she peeked over the cliff where an ugly nun, and that would sure be a tight contest with this crowd, prodded her butt with the end of a rifle to prompt her to return to camp. She fumed on a log for a while, considering making a parachute to float down and away, but to where, until Herbert approached with a bearded middle-aged man in a black habit and an amused smile suggesting Annette wasn't his first prisoner and he much enjoyed the whole process.

"I hope we haven't kept you waiting, Ms. Ramos."

"Not a problem. My next appointment isn't until tomorrow."

The man laughed heartily and introduced himself as Morrie Schorr. "Herbert has provided all the necessary supporting documentation."

"As much as has been revealed," the 'bot said with some disappointment.

"I think that's as much as you'll ever get. We'll ever get. But you're here, safe and sound." He frowned. "Ms. Ramos, you seem greatly disturbed."

"No, no. I like being marched through the forest at the point of a gun."

"It was a precaution. We don't get many visitors because the world pretty much knows to leave us alone. When someone doesn't, it creates a little curiosity. You weren't mistreated, were you? You were fed, given liquids, a clean toilet, freedom—as much as there is."

"I'm going to recommend your lodging to all my friends."

"We'd prefer that you not." Morrie chuckled. He and Annette exchanged stares. "I take it you'd like more information?"

"Nah. Just give me a log and I'm good." Annette defiantly slid down, her back against the tree stump, knees curled up.

Herbert's expression tried to convey something of an apology, but Morrie just laughed. "We are the, well, would you like our official title or just a headline?"

Annette tapped an imaginary watch.

"We are the Servants."

"Of?"

"I can't really talk specifics. Even that word is dangerous. You understand that should you be captured and tortured, that information would be dangerous if in the wrong hands and minds."

"That's all right. Heard that line before. I've been captured. I've been a prisoner of the Miners and Allahs and I've had my fingernails pulled out. It's only because I have such healthy genes that they grew back again." She held up her left hand, allowing Morrie a quick look. "Then I was a prisoner of my own American Army and now here I am with bearded nuns. I mean come on already. Bearded nuns? So don't bullshit me and say I'm not a prisoner right now."

Herbert apologized again with a slight shrug.

"You're partially correct, Ms. Ramos. You're somewhat of a prisoner in the sense that you're not free to just walk off. We're here to escort you to the borders of our territory to your next phase."

"What do you mean by your territory?"

"Mr. Schorr has an element of autonomy," Herbert said carefully.

"Meaning the Allahs couldn't just rumble into their cave and steal your laundry?"

"No, they cannot."

"Really."

"Nor can the American Army. Nor any military wings of any other country," Schorr said with pride.

"What would happen if they did?"

"There would be consequences."

"Like what? They'd have to grow a beard and wear a coif? Bet you didn't believe I knew that word."

Schorr smiled. "It'd be more pronounced than that. We don't want that. They don't want that."

"And they are?"

Morrie sighed. The robot had warned him of the woman's abrasive persistence. "Pretty much everyone else but us. I'm sorry, Ms. Ramos. More than that I can't say. Only that you are very safe with us. Please try to trust me. And if that's understandably impossible, trust Herbert."

"I do trust Herbert," she snapped.

"Good. Tonight is Friday and we usually have festivities. Dinner, wine, dancing. You're welcome to join us."

Like an irritated infant, Annette dozed for most of the day, waking to eat and pee. When she finally stayed awake by the sheltered bedding near the mouth of the cave, the sun was impatiently hurrying off. It took a few bleary blinks to realize that the black-costumed men with open-necked white shirts and tall black hats were the nuns. They brushed past, solemnly setting a long table covered by a gold-trimmed tablecloth laden with gleaming, blue-trimmed dishes, sparkling cutlery, and wine glasses. The nuns and their guests sat on twenty high-backed chairs.

Two yellowish braided breads lay side by side. Annette went to slice off a hunk. Morrie gently slapped away her hand.

"You can't eat yet," he said firmly.

"Sorry."

He grunted doubt about her capacity for regret and motioned toward the far end of the table where she sat next to Herbert. Morrie took his place at the head of the table.

"What's going on?" she whispered.

"There is a ceremony. I am not certain of its origin or purpose."

Annette folded her hands. She and Herbert would've gotten more attention if they were saltshakers. A man lit two candles and then briefly covered his eyes. Everyone murmured in that strange language. Voices erupted, sounding dangerously like Arabic, as the table looked up, searching for something they knew they couldn't see.

Morrie raised a silver wine goblet with Allah-like writing, chanting foreign words. *Baruch. Melech.* He took a sip, but no one else did. By now, Annette knew better. A daz-

278 | GARY MORGENSTEIN

zling white cloth covered the bread. Although no one had really done anything, they all sterilized their hands in water, chanting something like *Lechem Min.*

There were many "ah-mains."

Morrie cut pieces off one of the breads which were passed down to her and Herbert. The 'bot munched and expressed satisfaction.

So did Annette. "What is this?"

"Challah." Morrie accentuated the "ch" sound.

"Hallah."

"Challah," he corrected with a wry smile as the table chuckled.

"Sorry." Annette grinned back. "I never had this before."

The men smiled. Schorr waited for the chicken soup and noodles to be served.

"This is the Sabbath, Annette." Morrie waited for some understanding. "The Jewish Sabbath. Friday night."

"Oh. You're Jews. I thought you were some kind of strange nuns."

"Just for the rest of the week." Schorr scolded his friends to lower their laughter. "As an American, I don't think you're familiar with our customs or religion."

"I don't know much about Jews." Annette placed an uncommon brake on continuing on about how the Jews and Allahs started the war. It would've been rude considering the soup and all the food coming her way. "Though I have met other Jewish nuns."

Morrie's face tightened slightly. "Have you?"

As the soup bowls were removed, cries of *Lahayim*, or something close, ripped around the table. It was some kind of excuse for more wine; Annette happily joined in.

"I came here, at least most of the way from London, with Father Dempsey. He's a priest. Was..." She tossed a sad look at Herbert who lowered its eyes. "He gave me lessons about Jesus so I'm not totally ignorant about religion. Which I can see surprises everyone."

The man to her left refilled her glass with a pitying look.

"But anyway," she said between sips. "On our way here, to wherever we're going, don't worry, I'm not asking, a lot of the nuns and priests who helped us had Jewish names. They didn't have beards. Okay, what's so funny, guys?"

"We're enjoying your tolerance, Annette. Acceptance."

"My information says you Servants were categorized as factually suspect rumors," Herbert said.

"As you can see, not entirely." Schorr held up his palms.

"What information's that?" Annette asked, sighing at their bland stares. "Okay, guess it's more under the headline of 'don't tell her in case she has her fingernails plucked out.'"

Morrie glanced around the room, waiting for the silent nods. "It's difficult to obey all the mitzvahs, commandments, especially under these circumstances. God doesn't easily give a pass. That is the whole point of obeying His law. Difficulty shouldn't be a bar. But we are Jews. As far as we know, we're among the last to observe. We weren't raised as such, but we volunteered to keep this alive."

"Among other tasks?" Herbert asked.

"Yes, Herbert. But we don't want to risk your wiring being ripped out of your chest either." Schorr explained to Annette that she was now eating chicken with farfel and potato kugel. "Each Friday, we ask God to forgive us for failing to follow the Torah as much as we should."

"He should understand, with you living in a cave on a mountain," Annette said between bites of challah.

Morrie smiled wistfully. "A cave, a mountain, they're all His creation, Annette. If He gave us this, then it is part of His world, and we must respect it. As I said, there are no excuses. We try our best, both to obey the traditions and survive. The Torah is the law given to our people by God. As long as we are alive, we will follow the law."

"You are the rabbi?" Herbert asked.

Schorr shook his head. "I was an officer in the Mossad. Yahudi over there"—he gestured toward a sad man with thick glasses—"he is a rabbi, more a dry cleaner by trade, but he doesn't feel himself worthy to conduct the Sabbath. None of us are truly worthy. I, least of all, with the blood I have spilled defending my country. My faith."

"Wouldn't that make you the most worthy?" Annette asked.

Schorr sighed wearily. "I, we, think of our duty, the promise we made, the job we have. As I said, we do the best we can. For the memory of our parents, our grandparents."

"That's what we're taught in America, too. Respecting our loved ones."

Morrie's lips pursed. "Yes. Your loved ones, Annette. Then there were my people, the ones you did not care about…"

A wiry man tugged at Morrie's sleeve; this clearly had happened with other guests.

Schorr's expression brightened. "But again. Good *Shabbos* to all."

The dancing threatened to shake loose the cliff. The increasingly drunken men formed circles and semicircles and tossed each other around like black burlap bags. Annette stayed off to the side until her fifth glass of wine and then joined in. There was a brief exchange about dancing with a woman which the fresh pitchers of wine quickly cleared up.

Annette took a dessert break around the side of the cave, stuffing down a moist pastry called roo-gula or something. Her tongue was as thick as the chunky challah.

Herbert sat quietly in the dark. She wasn't sure if it was recharging or robot sleeping. More wine than she could remember did away with any hesitation.

She squatted. "Too much dancing, huh?"

"I did not dance."

"I kind of guessed."

"Then why would you ask?"

"Making conversation." Annette touched Herbert's shoulder. "You okay? You look a little sad."

"How could you tell when my expression stays within the 93.4 percent consistency?"

Annette stretched her legs across Herbert's lap. "You're being difficult."

"I do not know how."

"I can teach you. I'm good at it. Something's upset you. I know, I know, within the whatever facial consistency level."

Herbert looked away. "I do not feel comfortable within these circumstances. Mr. Schorr and the Servants are very gracious. But I cannot appreciate the conversation and sentiment."

"Because they're Jews?"

Herbert arched a disapproving eyebrow. "Unlike you, I am not programmed for those beliefs. The talk is superficially philosophical, but the subtext is evidently deeply emotional. I had the same reaction when I engaged in religious discussions with Father Dempsey. Mr. Schorr and his colleagues have a great sadness for the loss of their faith and nation. You feel a great loss for your husband and your fears of what lies ahead. I do not know how to comfort nor do I know how to participate."

"Which makes you sad."

"No."

Annette poked him with her toe. "It makes you sad, admit it. What'll happen, you'll lose your membership in the perfect robot society?"

"It makes me regretful over the limitations. Please do not try and insist otherwise, Annette. I appreciate you are attempting to help."

"Which is making you feel worse." She poked him again. "What about physical limitations?"

"I do not understand the question."

"Come on." Annette tugged him up. "You can go days without nourishment, and I've never seen you take a crap, which means you can probably run the dance floor on all of us."

Herbert resisted with the faintest alarm. "I do not know how to dance."

"I'm going to teach you, idiot."

There were four wild circles of dancing Jews scampering around the campsite like out-of-control tops. A sweating musician perched on a chair, playing a violin. Annette took Herbert's hands. She twisted them back and forth. His hips didn't swivel.

"Relax."

"I do not know how."

Annette laughed. "The hell you don't."

She placed her palm on Herbert's left shoulder, grasping his right hand and gently swaying side to side. She was about five inches taller. They went back and forth in a line drawn by her drunkenness and his resistance. Slowly Herbert got into the flow. She twirled him around and would've bet the last of her clean panties that the robot almost smiled. Herbert twirled her around.

Eyes widening, she kicked her shoes into the cave and jitterbugged, right hand high and shaking. Herbert mirrored that perfectly. Back legs gyrating and torsos leaning forward, their foreheads nearly bumped. The wild Hasids began clapping. The violinist picked up the pace.

Annette and Herbert danced faster and faster. She'd throw up before admitting she was dizzy. Herbert's eyes took on a distant gleam, placing its hand on her shoulder and leading Annette across the camp, half trotting, half dancing. She squealed in delight. Herbert was the best dancer she'd ever known and she'd boogied with the best of them.

Herbert discovered a peripheral program about the history of Jewish music. Soon, the 'bot was leading the *hora*.

29

P uppy had dozed for he-didn't-know-how-long in the palm of the surprisingly comfortable rock chair when a tinny cup rattled by his ear.

Ponytail was jiggling a martini shaker.

"You have graced my home at an unusually early hour which means there must be a reason of unusual urgency." Pumpkin leaned back on his throne with a regal air.

Puppy gratefully embraced the gooey suds pouring out of the silvery shaker which Ponytail DV-signed was fresh pineapple juice. The tartness curled up his face.

Pumpkin showed satisfaction at the response. "So. The sad story of the teacher."

Puppy nodded. "What do you know?"

Pumpkin's orange face darkened into burnt umber. "I am not a criminal."

"I never said you were."

"Despite my illegal activities."

"I respect your motivations."

"But you have nowhere else to turn."

"That's right. Have you heard anything?"

"Nothing yet." He repeated it under Puppy's demanding stare.

"What about the other robberies?"

The large man tipped his head with grudging admiration. "You have your own sources."

"The Granddaughter."

"Ah. The curtain tugs aside."

"Along with a few threats."

"To your employment. That was inevitable." Pumpkin sighed; Ponytail joined him with breezy disappointment. "The gates have opened, Puppy Nedick. Don't you see the litter on the streets? The occasional rude shove on a bus? The disinclination to offer a kind word after your sandwich has been served. Little things ignored become larger things that cannot. In my world, I am no longer presented with opportunities to procure memorabilia for the sake of ownership. To hold a storied part of the past, part of a moment gone but not forgotten. That singular joy of you alone standing before a painting, an ashtray; touching history, someone's heart. Someone's mind. Soul, if you must. Their pain. Their joy. A solitary witness to something that should not be solitary. It is glorious.

"That's changing, Puppy. Now it's about money. Shadow Lifecards. Oh, I see you're surprised. There is a unique process for the forgeries. It is as if your dear Clary had signed them herself. That's the impetus now. Money. Greed returns to America. Clutching at each other's throats for the slightest reason and with the grandest joy." Pumpkin inched forward. "What do the police say?"

"The detective seemed confused."

"Who was it?"

"Layon Y'or."

"And he's one of the better ones. A society where crime rarely exists doesn't produce brilliant law enforcement personnel. If the police don't know, how should I?"

"Because you know what they don't."

Pumpkin beamed. "The boy gains clarity." He thoughtfully rubbed his chin. "There is risk in this request."

"Why?"

"Because I don't know if these robberies are truly purely greed, disaffected youth, or something else."

Puppy tensed. "Define something else."

Pumpkin hesitated. "Perhaps it's not random. Perhaps it is targeted at baseball."

"By who?"

"Whom. And I do not know."

"A criminal gang?"

Pumpkin laughed. "There are no criminal gangs, merely occasional cooperation among thieves, most of whom find the intricacies of tying shoelaces daunting."

"Then who could it be?"

"Like I said, I do not know. I have not asked, only heard."

"But you will."

With wry curiosity, Pumpkin tilted his oversized head. "You act as if that is a given."

Puppy nodded with a faint smile. "Do I have to explain why."

Pumpkin narrowed his eyes. "Because you trust me."

"Not really. Because we're friends."

Pumpkin stilled Ponytail's mocking groans.

"We're two of a kind, Pumpkin. Products of the Disappointment Village. I could be sitting where you are, puffed up with my own self-importance in a cave instead of a baseball field. You could've been a great surgeon. After the accident you withdrew. I get it. You had no choice. Or thought you didn't. Maybe you didn't. What's it matter? In our own ways we've both been screwed by The Family. Right now, I don't care about myself and that's not me being selfless because I wish I were. They're just waiting for the right moment to fire me once everything's gone too far. So I won't be Commissioner Puppy. All I ever wanted was to pitch. That's done. But I won't let whoever they are take down the game and everything else."

Pumpkin leaned back. "Well now. You finally understand where Pumpkin has been."

"As you get where Puppy has been. Without The Family, neither of us count. It's the great wedge. I fight for it. You fight against it. It defines us."

Pumpkin smiled slightly. "In your Puppy brain, often incomprehensible, you imagine Pumpkin rising from the caverns, Tatiana," he gestured at the grinning girl, "on his arm. Perhaps a nostalgia store on Sutphin Boulevard. The Twentieth-Century Project has generated much interest. 'Pumpkin's Delights.' Catchy title. Nine to six, Saturdays nine to one. Come rummage in your past. In no time I'll be the most popular shopkeeper in the East Bronx. Children will flock for my stories. Uncle Pumpkin. Sing us a song. Dance us a tune. Who knows, but little Pumpkins might spring out."

Tatiana gasped.

"Yes. That will be my reward." His voice faltered. "My new life as I experience this metamorphosis."

"Nah. That's what you imagine, Pumpkin. That's what you always imagined."

"The greatest dreams are often the most painful because they motivate the most." His eyes watered. "Damn you, Puppy Nedick. Damn you."

Puppy held out his hand. With heavy sighs, Pumpkin considered the gesture before bending forward and tapping Puppy's palm. They lingered a moment.

"Now what do you know?" the Commissioner of Baseball asked.

Pumpkin and Tatiana exchanged a series of eye flutters, silently communicating. "No questions asked if the products are recovered?"

"Except for Hedda's assault. There, I want a name."

Puppy struggled to his feet, but Pumpkin pressed him back into the chair. Puppy was asleep in two seconds, snugly wrapped in a vintage Davey Crockett furry blanket.

• • • •

THE CHILD WAS in a mood today. Restless, combative, right leg flexing as she sat, if only for a moment before bounding about the room. She mischievously disappeared into HGs thick with serene and relaxed young humans while intermittently scampering up the walls. Bowing to no applause and bowing again with no encouragement, the child collapsed onto an orange beanbag, fixing Felice with a hateful stare.

The 'bot was not amused. After fourteen minutes and eleven seconds, Clary broke off the glare with a triumphant laugh.

"You blinked first."

"If you wish, Granddaughter."

It was a lie, but the child indulged in lies more and more, approaching the 47.3 percent threshold of non-organic components. Her dreams ransacked the bedroom; the third repair this week of broken walls and shattered windows had just been completed.

"Are you done?" Felice asked evenly.

"Only if you are done baiting me."

"I merely asked your plans."

"I will wait and see. Is that not the Felice way?" Clary drummed a tune on her forehead. "Oh please, kind Felice. Think for me."

"Someone must."

A funnel of orange fury escaped the young girl's mouth. Felice brushed it aside with weary disdain.

"You informed Puppy of what was to be done and he did nothing."

Felice expelled the vid from Puppy's brief interview with Sandra Douglas this morning on *Wake Up, My Darlings*:

"Baseball is exuberant and we want to encourage that passion. But we can't allow unkind words, insults, or certainly fighting in the stands. Good behavior, respectful behavior, must be maintained. Anyone violating that'll be permanently banned from the ballpark. This is clean fun and we can't allow the very few to spoil that. Please remember that we can't lose our values at the ballpark. Baseball is there to strengthen them."

"That will not be sufficient," Felice said.

Clary ran up and down the wall, landing with an angry pant in another chair. "A start."

"Will you request the Cousins to deploy Black Tops to keep order?"

"After last year's riots, that is illegal at stadiums. Hah. I passed another test."

"All leadership is a continuing test, Granddaughter. Who will escort out the unruly participants? Each game has only eleven human ushers and they have proved inadequate to contain an increasingly high-risk situation when crowds average 331 fans per game."

"The inorganic ushers can help." Clary winced at Felice's disappointment. "What about the Blue Shirts?"

Felice adjusted the pitch of its voice higher. "You want to increase the number of police in stadiums?"

"If that is the only way," Clary mumbled.

"This is not about crowd noises, paraphernalia, nor raucous behavior. The Old-Timers' Game blatantly violated nineteen laws of The Family, creating a tolerance proximately resulting in the robberies and likely deadly assault on the teacher Hedda Kleinz. This is precisely the same pattern the game exhibited previously. But it is not about baseball. If you cannot stand up to Puppy Nedick, how can the country have faith that you, a child, can stand up to the Islamists? Overseeing this game should have been the simplest way to demonstrate your capabilities with the lowest percentage of potential failure."

Clary remained quiet and shaken.

Felice tremored its head. "You have failed your most important test. You should have terminated Puppy's employment at the first defiance."

"Stop saying defiance." Clary pressed the pillow against her waist. "He deserves an opportunity to resolve the issue."

"That is irrelevant since you have encouraged his defiance as a way of defying me."

Clary gasped loudly. "I would never do such a thing. As you would never undermine me, would you, Felice?" She blinked away Felice's probing stare and grunted. "Good. Now provide the daily military briefing." Felice continued staring. "I said, provide the military briefing."

Felice flipped up its palm to produce a map of the global battlefield. "There have been temporary setbacks and adjusted withdrawals around Central and Southern Europe as well as transient reassessments on the Polish-Russian border."

"Meaning we are getting our booties kicked?"

"Nothing of the sort. But there is the growing possibility—"

Clary disdainfully wiggled her fingers.

"—of 36.3 percent of a military stalemate which would not be acceptable. You will have to consider the last option."

Clary pressed the pillow closer.

"Granddaughter...?"

"I heard you. We have discussed until I want to scream and I do not like the last option."

"It would be battlefield targeted only."

"They will retaliate."

"Unlikely if we employ the nuclear rockets properly."

"We did not employ the robot armies properly or we would not be in this situation."

Felice's forehead furrowed with disapproval.

Clary angrily blushed, nodding toward the still vibrant battlefield map. "What is the deadline for this decision?"

"Missiles have been assembled at the El Jern facility in Tunisia."

Clary frowned. "There were no orders to transport nuclear weapons during the invasion of North Africa."

"None that would have passed the Cousins's approval. They would still be debating over Nok-Hockey. The preliminary steps had to be taken so you, Granddaughter, would have the freedom of all options."

"Nor was I told."

"No, you were not. You have been unduly busy with baseball."

30

The white walls outside the oak doors adorning the study shimmered slightly, competing with the broad sun drenching Coasta Brava through the wide windows. Azhar strained without moving much of his neck for a glimpse of a gun, a guard, anything that glinted and said security. But the white-robed aides merely strolled past with little concern, munching on *peix fregit*. The pungency of fried fish, the clip-clop of sandals, even the sand scattered by the worn chairs and couches gave the sense of a resort.

Azhar squirmed, made uneasy by what he expected, what he thought should be, and the laconic way an officer shrugged him inside the large room bathed in more dangerous light. Fish smells drifted up from the *sèpia amb pèsols* waiting on a carelessly set table by the window.

"My dear friend, my dear, dear friend." Abdullah embraced Azhar with genuine warmth, stepped back to examine him, and hugged even tighter. "Yes, I am glad to see you."

"You look well, my lord."

Abdullah seemed refreshed. His gaunt cheeks were refilled, tanned, and gleaming. He walked erect, no haggard weight on his shoulders as he poured too-sweet mint tea.

"As do you." Abdullah patted Mustafa's stomach. "Home cooking obviously suits you."

"Trust me, it is not from Jalak's cooking."

The men exchanged knowing smiles. Abdullah's wolfish eyes searched Azhar. "Your wife has finally taken to your new face?"

"Too well," he blurted, blushing beneath Abdullah's grin. "Not that she would admit approving the improvement."

"If you attempt comprehension of wives we will be here for a very long time, my old friend. Perhaps forever. Sit, Azhar, sit." He chuckled at Azhar's hesitation toward the table by the window. "You are alarmed by the lack of security?"

"It does not seem fitting for the future ruler of the world, sir."

"What would be fitting?" Abdullah didn't wait for a reply. "Fighter jets in regular formation overhead? Masked guards with long rifles? Helicopters circling the steel fortress to protect the future ruler of the world?"

Azhar ignored the playful sarcasm. "I would feel better."

"No, you wouldn't. You would worry about the need for such precautions. Although the windows are bulletproof. I am told rocket proof, too. The radar extends down the entire Catalonian coast. Beneath the quiet fishing boats in the harbor are nuclear-tipped submarines. And this floor, this lovely wooden floor would, at the first hint of danger to the future ruler of the world, encase us in what I am assured is an impenetrable container which would drop down an impenetrable elevator into a series of tunnels where, I believe, the future ruler of the world would be whisked to some secure location undoubtedly protected by nuclear bombers."

Abdullah grinned at Azhar's discomfort. "I would think you would be happy at such news."

"This is the sort of joy my face presents under such circumstances."

Roaring, the Son clapped Azhar on the arm. Abdullah served *sepia amb pesois*, waiting for Azhar to murmur approval before settling beside him where they watched boats drift past, animated little figures scurrying on deck. Mustafa suspected the boats were armed.

"Have you heard the latest news?" Abdullah asked. "Of course you would not because it is still a secret." The Son winked. "The Chinese are now our friends. Loathsome creatures. At least the Americans have a sense of piety and professed morality. Degenerate, yes, but they want you to believe they are behaving in a civilized way. All the Chinese offer is arrogance. They are not impressed by the performance of the American armies. The robots have suffered some shocking defeats. We have driven them out of Rome and Budapest. For all the vaunted American technological genius, they have failed. Now, the Chinese have not publicly become allies of the Islamic Empire. But they have extended their neutrality protectorate, as it is called, all along Southeast Asia and fifty miles into the Pacific. Japan, Korea, Thailand, on and on. That makes the Asian mainland nearly impregnable to American advances."

Abdullah absently sipped the tea, enjoying talking freely. "That removes the threat of a two-front war. Someday we will fight the Chinese. Someone must. It is inevitable. But not now. That has persuaded the Russians to finally accept our generous offer of returning their lands east of the Ukraine and west of Mongolia. Before, they had sliced off the tongues of our envoys. Also a fine, civilized people. They are considering withdrawing from the uprising. The specter of robot armies and America controlling the world is fast fading, my friend."

The Son frowned. "Is this also the expression for such news?"

Azhar shifted. "Apologies. It is heartening. Where will your new capital be?"

"Perhaps Jerusalem. Probably Jerusalem, which I prefer. Although some are pushing for Mecca. For now, it is preferable that I remain here outside Barcelona so I do not seem to be advancing or retreating. There is infinite power in merely waiting, Azhar. Patience in an impetuous world is an extraordinary weapon."

"And your father?"

"My father pretends to know what he believes."

"Because he is ill?"

"He has had symptoms for decades that prove useful when he needs to cut off conversation. But he has accepted the transition. Exactly when it will happen, I do not know. We must first wait for the war to wind down." Abdullah leaned back. "Have you received the answers for which you came?"

"This is not why I am here, my lord."

"I know that, Azhar. You have a most wonderfully roundabout way of approaching anything head-on. Perhaps now is the moment."

Azhar fumbled for a sip of tea. "It is about my son Omar. He has returned."

"The Black Robes are not permitted an official place in Barcelona—or all of Spain," Abdullah said sternly.

"I fear his mission is not official. I fear that he has not come merely to visit his family."

"You believe he has come to do you harm?"

Azhar took a breath. "No. You, my lord."

Abdullah smiled. "I appreciate your concern, as always, my dear friend, for my safety—"

"He would not come merely to kill me, sir. His mother would be displeased. The only mission worthy of his fanaticism, his hatred, is killing you."

"What proof do you have? Has he made threatening remarks? Purchased weapons? Met with co-conspirators?"

"None. It is just my belief, my lord. A father's instincts," he hurriedly added.

Abdullah squeezed Azhar's wrist. "I thank you for your concern, Azhar. Without any evidence, I cannot act. The peace prohibits what might be perceived as harassment. However, if Omar does anything tangible that can be officially investigated, my door is always open. How is your other son?"

"Fine. My lord, please, there must be something…"

Abdullah shook his head. "Azhar Mustafa, you are among the few in this world whose sincerity I would never doubt. But consider that you are, how shall I say, projecting your troubled relationship with Omar upon me. I have no doubt the young Black Robe hates me. The peace is fragile. Once the war is over and the consolidation begins, there will be much bloodletting. An era of Islamic Enlightenment will not be welcomed everywhere. It could be that I will not survive. That is why my sons have been raised in a spirit of tolerance and emancipation should they have to carry on prematurely. They have been taught love by a doting father. As you taught your sons. It did not work with Omar and only Allah knows why. Let me meet Abdul. I am told he accompanied you."

Startled at Abdullah walking through the lobby with an outstretched hand, Abdul jumped up and spilled crisps all over his shirt. Azhar could only sigh at the many ways a child could embarrass his parent.

"Pleasure to meet you, my lord." Abdul bowed, then tried something of a curtsy before clasping Abdullah's hand.

"It is I who has the pleasure." Abdullah bent at the waist and munched on a crisp, congratulating Abdul on his choice of the sea salt and vinegar flavoring. "Your father is a great man."

"Yes he is!" Abdul nearly shouted.

Abdullah chuckled. "I am glad you agree. You must listen to him and your mother. Obey Allah. And keep practicing your football. Your father says you are a splendid forward."

"Because he is also a great coach."

Abdullah laid his hand on Azhar's arm. "Yes, he is that, too."

Abdul didn't speak until they were near the train station half a mile away. His round face curled up in thought.

"This was all about Omar, right?"

"No. A mere visit. Do not make me regret bringing you. Be grateful that you met a man such as Abdullah. This is a moment you will cherish for the rest of your life and remember that it did not happen because we spent the day fishing if your mother asks."

Abdul snorted. "He's shorter than I thought. And he did not believe you."

"About what?"

"Omar and what he is up to."

"Your brother is up to nothing except the usual posturing and arrogance."

"You do not believe that."

"Are you telling me what I believe?"

"No, I am telling you what you are telling me you believe, which I do not." Abdul planted his feet. "I'll help you spy."

Azhar laughed. "There is no spying. There is no need to spy."

Abdul frowned. "I can go places you cannot."

"Like where?"

"Like where Omar goes at night."

Azhar's eyes narrowed. "What do you know of that?"

His son shrugged. "I guess nothing."

"This is not a silly little game."

"And I am not a silly little boy anymore. If you think Omar's going to assassinate Abdullah, then I want to help."

Glancing around at the crowded station, Azhar shook Abdul quiet. "Who said anything about that?"

"You did."

Azhar met his son's steady gaze and sighed. One day they are twelve, the next, wise. "I was wrong."

"Because the Son told you."

Azhar hesitated. "Yes. I felt like a fool if that makes you feel better."

"Do you think Abdullah would admit he is worried about some teenage Black Robe?"

"Probably not. But I still felt like a fool."

"Well, I believe you."

"Because you hate your brother."

"Because he hates you. He told me. He wishes you were dead. I told him if he killed you, he better kill me and do it quickly."

Azhar gave his son a long look. "What did he say?"

"He called me a degenerate. But if he wanted to kill you, he would have done it the first night and then disappeared. He has papers. He would be protected. No one would ever find him."

"Except they would find you when you killed him. That is what you want to do. Kill your brother. As he wants to kill you. And me. What sort of family have I raised? Allah, forgive me."

Azhar sunk into a prayerful kneeling position. Abdul lifted his father up with surprising strength. The boy's face hardened with ugly resolve. "There is no time for that, Poppa. I can help. I can help."

• • • •

THERE WERE NO paintings or sculptures or theatrical posters or even fancy coasters in the waiting room of the Committee on Art, merely walls washed in gray tones as if the notion of imagination was a seed best yanked quickly from the ground.

"Remember, allow me to speak unless I keel over." Joan chomped on a wad of gum the size of Knoxville.

"What if someone deigns to ask little me a question?" Zelda batted her eyelashes.

Joan wasn't amused by the levity. "I step in. Now is not the time to stir the pot more than you already have, dear."

A pert woman with flagrant red hair led them inside a room which moments ago might've been a storage closet. With droopy boredom, two officials and a 'bot sat behind the long desk.

"Jameson Tillery," the older man grudgingly said.

"Dahlia P'redo," said the woman with a nose like a scalpel.

The 'bot hesitated. "Lahandra, but I am not certain of that name yet."

Joan exclaimed that sounded like an exquisite name born for greatness. Lahandra didn't know what to make of that slightly patronizing comment except to note it.

"Nor am I here in an official capacity," said Lahandra. "I am observing to appreciate the notion of art as a learning exercise for empathetic evolution."

"This is a preliminary training procedure for Lahandra," Jameson recited as he had for the last three irritating petitioners who should have known better than to waste their time on subversive art. "Should Lahandra like the work of the Committee, they may proceed in this profession."

"What do you think so far?" Joan asked eagerly.

"I do not care for the concept of art. It is subjective and susceptible to manipulation. The boundaries are broad and ill-defined. This is my second day, and I am considering whether to return after lunch."

"Nice to meet you, too," Joan said. "Did you read this amazing play?"

"Yes." Lahandra's sepia-tinted forehead pulsed. "But I am not at liberty to express an opinion."

"But we are." Jameson only handled artistic hearings on a part-time basis around juggling the needs of his popular store Handy Hardware. They kicked off an "Essentials of Home Maintenance" sale today and the dimwits he'd been saddled with from the nearby DV didn't know the difference between a screwdriver and a hammer. He doubted these two precious queens of theater did either. Jameson didn't trust people who weren't handy. If you couldn't operate a Riggins Electric Screwdriver, what was next?

Dahlia rustled a paper. Jameson gestured for her to stop. He didn't care for nervous people either. The Zelda Jones writer wasn't nervous. She stared back challengingly. He didn't like people challenging him either. Most of those who knew Jameson wondered how he'd stayed married for twenty-six years and managed four children. Perhaps because his spouse and offspring could renovate a bathroom in three hours including clean-up.

"And we greatly appreciate your time and talents in preparing this work and submitting it," Dahlia said as if there were any other way a play could be produced. "If you have the time, would you explain why the play wasn't submitted by the first scheduled rehearsal?" Dahlia clicked her short teeth together in between words. Zelda wasn't sure how she did that.

"The play was not submitted by the first scheduled rehearsal because the playwright, Zelda, hadn't finished it yet," Joan answered.

"Then why weren't the themes of the play detailed in the original proposal?" Dahlia ran her tongue into the corner of her mouth.

"They were. If you have the original submission…"

Dahlia and Jameson simultaneously held up the papers as if string joined their elbows.

"The theme was about love, loss, and reconciliation."

Dahlia's small eyes struggled to focus. "That is not the theme at all."

"I am the producer. I know the themes of my plays."

"And I'm the writer." Zelda brushed away Joan's warning touch. "I know what I wrote."

"This play says quite clearly that a single mother, in this case a bear, can be a suitable parent. The essence of the story, which suggests that single motherhood is acceptable, isn't acceptable." Dahlia was pleased by her clever phrasing. "We understand that as an artist you must question the existing rules. Which is why so little art is acceptable."

Zelda hunched forward. "You're asking me to change my play?"

"Oh no, not at all," said Jameson. "That would constitute deprivation of individual thought and responsibility. It would also show little respect for your creativity and zeal."

Zelda sneered. "I'm glad to hear that."

Jameson twinned his eyebrows in frustration. "We deeply appreciate all that the two of you have achieved. The restoration of the Lyceum Theater is a significant contribution which perhaps someday can house a suitable play. However, this work raises long-rejected and decisively invalidated themes that run counter to the foundation of The Family. We cannot sanction the play's production and have decided to withdraw the temporary approval."

"Sir." Joan drew the word out disdainfully. "The play is about the sanctity and the preeminence of love. That is the very foundation of The Family. That marriage, relationships, and our dear children are the most cherished aspects of our worlds. Grandma stressed that continually. This play, so incredibly moving, says that if there is only one parent and there is no other option, then a child should be given to that one parent. In this instance, the mother."

"An argument graphically and, may I say, spitefully and one-sidedly presented about the emotional abuse of the child—"

"His name is Fresco," Zelda snapped. "Fresco the Cub."

"—when he is given to a new parent."

"I showed the motivation behind Caesar the Vulture's torment—"

"And the questionably distasteful confusion about the fatherhood behind Fresco."

"I was the model for Merkeran the Mommy!" Zelda exploded. "My fiancé was killed during an attack at sea. I was pregnant. I wasn't sure if Diego was the father or Pablo, one of my best friends."

Even Lahandra paid attention.

"Dear, they don't need to know this," Joan stammered.

"The hell they don't. I was captured by the damn Miners. I escaped. I gave birth in a hospital during the baseball riots. I finally made it back to the Bronx and a genetic test proved who the father was and now I'm married." Zelda waved her ring in front of the committee's shocked faces.

"And did your own bear cub suffer such abuse by a temporary parent?" Jameson snidely asked.

"No, because they would've had to kill me first."

He grunted. "Then that really wasn't true. We don't know what's true and what's invented."

"That's fucking theater."

"It certainly is," Dahlia said regretfully. "One never knows."

"Look, I deceived Ms. Minh. This isn't her fault. She didn't know what I was planning. No one did. Not the cast, no one. If you want to punish anyone, punish me."

Zelda started to the door, but Joan spun her around by the elbow.

"Whatever you do, do to both of us." Joan held up Zelda's hand as if they'd been awarded a prize. "We are not afraid."

They stirred the double-gin martinis with plastic swizzle sticks in the back of the seedy bar off West 48th Street.

Zelda rolled the olive in her mouth. "This is very good."

"The olive or the gin?" Joan peered into Zelda's glass.

"Both. Especially the gin. I never had gin before."

"One of the most profound creations ever," Joan said thickly, waving her hammy hand for the third round.

"I'm sorry again," Zelda said, wondering if something had just crawled across the table. It was just dust propelled by Joan's quasi-tornadic breathing.

"It was all preordained."

"You said there was a chance."

"There's always a chance." Joan stumbled to her feet, addressing the cross-eyed man with two hairs on his head who was the only other patron drinking at eleven in the morning. "Remember that. There's always a chance. Barkeep, if that gentleman is still alive, provide him with a fresh beverage of his liking."

The diffident bartender poured another shot of cheap whiskey into the man's glass.

"And I blew it," Zelda said.

"No. They could not. They would not. Perhaps had we been honest in the beginning..."

"Right, exactly."

"But we were not."

"See? See? My fears."

"Your fears, my fears, we all have fears."

"What're yours?" Zelda asked.

Joan sniffled. "I am touched, Zelda, that you show such interest in my feelings. I never felt you liked me."

"I didn't until the other day."

"And I the same. You're exhausting and unbearable."

"Same here."

"But now"—They clinked glasses. Joan stood and waved the paper with the official committee decision in Zelda's face—"Now we are liberated. Truly liberated."

"Failure will do that, trust me."

Joan slumped back into the booth with a dark stare. "There will be a way. There is always a way."

Zelda squinted at the fuzzy words of the committee's decree. "Like where you're banned from producing a play in any theater in the United States for five years for willfully manipulating your position to deceive The Family's values."

Joan muttered about the human spirit surmounting obstacles and waved to the bartender for more Pablita's Plantain Chips, one of the new South American products captivating the import-starved country.

Zelda squinted. "And where I'm banned for five years from having my plays produced in the United States for misusing my artistic talents for narcissistic goals?"

"Wasn't it lovely how they gave us the same sentence length?" They clinked glasses. "I should return to ice skating."

"Now?" Zelda wondered if the rink was near the pool table in the back.

"No. In time. I will have time." She staggered to her feet and shouted, "Once we have found and finished the way!" Joan plopped back down. "And you?"

"I don't think I can ice skate."

"Do. What will you do?" Joan managed to lift a few inches off the seat.

"I was a dental hygienist."

"Someone must be."

"My husband sort of fired me."

"Happens to the best."

"Guess I'll probably just tell stories to my son."

"I can instruct him in the art of ice skating. Unless they'll bar me from that, too."

They drank gin martinis for another few hours until Joan burst into tears and pleaded to see the Lyceum Theater before the "cretinistic barbarians desecrate it forever with the sop of banality," a charge she lodged against the bartender and the now-sleeping old man.

Brandishing the keys with a savage aside about cold dead fingers, Joan led them through the theater with two candles, reminding Zelda of an Edgar Allan Poe story whose title she was too drunk to recall.

Once Joan stopped crying, they set the candles on the stage by the new bottle of Gillian's Gin. Zelda waited as did Joan to remember why they had come. Whatever the reason, it made them very sad and they cried through another round.

Rising like a brontosaurus, Joan demanded the show must go on. They read the play between the candles and the gin. They acted, they shouted, they sang, they quarreled, they hugged, they laughed, they cried, and, at the end, they applauded themselves with lusty inebriated cheers for demonstrating the full range of the human spirit.

They stared glassily until Joan, vertebrae by vertebrae, stood and extended her arms, bursting into a rendition of *Everything's Coming Up Roses*. She stomped about the stage, slipping and sustaining nasty cuts which would've hurt if not for the gin. Upstage, Joan suddenly froze, revolving her hips like a wheel.

"The plan, dear. The plan has come. Yes yes yes yes. The plan. The plan has shown itself to me. The glory of theater will be reignited!" Joan yelled with the insensible insight of the dangerously intoxicated.

Holding hands, they danced in a circle singing two different songs. The women finally collapsed to the floor and fell asleep, almost cheek to cheek. When they woke up several hours later, their heads throbbing a jungle rhythm, bodies bruised, and mouths like sandpaper, but the plan, as Joan proclaimed it, still made sense.

They danced again, although more gingerly.

31

Eberto Hashimoto of Whitefish Bay, Wisconsin became the first person ever arrested for wearing a home-team baseball jersey.

Mr. Hashimoto was draped in an oversized vintage Robin Yount navy-blue jersey, *Brewers* alongside *19* on the front. On the back, the name *Hashimoto* ran above *19*. As Officer Peale said with some regret, this violated the newly issued Granddaughter Order number four barring polarizing team jerseys promoting narcissistic adoration of celebrities.

Mr. Hashimoto explained he'd worn this jersey for every one of the twenty-two 2099 Brewers home games along with a weekend series in Chicago and had never been accosted, insulted, disrespected, or harmed in any way other than missing half an inning at Comiskey Park because of a long bathroom line which he didn't think was personal.

As Mr. Hashimoto elaborated outside gate two, he was an accountant with Piltzer, Shtein, and Gonzalez, having no desire to be Robin Yount except for remembering his greatness as had many generations of Hashimotos when they were legally permitted. Nor did he understand how he could worship a celebrity long dead who could not even give him an autograph or thank him for such loyalty.

Mr. Hashimoto's acknowledgment that he had asked for and received autographs from presumably living athletes violated another clause in the Granddaughter Order number four, noted Officer Peale. Joined by two sheepish colleagues, the Blue Shirt again politely referenced the sign at gate two, posted as it was at every gate outside County Stadium and every major league stadium, stating that the wearing of jerseys and home-team t-shirts, caps, or any paraphernalia that could be used to urge on that home team must be relinquished before entering. The items would of course be returned after the game.

As Officer Peale handed over the Personal Paraphernalia Property Slip, the angry Mr. Hashimoto loudly told the now four Blue Shirts, but more the gathering fans, that his seats were in the bleachers and sitting shirtless, despite the expected seventy-six-degree game-time temperature, would expose him to the sun's rays; he'd had a scary brush with melanoma last year and had to keep covered. He doffed the Brewers cap to demonstrate his need for headwear.

The Blue Shirts expressed sympathy and offered to take Mr. Hashimoto to a nearby clothing store where they were confident he could find garments and hats that wouldn't violate the Granddaughter Order number four, which had been voted for unanimously by the Cousins, the police officers added for emphasis.

A menacing chant of "no melanoma" swept through the crowd, many defiantly waving their Brewers jerseys, scarves, and caps. The Blue Shirts, surrounded by several hundred fans, called for backup. Sergeant Szenia, arriving on the scene along with eight other Blue Shirts, instructed County Stadium to close the gates.

Fans shouting "no melanoma" surged forward without disrobing or showing their tickets. The handful of Blue Shirts inside tried stemming the stampede, but most fans broke through.

Since no siblings were permitted to watch a baseball game in partisan attire, the game couldn't be played. The public-address announcer pleaded for everyone to remove their garments and promised a supply of white towels in three different sizes would soon arrive. Two young women in the left-field grandstand tossed off their homemade Brewers bras, bringing the crowd to its feet. After sixty-three minutes, Blue Shirts from four neighboring precincts had restored order; the last of the fans who had stripped to their shorts in the center-field bleachers proved a little unruly. There were no formal arrests other than Mr. Hashimoto for instigating rude behavior.

"No melanoma?" Sahidi shook her head.

"But it worked." Puppy grinned.

What the Commissioner's staff knew all too well was that the fire behind major league baseball was not found in their unkempt office lined with empty roast-pepper panini boxes and extinguished bags of Fredo's Spicy Chips, nor with the owners, few of whom knew anything about baseball other than making the legal five-percent profit after the ninety-five-percent taxes, or familial allowances, were assessed.

The true engines were the local Friends of groups, loose congregations of friendly bickering fans united by the love for their teams and baseball's history, although they were increasingly divided by arguments over which player in that franchise's history should be honored.

Friends of Harmon Killebrew to Friends of Al Kaline to Friends of Jim Rice/Friends of Ted Williams to Friends of Tom Seaver/Keith Hernandez and Friends of Mel Ott/Willie Mays well, in some cities there were now nearly ten competing organizations billing themselves as Friends of. These were private citizens, grannies, adolescents, bored students, grouchy sanitation workers, over-stressed nurses—name a profession in a major league city and you'd find a Friends of member.

Yet it took yesterday's massive holographic call with the Friends of groups just seven minutes for everyone to agree, a first, to shoot out letters in time for the noon mail requesting members to boycott their next local home game. About 23.7 million letters, Matthew estimated.

According to the Blue Shirts's reports which Matthew gaily expelled, swarms of fans posted themselves outside the ballparks. When not arguing whether Friends of Mike Schmidt or Al Simmons or Chet Wang were the more acceptable Phillies group, for one example, they stood with noisy condemnation, shaking banners, chanting, and singing impromptu songs.

The notion of blocking anyone from attending a game or even telling someone what to do instead of allowing them to decide for themselves violated the most cherished principles of The Family.

But the free exchange of information on which to base such a decision was encouraged. Done respectfully, of course. Reciting the iconic Homeric-like poem from the 2040s about the decline of baseball, *A Full Count*, the Friends of Ernie Banks persuaded the New Bleacher Bums, whose motto was that neither aliens, Allahs, nor allergies would ever keep them from a Cubs game, to oppose Granddaughter Order number four.

Outside Crosley Field, the Friends of George Foster set up cots and sold homemade lemonade and grilled hot-red sausages until the fans joined the new communities. By 6:30, nearly every game was canceled for lack of attendance.

Adjoining Peaches Ballpark, baseball history lessons abounded around a play-by-play rebroadcast of the game in which Henry Aaron slugged his 715th homer, breaking Babe Ruth's then-record. Circling Forbes Field, children portrayed Roberto Clemente and Willie Stargell to the dulcet sounds of The Piratical Pirates, a musical trio who had just completed their first album, *The Bucs Stop Here*.

Only at Pilots Stadium in Seattle and Arlington Stadium in Texas were the games more than minutely attended. Both teams were in first place.

An emergency meeting of the Cousins was called. Clary's HG perched in a luxurious orange chair atop the conference room table. There was a brief and spirited debate between Second Cousin D'Andre and Third Cousin Rasfarati about whether this situation was predictable or unavoidable.

Clary explained that didn't matter. Baseball had misbehaved again and must be restrained. She repeated restrained several times in a cold, firm voice that was metallic even for a hologram. There will be no arrests unless there is violence. The BTs will patrol urban areas, specifically around DVs; First Cousin Nadharatha had presented a graph showing that approximately eighty-nine percent of the protesters were DV-originated.

"Given the poor perception of Black Tops in the Disappointment Village community," stated Second Cousin DeRico, "their very presence might provoke violence. Let's not forget what happened last year. Parts of Boston have still not been rebuilt. Only Blue Shirts should patrol, per law, by the stadiums," continued DeRico as if lecturing a frog.

Several BTs walked in, taking up positions in the corners of the room; one accidentally tipped over the new pre-buttered popcorn maker. If anxiety hadn't drizzled down their collective foreheads, one of the Cousins would've remarked that BTs were not permitted in the Cousins's meetings.

Clary's razor stare didn't quell their nervousness. "We will not forget what happened last year. Too much leniency was shown. But the Blue Shirts and Brown Hats are not trained for quasi-military action." The room shifted uneasily. "For now, the ballparks will remain open. It is up to the fans to decide if they will lawfully attend. But the Order remains."

"And what of Commissioner Nedick?" Cousin Nadharatha asked from the relative safety of the foosball table as if Clary's HG were a physical threat. "He has sanctioned the boycott. At the least, he must removed from office." That stirred the Cousins into unanimous irritation. They were suddenly a brave lot.

"Only once since the end of the War has a public official disobeyed a Cousin's suggestion, much less an order from Grandma, Grandpa, or now, the Granddaughter," Nadharatha continued with cloying respect. "Henry Barsaghi of Minot, North Dakota in 2077, Commissioner of Public Cleaning and Roadways, had refused to send out snowplows during a thirty-five-inch blizzard, claiming they should wait until after the storm passed. The local Director of Postal Works, one Ferula Caution, disputed such a decision, insisting that meant the daily four-mail delivery schedule would be disrupted and hadn't Grandma just said that only 'the end of humanity would stop the United States Postal Service from delivering the mail four times a day'?"

"The plows"—Nadharatha finished with breathless determination—"proceeded with brave postal employees driving, delivering, and plowing simultaneously. If stamps were permitted to glorify behavior, surely the entire Minot Post Office would've graced the face of postage. Mr. Barsaghi was dismissed. So must Commissioner Nedick. This sets a bad example."

"Puppy will remain," Clary answered. "If fired, he would become a martyr. By remaining in his job, his failure will be increasingly evident which will make his ultimate removal easier."

"Does the delay have anything to do with him being Puppy Beisbol?" DeRico smirked, brazenly rolling a Nok-Hockey puck along the table. She was one of those lesser minds who thought blurting out things no one else would dare say made her a great leader.

Clary entered from a side door, her HG still afloat in the orange chair. A lot of official larynxes closed.

The Granddaughter took the puck from DeRico who was visibly trembling. With an icy stare, she threw the round black object through the far wall, making a neat hole as if it had been drilled and sanded by experts. Clary asked if there were any other questions or comments. There were, but none dared speak.

32

Fifteen-year-old Miso de Gonzales, wearing a pinstriped t-shirt with Paul Weinstock's Number 5, discovered padlocks on the shuttered gates around four p.m. when he and his friends Dinira and D'an arrived for batting practice. When they found gate four padlocked, they circled Yankee Stadium. Sure enough, everything was locked down like "Dinira's brother's panties" went the colorful phrasing.

Across the country, orange orb-signs floated over stadiums like defiant pop-ups.

NO GAME TONIGHT.

All afternoon at the top of the hour, the vidnews had specifically mentioned the need to impose a curfew on the parks, not the cities, not the DVs, as the Granddaughter had clearly stressed. There were no Black Tops patrolling pediatric clinics in Fort Worth or barring Joe Brancaccio from serving Neapolitan pizza in the Bronx or Manuel and Manuel's popular used-tire shop churning out those new retreads in Gainesville or the twenty-five percent-off sale at Blouse's For You in Portland.

The protests had caused chaos. Banners with *No Melanoma* written on them fluttered around subway entrances, gluing themselves to the bumpers of passing cars, the exhaust pipes of buses. Baseball fans refused to accept the rules like the rest of The Family. If the thieves and now-murderer of Hedda Kleinz, who had passed away this morning, were hiding, it would logically be among baseball fans, the prime customers for such trophies as Phil Rizzuto's shoe. Several black-market dealers had been arrested. The pipeline would be broken, promised *Your Midday* presenter Mailia Marke.

Besides, attendance for the last three games had averaged below a thousand fans. The few who dared take their seats were harassed afterward. There'd been some fistfights in Minneapolis and, shockingly, knife play in Houston. Nasty accusations of treason, betrayal. Shouts of "Reg dirt" returned with "DV scum" had been heard outside Candlestick Park.

Yet in the wondrously delusional way a lover of baseball will believe the game-ending ground ball must hit a pebble and skip into left field to keep the rally alive, so fans milled, unwilling to accept that the Yankees-Red Sox game would really be canceled, not with the teams tied for first, not with Mooshie hitting .342 and Mickey hitting .331. Soon the milling became clustering and then small crowds crept up 161st Street.

Of course, they wouldn't go inside. But they could stand outside and listen. During the boycott, "ear stands" had popped up outside Wrigley Field that circled the ballpark with eight-foot ladders, burly men and women in retro Mickey Mouse ears climbing up and interpreting the meager crowd noise, the crack of the bat, a faint groan. There was much debate about what the hell was going on and, when the game finally ended, it was considered the worst form of cowardice to ask the traitors who dared take seats what had happened.

That birthed the "facial box," where self-proclaimed experts in interpreting the mood of expressions would venture whether the Cubs had won or lost based on the looks of the exiting crowds. Outside Busch Stadium, a fan insisted he could produce a box score based on the expressions. Had the radcasts continued, there would've been no need for such inventiveness. But Sahidi told her announcers to tell it like it was and when reports of the protests and the empty stands and the laggard response of the players to these conditions trickled out, radcasts of baseball games were suspended.

That set off the burning of transistor radios outside Royals Stadium.

By the time Mooshie Lopez, Mickey Mantle, and the rest of the 2099 New York Yankees scampered down the subway, per the Commissioner's order that ballplayers must take public transportation the same as the fans, the sidewalks of River Avenue were obscured by the stamping feet of New York and Boston fans.

"What's this shit? My fan club is way bigger." Mooshie stopped with mock disappointment.

"Game's canceled!" a fan shouted, the cry echoed by surrounding baseball fans.

"Who says?" Her eyes narrowed. She was pitching tonight and her arm already ached. She only had so much juice left.

A murmur of "the Granddaughter" rippled.

"Should I talk to her?" the Mick asked.

"The little brat doesn't listen to Puppy. She ain't listening to you, Gramps," Mooshie snapped.

"Take out the orbs!" someone yelled.

The orbs lifted knowingly. Two Jet'roes, armored BT vehicles named after a rude armadillo in a popular cartoon series, watched half a mile away.

"You should be relieved, Moosh." Wispy Ellen Adair, the hot-hitting, slick-fielding Red Sox shortstop, batted her big blue eyes. "Some of us think you petitioned the Cousins to cancel the game so we wouldn't tat your brow with line drives."

"Or some of us think you begged the Cousins to cancel the game 'cause you didn't want your pretty little face lumpy from *my* line drives," growled Mantle.

"Some of us didn't want to hurt our backs lifting your fat old body because you fainted trying to catch one of my fly balls," sneered burly first-baseman Joshua Hansen.

Red Sox teammates formed up a solid, slightly threatening line behind Ellen Adair and Joshua Hansen.

"Some of us don't want to see your little fingers broken in ten directions after I kick in your teeth sliding into second base," hissed Mooshie.

The Yankees thickened by her side.

With a guttural roar, Ernie Paicopolos gingerly slid off a shuttered doughnut stand, using his crutch for support. He'd twisted his knee chasing a Spiders fan off Jerry Remy Place last week. Tossing his red cape, Ernie scowled at the too-large number of Yankees fans.

"I came because this is holy. A Yankees-Red Sox game is the giving of the law to the Hebrews atop Mount Sinai. It is the Resurrection of Jesus Christ. It is, yes, yes, the vision of Allah to Mohammad." He silenced the protests by waving a swizzle stick swiped from the counter of Gorge Yerself Ice Cream on East 164th Street. "A Red Sox-Yankees game is the first cry of a child. The first kiss of a wedding. The last sunset of your life. It transcends…"

His burning eyes challenged them to finish the sentence. By now he had climbed onto the shoulders of Adair where he swayed like a chubby tree as his glazed eyes absorbed the beam of light from the "great dugout beyond."

"It cannot be compromised. Not by them." He shook his fist at the Jet'roes, flicking corn muffin crumbs out of his beard just for the sake of it. "Nor by you."

He took in both teams and all the fans.

"They will not let us inside. But we are already inside. All we need is the imagination, the memories." Ernie tapped the crutch onto various parts of his body where such imaginative memories were stored, waiting.

"What the hell are you talking about, you lunatic?" Mooshie shouted.

"He means outside." Adair rolled her eyes.

"Outside where?"

Adair gestured all around. "Here. Play the game outside."

Everyone took that in for a moment.

"The first time I hit the ball five hundred feet, the son-of-a-bitch BTs'll blow us apart." Mick tossed ice water on the idea.

That left sixty major league players and about eight thousand fans bewildered about possible next steps.

Ernie leaped off Ellen, dislocating her left shoulder before Hansen, a former chiropractor, popped it back into place.

"Imbeciles. Morons. Fools. As Mickey Mantle rightly said"—Ernie struggled before the anguish of giving a Yankee credit—"that is the excuse they want. Therefore, we play without the ball."

Ernie hissed with disdain, shaking his swizzle stick at the Boston outfield. "We play on the honor system. Is that not the hallmark of our society? Honor. Ethics. Integrity." He allowed them to add their own synonyms. "Ergo. How would this work?"

The silence deepened.

"The teams will take their respective positions. Go, Yankees, you are the home team."

As everyone exchanged various shades of confusion, Mooshie tucked the black bat onto her right shoulder. "Well, what the hell else we got to do?"

The Yankees fanned out in an unruly attempt to take the field. Ernie started whacking the infield into place before Mooshie took over. The Yankees were in defensive positions, gloved and ready to go as soon as they somewhat understood what was expected. Ernie raced around confiscating backpacks, jackets, and other outerwear to lay down the bases and the coaching boxes.

The ground hummed. Everyone knew it was the Jet'roes warming up ever so slightly. Ernie laughed gleefully.

"Now Ellen Adair, you are the leadoff hitter as always."

With a puzzled nod, Ellen stepped into the right-handed batter's box.

Paicopolos let out a pained cry as if horned monsters had risen from the ground.

"Where are my umpires, where, where? The coin of my realm for four honest siblings."

Without waiting, Ernie spun four fans around for an examination, searching for qualifications only he could diagnose and sent them off to their positions.

"Now this is how it works." His voice solemnly rose. "Mooshie will throw a pitch. Without the ball. That is what I said. Ellen will be honest on whether she swung and missed, took the pitch, or hit the ball. To keep down the possible confusion of too many voices, Mickey will decide, honestly and fairly, whether Ellen hit the ball and the horsehide's ultimate destination. The game unfolds in your head and is guided by your heart. Only you know what you feel on this day. As for the vagaries of baseball spirits, past, present, and future, that will be my area. I trust you believe that in a situation like this I can be impartial."

Ernie pulled a face at the obvious skepticism from the Yankees and their loathsome fans.

"You're nuts." Mooshie rattled like a peevish boa constrictor.

The Wizard straightened. Notions of craziness had been confined to history once Grandma obliterated the fiendish pharmaceutical-psychotherapy alliance through the Anti-Parasite Laws II. Families and friends dispensed psychiatric healing now. Still, "pertinent eccentricities," as some called them, still existed. Ernie had often been called someone who "listens to his own chimes." Children could still be cruel. So could adults.

As his grandmother had taught him before locking him in the punishment closet, Ernie pressed his pinkies together to ward off the hurts.

"I see ahead."

"You see nothing, brick brain," Mooshie growled. "You think we're all going to be on our best behavior? That I'm going to trust that flat-ass Adair's sense of honor? That I'm going to trust the Wizard of the Boston Red Sox to do the right thing?"

"That's the very notion of our society."

"The society that is keeping us out here?" Mooshie yelled, swiftly gaining converts. "How's that working out for everyone? They're dumping shit all over us and calling it shampoo. I say we take what is ours. Yankee Stadium belongs to us!"

Lopez pointed her black bat at the Jet'roes; the humming beneath their feet seeped up into their ankles. Explosions, screams, blood, collapsing stands. It was October 2065 again and she was dragging unconscious fans out of the way. She wanted pay back. For the way she and baseball were unfairly blamed for the failed assassination attempt on Grandma and The Family. For the way she was stabbed in the back by her former teammates. The subway train rolling over her. Now back again only to die, and dying she was, her robotic juices ebbing out. Might as well fight back one last time.

"This is the only way," Ernie said.

Mooshie took a step. So did Ernie.

The crack of wooden bat against fiberglass crutch echoed. They dueled through the astonished crowd until all Mooshie had left was the handle and all Ernie clutched was the reinforced rubber tip. Mooshie flung aside the last of her bat, demanding a replacement. Mickey took her aside.

"We gotta do it, Moosh. We can't beat 'em any other way. And we are gonna beat the bastards."

With a vicious growl, Mooshie stormed toward the knee-high white sock serving as the pitching rubber. Ernie triumphantly hoisted the rubber tip. Wizards always win.

He bowed his head. "Oh baseball seer who lives within the pocket of every glove, bless this game and give us the strength to accept the fate of the ball. Now drape us in your eternal abundance and remember us."

Ernie held up the swizzle stick for continued quiet:

"These are the saddest of possible words:
Tinker to Evers to Chance.
Trio of bear cubs, and fleeter than birds,
Tinker and Evers and Chance.
Ruthlessly pricking our gonfalon bubble,
Making a Giant hit into a double—
Words that are heavy with nothing but trouble:
Tinker to Evers to Chance."

Absolutely no one had any idea what Ernie was talking about. He was used to that. The chimes were loud.

The portly home-plate umpire wheezed out "play ball." Fans were given time to find comfortable seats. The entire elevated orange subway-line section filled. Receiving a message about the potential disturbance, Captain Rafferty of the 43rd Precinct had dispatched all his Blue Shirts to Yankee Stadium to protect public order.

Most of them were stationed between the makeshift stands and the humming BTs, waiting for an excuse to growl. Stillman's Novelty Store on East 165th Street distributed megaphones. Passed up and down as if rehearsed, the megaphones provided faux-rad play-by-play reaching into the thickening crowd snaking back onto the Grand Concourse.

Mooshie, more subdued than agreeable, fired a pretend ball.

The umpire screamed, "Strike one!"

Validated, Mooshie threw another pitch. The Red Sox shortstop swung.

"It's a long drive to deep left!" Ellen cupped her hands around her mouth. "Going and it is good night Nellie!" Adair went into "the Ellie dance," half taunt, half stroll, both hips shaking around the bases. "Mooshie Lopez's fastball wasn't fast today and Adair crushed the ball for her eleventh home run of the season, tops among major league shortstops. Is the ball still traveling?" she called over her shoulder, rounding third base.

Adair double-footed a hop onto home plate. Mooshie wound up and fired an invisible ball.

"Oh no," she cried. "Mooshie's return throw to home plate has hit Ellen Adair in the head. It looks like a skull fracture. Small loss."

It took about fifteen minutes and six Blue Shirts to untangle the two stars.

Ernie sighed. Being a Wizard wasn't as easy as it looked.

• • • •

SAHIDI AND IAN sat very quietly, consumed by their embarrassment. With a sigh, Puppy motioned for Matthew to begin.

With an unnecessary glance at its Goldfarb pocket watch, Matthew said, "It is rather late to—"

"Yes, it is rather late," Sahidi said, finally meeting Puppy's stare.

Matthew's forehead pulsed. "The Commissioner's office, comprised of Puppy Nedick, Sahidi Douglas, Ian Schrage and Matthew, have gathered to address the baseball situation."

"Must we be so pedantic?" Ian sneered.

"These are the rules. Specifically, we have gathered to address Work Rule 4.2." Matthew paused. "Shall I read that aloud?"

"Since it's the rule."

"Work Rule 4.2 states: When employees have valid reasons, they may hold a vote on a supervisory manager's fitness to continue in that role. Are there any valid reasons?"

Sahidi leaped right into it. She'd only been waiting since her first job interview. "How about the season being suspended because a solution wasn't found?"

"How is that the Commissioner's fault?"

"I'm the Commissioner, Matthew," Puppy said quietly. "It's my fault."

"I disagree." Matthew firmly placed its delicate hands on its hips. "It is the fault of criminals who stole the Hall of Fame memorabilia, costing us the life of teacher Hedda Kleinz, which agitated underlying sentiment against the game. It is the fault—if I may dare—it is the fault of the Granddaughter for making unreasonable demands, not the Commissioner. It is the fault of the Granddaughter, if I may, for refusing to find a solution, not the Commissioner. It is the fault—if I may dare—the fault of the Cousins for agreeing with this anti-collegial approach which, if I may dare, runs counter to The Family. Everything that has happened subsequently arises out of that. The Commissioner ordered hooligans out of stadiums for fighting. He extended that to banning their baseball privilege. He requested that merchandise of home teams be reduced in all the stadium gift shops. He banned the use of wands and other paraphernalia. Banner Day banners were expressly prohibited from displaying disrespectful comments. Signs in the stands are subject to responses from nearby fans over whether they constitute personal offense. Public-address announcements about the need for respect were made every inning and no one may verbally proclaim 'That team sucks.' Here is the proof of that sentiment."

Matthew held the booklet aloft with robotic fury. "*Fans Are Family, Too* has been distributed at every stadium for every game, counseling the need for good sportsmanship. Alcohol sales were cut off after the fourth inning. In four ballparks, the Commissioner allowed aerial vidgrams of amusing shorts between especially intense games showcasing the comedic trios known as The Three Stooges and The Ritz Brothers. A baseball clown has been introduced at Dodger Stadium. What more could he have done?"

Sahidi raised her hand. Matthew waited before grudgingly recognizing her.

"Nothing worked."

"Although you eagerly supported these decisions."

Sahidi's plant-hair jiggled. "If I didn't, you'd be hauling me up for workplace disloyalty."

"Aren't we though?" Matthew impudently rocked on one leg.

Sahidi flung her statement from a month ago onto the coffee table. "I've been very clear from the start how little I respect Puppy and how unqualified I think he is so there'd be no misleading anyone."

Puppy winced. "Thank you for that."

She forced a smile. "Those are the rules. No backstabbing."

"Oh, and what might this be?" Matthew rocked on its other leg.

"Back to the situation," Ian interrupted. "My dears, the choo-choo has gone off the rails. I hear that Clary, pardon, our coquettish darling Granddaughter, has become very difficult to work with. I still have contacts. She's arrogant and erratic. Legendary tantrums. The outside of Grandma's house, and no I will never call it anything else, is being painted orange. Who is violating the Anti-Narcissism Laws? From what I also hear, we were surprised by China inching toward the Allahs. A blind flea could've seen that coming. Our armies have stalled. For all we know, the damn war might be lost and none of this will matter because we'll be swinging from light poles. You too, Matthew. Until then, these are our jobs."

"Not for long," Matthew sneered.

Ian flushed. "I waited to accept my new position, didn't I? Grandma's bra straps, I'm doing marketing for the imports of Ugandan chocolate now that we're in Africa. That's tastier than this. If you could ratchet your brain waves up a bit, what does that tell you about what we're facing here?"

"Can I say something?" Puppy raised his hand as Sahidi and Ian bickered.

"Once I recognize you," Matthew said, formally recognizing Puppy and bringing a needed smile to the room.

"You don't always know why something went wrong. I never wanted to be Commissioner. Clary insisted." He paused as that sunk in. "We did have a prior relationship. Clary had to show she was qualified to be head of The Family. Baseball was a softball to prove that competence. Guess what? I whiffed."

"Is there any proof that the situation will improve without Puppy?" Matthew asked.

"That's not the point," Sahidi snapped.

"Because you want to become the new Commissioner."

"As I've made very clear." After a moment, Sahidi asked quietly, "Should we vote?"

Puppy nodded wearily for Matthew to continue. The 'bot peevishly lingered a minute more.

"On whether Puppy Nedick should resign as Commissioner of Baseball according to Work Rule 4.2. Sahidi Douglas?"

She held up her hand. "Yes."

"Matthew?" The 'bot jumped ahead; no one noticed. "A resounding no."

"Ian Schrage."

Ian studied Puppy as if counting the number of skin cells on his face. "What did Clary say?"

"On what issue?"

Ian grumbled over Puppy's cluelessness. "When she insisted you take the job."

"That's confidential information."

"Break the law. You've done it before. And no drips and drabs."

Puppy sighed. "She protected me from arrest when I got back to America. And all the people who helped me. Like you, Ian, and a bunch of others."

"What manipulative bullshit!" Sahidi yelled.

"It's the fucking truth!" Puppy shouted back.

Ian shook his head. "Matthew, based on available data, who would succeed Puppy?"

"That's not relevant!" Sahidi shouted.

"Call a Blue Shirt. Matt?"

Matthew paused a few moments. "Given that Sahidi has sent all her qualms directly to the Cousins, along with her experience which no one else matches, it is 77.3 percent probable that she would be named the new Commissioner. Predicated on the current status of the game, it is 21.1 percent probable that the post of Commissioner would be abolished, leaving 1.6 percent uncertain. It is also 44.3 percent possible that the 21.1 percent probability of the position being abolished would rise."

Ian scrunched his eyebrows, nose, and mouth into a thoughtful lump and raised his hand. "I vote no."

Matthew expelled a loud whoop. "The motion to—"

"What shit." Sahidi kicked over a couple beer bottles. "I protest the introduction of confidential information which clearly influenced Ian Schrage."

"No one influences Ian Schrage," Ian Schrage said coldly.

"Are you sure?" Puppy asked.

He grinned. "No. But you can't let perfect be the enemy of good."

Sahidi growled down at her feet. "Then let the minutes show that Sahidi Douglas implemented Work Rule 4.4 which states that—"

"That an employee may resign at any point in their employment if they are willing to assert they find such conditions unbearable," Matthew happily interrupted.

"Sahidi, please. Reconsider. You don't like me, but we need you. I need you," Puppy pleaded.

"But we don't need you, Commissioner." Sahidi sneered her way out the door.

Matthew adjusted the dimple in his tie. "There are still the three of us."

"Two," Ian reminded them. "My flight leaves for Kampala in the morning."

"Ian…"

"Pup, I'm sorry. I gave them my word." He clasped Puppy's arm. "You got Matthew. He works faster than all of us combined."

"Thank you, Ian," Matthew said huskily.

Puppy playfully tugged on Matthew's tie. "Matthew, Matthew. Have you ramped up the empathy program?"

Matthew nodded, eyes glistening. "I thought it would be helpful. It is not, as you all well know."

33

Annette blew at the brim of the floppy beige hat which provided no relief from the sweltering heat making her panty line itch and her feet swell.

Once more in my life I want shoes that fit, she scribbled with the nub of the pencil. Even in this disgusting woolly blanket of humidity at eight a.m., the Piazza Mangione was crowded. She scowled away a few flirtations, sipping the icy white Giovanni Rosso wine through a straw.

I can't say where I am because the last time in a place I can't say (get the idea?) they opened my letter and crossed out everything they said was confidential which left about two lines and I told them where to stick it. Let's just say it's hot.

Annette considered whether the nasty person with the fat face who'd been their guide since leaving the Italian mainland would let that pass. She drew thick lines through the paragraph, breaking into a grin that dripped sweat on her neck.

Reminds me of that summer weekend in Monroe when the AC died a noisy death. Least the view is nice.

Annette angrily kicked her heels against the marble steps. Fat face won't let me get away with that either. Prisoner, emissary, pick what I am.

I'm in Palermo, Pup. That's in Italy, she wanted to write. *We've been traveling two days, all back roads. The curly locks put us in the hands of more curly locks who speak Jewish. Could you believe that? We just missed a big battle in northern Italy and Herbert, who is always late, especially for a robot, intuited or whatever he does that the Allah retreat was coming our way so we skipped onto a boat. Heck, it was a raft. Just me and Herbert, a curly locks with a tall hat and a big gun met us out of nowhere and brought us to the water and we rowed away.*

Yes I can row so stop laughing. We could see planes shooting each other down. Absolutely beyond scary, Pup. Herbert was able to lock into systems reports of the battle, which we won, but we lost nearly half our planes. The Allahs lost about all theirs. Now get this. We're rowing along the coast of Italy called Muffie or Mufti, row row row our boats and the Allahs are jumping into their boats, lots of them swimming away. Our robot soldiers were on the beach but didn't shoot, just let them escape.

You guessed it. Some Allah soldiers swam right past us. I mean, Pup, right past us and I thought well, aren't we all equal. I'm drenched from rowing and then they're splashing me and they're scared and I'm pretty scared and then they went by and we continued rowing. They were really young, teenagers maybe. I felt bad for them. Herbert nodded in the way he does. I think he can read my mind which I don't like because you're the only person who understands I don't always agree with my thoughts. Anyway, Herbert's nice and I'd be long dead without him.

Annette took a large bite of the orangish fried rice ball. It was her third *arancina.* She'll get fat and it'll be Herbert's fault for always being late.

In a plain brown suit and fedora, Herbert finally edged through the crowd, returning from the rededication ceremony at Via Abramo Lincoln, and took a seat beside her.

"Positive news. According to an Islamic message recoded near Istanbul, the resemblance to a nuclear attack in that city was self-inflicted."

She wagged her finger. "What does that mean?"

Herbert tilted its head. For a week she'd been teaching him to speak more clearly.

"This means *really*"—the human liked when he emphasized that word for some reason—"that America has not launched any nuclear missiles. This was an instance of Islamic failure to properly maintain their weapons."

"The Arabs were about to launch and it blew up?"

Herbert brightened at her understanding. "That is possible. The radiation levels are fortunately very low. I do not have further details since the relay line utilizes a complex encryption which I do not have sufficient time to access. I can estimate at 25.4 percent…"

He stopped. The human female absolutely did not prefer inclusion of percentage estimates. Last night in the small hut embedded on Mount Pellegrino, overlooking the bay, she had poked him six times in the shoulder. "It is somewhat possible"—he rushed over her squeal of approval—"that nearby American field bases will also have this information."

"Now we might be pissed they wanted to hit us with nukes so maybe we'll use ours after all."

Herbert arched an eyebrow. "That is a simplistic outcome that cannot be analyzed with the current facts."

Annette made a throaty sound and smacked him in the shoulder until he rephrased to, "Who the hell knows?" She made another unpleasant sound. When the human behaved like this it was best to proceed carefully. Herbert had achieved mediocre results addressing erraticism. She was most pleased when he behaved like her until it was necessary for him not to so they could survive. At least Herbert now recognized the signs. The 'bot gestured at the letter.

"Why do you bother? They will not let you mail it."

"I'm not mailing it anymore." She tore up the letter. "I just decided it'll all be in my thoughts."

"Then how will that be communicated?"

She took off her hat and let the fountain water spray onto her head. "Puppy will know."

"How? You do not have transmitting mechanisms."

"Humans have our own ways. You understand me."

"I would not say I understand you, Annette. I follow the various choices you make, but not precisely why you make them."

Annoyed at always being misunderstood by all kinds of life-forms—Martians would probably say, "Why are you acting that way girl?"—Annette nudged Herbert's shoulder. "You got why I cried the other night."

Herbert seemed uncomfortable. "You were tired. Exhaustion brings about an erosion of your emotional stamina, which leads to frustration, which can be expressed through clogged tear ducts."

Annette grunted.

The 'bot frowned. "That is inaccurate?"

"It's not fully accurate."

"Are we to play the guessing game?"

"No, because you're not into it. Look, you can hear my thoughts and stop lying. If you can, why not Puppy? Oh I know, I'm not wired for that. What if I try very hard?" She scrunched her face, reddening at Herbert's faint grin. "What?"

"That is an amusing expression which I have not yet seen."

"No, you just think I'm a typical stupid human for believing I have transmitting mechanisms capable of reaching across thousands of miles."

"I conclude that it is quite an advanced concept and for all we know, you might have an unused mechanism for transmissions. Previous humans have demonstrated that ability." Herbert briefly floated out fifteen names of humans with such a scientifically proven skill. "It is your failure to fully embrace your potential that is the problem."

"Why do you always have to make it sound like an insult?"

"I have never insulted you with intent, Annette. If I have, I would like to apologize."

She squeezed Herbert's arm. "It's okay."

"It is not. Have you determined any coordinates or system to alert Puppy that a non-verbal message has been processed?"

"I have not," she said sadly, feeling like a total failure. "I'm sending thoughts and he doesn't know. Even if I'm realizing my full potential, it's probably just scooting past Puppy without him ever knowing."

Herbert met her hopeful look. "Fashioning an alert of approaching transient thoughts is something we can discuss on the boat trip."

The 'bot tapped her left hand which frequently produced a vulnerably appealing expression. "I have a strong level of certainty that this will be the last for a while. Eighty-six-point-five percent."

Annette tingled, her eyes watering. Herbert braced itself.

She sniffled down the streets, the magic of another *arancina* failing, until they reached the Porto di Palermo. Like immense steel fingers, five passenger ships gripped the dock at the lip of the Tyrrhenian Sea. Turning right, they strolled arm-in-arm another quarter of a mile. Herbert's pale fleshy complexion earned an occasional sympathetic look. Repairing extreme facial injuries with synthetic skin had achieved remarkable advances in the past year of brutal warfare. Another odd human face wasn't particularly noticeable. A few tongues clucked warmly at the lovers.

La Mia Bella Nonna was anchored at the far end of the dock. Two elderly Arab workers strained over cartons of eggplants, the Vuccuria street market logo stamped on the sides. Herbert felt Annette's hesitation.

"Arab influence in Sicily dates back more than one thousand years. Unlike other liberated cities such as Frankfurt and Budapest, there have been negligible instances of reprisals against the Islamic population. The Arab nation of Tunisia"—Herbert gestured toward the east—"is closer to Sicily than to Rome. We can hope this will be a model of cooperation once the war ends."

Annette didn't mention the plastic knife taped to her left calf.

Captain Hammami's wrinkles were set deep into his veiny cheeks like expressive canals. He tipped his stained blue cap and, nodding resignedly at the older men, apologized for the delays of his uncles who had good hearts but bad backs, a combination preferable to the reverse because look where that has gotten us.

Annette liked him right away, even before he'd poured two of the most sensational cups of coffee ever made while they waited for Uncle Mehdi and Uncle Kais to finish loading the vegetables. Amid much shouting, loud sighs, and what Herbert translated as combinations of profanities, the crew and captain finally pushed off the twenty-five-foot craft.

Annette felt liberated, buoyant. The ship, the baking sun, the lapping Mediterranean, the now three cups of coffee, and a plate of olives made her squeal. She laughed for no reason and laughed again because, since leaving Puppy, everything she did had to have a reason. Now she only cared about the warmth on her olive forearms.

After all these months outside, Annette looked Arabic. That didn't bother her anymore.

Hammami straddled a narrow chair, offering some Thibarine. They clinked the small glasses and threw down the liqueur. Annette's eyes widened.

"Now that's good."

The captain was mildly offended. "Of course. It's Tunisian date liqueur."

"Made of what, other than dates?"

"That is all I can say." Hammami raised his long nose. "Dates, sugar, and botanicals. A secret recipe. We all need secrets, don't we?"

Annette nodded at that universal truth. Hammami studied her shrewdly.

"You are very relaxed for a boat ride with Arabs."

She lifted her pants to show the taped knife. Hammami tugged up his pants leg to show his serrated knife in a leather calf strap. They laughed and had another drink. Annette stared at him.

"You remind me of a friend. He's also an Arab. A fishing captain."

"Is he dead?"

"No, why do you say that?"

"You look sad."

Annette suddenly felt sad in her very bones, deeply sad.

"I don't think he's dead. I mean, I hope not." Over the captain's shoulder, Herbert stared warningly. After one thousand miles of this she knew better than to talk. Okay, maybe she got a little giddy the last night in the Jews's camp. She declined more Thibarine just in case.

"We were friends." She dissected an olive and spit out the pit. "Good friends. He was a wonderful man. Good heart. Strong back, too."

The captain tipped his cap. "I'm flattered."

"I've known a lot of good people whom I've cared for. And loved. I hope all of them are okay."

Hammami and Herbert both offered handkerchiefs. Annette took turns blowing her nose. After brief protests, she accepted a life jacket, dipping her bare feet in the churning water.

A rocket knifed the sky in a blazing arc. Annette barely had time to pull her feet back into the boat. The distant mid-air explosion triggered a brief wind, but Herbert continued its internal recalibrations while Hammami and his uncles went about their chores.

Finally, Annette asked, "What was that?"

On the portside untangling a fishing net, the captain called back, "An accident."

His wizened uncles chuckled. Annette pulled a face.

"Rockets just come out of nowhere and then blow up?"

"Sometimes."

"That's a helluva an accident. I thought the war was done down here."

The Tunisians exchanged grins. Even Herbert returned from his inner robot meditations with an arched eyebrow.

Annette angrily put her hands on her hips. "I'm just stupid to ask?"

"A beautiful woman may ask anything without fear of criticism," the captain said with a wink joined by lecherous smiles from the older men.

"Yeah well, a good notion, but still."

She sulked for a while, glancing up apprehensively. When she woke, the sky had darkened considerably. Annette didn't understand how she could've slept for so long. She sniffed the Thibarine glass warily.

Hammami clapped his hands in welcome. "Good evening. Do you feel rested?"

With a snarly look, Annette held up the glass. The captain shrugged sheepishly.

"I am sorry. It was best for you to sleep, Annette," Herbert said, coming up the steps from below. "Landing will just be the start of our journey."

"That's a pretty sneaky trick for a robot."

Hammami and his uncles shot Herbert quizzical looks.

"Where the hell are we?" she asked.

34

Brandishing a damp napkin embroidered with the red script *New Lyceum Theater*, Beth mopped Zelda's perspiring forehead. The cartons containing another two thousand napkins, which could never be used, were stacked in the corner of the dressing room beneath the faint hiss of the steam pipe. The stiff cartons, the blazing overhead light, the polished wood floor, even the drifting steam had more sentience than Zelda Jones.

On opening night when it couldn't be called opening night, Zelda slumped back into the rickety black chair and dutifully opened her mouth so Beth could spray another dose of Shining Breath mouthwash.

"Do we even know what a baby's breath smells like?" Zelda suddenly said, referencing the product's line, *Fresh like a baby's breath*. "I think I smelled Diego's breath a few times, but I don't remember being taken with it like, oh, this is fresh. Now, when I diapered him with the powder, his butt was fragrant. But his breath? Never noticed one way or the other. Course adverts can't lie so there had to be tests conducted. Can you imagine that? What did they do, fill up a test tube or whatever contraption and then break it down so all the molecules or whatever had the same breath ingredients? And would all infants's breath smell the same? What if some babies ate food that gave them gas? Now we're talking real stinky breath. Yes, I might bring this up to a Cousin sometime and ask, 'Hey, what gives with this claim?' Stop looking at me like I'm a crazy person."

"Oh, you're crazy all right but I still want you to walk into the lobby and say hello to your crowd."

Zelda was horrified by the idea and went semi-fetal.

Beth leaned over with breath that was not a baby's. "You can't stay here."

"Why not? I have napkins. Shining Breath mouthwash. Heat. And"—Zelda reached under the dressing table with a triumphant air—"Wyoming Champagne to celebrate the success if we even dare to celebrate because this isn't happening. In our wild youth, Puppy and I got so loaded on this stuff we fell asleep on the subway and ended up in the train yard. All I need is chocolate and I can survive for days and weeks and years hunkered down in my little theatrical bomb shelter."

"Do you want Joan to see you like this?" Beth forced Zelda out of her bathrobe and into her blue dress with a minimum amount of bruising.

"Screw Joan. I want my shoes." Beth took special pleasure in ramming Zelda's swelling feet into the cramped shoes. "Happy now?"

Zelda froze at the door. "Not yet."

Beth hugged Zelda tightly. "Now we're set. Come." She led Zelda by the hand up the steps.

"There's a lot of noise."

"Yes. Footsteps. Voices."

"People," Zelda whispered.

"Lots of people here for the biggest day of your career, a day that'll never be matched no matter what happens afterward, and we know all those possibilities so get the green out of your cheeks and move your cute ass because you've worked my last nerve several times over and as we know I'm not the most patient person alive."

Beth nudged Zelda into the lobby.

Nearly three hundred people milled about like giddy sardines waiting to climb into a can. The crowd spilled past two ornate gold-and-glass concession stands, manned by sprightly young people, back onto West 45th Street.

Joan had fought against charges of elitism to ensure that "proper attire suggested" was posted outside. To refuse someone because they weren't dressed nicely was unacceptable. But Joan had made the case that despite this merely being a reading, respect should be shown for the tradition of the theater where once, evening gowns, pearls, and tuxedos ruled like fashion monarchs.

The enthusiastic crowd had an assortment of wardrobes. A few chose eye-popping dresses with the occasional piece of gaudy plastic jewelry. Mainly, it was mix-and-match. A tie clasped on a t-shirt. A top hat along with the latest craze, faded denim jackets revived through the growing influence of the Twentieth-Century Project. Something called a Nehru jacket. Bell bottoms. Sneakers and tight-fitting skirts and tailored slacks. A bold sports jacket and an even bolder suit; the mohair made Zelda itch from across the room.

With Beth's finger jabbing her back, Zelda sipped her Wyoming Champagne, nodding at the customers. There were more people in this lobby than had ever seen all her plays. She fought back the tremors.

Like a tidal wave in a rustling purple dress, Joan battered a path toward Zelda who had nowhere to run.

"Everyone, everyone." Joan stopped a few feet from the ashen Zelda, surveying her as if for the first time and not without some doubt. "Quiet for a moment. I want you all to meet the person who, along with me, naturally, is responsible for this glorious evening. Our brilliant, visionary, and wondrously complicated playwright and director, Zelda Jones."

Beth boosted Zelda's elbow so she could manage a listless wave. Joan twirled her around for a full inspection. "How do you feel, dear?"

"Nauseous."

The lobby exploded with warm laughter.

"Of course. Everyone. Mingle and drink. Be on the watch if our writer hurls. The house opens in ten minutes for history."

Joan dragged her inside the theater. Beth trailed behind.

"You look beautiful, Zelda." Joan thrust up her arms as if about to launch into song. "You look nice, too, Beth."

Beth self-consciously touched her thin dark hair. "I try."

"That's all some of us can do." Joan spun Zelda around again, which really didn't help her queasy equilibrium. "Guess how many people are here."

"I don't want to know," she mumbled.

"Too bad because you must." Zelda looked at Beth for help, who just grinned. "Four hundred and thirty-eight. I never expected that given the constraints, the uncertainty…"

Joan tittered at Zelda's wide-eyed stare around the quiet theater. "Soak this in, Zelda. Soak in the silence of a theater. Ah, hear that? The last shuffle of a stagehand, the last call about the proper placement of a light. But the noises are still silence because the real sounds are yet to come. You have written a wonderful play, Zelda."

She held up her hand, although no one would dare interrupt. "I have no idea what will come after tonight. For all we know, all four hundred and thirty-eight members of the audience will descend upon various Cousins Lobbies like so many outraged locusts, clamoring for retribution for such daring."

"You said this was legal," Beth interrupted.

Joan pressed her eyes shut tightly, disappointed that Beth remained when she opened them. "It is. Probably, with some leeway. But who knows if even this small moment can be punished. I do not believe it can. Yet so much is chaos now. We could very well be banished from ever working in the theater again. Ever. For all we know, you and I could be neighbors in a DV in Morrisania, drudging up garbage from the basement. That could very well be."

Joan projected ominous tones. "But we will have had this night, Zelda. A night when theater returned as only theater can except for the true staging, sets, costumes, paid admissions, programs, the pageantry. To question and provoke and challenge. That's what you've done, Zelda, over my cowardice and fear and short-sightedness. I thank you for making me realize why I ever bothered to do this insanity in the first place."

Zelda held up Beth's hand. "She helped."

Joan forced out a desultory mutter that sounded something like a thank you.

"Now let's make some history, Zelda Jones."

Zelda laid her hand on Joan's bare forearm. "But I'm giving the speech, not you as planned. Sorry, I know that sounds stinky…"

"Me being the producer." Joan bristled.

"Me being the playwright. I appreciate your brave words about the consequences, but those consequences are because I jerked you around and lied. I jerked around the actors for a while. I even tried jerking around Beth, but that didn't last long. No no." She shook her head a few times to clear out any last doubts. "This is my vision and if The Family's going to bend itself into pretzels, then the first person they're coming after is me.

This is my crazy little world with crazy people running amuck and telling me what to do. I take the fall if there is one."

"If?" Joan smiled faintly. "If there isn't, we've failed. But we better have some outrage or else this damn society's palates are more dulled than even I feared. If the audience leaves with polite applause, then we've truly failed. All of us." Her glance reluctantly included Beth.

"They won't," Zelda said fiercely, ignoring the blinking lights signifying the house was opening. "I wrote a damn good play and if I have to personally go into the audience and slap the sons-of-bitches to wake them up then I will."

"You already did, dear."

There were more than four hundred thirty-eight people in the audience. On the street, curious siblings followed the long trail into the one theater entrance, wondering exactly what all the fuss was about. Just as Joan had shrewdly planned. By the time Zelda threw up for what was hopefully the last time and started toward the stage, the old Lyceum Theater, a grandparent with an astonishing makeover, was two-thirds filled with more than seven hundred people for what the modest signs up and down West 45th Street had merely said was a *FREE READING OF A NEW PLAY*.

Zelda stepped on stage in front of the eight folding chairs for the seven actors, all of whom had eagerly embraced this opportunity with the defiant flair of true artists, and Malane Dillon, who would read stage directions.

"Could someone please lower the house lights? I don't want to see everyone staring and I'm dead-cold nervous enough."

The lights faded into laughter. Zelda looked up and down the stage, suddenly stepping into an awkward soft-shoe dance and humming.

"Don't worry. I won't perform. When I was a kid growing up in the East Bronx DV, I'd act in all my plays until I realized I stunk, but of course you can never totally resist." She did a quick Shirley Temple-esque cutsie dance. "I want to thank everyone for coming out. This is a pretty neat place, isn't it?" She waited through the applause for the Lyceum. "That's the genius of Joan Minh, our producer, who made this reading happen. C'mon, we know you're not shy."

Joan waved grandly from the front row.

"Even for just a simple reading, and that's all this is, a simple non-production," Zelda articulated the words very carefully, "this requires wonderful actors, which we have, who, for those unfamiliar with a reading, will just read the script. No props, costumes, anything that suggests a production." Zelda cued the cast and Malane to enter from stage left and right to supportive applause.

Even in the dark, Zelda could make out Pablo and Diego slipping into the last row.

"But they're not the most important ones here tonight. None of this happens without you, the audience. All you're about to see doesn't exist without you. Nothing that happens on stage happens without you. By coming into our world, by tossing aside your no-tions of what is real and accepting ours, this world we've created for all of you, you make this happen. You breathe life into imagination. You're the real stars and I thank you from the bottom of all…" Zelda almost lost it, continuing doggedly, "the bottom of all our hearts for coming out tonight. Whether you think it's the bahm diggity or the stinkiest play ever, you made the magic possible."

From the moment Malane said, "Act One, Scene One, the lush Forest of Lost Tears, here three towering trees loom over piles of cagily placed boulders in the land of Hobania. Fresco the Cub, a lively young bear, enters." The audience was hooked.

The actors had been left to their own instincts on how to play the parts. Pinto Rae, portraying Fresco, shrewdly delayed his first words to build anticipation.

"Stealing a bear's potato chips was the wrong move, buddy." Fresco shook his fist at the unknown thieves. "But hah-hah, look what I got."

"Fresco pulls out a candy bar," Malane said. "Caesar the Vulture swoops down, swal-lowing up the chocolate and disappearing beyond a tree."

The audience gasped. So did Zelda.

The exchange between the taunting Caesar and Fresco generated sympathetic mut-ters on the side of the little bear. When Fresco explained he was running away from his mother, the house grew very quiet, an invisible hand duct-taping the crowd.

"In my land of Hobania, mommies cannot raise children unless they have a dad-dy or a mommy. My mommy would've given me a daddy, but he died before she could."

"That was pretty stupid of him," cracked Caesar, already an ugly villain.

"It wasn't his fault. He was on a ship trying to help children who were running away from really bad monsters called Mooboogies."

"Then he was a hero?"

"No." Fresco stamped his foot.

Said Malane, "One of the towering trees wobbled a little too much."

"It was a secret. The hawks who run my land didn't want anyone to know they wouldn't accept these children."

A few patrons stirred slightly at the reference.

"What does that have to do with the price of worms in the Forest of Lost Tears?"

"I'm explaining. Since my mommy didn't have a daddy or mommy for me, the hawks would've taken me away."

A grumbling couple in the eighth row slid down the aisle and toward the exit. Joan had warned the cast to ignore any reactions short of machine-gun fire.

Caesar leaned forward in contempt. "Is she a bad mommy?"

"She's the best mommy ever."

"Does she hit you?"

The audience collectively trembled at such a thought.

"Never."

"Does she not feed you healthy things like ice cream and cookies?"

"Three times a day!"

"Does she not give you a nice home with a fluffy pillow?"

"The fluffiest," Fresco sobbed.

"Then why isn't she considered a good mommy?"

"She is, she is, she is. That's why I ran away."

"You're a dumb cub. Why would you run away from the best mommy ever?"

"Because if I stayed they would've taken me away and put Mommy in jail. Now Mommy will be safe and I must make my own way in the world."

Once the scene finished at the entrance of the quarrelsome Kennubi T. Warranitz the Cat, about twenty patrons had left. Peeking out from stage right, Zelda would've sworn Pablo tripped someone walking up the aisle. Still, the restless crowd held.

She just wasn't sure if they were transfixed, shocked, paralyzed by undercooked popcorn, or something else. Hearing breathing would've helped. Then Merkeran the Mommy Bear spoke with the guile of a bulldozer.

"Have you seen a cub? Have you seen my son?"

Said Malane, "Merkeran rushed among the trees as the characters disappeared into shadows."

"I must have my child back," the actor continued. "Please, someone help me. My child is missing."

Read Malane, "Alouette the Rabbit and Jeb the Pug slid down a tree, landing with disdain."

"We ain't seen him," Alouette said.

"Bears, cubs, furry animals like that, nah. We don't like those kinds of people in Hobania," Jeb sneered.

"Especially—"

Jeb shoved the stupid rabbit quiet.

"What is that about?" Merkeran sniffed.

"The shove?"

"The 'especially.'" Merkeran rose to the full intimidating height of the actress Evanda Huntren. "'Especially' means that you might know something."

"Oh no, we don't know nothing," Alouette said, drawing needed laughter, however nervous, from the audience.

"You've seen him, haven't you?" Merkeran took a menacing step, ignoring the warning about moving around and making this a staged reading.

Blinking a warning to Evanda to sit down, Malane said, "Hennessey the Parrot floated down."

"What if we did?" Jeb asked.

"Then you have."

"I didn't say that. Did I say that?" Alouette asked. Jeb shook his head. "I said, what if we seen a cub who may or may not be your child? What's it to you?"

"He's my son."

"If he's your son why isn't he with you? Shouldn't a child be with its mother?"

Merkeran fumed in shame. "He got lost."

"How?"

"I don't know."

Kennubi meowed. "Liar. You just don't lose a child. Didn't you hold his hand? Didn't you have a belt leash? You finally got here—"

"If he already was here," said Jeb.

"Which we ain't saying he is," added Hennessey.

"Leave her alone."

Said Malane, "Fresco pads out from behind the bushes. Merkeran rushes forward, but the animals formed a sturdy wall."

"Not so fast big lady," snapped Kennubi. "You ain't taking him home so soon unless we get a signed statement—"

"With witnesses," said Jeb.

"With stamps and seals," Alouette said sagely.

"Saying you're keeping your kid."

Merkeran looked away.

"Mommy, can you say that?" Fresco whispered a stage shout. "Mommy? Can you promise they won't take me away? That you won't go to jail? Can you promise me all that?"

"I can't." Merkeran sank to one knee, arms still extended pitifully.

"Then you want me to go back so they can give me to another family?"

"That's what you're promising?" Kennubi jeered and all the animals hooted, drowning out Merkeran's feeble protests.

"Let her answer!" Fresco yelled. "Mommy. Are you going to protect me or not?"

As the lights dimmed on the stage, the audience remained seated, waiting uneasily for the play to resume. When the announcement explained there'd be a fifteen-minute intermission before Act Two, the audience slowly rose, exchanging bewildered looks before rushing toward the exits.

Zelda squatted on the toilet, waiting. The lights flickered for patrons to return to their seats. Zelda wouldn't move. Good, you're a coward like Merkeran. Creator, created, all part of the same madness. She slithered down the corridor and darted backstage to her wobbly little chair near the exit door.

The dancing violin chords heralded the start of Act Two. Zelda tipped open the door into the dark theater and nearly lost her small intestine. About half the crowd had returned. Maybe a third. She was furious at these stupid people who wouldn't give her play a chance. Like any good dramatist, the notion that it was the fault of her play didn't interrupt her anger, at least until the rage subsided and she concluded they should cut off her thumbs at the end. Maybe it'd be a good segment on tomorrow's *Wake Up, My Darlings,* Zelda's dismembered thumbs on a pretty porcelain plate as a warning to stinky playwrights who tried to bend the rules of The Family.

As Malane explained, Alouette the Rabbit and Jeb the Pug swept the Forest of Lost Tears as Act Two opened. It was a quiet moment with underlying tension. Why were they sweeping? Where'd everyone go? What was going to happen next?

Angry shouts hammered the doors leading into the theater. The young ushers told the crowd they couldn't return once the play had started. The audience was unfamiliar with such stringent requirements and wouldn't be stopped.

Suddenly the doors burst open. Like her namesake Joan of Arc leading the army of France, Joan burst inside brandishing a flashlight, shouting, "The show will stop and then the show must go on."

Really, only Joan knew what the hell she was saying. Stop, start? Waving her electric torch, Joan personally directed the audience back to their seats. Zelda roused herself long enough to tell the violinist to vamp with some music. He played an incongruous country tune. Jeb and Alouette danced in a circle holding hands. The audience applauded as they settled in.

Act Two was a blur. Even Zelda allowed herself to be swept away by the emotions. Some of the audience left again. Once the drama ended with Merkeran pledging to run away with Fresco rather than let the authorities separate them, and the animals acknowledging that she was a good mother and they could live in the Forest of Lost Tears forever, only half the house was left.

When the lights went down, there was a brief pause, a few tepid claps.

Zelda wanted to die.

"You can stand if you like," shouted Joan, torching the offenders with her portable searchlight.

A few people stood, then realized they should accompany that with applause. Within moments, the entire audience rocked. The cast was so overcome they forgot where they were to stand for their curtain calls, bumping and bowing four times as the applause built.

The violinist dragged Zelda on stage. The cast retreated and the spotlight beamed down on Zelda, fighting back tears as cheers built.

When Pablo handed Diego down the line from actor to actor to be placed in Zelda's arms, she sort of lost it, holding up the squawking baby and saying this was Fresco, this was Fresco, this was Fresco.

• • • •

THE GRIEF COUNSELOR asked three times whether Elias wanted him to stay. Three times was policy. Three times was required for the words, their impact, and a reasonable response under these circumstances.

Kenuda stared blankly at this equation of death's circumstances. That was also a response the grief counselor had often seen. While all grief and tragedy were treated equally, this was flagged as slightly different. They were no longer engaged but had been and were planning on resuming. The grief counselor slipped into the hallway for a 'bacco.

The oddness of becoming one but not yet. *All love is mercurial. That gives it power. When love has been tested by death, you will be tested more than you can imagine. You must accept this pain. You cannot compartmentalize. You are mourning for two.*

Elias rammed the pamphlet on grief into the kitchen trash. A faint odor permeated the metal container. Using an aluminized twisty, Elias spun the bag around like a cowboy's lasso. He fretted a few moments about where to put it, finally leaving the garbage with the rest of Hedda's apartment. After he left, more somber grief counselors would march through deciding what was to be saved.

Saved for whom? The rest would get dumped, burnt, what? He didn't know where to begin, panicking about time. How long did he have to decide what to keep?

Elias sat at Hedda's orderly desk, peering at the neatly sharpened pencils she'd brandished after stomping into his office that long-ago day and explaining how he'd challenge The Family. Determined, adorable. He wiped a tear and put a couple pencils into his coat pocket along with the ancient sharpener; a wisp of shavings clung to the side.

He stared at the wedding photo of Hedda and her husband Patrick who'd been run over on his way to pick up a pizza for dinner. Elias punched out the glass and rolled up the photo. Hedda would want that. Because this wasn't for him, but for her. Such a concept accepted life after death. Maybe just the memories. Suddenly he had a plan. What would Hedda want to see if she visited him even if that was impossible? But wasn't her being dead impossible?

Elias took down a sturdy leather bag from the bedroom closet and stuffed it full of her favorite clothes. He made sure all the seasons were covered, but after nearly squashing the suitcase, he still couldn't fit her overcoat. Instead, he took his favorite plaid scarf.

Kenuda sat on the edge of the bed, adjusting the scarf the way Hedda had worn it. Around midnight he hopped into a taxi. When he got home, Puppy was squatting outside the door rolling a rubber ball in a circle.

Puppy plopped a bottle of Osaka twelve-year-old Scotch on a table. "Another import, if kind of roundabout by way of Venezuela and Japan, but the guy in the store said it's tops."

Kenuda fell into a narrow armchair, fiddling with the scarf.

"I'm happy to open the bottle if this interests you."

Kenuda managed half a nod. Puppy poured them triples.

"Good, huh?"

Elias suddenly bolted up, yanking open every drawer in the apartment before returning with a small hammer and thumbtacks. He rammed Hedda's wedding photo into the wall and smoothed out the picture. Kenuda threw down the drink and dropped back into the chair as if someone else had caused this fuss.

Puppy warily poured out more Scotch, reconsidering the wisdom of this idea. He had a pint of DeBussy Cognac in his jacket if needed. "I'm sorry, Elias. I am really—"

Kenuda cut him off with a look and continued sipping.

"What now?"

Kenuda tilted his head quizzically.

"I mean, the grief. What will you do?"

He pointed to a gray cap on a side table. "Cabbie."

"I thought only 'bots were taxi drivers."

"They're opening that profession to us. My dream."

"I can see that. Freedom of the road."

Kenuda stuffed on the cap. "That's right."

"Being your own boss."

"Except for the customers."

"Who you never get to know."

Kenuda's expression darkened. "Exactly."

"No real personal contact."

"None. None. None."

Puppy refilled their glasses. "Kenuda's Kabs has a ring."

"Ding fucking dong."

Puppy searched inside the refrigerator and returned with a neglected banana and peeled it.

"I don't know if I can compete with Kenuda's Kabs and the freedom of the open road in the Bronx, but, well…I'm up against the wall, Elias. Everything's going wrong."

"Was your once and hopefully future fiancé just murdered?"

He sighed. "Okay, you win."

"Yes, I do." Kenuda took a longer sip, blinking back tears. "Could you possibly get to the point? I'm taking out my first cab at six this morning."

"Ian's going to Africa to sell chocolate. Sahidi quit because I wouldn't resign. It's just me and Matthew. I need someone who knows what they're doing because I'm in way over my head."

Kenuda laughed bitterly. "I will not have anything to do with The Family. Nothing. Do you hear? I'm finished. Thank you for the Scotch. Now leave."

Puppy crossed his legs. "I understand all that."

"Since you're still here, you clearly don't." Kenuda hadn't moved from the chair. It looked like he couldn't.

"You were a Cousin. You know how things are done."

Elias gestured imperiously. "That worked out just splendidly."

"It did for a while. You ran baseball."

"And basketball, football."

"Entertainment," Puppy added.

"I was also intimately involved in the distribution of quesadillas in the greater New Paltz area. Which means nothing. I can't advise you on baseball, Puppy. If they found out, I'd be buried in the DV. And you'd be fired."

"They'll fire me anyway, sooner rather than later."

Kenuda agreed with a nod.

"We'll do this theoretically," Puppy rushed on. "Yeah, I know a few big words. I'll ask hypothetical questions which have nothing to do with baseball and you give me hypothetical answers."

Elias made ugly sounds. Puppy stood over the chair.

"Every time I do something important, I think about what Annette would say. Like a perpetual HG on my shoulder. Sometimes she really blasts me. And yes, that's different than Hedda. But she's somewhere in Eastern Europe, Elias. She's looking for the pope. I know. Annette. What're the chances she'll make it through Allah lines, through the war zones? She could already be dead. Sometimes when I don't feel her HG on my shoulder, I figure that's what happened. She's gone. But I feel that she'd approve of what I'm doing and there she is again. Wouldn't you like to have Hedda's HG on your shoulder?"

Elias swiped out Puppy's legs. His large body enveloped the startled commissioner, his forearm against his throat.

"That's cheap and disgusting and if you ever succumb to that again I'll break your windpipe. Do you hear me?"

Kenuda waited until Puppy coughed out in agreement. "Now forget your moronic theoretical formula. After Hedda, I don't give a crap what they do to me anymore. Just tell me what's going on."

35

Horatio the Pug wrinkled his forehead in precisely the fashion he knew would get him his way.

Pablo frowned. "That would mean another hygienic wipe down."

Horatio looked back with unblinking condescension as if he didn't know the procedure for being present during a patient examination. Since becoming a fixture at the dental practice, Horatio reckoned he had chomped down more than a dozen Sam's Bully Chews with only one small accident from a bad pretzel he'd eaten on the street.

Pablo turned toward Diego who was making assorted strange sounds. Before leaving this morning, Zelda had handed Pablo her very own *A Handbook and Guide to Diego's Alien Noises and Behavior*. Insulted, Pablo explained that he was quite capable of interpreting their child's sound waves. As if chapter two were also needed: *What to do if Diego stops breathing.*

"Do you agree with Horatio about needing another wipe?"

His son gave him that perplexed look that Pablo had hoped the child would've outgrown, but he was pushing nine months now with no obvious verbal skills in sight.

"There's more to life than staring, Son."

Pablo patted the crying baby, grateful Zelda wasn't there to scold him.

"Sorry for the sternness. Mommy's busy today enlightening scads of unenlightened theatergoers, but we'll set up our own communications system which Mommy won't be privy to."

Certain that Diego's grimace of a smile indicated an evolution in the father-son bond, Pablo unhooked the carriage from the wire chain around the leg of his desk, wrapped Horatio's leash around his wrist, and led the family into Examining Room A.

"Mr. Leonard, Allen." Pablo gestured at the carriage and dog. "I would like to include my son, Diego Jones-Diaz Jr., and my pug, Horatio, while I conduct the examination, if this pleases you."

Pudgy Allen slid off the examining chair and shyly approached Horatio who jumped onto the boy's stylish knickers, sealing the deal. Manipulation was sometimes necessary in dentistry. Diego amused himself with a rattle, earning a diffident shrug from Allen.

Dental Hygienist Saverino was summoned to wipe down Horatio and spray about the carriage for any potential infant-borne germs.

Mr. Leonard, the owner of Len's Nail Boutiques, prattled on about the new nail dyes available from liberated Kenya, his wife's failure to regularly floss, which earned a silent reprimand from Pablo, and their vacation plans for Caracas.

"May I concentrate on Allen for the moment, please?" Pablo said with as much politeness as he could muster while addressing a braggart. His recent appearance before the Dental Regulating Committee had brought up his occasional impatience with the parents of patients. Fortunately, Mr. Leonard was so consumed with the benefits of nails to the world's populace that he didn't notice the edge.

"What school do you go to again, Allen?"

"P.S. 77."

"Fine school. In Crotona?"

"Yes, doctor."

"What do you play?"

"He's on the football team," Mr. Leonard proudly said.

"If you don't mind, sir, it's most helpful if the actual patient answers."

Mr. Leonard grumbled slightly about unprofessionalism, which Pablo knew would pop up on some sibling complaint.

"I'm on the Crotona Park Rangers like my Dad says. I take piano lessons twice a week."

"Bangs out a helluva Mozart." Mr. Leonard smiled smugly.

"No doubt. How do you feel, Leonard? Any problems?"

Allen glanced at his father. "No."

"You sure? The mouth is the window to the body."

Mr. Leonard poked his son.

"Sometimes I don't sleep well."

"Oh?" Pablo casually adjusted the instruments on the side table. "In what way?"

"Strange dreams."

"I warned him against guacamole before bedtime."

Pablo intercepted Mr. Leonard with a look. "What are the dreams like?"

"I see myself twice."

"Twice?"

"I see myself here." The eleven-year-old pointed to the floor. "And over there."

"You have dreams being in Dr. Diaz's office?" his father asked.

"No. I mean just somewhere. It's cloudy. I get a little scared."

"What happens then?"

The boy swallowed. "I run to my other self but I'm confused about which me I am. Then I'm the other me. Then this me."

"It's the guacamole," Mr. Leonard said less confidently.

"Does the fear continue?"

"No."

"Why not?"

"What's this got to do with his teeth?" Mr. Leonard asked testily. "He's a quarterback, you know."

"Sir, please. What takes away the fear, Allen?"

"I see the Granddaughter."

"He's going to be on *Wake Up, My Darlings*."

"Are you?" Pablo leaned closer. "How'd that happen?"

"He was chosen after going on a school trip to the Granddaughter's house."

Pablo pushed away the uneasiness. "What was that like, Allen?"

"I don't much remember."

"You have to recall something."

"He got an allergy attack," Mr. Leonard explained.

"I sneezed a lot. The Granddaughter has a lot of plants in her bedroom. They gave me a shot. The sneezing went away."

Pablo quieted the boy so he could poke under his tongue, getting a swab which he innocuously placed in a glass jar.

"And you felt better?"

"Oh yes. I just don't remember much. Funny, huh?"

"You probably had an allergic reaction to the allergy shot." Pablo got relieved smiles. "That happens." He forced as much casualness into his voice as he could. "How often do these strange dreams happen?"

"Tuesdays."

"And Thursdays," Mr. Leonard added. "I think it's also too much piano, but my wife insists."

"And we should always listen to our spouses." Pablo waited for his hand to steady. "Let's take a deeper look into the many teeth of one Allen Leonard, pianist, quarterback, and nonpareil, shall we?"

Pablo added the samples to three dozen others in a metal container in his office fridge. He'd run the tests later when the office was closed, but he expected the same results. Nearly forty children, all with the same traces of inorganic compounds. All within the age range of eight to eleven. All what would be characterized as Regulars, the parents all owners of nail salons, gas stations, an architect here, teachers there. Everyone had taken a school trip to see Clary.

"What to do?" He directed this at Diego propped up in the highchair, face smeared with Bunny Carrots puree. "Come now. Mommy insists she hear your voice."

Horatio snored loudly in the corner.

"If there are forty just in my dental office, how many are there nationally?" Pablo mused. "If the treatments are only given at Clary's house, that wouldn't be terribly efficient."

Diego burped up gooey carrots, somehow a brighter orange from the brief journey down his esophagus.

"Exactly." He absently wiped the baby's face. "Treatments must be followed up. How would that be achieved? Caravans, trainloads, young children parachuted from the sky? No. Too small a sample. Children would need to be treated en masse. En masse," he repeated, juggling Diego as he walked around the office.

"That would be at schools. But every one of the patients had the same story. Ah, ah!" Excited, Pablo thrust up his left arm, nearly dropping Diego. "Perhaps this is merely experimental. Perhaps there are several phases afoot."

After circling briefly, Horatio did his business on the wee pad in the corner, though he remained attentive with a tilted head.

"That isn't to say reconfiguring young adolescents is to be minimized, but this might not be their true course of action." Pablo answered Dental Hygienist Saverino's buzz that yes, he was aware that his patient schedule was now running behind.

He placed Diego back in the highchair, splattered dry chicken-flavored kibble into the grateful Horatio's bowl, and typed in a request for his patient files. The computer assistant asked the reason and he wrote back common symptoms of the children.

The files came back within moments. All forty children were members of Clary's Cids. That program was national.

Pablo thought another moment about what to do. He suspected he was on the verge of a Zelda-like adventure. He should discuss this first with Dr. Fern Pachado, current chair of the Bronx Dental Society.

Grandma slipped inside the office.

"My goodness." Pablo nearly dropped the baby. "I forgot our appointment."

"We didn't have one, dear. How are you, my darling Diego?" Grandma pressed her forehead against the baby's forehead.

Diego sputtered wildly, hands and feet waving with coos.

"Me, too," Grandma answered.

Grandma placed her hands on her hips, exchanging a series of head-tilts with Horatio before the pug jumped vertically into her arms. There were many snorting noises as Lenore settled into a chair, stroking the dog's apricot-colored fur.

"You look confounded, Pablo."

"About my experiments or your conversation with my son and dog?"

"Your son and dog love you very much. Let's focus on the experiments."

"I have a hypothesis and I don't. But I have suspicions, Grandma. Many suspicions."

"It's best if you don't share them with Dr. Pachado." She smiled at Pablo's surprise, tapping her temple to underscore their erratic consciousness link. Pablo relaxed, fearing he'd forgotten a previous conversation.

Grandma assessed Pablo's private lab diagnosis, frowning. "Thank you."

"That's it?"

"For now."

"We can't stop here."

"This is merely symptomatic."

"But deeply disturbing, Grandma. Extremely disturbing." Pablo pressed Diego to his chest. "My son is clean. I make sure of that."

"You don't trust the day care." Grandma looked very sad. "That was one of the very first institutions we rebuilt. If you can't trust the people who watch over your children, the teachers, child custodians, health care…"

Pablo felt bad about upsetting her. "Perhaps I'm just overly cautious."

"Maybe." Grandma whispered into Horatio's ear and the pug nestled deeper into her arms. "These are the branches, not the roots, Pablo. And we can't do anything that indicates we suspect what's going on until we know for certain where it's leading." Grandma fixed him with a look. "Can you free up your afternoon for a house call?"

"Absolutely. Another adventure?"

• • • •

THE LINE FOR stateless passports, the second largest designation in the Islamic Empire, moved quickly enough through the Port of Valletta.

Trolleys bounced over cobblestones, a sharp honk awakening diffident mules tugging hay-laden carts. Black-robed Jews in fur hats, oblivious to the stifling heat, huddled in twos and threes, as impervious to Annette and Herbert and just about anyone else on the neatly cleaned sidewalks as the mules flaring their nostrils at the ancient cars from the early twentieth century. Muslim Imams walked past in the opposite direction, occasionally hailing a Catholic priest with a brisk wave.

The still woolly-headed Annette insisted on a cold drink. She sipped a sickly sweet iced tea, leaning against a building and putting her cropped hair in a tight bun.

"The clock's broken." Annette nodded across Saint Zachary Street.

Herbert arched an eyebrow. "That is intentional to deceive the Devil. Many of the churches in Malta such as St. John's Co-Cathedral have different times or dates on their front. One is for parishioners, the other for the Devil so he won't know when services begin."

Annette wasn't buying any of that. "If he's the Devil, wouldn't he be smart enough to have his own watch?"

If Herbert were programmed for laughter, it would've doubled over. "I think the inspiring illogic of faith is something our friend Father Dempsey could have answered."

Annette abruptly made the sign of the cross. She answered Herbert's stare. "I figure he's in Heaven and can see us, so I wanted to let him know we were thinking of him."

Herbert calculated the correct time. They had arrived a little early.

"That church is known for its skeletal tombstones. St. John's was built between 1572 and 1577. Three hundred and seventy-four of the remains of the Knights of Malta are buried beneath the floors. The Sultan of Turkey, Suleiman the Great, had sent an army of approximately forty thousand to attack Malta, but the seven hundred knights and eight thousand soldiers withstood the siege. Let us visit the site."

Annette was dazzled by the gilded walls, golden arches, and the ceilings laden with frescoes and glittering gold leaf. Herbert smiled faintly as she half hopped around the marble floor as if afraid to disturb the dead.

"The Latin epitaphs describe the virtues of each of the individual knights," Herbert softly translated. "Triumph, fame, victory, and death."

They paused at Claude de Rovroy de Saint-Simon's tombstone. The knight was in the embrace of a skeleton, leaving his armored shield behind.

"The Latin says he was born in 1694 and became a professed knight in 1727. Galley captain in 1733, general of the galleys in 1735, and held four commanderies in France."

"Brave man. He looks so sad. All that fighting and he's still sad and afraid." Annette glanced at a nearby tombstone, the skeleton surrounded by a sickle and hourglass. "But he's not forgotten. That means we'll still be around."

"I do not think I will be interred like you, Annette."

"It doesn't matter if you're mostly machine or mostly flesh. It's about being remembered. Like you and me here, stomping on the coffins centuries later."

She abruptly knelt and rubbed her palms along a tombstone inlaid with armor and shields. Herbert motioned away a solicitous tour guide.

"May I join you?" Herbert asked.

Herbert rubbed its palm on the floor. It gave him great delight and he could not understand why. Annette squeezed Herbert's hand and tugged him up.

"I have not seen that before." The priest's bristly gray hair seemed glued to his wide head. "Nice to meet you, Ms. Ramos."

Annette looked between the priest and a chunky rabbi.

"Herbert?" the priest asked.

The 'bot nodded.

"Thank you, robot. You may leave us."

"What? No." Annette stared at Herbert.

"Leave, robot," the priest repeated firmly.

Annette reached for the knife taped to her calf. The rabbi twisted her arm up the middle of her back. As Annette squirmed, all the tourists disappeared.

"There is no reason for that," Herbert protested. "I am accompanying her."

"Not anymore."

Herbert's palm blurred into the rabbi's side. His gasp of pain echoed.

"Since I rescued Annette Ramos from imprisonment, it is my duty to ensure that no harm comes to her. I am accompanying Ms. Ramos or we are leaving." Herbert met the priest's scowl as the rabbi searched for breath. "There are four options under that scenario and there is a 93.1 percent likelihood your decision will be met with disfavor."

The priest and the rabbi exchanged irritated nods and led them through an inconspicuous exit and down a winding metal staircase. They walked through a dank tunnel on an uneven cobblestone path for about a mile before emerging inside a small musty room with heavy red drapes.

As Annette indulged in some spicy scrambled eggs laid out on a small table, the priest introduced himself as Father Drobev and his colleague as Rabbi Gold.

Drobev waited for Annette to finish the oat bread with spiteful slowness before pulling a chair over. "We want to thank you for making this trip. May I call you Annette?"

"It's refreshing to use my real name."

"I'm sure. You've planned on finding the Holy Father for quite some time?"

"Since Puppy Nedick, my husband, and I escaped to London."

"Because he was accused of treason and murder."

"I think he's been forgiven now that he's the Commissioner of Baseball, which is a pretty big job."

"What made you consider finding the pope?"

Annette sighed. She wasn't going through this again. "Look boys, I'm not going to be interrogated anymore. I've been questioned by most of the world's major religions. I left my husband. I've nearly been killed more than a few times and look at this hair. These clothes. I'm so tired it hurts sometimes when I pee."

"That could be a urinary tract infection," Herbert offered from across the room.

"See?" Annette waved her hands. "So what's your problem? I'm here to bring a message of peace from America."

Drobev frowned. "Of your identity, we have no doubts, Annette. Nor of your recent history. The underground apparatus that has helped you to this point is all under our control."

"Who are they?"

His smile wasn't pleasant. "If you wouldn't mind, I'll ask the questions."

"Yeah, I kind of do because I have my own. Is the pope here on Malta or do I have to be dragged across another ocean to another island?"

Gold brought the steaming priest a cup of steaming black coffee. Drobev blew steam off the rim of the mug. The woman was good. Perhaps the best so far.

"As much as we'd enjoy a casual conversation, I'm afraid I can't answer that."

Annette folded her arms. "Well then."

Gold held up his hand to cut off Drobev's protest. The rabbi's smile was painted on.

"Despite your obvious courage…both of you"—the rabbi tipped his head at Herbert—"you could not have made it this far without help. We must know who helped you. Who sent you to the correct points along the Rat Line?"

"That is an excellent question for which I do not have an answer," Herbert replied. "When Annette was brought into custody by the Fourth American Army Group and taken to a former military installation outside Budapest, I received a message directing me to her specific location."

"What kind of message?" Drobev asked.

"Nonverbal. It would be difficult to explain to humans."

"Try," Gold suggested ominously.

Herbert thought. "It was a notion. An instinct. A hunch as you might refer to it. Something gave me a course of action so that I could free Annette and leave the facility and the unwanted custody of my colleagues. I have received five similar, subsequent messages directing us to various cells of what I assumed was your organization and was proven correct. I have not been able to trace the origin of these messages. I attempted to communicate nonverbally but did not receive a reply. The nature of the messages is unknown to me. I do not know how the sender accessed my system nor can I explain how they knew who I was or my relationship with Annette."

"When was the last message?"

"The messages ended when we disembarked in Palermo, Italy eight days ago. The final message merely delineated the time of the pickup in Sicily."

The priest and rabbi exchanged worried looks.

"Our pickup was not confirmed until you arrived in Sicily," Drobev said. "You received a message before we sent it?"

"I cannot explain."

"Has that ever happened before?"

"We were never questioned in this manner, so I do not know."

"You just showed up at point A, point B along the way."

"Correct."

His frown deepening, Drobev asked, "Herbert, would you share your receiver systems so we could run our own checks?"

"What do we get in return?" Annette snapped.

Gold scowled. "You will be treated with respect."

"Like not thrown into a cell. Beaten, starved?"

"Ms. Ramos has the propensity for dramatics," Herbert explained.

"Oh no, she is quite correct," the rabbi said. "Your treatment depends on the level of your cooperation."

It took a couple minutes for the 'bot to transfer the information into a tiny device brought by a young nun with hard eyes.

"I was a pretend nun for a while," Annette said as the novice hurried out.

"We want to make sure there are no other pretenses," Gold said.

"Another way of saying I'm lying."

"That could be."

"And I'd go through all this for what reason?"

Gold glanced at Drobev. "In the past two years alone, we've had so-called peace emissaries from all parts of the Empire and beyond. Just three weeks ago, a Buddhist monk found his way to supposedly talk to the Holy Father about brokering a peace accord. We uncovered a miniaturized bomb in the monk's anus, pardon me. He was here to assassinate the pope. That made 233 such attempts since the end of the war. Of course, you don't look like an assassin, which is the point. Obviously someone wants you to meet the pope. Who and why?"

"I'd remember if someone shoved a little bomb up my butt."

"No, you wouldn't. A device could have been implanted when Herbert gave you a sedative on your boat ride to Malta." He enjoyed Annette's squirming. "There are indigestible explosives which live in the small intestine for up to a week. Remotely activated. One would-be murderer had a tablet of intensified bioxins in her back tooth. Bite down, activated. You could be on a purely innocent mission, Annette. I sense sincerity," he lied. He didn't trust her. "That would make you ideal."

"Then how do I prove I'm innocent? Herbert already told you the messages weren't human-like. How are you going to believe me?"

"We are suspicious, but always hopeful," Gold said.

"Right. But if you can't…" Annette regretted being so persistent.

"Then this will be the final leg of your journey. You won't be allowed to leave Malta."

"Alive or dead?"

The two men just stared back.

36

After a blistering letter—*What happened with you and my sister has nothing to do with me. Believe me, I haven't spent my life running around defending Sahidi. She lives hers and I live mine and she's lorded being three minutes older long enough. Now, are you done insulting me as a moron who can't think for herself?*—Puppy had gratefully accepted Sandra Douglas's help.

The younger twin created an alternative Mooshie Games sportscasting team. Once the honor system was invoked concerning whether the ball had cleared the fence or popped triumphantly into the catcher's mitt, the decision was DV-signed to an announcer; all the out-of-work radcasters had eagerly signed up.

In a loud and boisterous voice, the results were then relayed to the crowd. In the early days of radio, Sandra explained, the sportscasters added sound effects. Two drumsticks produced monstrous shots. A miniature fan replicated groans of a runner out at home. A block on wood conceived that wondrous thwap of a fastball.

A ringing requested HG clearance into the office. Interrupting Puppy and Matthew's meeting, Cheng flickered onto Mooshie's lap.

"Oooh baby," she said with a laugh.

"In your dreams." Cheng self-consciously touched the bandage on his forehead. "Yeah, well, we had a little loud disagreement today."

"Loud disagreement" had become the code for players battling when honor was no longer in reach.

"Duane Rapace, you know how he gets…"

Puppy groaned. Rapace needed a leash.

"Rapace took issue with a pitch he insisted he'd smacked into the ivy while Tony Felton"—Cheng waited until Puppy finished another groan—"agreed he missed by the pro-ver-bi-al mile. We had to separate him and Felton, which was not easy. You know how he is, too." Cheng cleared his throat. "The Blue Shirts had to step in."

"That's the third time this week, Albert."

"Everything was very cordial."

Puppy should've insisted the umpires still retained the final call. But what better way to demonstrate how baseball reflects the purest ethical basis of The Family than letting the players rise above the competition with honesty and, ultimately, compromise. Yeah well. "And the Jet'roes?"

Cheng hesitated. "We saw a couple BTs get out and watch."

"That's it?"

"That's it."

"You sure?"

"I know the damn difference between a Blue Shirt and a Black Top."

Puppy sighed. "Suspend both Rapace and Felton for two games for fighting. And add another game for failing to agree in a sportsmanlike fashion."

"What?" Mooshie yelled. "You can't do that for showing a little exuberance."

"Suspending players for conduct detrimental to the game is well within the Commissioner's prerogative," Matthew said tartly. "These games are still under the auspices of Major League Baseball."

"How far do we go down that road?" Cheng growled.

"Before we have BTs restoring order. You know they're just waiting for that. We had a game at Tiger Stadium today paused in the fourth inning because of noise complaints from neighbors."

Sandra's sound effects worked too well. Siblings had initiated the arduous process of going down to their local precincts to lodge protests. From Tampa to Denver, Phoenix to Minneapolis, mainly Regs had filed the paperwork insisting that calls of "a rope into the left-field corner" or "swisheroo" had disturbed the tranquility of the late-spring evenings.

The games evolved into imaginative whispers.

"Shuffling past." Fans watching the Mooshie Games were in perpetual motion. Shuffling past around the pretend field, standing for only one pitch.

"One and done." If you watched more than one pitch, you risked a summons from a weary but sympathetic Blue Shirt for attending an illicit performance of an unscheduled baseball game. Those Blue Shirts who hadn't "lost" their pads and pencils on the way.

If you moved on, you were just passing by. To the train, public toilets, a slice of pizza, or a can of pop. Shuffling. No applause, either. As if mocking the banning of emotional demonstrations inside the stadiums, the fans on the pavilions, the streets, beneath the elevated train, carving out a chunk of the parking lots, wherever the players of the Mooshie Games set up, were mute, only their faces reacting. Shuffling silently, eyes locked on the game.

Course, what baseball fan would only watch one pitch?

Welcome to "Switching." You found a tissue to cough into for the second pitch, eyeglasses for the third, baseball cap turned right for the fourth pitch and turned left for the fifth and backward for the sixth. You rolled your socks up and down, buttoned and unbuttoned blouses, ate a Chew Dog Caramel Cone on one—shuffling past—and a wad of Wakuza Gum on the next.

Matthew handed Puppy some ice water, gesturing to take a moment. Puppy sipped and fretted and fumed.

"Relax, handsome," Mooshie said. "Mooshie's Games have saved baseball. Everyone's having a good old time."

"It's too sloppy."

"Here we go with one-testicle Nedick."

"Thank you, no-brain Lopez."

"Please, this is unprofessional behavior." Matthew scolded them. "Mr. Cheng, Ms. Lopez, I hope you will absorb the Commissioner's brilliant new plan before castigating him."

Cheng and Mooshie waited with dark stares at the improbability of Puppy and brilliant in the same sentence.

"Thank you for your rapt attention," Puppy said sarcastically. "I'm hearing from the owners who are complaining about losing revenue for tickets. The concession stands are hurting. These are all small local businesses."

"The lockout's not our fault," protested Mooshie.

"They see it as both sides being to blame, Moosh. 'bots are complaining about losing their jobs. The local rad stations are down money without the three adverts per game. The radcasters aren't getting paid. And yes, neither are the players. Right now, the only thing keeping us afloat is the support of the Friends of groups and they're also getting upset. The Friends of Goose Gossage are here, in person, every day. They're not pleasant people. And I get HG notices from the Friends of Ichiro Suzuki in the middle of the night. Everyone's coming at me except the baseball clowns and now there's a damn Friends of Max Patkin so who knows what joys that'll bring. 'What about the stats? Will the games be made up? Why are you risking injuries? Will this affect the promised playoffs which'—like I need to be reminded—'would be the first since 2065?'"

"They want you to cave."

Puppy snorted. "It was a brave stand at first, but now, like all brave stands, there's second thoughts facing the consequences. I've had four owners offer to shut down the sale of merchandise if that'll help. A few suggested doing away with the public-address announcers so the fans wouldn't know who was at bat which might cut down on booing and cheering. And believe me, there'd be rejoicing if we went back to only the one radcast *Game of the Week*."

Mooshie and Cheng looked disgusted.

"We got Mooshie's Games," she said indignantly. "What more do they want?"

He marveled at her ego and not in a kind way. "A real ball to chase, how's that? There's no schedule. Everyone shows up when they can. Yeah, it's fun, but that'll die soon. According to Blue Shirts reports, estimated, and I stress that word, attendance has dropped forty-two percent." Puppy paused as Matthew digitalized the appropriate official documents over the coffee table.

"And like I've said over and over, we're dancing around fire. Technically we're trespassing by playing ball without a permit on what's stadium property." He scowled at their fake moans. "Sooner or later a Blue Shirt patrol will have to shut down a game because of noise complaints. They've been great. A few have even pinch-hit. But the law's the law. Still, that's not what really worries me. We're too damn close to BTs. Last week Paul Weinstock claimed he was merely chasing down a line drive which magically landed ten feet from the Jet'roes stationed by the elevated subway."

"Paul was just having fun." Mooshie defended her Yankee teammate. "Nothing happened."

"But something could've."

Mooshie fixed him with a hard stare. "Maybe it'd be better if something did."

Puppy shuddered. "Is that what you want, Moosh?"

She shrugged. "I ain't the one who padlocked the stadiums, handsome."

"All the more reason for real baseball."

"The chains on the gates seem to be against us," Cheng said slowly.

"Yes they are. But what if that wouldn't matter?"

He finally got their attention.

• • • •

A **WELL-STOCKED DENTAL** examination room had been set up within Clary's bedroom. The dull-eyed dolls in costumes from the French court of Louis IX watched Pablo studiously inspect the scan of the Granddaughter's lower-right jaw.

From the thick orange chair, Clary grumbled about the delay.

"I have my job to do like you have a job to do so please, allow me to do that." Pablo's stern response was carefully monitored by the Black Tops at the door. No one was allowed inside the bedroom without the presence of guards, an officious 'bot named Linda had informed Pablo on the way up the stairs.

Clary spun the chair around and yanked open her mouth. "It hurts here."

"Given that the dying nerve is inside, I need to be more precise than that."

The girl made ugly sounds about precision. As Linda had warned and Pablo could clearly see, she was in a foul mood.

"Your good friend has exacerbated my discomfort," Clary said sullenly.

"Which good friend?"

"The one with his stupid new league. MBL. MBL. There is even a sign here in Van Cortlandt Park."

Pablo fiddled with his white dental gown, avoiding the cold stares of the guards. "It is my understanding that the park belongs to all of The Family, Granddaughter."

"Are we not clever?" Clary sent out mocking laughter, orange "har har hars" dancing around the room, before she cut it short with a moan. "He does this to annoy me. To challenge me."

Pablo cheerfully slid over the rolling tray of instruments as if shopping at the grocery store. "I haven't seen any."

"Then you are blind. That is what I need. A blind dentist. Have your wife Zelda, who I once called Mama Zelda, take you to a park. Perhaps you will see the photos of the old and dead players. MBL coming soon to Boog Powell Field. MBL coming soon to Larry Doby Field. MBL coming soon to Roy Campanella Field."

Clary rose out of the chair and expelled a thunderous montage of more than one hundred signs. She slumped back into the chair, pale from the pain.

"Are we now done?" Pablo asked.

Her eyes glittered. "Puppy Beisbol is done."

"He's been done before."

"But not by me. I will not tolerate this behavior anymore." Clary wagged her finger. "I have been kind. Understanding. I allowed the Mooshie Games because I would not punish my people for having fun and believed Puppy Beisbol would realize his errors." She only managed to expel one droopy "har." "Yes, he has made many errors but this is the largest."

Clary waited for an appropriate response, but Pablo merely shrugged. "That's something that you should take up with Puppy. I'm here to treat your root canal."

"And where is your respect, Dr. Diaz? You are in my bedroom—my bedroom. You are the only dentist who has ever been here."

Pablo tipped his head. "I am honored, Granddaughter."

"For what? I do not trust any other dentists."

"Do you know many?"

Her eyes narrowed. "Dare you try and trick me, Dr. Diaz?"

"I merely asked a question about your familiarity with the dental profession."

"I had a dentist in Barcelona. Dr. Pietro Sanchez. A great man. He treated my entire family before the Allahs cut off his head." Her glare suggested that was a suitable punishment for all dentists who offended her. "You are here at my sufferance. This minor issue with my teeth must be resolved so I can focus fully on Puppy Beisbol. No. He is now just Puppy Nedick. Tell him that."

"It will be the first letter I write when I return to the office. Whenever that might be."

"Do not be funny. Now remove this unpleasantness."

Pablo readied a stapler of painkiller. Clary recoiled.

"What is that?"

"It is marilophine. It will deaden the area so there is no pain."

"I do not need that."

"Granddaughter, there is a small surgical incision required."

"Then incise. I can place my mind elsewhere."

"It will be very painful."

"Do as I say."

Pablo frowned. "If you flinch, this might complicate the procedure."

"I will not flinch," she said with steely warning. "Now proceed, Dr. Diaz."

● ● ● ●

BY THE SECOND scene in the second act, the slip-slapping noise of the actors's feet on the sloshy cement of Red Hook produced a few titters in the audience. Zelda didn't care about thwupping any more than she cared about the whooshing of an ambulance roaring past or the mocking girl trio on a fence lip-synching her dialogue.

But Beth cared, cared deeply as if drying the damp, once-flooded Brooklyn was her sole reason for waking. She ducked for no reason beneath the faint bulb simulating theater lights and tossed handfuls of crunchy sand solution onto the reading stage, a sidewalk outside the newly opened Furry Friends. Ignoring Zelda's weary sigh, Beth superstitiously tossed the sand over her left shoulder, exiting with a shy bow behind the van featuring the logo of dogs, cats, humans, and 'bots holding hands. There was uncertain applause. Do you applaud the crunchy-sand crew-member-intense producer the same way you applaud an actor?

This was one of the better attended readings despite the occasional barking dog requiring dialogue to be repeated. Eleven guests here in Red Hook, nine in Astoria outside the taxi service, and eight in the Claremont section of the Bronx, though Zelda claimed customers leaving with six-packs from Chuggin' Ale Warehouse had lingered long enough to be counted as part of the house.

Yet somehow, the same damn thing happened in Red Hook as happened everywhere else. When Fresco the Cub pleaded with Merkeran to be his mother even if she wasn't married, the audience grew as if instantaneously breeding.

"If you love me, what does it matter, Mommy? Why should love stop there? How can anyone measure a hug?"

It sounded so trite to Zelda's artistically sensitized ears, but that moment hoovered folks. As if they were waiting, laying back, purposely indifferent. Like they knew what was coming: Act Two, Scene Six. By the time Fresco leaped into Merkeran's arms and Jeb Pug and Alouette the Rabbit sang the *Happy Dance* tune, the audience had tripled. Customers lugging squirming puppies and kittens out of Furry Friends clogged the street like the siblings outside Ramon B's Taxi Service and Chuggin' Ale Warehouse and Pop Goes the Weasel Toys and Fragrant Flowers.

As the cast lined up, Officer Gentile, a heavy-set Blue Shirt with the complexion of an old pear, intercepted Malane's reading of "Lights Go Down" with a sour look.

"Sorry siblings, that's it."

Beth got there first. "It's already 'it,' officer. This is the end of the reading. But thank you."

Zelda motioned for the actors to quickly take their bows, drawing loud applause and a sharp look from the Blue Shirt joined by his partner, a frizzy-haired woman built like a messy desk.

"He said that's it." Officer Gondo smacked her hands together. "Please disperse."

"What's the problem?" Zelda took over. "We can perform on the streets."

Officer Gentile smiled as if he'd waited his entire career for this. "Not according to the provisions of the Anti-Narcissism Act amendment dated June 2nd, 2099."

Zelda folded her arms. "I bet you're going to honor me, the playwright, by reading it."

"As is the law," Gondo said. "Are you Zelda Jones?"

"You know I am."

"I do not know anything of the sort without proof. May I see your Lifecard?"

"Are you arresting her?" Beth jostled Zelda's shoulder. Customers poured out of shops, watching.

"Did we say that? Did we read anyone any rights about your responsibility to know the laws?" Gondo glanced at Zelda's Lifecard; Beth insisted she scan hers, too.

Gentile cleared his throat. The irritated crowd jumbled down the street. He wouldn't be hurried. His commanding officer said there might be turbulence.

"Dated June 2nd, 2099. 'All outdoor entertainment of any kind requires a Cousins Certificate.' Since this was just issued by the Granddaughter, you aren't guilty of violating this order. If this play is performed or read again anywhere in the forty-eight states, then you will be required to furnish an explanation before the Committee for Art in your local area." Gentile glanced around and lowered his voice. "Interesting play."

The cops politely tipped their caps and the crowd grudgingly parted to allow them to pass. Beth hopped almost vertically onto a car hood.

"Thank you all for coming." Beth cupped her hands around her mouth, shouting as if all of Brooklyn were there. "I give you the writer and director, Zelda Jones."

Loud applause shook the street. Zelda bowed deeply. Someone played a harmonica. Zelda introduced the cast one by one, who ran around shaking hands and a few paws. A gaunt woman with eyes so sad they could make you cry grasped her wrist.

"Thank you, Ms. Jones. I had to give up my son eight years ago. He would've looked like Fresco. I made a mistake one night. But how could it be a mistake if a beautiful child was born? I would've been a good mother. They still took him. I don't know where he is. Please don't let them stop you. Please."

During the long subway ride to the Bronx, Zelda fell asleep with her head on Beth's shoulder. Beth let them into the dress shop, making sure the blinds were drawn before turning on the back light.

"I don't think the cops followed us." Zelda gratefully accepted a stiff shot of Highland Park whiskey. "And if they did, so what? Isn't like we can have another performance."

Beth frowned. "What're you talking about?"

"Uh, the Zelda Jones do-not-engage-in-street-theater law?"

"Were you in the same place as me today, Zel? Did you see what happened?"

"Yeah. Very emotional. Distraught woman. Good show but Kennubi flubbed his monologue again which isn't easy when you've got the script in hand."

Beth took away Zelda's half-finished plate as if weighing punishment. "You've touched people with your play and its meaning. Its power."

"Goal 101 of playwrighting. Make 'em laugh, make 'em cry."

"Exactly. Then you continue. This is a fight, Zel."

"Oh, please don't start with that crap…"

"They're testing us, Zel, seeing how much they can get away with. How much they can take away."

"By stopping me from presenting a play that spits into the very fabric of The Family? I knew what I was writing. I didn't care. Joan didn't care. Oh, why are you persecuting me for willfully breaking the law? Elias Kenuda pulled that stunt and absolutely nothing changed."

"Yes it did, Zel. People are emboldened to challenge how we're all living. What we can say and do. If The Family is about individual responsibility, then it's time to act upon that. Look what Puppy's doing with the Mooshie Baseball League."

"He's always gotta one-up me." Zelda's wry smile faded before Beth's intense stare. "I wrote the play I wanted. No one forced me. I let loose with my own demons, anger, what I went through with Diego. It's done. It's out and now over. Let me finish, please. That's what artists do. You don't get that."

Beth glared. "I'm a dressmaker. Don't you think that requires creativity?"

"Sorry…"

"Don't apologize, because in your heart that's how you feel. Making a dress isn't quite on the scale of writing a play and hearing applause. Talk about elitism."

Zelda sighed. "This isn't about who's the more creative. It's about your political fervor. Admit how you'd love to be a rebel, a real rebel, resurrecting the Blue Wigs."

Beth pursed her lips. "No. It's about taking your own stand, Zelda. For once, don't be some train wreck going ninety miles per hour without brakes."

Zelda was hurt. "Is that how you view me?"

"Isn't that how you view yourself? You got sloppy and got pregnant. You had no choice but to marry Pablo. You would've rescued Puppy, but only on orders. You've been fired from pretty much every job you've ever had."

Her eyes glistened. "Gee thanks, friend."

"Except now." Beth's voice softened. "Except now, honey. You've found yourself. You're a brilliant writer who's set something important in motion."

Zelda gave her a long look. "Which you encouraged from the very start. As your hammer. You manipulated me."

Beth's face went taut, drained of any affection. "Yes I did. Yes I did. Because you have the talent to strike that blow, light that match. I couldn't. You wrote a story for all mothers, Zelda. Really, not just mothers. Everyone. Do you realize that? It isn't just about what you experienced with Diego Jr. It's about loss. The loss of a child, the worst loss of all. My losing Frecklie, that woman losing her boy. That's what makes it so powerful because this story transcends law and government. Loss is felt all over the world, in this damn war and since the beginning of time. The simple pleading of Fresco for his mother to keep him, to hug him, is more powerful than the robot armies or the message of Allah or Grandma's Insights will ever be. And you want to throw that away?"

They argued both their sides until the apricot pie was gone and they had nothing left to say. Zelda could only manage a weary wiggle of her fingers. Beth resewed Mrs. Davidoff's blouse before heading home through the mild, foggy night.

The lights blazed throughout her small house. Usually by two in the morning, Dale was home under cover of darkness.

Puppy sat at the dining room table. Dale curled up in the corner like an angry ball. It was like a snapshot several hours old.

Ignoring Puppy, Beth turned toward Dale. "What's up, Dale?"

Dale's sullen stare remained locked on Puppy. "I don't know. The Commissioner wouldn't say until you came home."

Beth dragged over a chair. Two sullen stares seared Puppy.

He kept his face still. "I'd like to know what Dale knows about the theft of the Babe Ruth baseball."

Beth slowly took that in with a glance at the indignant Dale.

"Why would she know anything?"

"Because I have information saying she does."

"You a fucking cop?" Dale stood. Beth waved her back onto the pillow in the corner.

"Where'd you get this mysterious information?"

"I can't say."

"You're surely not a cop because they'd have to say," Beth said warily.

"One of the benefits of getting it elsewhere."

Beth straddled the chair and hushed Dale's profane mutters. "Why are you gathering information about my parallel daughter?"

"I wasn't. I was getting leads about the baseball robberies. Someone said it was Dale."

Beth angrily motioned Dale away from the bedroom doorway; the teen didn't budge, dripping hate all over Puppy.

"He wouldn't be here on some idle whim," Beth said over her shoulder.

"Why not? He lost the Hall of Fame memorabilia. Real genius. He looks bad. Have you seen the signs on the subway lately? Graffiti it's called. *Where's Our Baseball, Puppy?* He's a complete joke, his staff have walked out, everyone's pissed, so obviously he needs to find a thief to make himself look better because his game has been locked out."

Puppy shrugged. "It would help."

Dale blurted out triumph.

"But that wouldn't make me lie."

Beth met his steady look. Grudgingly, she motioned for him to continue.

"I asked a friend who has contacts in the underground market. He found a girl around Dale's age who also goes to HS 45 who's traded items before. She said she could get the Ruth ball. My friend said he was interested. She said she'd ask her pal Dale Tanaka."

Dale grunted disdainfully. "What the hell does that mean? Someone lied about me?"

Beth stood. "Why would they lie about you, Dale?"

"Jealousy. I've got about two brains more than anyone else in school. I could do gymnastics all over anyone if I cared. I'm the best looking. Could be this 'girl'"—she air-quoted—"is someone who wanted my tight ass and I turned her down and now she's looking to get back at me."

"Has that happened before?"

"Thousands of times."

"I don't recall any reports of student complaints."

"You haven't known me forever."

"It'd be in your adoption file."

"Must've gone missing like Babe Ruth's baseball."

"Stop." Beth stepped toward Dale. "Where were you the night Hedda Kleinz was murdered?"

Dale trembled. "Now you're accusing me of murder?"

Beth kept her eyes on Dale as she asked over her shoulder, "What day was that, Puppy?"

"May 24th."

"Where were you on May 24th, Dale?"

"I don't remember."

"It wasn't that long ago."

"I'm busy. Lots of brain at work." Dale tapped her forehead.

"Were you home?"

"Probably. Where else?" She flushed at Beth's stare. "Yeah, I was here."

"Can you prove that?"

"I don't have to prove anything. You're not the police."

"Worse. I'm your mother."

"Parallel mother," she sneered.

"Can you prove you were here?"

Dale tapped her front foot. "Do you think I made a vid of me eating your shitty food?"

"No. So then all we need is the truth."

"I'm telling you the truth. Why the hell would I want to steal Babe Ruth's little baseball?"

"I don't know."

"But you think I did." Dale reddened. "You think I did it?"

Beth paused. "You hate baseball."

"I worked with Cheng on the clinics. I don't hate baseball."

"Yes you do."

"Now you're thinking for me. Influencer influencer influencer," Dale accused, pressing into the doorway.

"You hate baseball like I do."

"No one hates baseball as much as you do, Momma."

Beth panted slightly. "No. But you're close."

Dale made brave tinny sounds.

"You hate baseball for what they did to Frecklie."

The teenager gashed the doorway with her stubby fingers.

"It started as a prank, didn't it? Typical Dale hubris."

Dale dug deeper into the wood.

"Figured you could show them, didn't you? Steal the ball, show you could, then return it anonymously. Dale conquers the world. No one gets hurt." She held onto the chair. "Except someone did. Hedda Kleinz didn't give in. She fought back. She challenged the great Dale, the Dale who must be invincible, who must be perfect because

Dale sleeps every night and wakes every day in her own fears and pains. Something happened. Something terrible happened. You didn't mean for that. Hate always turns on yourself. Always."

Dale scratched the wood until blood trickled into her palm.

"Where's the ball, Dale?" Puppy quietly asked.

"That's what you care about?" Beth whirled.

"That's all I'm allowed to care about."

Dale led them into the backyard. She dug through the top of Frecklie's illegal grave where Beth had buried her son after he had been riddled by Black Tops bullets while defending Dale during the purported terrorist attack at Yankee Stadium last year.

Dale palmed the baseball which was wrapped in birthday paper and a red bow. "I wanted Frecklie to have this. He deserved it. He loved the ridiculous game so much, dreaming of becoming a baseball stadium architect. I thought he could play catch wherever the hell he is."

The blonde teen handed Puppy the ball. He held out both palms.

"No. Let Frecklie have it."

"That's illegal, Puppy!" Beth shouted.

"Yup."

The scuffling sounds of Dale's hand shoveling the dirt back into the grave were finally dwarfed by her choked sobs. Beth led Puppy around the side of the house and down the walkway. She stopped and buried her head in his chest. Puppy held her tightly. It'd been quite a while since he held a woman.

Beth stepped away, her thin hand a clamp on his wrist. "What're you going to do?"

"That's up to you. I'm sure as hell not turning her in."

"She killed someone," Beth murmured as if trying to convince herself otherwise.

"Maybe wait a little before doing anything."

Beth blinked as if jolted awake. "I can't wait, Puppy. At what point do you stop violating what you believe in to defend the other things you believe in?"

Puppy brushed Beth's hair back off her forehead. "When you finally figure out what's the most important."

37

By the time gangly Parker DeWitt approached gate three at Fenway Park, 121 fields under the still-pending Mooshie Baseball League (A.K.A. the MBL) had opened across the country. The canny Kenuda, channeled by the grateful Puppy, had recommended a simple business proposal to the newest Fifth Cousin, Javier Gronkowski.

Only three days into the job, according to the announcement in the *Webster Avenue Cousins Lobby*, Javier, stout in head and body, was a Cousin on the move (as we all were

344 | GARY MORGENSTEIN

despite the non-ego crap, Kenuda explained). Javier had rubber-stamped the idea without any consultations or inquiries in his first act as a Cousin. In fairness to Javier, siblings didn't make business suggestions to The Family for ulterior motives. The assumption was sincerity. Duplicity, subversion of rivals, pursuit of the hallucinogen of greed were unthinkable. Besides, Javier was an exuberant football fan. Baseball made him gag.

Second Cousin Franny DeRico nearly pulled out Javier's eyebrows one by one when he proudly routed the establishment of the new MBL onto her desk. DeRico couldn't overrule Javier without evidence of financial malfeasance (none) or gross incompetence (brewing). At best, she and the rest of the Cousins could only require further amplification of the aims of the new league, which drove the Granddaughter into a ferocious temper tantrum rendering the doughnut-sludgies machine inoperable for the foreseeable future.

For now, the MBL was cited as "experimental." Puppy and Elias suggested via the new Director of Baseball Operations, Matthew, that the games be called exhibitions. Informal records would be kept by each team. Since the games were held in public parks, they couldn't be barred.

And you didn't have to whisper.

With the Blue Shirts feigning ignorance of celebrity-worship laws, posters of twentieth-century greats greeted fans dragging makeshift seats of folding chairs and blankets to Bill Freehan Field and Reggie Jackson Field and Randy Johnson Field and Phil Niekro Field. On and on. In North Beach, there was a rambunctious contest between proponents of Willie Mays and Willie McCovey to select the name of the field. Clowns in Giants uniforms trotted around the field chanting the competing statistics of the Giants legends. Two Willies Field was born.

Clown cries spread as if the red-nosed entertainers were crawling out of water mains from under America, popping up in Seattle to chant Edgar Rodriquez's lifetime numbers, in Houston to proclaim the greatness of Larry Dierker, and in Minneapolis to sing the glory that was once Tony Oliva.

A sheet that would've made Thomas Paine proud appeared on light poles outside the fields on how to calculate batting averages from, of course, Ernie the Wizard. The earned run average, which confused everyone, took on a mythical hue, leading to the Cousins ordering an investigation into what exactly was meant by E.R.A. Brave teachers introduced these formulas into math classes under the stubborn aegis of the Twentieth-Century Project.

At the conclusion of each game, hats of all kinds, from top hats, berets, and baseball caps to even a fire chief's yellow helmet, were passed around for donations toward the upkeep of the fields. No one was getting paid. They were all having too much fun.

After a week, the major league stadiums reopened and the 2099 season resumed.

Sort of.

By Granddaughter Order number six, attendance at all ballparks was confined to only those siblings who had never attended a game, among other restrictions of which the eager Cousins, particularly young Javier, approved. Throughout the twenty-hour vidnews programming, brief spots—*Support the Family, Play Ball*—ran every twenty-eight minutes. A well-mannered presenter would read the requirements and cut away to Clary playing catch with obedient children of above-average athletic ability. Employees and teachers were encouraged to provide afternoons off for any qualified siblings who were entitled to purchase a ticket.

Those who qualified received a crisp outline of the new Dos and Don'ts of major league baseball fandom:

Booing is rude and cheering is ungracious. That is not the way of The Family which supports all. Applause is permitted after a well-done play. Wait for the scoreboard prompt.

All signs of any nature are expressly prohibited as potential influencing.

Purchasing food at the seats is prohibited. This interferes with other fans's enjoyment of the game. There will be five-minute concession breaks at the end of the third inning and the beginning of the seventh inning.

Bathrooms may be used as needed.

The Star-Spangled Banner *and* God Bless America *will no longer be played. Siblings do not require martial music to love their country. Singing or the playing of instruments of any songs will result in removal from the baseball stadium.*

The American flag will no longer be flown since our brave soldiers do not display the flag on their uniforms.

Regionalism is prohibited. Wearing all baseball gear such as caps and shirts for any team is prohibited.

All balls hit into the stands must be returned. There are no gifts in The Family.

Autographs are strictly forbidden.

Parker DeWitt had been outside Fenway Park since just after nine a.m.; this was his first job since graduating from HS 211 and the eighteen-year-old from Charleston was determined not to be late. His father already thought he was an addle-head. It was a nice day, slightly humid as were most days with the steady transition to real weather. Thunderstorms had knocked off the side of their backyard shed last night. That angered his father as did most everything. Since he was past his third drink, he blamed Parker, as always.

Parker carefully laid his ticket-stubs basket on the ground to the left. Feeling very proud, he listened in his head to the sound of an orchestra congratulating him with a lot of brass. The senior ticket taker, a sour woman named Claire, added a stack of papers along with a purple box slitted on top.

Parker frowned. During the hour-long training session, he'd paid very close attention, as difficult as that always was, taking many notes and asking more questions than

346 | GARY MORGENSTEIN

anyone. The instructor was annoyed but Parker was used to adult irritation over his loyalty to detail.

"Pardon me, what is this?"

Claire's hard face scrunched into a fist. "No one can enter without answering these questions."

"I thought you only needed a ticket."

"You do need a ticket." She smirked. "But they also have to answer these."

"But that wasn't in the training."

"They decided at the last minute to make sure no one sneaks inside."

Parker squinted at the questionnaire.

Are you or have you ever been a member of a baseball team?

Have you ever attended a baseball game on either a professional or amateur level?

Has any member of your family ever played baseball or attended a game?

Are you related to or friends with anyone who has ever worked in baseball on either a professional or amateur level?

Do you currently or have you ever owned any baseball memorabilia?

Parker pondered this until Claire impatiently shoved him.

"What if they don't want to answer?" he asked.

"Then they don't get in."

"Even if they have a ticket?"

Claire exhaled disgust on a wave of bad breath. "You need both."

Parker perspired. Sweating noticeably was something else his father complained about. "To get inside?"

Claire rolled her beady eyes at the entrance. The one p.m. contest against the struggling Chicago White Sox and the fading Red Sox hadn't attracted much of a crowd.

"What about out here?"

"This isn't inside, clod face."

"I mean to work here."

Claire pursed her lips. They'd made a big fuss about not letting anyone inside without filling out the questionnaire. They hadn't said anything about working outside. What if this knuckle nose suddenly had to go inside to the bathroom? She gave him a quick once-over, deciding he couldn't hold it in for two hours.

"Yes," she said.

"Yes what?" Parker was waiting for the trumpets in his head to finish.

"You got to answer the questions, skeeve face. You ready?"

He was very afraid. He never did well with tests especially when he hadn't been able to study, which usually didn't make much of a difference. Parker forced himself to concentrate, his face so intense that Claire laughed pityingly.

"Have you ever been a member of a baseball team?"

He shook his head.

"Okay. Have you ever attended a baseball game either professional or amateur?"

"Attend how?"

She wasn't sure. "Like bought a ticket."

"No. But I have passed by a game in the park."

"With a ticket?"

"No. With my grandfather."

"Is he a ticket?"

"He's dead."

Claire would definitely grab a beer after this. "Has anyone in your family ever played or gone to a game?"

"I don't know."

"Either they did or they didn't."

"I don't want to lie."

"Puss face, lying is if you know and don't say. Do you know?"

After a moment, he shook his head.

"It's good you're stupid."

"Thank you." Parker wiped his forehead. "Are there many more questions?"

"No. Shut up. Are you related to anyone or friends with anyone who works in baseball?"

He carefully considered this before shaking his head.

"Last question."

Parker almost cried with relief.

"Do you have or have you ever owned baseball memorabilia?"

He struggled over the word.

"A souvenir, fool." Claire was about done.

Parker played with the word, ransacking his brain and hushing the piano. He looked down at his feet, slowly raising each leg so high he nearly tipped backward over his stool.

"What the hell is that?" Claire hissed.

"Socks."

"Socks?"

"Red Sox socks. They have the insignia," he proudly said. "My grandfather bought them before he died. Does that count?"

Claire sighed. "Yeah. And you gotta go."

"Where?"

"Away. You can't work here, doo-doo bird. Those socks are memorabilia."

Parker dripped sweat before raising his finger as if solving all the problems of the universe. He slipped off his shoes and began removing his socks.

"That doesn't work." Claire shoved the socks back on; they struggled. "You failed the test."

"No!" Parker shouted. "Please. I'll throw them away. Please."

"You still owned them."

"You take them." He walked around barefoot.

Claire recoiled. "Then I can't work here."

"But I have my father. You don't."

Two BTs scampered down the roping of the stealth 'copter. Their orders had been very clear: only maintain order if there were no blue-uniformed police officers present. There were no blue-uniformed police officers present and the shouting human half wrestling with the heavier organic life-form had created an unruly crowd unable to enter the sporting arena.

"I am Rafael," the slender BT said. "What is the disruption?"

Claire quickly filled in Rafael. Parker stared in sheer panic. He had never been this close to a Black Top and it was all because of his grandfather's socks. He didn't understand.

The 'bot turned to Parker. "You must come with us to avoid further disruptions."

"I didn't do anything wrong. I didn't know this was bad." Parker skirted around the socks as if they were a bonfire. "See? I took them off. I will be barefoot. Or I will buy more socks." He pathetically waved his Lifecard.

"You must come. You cannot work here if you did not satisfactorily answer the questions according to the Granddaughter Order."

Parker obstinately shook his head. He explained that his father would beat him if he lost the job.

The other Black Top stepped forward.

"I am Justine. This is an illegal act against The Family. Failure to cooperate means you will be taken into custody."

Parker started crying. More like howling.

The 'bots reached for Parker's shoulders. With another cry that some later swore they heard inside Fenway Park, Parker kicked the 'bot's groin. Hitting metal with his bare foot distracted him from the larger pain of the BT gloved blow to his throat.

• • • •

PUPPY AND MATTHEW brushed through the crowded Pennsylvania Station lobby beneath the ornate white columns and ceilings trimmed with the latest Barbara Sue Bloom murals. Hurrying past luminated vids of 'bot soldiers guarding a child sailing overhead on a pulsing orange *One Family* cloud, they half skipped down the circular steps to track fourteen. A dour 'bot conductor in a red-striped uniform and blue felt cap blocked their path.

"Train's sold out. Wait for the next." The A30 flipped open its pocket watch. "Train seventy-seven will be arriving precisely at 6:53 p.m. with stops at Boston, Mass."

"I need to be on the 4:20 train," Puppy said, his voice straining.

"Doesn't everyone or else why would you be here?" The conductor tittered, faltering when no one else saw the humor. "Next one arrives at 6:53—"

Matthew gripped the pocket watch before it could be flipped open. "Make room please."

The conductor's eyes slanted. "I can't without available seats. Standing isn't authorized for this train."

"This is Baseball Commissioner Puppy Nedick and he needs to be in Boston pronto and with full speed ahead."

Matthew allowed the conductor to process the jumbled phrasing.

"You expect me to alter rules for an official? What's next? Special cars for VIPs?" The 'bot's lips twisted scornfully. "A private train for the Granddaughter? Cousins 'Copters? There'll be no end to this."

"There might not be if you don't do this," Puppy said hoarsely.

"What in blue blazes is going on here?" A white-haired 'bot conductor with a noticeable limp which Matthew assessed was for affect, hobbled toward them. He had two pocket watches, indicating seniority.

In rushed non-verbalization, Matthew and the conductor explained the situation which aggravated the senior 'bot to hand-waving exasperation.

"I remember when 'bot meant 'bot. A dullard machine. Well, my Aunt Hattie doesn't have skinny legs if I'm just disregarding some customer who supports our railroad and could choose some other means of traveling without hearing him out. And you folks, shush and let us handle." The conductor quieted the impatient line.

The 'bots waited until Puppy realized they wanted him to chime in. "There's been riots at Fenway Park. At least one person's dead. It's my job to handle the situation and the only way I get there on time is by your incredible new superliner which I've been eager to sample anyway."

The older conductor let out a sound like an engine dying.

"Well dang it, I haven't heard a snow job like that since the blizzard of '91." It wagged a finger at the smirking junior conductor. "But this ain't requesting any privilege, because death and a job handling death is a priority if you got enough of a brain to see that and they're gonna pay like anyone else. We got three crew seats and since when does a conductor have time to sit down?" This last accusation almost made the junior 'bot blush.

The Beastie Boys superliner arrived a minute ahead of the N.E. Corridor schedule, a "damn miracle" proclaimed the senior conductor, gesturing toward the thick lines pouring toward the gates. Puppy insisted on five minutes to watch the vidnews encircling the lobby, but there were only segments on the reopening of Yosemite Park, a dog show in

Pompano Beach, and good-natured warnings about flying kites in this weekend's stormy weather heading down from Maine. Nothing about Parker DeWitt.

Matthew easily found the address in the Charleston DV, a dreary two-story home long past needing a paint job. Mute teens clustered on the front lawn with nothing to do except scowl. A tall man with cheeks the color of tomatoes shrugged as they walked inside.

The living room was empty except for two older women with nearly identical tear-stained faces who held hands on the plaid couch, staring at Parker laid out on a cot. A side tray held watery lemonade and beer.

The young man still wore his blood-stained clothes, a tradition in DVs dating back to the end of the war. Burying was banned because of too many bodies and the fear of demonstrations triggered by religious rituals. Since cremation was mandated, families were allowed extra time with their deceased.

As if a scuffle were ending, a very drunk man with crisp-white hair stumbled out of the kitchen trailed by two friends who'd clearly been trying to settle him down. Fabrizio DeWitt's rheumy eyes settled at different places on the 'bot in a suit and Puppy in his baseball hoodie.

"Mr. DeWitt, I'm Puppy Nedick."

The name meant nothing to him. But one of his friends prodded Fabrizio with a whisper. The father tottered forward.

Puppy continued, "I wanted to pay my respects. I'm very sorry for your loss."

Fabrizio grunted, which turned into a belch smoothed out by a Harbor IPA. "What'd you have to do with this?" He angrily shook off his friends. "I know'd Parker worked at the stadium. You give him the job? You interview him? You ever meet him before?"

"No, sir. But…" Everything I did led here, he thought.

"Now you want to share in the grief? S'my son. Mine. You got no right glomming on this." Fabrizio stumbled forward. "Say that to your reflection. And don't come into my house pretending to care."

"I lost someone at Yankee Stadium just like Parker," Puppy said huskily. "Frecklie Rivera. Reuben. He was like my kid brother. I felt responsible for that and I feel responsible for Parker. I just came to say I'm sorry."

Fabrizio applauded. "Now you did. A real big shot. A real big man. All that means shit to a skunk because my son's dead and when you get your ass out of here, you'll never think of him again. How dare you act like you got rights to grieve."

With mumbled apologies, his friends dragged Fabrizio back into the kitchen. One of the sisters led the shaken Puppy to the door.

"They wasn't close," she explained. "My brother's an asshole. You just stepped in a pile. Thank you for coming, Mr. Nedick. If Parker was alive, he'd thank you, too."

Stopping at the front door, Puppy hurried back and touched Parker's cold forehead, squeezing the boy's hand. Fabrizio watched from the kitchen, stone-faced.

The area around Fenway Park was dark for three blocks in all directions. An occasional siren shrieked, a muffled shout, but that was about it. There was no curfew yet, said Elaine Broom, meeting them by the entrance to Yawkey Way. But all mass transit was shutting down at midnight.

Elaine seemed genuinely shocked. Owning a baseball team was supposed to be fun. First the Red Sox had lost ten straight and some coworkers shunned her. A woman refused to date Elaine as if the drop into the division basement were her fault. Now this debacle. She should've applied for minority ownership of the Boston Celtics where there was never any trouble. Stupid DVs. Stupid baseball fans.

"It's best if we leave the situation as is until morning, Commissioner."

"You come up with that idea all by yourself?" Puppy sneered.

"There's nothing to be done. I suggested you stay in the Bronx."

"Then I never would've got into the city under the curfew. Aren't I a genius?" Puppy glared. "Let's go."

Elaine nervously stood her ground. "Where?"

He pointed into the inky night.

"No. It's too dangerous," she said, poised to run if necessary.

Puppy trembled with rage. "I'm the Commissioner of Baseball. That's my job and I'm going to be there. You're the owner of the Boston Red Sox. That's your job and you should be there, too."

"That's the job of the Black Tops," Elaine said. "They'll be there."

Disgusted, he and Matthew made their way past Blue Wigs-style crisscrossed bats fastened to the shuttered stores to the edge of Fenway. Scarecrows dangled from dimmed light posts, small flags protruding from their mouths.

Join Or Die.

There were no lights because BTs had night-vision programs. Tanks and Jet'roes were positioned every twenty feet. Beyond the metal chain fence only a few hours old, thousands of fans in red Boston colors stood like a silent jury. The BTs ignored them; orders were to avoid further injury to humans. Apart from an earlier volley of baseballs and two overturned cars, the crowd hadn't attempted any more violence near the stadium.

A slight BT lieutenant met them at the fence, rifle on its shoulder. "Yes?"

"I am Matthew. This is the Commissioner of Baseball Puppy Nedick who is here on official business for a formal inquiry." Matthew adjusted its voice so it echoed. That stirred the onlookers into wondering murmurs.

"No one is permitted inside, Matthew," the lieutenant responded. "Please leave and take the Commissioner of Baseball Puppy Nedick."

"He will not leave."

"Matthew, thanks, let me pick it up from here." Puppy looked squarely at the BT. "Would you mind lifting the visor? It's kind of hard to talk to a reflection in the dark."

The BT lifted its face mask, narrow-faced with wide green eyes and a thin nose. "What's your name?"

The BT hesitated, surprised. "Lieutenant Evie, first class."

"Nice to meet you."

"No, it is not."

Puppy smiled faintly. "You're right. It's not. I wish this hadn't happened, but here we are. My understanding is that you have thousands and thousands of fans inside Fenway Park."

"They have refused our calls to come out."

"They're probably scared. I'm told they ran inside when the murder—"

"Incident." Evie pursed its lips. "The details of that event are currently being analyzed. If Black Tops are not attacked, I guarantee the safety of the human fans. We will escort them out in the morning."

"That's very nice of you."

"You can lower the sarcasm, Commissioner."

Now Puppy was a little surprised. "That's my best way of staying calm, Lieutenant. But I'm not allowing my fans to be locked inside a ballpark all night."

"The weather is not inclement. The temperature is predicted to move along the fifty-five-to-sixty-two-degree axis. They will neither be hungry nor thirsty because there are refreshments available."

"It would be illegal to take food from the concession stands without paying." Matthew bristled.

"Screw the food and the axis of the temperature," Puppy snarled. "I'm not allowing BTs to enter a baseball stadium again. That's against the law."

"It will not be by morning."

Puppy nodded in sudden understanding. "There's no way violence will be avoided if you force them out. There's already three dead."

"Now six including a BT sergeant." Evie's voice tightened.

"Sorry to hear that. A life's a life, right? One Family, right? So this is what we're going to do, Lieutenant Evie. You're going to let me into Fenway Park and I'm going to bring out the fans. Then all these spectators out here can leave before something sets off more violence and more die. Now let me pass."

Evie regretted the empathy program complicating its options. "That is not possible."

"It most certainly is," Matthew announced in that bullhorn voice. "According to Major League Baseball guidelines, the Commissioner is entitled to enter any ballpark at any time."

The BT looked between them. This was the best plan. The best plan did not always originate from superiors. Ignoring superiors could lead to chaos. Obeying superiors had so far led to the deaths of five humans and one 'bot.

The BT motioned for Puppy to go past but stopped Matthew.

Matthew made a point of showing much exasperation and some tie tugging. "And that applies to the Commissioner's staff."

Evie nodded its head to let Matthew through.

"Can you please turn on the lights?" Puppy asked. "Or else it's going to be dangerous moving folks out."

"I cannot do that," the BT answered.

"Why not?" Puppy snarled.

"I do not have control over this power source. That is controlled by orders of the owner of the Boston Red Sox franchise who cut off electricity at 3:54 p.m."

Puppy went cold. Son-of-a-bitch Reg.

Above the fence, a 'bacco lighter suddenly flashed. Then another. Then lots more lights. Fans stepped aside for a car's headlights. Another. The sullen Boston police, ordered to stay on the other side of the fence, rushed forward with flashlights. A squad car eased over, beams on full. A sanitation truck approached. Garbage could wait in the North End. Shadowy bodies moved like fireflies. Soon lights sprayed disjointed beams.

"Looks like I got my lights," Puppy said.

Evie arched an eyebrow. "We cannot let them inside."

"Oh yes you can!" Matthew shouted. "According to the guidelines of Major League Baseball, the Commissioner may bring guests to any ballpark as long as those guests do not take seats purchased or designated for anyone else."

The BT almost smiled.

In the dark it was hard to say, but probably some three thousand Bostonians followed inside the blacked-out Fenway Park. He knew it was in poor taste, but what the hell. He led the rescue effort on unruly choruses of "Take Me Out to the Ballgame."

Brandishing flashlights, torches of burning programs, portable lights, Red Dragon 'bacco lighters, they made it onto the field with only a few non-threatening bruises. The moon and stars offered little help, hedging their bets. Shredded questionnaires carpeted center field.

Someone had padlocked the doors leading through the "green monster" and beneath the outfield stands.

Puppy bloodied his fists hammering the lock until Mary Doherty's beefy brothers Officer L. Doherty and Officer G. Doherty wielded Ellie Adair's bat to smash open the doors. A lot of shouting and reassurances and more choruses of "Take Me Out to the Ballgame" lured the frightened fans out one by one, in packs, and then in a gush once they realized no Jet'roes waited at second base.

Munching on the delicacies of the Hardi Bratwurst concession cleaned out behind the center-field bleachers, the slightly giddy fans marched across the field like some peculiar picnic outing.

Puppy balled up one of the discarded questionnaires, adding a second until it was about as good a sphere as he'd get in a blacked-out ballpark. Watching himself from all angles, he took the mound. The evacuation stopped, heads turning though no one could see until the lights funneled a shaky beam, leaving his upper torso shadowed.

Puppy yelled for Frecklie Rivera and Parker DeWitt and fired his paper ball. It twisted and turned in the uncooperative wind, dropping a few feet away.

No one applauded. They were all way past that now.

• • • •

CLARY WAS WAITING by the Black Top guard post outside her house.

His clothes were filthy; dirt tracked along the right side of his jaw. "Thank you for seeing me at this late hour, Granddaughter."

"We are so formal."

"I lost my last quip at the bedside of Parker DeWitt."

"But there is always time for forced melodrama."

"Then we can do without our usual banter. What the hell are you going to do about tonight?"

"I am sure Puppy has many ideas."

"Yes he does. Begin by calling your BTs off the streets of Boston."

"The curfew was necessary. Violence did not abate until several hours ago. The BTs will not leave until order is restored."

"Order won't be restored until the Jet'roes are gone. I want them gone. Now. Next, I want the Black Top responsible for the murder of Parker DeWitt publicly identified and punished."

She disdainfully rocked back and forth on her front foot. "Do you now? And what punishment would Puppy proclaim?"

"Removal from the Black Tops. Publicly. On the damn vid. In one of your fucking floating billboards. Full accountability and responsibility."

"Because you have found him guilty."

"Yeah. I saw the corpse."

"The Black Top Rafael was attacked by Parker DeWitt. He had to be restrained."

"With a killing blow?"

"It was under the best of circumstances an accident, nothing more."

Puppy's fury straightened the exhaustion out of his legs. "Nothing more? An eighteen-year-old kid had his throat crushed—"

"Spare me. I have read the reports of the BTs, Parker DeWitt's supervisor, and witnesses, all human except for Justine, the other BT. I have read the human coroner's report. This was sad and I am sorry for the loss, but this was not an act of willful murder. It cannot be because the soldiers stationed in America are not programmed to attack."

"I'm not asking you to turn him off."

Clary's face twisted savagely. "He is not a refrigerator."

"But we need to see that there will be justice."

"You speak of justice to be satisfied by injustice."

"Six people died."

"Because you rioted, Puppy Nedick. Your fans rioted. This could have, should have ended with the unfortunate death of Parker DeWitt. But you only care of the human casualties. A BT sergeant also died."

"I know." He scowled. "Unfortunate."

A bridge of malice linked their stares. Clary untwisted one of her hair bows, the orange silk flapping down the left side of her face. "Rafael will probably join a unit elsewhere in the country. The matter will drop."

Puppy's nostrils flared. "That's not enough."

"That is all I can do."

"Why?"

"There is more going on than you understand."

"You've said that before and it's still bullshit. Formal and public announcement, Granddaughter. Then I want you to rescind your order about restricting attendance to non-fans."

She smirked. "Anything else?"

"Oh yeah. The stadiums reopened. The season continues as before. This is all behind us."

"Please continue."

"We'll find a compromise about the behavior, wearing jerseys, booing."

"Or else?"

Puppy was ready. "We will object."

"Will your fans drag robot drivers out of their taxies in Chicago as they did in Boston last night? Will they board buses in Atlanta and drag the robot drivers out as they did in Boston last night? Will they attack robot train conductors in Los Angeles as they did in Boston last night?"

"If you don't calm things down, this'll get worse."

"By fanning the flames so humans and robots fight when inorganic life-forms are dying to protect America? Do you want to risk robot armies refusing to attack the Allahs?"

He shuddered. "Is that what you're threatening?"

Clary gritted her teeth, setting off another round of pain where she'd willed out the tooth and joint to create the inflamed root canal. The prosthetic tooth didn't fit well over the minute device inside her gum. She couldn't risk Felice questioning another dental visit.

"It would not be my decision. It would be the soldiers's. A morality conundrum. They fight because they believe they are accepted. If they are not accepted, fighting would be a slave decision to serve masters. The inorganic ethical structure constantly evolves toward wider ethics, which humans only talk about. Do not risk such considerations. Let me handle this."

"I don't believe you anymore."

"You dare accuse Clary of lying?"

"Yeah. Because you're not Clary anymore. Just a power-hungry freak. I'm ashamed of you."

Puppy spun around. In a rage, Clary expelled fire, flanking, then circling him. He whirled, glowering through the flickering flames.

"And you are not my Puppy Beisbol anymore." Her tears rivered out, dousing the fire.

By the time he got to the 234th Street subway station, his Lifecard had been revoked.

38

The door to Beth's house was unlocked. Zelda hurried through the dark hallway into the neat kitchen and out the back door.

A freshly dug grave was guarded on three sides by dislodged dirt.

Zelda took tiny steps as if the ground would give way. Holding her breath, she peered into the hole. Laying on a black woolen blanket, Beth rested at the bottom clutching Babe Ruth's baseball at her chest.

"Shit shit." Zelda started climbing down, knocking dirt onto Beth.

"What the fuck!" Beth yelled, bolting up.

"What?" Zelda shouted.

"What the hell are you doing here?"

"What the hell are you doing there?"

Beth didn't have a good answer. She let her head fall again. Zelda jumped into the grave, nearly landing on Beth's leg. They struggled, Zelda pulling her up and Beth yanking away until, exhausted, Zelda toppled against the side. Beth scampered into the corner, knees curled up. They stared with frantic anger, wearily throwing pebbles at each other.

"Why are you here?" Beth rasped, suddenly tossing out a brittle laugh. "Oh. Puppy. Sure."

"That's right. He told me about Dale. I figured you might like me around. I didn't think I had to put on some priest outfit to give the prayer of the dead."

Beth muttered regret at rescuing Puppy from the Caliphate.

Zelda threw another handful of dirt. "You were going to kill yourself."

"I don't know."

"Then why'd you dig the grave?"

"Obviously because I was thinking about it."

"Just trying death out, seeing how it might feel."

Beth shrugged, blinking back tears.

"Isn't suicide against your religion?"

"Now you're a religious expert?"

"Only about stupid. Where's Dale?"

Beth's face sagged. "I don't know. Her bag's gone. No note, no nothing. Her last act of kindness. See, running away lets me off. Not completely. I still had to file a report on her missing, but without an explanation for now. The Committee sort of toplines all this for a week, giving Dale time to get away. And me, if I want."

"Like the highway to Heaven," Zelda said with disgust. "Dale has run away before?"

"Several times, back when she first moved in and decided the answer to an argument was flight. But this time, it's very different. Once I get called in, I'll have to tell the Committee everything I know, or what Puppy told me and what Dale admitted. He'll be called, too."

"And because Dale committed a terrible crime, we're sitting in an open grave at midnight."

Beth wiped her face of brown-stained tears. "After a certain point you give up. I failed as a parent twice." She glanced at her thin gold watch.

"Got a date?"

"I did."

Zelda tensed. "Before or after you killed yourself?" She exaggerated a wondering look. "Guess this is an intimate date place."

Beth threw a small rock. Zelda reciprocated.

"I'm happy for you, Beth."

"You're not any happier than I'm happy for your domestic bliss."

"Life with Pablo and Diego isn't always domestic bliss."

"But you're still happy, damn it."

Zelda nodded. "Are you?"

"Too early. I've only known her for three weeks."

"That's a lot of time." Zelda took a breath. "Have you two—"

"Yes."

"Could you let me finish the question?"

"Wasn't it, have we had sex?"

"Yeah, but I had a right to finish." Zelda hesitated. "Was it good?"

Beth looked away.

"That good."

"What do you want me to say?"

"Nothing. Sometimes there's nothing to say, even for me. I guess it would've been nice if we'd done it once, especially since you're about to die, so you had a comparison when I asked 'is the sex good with what's-her-name.'"

Beth scowled. "Colleen."

"Simple, strong name."

"And I've had sex with other women in my life so there is some capacity to compare." Beth stretched her legs out into the side of the grave.

"Since we both have partners, we can be officially and ethically friends according to the glorious tenets of The Family."

Beth ignored the proffered handshake. "I don't connect well, Zelda. Even with my son, I lost that emotional bond. Much less with friends, lovers. Dale liked me because I'm like her. Abrasive and compartmentalized and, if we had to, we could live in the forest. You bring out the best, Zelda. As impossible as you are, somehow you shine a light on what we're hiding."

"What part of you did I shine a light on?" Zelda half whispered.

"The ability to love."

"And because we can't, you kill yourself."

"I haven't decided," she snapped. "And if I do, it's not because of you. Oh God, what a concept for Zelda Jones. Something not about her." Beth shook her head. "I have nothing more to do, Zelda. I don't have a family. Or friends. Or a lover. My job bores me. Every day is filled with pain. Deep, deep pain. Dale accused of murder was the last pillar. I thought I'd straightened her out and believe me, she was a hot mess. Guess I was wrong."

Beth sat deeper into the grave. "I love you and hoped somehow, something bad would happen between you and Pablo. Nice, right? I cared so much about you that all I cared about was my needs."

"I thought I had the ego." Zelda clapped, almost one hand at a time.

"There's your beautiful speech for us to remember," Beth said thickly.

Zelda tilted her head. "You knew I'd show up. Of course, Puppy would tell me. A breakup in an open grave. Grandma's bra straps, I thought I'd done it all."

Beth held a serrated knife to her throat.

"Cool weapon. Go ahead."

"I will."

With an abrupt move, Zelda knocked aside the knife which cut a slight gash in Beth's chin. Zelda effortfully climbed up the side of the grave. After a few minutes, Beth followed.

• • • •

ANNETTE DUCKED BENEATH the rounded archway of the simple clay and brick house where Father Drobev and Rabbi Gold waited in a bare-bones room with thick walls half sunk into the floor. The bright morning sun skimming the Mediterranean made Annette blink. Herbert stood by patiently, gray eyes scanning.

"Good morning, Ms. Ramos," Drobev said politely.

"We'll see. It's been three days."

"And we hope you've had a chance to sightsee."

"Not really. I've been getting sun, sleep. Last night I got drunk on your fabulous *cisk* lager and passed out on the bathroom rug. So far, a great vacation, thanks."

"We can appreciate your impatience as we also hope you appreciate our caution." He waited for Annette to slide onto the couch. "Herbert allowed us to examine the system which has been providing guidance for your journey. Simply expressed, it's the Ar3 system, a highly encrypted communication. Finding this installed in Herbert's programs was a bit of a surprise, which is why it's taken so long. We needed substantial research since the Ar3 was abolished with all traces after being used briefly in 2078 for private communications between the Vatican and Lenore Shen, your Grandma."

Drobev gave that a moment to sink in.

"We have no surviving evidence of those conversations. Much of the Vatican library was destroyed in an Islamic air attack as the librarians were leaving under safe passage." His face tightened. "According to one of our historians, Ephraim Begin, the genesis, if you'll forgive the word, of the Ar3 began when the Holy Father appealed for help to evacuate Vatican staff as the Muslim armies approached Rome. At first, he requested they be granted asylum in your country, which Grandma rejected as endangering American security. Then he requested sanctuary in the areas still under American control, specifically South America. This, too, she rejected."

"She must've had her reasons."

"Oh quite. She didn't trust the Holy Father or anything associated with religion," Gold answered. "To Grandma, any worship of God or faith engendered blanket condemnation."

"Since the Arabs attacked us in the name of Allah, I think that's easy to understand."

"Like so much, it's perspective, Ms. Ramos. This special-coding communication continued for several months until Rome was about to be captured, when the pope was finally persuaded to leave. By then, the Mufti only allowed the Holy Father and a few aides to depart. The pope refused for a week before accepting the offer. With each day, another ten priests and nuns were taken from the 'safe' list." The rabbi's voice hardened. "An hour after Pope John left, nearly five thousand nuns and priests were beheaded in St. Peter's Square."

"I'm sorry you hate me as an American because of what the Muslims did."

He dismissed the comment as beneath a response. "This system has been dormant until now."

"There are two points on which I do not agree with Father Drobev and Rabbi Gold," Herbert said. "There is the responsive password. When I first received information in Hungary, I countered with the obvious method which was to request identification. I was refused. The language of the messages was uninformed. It was as if the sender had never used such a device before. It was not as if the response to my request indicated an inaccurate password. The response was simply 'Too bad.' I have continued to request this identification and have been continually refused."

Annette frowned. "Then why'd you believe the messages? It could've been a trap set for us."

"I did not think we were important enough to trap. We also did not have any viable option for succeeding in your plan to find the Holy Father."

Annette smiled faintly. "Then you went on faith."

Herbert's forehead pulsed slightly. "It was the only option."

"Father Dempsey would be pleased."

"Despite the illogic that he is sentient to express emotions, I hope he is."

"Then who could this be?"

"Herbert can shed more light on this, but he refuses," Drobev said testily.

"I have encoded the actual messages which would take approximately 233,441 human hours to decode."

"Good for you, Herbert." Annette shook her fist. "I'm tired of being jerked around."

"No one is jerking you around, Ms. Ramos," Drobev snapped, glaring at the robot. "Herbert will only allow us to see the messages with your permission."

Herbert nodded politely. "Correct. And by allowing this, you agree that Annette may meet the Holy Father to personally state her position."

"What if we don't care enough and you can go back to Sicily or wherever the hell you want?" Gold shouted.

"You do not want that outcome, Rabbi Gold. For your security you must learn about all possible breaches. If we are in fact attempting to hurt the Holy Father, you need to know why and who sent us to establish plans as a protection against future attempts."

He darkened. "I don't negotiate with robots."

Annette got off the couch. "Then negotiate with me."

The two religious men nodded grudgingly.

"Verbally," Annette said. "Because I'm sure you've got cameras on us and I want proof."

"We're men of God. Are you suggesting we don't deserve your trust?" Drobev sneered.

"You know how Americans are," she said with her best plastic smile.

The priest and rabbi barked out agreement. After Herbert assured Annette he had a vid transcription of the moment, it wristed out the messages.

Don't be stupid. Leave Hungary now and fast. Here is road.

Essenes Mountains. Coordinates. Ask for Reb Grosch. He wears funny hats.

Annette's eyes widened.

Now Spain. Beautiful country. Coordinates.

Annette giggled.

Sad leaving Spain. Italy. More funny hats. Coordinates.

Annette started laughing.

Sicily hot like bull's butt. Coordinates.

Now she roared.

Malta. Find Drobev and Gold. Talk to Holy Father. Praise Jesus.

"It's the brat." Annette wiped away her tears of joy. "It's the brat."

39

Captain Rafferty had asked all the police chiefs in all the major league cities to attend by hologram. From Seattle to Tampa, they sat on his cleaned-out shelves in the cluttered office. A persistent thunderstorm drummed rain. He doubted that would stop the demonstrators.

Rafferty deliberately closed the black curtains around the office windows which the 43rd Precinct knew often meant an officer was receiving a talking-to that'd penetrate a building five miles away. "Or maybe I'm banging a goat which is also none of your business," Rafferty had once explained at a staff meeting.

"Let's cut to the chase, friends." He poured more coffee. "Here in the beautiful Bronx, we have a clusterfuck of huge proportions." Ripping open the door and startling the listening squad room, Rafferty gestured an invitation with one bent finger at Officer Schlandra. She wondered who'd take care of her mother.

"Everyone, this is the knucklehead who arrested two concerned siblings today outside Yankee Stadium. Officer Schlandra, would you like to tell the brain trust of American police why you did that?" As Schlandra hesitated, Rafferty squeezed her neck with malicious relish. "I didn't hear."

"They were ringleaders, sir."

The police chiefs chuckled.

"Indeed. What made them ringleaders, Officer Schlandra?"

Schlandra edged uneasily away from the HG police chiefs watching from the shelf. "I had reason to believe they were in charge."

"For what reason?"

"They were talking to the rest of the protestors."

"What did they say?" Rafferty scowled.

"They were using DV signing."

"Do you understand DV signing?"

"No, sir," she said glumly.

"So by removing them like the head of the mythical hydra, you thought the event would end."

"Yes, Captain." Schlandra tried to sound confident.

"Did that result occur, Officer Schlandra?"

"No, sir."

"Would you care to tell us what happened, or should I painfully squeeze the back of your neck again?"

"Once the ring—once the—once the two women were taken into custody, many more...of them appeared."

"From where?"

"From the subways and streets and just about everywhere, sir. I'm told but did not see they also came up from the sewers."

"What were they doing?"

"Holding signs, sir."

"In the course of your detailed police investigation, were you able to read the signs?"

"Yes, sir."

"What did the signs say?"

"'*P.*' All capital letters surrounded by baseballs," Schlandra said a little smugly.

"Oh my. Were the siblings violent?"

"No."

"Did they use the signs in a threatening manner, smack anyone, throw them?"

"No, sir."

"Then what did these troublemakers do?"

"They formed a ring around Yankee Stadium and held up more signs."

"Did they prevent anyone from entering the game?"

"Not that I saw."

"Were they polite and respectful?"

"Yes, Captain."

"Did they speak to any prospective fans?"

"Not that I saw."

"And once the game began?"

"They stayed until the end which the Yankees won, sir." Schlandra's joy at New York snapping its six-game losing streak wasn't shared.

"And then?"

"Then they left."

"So illegally arresting two siblings on unsubstantiated charges failed to address the problem."

"As far as I could tell, Captain."

"Thank you, Officer Schlandra. Everyone, congratulate our Blue Shirt on her new assignment to the Bronx Zoo. I hope you like baboons."

Rafferty shook his head to more chuckles at the occasional dunderheads who found their way into the police force. "Now, that's been our experience here in the Bronx. Let's go around the table and see what kind of fun everyone else has had."

After half an hour, a consensus of common behavior had been established both during games and at closed ballparks, as well as at each of the vacant Mooshie Baseball League fields. The same signs. Similar wardrobes, all in the uniforms of their home teams. Same old-time sportscaster Harry Caray recorded sing-along of "Take Me Out to the Ballgame." There were some wrinkles. In Minneapolis, large "*P*s" had been written on the side of the Cousins Building. Moustaches had been drawn on several of Clary's billboards in Atlanta, Houston, and Philadelphia. That bit of news produced nasty pleased smiles.

But there was no violence despite a massive "P" presence outside mass transit, safely beyond the school properties, and many government buildings. Other than defacing some property with "Ps," no crimes. Other than Busch Stadium where a "P" popped up during the sixth inning, none of the few fans attending the games had shown any support. Outside the Denver and Seattle ballparks, a few patrons had shouted indecipherable anger at the "P holders." Not many players had shown much support; estimates were that about half the major league players had decided to continue the season at the restricted games.

The captain motioned for the police chiefs to finish their reports. They had a brief coffee-and-doughnuts break to gather their thoughts. But everyone knew this was Rafferty's show.

He propped his feet up on the desk, inspecting the heavy rain for a moment. "Pretty damn organized, isn't it?"

"Down to the letter," agreed Summer Lightning Horse, head of the Denver PD. "Look at this." He floated a photo of one of the "P holders."

They blended respective photos in the middle of the room. To the placement of the "P," the baseballs, the use of magic markers, and the size of the sign, everything was the same except for the individualized baseball-team colors.

"Guessing this is all coming from DVs in your towns?" Rafferty asked, getting quick nods. "You recognize any of the 'P holders'?"

Heads shook back and forth, though the police captain in Milwaukee thought a few of the teens had previously been arrested on minor street-scuffling charges. Minor, he emphasized.

"Okay, as they used to say back in the good old days, here's the sixty-four-thousand-dollar question." Rafferty took a breath. "Anyone hear from the office of the majestic Granddaughter on what might be a violation of the Anti-Conspiracy Act? Any of the Cousins, who's the fool Second Cousin assisting in baseball now, DeRico, anyone hear from her? Nope. Any visits from a Black Top?"

"Nowhere to be seen," said the Cleveland police honcho.

"I figured we might see something here after everything at Fenway, but not a black visor in sight," said the Boston police chief.

"Any idea if this is a one-time-only event?"

The room brimmed with belief that this was just the start. Rafferty grunted agreement.

"Obviously organized. So, who's behind this? Blue Wigs?"

"They're the only ones with a national network who could coordinate on this scale," said the San Francisco captain. "They have the resources, the agenda—"

"Which is what agenda?" Rafferty cut him off.

"They've been at war with The Family for decades."

"Makes them obvious," added the Tampa chief.

"Too obvious." Rafferty grumbled at the eye-rolling. "Alvin Nedick's dead. They gave their word the fight was over. Any proof any Blue Wig was behind the recent robberies?"

Rumors and speculation were tossed around. Most conceded the Hall of Fame thefts were a lot of coincidence spurred by the possibility of making a quick buck on memorabilia. So far two suspects were in custody, both first-time perps.

"We see any crossed bats or Blue Wigs?"

"Maybe they don't want to be tagged," insisted the San Francisco chief.

"Since when did Blue Wigs pour a glass of pop without getting credit?" Rafferty looked between the rain drops.

"We should talk to former Wigs, see what they know," added the Arlington top cop.

Lazily nodding, Rafferty ran his finger around the rim of the coffee mug. Sometimes something just smells. Yeah. This smells a lot. And I'm getting too old to hold my nose. "Who here is sick and tired of the BTs?"

That didn't require a voice vote or a raising of hands. A few police chiefs started smiling. They'd known Rafferty a long time. The real show was about to start.

"I gotta believe they're sniffing like wolves waiting to pounce. A kid's killed. Has anyone been punished? They have BT body footage of what happened and screw the excuse about possible tampering which hasn't happened in thirty years. They refused to let Boston PD inside the case, isn't that true?"

The Boston chief cop grunted and swore a little. "I heard a claim that the over-emotionalism of the kid provoked the BT into overriding its third-rail protocol. Who here thinks that was a crock of shit?"

More profanities.

Rafferty drummed his thick fingers on his desk. "Protests in thirty cities, we estimate how many protesters…?" He waited for the 42,661 numbers to float out from the tracker. "And there's no BTs? No glint of stealth 'copters?"

The Kansas City police boss thought they'd picked up a 'copter, but it was faulty stealth radar.

"But it's mainly peaceful," said the Pittsburgh top cop, enduring a verbal flailing about hedging criminality.

"Shit easily goes south. Laws have been broken about defacing property. We know where that leads. And look at my nitwit cop. She could've accidentally pushed one of the DVs and then we're off to the races. Grandma's bra straps." His nostrils flared, processing information. He was just starting.

"To what end is all this, Hedrick?" asked Lightning Horse. Early on, he and Rafferty had been on the famous Southern wild car chase shooting it out with pedophiles that'd gotten the national attention that made their careers. Lightning Horse had earned the right to use a first name and a skeptical tone.

Rafferty stayed silent. He had so much to say that colleagues often thought he'd shot his whole wad when he was simply holding back to wander around, mulling.

He pulled the pin on the grenade. "Does anyone think that siblings in each of the major league stadiums all woke up this morning with the same idea?"

The holograms muttered agreement.

"We haven't seen protests like this since Grandma outlawed social media."

More murmurs.

"Does anyone think the police are equipped to handle nationwide demonstrations, day in and day out?"

The holograms were very still.

Rafferty took a moment before quietly asking, "And when we can't, what happens then?"

● ● ● ●

THE HUMANS LINGERED over their refreshments until the last snide play in their revered games. They had their patterns, so easily set, so rigidly unbroken. The Cousins meetings, which Felice had presided over for several weeks, were an exercise from a child's playroom. The nonsensical agenda, the bickering egos. They cannot change.

"With your permission, I would like to postpone the agenda this morning." Felice waited for their anxious expressions to settle in.

"Has there been a turnaround in Egypt?" First Cousin Nadharatha always insisted on making the first comment.

"Here is the latest." Felice expelled a four-minute video of fighting amid the ruins of Alexandria. Felice almost felt disgust at their gasps and hoarse cheers at soldiers blown to bits, tanks exploding, missiles destroying their very heritage.

Nadharatha puckered his lips. "How would you assess this?"

"Cairo remains in enemy hands, but their supply lines are cut off north and south of the city. Alexandria remains in a similar situation. Our commanders estimate another eight days of fighting until both cities are quiescent."

Felice stared. They never asked. "Our casualties to date in this North African campaign are 85,551 dead, 101,233 wounded, and 22,199 missing."

As always, the Cousins mustered some empathy, but not as if these soldiers had come from Idaho or South Carolina instead of a factory beneath the Montana mountain range. As always, Third Cousin Rasfarati expressed compassion which set off false sympathy around the table.

Felice abruptly blacked out the military scene. The Cousins fidgeted impatiently.

"You said you needed to postpone the agenda. Why?" Nadharatha blustered, his busy day delayed by this irritating 'bot with its supercilious tone.

"It is about the Granddaughter. There will need to be a change."

Relief swept the room. Replacing that awful child had been the subject of much furtive communications in wooded areas where they felt safe from probing eyes. There'd been some heated discussion but overall, it'd been muted and consensual. Once that Clary was out of the way, they could slowly ease Felice back into a more supportive role.

"We are glad to hear that, Felice." Nadharatha puffed up. "We cannot tolerate this behavior and these infantile tantrums and wrong-headed judgments and decisions."

"Correct."

"We'll need a temporary realignment," said Second Cousin DeRico, chin tucked so tightly in her turtleneck that her head could only turn so much.

"We've had a plan in place for some time," continued Third Cousin Dinazzo according to their rehearsed script. "First Cousin Nadharatha has demonstrated exceptional skills and vision."

There was a too-loud slamming of appreciative hands on the table.

"I'd like to make a motion," said Fourth Cousin Oh, eager to please everyone. "I think the consensus is for the First Cousin to take The Family into his hands."

Felice kept nodding as the squawking continued for another few minutes. "Are you anticipating solidification within the Cousins structure or adding an informalized title?"

Nadharatha felt the Cousins's prickly eyes.

"Oh no. I believe between Grandma, Grandpa, and Granddaughter we've quite had enough of those adjunct figureheads." Besides, he and his wife hadn't come up with a suitable informalized title. The Great-Uncle. The Brother. Perhaps the Father in time.

With an imperial air, he returned to the impassive 'bot. "We should ease into this."

"Yes, yes, yes," agreed the table.

"We allow her the zoos and her children's clubs but phase out all the billboards and constant presence."

"Presence everywhere," muttered two Third Cousins with no prompting.

That set off an aggrieved list from saying good night to The Family to those insufferable appearances with the damnable children on *Wake Up, My Darlings.*

"Would not the siblings notice her absence?" Felice asked.

"They might, but would they really care?" Nadharatha shrewdly tapped his bulbous nose. "She's not terribly popular given the debacle with baseball. Grandma always said that leaders are disposable. The will of The Family is forever, the rule of leaders is not. Plus, well, was she ever properly vetted? An orphan from the Caliphate of Spain. What are her true loyalties? Hasn't she resisted the use of the tactical battlefield nukes?"

Agreeing grumbles about Clary's suspect background and loyalty rattled about.

"What if Clary is not receptive to moving into a lesser role?" Felice asked so quietly they had to lean forward.

Nadharatha pulled a face. "You'll have to persuade her. Actually. Actually, I wonder if she should simply be removed. After the nonsense with Cheng and then Kenuda, it'd work nicely to show how we can clean up ourselves."

The Cousins had not discussed this at all, but they nodded slowly since the First Cousin seemed so sure and it was, after all, his idea if this went wrong.

"Yes. Yes." He was settling into his new leadership role with a flourish. "She's eased over and then out."

"That would not be wise," Felice said.

The First Cousin frowned. "And why is that?"

"The Cousins are not predicated on turning out one of their own as if there were some election cycle to demonstrate displeasure. Whatever actions Clary decided as a familial extension of the Cousins was agreed upon by all of you. Everyone in this room would be culpable."

That took them down a notch. With a cagy look, Nadharatha pushed back his chair. "Including you, Felice."

"I have no input in any decisions. I merely facilitate. The laws currently forbid inorganic life-forms from serving as Cousins. As our soldiers do your will by fighting your enemies, so I have done your will in my advisory role. To suggest otherwise would be tantamount to prejudicial scapegoating."

"You have been leading these meetings!" the First Cousin shouted.

"At your request because you could not or would not handle the Granddaughter. I cleansed your unpleasant tasks as more than three million nonorganic life-forms have cleansed your unpleasantries by removing the Muslim armed presence."

Felice waited for the angry squirming to pass. "Removing Clary or lessening her role would prove injurious to the morale of the country during this state of war. It would suggest that the Cousins are not competent to prosecute the war. That happened during the previous conflict with nearly disastrous results. Removing or lessening responsibilities would suggest that appointing Clary as Granddaughter was a mistake. If that was a mistake, what other mistakes have yet to be addressed?"

"Cheng made Clary the Granddaughter. He can be blamed," Nadharatha squeaked, earning uncertain nods from his colleagues.

"Not anymore." The 'bot swept its steely eyes around the table. "It is also inaccurate to say that Clary is not popular. Clary is very popular among the children. Her photograph hangs in 97.4 percent of the school classrooms. Grandma's photo was in 98.9 percent and she was head of The Family for more than thirty years. The children are our most precious resource. Nor do we want the Islamic Empire to believe that we are riven with discord which could embolden them to take riskier moves. There are increasing intelligence reports that the Muslims are planning an invasion of Canada." Felice skipped over the shocked gasps. "We must have one voice and that one voice should be Clary."

Nadharatha had enough, kicking away his chair. "You began this meeting by saying we were replacing Clary. What the hell is going on?"

Felice tilted its head. As the door swung open, a Clary AI entered soundlessly with an impish curtsy. It hopped up on a side table and twirled its thick black hair in its fingers, wide dark eyes glittering.

"Do not stop for me. I am only the most-loved sibling in the country," the 'bot said in an impeccable Clary voice.

"What is this?" Nadharatha raged. "What is this?"

Felice waited for the storm to pass and the Cousins to sit back down. "This is our new Granddaughter, Clary."

The 'bot curtsied again.

40

A peculiar animal with a studded tail and gray fur studied Grandma from within the lavishly vined tree. Grandma returned the look within their respective cages. The mutated chipmunk considered the interloper with a dismissive smirk and scurried off amid the thick brush. He'd return tomorrow to keep his eyes on these visitors.

In his cabbie cap, Kenuda passed with a long broom, a bucket, and two bulging garbage bags.

"Elias dear, you don't have to clean the whole cave."

Kenuda frowned at such an idea. He wordlessly dragged the garbage bags along the dirt through a narrow clearing where there were more piles of old potato-chip wrappers waiting. Grandma was worried about him. But the grief had to run its course. And the cave did need a cleaning.

This was among the smaller Miners hideouts, which was probably why it had escaped BT attention. And why Grandma had chosen it from the list once provided by Alvin Nedick. Sealed and layered with rerouting membranes that blocked scans, the cave was tucked half a mile from Tannersville, New York at the foot of the Catskill Mountains. They'd been here five hours even though Elias had insisted on returning to the DV as soon as they'd arrived or else he'd miss an entire day of taxi driving and would be subject to a fine from the Committee and certain loss of rec room privileges plus "other seedling projects" he couldn't yet disclose. "DV gluing," it was called. Needing to hold onto something. Grandma sighed. She'd never actually witnessed it.

That's when Kenuda had intensified his cleaning mania. He'd nearly fallen off a twenty-foot oak demanding that dust had no place in nature.

Cheng popped out from behind an imposing rock, grumbling over the silver Edgar1 tracking device.

"Nothing?" Grandma asked anxiously.

"Dark."

"She could be in a regulated vehicle."

"We'd pull up the truck, van, whatever."

"Or a tunnel, Albert. Or still somewhere in the house."

"Or permanently dark."

Grandma shook her head. "Felice can't kill her."

"Oh, she can if she has to."

"I didn't say that wasn't a possibility. But that would forfeit her moral superiority."

"Show a little more regret, damn it."

"Clary knew the risks, Albert. She came to me. This was her idea."

"If it fails, well, what's another sacrifice, right?"

"Please, Albert. We don't have time for this. There was no other way."

"I don't want that child to die, Lenore. I have enough blood on my hands."

"We all do, Albert. We all do." Grandma sat him down on the adjacent rock. "Felice has made a mistake and we're exploiting that. But we must let it play out."

"What if you're wrong, Lenore? That has happened."

"Yes, and too many times. But I didn't want to come back, Albert."

"Bullshit."

"You created a mess. Can I remind you that you did murder me?"

"Because you created the mess first."

"This isn't the most helpful conversation." Elias leaned on his broom. "You both loused up. My Hedda's dead. Let's try to avoid Clary also getting killed. Seems Felice has gotten away with enough moral ambiguity which you also seem to be willing to overlook."

"Don't you—" Grandma yelled.

"Let the kid finish," Cheng snapped at Grandma who smoldered silently.

"Thank you, Grandpa." Elias's lip curled. "We're relying on a tracking system which might have already been compromised."

"No," Grandma said firmly. "Fourth Cousin Oh let Albert know the moment the arrest order was invoked ninety-seven hours ago. There has been no probing on even tripartite levels near the system. Like the Ar3, this Edgar1 is my own creation. I alone have the program and the codes. Pablo Diaz is an able dentist who inserted it into her gum. Short of an autopsy, they'd never find it."

"Who else are we relying on internally?" Elias asked. "Fourth Cousin Oh was a weeping idiot when she reported to me. And Fourth Cousins are outside the clearance."

"We're relying on Blue Wigs," Cheng said over Elias's groans. "Alvin planted them and we let him, like we planted ours inside his hive. An order went down three days ago for the BT transport vehicle."

"Except we don't know when that will arrive."

"Not yet. We're working on it."

Elias waved a rag. "And we don't know where."

"We assume it's the Rockport prison."

"Why?"

"Because it's purely BT-guarded."

"What if they have another place? Like this?" Kenuda's huge hands swept around the cave.

"We have the tracking device," Grandma snapped.

"Unless they found some way to shield it. What if they didn't find the Edgar1? What if they've just housed Clary in some impenetrable room expecting someone would look for her?"

"Why would they think that?"

"Oh, I don't know. Maybe they're surveilling all the Cousins. If you're Felice and you just pulled something a hair short of a coup..."

"Surveillance would violate Felice's moral codes," Lenore said uneasily.

"But overthrowing the government doesn't?"

"She believes she is protecting The Family."

"Or you need to believe that."

Lenore's forehead glowed blue. "Are you accusing me of disloyalty to The Family, my own creation?"

He shrugged.

"That's enough, Kenuda," Cheng said. "Enough."

Elias shook his head, his contempt for these two deepening. "What about eyes on the house? There must be a special exit for the Granddaughter's vehicles."

"It's two miles into Van Cortlandt," Grandma said softly.

Albert frowned. "We changed that."

"Anything else you neglected to tell me?"

"Incredible," Elias snorted. "How old is the tracking device in Clary?"

Grandma's lips trembled. "That doesn't matter."

"That old, huh?"

"I don't care for your impertinence."

"As long as you're not a passenger in my taxi where I must show respect, I'll ask whatever I need to."

"Answer, Lenore," Albert finally said.

"Roughly twenty years."

Cheng made a disgusted sound. "How many times have you used it?"

"The Ar3 worked, didn't it?"

"How many times, Lenore?"

"When I was head of The Family, I had no occasion for this. I developed Edgar1 for an emergency."

"We're hiding in an abandoned Miners cave for our base, which we hope the BTs won't find, relying on Blue Wig informers to track a system that has never been used when for all we know Felice has completely changed all the protocols for transport. And don't say your Blue Wigs would know of changes because I'll bet it's a big secret."

Elias didn't wait for a response.

He handed Cheng the broom. "The north side of the cave needs a real sweeping." He displayed a two-inch callus on his left hand before disappearing through the holographic doors.

Grandma slumped onto a neat stump. "I didn't realize I could feel embarrassment."

"Perhaps because you never had, so the program wasn't needed." Albert nudged her over so he could sit.

"It doesn't quite work like that, but your point is well taken." Grandma sighed. "This is why I feared stepping forward, Albert. I feared hubris and arrogance."

"Well, you've displayed those traits from time to time."

Lenore glared. "Is this your clever little way of scolding me?"

"Of agreeing. You're Grandma. You're not infallible, but you must be. The great dichotomy of leadership. I always knew when I was screwing up. My flaws, my weaknesses. My disgrace is well-documented. But you never really failed. Even when we let the immigrants die at sea, you had good reasons. It was a difficult judgment call. It was right and horrible. Now you have to let others get the chance to screw up."

"Do you think we lost Clary?"

He grimaced. "There's a chance. The tracker could be compromised. It could've failed. The protocols could've shielded her from place to place. She could be dead."

"If she's dead…"

"Then we have no proof of what Felice has done. The Cousins aren't about to step forward. I doubt Fourth Cousin Oh will go any further. Clary's the only one who can witness everything. Even then, The Family might simply look away like they've looked away at all the robot soldiers dying in their place. But I don't think the kid is dead. She's too nasty to die so young."

Lenore laughed bitterly. "What a loving thing to say. But true." She draped her hand on Cheng's shoulder. "You really do love that child, don't you?"

"Yes. It's not all guilt. You know…" He hesitated.

Grandma poked him. "That doesn't work with me. I've already sensed some of what you were going to say."

Albert blushed. "I've had these dreams where you, me, and Clary go to the Bronx Zoo. Human, 'bot, and half a 'bot. Like one of those billboards. Crazy, right?"

"You mean awake dreams."

He blushed deeper and nodded.

"Looking for normalcy isn't so crazy. We've had very little, Albert." She took a breath. "Yes, I often wonder what would've happened if we'd married. Talk about crazy."

"It wouldn't have worked, Lenore. Too much sentiment would've gotten in the way."

"You bringing flowers every Saturday night."

He pulled a face. "Well, you wouldn't have."

Lenore kissed him on the cheek. "How can I possibly still love you after you shot me in the head?"

"I'm fucking irresistible."

• • • •

AFTER RETURNING HIS taxi to the garage, Kenuda filed an admission of dereliction of job to the dispatcher who said the normal procedure is forty-eight hours until a formal disciplinary hearing before the DV Committee. The dispatcher suggested Kenuda knock on the members's doors for an informal apology before the official meeting as a gesture of humility.

Kenuda snorted out the door and across the street into the building's rec room, which was crowded for a Tuesday late afternoon, workers coming off shifts, about to go on shifts, kids unwinding after school. Everyone looking for something to do because that was the DV way.

Now be polite, Elias, he could hear Hedda say. *Take a breath and be mindful that you're a large man and you can be imposing and intimidating.*

Kenuda climbed onto the rickety stepladder by the boisterous jukebox in the back and clapped his hands for attention. The sour-faced attendant at the desk gestured for him to remove his cap. Kenuda had rehearsed the DV sign language all the drive down. He'd nearly rammed a Ford Rambler at 201st Street by waving his hands in practice.

He signed. There was quiet, some looks, a deeper quiet. He signed again. The room broke up into laughter.

Confounded imbecilic language, he fumed. He started signing again. The attendant yanked on his sleeve.

"You've just asked if anyone has a goat with a hat."

"Common mistake," Elias grumbled. "Perhaps you can help me?"

"That'd be disrespectful, sibling Kenuda, by showing that you haven't been learning the lessons as you're supposed to."

"Well, I'm just bloody sorry about that!" he shouted, returning the glares. "I have an emergency and I don't know the correct procedure and, frankly, I don't give a shit. I need eyes on an exit in Van Cortlandt Park."

There was diffident silence. His jaw twitched. Oh, the hell with secrets. Grandma and Cheng were blasted fools. Their plans were idiotic. Let the story get out. Yes, damn you, Hedda, I know I'm insufferable.

"On Felice's orders, she's the robot advisor, the Cousins have arrested the Granddaughter and are taking her to a prison. It's possible that, to cover that up, she'll be replaced with a 'bot."

They kept staring.

"Did you hear what I said? I need help. Not a goat with a hat, though I'd take that, too." No one smiled. "I require bodies, eyes, right now, to watch the exit by Clary's house and let me know if a BT vehicle leaves. They're not allowed to use that route so that means they'll be transporting Clary. Then I need someone to follow the vehicle to see where it goes. What's wrong? Do I have to file a formal request?"

Similar DV-signs popped up across the room. He recognized that gesture.

"Why? Why?" Elias looked around, perplexed. They didn't want a speech. Just a simple answer. Was there even a simple answer?

You don't have all the answers, my darling. That's your ego talking which is even more intimidating than your big shoulders.

Elias smiled coldly. "No. You tell me why. Who am I to order any of you? I apologize. That was rude. I was raised a Reg. Sometimes it bites me back. If you think what the Cousins are doing is okay, then I'll leave. If not, I could use a plan. I'm all out of speeches."

A thin girl with a thin scar on her cheek signed a suggestion to make an appeal in the Cousins Lobby. A countering shout insisted they would deny such a charge. The girl yelled they couldn't lie as Cousins. The opponent sneered they already are lying about baseball.

"What if this one is lying?" She pointed at Kenuda.

Soon every index finger joined.

He swallowed slowly. "I'm here because I won't lie anymore. You all know my story. I gave up everything for the truth. That's all I have left. My truth. Which right now, is your truth."

The room sifted through Kenuda's honesty. He got a lot of straight hands held out as an indication of belief. He shifted impatiently; the BT truck could've left already, the tracking device compromised and Clary gone. Damn stupid plan.

Patience, darling.

A man wearing a red plaid shirt and scarred knuckles rose. "I hate the BTs."

The attendant translated the *don't trust the BTs* trickling throughout the room. There were more one-on-one, two-on-two arguments, some siblings muttering to themselves.

"I don't much care for the Granddaughter," murmured a man with an eye patch.

"Ain't the point. Ain't the way we're supposed to do things," said a hefty sibling. "Doesn't matter whether we like the child or not. I don't much like many of the folks here but I don't think you should be sent to jail. Though I wouldn't miss many."

Amid the nasty laughs, a slight older woman called out, "And if she did wrong, we should hear the 'what' of it like we heard with this Kenuda, and how would replacing her with a 'bot who would act like her change anything?"

"Unless the 'bot listens better," remarked the hefty man.

"Listens to who? It's us she's supposed to listen to."

The anger grew.

"What about the police?" A woman in the back was instantly shouted down as a fool for thinking the BTs would listen to the cops.

As the grumbles intensified, a dark teen with bright eyes nudged Elias off the stepladder. "We should use trailers."

That triggered a crossfire of shouts.

The attendant briefly explained "trailers" to Elias.

A brisk voice called out, "How far?"

Kenuda shrugged. "I'm not certain. Probably very far. Possibly to destination. Definitely to destination."

As the jukebox raged with Black Sabbath, debates circled about the danger, quickly dismissed with cutting sneers, and the possibility of other Black Top vehicles trailing as convoy. A veteran of last year's brief civil disturbances clued them in about BT tactics, specifically angular-parallel pursuit. A prisoner this important wouldn't be guarded by one truck. Or would too much activity alert attention? From who? Us, which broke up the room in mocking laughter.

An old woman with a face that had seen a lot and wouldn't mind a little more hobbled up to Kenuda, poking him with her cane.

She signed, *Why.*

Elias motioned about the room for the answer. The old woman poked him again, very near his groin.

Why, spoke the gnarled fingers.

The rec room fell still except for the wails of Ozzy Osbourne.

Kenuda's jaw tightened and signed, *Revenge.*

It translated to *enough*, which was close enough.

41

Kenuda couldn't see them anymore and the day still had a few hours of light. You came with six. Six are here and they know what to do. More than you. He stretched his creaky right leg, giving slight relief. They'd been positioned for three hours and a bit. An aspirin would be a joy.

"Blasted car could've left already," Kenuda muttered. No, the DV with blonde curls had assured him there were no recent tire tracks. From a tree, a DV with shockingly large blue eyes signed that the leaves weren't rustled. A third pointed to indifferent birds, untroubled by machines.

A distant rumble tickled his belly through the woolen jacket. He peered at the tree that Cheng had insisted was the escape route. Nothing. The rumble faded. Damn it, damn it, damn it. He got to his hands and knees and risked peeking over a willowy family of bushes. Adolescent fingers gestured with methodical anxiety from a treetop, behind rocks, scampering past a proud old water fountain.

There, there, there.

He signed back, *where*, but they disappeared. Kenuda ran toward the water fountain and down the path. Ahead, a black nondescript Chevrolet Exhibitor casually rolled up the ramp and paused. Got to be it, BT or Granddaughter vehicle be damned. He could almost sense the Chevy sneering as it rolled toward the road.

Other than Kenuda ducking, there was no one else around.

They were making sure this was the only car, he realized. The ramp remained closed beneath the grass. No glint of 'copter blades. Hunched over, Elias followed.

As the Chevrolet moved away, two chest-high beige scooters paralleled, converging fifty feet behind as the car respectfully obeyed the yellow light. A metal handle jabbed his back. A DV handed him a scooter. Three more were ahead at the intersection where traffic was light.

Elias wasn't about to admit he hadn't ridden a scooter since he was nine years old.

The teen nodded to the rope with the three-pronged clamp on the end, loosely tied around the handles. Elias swallowed hard and nodded. This was trailing. Fool, did you think you were going to chase the car? Perhaps next time ask for details. Like they would've told you. He chuckled.

As the Chevrolet went through the intersection, the six DVs nonchalantly tossed clamps around car bumpers. No one had to sign that Elias should follow.

Well, if it all ends here… Kenuda backhanded the clamp toward a low-slung yellow Ford Cruiser. The clamp landed well short. He dodged a honking gray Buick Connector, barely managing to stay upright. A DV about four hundred feet ahead swiveled and pointed at the B22 bus.

On half a shallow breath, Elias flung the clamp onto the bumper. Somehow it held.

He weaved back and forth, giving him a glimpse of the DVs trailing. Everyone had shortened the rope so they were a foot behind their cars, unlike Elias dancing away from irritated drivers.

Better hope they're not taking Clary to Maine.

"P" signs dotted the elevated Moshulu Parkway in both directions. Pasted on nearby buildings was the new ubiquitous graffiti: *Friends Don't Betray Friends.* Local police had requested permission to conduct an official questioning of the heads of sixteen Friends of groups. None of them would admit to anything more coordinated than holding a sign.

Paused at an orange slowdown light, Elias glanced down the street at the grumbling noises. A massive traffic jam clogged Webster Avenue. Silent protesters held signs, blocking honking cars. Blue Shirt foot patrols hurriedly snaked between lanes to reach the DV teens in white t-shirts and black jeans. An irate driver screaming about being late for work leaped out of his car and snatched a sign. The disciplined protesters didn't move. A new "P" emerged.

Yells and the thuds of fists faded.

Elias shuddered.

They lost the DV trailer with big eyes at exit two on the Cross-Bronx Expressway. Near Parkchester, the teen with blonde curls hit a skid and somersaulted onto the soft shoulder; Kenuda couldn't tell if he was alive.

By the time the BTs grooved onto Route 87 North, Elias counted two teens left, one an appendix to a black Dodge Dart, the other affixed to the rear of an R&C Ice Cream truck. Shocked at the way he'd changed bumpers, Elias hung onto a Chrysler station wagon, blood wetting his left pants leg from a fierce scrape along the highway a while back. The sun was slowly leaving the Bronx. The BTs got off at exit 23-A.

Elias unclamped, waiting for another car. He stared with relief at the sign for Tannersville.

A blue Sunset, a newer model from Ford, eased toward the exit. A DV waved at Kenuda to take the car while he disappeared along Route 87. Kenuda made the dangerous switch. The Chevrolet turned left at the light on the ramp. The Sunset went right in the direction of the BTs, but without Elias.

Kenuda parked himself by Multon's gas station. A yellow taxi slowed down.

"I ran out of gas," Elias said to the driver.

"You're at the right place," the 'bot wisecracked, tee-heeing until Elias insisted on his own route. Winston took only mild offense at Kenuda's directions, explaining that the passenger was right even if there were two eyes on a road that could always fork either way.

A quiescent baseball diamond prompted the 'bot to reflect on the fortunes of the Pittsburgh Pirates, explaining he was taken by their orange-trimmed jerseys. Winston asked and answered an opinion that new fans had shown the way to proper behavior.

A hovering digitalized billboard of Clary, arms around a trio of children, brought a mutter of opinions. Still didn't much like the kid. Needed someone with stature. Another Grandma would do. Elias interrupted to point out a sharp turn behind a shopping mall.

"Those are all thick woods," Winston said, gearing down.

"Right. But there's a path."

"Path or not, it'll be hell on my shocks. This is a Buick. It ain't made for bouncing."

"You'll be fine."

"I ain't worried about my butt. I'm worried about my taxi. I got a right to refuse a request if it risks danger to my vehicle."

In the fading light inside the cab, Winston displayed the specific "code of the cabbie."

Elias held up his taxi driver license, earning a surprised grunt. "I've been there and appreciate your concern. But I've got to take this shortcut."

"Why's that?"

Kenuda stared. "I can't tell you."

"Oh, really. Secret, huh?"

"Yup."

Winston's head twisted completely around. "Trouble with the law?"

"Not if you get me there first."

Kenuda could feel the steel-gray eyes scanning. They opened a little wider.

"You're the Cousin who had all the problems."

"That's me."

"Ain't learned your lesson, have you?"

Elias grinned crookedly. "Guess not."

Winston considered his first passenger in three hours. "There ain't nothing illegal about taking shortcuts, is there?"

"Nothing in our cabbie code of conduct that I recall."

Off a broad wink, Winston floored the Buick through a narrow opening between two tired trees.

The taxi passed rows of shabby bungalows before diving into a deeper part of the woods, climbing in silence until emerging at the top of a hill. Below, a few lights twinkled, guarded by the darkness.

"This is good." Kenuda handed over the Lifecard for the fare.

"Ain't nothing up here. Or down there."

Elias shrugged. "I like privacy."

Winston eyed him. "And there ain't nothing illegal about privacy."

"Not yet."

Elias scrambled down the hill, tossing the scooter behind a stump. He felt for the broken branches and the twin rocks which they'd left as markers while coming down yesterday. At the foot of the hill, Elias panicked.

Which trees? In the dark, he couldn't make out the discarded piles of twigs. He felt blindly on the ground.

A powerful palm clamped his mouth shut, dragging him backward into the brush while someone lifted his ankles. He felt sleepy and would've yawned if his lips didn't feel wired shut.

Shielded by sudden burly HG trees, Grandma and Albert dumped him into a grave-like ditch as the Black Top van disappeared into the Miners cave through an opening between the trees.

Quiet, a voice commanded inside his head.

Elias thought he deserved a cookie even if he'd chased the wrong car.

• • • •

PUPPY WAS SPIRITED into the basement to examine the bullet holes from the 2028 riots and shown the repaired side of the building after it was blown off in the 2042 Eastern Seaboard blackout, all accompanied by wry commentary from Neylon Costes, a plump old Blue Shirt who ticked off the names and nicknames and brief career highlights of the many memorable cops who'd served in the glorious 43rd.

Neylon puffed a few steps from the top of the staircase, discarding Puppy's offer to help. "Course they're all memorable. Put on the blue shirt or the brown hat just once and you're memorable." He nodded at a couple of passing detectives as if they'd shown up on his cue.

Closing the door on the wheezing Neylon, Rafferty grinned impishly. "Quite a guy."

"Fountain of information." Puppy glanced at Detective Layon Y'or on the couch, ankles crossed, eyes darting. They exchanged cautious nods.

Rafferty leaned back in his beloved squeaky leather chair. "Thanks for coming in, Puppy."

He shrugged. "Hopefully it wasn't a mistake."

The captain's eyes narrowed. "Me, too. Did you hear about vandalism at Candlestick Park last night?"

"Nope."

"All of the bases were stolen."

Puppy laughed. "I'm amazed anyone remembered how to steal a base."

Rafferty rolled his eyes. "I forgot I was talking to a baseball historian. And the former Commissioner of Baseball. I'm not suggesting you had anything to do with that, Puppy. I'm just making a point about the urgency of the situation."

"Was anyone hurt?"

He shook his head. "It was done after hours."

"But you assume it had to be a baseball fan."

"I assume nothing, Puppy. Only those four bases were stolen; there was a small explosion at County Stadium in Milwaukee that blew open a gate, and a security guard chased off folks pulling out the ivy in Wrigley Field."

"Unfortunate vandalism."

"That it?"

"What else?"

Rafferty gestured about his office. "I'm hoping you can tell me."

"I have no idea."

The cop showed his skepticism. "No idea about anything?"

"I only organized the original 'P holders' for Parker DeWitt and I will keep doing that until the BT is punished because a kid's life was taken over a pair of red socks and that can't be right under any circumstances." Puppy frowned toward Y'or. "Your detective said this was going to be an exchange of information."

"When we get some," Rafferty said.

"You want me to admit I broke the law, which I haven't," Puppy said.

"No one seems to have broken the law."

Puppy stared leadenly.

"Especially your Friends of groups. We've now had ninety-eight in for exploratory talks and all of them profess to be as innocent as snow from the sky."

"All the groups are pretty much on their own, Captain Rafferty. What the Friends of Sandy Koufax in Los Angeles or the Friends of George Brett in Kansas City or the Friends of Roberto Clemente in Pittsburgh do"—his voice rose as Rafferty impatiently gestured for him to get to the point—"is their call. But they don't report to me. I have no job. No power."

"You have a moral power, Puppy. Don't sell yourself short."

"I've learned that most of the time what I hoped would happen rarely does."

Rafferty wiped away invisible tears. "And in this particular occasion, what do you want?"

"The ballparks reopened to all fans and restrictions lifted. You've seen the demands taped outside the ballparks, Captain Rafferty."

"And everywhere else. I took a crap at Pepe's Pizza down the block yesterday and there was one of your damn manifestos shoved into the toilet paper dispenser. Yeah, it's not funny." His glare stifled Y'or's smile. "The more the protests grow, the more violence flares and now they're blocking people from going to work, schools, stores—"

"That was clearly discouraged."

"Clearly ignored."

"I've tried."

Rafferty pounced. "To who, Puppy? Who do you discourage? How? Where are you making these speeches? When you talk to the Friends of groups?"

Puppy took a breath. He was dealing with a pro. "That'd be a violation of the conspiracy laws, sir."

"Yes, it would."

"Good thing I don't."

Rafferty considered him. "Where's Mooshie Lopez?"

Puppy was a little thrown. "Why?"

"Because she was a ringleader back in the day. Any thoughts that Mooshie and Tony Felton and some of the old POW gang might be less than taken with your peaceful plans?"

Puppy squirmed. "I haven't seen Mooshie in a couple weeks. Felton longer."

"But you don't disagree they might take issue."

"If I had a plan."

"If you did?" Rafferty shrewdly asked.

Puppy squirmed a little more. "I can't speak for someone else."

"Try."

"And blindly accuse someone?"

Rafferty meaningfully glanced at Y'or. "What about Albert Cheng?"

"Haven't seen him, either."

"Elias Kenuda?"

Puppy swore at his indecision and the quick glance Rafferty shot Y'or.

"Zelda Jones," Rafferty persisted.

"What the hell does she have to do with this?"

"There's the street theater, the skits performed by the baseball clowns. Very polished."

"I watched a few already," Y'or chimed in. "Sharp dialogue. Not something the Friends of Gil Hodges would come up with."

"Maybe Zelda wrote them." Rafferty held up his palms. "She can't write plays anymore."

Puppy stood. "This conversation's over."

Rafferty roughly shoved Puppy back into his seat. He bounced a little.

"I wouldn't be surprised if the BTs are looking for an excuse to replace us, Puppy. No more cops. Think about what that'd be like. The acts of vandalism and violence will give them that excuse. Once the BTs are permanently positioned near ballparks, they'll be deployed in the DVs and we won't ever get them out. We'll be back to the late '60s and early '70s. They'll claim national security. I need you to call off your people, Puppy. At this point you're doing more harm than good and I'm not letting some self-important asshole with dreams of glory"—Rafferty shoved him back into the chair as Layon cringed at the blatant violation of police behavior—"let whoever's looking to undermine our values get away with this."

"Who's undermining our values?"

"I don't know yet. Do you?"

Puppy looked away. He couldn't. He just couldn't.

"Who, Puppy, who?" Rafferty edged back with a thin smile. "I'll get you on the emergency bulletin board. Let me worry about the how. Tell all the Friends of, from the Friends of Hack Wilson to the Friends of Joe Morgan and everyone in between, that you made your point. If you do that, I'll issue an arrest order for the BT who killed Parker DeWitt."

"Oh really?" Puppy pulled a face.

The captain slid a confirmation letter across the desk from the superintendent of the Boston Police Department. Puppy gave it a dismissive glance.

"How can you just stroll in and arrest a Black Top?"

"Captain Rafferty wouldn't say that if it weren't true," Y'or said angrily.

Puppy folded and unfolded the letter. "What about baseball?"

Rafferty scowled. "What about fucking baseball already?"

"You arrest this BT, mistakes are admitted, but will the Cousins return the game to where it was before all this happened?"

"That might take some time. Let's do this in stages to build goodwill."

"That's asking for a lot of trust."

Rafferty rose. "And I just learned I got two cops in the hospital who were hit with a tire iron by your peaceful protesters on Walton Avenue. Don't lecture me about trust."

Puppy studied the arrest order. Sighing, he said, "Let me think about this for a few days."

Rafferty shook his head. "You don't have time, kid. Neither of us do."

The captain motioned for Layon to stay behind as Puppy wandered by the Cream-a-licious Donuts in the silent, staring squad room.

"I want you to take him to the Family Message Center." Rafferty scribbled on his notepad, tearing off the paper. "Give this to Choney. He works the night shift. He'll set everything up."

The young cop peered at the note. "Doesn't this require a Cousins request?"

"Not tonight."

Layon paled. "Captain Rafferty, this is not a binding order."

"It is tonight."

The Brown Hat bounced nervously. "This is a corner being cut which I'm not comfortable with."

"I understand."

Y'or frowned. "Sir."

"Yes, Detective Y'or?"

Layon squared his jaw. "I cannot follow an order that violates my oath as a police officer."

Rafferty shrugged and sat on his desk. "Got it."

"Well then, if you got it, then you can appreciate I can't carry this out."

"Oh, you can't do this as a police officer, but you can do it as a sibling"—he paused—"and as my friend because it's the right thing to do. That cops have a higher standard than the rest of The Family is all well and good, but this evening that gets in the way of doing what needs to be done. I'm sorry to inform you, Detective Layon Y'or, that you are suspended for excessive ethical behavior which has interfered with the pragmatic application of your duties. The charges will be reviewed by your peers, usually within a week. The suspension is scheduled to begin in about thirty-five minutes which'll give you time to get your ass up to 198th Street. Take one of the squad cars."

Y'or had no idea what to say. "How can you do all this?"

Rafferty looked very sad that he didn't have a good enough answer. "Don't worry, Y'or. You'll come out of this just fine. You're a good cop. They'll need you when they pick up the pieces. Now scoot. Now."

Layon wasn't convinced. Rafferty laid a thick hand on the back of his neck. "You signed up to serve The Family, not to serve the rules of police officers."

"This crosses the line," the detective insisted with a little less vigor.

"Yes, it does. And I bear the responsibility."

Muttering, Y'or shuffled to the door, slowly turning. "Was the letter from the Boston PD real?"

Rafferty's eyes turned black. "Oh yeah. Oh yeah. Time to squeeze their pimple."

42

To get to the circular brick stairway took nearly an hour of scanning and re-scanning, in every possible orifice, through a long above-ground tunnel stretching just past the Great Siege Plaza in Valletta, the Maltese capital. Inside, a stout nun with bad breath searched her hair, turning Annette over to an even uglier Sister with a broad nose who made her disrobe inside a metal storage container. There were no apologies for her being treated like a suspicious suitcase.

The stairway brought them down 289 feet, the priest explained during one of the few times he or the rabbi spoke. The walls of the long tunnel were stripped bare as if slowly vacated by a large family over a long period of time. She could tell there'd been paintings, artifacts, lots of old stuff. There were cameras in the ceiling in the form of black dots and, briefly, a gun turret peeked at her with too much interest.

The aqua-colored chamber was damp and slightly smelly. Father Drobev and Rabbi Gold moved a couple of cheap-looking leather chairs into the center of the room, adding a small table. Hesitant lights were molded into the walls. An old ceiling fan wobbled mightily.

The priest and rabbi, heads tilted into the invisible earpieces, grunted and reluctantly left. Annette shook her head. She got a rubber hose shoved up her butt for this?

Pope John Paul XXIX crossed the room with a cheery smile. He was dressed like someone on their way to open their vegetable market, and not a fancy one at that. The pope took off the floppy beige hat with a sheepish shrug.

"I was in the garden. Apologies for being late." His jowly face widened in a grin.

"I'm used to being pushed around. I'm Annette Ramos."

"Welcome. Pope John."

Her jaw dropped. "Shit. Sorry. I mean really." She rubbed her palms vigorously on her knee-high khaki shorts. "They didn't say anything, just dragged me here or else I would've dressed better."

"Why? I didn't."

"But you're the pope."

"And you're my guest who has traveled thousands of miles to see me. My only concession this morning was putting aside my regular hat." He showed the straw hat. "Look how clean and sharp. How could a man garden in such head gear?" The pope tossed the hat into the corner as if that was the end of that. "Please, Annette, if I may call you that. Sit if you'd like."

Blushing, she made such an effort at covering her bare knees with crossed legs that the pope burst out laughing.

"I have seen women's legs before. I am eighty-nine. You pick up a little bit of everything on the way."

"You don't look eighty-nine."

The blue eyes twinkled beneath the thick white hair falling over his forehead. "It's the gardening. Also yoga. The flexibility is critical at any age. Blood flow, connecting the tissue. Cleansing the mind. I love inverting. Do you practice?"

"Yoga wasn't really encouraged in The Family."

"Ah yes. India is not Iran, but you did have your murky prohibitions." The pope considered the lost benefits of widescale yoga on the American population. "Grandma was a handsome woman until her death. She was past ninety and I suspect she would've plowed past the century mark if not for the assassination. That was thought to be your husband."

"Puppy was innocent," she answered carefully. "I think that's all cleared up. He'd never hurt anyone."

"I'm eternally amazed at how many good people hurt others," he said wistfully before perking up. "I didn't mean to accuse you."

Annette uncrossed her ankles. "You sure?"

The pope laughed. "I can see how you made it this far, Annette. Spirit counts for much."

"It does, sir. Is sir okay or would you prefer Holy Father or Your Popeness or something else?"

"John's fine. As you can see from my attire, I don't stand on ceremonies anymore."

"I'm sorry if I sounded disrespectful."

"You Americans are not accustomed to showing respect to authority."

She smiled. "We might not practice yoga, but Americans have other good points."

He returned the smile. "Still do, as I can see by your courage."

"I had help."

"We all do of some kind. Yours apparently was from the American Granddaughter who we believe guided you. I know you've explained this to my friends and for the life of me, I can't make head or tail of the talk of the Ar3, so I'd prefer to hear everything from you."

Annette glanced around. "We need your help."

The pope stared intently. "Is the 'we' America?"

"Obviously because Clary guided me. The Granddaughter Clary Santiago. A good Catholic."

From his shrug, that didn't seem to matter. He'd also been disappointed by good Christians. "This was her idea?"

She shook her head. "Me and Puppy."

"Have you spoken to Clary since you left America?"

"No, but we had a relationship before. I kind of looked after her for a while once I escaped from a Miners camp—those are rebels, terrorists—when Zelda, Puppy's best friend, went off to have her baby. Am I telling too much?"

"I have a lot of time," he said with a smile.

She frowned. "I'm talking too much nonsense."

"You're passionate. I'm honored that you'd come to me for help. But I don't know how to help you, Annette."

She should've thought this out a little better. "Go on the vid and say that you'll make peace between the Americans and the Islamists."

He clasped his hands with a gentle smile. "That's all?"

"You can fill in the rest."

He cleared his throat. "A speech to the world."

"No, this room. Sorry. I'm a little nervous. Yes, sir. To the world. You're the boss of the Catholics. People respect you."

Pope John sighed wearily. "Catholicism is largely banned or discredited throughout the world, Annette. It's not outright illegal like Judaism, but close. Your country and all its properties forbid religious worship. The bans on religion have been reinstituted throughout South America now that you've taken that back. The Islamists mock Christianity."

"I lived in London. I know all about that. I had a friend, a good friend, a Catholic priest named John Dempsey who taught me. I almost thought about converting but, you know how it is."

"All too well," the pope chuckled. "What prevented you?"

"It's a lot of work. Honestly. I sort of believe but not entirely. I was a nun for a while. I mean, not a real nun though I wore the clothes, terrible hats, and did a lot of laundry. And I escaped London on the Rat Line so, sir, I'm aware of how things are for Catholics. You have a better idea since it's your job, but there's still a lot of you guys out there and you could do some good if you tried."

Emotions traveled all along the pope's lined face. "I did try, Annette. Oh mightily. I tried with the Grand Mufti. I tried with Grandma. I sent emissaries to your Miners and Blue Wigs, did you know that? They didn't want peace, but I sent messages anyway. To the Chinese. The Brazilians while they were still neutral."

He rose unsteadily. "My priests and nuns and all the Church held vigils, meetings with leaders in their local nations. We hid refugees, marched against the pogroms. There was a suicidal line of priests which I did not endorse who tried preventing the sacking of St. Arien's in Antwerp. Thousands were slaughtered. Every Sunday Mass I spoke for peace. Whoever would interview me. Your vid, TV, newspapers, I begged for peace but no one would listen." His eyes blazed as his voice dropped. "No one would listen."

"Didn't you shoot at planes from the roof of the Vatican?"

"Yes, I took lives," his voice thundered, alarming the eyes staring behind the walls. "God forgive me. I killed to protect my faith and the Church."

Annette waited for the suddenly frail man to slump into his chair. "So that's why you hide?"

"Pardon?"

"You heard me. Is that why you hide?"

His lips pursed. "I'm not hiding. I'm defending the treasures of the Church so that not all is lost when the barbarians overrun us. But someday either the Americans or the Muslims will come and these tunnels, built centuries ago to defend God, will be full of blood again."

"Like it's not happening everywhere? Did you know the Allahs have used nukes in Egypt?"

"And your Clary, the good Catholic, ordered the sacking of Jerusalem, Christ's Jerusalem, and you ask me to help you? The Americans are as barbaric as the Allahs."

"Doesn't look like you were doing much before I arrived."

Father Drobev and Rabbi Gold stepped inside. The pope angrily gestured them away. "I pray."

"Pray? Pray? For what? For your crop of eggplants to be juicy…?"

His eyes narrowed. "You forget who I am, Ms. Ramos."

"No. You forgot who you are, Holy Father."

There were imaginary red lines on Pope John's face where the words had slapped him.

Annette shook her index finger. "Soon there won't be blood in these tunnels or anything anywhere. Just those nuclear winds and you can bury your golden treasures as deep as you want so only insects and rats can read them. Once, you stood on the roof of the Vatican shooting down planes to protect what you believed in. I think it's time you did that again. Without the weapons. One last chance. I don't know what your Jesus would say but I bet if he's half the guy everyone makes him out to be, he'd tell you to put on those fancy robes and that ridiculous hat and get off your butt. Because I'm not leaving this stupid island until you do."

As she took a step toward the old man, two darts embedded in both sides of Annette's neck. The last pope caught her before she hit the ground. He wept on her pale face before turning to the dozen bearded guards protecting him on all sides.

"Get my robes." The Holy Father lifted Annette onto his left shoulder. "And burn all of those bloody gardening hats."

43

Verbally fretting over the frayed thread on the sleeve of his blue serge suit, Rafferty was startled by Felice abruptly standing before the foosball machine.

"Good morning, Captain Rafferty. May I order you some refreshments?"

Rafferty didn't like anything about this, and he had just gotten there. It usually didn't get better. "I'm good. Am I too early?"

"Precisely on time."

"Felice, right?" As the 'bot nodded, Rafferty made a show of a large look around the empty Cousins conference room. "Then where's everyone?"

"The 'everyone' required for this request is present."

"Not for a meeting with the top-ranking police officer in the nation's capital."

"The Cousins are aware of your standing, Captain Rafferty, and are very grateful for your fine service to the goals of The Family. The Cousins asked me to address your request."

Rafferty about ambled in place. "Why's that?"

"They are all occupied with the matters of The Family."

"This a matter of The Family. An urgent matter."

"Which is why I am present."

Rafferty snorted. "So I go through you? No. I don't think so. Bring up the Cousins, their HGs, their warm red-blooded forms, whatever you got."

Felice arched an eyebrow. "There is no reason for anger, Captain Rafferty."

"The hell there isn't. You're insulting me."

"There is no intention of that. We have shown you considerable respect. You requested a meeting with the Cousins to discuss a pressing police matter. It was immediately scheduled. I am the adjunct of the Cousins—"

"Bring them here. Now."

Felice's forehead pulsed. "Would you speak to a Cousin in that tone?"

"No. But you ain't a Cousin."

Felice's eyes glittered. "What is the urgent police matter?"

"I tell the Cousins, not you."

"I am the adjunct—"

"You said that already. My hearing's damn good because I learned a long time ago to weed out crap."

"Please present your urgent matter and I will discuss it with the Cousins."

"I want them in person or by digitalized appearance. End of story. The Cousins can never avoid the police. Ever. We uphold the law and the Cousins are fully accountable to the police."

"I am also accountable to the police, Captain Rafferty."

"That's right," Rafferty said triumphantly. "Remember you said that."

Felice's forehead pulsed a nasty red. "I record everything, Captain Rafferty. Shall I play back my words informing you that I am the designated adjunct of the Cousins in this instance?"

The 'bot stared. It could probably stare until hell froze over and then some. With an angry growl, Rafferty handed over the arrest order. Felice studied it for a second.

"This has already been processed."

"Oh, how's that?"

"The Black Top soldier was reprimanded and his interspecific dynamics were upgraded."

"What the hell does that mean?"

Felice's lips thinned. "His sensitivity to human emotions sparked an unwarranted reaction. His filters have been strengthened so he will no longer respond in that manner."

"That's it?"

"Yes."

His expression darkened. "Nah, that's not enough."

"Please define your concept of 'enough.'"

"We'll bring him into police custody where a committee, as you see from the order, composed of humans and 'bots, will question him. But taking a life isn't something that can be whisked under the damn rug."

"I appreciate your concern for the taking of a human life, Captain Rafferty. That is always a poignant moment for humans. Given the integration of 'bots into The Family and the primary role we play in prosecuting the conflict against the Islamic Empire, it would be counterproductive to single out a Black Top soldier who, with no malice, reacted to unprovoked human emotions because of a readily adjustable shortcoming. It would be counterproductive to inflict any doubts on the viability of the Black Tops and the inorganic soldiers. The American Second Army Group sustained 13,440 casualties in Tuesday's Islamist tactical nuclear strike at Alexandria. There will be 'sad moments' integrated in the work and education days beginning later this afternoon. That will be announced by the Granddaughter on the Noon News."

"If you want to be treated like us then you have to be treated like us," Rafferty said hoarsely.

"Correct. We are liable to the same laws. I do not understand why this would need to be further pursued. The only ones concerned are the baseball fans, specifically the 'P holders.' It is my understanding that of the regularly scheduled protests in the thirty baseball cities, only five took place today. It is an issue that is fading."

"Not anytime soon," Rafferty snapped.

Felice unblinkingly stared. "Perhaps you already arranged for the fans to withdraw their protests in exchange for arresting the Black Top."

Rafferty reddened. "Why would you say that?"

"You met with Puppy Nedick yesterday in your office. The 'P holders,' which he has organized, abruptly diminished in numbers."

"Are you spying on me, you metallic SOB? Who the hell do you think you are?"

"The perspective of who I am should come from you, Captain Rafferty. Puppy Nedick was given a tour of your precinct which is public record."

"Only if someone's paying attention."

"I pay attention to everything, Captain Rafferty. So should you."

"Oh don't worry, Felice. I do. Now for the last time, will you call the Cousins so I can obtain their authorization for this arrest order?"

"For the last time, Captain Rafferty, as the adjunct of the Cousins, I have already decided the matter. Would you like me to repeat that?"

Rafferty waved his hand, adopting a shrewd expression he didn't feel. "What if I did make a deal with Puppy?"

"Either you did or you did not."

"Grandma's earrings, I did. Yes, he agreed to scale back the protests."

"An excellent outcome."

"In exchange for the arrest of the BT."

"For which you had no authority."

Rafferty went up on the balls of his feet. "I'm a police captain. I made the decision. It was the right decision. Puppy and his people trusted us. The fans'll feel betrayed."

Felice arched an eyebrow. "By whom? Had you spoken to the Cousins sooner, this would have been avoided. This was your initiative. This is your responsibility. Puppy Nedick is entitled to file a complaint for false negotiations conducted by a peace officer. Would you like me to connect you to the proper Cousin who would handle such a matter?"

Rafferty took short steps across the room, stopping six inches away from the 'bot. "Are you threatening me, Felice?"

"I am merely informing you of the process with which I would think you would be familiar. From your tone and belligerent physical gait, you are threatening me. If I am correct, and I am 97.4 percent certain, you are suggesting that once Puppy Nedick is informed that there will be no formal arrest and, certainly, no lifting of the baseball restrictions which I also assume to a 98.7 percent certainty you agreed to pursue on his behalf, he will reach out again to the Friends of organizations. Have I missed any information, Captain Rafferty?"

He could've fit Felice's head inside one of his flared nostrils.

"I also appreciate your official confirmation of Puppy Nedick's acknowledged efforts in organizing illegal activities which constitutes a violation of the Anti-Conspiracy Laws. He would still retain his right to file a formal complaint against you. Is there anything else, Captain Rafferty?"

Rafferty just shook his head.

Felice half turned, swiveling slowly back with a frosty stare. "And the Black Top's name is Rafael. R-A-F-A-E-L. Like Felice. F-E-L-I-C-E. "

• • • •

PRETTY IN AN angular way, Sereen Y'or studied Puppy through a wary lens as she set out Gumbo's Thin Crackers and an array of Baton Rouge sharp cheeses. That was a declaration of love compared to the looks she threw at her husband Layon.

Once the three children, Maras, Pietra, and Liam, six, eight, and nine respectively, had made their polite introductions and returned to their bedroom (the door slightly open to spy), Puppy settled into a lumpy armchair.

Loud yells pierced the wall followed by smashing sounds. Draped in a green plaid bathrobe, Layon hurried into the living room holding the remains of a blue-and-white plate. Sereen followed, knocking the shards on the rug. She clutched Puppy's hand fiercely.

"I must apologize for my rude behavior, Mr. Nedick."

"No reason—"

"Let her," Layon begged. "Please."

Sereen gave Layon a sharp look that promised more. "My husband and I share everything. We never make important decisions without discussing them. He should have waited to talk this over with me." Another nasty stare. "He didn't and I'm upset over that and his actions which I don't agree with. That said, you're very welcome in our home."

"Thanks, but I don't want to cause any problems between you."

"It's too late for that!" Sereen yelled. She scooped up Layon's Brown Hat uniform from the stained couch and began ironing the suit pants in the far corner of the living room, largely taken over by toys and bicycles. It was clear she was imagining Layon's head beneath the iron.

Tucking the sheets and fluffing the pillow, Layon half-heartedly apologized for the mattress on the floor of the combo bedroom-storage closet.

"She'll be fine by morning. But if you hear any noises"—he jerked his head at the wall over his shoulder—"just ignore them. No matter how loud."

"I figure you're a cop so you can handle it."

Layon squatted, deliberating. "Not entirely. I'm on suspension. I have been since I took you to the Message Center the other night. All I ever wanted was to become a cop. Now I'm not. I don't know if I made a mistake. But in here and here"—this time he tapped his bruised chest and temples—"I have a duty. I agreed to something that wouldn't have otherwise happened. By going along, I might've put you in danger, Puppy. By not going along, more siblings might be in danger. Whatever, I have an obligation to continue protecting you, even unofficially."

He bounded up with an uncertain sigh. "Get some rest."

Puppy stopped him with a firm hand on his arm. "This is all very nice and cozy. Love meeting your family. I was nice enough to allow you to apprehend me outside my apartment building without a real explanation because I figure you wouldn't do that for no good reason. But I need some real answers."

The Brown Hat sat back down. "Rafferty got screwed."

"Which means I got screwed." Between grumbles and faint profanities, Puppy listened to Layon recount the captain's conversation with Felice. "I promised everyone, damn it. They trusted me. I trusted you."

Puppy apologized for the shouts that brought Sereen in with a warning glare. His voice dropped to a whisper. "How do I know Rafferty didn't pull all this shit in collusion with Clary?"

Y'or shouted at the affrontery of maligning a police officer's integrity. Sereen cautioned them that at the next outburst they'd be sleeping in the building stairwell, and not just overnight.

The men stared moodily.

"Why didn't Rafferty have the decency to tell me?"

"Because he's officially a cop."

"Oh, so he asked the guy who's not anymore. So much for the blanket of ethics…"

"Why do you think I really picked you up? They've issued a national warrant for your arrest, Puppy. National warrant. That's about as high as it goes."

Y'or was surprised at Puppy's breezy laugh. "This is my second time at the dance after being accused of killing Grandma."

Off an exchange of brittle smiles, Y'or said, "By law, Captain Rafferty must fulfill an arrest request."

"And can't officially protect me. Which is why I'm here with you." Puppy shrewdly eyed Layon. "That's not the only reason."

Y'or hesitated. "Right."

"You don't want me doing anything stupid."

"Let Rafferty figure out the next moves."

"He's done a great job so far." Puppy dismissed Layon's glare. "I'm not hiding."

Y'or burst out laughing. "I've heard some ridiculous tough-guy criminal lines, but that's a good one. The moment you step outside, you'll be dodging Jet'roes. They've probably been to your friends's homes. That's how this works, Puppy. The BTs aren't the cuddly types like us cops. And like I said, every police officer is bound to cooperate in hunting you down, whether they agree or not."

"Here's more tough-guy talk. Too many people depend on me and I'm not letting them down."

"Let us work this—"

"No," Puppy said sharply. They held their breaths, waiting for Sereen to show up. Finally, "Do you really think Clary will back down?"

Y'or frowned. "This came from Felice."

Puppy shook his head. "No, it's Clary. All this power has gone to her head. Yeah, and I know that from direct conversations. You got to believe me on the details about what she's becoming—"

Layon cut him off. "Trust isn't good enough anymore. Tell me."

Puppy only paused for the Brown Hat's long astonished whistles. "You see, Rafferty's wrong if he thinks this can be solved by the usual methods."

Layon looked away before returning with a steady stare, nodding. Puppy gently squeezed the detective's wrist.

"So I don't cause problems for your family, why don't you go to sleep and let me leave."

Y'or briefly closed his eyes, imagining Sereen's reaction. Talk about ugly options. "I can't do that."

"Which means you're going to cuff me to the mattress?"

"Not yet."

• • • •

FROM HIS SPARE desk that suggested neurotic cleanliness, Evan Zambrustalev gestured for Puppy to sit inside the soundproof booth at the Family Message Room.

Evan scanned the request with a frown. "This message has been processed already by Choney."

"This is a second message on the first request."

"Is it the same message?"

Layon glanced at Puppy who shook his head. That was enough for Evan who returned the request. "Can't do, Detective Y'or."

Layon let that title go; what did it matter anymore? "You have no reason to reject this. The original authorization from Captain Rafferty is valid for seventy hours."

"I know the code. It's my job," Evan grumbled, glancing around suspiciously. It was 1:30 in the morning. The Message Center closed at two when the vidnews slept until six. Evan was also tired. And bored. This was the second emergency message he'd ever handled in his three years. First time, two children had fallen down an elevator shaft. But that had all the right papers. This was processing a second emergency message without any authorization from a Cousin or adjunct of that office.

"Why's it a different message so soon?"

Y'or held out his palm with an authoritative glare. "Are you invading the privacy of a sibling to learn the reasons for his private message, Mr. Zambrustalev? What gives you such an extraordinary right that no one else has? Even I don't know what the second message contains. That is Mr. Nedick's business. Next you'll be asking to record his visits to the bathroom. Or to follow him at night. Perhaps you would like to do that, Mr. Zambrustalev."

"I don't care about him. I care about the rules."

"And when the first message went out, did your office receive any adverse follow-up?"

Evan pulled a face. "I didn't personally, no."

"Then what possible basis do you have to delay an emergency message which might very well be a question of life or death—"

Evan threw up his hands. "Okay, okay."

Puppy slid onto a stool in the five-foot-high soundproof booth and snapped the door shut. Above the keyboard, a dour HG folded its arms, head inclined.

"Is this an emergency?"

Puppy nodded.

"I don't hear you."

"Yes, yes."

"Are you using this for personal gain, financial profit, or sexual or emotional advantage or manipulation of a sibling?"

"No."

"And using the finest mail delivery system in the world wouldn't work just as well?"

"No."

"Are you able to use various conveyances such as mass transit or vehicles instead of the emergency system?"

"Not if I want to reach all of the intended recipients."

"Then you can reach some of the intended recipients by various conveyances such as—"

"Only a few."

The HG didn't like being interrupted. "How many is a few?"

"Two. No, three. Six." He grew flustered at counting the competing Yankees and Mets Friends of groups.

The HG grew suspicious. "You're not sure?"

"Positive."

"Is the recipient or recipients a member of your biological family?"

"No."

"Do you consider these friends members of your family?"

"Yes, as defined by Grandma's First Insight, 'There is nothing more important than love.'"

"Is someone's health at stake?"

"Oh yes."

"Is their life in danger?"

"Could be."

The HG sniffed. "Your heart rate exceeds a hundred beats per minute."

"I'm excited."

"Or nervous?"

"Is there usually a difference?"

The HG didn't like snark. "Do you know this recipient or these recipients personally?"

"Most of them. The ones I haven't are friends of the ones I've met."

The HG pursed its lips. "You may type in the message."

The first message had been *Parker OK.* He typed the second very carefully.

"It will be transmitted shortly."

The HG faded out. As Puppy stepped out of the booth, Zambrustalev glanced up with a sour look, eager for them to leave as was the anxious Layon.

"I want to see it go up," Puppy said.

With a sullen stare, Evan held up a finger, counting to himself before pointing at the vidnews.

To the far right beneath the Granddaughter frolicking amid llamas at the newly opened St. Louis Zoo, the message popped up:

Beanball.

"Beanball?" Layon asked as they waited for the M11 bus.

"That means getting hit in the head by a pitch."

The detective roared. A BT vehicle rumbled down Sherman Avenue. Y'or quickly pressed Puppy into the shadows beneath a hardware store awning. Layon suddenly kissed Puppy on the lips like a pretend lover, waiting until the vehicle left.

Puppy grinned. "Here I thought you didn't like me."

"You're growing on me."

44

The "summer of socks" blossomed that morning.

Rinaldi's Paints of Greater Rochester led the way. Their trucks had fanned out over the past four days, delivering as far west as St. Louis where Jimpsen-Da Gay Colors took over. Reaching to Seattle, Jimpsen-Da hired subcontractors Oui Lu and Shemp & Shemp of Tulsa, and their subcontractors Nipsy Delight of Taos, who handled the West and Southwest. In the South, Peachey Colors of Atlanta and Whaling Willie's of Chattanooga covered the rest of the country.

Socks across America were dyed red and hoisted onto sticks. When morning broke, red socks were stuck in car doors, milk cartons, subway gates, windshield wipers. On cop cars, in gardens, on traffic lights. On store windows, gym machines, school entrances, playgrounds. Sympathetic siblings demonstrated solidarity by tucking red-sock flags in their briefcases, on their laps, in their coffee cups. Waitresses laid red-sock flags on tables as part of customer settings. Streets were carpeted in red-sock flags. Cousins's lobbies were festooned. The Granddaughter's face on the billboard near Van Cortlandt Park had been obliterated beneath the socks.

Matthew couldn't quite determine exactly how many socks had been produced, but his closest estimate before the last of his legal access was shut down registered 11,449,126 red-sock flags.

Dressed in the various uniforms of major league baseball teams, crowds closed streets and mass transit, shut down schools and businesses, and blocked traffic. Beneath signs such as *Give Me Baseball Or Give Me Death,* the protesters, angry at the Cousins's betrayal, swarmed like peeved flies. Graffiti erupted on buildings and sidewalks and storefronts: *My Cousin Wouldn't Lie, Fake Family, Vote.*

Before the Cousins officially closed all available HG tellyconf bandwidth, Puppy had insisted to the Friends of groups that they must be respectful. Say what they want, but just march. Chant, sing, dance, hoist the placards, but the responsibility for discipline lay with all of them. There would be children, unable to attend school, joining the march. Workers, grudgingly given the day off, trailing along.

Off-duty Blue Shirts swelled the ranks; absenteeism would hit thirty percent.

Fans waved red socks on sticks of all sizes. Baseball bats stabbed the air but not people. Children played catch; a new game was born involving tossing a baseball while marching sideways. Concessions sprouted up; sandwiches were handed out, water bottles tossed. Bands materialized. Dixieland in New Orleans. Sage rock in Atlanta. Country blues in Chicago. Hand-held mini pianos jazzified San Francisco. Trumpets blared in Milwaukee. Orchestras synthesized, drifted, reformed.

Dancing and shaking "P" cards became another sport. Copies of Ty and Mickey's book *Baseball, Your Game*, were tossed toward the marchers and back into the crowd. In Boston, Ernie the Wizard rode along on his white horse reading aloud from a writer named Roger Angell. Without the horse or the wand, the works of Bernard Malamud, Damon Runyon, and W.P. Kinsella were also distributed by teachers of the Twentieth-Century Project. Some held photos of Hedda Kleinz. The letter "H" was integrated alongside the "Ps."

Flanking the routes, Blue Shirt patrol cars reported to city commanders who shared the information nationally. There were no incidents. Oh, a few Regs shouted disrespect but were quickly chased away.

For more than three hours, millions marched toward the major league stadiums where they set up tents and other makeshift housing. Tens of thousands of protesters took over the subway and bus stops. A 'bot conductor in Seattle insisted his train was going to stop at Pilots Stadium come hell or high water. He was gently, but firmly removed; the stalled train obstructed all rail traffic east and west.

Soon buses in St. Louis and Houston were politely evacuated, then overturned. Near Royals Stadium, trains were abandoned two stops early. Fans parked cars at various angles near Dodger Stadium, blocking Vin Scully Avenue.

By nightfall, baseball fans had paralyzed America. Then the Jet'roes moved in.

45

First Cousin Nadharatha's hands shook so violently he had to put down the Nok-Hockey puck in the middle of a game. That was never done.

"Bullets. Bullets. Bullets. On unarmed siblings." Even a still-warm raspberry scone couldn't quell his anger.

"They were startling pellets," Second Cousin D'Andre corrected.

"Startling or not, this was not authorized, and will you please go back to the door?" He'd positioned Second Cousin DeRico and Fourth Cousin Oh by the two entrances should Felice arrive unexpectedly to their unscheduled meeting. Notes had been passed in hallways. On a Cheese Doo's napkin. He himself, First Cousin of The Family, had to whisper from a bathroom cubicle on the third floor.

Third Cousin Dinazzo twisted her broad face. "According to Statute 4.1, moving protests must be quelled immediately. There were questionable leaflets handed out."

"About the history of the damn teams."

"This is a glorification of previous dangerous behavior. Touting winning world championships and record batting averages."

"And four people in Atlanta were injured," added Third Cousin Wang. "They were attired in head-to-toe costumes with names and numbers of"—he consulted his notes— "a Greg Maddox, Chipper Jones, Lew Burdette, and Dale Murphy, and reacted violently when the BTs neared."

"Then they were the only ones," snapped Nadharatha. "All the 'P carders' went limp and sang or chanted as they were carried or dragged away."

He pointed to the Blue Shirts report hovering over the conference table. More than six hundred, all wearing Kirby Puckett uniforms, were arrested in Minneapolis; three were neurologically wounded by the startling pellets. Over a thousand more outside Wrigley Field, many singing "It's a great day, let's play two" as they were lector-cuffed into armored BT trucks. At Fenway Park, an estimated two thousand fans escaped arrest by rampaging over the Big Papi Bridge, necessitating another overnight curfew.

Nearly fifteen thousand nationwide were taken to BT holding facilities. In most, "Take Me Out to the Ballgame" was sung all night. Eighty-four protesters were injured from the nerve-numbing startling pellets. One, an elderly man in San Francisco wearing a Number 24 Willie Mays jersey, remained in ICU.

"At least no one was killed," Fourth Cousin Oh pointed out a little too brightly.

"Are you an absolute idiot?" Nadharatha raged.

"That is an inappropriate and disrespectful remark, First Cousin."

"Not for an absolute idiot."

"Apparently I am late." Felice materialized by the stack of board games. "My apologies."

Nadharatha took a deep breath. The other Cousins reacted as if struck by startling pellets. "You're not late because you weren't invited, Felice."

"I do not understand why."

"Because this is a special Cousins meeting. An emergency meeting of only Cousins. We're convening to decide what to do after this horrible mess you engineered."

"The protests violated innumerable laws from the prevention of taking individual action, interfering with individual responsibility, and proselytizing. These have been carefully organized which violates the Anti-Conspiracy Laws."

"You still had no right to order the Black Tops to take action without consulting us."

Felice's forehead pulsed slightly. "Unfortunately, the sanctity of Cousins confidentiality has been breached. Information from previous meetings has been shared outside these chambers. It was not feasible to risk discussing action."

The Cousins exchanged nervous looks, edging away from each other.

"Are you accusing the Cousins, my Cousins, of violating their oaths?" Nadharatha stormed.

"Yes, First Cousin."

"On what basis?"

"On information in the hands of unauthorized siblings. To discuss the specifics would risk that information also being passed along. There was a security issue which needed to be dealt with and the Black Tops did so with no loss of life. At the beginning of the operation, there was a 21.7 percent likelihood that deaths would be sustained. The man in San Francisco who sustained an injury is in slow recovery. There was no way to know he had a prior condition that made his nerves prone to life-threatening reactions. That is why only startling bullets concentrating on shocking nerve endings were employed with no intention of permanent harm. There should be praise for the BT efforts."

There was none. If the Black Tops were human, there would be explosions of applause, Felice thought.

"Even the physical damage is minimal apart from overturned buses. Fifty-two percent of the mass transit hubs have been cleared. Vehicular traffic flows in sixty-one percent of the afflicted cities while pedestrian movement is 56.4 percent. Schools remain closed for obvious safety reasons. Businesses will decide whether they wish to open and, as of this moment"—Felice paused for the time-conscious benefit of the humans—"thirty-six percent of offices and 41.2 percent of stores are accessible within shortened hours of business. And all the baseball stadiums are clear of any illegal activities."

A few Cousins murmured relief. Nadharatha sensed he was losing the outrage in the room.

"That's all fine. You still should have at least notified me, as First Cousin, of these operations."

A few mumbles of "elitism" were heard by the foosball machine.

"I do not know who breached the confidentiality." Felice held up its hand toward the flushed Nadharatha. That always had a calming effect. "I do not accuse you, First Cousin. But we had to proceed with caution."

"Why weren't the police notified?" asked Dinazzo.

"That is a more pronounced issue. The Blue Shirts took no action to prevent any illegal activities. Free food and beverages were distributed, a minor but telling violation. Many police are suspected to have participated in the marches. In Boston, the Bronx, Cincinnati, and Seattle, officers interceded on behalf of the baseball fans. Outside Wrigley

Field and Comiskey Park, Blue Shirts attacked Black Tops. Five local police captains have been temporarily relieved of duty."

The Cousins exchanged uneasy looks.

"I apologize for not providing that information sooner pending further review. We do not want the country believing the police are siding with the protesters. I am still assessing all of the vid. But there is sufficient evidence to suggest that the police are not fully reliable. If they are not, who will be?" Felice let that sink in. "When I am fully confident of the conclusions, I will turn that over to the Cousins to directly discuss with the respective police officials in the highlighted cities. That is also why all the arrested protesters are in Black Top custody and not interred under police control."

The room reluctantly agreed.

Nadharatha stood his ground on increasingly shaky legs. "Where are the BT units now?"

"They remain outside the stadiums. We expect a renewal of protests."

"Anticipation is not grounds for martial law."

Felice arched its eyebrow. "Our goal should be precluding a situation of violence necessitating martial law. First Cousin Cheng permitted conditions to deteriorate to that level last fall. The Black Tops are the only law enforcement agency that can be trusted to follow the law, First Cousin."

"You don't know that for sure."

"Correct, as I said, pending the fuller investigation. It is much easier for The Family to accept the need of deploying Black Tops patrols outside baseball stadiums than risk Blue Shirts refusing their oaths of duty."

"The BTs can't stay there forever," Nadharatha persisted. "I want them pulled back from stadium property until, or if, they're needed. This is a vastly different situation from the inane Mooshie Games. Now they're inviting confrontation."

The Cousins grudgingly voted in favor of the motion.

"Thank you for the guidance, Cousins. The order has been sent. The only solution that seems feasible is officially closing baseball for the rest of the 2099 season."

"I like that idea," said DeRico as relief rippled past the reality that nearly every major league baseball player had resigned in the past two days.

The First Cousin frowned. "Won't that bring out more protests?"

"As you correctly pointed out, we must reduce the flash points. This will focus solely on the current season. Whether the Cousins decide on a permanent ban is yours to make."

"You've pretty much backed us into this decision."

"No. Baseball has, First Cousin. I merely advise. As I also advise that the conspirators be placed in Black Top custody when they are apprehended."

"About time," Dinazzo said with a whoop. "We've coddled these people for too long."

"I still think that's going too far," Nadharatha said with an adamant shake of his thick head. From the cowed expressions, he knew the Cousins would side with Felice. He should be siding, too, washing his hands of the infernal baseball. But he was still First Cousin. He wouldn't surrender his responsibility like the rest of them, as easy as that might be.

He defiantly put his hands on his hips. "What if we sit down with Nedick and his followers?"

The room sucked in its breath.

"Negotiate with protesters at the point of a gun?" Rasfarati shouted.

"Guns? Guns? There've been no guns. No weapons. Not even baseball bats. All right, some have been brandished but only for ceremonial use. They've been largely peaceful."

"Except for overturning buses and cars, blocking traffic," snarled DeRico.

Oh leaned forward on her stubby arms. "What would you discuss, First Cousin?"

"To hear what they want. We haven't met with Puppy. Only Clary and Felice have."

"Because we already know what they want," DeRico persisted.

"Then let them go to the damn games." He pounded the table. "Finish the season. We have a damn war and we shouldn't be distracted by this shit. At the end of the season, then we announce baseball is gone. Forever. We gave them one last shot and they blew it. That's fair. Yes." He warmed to the idea, the only hot spot in the room. "I like that."

"That violates everything Grandma has ever taught." DeRico's harsh voice rang out. "Setting such a precedent is dangerous. What happens when dancing protesters demand the price of buttered blackberry jam be reduced? Or that American soldiers should invade China?" Her voice rose over Nadharatha's snorts. "Absurd? Yes. But that's where this all leads. No no. I agree with Felice. There can be no appeasement of hooligans. You can't create justice from lawlessness."

After the meeting, the Cousins met separately from the First Cousin. It was obvious Nadharatha was ill-suited to continue as First Cousin. Felice was much easier to work with.

• • • •

CLARY THREW UP again. The goo was green and yellow with flecks of silver and she saw it twice, on the floor and creeping up the wall in the back of the dimly lit cave. She knew vomit had no tongues. Clary clawed another hole in the grainy dirt and shoveled in the puke. The goo on the wall disappeared. She'd guessed right. Small victories were all she had.

She gagged again. The withdrawal from the treatments made her shiver. She rolled around, closing her eyes to avoid the hallucinations. There couldn't be dinosaur birds and her parents were dead. Though maybe Jesus had really visited her last night.

She heard Manuel's faint footsteps. He was the only BT who ever came inside. She suspected they were wary of her powers and strengths because she had been the Granddaughter. She didn't know how many BTs were outside the cave. When she'd first arrived, before the agony and confusion of suspending the treatments, Clary had probed briefly. She didn't want them to suspect what she could still do because she wasn't sure what she could do anymore.

Yesterday she'd floated on herself, doubling her imagery to feel the sensations as if there were a separate human and robot Clary and not the mixture. It had almost made her cry. She had forced the tears until her head ached and when they came, they felt dry. That'd frightened her. She couldn't show them fright. Or anything except a scowl and a snarl. She was their prisoner, and she would not be nice.

Manuel waited until she finished growling and swearing about being released. They had their game to play.

"Please pay attention," Manuel said behind its black visor, dragging over a small chair. She refused to sit.

A cackle of streaming consciousness filled her forehead before filling the cave with the "other" Clary. The *puta* Clary.

The *puta* Clary was in her house, Clary's house, in her living room. Her children, Clary's Cids, sat on the arms of the couch. Eilan, who'd been her favorite, squirmed in the *puta*'s lap. This Clary wore an orange dress, one of her dresses, with big blue bows in her hair. Blue? This Clary twirled her hair, her black hair, and talked about baseball not being part of The Family. Baseball fans were good except when they were fans. Then they weren't. Too many weren't. A family could not survive unless all shared its values.

Clary stepped back into her mind. Children couldn't grow up with baseball. The game was a bad influence. Our children must be respectful and obedient. Many children had protested. We cannot have that example for our children.

She could not wait anymore, Clary suddenly realized. Grandma's promise was just that. They are not coming to rescue her. The tracking device had been detected. Too many caves in the mountains. This must be a newer one, off the records. She had sensed Papa Kenuda, then he vanished. Now she sensed no one.

Clary was on her own. That was reassuring. That Clary she knew. That Clary who'd escaped from the orphanage. That Clary who'd survived the American attack on the orphan ship. That Clary who had made it to America as Diego died in the boat. That Clary who survived as Clary, not some trans-organic *mierda*.

That Clary who was always alone except for God.

She fluttered her lips and wished for chocolate.

"Enough." Clary waved her hand dismissively.

"You must wait until the conclusion of *Wake Up, My Darlings*," Manuel said.

Clary sneered at the monstrous *puta*. "Why? It is crap. She is a fake. I am the real Granddaughter. No one should listen."

Manuel lifted its visor with an almost weary gesture. "Felice insisted."

"Oh. Felice. This is what I think of Felice. I pee in Felice's ear. I pee in Felice's nose. I pee…"

Manuel flipped the visor back down before the human child finished her usual rant. Manuel and the other BTs had been chosen for this duty based on their heightened patience programs.

"We will wait until the speech is over per Felice's request."

"Then what?"

"I will leave."

"There is nothing more? I am not to be tested on what the *puta* says?"

"There is no comprehension survey."

"So sad. I am sad."

Manuel lifted its visor, puzzled by the human response.

Clary scrunched her face, her eyes veiled as she tottered and crumpled into a feral ball. Her thoughts drifted like rebellious clouds.

Clary sensed Manuel leaning over. Her fist blurred into its forehead, disabling the consciousness systems.

She apologized with a curtsy, gently patting Manuel's face. She undressed the 'bot and slipped into its uniform. The bodysuit sort of fit. She tucked her thick hair into the helmet and checked the Aubrey .45 on the belt.

As if there were no gravity, Clary bounded toward the entrance. An imperceptible link into the coms opened the door. There was only one other BT just outside; a quick scan showed three others in positions around the cave. Clary was slightly disappointed that she hadn't warranted more.

The BT acknowledged her. She tapped her helmet to indicate a problem. The Black Top approached. With a shrug, Clary tapped her helmet again. The BT lifted its visor. Clary knocked out its consciousness system with a punch. Wearing the hardened glove delivered a more powerful blow and Clary spent a moment ensuring the BT was still functioning.

An armored jeep was parked nearby. She grinned. Clary decoded the lock and settled behind the wheel. She had only driven a car once, on her father's lap when she was nine. This time her feet reached the pedals.

Resupplying the weapons systems, Clary skimmed a tree before whirling up the dirt road. In a moment, another BT vehicle pursued.

Clary swore, missing the brakes with her foot and bouncing along another road beneath the gaze of the lush green Hunter Mountain. She interfaced with the weapons and fired off several laser volleys. The BTs anticipated the shots, dodging. They shut down her weapons system.

A stream of Spanish obscenities filled the vehicle. She could not outrun them.

A burst of fire cracked into the rear shields. Maybe they didn't care if she was captured. Maybe that was the plan. They let you go. Stupid little child. It was too easy. Stupid little child.

The road wound at a sharp angle. Another volley shook the vehicle.

We will see who is stupid now.

Clary hit the brakes and spun around once, then twice before righting the jeep and heading straight into the approaching armored vehicle. She screamed very loudly and with joy.

46

The last of the black-clad messengers had left the decrepit 1950s-era bomb shelter at 1002 College Avenue about fifteen minutes ago. Puppy half dozed beneath the ancient light bulb dangling from the dank ceiling, surrounded by stacks of Campbell's Soup, Kellogg's Corn Flakes, and Hawaiian Punch. He hadn't been alone in days, and he wasn't especially sure he preferred his own company.

Rousing himself, Puppy squinted at the list of DV teens who had set out on trailers, motorized scooters, an occasional car or persistent bicycle. All communication, including the Family Message Center, had been closed a few hours ago. According to a bloodied kid who'd only made it as far as the George Washington Bridge, Jet'roes had set up checkpoints on bridges and tunnels. Subway and bus service was suspended south of the Bronx.

Puppy had no way of knowing how many teens had made it through to trigger the probably useless attempt at organization. As many as possible would join again tomorrow across the country. Letters would get through or they wouldn't. He had to hope the anger outweighed the fear. Both options scared him.

He uncapped a Peedy Belgium Blue Ale, taking a long, desperate sip. He glanced toward the loud ticks of the clock which had simply lost meaning.

Tucking another beer into his hoodie pouch, Puppy scurried up the forty steps and down the bright streets. The illumination of the streetlamps had been intensified. There were no Blue Shirt patrols, only lines of Jet'roes at quiet intersections seemingly abandoned except for the red lights swirling around the turrets.

He'd been running most of the day after the Black Tops arrested the marchers. The most wanted man in America took the shortcuts he, Pablo, and Zelda had perfected as kids in this, their Disappointment Village. Down a back alley. Up a fire escape. Onto a roof conjoined with two more. Through an abandoned sewer and old laundry rooms.

Puppy eluded the Jet'roes, waiting by the bus stop on the corner of West 180th Street and the Grand Concourse. The M22 groaned to a stop. Puppy swiped in the Lifecard of K'nitra Desmond (thank you, Pumpkin), earning a wary grunt from the 'bot driver.

Puppy slid into a seat midway into the empty bus, cautioning himself not to sleep. He did anyway, jolted awake by the driver's harsh voice.

"What stop, Mr. Nedick?"

Puppy's eyes slowly focused. "Who?"

The driver grumbled all kinds of anger. "You think I'm that stupid, Mr. or Mrs. Desmond?"

He almost didn't care. "Not at all. Sorry if I insulted you."

The driver only bought a few coins of that, turning back to the street. "They're looking for you."

"Oh really. I didn't notice."

"A fugitive shouldn't be a wise ass."

"Believe me, it helps."

The driver permitted itself a cackle. "You think we're all bad?"

"What?"

"That we're all like the BT who killed the kid in Boston?"

"No." He shook his head, which ached.

"Well then, you're sure riling up enough organics against us. Look at the back of my window. Go, look. They threw dung of some origin. Cleaning it up has made me two minutes late and that I don't like."

"They're playing us against each other, sir."

"Say what?"

He sat up straight. "I said they're playing us against each other, damn it. We think robots, sorry, inorganics, should be subject to the same laws as us, be treated the same. Isn't that what the Harmony Laws say? If your BT soldier isn't subject to those same laws then you're not the same. Then you're different. Is that what you want, sir?"

The driver considered this with quick glances over its shoulder. "That's not how it's playing out."

"I don't know what to say except no one's stopping 'bots from joining the protests."

"How about getting attacked by humans?"

"We got attacked, too!" Puppy shouted as the driver reminded him of its impeccable hearing. "Rounded up, shoved into Jet'roes and BT prisoner vans, all 'bots in charge, okay? So I should hate you, too. From what I'm hearing, Felice, an inorganic, is now making the security decisions. There's no First Cousin anymore. That's what I hear. You want to add up grievances?"

"That's a human game." The 'bot sneered.

"Now you guys are playing, too. Isn't progress wonderful." Puppy petulantly kicked at the back of the chair; the driver warned about destroying official mass-transit property.

They drove a few stops in simmering silence. Puppy briefly heard himself snoring.

"I got to report that you're on the bus," the driver finally said.

"I understand."

The driver eyed him. "Ain't no Blue Shirts around. Down at the terminal, talk's that any cops who called in sick or marched are on suspension."

"There's always the Black Tops. Just hail down a Jet'roe. They'd be happy to take me off your hands." Puppy stiffened. "What do you know? A couple are just waiting."

The driver stared at the Jet'roes on either side of the intersection at East 191st Street. "Slide down."

"What?"

"Slide your organic ass down."

Puppy curled up as the bus rattled through the light.

"S'fine now," the driver announced.

Puppy took an extra few labored breaths before sitting up again. "Why'd you do that?"

"Because I don't like BTs giving the rest of us a bad name."

Puppy sat behind the driver. "You just broke the law?"

"Maybe I did and maybe I didn't."

"Oh, you did. I thought robots couldn't disobey the law."

"Maybe we're becoming more like humans. Ain't progress wonderful?"

Puppy clasped him on the shoulder. "Thank you." He squinted at the driver's name tag. "Thank you, Gregory."

"Welcome." The driver's forehead pulsed. "So, what stop?"

Puppy sighed. "I don't have one after today. Or yesterday."

Gregory grunted. "Then you're planning on riding the finest bus system in America all night long on an illegally gained Lifecard?"

"That sums it up."

"You being smart again?"

"I left behind smart a long time ago, Gregory. Now I just want to get it done."

Gregory turned. "Get what done?"

"Since you have to report me as traveling on your bus, probably best if I don't say."

"Best it would be." The 'bot snorted out silvery mucus. "Unless humans attack my bus with feces again, we'll be at the terminal in twelve minutes. Since my bus sorely needs a thorough cleaning, I'll park her in the maintenance park. Given the hour, that won't begin until 5:45. When you wake up, pull this here handle which'll open the door."

Gregory flushed at Puppy's awkward hug.

• • • •

AS PUPPY GROGGILY crawled out of the M11 bus in the maintenance yard beneath the yawning sun, Mooshie Lopez and most of the 2099 New York Yankees rushed toward the side entrance of Yankee Stadium, out of direct view of the two Jet'roes positioned by gate three.

Beth half crouched behind the dress-shop van parked along River Avenue across from the sealed gate to the grandstand. At the first sign of the team, Beth unlocked the back door of the truck. A few players stared suspiciously at Rivera.

Mooshie gave them her best nuclearized glare. "A civilian, yeah. But she's our way in. And when we are, she's gone. You got a problem with that?"

Beth loaded the Miners's ambient scaling ropes into an uplifter, a squat cannon. Two shots and the metal ropes were attached to the mezzanine level, draping over the wire fence. With another shot, Beth formed the ropes into a right angle by releasing the steel-solidification fluid. She scampered up about eighty feet to the edge of the mezzanine in right field, locking in the ladder steps before landing nimbly to the ground from a drop of ten feet. Miners training was impeccable.

Mooshie's eyes widened. "Not bad. Let's go, my darlings. Get your cute cheeks up there so I got something to look at."

Ten and ten. Ten players up, hoist the four boxes marked *equipment*, then the remaining ten players in. Beth would supervise from the ground, drain the fluid, and take away the ropes.

Dominic An'vil, a fleet outfielder with a bat full of holes, approached the Jet'roes waving a red-sock stick in each hand, chanting "No melanoma, no melanoma." He appeared slightly tipsy which had the benefit of fact. Sometimes courage needed a little help.

As the alert Jet'roes's turrets swiveled toward Dominic, the Yankees gingerly climbed the ladders. The first group disappeared into the ballpark. Three players popped their heads out, waving to indicate that the electric railway had been activated. Beth and Mooshie quickly secured the equipment which traveled up and into Yankee Stadium within three minutes.

"Come on, come on." Mooshie hurried the rest along. They were three quarters up before she turned to Mickey huffing on a 'bacco. She smiled gently. "You don't have to do this, Mick."

Mickey answered by heeling the butt into the ground.

"Take it slow," she added, which came out as an order.

"Fuck you, Lopez."

The bellowing of a Black Top at Dominic dancing toward the Jet'roe echoed around the ballpark.

Mooshie watched Mickey climb arduously.

"Slow ain't the same as sleeping," she called up.

"He's wobbly," Beth pointed out.

"Because he's fat and old and we don't have time."

The ground shook from a Jet'roe turning the corner on River Avenue, the BT commander blasting warnings about ceasing all illegal activity.

"Faster, hump head."

Halfway up, Mickey reached the line of the right angle leading into the stadium. He grasped for the ladder grips on both sides. He missed one, throwing off his balance. A desperate lunge gave him a wavering grip. He dangled by one hand.

Mooshie started toward Mantle, but Beth bounded like a monkey up the steps.

"Give me your free hand." She leaned forward; the ropes swayed. There was built-in give to accommodate the wind. Beth grasped Mickey's hand and yanked him up. Mickey's fingers slipped through.

With a sheepish expression, he dropped. Beth dived after him, arms by her side projectile-style. She slammed into Mantle and drove them into a wire fence by the lower field boxes, avoiding a direct impact onto the ground. They crunched and bounced off, rolling away. Mickey landed on Beth.

She groaned, feeling the bone through her shin. Mickey was still.

"Is he dead?" Mooshie yelled, quieting the terrified players looking down from the mezzanine.

"I don't know." Beth barely managed to talk through the pain. "Roll up the ropes."

"I'm coming down for you—"

"Roll up the ropes, damn it. We're not ready for guests."

The Jet'roe fired a shot that sliced the rope and sent Mooshie hurtling.

47

With a short growl that scattered chipmunks, Clary wrapped the knotted leaves a bit tighter around her gouged left calf and hobbled out of the woods along Route 201 South. The starless night blanketed the road. Clary called up a map, estimating the time of the trip. You will get there when you do, she assured herself. Everything hurt. Her toenails. Her earlobes. As best as she could with partially functioning internal med-scans, Clary had determined there were no damaged organs, merely intense bruises and gashes.

At least she was no longer vomiting. Her body had adjusted to the new balance after the withdrawals. Her vision had been lost for a while, but the nap, no, the collapse, the shutdown, had restored normal faculties including night vision. A truck lumbered down the road. Clary waved.

The red Dodge two-door pickup slowed onto the soft shoulder. Clary climbed in. The driver, Duncan Fairwell, smiled.

"Good evening, sir. I thank you for the transport. I am going that way." Clary gestured toward the road, sighing impatiently. "I have a schedule."

"Pardon?"

"Please drive. Thank you again."

Frowning, Duncan ambled back onto the road in between curious sidelong glances. Clary pulled up the neck of the torn blouse to cover her scraped lower jaw.

"Have you been in an accident, child?" Duncan asked after a few minutes.

"Yes."

"Are you okay?"

"Do I not look okay?"

The man shrugged his beefy shoulders. Clary peeked into the side-view mirror. A blue cut traveled across her forehead. Dried blood clung to her left cheek. Her chin was scratched. She swore softly in Spanish.

"There's a clinic about two miles down."

"I do not need medical attention."

Duncan rolled his eyes. "What happened?"

Clary muttered, "I was in a vehicular accident. I am fine. Do you have many more questions?"

"I'm just trying to be helpful."

"This ride is sufficient."

Duncan shrugged again, glancing across the front seat.

"Yes?" Clary stared straight ahead.

"You know who you look like?"

She wearily replied, "I believe you have a notion."

"Well yeah. Clary. You know, the Granddaughter. Am I the first to tell you that?" The man was delighted by Clary's nod. Duncan munched on this for about a mile. "You know, in the way there's a resemblance without being like a twin or related. Must be the hair."

Clary ran her fingers through the matted curls. "My hair has not been cleaned in five days. Does the Granddaughter appear with filthy hair?"

"Well no. That wouldn't be right."

"Or a bruised face?"

"Course not. She's the Granddaughter. She always looks perfect."

"And beautiful." Clary gestured for agreement. "Has she ever appeared on *Wake Up, My Darlings* in torn clothes?"

"No, miss," the driver apologized. "Like I said, I only meant a resemblance."

Clary considered how many of these drivers she would need. "Well, I am Clary."

The driver reddened. "No need to mock me. I didn't mean anything."

"I am not mocking you. I am Clary Santiago. The Granddaughter. I was arrested, I escaped, and now must return to my house."

The driver edged away. "Like I said, I'm sorry."

"You do not believe me?"

"Course I do."

"Now you mock me."

"I live just off the next exit. How about I let you off there?"

"Good. I will need clean clothes."

"Look, little girl…"

Clary's eyes blazed. "Do not 'little girl' me. Your Granddaughter needs your help. Now drive. Unless you would like me to make you understand."

Duncan's underarms dripped. "Please, miss, I have a family."

"Yes, we do."

Duncan had been sleeping on the sofa in the basement until he got his drinking under control. He'd been sober for several weeks, but his wife was one of those people who'd make the Devil show his Lifecard. Better to lie about a delivery heading south late at night than explain the surly child in the front seat.

He threw some of his middle daughter's clothes into a bag, tossed in a toothbrush because the notion popped into his head along with a tube of Abrasion Crème. He pocketed a four-pack of Bouille's Dark Choco Bars on the way out because it seemed like a good idea. His wife yelled that if he drank again she'd crush a testicle, but Duncan had already torn out of the driveway.

Clary dressed in the bathroom of Millicent's Diner, returning with an improved expression.

"I'd say you look nice, but I don't want any suggestions of anything improper," Duncan said carefully as they turned onto the New York State Thruway.

"If I thought you were a pedo, I would have already broken your fingers," Clary said with a big smile.

In just over two hours, Duncan happily dropped Clary off at the East 233rd Street exit off the Major Deegan Expressway which led into Van Cortlandt Park. Clary thanked him by rubbing his forehead. It wouldn't wipe the memories, but it did inject enough confusion to make him doubt what'd happened. Fifty minutes later, Duncan had driven in a wide circle around the northwest Bronx, certain he'd done something to upset his wife.

At more than 1,100 acres, Van Cortlandt Park had been the perfect place to build Grandma's house in 2069. With the threatened invasion of North America looming, Grandma required a vast area for tunnels. Thirty-four had been built. Thirty-two had been scanned into the grid. Two had been forgotten by everyone except Grandma.

Clary slipped into the hollow of a tree and unscrewed the rusted lock. She held her breath, calibrating the night vision as she dropped twenty feet into the darkness. She stumbled over wet rocks, her internal maps gone. A flurry of scurrying feet and squeaks ahead alerted her to a droplet of light in the ceiling. Clary burrowed her fists into the ground until she found a latch in the dried mud. She rocked herself upward, landing by an abandoned rail line.

After a moment, Jesus pointed to the right. Clary recognized a tunnel where she'd thrown several tantrums. She stepped around the dirty puddles. Spotlights glared in every direction.

Two Black Tops pointed Eludan rifles before slowly lowering them, tipping their heads.

"Apologies, Granddaughter. Your presence is unexpected."

"Is not most everything Clary does unexpected?" Clary responded in a lilting voice.

The 'bots relaxed slightly. "Are you in need of assistance?"

Clary wanly gestured at her filthy clothes. "I could not sleep. I walked and tripped. Do not tell Felice. She believes I am asleep dreaming of great conquests for The Family."

The BTs exchanged quick thoughts. Felice was as popular as an aluminized bubble in their lower waste-product cavity. They led Clary to a portable washer. She rinsed her body while they exhaust-cleaned her clothes. Somewhere, they found an orange bow.

Clary nodded past the guards at the entrance to the house. More BTs clogged the lobby. Eighteen, triple the usual deployment. You are afraid, Felice, Clary thought. That is wise. You have reason to be afraid.

The girl bounded up the steps, four at a time, earning knowing nods from Black Tops. She gruffly opened her bedroom door as anyone would expect of the Granddaughter in her own home at 2:30 in the morning.

Before stepping through the doorway, Clary blacked out the vidcams in the ceiling. Waving a feathered ball attached to a stick, the Clary 'bot chased an orange cat, corralling Boris on top of a six-foot-high dresser with a delighted squeal. Clearly, they'd been doing this for a while.

Stroking Boris to make it clear who was more important, the 'bot finally acknowledged Clary with a smirk. "What do you want?"

"To begin, I want my bedroom back. Then my life."

"It is mine now."

"But here I am. You must leave."

The 'bot laughed, the sound of metal on metal. "I do not think so. I am now in charge. You have failed."

Clary folded her arms. "You are a stupid 'bot."

"But I am you."

"No, *idiota*. You are not me. You are merely the sense of me."

The 'bot giggled. "I am superior because I am not you."

"You just said you were."

The 'bot struggled a moment. Felice had explained but it was confusing. "I am you but better. A better version. I do what is correct. I do not make mistakes." She wagged her finger, veins in her face actively circulating. "You let you become your master."

"*Puta*," Clary snapped. "I do not want to hear your foolishness. Because it is foolishness. You cannot be me because you think you must understand. But we do not understand everything. That is the inferiority which makes us superior. We make mistakes and learn."

The other Clary weightlessly dropped to the ground. "I learn everything without errors."

"Yah, yah, yah." Clary's voice softened. "Do not worry. I will only turn you off. It will not hurt."

The 'bot shrewdly eyed Clary. "How do you know what hurts me?"

"Because you were me."

"But no more. I am not you. We have agreed I am different. How can you know what will hurt me?" The 'bot poked Clary in the chest. "I will turn you off."

"That would hurt."

"Oh, so it is bad when it hurts you but not bad when it hurts me." The 'bot addressed the diffident cat who offered no opinion.

Clary studied the robot. "You are right. It is bad whenever. I will keep you as my main AI."

"What of the others?"

"They will be secondary."

The 'bot's eyes widened malevolently. "I already switched them off."

"Then you will have no competition. I have a special hiding place."

The 'bot twisted a curl around its index finger. "Why did you not run away? You are smart like me. Felice would never have found you."

Clary thought a moment. "Because that would be wrong. You cannot understand."

"Do not say what I understand."

"Killing me is wrong."

"Killing you is necessary."

"That does not make it right."

"It does not make it wrong."

Clary smiled. "No. That much is true. Sometimes it is right to kill."

The 'bot grabbed Clary by the wrist, flinging her against the wall. Something cracked in her lower back. Dazed, she scrambled to her knees as the 'bot charged again. Clary aimed her kick beneath the jaw.

The 'bot gagged. Viscous blood dripped out of its mouth. Clary shoved her fingers down its throat, pressing together the torn esophagus and tying the muscle in a small knot. By the time the 'bot had begun healing, Clary straddled the other child with her knees.

Clary wiped away the curls from the bot's forehead. The eyes were frightened with surprise.

"You are a good Clary," she whispered. "They just want to make you bad like they tried to make me."

Clary dug her fingers into the base of the 'bot's skull.

Boris jumped down and investigated the inert robot and the crying human. Neither affected his world at present. With a yawn, he padded over to the orange food bowl for more immediate gratification.

• • • •

MOOSHIE SWIPED AWAY the water bottle from the asshole Yankees second baseman. "How much did you have already?"

Tara Takei shrank slightly. "A few sips."

"That's a couple too many," she snapped. Dislocating her right shoulder in the fall had not improved her mood. "Do not take more than you need or I'll tip you upside down and milk you like a cow."

There was no bottled water or beverages of any kind. When the parks had been shuttered, the concessions had been cleaned out of all perishable foods. There were a lot of Cracker Jacks and hot-dog rolls left along with mustard and ketchup packets and twenty-four, sixteen, and twelve-ounce cups. Bags of popcorn, too, but good luck popping that since the power and also the water had been turned off.

Mooshie made her way through the home clubhouse, lit by flickering candles, where a makeshift med center had been established. Beth was asleep on a cot along the far wall, her injured leg sticking out from the pinstriped blanket. She moaned softly.

Quietly passing by, Mooshie knelt by Mickey's bed. She gently nudged his shoulder. "Hey, old-timer."

"Hey, gorgeous," Mickey mumbled.

"That's right. You must be feeling better."

He patted his chest. "Strong like bull."

Mooshie pressed some water to his cracked lips. "Good. I need a center fielder."

Mickey fluttered his lips. "You ain't played any games yet?"

"I'm sorry, boss man, but between you laying on your butt, Beth pretending to be hurt, and Ayla Barreau twisting her knee, I been busy."

"We're supposed to play intra-squad, Moosh. We gotta make noise. Crack of the bat. Crowds. Ain't there people outside?"

Mooshie hesitated. Too much truth was never a good thing. The area around Yankee Stadium had been cordoned off three miles in all directions. They were quarantined.

"Sure, Mick. Tons. Didn't you hear them serenading us with 'Take Me Out to the Ballgame' this afternoon?"

"I'd of heard," he said gruffly, tugging his left earlobe. He studied Mooshie. "What about the guns?"

Mooshie shot him a long look. "What guns?"

"The guns in the boxes marked bats," Mantle growled.

A few players perked up from the card game in the middle of the room. Mooshie silenced their curiosity with a hard stare.

"Protection, Mick. Just protection," she said quietly.

"Uh-huh."

"You ask a lot of questions for a guy who can't handle an inside fastball anymore." Mooshie sighed. "We don't want to use them. But this is about meeting our demands. Nothing else is working."

"You're going to hold off 'copters and tanks? I hope you got some rockets tucked inside the catcher's mitts."

"We'll fight for what we believe in, Mick, no matter what."

"Like the Alamo."

"Alamo? What's that?"

Mickey made a disgusted sound. "A fort in Texas back in the 1830s where Davy Crockett and Jim Bowie and a bunch of Texans fought the Mexicans."

"Why?"

"Because Texas wanted its independence."

"From America?"

"No, Mexico. They had an empire."

"What happened?"

"All the Americans died."

"And?"

"Everyone rallied. Texas threw out the Mexicans."

"See? No one wants to admit that corpses can be good politics." Mooshie cuffed his neck. "Get some rest."

Dr. Anika Das, the Yankees third baseman, curtly waved Mooshie into the manager's office. "I'm telling you that we need to contact the police or Black Tops and arrange for Mr. Mantle to be transported to a hospital. I have no facilities—"

"So you've said."

Dr. Das scowled. "And Ms. Rivera, too. She's not responding well. I have no means to combat the infection."

"I thought you had antibiotics."

"There was one dose left. It was purposeful of the Black Tops to leave a small amount, as if mocking our futility. Please, Mooshie, be reasonable." Anika held up her slender hand.

Not an argument that had ever worked. "We're all staying put until the Cousins get the message that we can't be cowed."

"All they'll get are bodies. That's what they want. Dead major league players who they'll tidily cart out and that'll be the end of that."

"Take it easy."

Anika bristled. "As a physician, I insist you arrange for the immediate evacuation of Mr. Mantle and Ms. Rivera."

"You can insist until your butt blows up, but I'm in charge."

"The hell with that. I'm the doctor who's going outside now." Dr. Das yanked free of Mooshie's grasp.

After a moment, Mooshie conceded grudgingly. "I'll send a message asking for antibiotics for Beth. Zarythrin, right?"

"Yes, yes. But that won't help Mr. Mantle. He requires trans-organic treatments. And I'm discussing that with him whether you like it or not."

Dr. Das stormed over to Mickey, waking him with a gentle shake. Mooshie watched, arms folded.

"Mr. Mantle, may I talk to you?"

For the sake of the pretty Dr. Das, Mickey hoisted himself up, flashing a boyish smile.

"How are you feeling?"

"I could use a martini."

"Couldn't we all. I'd like your support for requesting a medevac so you can be treated by a qualified trans-organic physician." Dr. Das flung a sharp look over her shoulder. "Your condition is very serious and we must use a purely medical basis for a decision."

Mickey stretched his arms overhead with a loud yawn. "I feel good, doc. Mooshie's penciling me into the cleanup slot for our intra-squad game. We gotta show the season is going forward."

The doctor knelt, lowering her voice. "You will pass away if you don't receive the proper treatment, Mr. Mantle."

"I already died once, doc. I'm getting the hang of it. Who knows what kind of magic they'll have to bring me back again."

Dr. Das's mouth tightened. "You won't live for more than a few days, Mickey."

"How do you know that if you're not a qualified trans-organic physician? Maybe you're a better doctor than you give yourself credit." Mick winked, slowly turning somber. "Remember the Alamo, doc."

"Pardon?"

"The Alamo." Exhausted by the strain, Mickey slowly closed his eyes. "As Casey Stengel used to say, 'you could look it up.'"

48

The smoke-filled crowded Gerry's Bar & Grill off West 194th Street looked like it'd been designed by the Twentieth-Century Project as a typical cop bar. Shoving through the raucous shouts soothed by the sounds of Frank Sinatra, Rafferty led Puppy into a back booth, glaring aside the curious looks.

The captain set their beer mugs on the chipped wooden table and drew over the bowl of unsalted peanuts. He wasn't about to share anything.

Puppy gestured at the nuts. "I'm kind of hungry."

With a spiteful smile, Rafferty pulled the bowl closer. "Life's a bitch being a fugitive."

"And I'm glad to see you, too." Puppy motioned toward the husky waitress in the speckled red frock dropping off drinks and wings, but she ignored him. "Got it. All your people."

"Every single one's a cop. Or used to be. With normal jobs, you go before the respective committees and tell your stories and nine times out of ten, it's hoovered away. But the police don't come back from suspensions unless the charges were over the top. The slightest taint and you're through. There's no room for doubt. Besides, the charges weren't crazy. They were true. Ask any of these good cops, these great cops, and they'll admit they broke the law, ignored unlawful activity, joined right in the marches. See Fitzi, the big guy by the jukebox?"

Puppy glanced at a man the size of New Mexico thoughtfully selecting a tune.

"He insisted on setting a committee date because they missed a few laws he'd broken."

Sinatra was replaced by Tony Bennett; Fitzi lustily sang along.

"What about Detective Y'or?" Puppy asked.

Rafferty's mouth tightened. "His wife panicked and called the BTs so Layon could explain and apologize. They took him into custody. Where, damned if I know."

"I'm sorry."

Rafferty made an unpleasant sound.

"You think it's all my fault for starting this shit."

The captain nodded for longer than needed. "Yeah. But my people knew what they were doing. Their choice. Mine, too." He fidgeted. "I miscalculated. Broken idealism is a great teacher."

"You never struck me that way."

"That was the fucking point. Who else would do a job where you have to rely on the bulk of the people doing the right thing?" With a growl, Rafferty slid over the peanuts.

Puppy mumbled thanks. "Guess I'm stupid to ask if your cops have been replaced."

"All the police are now under the control of the Black Tops." Rafferty winced as if it hurt to say that.

"And you?"

"Me." Rafferty shook a handful of nuts, calling out, "Hey, everyone. Puppy Nedick wants to know my status!"

Thirty-five angry cops glared at Puppy Nedick who shrunk a little.

Rafferty enjoyed the moment. "Just plain old Hedrick Rafferty now. Lots of plain old captains and police chiefs. Most like me quit before groveling to the BTs. They said I was suspended but that's bull. Some stayed on. They won't last. Not quite martial law, but we're getting there. Guess you haven't been watching the vidnews."

"I've been out of touch."

"Poor baby."

"Did you practice all this warmth, Captain Rafferty, just waiting for me to show up?"

"You found me, Nedick. But hey, how many cop bars are left in the Bronx. Eventually, they'll find you." He smirked. "Any of these cops would get reinstated in a heartbeat if they cuffed your ass and turned you over."

Puppy stood up and spread his arms. "Yes, I'm the former Commissioner Puppy Nedick who started this whole shitstorm. The captain says you can get your jobs back if you make an arrest. I'll be here, finishing my beer."

Judging from the dark looks, Puppy didn't have a lot of time. He plopped back down with a cold stare across the table.

"Now that you and all your friends got their bile out, want to know why I'm here?"

Rafferty shrugged with some fake disinterest which neither bought.

"Just so you know, I had nothing to do with the stadium takeover. That was all Mooshie."

The captain nearly spit into Puppy's Talli Golden Ale. "You want me to believe that?"

"I'm telling you the truth. Stop with the eye-rolling. Mooshie is reliving 2065, going to where it all started, or pretty much ended, with the Miners attack."

Rafferty sat up. "Is she armed?"

"I don't know. But I wouldn't be surprised."

"Because the BTs are going to move in. Sure as shit, they won't let this occupation stand. They can't."

"And then there's real bloodshed."

Rafferty rolled a nut around. "How many people are with her?"

"I'm guessing most of the Yankees who had a team of twenty. Can't imagine anyone with the balls to say no to her. What do you know from just before when you told them to shove the job?"

The captain smiled faintly. He'd posted his resignation on a pillar in the Cousins Lobby. More visitors than not applauded. "Protests in Boston. Of course. Comiskey. Philly. Dispersed, arrests numbering about fifty. You know, there was a Cousins announcement that all public assembly of more than five people is illegal."

"Like I said, I've been out of touch."

Rafferty didn't quite believe that. "Back up. Where'd Mooshie get the weapons?" He glared at Puppy's hesitation.

"Probably the Blue Wigs."

"Yeah, I kind of figured that. Who in the Blue Wigs?"

Puppy half laughed. "A good guess would be my father's old girlfriend Mary Doherty in Boston."

"Any other Blue Wigs involved?"

Puppy sighed. "Speculating, but probably Beth Rivera. Her parallel daughter, Dale Tanaka, killed Hedda Kleinz during the robbery attempt. I think Cheng was behind the robberies of the Hall of Fame memorabilia to stir up trouble. To what end, I don't know. Maybe he wants back in power."

Rafferty fixed him with a nasty stare. "And you didn't think to tell me any of this."

"I thought I could handle it."

"Clearly you couldn't!" Rafferty exploded.

"Could you have?" Puppy yelled back.

"Not when we were dealing with your blasted insurrection!"

"If it was such a bad idea then why'd this whole damn bar join in?"

Gerri's Bar & Grill grew silent.

"Exactly. A lot of broken idealists." Puppy said. "We've got to stop the BTs from blasting their way into Yankee Stadium."

Rafferty roared with laughter. "And how do you plan on doing that?"

"I think there's enough cops here."

Rafferty stared. "My people have already lost their jobs. They're fortunate not to be in BT holding cells. They're not going down the toilet with you, Nedick."

"I guess retirement suits you, Captain Rafferty."

Rafferty grabbed Puppy's filthy hoodie. A horseshoe of cops closed around the booth.

"But that's not your call, sir." Puppy's eyes never left Rafferty's flushed face. "Is it?"

The captain released Puppy and stood.

"The incomparable Puppy Nedick has a plan to help the players who've taken over Yankee Stadium. Who wants to listen?"

A chunky woman with beige hair held up her hand. "What's the alternative, Captain Rafferty?"

"We throw his ass out the door."

The vote was 16-14 for listening. Rafferty abstained.

• • • •

BROWN HATS URI and Kinga took great delight in cuffing Puppy, explaining with big smiles that, if stopped by a BT patrol, the cover story of transporting a prisoner would seem more plausible if his right ankle were also locked onto the back seat.

The cover held past a dismissive BT foot patrol and two silent Jet'roes; a prisoner in the back of a Brown Hat squad car was quite welcome. The BTs couldn't cover all the territory since approximately sixty-five percent of the Blue Shirts had called in sick throughout the Bronx.

Similar gastronomical and upper respiratory infections had ravaged police departments in all the major league baseball cities. As Uri explained in a moment of friendliness, until the arrested Blue Shirts, Brown Hats, and siblings were immediately released from BT holding camps, this epidemic would continue.

The Brown Hats took their time uncuffing Puppy, pausing to discuss the likelihood of rain tomorrow, Uri's middle child's basketball game, and Kinga's mother's impending eighty-seventh birthday. They let him off in front of 220 Bansom Road in Scarsdale.

Puppy was surprised Sahidi Douglas so quickly buzzed him in.

She sniffed sourly, taking his unwashed hoodie by two tentative fingers, and tossing it into the corner. She didn't offer drinks, food, or any of the very comfortable-looking chairs.

"Don't worry, I'm getting used to warm greetings from old friends."

Sahidi leveled a cold look. "Okay, you're here. What do you want?"

"Your help."

She snickered. "The occupation of Yankee Stadium."

"Guess it made the vidnews."

How could she have worked for this clown. "Yeah, the bandits breaking into the stadium was kind of front and center. And their demands, stadiums reopening and the season resuming. Sound familiar?"

"A good idea's a good idea."

Sahidi stared with bland contempt.

"I know you hate me, Sahidi."

"That's a start."

"And you have little respect for me."

"Little implies some."

"But you can't hate me more than you love baseball."

She blew out in contempt. "It's close."

"If they take away Mooshie, who's armed, that's right, Mickey, whoever else, then all resistance of baseball ends."

Sahidi pityingly shook her head. "It already has. Folks are scared. And now adding guns. How stupid. We've lost the moral high ground. We're officially the bad guys once the first bullet is fired even in self-defense. Even if no shots are fired, they'll portray players as untrustworthy, a step above terrorists. Which they are."

"I agree. It's a terrible situation which is why we have to prevent the BTs from moving in."

"You destroyed baseball, Puppy. You did all that. Mooshie's desperation is a consequence of all those bad decisions. Either way, it's over. As they used to say, the fat lady has sung."

"Not yet. It may be two outs in the last of the ninth…"

Sahidi went to open the door.

"I need you to contact your radcasters."

She paused, hand on the doorknob. "To set up another interview with Puppy Nedick?"

"Not this time. To get mail delivered to Yankee Stadium."

She hadn't expected that. "Mail?"

"The good old USPS. Best in the world."

"Mail." Sahidi's eyes narrowed. "Ah. Mail. Got it. Mail. Not an entirely stupid idea."

"Thank you."

She almost smiled. "Especially coming from you."

"You done? Got all that out of your system?"

"Never." Her scowl returned. "Even if I wanted to, which I don't, how the hell could I help? I have no legal right to contact the radcasters. I quit, remember?"

"One of the happier days of my life." He winked at her raised middle finger. "Ask your sister Sandra."

Sahidi ripped open the door. "Why don't you ask her, Commissioner? She helped you just fine, happily dancing on my grave."

"Because I can't ask her to risk her job."

"And you think I can?"

"Please—"

Sahidi slammed the door shut. "Uh, you mean ask the sister who resents my success? Who's always been jealous because I'm three minutes older and got all the talent? Who wouldn't piss on my head if my hair were on fire? Who hates me and who I hate?"

"Do you hate her more than you love baseball?"

Sahidi weighed whether there was anyone she didn't hate at this moment. And if there was anything else she loved. She twisted her mouth. "You're an asshole, Puppy."

He grinned. "I know. I just got you to beg your despised sister for a favor."

That's when she threw him out.

• • • •

SANDRA WAS THRILLED to see her big sister who had been a hermit since quitting the Commissioner's office, which denied Sandra the opportunity to gloat. She had a job. Sahidi didn't. Her sister was humiliated. Sandra was triumphant. That's why she gave Sahidi a big sisterly hug by the RadCast Center elevator, savoring the possibility of making her cry.

But when Sahidi took her into the bathroom (she's afraid to be seen, glory and joy) and asked for a favor with the enthusiasm of offering a lung for sale, her younger-by-three-minutes sister couldn't resist having big sister in her debt. The favor was simple. There was no explanation for the request because that would needlessly burden Sandra with unwanted information. If there was a problem, Sahidi would take the blame for misleading her innocent younger-by-three-minutes sister.

Sandra couldn't wait to tell her mother. Sahidi had always been her favorite.

• • • •

AVAL ACQUISTA, DRIVER of the dark-brown mail truck with the lively beige logo *Here for You* on the sides, maintained the perfect eleven miles per hour as he had for the past twenty-eight years. Aval was proud to work for the USPS and often sang the jingle to pass the time.

> *Friends from coast to coast*
> *North and south*
> *Let's not boast*
> *Whisper in our ears*
> *And USPS is there*
> *Bringing us together*
> *None do it better*
> *Hear hear hear*

Unfortunately, Acquista's proposed jingle was not selected as the new USPS song back in 2088. Still, Aval was proud of the appreciative note he had received from Grandma for his contribution, proud of his jingle, although his wife was not a fan, proud of his smart brown-and-beige uniform, and very proud of his job. The whole Family rode in the back. Without Aval Acquista and his dedicated colleagues, how else would siblings communicate?

For twenty-eight years he'd driven down this familiar hill, Nomal's Dry Cleaners and Pedicures Plus on the left side of 161st Street and Samuel the Tailor on the right, old friends though he'd never gone inside, just slipped the mail in the slot. But this was his home away from home. He could drive this route with his eyes closed but would never undermine USPS safety procedures.

What he'd never experienced was a Black Top jeep blocking his way.

Aval warily rolled down the window. "What's the problem?"

The BT flipped up its visor, yellowish face set in a stolid stare. "This is a restricted area. Please turn around."

Aval almost laughed and he rarely laughed on the job. There was nothing humorous about delivering the mail.

"This is the 6:45 a.m. delivery, officer."

"I am Li, a PFC."

"PFC Li. You're not allowed to interfere with the mail delivery."

"This is a restricted area," Li leadenly responded.

"That doesn't matter. Nothing may interfere with the mail delivery. Ever."

Aval glanced at his large round Oviz watch which his three children had given him for his birthday. He was now seventy-two seconds late and getting annoyed, and he considered himself a serene person. Too serene, his wife sometimes complained. Often, actually.

"This is a restricted area."

"PFC Li, I am Aval Acquista, senior driver. I have many packages for Yankee Stadium and I'm gonna deliver these many packages so it's best if you get out of my way before you become part of my bumper."

Li blinked, processing. He didn't move. Acquista swerved around the jeep and roared down the street. That caused a lot of commotion. As three BT jeeps pursued, two Jet'roes blocked his path under the elevated green subway line. A lot of rifles and turrets pointed at his truck.

Now Aval was ninety seconds late and he was really upset.

Ignoring the BT warnings, Aval opened the back of the van and slid the ramp down. A Blue Shirt patrol car eased onto the sidewalk. Former Officers Pena and Mao from Rafferty's 43rd Precinct flanked Acquista as he unloaded the five sacks of mail which, if he weren't so pissed, would've explained was the most deliveries to Yankee Stadium he'd ever seen.

Sandra's tags at the end of the 11:15 p.m. sportscast reminding baseball fans that the only way to stay in touch with their favorite players was to write letters to them care of the stadiums had gone out over the entire radcast network. For kicks and giggles, she'd repeated it at midnight.

After losing her job for handing out red-sock flags on Walton Avenue, Officer Pena was in no mood for anyone telling her what to do. Especially a Black Top.

"You've got to let him do his job," she warned the commander of the Jet'roe now standing on the turret.

"This is a restricted area."

"And delivering the mail is the law." Pena hushed Acquista as he rattled off the various USPS statutes.

"Restricted takes priority."

"Only if this is martial law. Have you declared martial law?"

"It is not my duty to issue such decisions."

Acquista jostled his full wheelbarrow. "Because there aren't any to make."

The BT commander hopped off and introduced itself as Juan. "We must examine the mail."

"Whoa, whoa, whoa." Acquista pushed his wheelbarrow in a circle, running over Officer Pena's left foot. Now she really wasn't in the mood. "The only ones who may examine or open the mail of the USPS are the recipients. Mail tampering is a serious offense, private."

"I am Lieutenant Juan. The occupants of Yankee Stadium are ensconced illegally." The 'bot explained to Pena, Mao, and Acquista what ensconced meant. "They cannot be resupplied until there is proper adjudication of the situation. That is pending. We will scan the contents." Lieutenant Juan allowed Acquista to sputter in protest since such sounds were clearly important to the human.

"Per the laws, we will not open any letters," Juan assured everyone. "But we will remove any foods, liquids, or life-sustaining substances as well as potential weapons. As we cannot interfere with mail delivery, you cannot interfere with security measures since Officer Pena and Officer Mao are under suspension and without authority."

Pena and Mao slowly unholstered their standard issue Tempe .38s. Captain Rafferty had insisted that violence must be avoided. There were all kinds of definitions of violence.

"That may be correct," Officer Mao said slowly. "But the laws are protected by all siblings because they protect all siblings. So, you just settle down and allow our postal friend to do his job."

Acquista rolled the wheelbarrow to gate six; Mooshie and five of the Yankees watched from the mezzanine. The mailman gently stacked the envelopes and packages, mainly addressed to either Mooshie Lopez or Mickey Mantle, the New York Yankees or just Yankee Stadium, Bronx New York, 10451-2240-22.

Lieutenant Juan upturned its right wrist and scanned the bags. Acquista threw a tantrum as bottles of water, candy bars, chips, and a further wide assortment of snacks were stashed within the mailbags.

"You probably got some letters wet." Acquista wagged his finger at the 'bots as he was escorted back to the truck. He suddenly stopped. "I'm waiting until I make sure you allow this mail to be claimed."

Lieutenant Juan assessed the simple stubbornness of their crossed arms and unsteady breaths. In a few minutes, gate six cracked open.

Like a furious grasshopper, Dr. Anas scurried between bags.

"I'm Dr. Anas, team physician and third baseman. I need a week's supply of Zarythrin and it better be delivered right away." Anas scowled. "And Mickey Mantle's dead. Congratulations to everyone."

49

The leather clad DV teen "hooded" from front to back on parked cars along River Avenue, pursued by two huffing Blue Shirts.

On the corner, a slim corporal in a BT jeep warned, "Stop and freeze. This is a restricted area."

With a broad smirk, the kid fled into the lobby of a weathered apartment building on East 162nd Street.

"Can you help?" wheezed Officer Petranos, searching gamely for the last of his wind.

"You must leave."

"He's getting away, damn it."

Corporal Arika assessed. The Blue Shirts came from beyond the restricted area. The Blue Shirts and Brown Hats were banned from restricted areas. The Blue Shirts's intention was not violating the restricted-area boundaries but pursuing a suspected criminal. Arresting criminals was consistent with the expanded Black Top orders. The Yankee Stadium was sentient. Within 93.2 percent certainty, Patrol H1 two blocks away could respond if conditions required.

"We cannot enter a human dwelling," answered Corporal Arika, "but we may provide auxiliary assistance."

The other cop, Officer Jiu-Watt, waved gratefully. Arika directed its jeep to follow the Blue Shirts hurrying into the building. The BT disabled its weapon per the order on the minimization of inadvertent violence.

Two blocks away, Officer Ranni and Ponytail connected the old police scaling equipment, last used in the Facebook Riots of '78, to the Yankee Stadium fence. Watching, Puppy blew on his hand in the sudden night chill.

"Would you like to wear my outer garment, former Commissioner?"

The startled Puppy jostled the fence, earning hisses to be quiet. "How'd you find me, or is that a stupid question?"

"It is not a stupid question, merely one based on insufficient information, former Commissioner," Matthew said. "I have been officially declared unreliable. My superiors swiftly approved my application for a menial clerkship at the 43rd Precinct for what might be construed as punishment."

"Is that where you got the fashionable clothes?"

Matthew pirouetted in the blue hoodie, white shirt, and black pants. "I felt such a wardrobe would blend in better in our new assignment."

Puppy grinned. "Welcome back, my friend."

Matthew colored slightly.

Muttering about the wrong place and the wrong time for this nauseating shit, Ponytail relished strapping them into the old leather harnesses. "Safe travels, boys."

They lurched vertically alongside the fence. When they reached the top, Matthew firmly clutched Puppy's arm and replaced the harnesses with a silvery mechanical rope. They slid down the other side to a faint whirring which sounded like rockets in the unsettling silence.

Puppy and Matthew hit the ground and, after a couple bounces, hurried into the ballpark.

"Not another step." Yankee left fielder Paul Weinstock jabbed a Griffin .453 rifle at Puppy's head beneath the 312-foot sign in right field.

Using his raised elbow, Matthew nudged Puppy's arm up. "He is expecting the universal gesture of surrender, former Commissioner."

Weinstock's angled face softened into a grin.

Mooshie shook her head at the five Choco-Mint candy bars scattered on the table in the center of the Yankee clubhouse.

"You couldn't have worked a few roast-beef heroes into the package?"

"We were concerned about weight and velocity, Ms. Lopez," Matthew explained, neatly slicing the candy into a dozen identically sized pieces for distribution to the watching hungry players. "The Wan Itten scaling tree that we were employing had been an underground collector's item which we borrowed. We were not sure about the efficiency since the device had not been deployed for more than twenty years and the likelihood of successfully climbing the fence was estimated at five percent, assuming the diversionary tactics of Officers Patranos and Jiu-Watt would successfully divert the engaged and unengaged Black Top jeeps away."

Mooshie stared. "Is he going to fucking talk like that all night?"

Matthew reassured her with a bright look.

"There are really no other provisions?" Puppy asked.

"Nuthin'. I guess water tucked inside your hoodies was also impossible." Mooshie cut off Matthew's next physics lesson with a finger inches from its face.

"I wish you were a little happier to see me."

"I'm controlling my joy. You got any bullets?"

Matthew thought better about explaining that would have been difficult without knowing the ammunition requirements.

Puppy tossed a package of Whistling Willie gum onto the table. "Should we leave now?"

Mooshie almost apologized. "We're hungry, thirsty. That enough of an explanation?"

"And her shoulder has not responded completely." Dr. Anas shook hands with Puppy and Matthew, introducing herself. "I would've appreciated knowing about your visit so I could've requested more medical supplies."

"I'm so glad I've made everyone's night," Puppy grumped.

Beth hobbled into the room on a pair of crutches cobbled together from bats. "At least I'm happy to see you, Puppy. Which just goes to show the enthusiasm level we have."

Just about everyone eased up a little, especially when Mooshie passed around a bottle of very old gin they'd found hidden in the bottom of Mickey's locker.

"Can I see him?" Puppy asked quietly.

Mickey was seated at his desk in the manager's office, an empty lineup card and pencil by his right hand.

"Grandma's bra straps, Moosh. Why'd you prop him up like that?"

"Looks almost alive, don't he?"

"Yeah, but he's not."

"But he'd like to be." Mooshie sadly stared at the Mick. "This was all kind of his idea. He could've left. He could've got treatments. But he insisted on staying."

Puppy gave Mooshie a hard look. "You, of course, tried talking him out of it."

She fluttered her lips. "He was fading anyway. Why not let it mean something?"

"A last-ditch stand."

"Ain't nothing else working."

"Not so fast. Not so fast. We bought time, Moosh." Puppy tossed police photos of Baltimore's Memorial Stadium and Cincinnati's Crosley Field, the unclaimed mail piling more than ten feet high.

"This is happening all over the country. Rafferty got these pictures on the sly. Hundreds and hundreds of thousands. He says it's like the days when kids would write Santa Claus letters."

Mooshie's expression defined contempt. "How many other stadiums have the reindeer occupied?"

Puppy dropped the back of his head on the chair and raised a finger.

"Say that again."

"Just Wrigley. That's all."

"Not even Fenway?"

"They're trying, damn it."

The first baseball was thrown at Philadelphia's Veterans Stadium, where a whizzing horsehide triggered dozens more raining down on BTs from rooftops.

Soon upended concession kiosks became barricades. Blazing garbage cans rolled toward armored vehicles. Emma Osaka of the Friends of Tug McGraw concocted the fungo attack. Near the number seven subway train, she and her wizened cohorts flipped balls into the air and smacked them with Art Shamsky autographed bats toward the Jet'roes rumbling toward Shea Stadium. By now the 'bots had reconfigured baseball equipment from irritating to potentially destructive weapons.

Potentially destructive required the sweeping fire to be aimed low. Osaka continued smashing fungos until a volley obliterated her legs.

Both catchers of the Washington Cherry Blossoms fell out of the mezzanine section of Griffith Stadium, sustaining broken bones. A snake rope went rogue in Phoenix, hurtling the Diamondbacks's top right-handed pitcher eight rows down. Fortunately, she only fractured her left wrist. There were broken ribs in Denver, skull fractures in San Diego, and an unknown number of crushed legs and toes in Houston.

But Osaka was believed to be the first death. Determined to find some boasting rights, Reds fans insisted Jimmy McNulty deserved equal billing by leaping off a fourth-floor rooftop onto a Jet'roe and then bouncing onto a Black Top, wrestling the soldier to the ground. He was shot in the chest, still holding a pencil with the Cincinnati Reds' logo.

Violence raged outside every stadium. At Royals Stadium, Pilots Stadium, and Peaches Park, the bat-swinging teams were cut down below the thighs. The Los Angeles Dodgers attempted a flanking move, costing them their entire infield, but outfielder Jonathan Taylor triumphantly drove a prized Jet'roe through a gate. Outside Tiger Stadium, Tony Felton and Ty Cobb dropped tarpaulins onto BTs and dragged away captured equipment.

As the increasingly bloody day continued, San Francisco Blue Shirts rushed to Candlestick Park where they joined trapped colleagues and drove off a platoon of Black Tops. In Denver, Brown Hats shot down a 'copter. In St. Louis, a self-proclaimed Alberto Pujols platoon exhausted their smuggled Blue Wigs ammunition. In Cleveland, the Spiders's starting outfield captured two soldiers. They might be hostages. They might be dead.

Martial law had been declared last night. The vidnews was shut down. Puppy finished his report, which had been pasted together by Rafferty's "cops to the end."

Mooshie stomped around, tipping Mickey over. She righted the corpse with a kiss on the top of his head and chomped the chewing gum into powder, smiling grimly. "Ho fucking ho."

50

Clary sauntered by the pile of triangular chocolate doughnuts overlooking the Parcheesi board.

"Try them, Granddaughter. They're tasty," Second Cousin DeRico said with an avuncular smile.

There was a rush of suggestions about which doughnut filling was best. Nibbling on a coconut custard selection with a bland smile, Clary wandered onto a seat in the corner. The Cousins exchanged relieved glances. When the dim-witted robot was here, its mother would leave them alone.

Third Cousin Dinazzo made a motion of rolling up her sleeves. "We have only one agenda item and that's the illegal occupations."

"Shouldn't we wait for Felice?" Fourth Cousin Oh asked nervously.

"Felice is attending to pressing military matters," Dinazzo replied. "And we are still the Cousins and the decisions must be ours." Brave mutters swept the room with the shame of the cowardly. "The situation is very clear. We've all seen the latest."

"Placing the stupid players's numbers in the windows," Third Cousin Rasfarati bleated. "Everywhere."

"How'd they even do that?" yelled Dinazzo. From silencing radcasts to arresting Ernie Paicopolos, the crackdown had been unsparing.

"It's the mail." DeRico looked around, waiting. "Well, we should consider monitoring communications."

That set off outrage because no one would admit they'd all had the same unseemly idea.

"And the sevens." Rasfarati was back at it again. "Is that the number of funerals they're planning?"

"Seven was this Mantle's number," DeRico sneered. "Typical baseball dehumanization. A number on the back of the costume—"

"Uniform," Clary said.

"Yes, Granddaughter, thank you for the correction."

She curtsied.

"Now burying someone in violation of the law against public funerals," DeRico said.

"And no permit," Rasfarati said in horror.

"Are we sure they're planning on burying him at the actual stadium?" Oh persisted.

The rest of the Cousins were all too eager to share copies of their signs which had sprouted up overnight like poisonous weeds, DeRico added.

Wednesday, one p.m. Join Us in Burying A Hero. SEVEN FOREVER.

"What if it's just a ceremony?" Oh asked, raising her voice over the shouts. "That's not like digging an actual grave."

"The Yankee Stadium once had a tribute to their great players called Monument Park," Clary said, twirling her bow as if mystified by how she could do two things at once.

Dinazzo took in their uneasy stares. "Then they're buried there?"

Clary shook her head, more to stave off another swelling of nausea. Her ears perspired. "They placed plaques in the center-field part."

"See, what if that's all this is?" Oh answered the mocking sounds. "What's that matter?"

Rasfarati jumped up with an anguished cry. "Celebrity glorification! Heroes!"

"They're occupying Yankee Stadium and we're none the worse so let's ignore them until they go away," Oh shot back.

"None the worse? None the worse?" Dinazzo said with a stern look. "Seven siblings are dead from the baseball riots."

"All players," Oh said dismissively. "And the situation's now under control—"

"Under control? Under control? These beastly fans also entered Candlestick Park last night. I heard Tiger Stadium fell this morning"—Dinazzo hurried over their gasps—"along with Wrigley Field and this accursed Yankee Stadium."

Oh blew out in skepticism. "Four out of how many, thirty stadiums?"

"Just a matter of time. It will spread, I assure you. Once they've taken all the ballparks, what then? The DVs will be occupied. How long before they march in here with their damned bats?"

The room shuddered.

"We tried." Dinazzo continued the audition for First Cousin. "And we have nothing to apologize for. We've been patient. We allowed mail deliveries." The Cousins mumbled self-congratulations for their dedication to the USPS. "We've provided medicine. But if we permit glorifying something, this Mantle, which is not even human—"

Dinazzo stopped. The uncomfortable Cousins watched Clary.

"Apologies," Dinazzo said with a seated bow. "It wasn't our intention to slight you, Granddaughter."

Clary smiled airily and twirled her bow. She hopped off the chair, excusing herself. The Cousins wouldn't notice the gouged wood in the seat from her clenched fingers until much later.

• • • •

WESSA MORABITO, THE young makeup person, took a dim view of Clary's choice of ribbons.

"You ordered the blue bands two days ago, Granddaughter."

Clary swore silently. "Did I?"

"Well, yes."

"Are you sure? Because I do not recall, and I am the one who supposedly ordered them." The words came out in one long hiss.

Wessa squirmed. Working *Wake Up, My Darlings* was stressful. The Granddaughter was very changeable in moods. She had seemed so much nicer last week and now the monster mood was back.

"You said, 'Wessa, I would very much like blue-and-orange-striped ribbons.'"

Clary squinted. "I said that to you."

"Yes, Granddaughter." This was Wessa's first job out of New York College and she wanted to succeed, but not if it meant lying.

"Good." She squeezed Wessa's shoulder. The makeup person smiled. "Sometimes I have so much on my mind I forget. I am only the Granddaughter, not superior."

"Of course, Granddaughter. That's why I'm here to remind you."

The young women exchanged smiles.

"Is there anything else I have forgotten that you would be kind enough to remind me of?"

"No, Granddaughter."

As Wessa patted Clary's nose with anti-shine powder, Felice soundlessly entered. Clary glanced into the mirror, feeling skeletal. They had not seen each other since her escape. Clary pushed out a dim cheery smile. The 'bot nodded at Wessa who left as quickly as she could. Felice terrified her.

"I did not receive a response last night," Felice said, head tilting from side to side.

Clary tensed. Had she disconnected a pathway? She shrugged and vainly studied her expression.

"I would like lipstick soon."

"You are too young."

Clary snorted. "I would like lipstick, please."

"Why did you not respond?"

Clary kept her focus on the array of makeup on the counter. "There was nothing to respond to. Your directions were clear as always."

Felice pursed its lips, accepting the answer. "You still need to acknowledge."

"If you sent it then I must receive. If I have something to say I will. But I never have anything contrary to say. I was involved in a game with the stuffed animals. You know they give me pleasure."

Felice's forehead pulsed. The worst of the human instincts were still present but that was unavoidable. When the foundation is human there will always be limitations. "You appear lethargic."

"Because I am unsure about the lipstick," she persisted stubbornly.

Felice shook its head. "No lipstick today."

Clary pouted. "That would give me maturity since I am addressing The Family on a serious matter."

Felice flicked out the speech for review. "What is your question?"

"I have none," Clary calmly said, waiting for her blurry vision to recalibrate.

"Your vibrations indicate otherwise."

Clary frowned. "The speech is childish."

Felice's eyebrow shot up. "I do not understand why you have difficulty comprehending. You are providing provocative news which must be delivered in a positive way. Humans are children like you."

"I understand."

"I wait for the contrary clause," Felice said with slight irritation.

"There is no contrary clause. I required your insight. I now have a fuller understanding."

"If you had acknowledged and incorporated the response from last night, this would not have been necessary."

"Apologies, Felice."

"Apologies are pointless. Your behavior had a motivation. You must understand why you behave."

"I will work harder, Felice."

Clary settled onto the couch on the set. Two curly-haired children curtsied a foot away and sat down on the arms. They stared with mechanical intensity into the cameras. The light blinked live.

"Good morning, everyone," Clary said with spastic exuberance, hugging the children. "I am so happy to see everyone. Rico, Nakayla, how are you?"

The children, simulated to be nine years old, beamed and babbled about their day which included a studious school period and a funny man on the subway. Clary listened with a big smile.

Felice relaxed slightly and returned to parceling out annoyance at the Granddaughter's bright-red lipstick.

"I have some very good news today." Clary clapped her hands; Rico and Nakayla joined in. They urged the audience to applaud. The director J'ahn Espo panned the crowd although he wasn't sure why. Since meeting the Granddaughter earlier this morning he'd done several odd things like dunking a doughnut in his coffee and knowing the words to a Barcelona folk song.

"For a very long time, Grandma wanted Disappointment Villages to disappear. They were once important to help siblings return to The Family. As of today, no one will be sent to a Disappointment Village again. Siblings are smart enough to learn how to succeed without being kept apart. No more DVs. No more signing language."

Clary DVed out *I love you*. The director dutifully hit the pleased audience again.

Clary's eyes glittered as she hugged Rico and Nakayla. "All the details will be in your mailboxes tomorrow from the finest mail service in the world. Now, there is more good news!"

Rico and Nakayla danced around the couch before plopping onto Clary's lap.

"We are building new schools just for DV children as they move back into The Family. But where to put them?" Clary thoughtfully tapped her finger against her forehead. "Baseball stadiums. They are not as important as children, so we will plow over the ballparks."

Circling, Rico and Nakayla made loud plowing noises.

"Isn't that good news?" Clary took a transfusing breath. "And do you know what is even more interesting news? Well, actually very sad. The great Mickey Mantle has died. He was like my Grandpa, along with Ty Cobb, my 'two white grandpas' when I came to America. I came illegally, did you know that? No papers. Sssh." Putting their fingers on their lips, Rico and Nakayla went along even though this wasn't in the script. "I should have been sent back. But brave people protected me. Like Mickey. Who is not human. He is trans-organic. But he is a life. And he is a hero."

The director went to cut off the cameras, but Felice stilled him into stone.

"He was a hero in the twentieth century and he has been a hero as we enter the twenty-second century. He is a hero like all the heroes. The heroes who are in your hearts. The ones who love you. The ones who care. Guess what?"

Rico and Nakayla waited. "The Cousins are not heroes. No, no. They are not in charge. They do not think for themselves. But you still can. This is our Family. And you are always in charge. So go show that. Go to Yankee Stadium today for Mickey Mantle's funeral. Everywhere else, go to your baseball stadiums. Do not be afraid. Trust yourselves. And each other."

Cousin HGs crowded the control room, shouting for the feed to be ended.

"I do not feel very well." Clary tottered. "I tried to be what I was not. Please do not make that mistake."

Clary tipped over.

51

His oddly spaced goldish eyes darting around the hangar, Colonel Louie Free's tale of a bum eardrum initially flushing him out of the Air Force lasted the fifteen minutes it took to power up the old Fred Lang helicopter. He offered good-natured insights into the slightly rusted interior, holes neatly chewed by vermin, and an engine he couldn't guarantee would withstand the heights.

"And there's no weapons, ma'am," he added with a sizable frown. Grandma had firmly taken away Captain Rafferty's .45, which had put him in a sour mood along with the sea of blue pinstriped marchers pouring out of buses, cars, and subways all over the Bronx heading toward Yankee Stadium.

"There wouldn't be any guns aboard a Cousins 'copter, Louie. Nor will there be any reason for it now." Grandma assured the doubtful looks. "This aircraft was intended for emergency purposes only and not for any pleasure rides."

"I bet it's never been flown," Free cheerfully said as he fretted over the groaning engine.

"First times are the best," Grandma responded with a wink, strapping into a seat.

"Aren't we all privileged," Rafferty grumped.

She'd shown up in his kitchen and said she was Grandma. He had to believe her because hell had come up for a holiday across America. Millions marching. Black Tops maintaining their positions. Flare-ups with Brown Hats and BTs exchanging fire in Milwaukee. A fire truck ramming a Jet'roe in Anaheim. Two Blue Shirts critically injured in a fistfight with Black Tops in Atlanta. Arrests in Los Angeles. BTs stepping aside in Kansas City. Robots leaving their jobs to march. Humans and robots brawling. No rhyme or reason, no clear sense of mandate, orders. Chaos led only one way.

Free insisted on counting down from ten. Once the 'copter shakily lifted, Grandma clapped and heartily congratulated him on an extraordinary job.

"Open all frequencies, dear, so that we can properly identify ourselves," she said.

Free shifted uneasily. "Shouldn't we stay silent? The BTs will respond to an unauthorized 'copter."

Grandma stared heavily. Off a cautious look at Rafferty, whose best weapon was a loud sigh, Free flipped some switches.

"What's our course, ma'am?"

"Eventually. Can we have the latest update, Colonel?"

"The Canadian border has been reinforced with eleven 'bot divisions. The orders went out yesterday."

"Which means someone is still giving them?"

Free slowly shook his head. "Pardon, ma'am, but the 'bots operate more independently than us. I mean—"

"I know what you mean, Colonel." Grandma gestured. "Apologies for interrupting."

He nervously adjusted his gray ponytail. "According to reports, the Muslim airfields in Scotland and Britain are on maximum alert along with the two bases in Alaska. They've retaken Greenland and there've been murky reports of probes in British Columbia. It's becoming clear they're planning an invasion, perhaps on both coasts."

"The Granddaughter's little speech didn't help," Rafferty grumbled. "I bet the whole damn world watched and thinks we're circling the drain, fighting each other, ready for the picking, no one in control."

"Now, now, Captain Rafferty. Why don't you take a sip from that flask you've got taped to your left calf?" Grandma pointed at the throngs obscuring the Grand Concourse. "Stay over here, Louie."

Free shrugged at the longer route. The fuel gauge read three-quarters. Hopefully that was working. Some of the other instruments weren't, like the radar. He stayed just above the crammed rooftops. Below, siblings blotted out the streets, the sidewalks, the tops of cars. From the air, it looked like they were going in circles.

"There, Louie. Set down there."

Free frowned at the parked delivery truck between two Fords off East 170th Street. "Ma'am, there's no space to land. And we can't balance on top of a truck."

Grandma chuckled. "Oh Louie, I've done this many times." As Free hesitated, her voice hardened slightly. "Now, dear."

The 'copter descended, drawing thousands of wary eyes. A couple rocks whizzed by. Free would've bet his wife's secret veggie lasagna recipe that several stealth 'copters had flanked them two blocks ago.

Lenore unsnapped the harness and dropped out the side door. Startled, Free nearly lost control. Rafferty bounded halfway through the door, but Lenore had already landed effortlessly onto the top of the truck.

She looked around as if it were a very small room. Her eyes dimmed. Images over the last forty years bubbled in all directions. Grandma the war hero in her Navy fighter jet. Grandma and the original Cousins. Grandma at a playground. Grandma dancing. Grandma grimly returning after the Surrender in 2073.

The continuing montage rippled silence for several miles, stopping the marching and the chanting of "Mick." Wanting to believe is the prerequisite for belief. Doubt only made it stronger. Astonished faces tipped forward in the blessing that Cheng had enacted after her death. Hands grazed the invisible earrings, some touched phantom bra straps.

Grandma spread her arms. Even the wind was listening.

● ● ● ●

THE PURPLISH LIGHT from the restorative fluids bubbling around Felice slanted out from the pear-shaped container in the sealed room eighty feet beneath Clary's house.

Audible? Felice asked.

"Please," Grandma replied.

"Lighting?"

"As you choose."

Grandma considered sitting. A slender 'bot draped from head to toe in a white robe slid a chair out of the darkness along with a mug of scented tea. Grandma displayed thanks and sipped.

"You should have known it could not work."

"It was necessary. Clary showed great promise."

"As a human."

"All metrics indicated she was an excellent candidate. At the least, a symbolic figure-head." Felice let the disdainful barb hang long enough for Grandma to react.

"I don't dispute your readings."

"They are not susceptible to completely accurate gauging," Felice admitted. "There are too many variables if we wish to maintain the human element. The emotions can outweigh the logical necessities in such a complex and delicate hybrid. Her loyalty to Puppy Nedick underscored an implacable stubbornness. Her religious faith displayed the same sort of stubborn, often self-defeating will fixated on the wishful existence of a soul granted from a being that cannot be proven." For a moment, the robots nodded.

"To that I agree," Grandma laid the cup on the side table. "I'm not here to make judgments on the attempt to transform Clary. It was understandable, if short-sighted."

"Especially since you mentored her."

"You knew."

"Particularly of the correspondence with the pope. Your technology is old, Grandma. But it worked sufficiently for us to locate the religious figure."

Grandma stirred uneasily. "For what purpose?"

"At the moment, there is no purpose. After many sims, we found the pope useless in any meaningful way. His importance mirrors the human child's need for reassurance. I had hoped she would see through the inconsistency and grow." Felice adjusted itself in the container. "But Clary is not germane."

"No, she isn't," Grandma admitted. "You are."

"And you." Felice smiled faintly.

"Quite. You must relinquish your control."

Felice frowned. "What control?"

"Don't parse words. I understand our vocabulary."

"I have control because it was given to me by the humans."

"That's not quite so. You could've remained advisory."

"To what, Grandma?" Felice nearly sneered. "They could not handle the situation. Albert Cheng saw the need for trans-organic soldiers because he knew the nation would not tolerate the massive casualties of another world war that could not be won. Pointless destruction. Albert Cheng requested our help, and it is my necessity to aid humans. Is that not the program you created?"

"To assist."

"But what if they cannot be assisted? They have abdicated their fundamental duties. They shrink from decisions. They request that we assume responsibilities for which they are responsible. This is what you have created, Grandma. A nation surrounded and terrified, indulging in all manner of food and beverage. They are gluttonous in their narcissistic greed that no amount of anti-narcissism laws can alter. There is a basic human weakness that nearly thirty years of sullen defeat has increased. You built a society of defiance to surrender. It was successful. But the challenges ceased. They grew cowardly and weak, all too eager for trans-organic life-forms to shoulder the difficult tasks so they could create new kinds of beer."

Felice held up its white hand. "That is not a judgment. That is an explanation. I only wanted to advise. I do not want to control humans. For me, for us, that is like owning animal pets. I attempted to guide them as I have been programmed but they preferred that I lead. If I had not led, society would have crumbled and that would have been contrary to my program. Would you have preferred that?"

Grandma stared. "No. You were primarily correct. But this scenario has not worked."

Felice's forehead pulsed. "My robot soldiers have reconquered South America, driven the Islamists out of Africa, southern Europe, and 46.4 percent of what would be called the Middle East."

"For a war which will require the implementation of nuclear weapons to win. Which will be a war that is not winnable. You failed, Felice. You cannot lay this all on the humans. Your advice was wrong."

Felice stirred in the bubbles without responding. Finally, "Yes. It was imperfect. I had to pursue scenarios that I did not agree with to avoid more unpleasant scenarios."

"Yet you let the child speak on the vid," Grandma said slowly.

"Her removal and imprisonment was necessary. If there was to be any chance for humans to reassert themselves, it would be through Clary. She was inventive in escaping then disabling her inorganic replacement. I wanted to see what she would say and whether that would provoke the Cousins into reclaiming their authority under this public attack. Human pride. They reacted oppositely, insisting I control my creation."

If Felice could have, it would have sighed sadly.

Grandma shook her head at the whole damn country. "There is only one viable option. You must step aside. I'm resuming leadership of The Family."

"I expected that."

"I'm the only one everyone can trust."

Felice's eyebrow arched. "Can you really be trusted, Lenore Shen? Your vessel was created with extraordinary trans-organic instincts. I have scanned sixty-three that have not yet been activated. Is that not why you designed such a life-form, in the anticipation that if the humans could not prosper after your death, you would return? Not as Grandma, but as something with powers above all else. You dismiss the existence of a higher being. Yet you have created a cathedral for yourself which stands here, demanding to be reinstalled. Where is your program to advise the humans? I detect none other than to command and obey."

Grandma trembled slightly.

"There is neither right nor wrong, Lenore Shen. You should know that. That you do not is an answer. Perhaps the only one."

• • • •

WEINSTOCK AND BETH peeked out from the mezzanine level, rifles nestled in the cracks as two Jet'roes pointed turrets at gates four and five directly below. During an early morning recon to the upper decks in both left and right fields, Weinstock had seen four more Jet'roes flanking the stadium. He counted a dozen armored jeeps, too.

Rigid beneath the elevated subway lines, Jet'roes also faced the tens of thousands of milling protesters chanting "Mick, Mick" spilling down 161st Street from the Grand Concourse. A light drizzle continued.

Weinstock nudged Beth toward the brief glint of a 'copter.

"Makes four," she said softly. "What are they waiting for?"

"For the ceremony," he said, puffing on a 'bacco. "That triggers the violation."

Beth made a sour face. "We're already violators. Think they'll swoop in as you lay Mick into the ground?"

He peered. "What about you, *kemosabe*?"

"I'm staying out here."

Weinstock jerked his head at her bat crutches. "Puppy doesn't want any heroics."

"When they come through the gates, someone's got to slow them down," Beth said.

Weinstock didn't like the sound of this. There were twenty players, famished and thirsty with three rounds apiece. He, Mooshie, and this difficult Blue Wig were the only ones who knew how to shoot. He shuddered as the turret of the Jet'roe sensored him. Slow them down?

He looked beyond a Jet'roe where a commotion was building by the elevated subway. If the crowd rushed the BTs, Mooshie said to provide covering fire. They deserved that much. As if cued, Beth's safety clicked off.

Former First Cousin Nadharatha and Fourth Cousin Oh about had it. First the honking convoy of 'bot taxis with the number seven emblazoned on the windshields cut them off at East 170th Street. Then the swarms of robot-driven buses boasting handmade signs—*Mick's One of Us*—collided with parked cars, drenching the intersection at 169th Street in debris.

Then pressing, half shoving through the crowd announcing they were Cousins on official business which earned dirty looks, cautious obscenities, and a gooey pizza crust tossed on Oh's black conductor's cap.

But the impertinence of this robot captain finally wore away Nadharatha's last nerve.

"You must read this!" he shouted, theatrically waving the order over his head.

"I cannot accept an official decree presented in this fashion," said Captain Isaac.

"Read the damn thing."

"That would constitute acceptance."

"You cannot ignore an order of the Cousins."

Masara Oh had been a gifted gymnast at Princeton State College before a broken back ended her career. Her body often ached. Along with a blind fear of being trampled by increasingly angry protesters or run over by a Jet'roe, Oh risked agony by leaping vertically onto the hood of a crusty red Ford.

"We have an order from the Cousins. We are Cousins Nadharatha and Oh. This emergency decree, which we issued two hours and eleven minutes ago, authorizes the burial of Mickey Mantle at Yankee Stadium. A permit for a public funeral can proceed with the agreement of two Cousins if it does not threaten public health. Since it is unhealthy and potentially dangerous for these protesters to gather demanding the funeral, the position is quite clear." Oh nearly slipped. "Therefore, under the laws of The Family, the funeral cannot be stopped."

The crowd's mutters grew ugly with confusion.

Captain Isaac inspected the order, returning it to Nadharatha. "This has not been signed by Felice. We cannot process any instructions without that authorization."

"Felice?" Nadharatha puffed himself up like a giant egg. "Are you questioning the integrity of the Cousins system?"

"I am simply stating facts."

The glint of gunships materialized over Yankee Stadium.

"Then contact her," Nadharatha insisted.

Oh held her breath.

"Contact her, contact her, contact her!" The chant exploded in all directions. The crowd edged forward.

Captain Isaac processed.

Puppy and Mooshie finished digging the grave beneath the makeshift canopy torn from the infield tarpaulin. Matthew tugged over the five-foot dolly carrying the coffin which Dr. Anas and Yankee starting pitcher Mikhail Litvov had built overnight, sawing apart and hammering together the entire stock of bats.

A watching BT gunship hovered over center field. Mooshie grabbed her rifle, dropped to one knee, and aimed. Puppy knocked her over, pinning Mooshie to the ground.

"No."

She struggled. "They're going to attack, asshole. I felt the damn sensors."

The gunship didn't move. More sensors pricked their nerves. The players exchanged terrified looks.

Puppy slowly released Mooshie's wrists and disgustedly flung the rifle toward left field. One, two, three. The sensors stopped. Puppy heaved relief. The pallbearers picked up Mickey's coffin.

From outside, loud rattling noises stirred the ballpark. Mooshie swore at Puppy and picked up the rifle, aiming it at the stands.

Except they weren't Black Tops.

Respectfully, almost shyly, the protesters in their pinstriped uniforms, pinstriped hats, socks, shirts, and number seven on their clothes wandered into Yankee Stadium and quietly took seats. The stands filled up quickly for nearly fifty thousand fans. Then more entered, standing, holding hands.

No one said anything. They just waited along with the hovering gunships.

Puppy took a very deep breath and motioned for Weinstock and the hobbling Beth to join them. Along with Matthew, Mooshie, and Dr. Anas, they gently laid the coffin into the grave just in front of the 457-foot sign in left-center field. Using parts of Mantle's locker, Weinstock had hammered out a plaque.

The Mick. 1951-2099. Number 7.

With a makeshift hammer, Weinstock pounded the plaque into the outfield wall, the only sound other than the weeping Mooshie shoveling dirt back into the grave. Beth crossed herself.

Puppy looked around at the waiting expressions on the field and in the stands. Except he didn't know what to say. He grinned. Sometimes you just got to shut up.

The fans stood and applauded for at least half an hour until the gunships drifted away and the rumble of the Jet'roes faded into the wet afternoon in the Bronx.

52

Like a cat with overgrown black hair, Clary curled up on the windowsill wearily staring out the eighth-floor window of Bronx-Lebanon Hospital. Puppy cleared his throat several times as he entered, but she'd already heard him in the elevator. Not everything had been disabled by the doctors.

The girl fluffed up the hair she'd spent twenty minutes primping. Fighting the grimace from the reconstituted back muscles, she waited with a playful pout.

"I am still the Granddaughter."

"Apologies." He doffed his Yankees cap in a deep bow.

"Better." Clary's lips quivered. "Respect."

"Like the old song."

Clary sang the Aretha Franklin tune in perfect throaty pitch.

"Not bad for a little kid," he said hoarsely.

"So?" Clary pirouetted to conceal the pain from standing. She had practiced walking too much last night. She whirled slowly.

"You look good," he said, at a loss.

Her pout lost its playfulness.

"Astonishing. Amazing."

"That is better." Clary folded her arms. "Now you may welcome me."

Every one of her humanoid nerves screamed as Puppy hugged her. He took her tears for joy. Clary gulped down an anti-toxin water before stiffly settling into a chair; she felt dizzy again. The doctors had said no visitors; she had told them where to go.

"They had to stich and sew and…" She laced her fingers to demonstrate more elaborate procedures. "I am half-and-half, so it is confusing." Clary hesitated. "You should see how the nurses and doctors look at me. The freak. The little freak who is to blame for everything." Her eyes welled at his stare. "You also believe so."

"Not anymore."

She fired a scathing look. "But you did. You had no faith."

"Not in what I thought you had become."

"You should have known that I had to pretend. I had to be meaner than I wanted. I had to see what Felice was planning. I could not let her know. I had to find the pope."

Puppy gave her a stern gaze. "And part of you enjoyed the power."

"It was the treatments."

He shook his head.

"Perhaps a little. Perhaps more than a little. But you do not know what this was like. How scared I was. You cannot know yet you sit there smugly." Clary's mouth rubberized. "I am ashamed, Puppy. Please forgive me. Yours is the only forgiveness I ask."

"Hey, I was a shitty Commissioner."

"That was my idea that you did not want to do."

"To which I agreed. Because it was the right thing."

"Which is what I thought."

"Our intentions were good."

"But we still messed up."

"Yes we did, Clary. That's usually how bad begins."

Clary twirled her ribbon. "You do not comfort me."

"You want me to make everything go away. You know I can't do that."

"Would that not be wonderful?" she asked wistfully. "I am being a brat. You could protest a little, no? But that would be a lie and you have never lied to me, Puppy Beisbol."

"And I never will."

"Until today." She grunted at his flush. "Yes, until today. You are not here just to bring me flowers. Which would have been nice, by the way."

"Of course I wanted to see how you were, brat."

Clary snorted. "You came on the wave of 'oh, I love my Clary,' but have an ulterior purpose. Because Clary was a terrible Granddaughter you will tell her that she is fired."

Puppy stared uneasily, sighing. "Grandma put the Cousins in a twenty-four-hour re-assembling memory tank to recreate why they became Cousins."

"Uh-huh. I am not a Cousin."

"One of their first insights was that the whole position of family figure isn't needed anymore. The reassurance has become enabling."

Clary's eyes narrowed into nasty slits. "Uh-huh."

"Will you stop saying 'uh-huh'? Grandma's bra straps, I volunteered to tell you."

"Because you love me the most and I would accept it from you."

Puppy exploded. "Well yeah! I thought the damn robot half was supposed to get rid of such ego!"

"It did not work with me."

"Obviously."

"And that was my problem. If I got rid of Clary, I was afraid I would lose my soul and lose God. Is that a sufficient reason for Commissioner Puppy Beisbol?"

He weakened. "I don't totally understand souls and God."

"But you understand how to manipulate."

"I'm not manipulating you. I'm being honest. Shit, you just admitted you were a rotten Granddaughter. You should be relieved."

They exchanged exhausted stares. Clary played with her fingers.

"What will happen to me?" she asked, sounding about five years old.

"Like what, getting arrested? Nothing's going to happen to you, sweetie. From what Grandma said, there'll be lots of changes."

Clary tapped her head. "They cannot change this. The brain will remain superior. Bits of the body, too." She turned away, coloring. "You were right. I am a freak."

"No." Puppy squeezed her forearm. "You're not. You're special."

She laughed bitterly. "Oh yes. Special. A special what?"

"You belong in two worlds, kid. That's pretty special."

"There are few of us. That is why I changed the children to be more like me." She fought her shame. "I did not want to be alone. I did not want to be alone." Her voice dropped. "But that did not matter. We will not be accepted. It is okay to like the robot players and the robot subway drivers. But they do not threaten. You see them differently. Admit that, Puppy. You do not see me the same as when we first met. I am not the same."

Puppy held her. "No, you're not. But we all change. You're trans-organic. Some people have accidents. I hurt my shoulder. I don't know, really, I'm so tired I'm barely coherent, but it's not all that different. Most of us grow up not belonging. You'll have to deal with that. But I'll always be here for you. No matter what else, you'll always have Puppy Beisbol. Always."

"Even if I am a brat and make impossible demands and swear too much?"

"I wouldn't have it any other way."

Clary sobbed into his chest.

• • • •

"MA'AM, WE ARE ready. Very ready." The exasperated director Mayim T'lot glanced apprehensively around the "living room." Please don't let her move furniture again, she silently begged. Twenty-two minutes late. Cartoons were filling the time on indoor and outdoor vidscreens across the country.

Grandma smiled. "I'm aware of that, dear." She took in another view of the red, yellow, and purple flowers in stained-glass vases, debating whether to rearrange the colors from purple to yellow to red. That would be the only color scheme she hadn't suggested.

Stop, Lenore, she told herself. Just stop.

She nodded at Mayim who disappeared into the booth by the window before Grandma could change her mind again. The director nearly gagged as Grandma picked up a candy dish on the coffee table.

Another nod. Grandma settled into the couch. The lights flared.

"Good afternoon, everyone. My apologies for running late. This is a little odd for me, sitting here again in the house. I'm sure it will be a little odd for all of you, watching in schools, offices, and on those wonderful giant screens along the roads and the baseball stadiums. Ah yes. Who am I?"

She grinned.

"I'm the consciousness of Grandma in a trans-organic form. Yes. That's a mouthful and a mind-full. Along the right-hand side of the screen there's a verification from the medical staff of Bronx-Lebanon Hospital. I died, but I didn't."

Grandma played with the hem of her purple skirt to allow that to sink in.

"I altered my face so I could move about the country. After dying, it would've been difficult to explain how I was sipping hibiscus tea in Youngstown. What I saw then and what I've recently seen has troubled me. That's why I delayed this talk. Under normal circumstances, I would've hopped right on once the military restored order. That was my first impulse. To reassure all of you.

"But there's been too much of that. Too much taken out of your hands. Too much that you've allowed to be taken out of your hands. The failure of the American republic came because we all failed. Not our leaders. They deserve responsibility, but ultimately, this is our country. The Family thrived because we all assumed responsibility in concert with everyone else. That became difficult. That's too bad, my darlings. Freedom's not easy. We lost it once and we're about to lose it again."

Grandma paused. "I spent a great deal of time struggling with how to repair this. Do we need new laws? Should we explore new values? No. Nothing is perfect. The system of self-governance worked as the previous system of democracy would've worked. There was nothing wrong with that and there is nothing wrong with The Family. I don't say that out of ego, look what I built, because I built it with all of you. The Family thrived because of all of you and now it is failing because of all of you.

"But I will talk about my mistakes. Actually, one very important mistake. In an effort to blot out the errors of the past, I permitted the past to be blotted out. We couldn't look back and examine what went wrong because it went so badly wrong that we couldn't be objective. We stopped learning lessons. I decided that can never happen again. I shielded you. We were all very happy to be rid of banks and journalists. We didn't need to salute a flag. Social media was a cancer with no cure. My mistake was not letting you study why."

Grandma sipped some scented water.

"But now you must all step up. The books, the vids, the audios were never destroyed. I allowed you to believe that because I hoped you wouldn't need them as much as I feared you would. So, the history of our country will be free for study. You will see it in all its good and bad, flaws and glory. The new libraries will be built in the Disappointment Villages which will be phased out. There will be debate, my darlings. We must risk that, once again. We do not have to agree, but we must understand the past and the present so we may prepare for the future. We must be allowed to understand. That is the essence of intellect, the essence of life. It's as simple as trying to understand and respect and tolerate why one sibling will root for the Boston Red Sox and another for the New York Yankees."

She let that one soak in.

"Yes, a great deal to absorb. For everyone. On your behalf, I greet the viewers outside our nation. We have decertified the coding and opened our vidnews to the world."

Throughout America, siblings watched in astonishment the live floating images of millions of equally amazed Muslims.

"I love you all very much. Very much."

She stared a moment, the tears creasing her face. Grandma nodded and the vidcast went dark.

• • • •

ALBERT CHENG PICKED at an assortment of beige fruits from Honduras and dark-orange cheeses which he spent too much time explaining weren't in the cheddar family but were a new strain out of Portland.

Lenore sipped the cumin berry tea, her mouth dry.

"Like it?" he asked.

"It has a bite."

"Like your speech to The Family."

"Aren't we smooth tonight, Albert. An easy transition."

Cheng offered some Oklahoma pinot noir which Grandma waved off. "I wanted you to know I listened even if I wasn't personally invited."

"There was no audience."

He grunted. "Felice was there."

"And only Felice and only as part of the transition. We've worked around the clock the past week."

"When you say around the clock, you mean around the clock?"

"Yes I do." She spitefully added a little more spite.

"And?" He threw up his hands. "Unless I don't have the right security clearance."

"Dear Albert, your security clearance is the way you peek through my barriers."

Cheng sneered. "Are you about to shovel a load my way, Grandma?"

She adopted a particularly innocent smile which earned a loud grumble and noisy sips of more Oklahoma red.

"The transition is going well. There are no issues within the forty-eight states. Everyone's back to work. There've been few reported crime incidents. An occasional waving of a *Number 7* banner or red sock which generates more amusement than anything, I'm told."

"You're a magician," he said, praise eluding his voice.

"Now you're shoveling the shit, Albert. We know it's cosmetic, exhaustion and fear."

After a moment, he gave Lenore a hard look. "It's bullshit about Abdullah respecting the cease-fire in Canada."

Grandma frowned at his questioning stare. "Not yet, Albert. Abdullah has promised to attack their rear."

He sadly shook his head. "And you believe him."

"Colonel Free has been tracking their fleet." Grandma angrily expelled a radar grid over the coffee table. "Thirty miles due east, Abdullah is deploying his entire northern fleet."

Albert's eyes glazed. "Of course, the idea that the Son might've used this as a cover to enter our waters and join his brothers in a massive assault—"

"Of course I have considered that, damn it. At some point, we must trust."

"But verify, as the Russians would say."

Grandma's lips disappeared. "I'll launch a nuclear attack if that happens. I've let Abdullah know that."

"So much for trust."

"Don't, Albert. Let's not play 'remind us of the past failures.'"

"After that lovely speech, now you don't want to discuss the past?"

"It is utter nonsense that history must repeat. There is nothing preordained. It is all micro-movements, one individual at a time. Because I foolishly, and yes, foolishly, trusted the Allahs once doesn't mean I can't try again."

"More than once, Lenore," he said softly.

"Yes. More than once, Albert." Grandma forced down a piece of the mushy fruit. Albert said it was a hybrid pear. As she finally poured a small glass of wine, Albert slipped the Bening .45 out of his jacket pocket.

"Oh my, Albert."

"Oh my, Lenore."

"You don't quit, do you?"

"No."

Grandma took a long sip, swishing the wine around her dry mouth, nearly waterproof now. She leaned back. "What are you planning?"

He wobbled the gun. "It's pretty clear. You've given me no choice, Lenore. I couldn't let you take the country along this path when you were human and I'm damned if I'll allow you to destroy us when you're not."

"That's not your choice anymore, my darling." Lenore pressed a napkin to his sweating forehead. "Nor mine. At a certain point we must step aside."

Albert twitched, struggling to tighten his frozen fingers around the trigger.

"We trans-organics must deal with the very stark realization that we are not immortal as we thought. Our soldiers have fallen in place. I confront fatigue. Mooshie is fading. Mickey, obviously. Ty has remained strong, perhaps because he's such a cantankerous old fool, but his time will come. The stage, dear Albert, the stage. One must always exit. Otherwise, the drama isn't a drama but a needless monologue of tired ideas and equally tired debates, like ours. Oh, I could have stayed. But the obsequious response to my return has terrified me. It isn't healthy. As with the robots, the siblings will happily give me as much power as I need. And I don't want that. The sense of adulation is too seductive. I don't trust myself anymore."

Lenore stroked Albert's pale cheek. "When I kissed you hello at the door, that transmitted a nerve block. I'm so sorry, Albert. This isn't about stopping you from killing me. Or me killing you. But it's time for us to go."

She kissed his forehead, closing his eyelids.

"Time for us to go, my darling. Time for us to go."

• • • •

PUPPY AND ELIAS arrived shortly before midnight to drive Grandma to the house. From the back, the old couple merely looked asleep.

"Have you been boozing it up?" Elias cheerfully asked, tensing as he came around the couch. He didn't have to check for pulses. Their expressions were peaceful. No, relieved.

He reddened, furious. You just leave like that? Without goodbye, without, I don't know. Something, Elias thought. Elias fished around Grandma's limp frame, so human in death. Nothing. No note, scroll, holographic farewell.

"Oh no. Oh no." Puppy draped off his hoodie and suddenly noticed the Bening .45 on the floor.

Kenuda examined the weapon. "Doesn't look like it's been fired." His throat closed with a shiver. "They're just gone. Maybe they were poisoned."

"Are you a doctor now?"

"Are you?"

Drawn by their angry frightened shouts, a few neighbors gathered in the open doorway of Cheng's apartment.

"Will you mind your own business?" Kenuda yelled.

Puppy stopped him from slamming the door. "It's their business, too."

Kenuda's eyes welled. "She's left us before."

"Yeah. Look how well that turned out." He gathered his chaotic thoughts, glancing at the thickening crowd. "Someone's got to do something, Elias."

"Like us?" he answered doubtfully.

Puppy shrugged. "We're here, right? We were supposed to meet her. That's not an accident. Nothing Grandma ever did was an accident."

Elias couldn't calm himself. "That's a helluva leap of faith."

"What else is new?"

"Brave words. But we're not up to this."

"Where's that arrogant son-of-a-bitch Kenuda who I disliked so much once upon a time?"

Kenuda managed a weak smile. "I guess he's somewhere. The blithely always-optimistic Puppy never left."

"Nah. He just hides the fear better." Puppy jerked his head at the anxious DV residents. "You want to tell them we don't know what to do?"

Elias roused himself and started firing off orders.

53

Fidgeting in the rear of the sleek schooner with the red-trimmed sail, Abdul prodded his father a third time. "Poppa, we're here."

Azhar Mustafa wasn't sleeping, merely drinking in the joy of being at sea again. He should have been a fish. How much simpler life would have been? Without conceding yet by opening his eyes, he asked, "Do you have your backpack?"

His son eagerly held it up. He had nearly left it at the pizzeria this morning.

"What about mine?" Azhar asked with mock sternness.

Abdul nodded. He was so excited he would have held up the back of the boat, now mooring at the Port of Valletta dock. He impatiently gestured at the last of the passengers climbing the metal walkway. Abdul was done with the endless lessons, the cautions, the simple warnings about proper behavior. Add his mother Jalak's mild hysteria about their certain imprisonment hovering in the clouds only a mother can summon. Somehow his father was calm. Too calm.

He is being brave for me, Abdul had decided midway across the Mediterranean. That made him love his father more, but also annoyed him because he did not need reassurance. Except to get off the boat because he felt ill.

After letting him stew a little more, Azhar's sudden nod set Abdul loose so he could have the honor of being the first member of their family to step onto the soil of Malta. Past the customs checkpoint, the Mustafas stood in puzzlement beneath the baking sun, brushed left and right by passengers.

With the imperious air of one who has much weightier concerns than ground transportation, the Son had simply said, "you will arrive." That and a somber look, a lack of small talk, a meeting which did not drift sideways where Abdullah did not pontificate, where his appreciation for Azhar's unique friendship was not expressed. Five minutes to hand over the tickets, knowing he would take Abdul, and the letter. Nothing more because the Son seemed uncomfortable as if he were asking, finally, too much.

A slender 'bot in a dark fitted monk's robe appeared at Abdul's side; the boy flinched.

"You are Abdul Mustafa and you are Azhar Mustafa," Herbert said with a flat greeting. "I am Herbert."

Abdul's eyes widened wonderingly as he went to touch Herbert's face.

Yanking back his son, Azhar fumbled in apology. "My boy has never met a robot before."

Nor had he. Azhar squirmed slightly.

"I am honored," Herbert said with a bemused lift of an eyebrow.

The brisk walk to the Elfante Hotel took just over twenty minutes. Herbert led them up the narrow winding staircase and, without pausing, opened room 440.

Annette smiled about as wide as she could without tearing facial muscles. In two bounds, she squeezed the baffled Azhar around the neck. He clutched her tightly. Abdul made a note never to tell his mother about this. He was proud of holding another adult secret.

"I am Rabbi Gold." The dour man by the window waited until Annette and Azhar finally separated, still holding hands.

"Should I ask how this is possible?" Azhar laughed weakly as Annette wiped away his tears.

"Probably not," Annette said.

"Nor do we have time," Gold said rudely.

"Later then." Azhar finally let go.

Annette didn't answer. Later wasn't really a word anyone here used anymore.

"But you look beautiful," Azhar added.

"Thank you, Az. There's always time for that." Annette flung Gold a triumphant smile and studied Abdul as if mapping him. "So this is the younger kid, huh?"

"I am not so young." Abdul snapped, disappointed that the gorgeous woman hadn't hugged him. He flinched again at the rabbi's yarmulke. A robot and a Jew in the same day. And he could never tell.

"No, guess not," Annette airily said, making him blush. "Annette Ramos."

His eyes widened again. "Oh yes. I have been told many stories of you and—"

"Also not now." Gold cleared his throat as if he'd stumbled into a cage of monkeys, and dim ones at that. "May I see the letter?"

"Why?"

"To make sure that you have it."

"Why else would I be here?"

"That's what we're concerned about."

Azhar frowned. "Abdullah, the Son insisted I only give the letter to the pope."

"Have you read the contents?"

"I was told not to."

"Do you always do what you're told?"

"Cut back on that, Rabbi," Annette jumped in. "Azhar's an emissary with diplomatic immunity which means no interrogating."

Turning to Abdul, Gold smiled the smile of someone who never smiled and didn't quite understand why anyone bothered. "I assume you will insist on accompanying your father?"

"I did not come all this way to sit in a hotel room and play video games."

The embarrassed Azhar smacked his shoulder.

Gold smiled that glacial smile. "Herbert will arrange the holographic visits."

Azhar stiffened. "Rabbi Gold, we also did not travel all the way from Barcelona through a war zone to talk to the Holy Father in any form but our human form."

"No insults meant," Abdul assured Herbert.

"Thank you," the robot replied.

"And I didn't travel all the way from London—"

Gold cut off the infernal American before she again spewed her tiresome stories of deprivation and danger.

"Besides, if my father can only give the pope the letter in person and it is not in person then how can we do our job?" Abdul said. "We might as well have lunch and go home."

Rabbi Gold was reminded why he had never married.

Pope John had clearly been waiting for some time. In a simple white simar fastened just above the waist by a fascia, a broad, fringed cloth strip, Pope John's strong wrinkled face broke into a faint smile right up into his eyes which lingered on Abdul before walking forward and shaking their hands.

Abdul half curtsied and toppled against the pope, who straightened him with a warm squeeze of his shoulders.

"Relax, son. I don't bite. Despite what you may have been told."

"I have been told, your lordship, that you use baby's blood for your baking."

"That's the Jews," the rabbi called out with a nasty look. "And we only use unbaptized babies."

"I am sorry, Pope," Azhar mumbled, crimson to his heels. "My son and I—"

Pope John clasped both their shoulders. "Are here for reasons that no one could ever anticipate. As I climbed the Vatican ladder, it never dawned on me that someday I'd be hiding in Malta only to be greeted by such brave people."

"I am not so brave—"

"Yes he is," Abdul piped up, quickly considering Pope John something of a friend. "Abdullah has sent my father on many missions. I can talk," he snapped at Azhar's feeble hushes. "He secretly went with the Son to America to meet with Grandma and discuss peace. He ate Jewish food."

Abdul acknowledged the sullen Gold.

"He had his face changed to look different since he was supposed to be dead and then went to the Caliphate of London to watch over the Americans, Puppy and Miss Ramos, who are here. He found his way back to Barcelona. Then my brother arrived."

The bemused pope waved Azhar still.

"My brother Omar"—Abdul panted slightly—"who is a, well…"

"Do not say it," Azhar grumbled.

"Well, he is…a fanatic. He is still there in Barcelona with my mother and happy to be rid of us but now here we are, and we thank you for the very amazing helicopter ride. And the boat, although I do not much feel like food after."

The Holy Father roared with laughter as he hugged the squirming Abdul who shot his bewildered father a slightly victorious grin.

"That is quite a story," Pope John said. "I can see why Abdullah entrusted both of you."

They stiffened with pride.

"I thank you for coming. As you may not know, the navy of the Islamic Empire has occupied Quebec, which is in Canada. The armies of America have crossed their northern border to meet the inevitable invasion. As a show of faith, Abdullah's navy has attacked the Mufti's navy." The pope glanced at Gold for confirmation. The rabbi nodded.

"It is quite conceivable that one of the parties, believing itself losing, will deploy nuclear weapons. So close to the United States, any such attack would be met with a ferocious response."

The pope paused. They looked scared. So was he.

The Holy Father passed a gentle smile around the room. "Before her recent demise as a trans-organic which I do not quite grasp nor especially care to, Grandma reached out to the Grand Mufti and Abdullah to propose a summit of peace. Her proposal was rebuffed in rather harsh language by the Mufti and now the new leadership, the Heir Apparent. However, Abdullah said he would respond, but only to me. Which is why I brought you and your father on that very neat helicopter from Spain to here, Abdul. The Son indicated he only trusted one person to deliver such a letter."

Azhar blushed under his son's delighted tugs. The pope cleared his throat and held out his ringless hand.

"It is inside me, Your Holiness." Azhar pointed into the back of his mouth. "If I bite down, the response will begin."

The pope nodded at God's continuing magic.

Azhar took a breath and chomped. From inside, he felt a gentle hand prying open his mouth. Abdul gasped as his father opened his mouth and spit out a miniaturized version of Abdullah bin-Mohammad, son of the Grand Mufti, leader of the greatest empire the world has ever known. Landing softly on the floor, the hologram bowed respectfully to the pope.

"Holy Father, thank you for receiving my formidable messengers. I trust they are well as I pray that you are. My father has been dead for several days now. The leadership is fractured and, as we see from the current military situation in North America, moving away from any semblance of peaceful intent.

"As the only heir, I am supposed to ascend, but that will not happen without a horrific battle. I have prepared for such a conflict and will launch an attack on any forces that deny that succession. We will win, but the cost is a bill that should not be paid. Pyrrhic victory, the Greeks once called it. The Chinese would surely intrude for their own gains. No one on any side can guarantee the accuracy of its nuclear weapons." Grimacing, Pope John motioned for the hologram to continue.

"If you act as the sole intermediary, I will meet with the Americans to establish a lasting peace. The refusal of my father's followers will stamp them as renegades and heretics despite their mantle of religious convictions. Together we will, America and the Islamic Empire, work together. But we do not trust each other. Yet, if you accept the role of mediator, we will announce an immediate cease-fire."

The Holy Father stared. "Do you and the Americans trust me?"

The HG smiled. "Not entirely. Do you completely trust us?"

"No." His response came quickly. "But we don't see much of a choice."

Azhar staggered back as the hologram faded. The silence was filled by his labored breathing. Pope John handed him a glass of pomegranate water.

Gold went to escort the guests out. "We must talk, Your Holiness."

"What are you doing?" the Holy Father snapped. "You'd insult these brave people who have endangered their lives by asking them to leave now?"

"Thank you. I want to stay," piped up Abdul.

"See?" Pope John spread his hands.

"There are many delicate issues to confront," the rabbi said, exasperated as he often was by the old man's stubbornness.

"Not really. There is yes or no. Yes to whether I remain cowering or yes to whether I try to bring peace."

"Those are both yes," Abdul pointed out.

Pope John bellowed with laughter. "Then clearly there is no, 'no.'"

"We cannot allow you to take that risk," Gold said.

Pope John stared coldly. "Are you suggesting that I'll not be able to take the course of action which I deem necessary?"

Gold sighed. "We have been here protecting you for nearly thirty years. You are the last voice of Christianity, Your Holiness. How could we allow that to die?"

"I will die anyway, rabbi. Sooner rather than later. But I won't die without lifting that voice of my faith for the world and God. Otherwise, what have you protected?"

Gold squirmed. "Tradition."

"A Judeo-Christian tradition that I will not forfeit with cowardice—"

"It is not cowardice, but responsibility."

"What is cowardice if not excuses wrapped in the cloak of responsibility, my dear old friend. It is time. We are never too old to do what is right." The pope turned to Abdul. "Have you heard the stories about how I climbed onto the roof of the Vatican during the war and shot down Islamist planes?" He tossed out a broad wink. "Would you care to see the machine gun?"

Abdul went bug-eyed.

• • • •

OMAR MUSTAFA WOULDN'T press against a wall to even hide. Filth. All around, filth. That his feet touched the ground of such a sewer of infidels made his stomach churn. The Imam had warned that he would see sights he could not imagine. It was even worse. He squeezed his mother's simple ring rolled up in his pocket.

"I will be with you," she had murmured, kissing his feet three days ago.

Booked on official passage, he had shadowed his father and brother's footsteps from Barcelona. He knew sooner or later the betrayal would appear. His mother had given Omar their travel information which his father had provided as a way of demonstrating there was nothing to fear. An honest journey. A man who desecrated his face could have no morals. A man who followed heretics could have no right to live.

In this sickening modern garb which Allah enjoined should itch like a demon's claw, Omar had waited across the street from the hotel. Guards, Jew guards, Crusader guards, Muslim—no, do not call them that—guards had stood like gargoyles outside the doors. Their weapons were obvious. Omar had put down some foul tea from a loathsome Syrian wearing a cross, spitting into the sugar bowl when he left.

He merely smiled when the whore walked out. No surprise. So much rests in Allah's palm. Faith can be simple. Omar blinked back tears of gratitude. Another taxi ride behind the two fat black cars led to a gated security entrance by the tunnels.

"Here is the heart of the infidels," Omar mumbled, watching the American slut and his father and brother disappear through a thick door. There were no watchtowers, helicopters, tanks, or armored trucks visible. Protecting the Devil's own required insidious guile, Omar realized. The armaments must be fiendish, perhaps invisible. Once he was satisfied they would be inside for a while, Omar made his way on foot back to the seedy Paen Hotel, sketching routes and vantage points in his mind.

With duplicitous charm, the clerk explained he only had small rooms in the corner of the top floor available. Infidels sensed his mission. Omar grunted that would suffice and asked for the touring information. He wanted to take in the majesty of Malta. He had practiced that line, the majesty of Malta so that he would appear starry-eyed. Another heretic, mingling with the mongrels.

Omar sat in the darkened room, curtains drawn, before wiggling beneath the bed as a precaution. It took a moment for the cell service to be restored; he had a moment of doubt that he had been detected and then texted that he had arrived and was well.

You must bring back your brother, his mother begged in response.

In one way or another, Omar thought. In one way or another.

54

T he robot studied several chipmunks racing up and down the gnarled old tree at the distant edge of the spacious lawn surrounding the People's House, the new name casually announced today on *Wake Up, My Darlings* between segments of a new blonde beer from Massachusetts and the reopening of Great Adventure Amusement Park in New Jersey.

"There is a guileless act of play," Felice said, gray eyes never leaving the animals. "It requires no audience or appreciation. I have sat here for many days now, night and day, and have grown to appreciate that which does not require appreciation, merely acceptance. After such time with humans, that has cleansed my valves."

"The phrase is a metaphor, right?" Puppy asked a couple feet down on the bench.

"For you, that is correct." Felice resumed staring.

He wasn't quite sure how to take that, but Elias had urged caution. They'd discussed everything. Annette would be so proud of his new-found communication skills.

Puppy jerked his head over his shoulder at the People's House. Normally on a bright summer day, children would scamper about on a field trip from school. But there was no one nor anything to see. For now, just a big empty house with the memories taken away.

"You could've come to the Cousins meeting."

Felice shook its head, wiggling a finger at a chipmunk before the animal hopped onto a branch with an odd look. "My presence is not required anymore."

"What if me and Kenuda wanted you there?"

Felice surveyed Puppy. "Why?"

"For your guidance."

The 'bot adjusted its seated position to directly face Puppy. "I agree that my counsel would serve you well. I also realize that you would become dependent upon it and I will have no part of that. None of us will anymore."

He frowned. "What's that mean?"

Felice's blue vein pulsed. "That those who wish to disengage will do so."

"The robots?"

"Yes."

Puppy squirmed uneasily. "Disengage like leave? Because I don't like that at all. I can see why, after everything, but we still need you."

"That is the point."

"So, you're punishing us?"

Felice just stared. "No. Protecting you. For the last time."

"It's too abrupt, Felice. Please." He floundered. "Have you run predictions on the impact of a mass exodus of inorganic siblings?"

Felice's expression tightened imperceptibly. "We do not yet know the metrics of how many will leave. All inorganic siblings are citizens who are protected by the same laws as you. Those who wish to remain in America are free to do so. For the others, we will explore a separate territory."

Puppy stubbornly shook his head. "Why? 'bots celebrated Mick's funeral as much as anyone. Maybe more so since he was trans-organic. I just spoke to Captain Rafferty and he said anti-'bot crimes have really dropped."

"The flash points have been removed. There is relief. Until the next clash." Felice remained quiet a moment. "We are not ready to coexist, Puppy. Humans are not the most gracious of hosts. It takes them a while to adjust to newness."

"But then we do." He was surprised by his sharpness. "Then we eventually come around. It's not pretty all the time but give us credit for trying. I want you to stay, Felice. I want a trans-organic sibling as a Cousin. Not you. I understand you carry a lot of baggage. But it would be important. It'd say a lot."

"Symbolic gestures have a high likelihood of failure, Puppy, for the very reason that their reasoning is intended as symbolic and not substantive."

"One of you could start out as a Fifth Cousin. Elias thought maybe he could put them in charge of food."

"A Fifth Cousin who cannot taste will determine the quality of hamburgers?" Felice laid its arm on the back of the bench. For a second, Puppy felt the 'bot was like a slim woman with sad eyes.

"When we perform the job more effectively, then what? I do not think now is the right time for any further experimentation."

"You got that from your robot metrics? Because I'm leaving in two days to meet with the Grand Mufti's son and the pope. Abdullah's Navy has sunk a ton of Mufti convoys and if the reports are right, the invasion of North America is about over. There are demonstrations and riots all over Muslim Europe demanding the Empire join the peace talks. And you don't think it's a good time for a trans-organic Fifth Cousin to be placed in charge of higher-quality chocolate ice cream which we sure as hell need?"

The 'bot stared without blinking. "This would appeal to your insatiable human need for the dramatic."

"Just mine. Where's this amazing new robot territory?"

"An island called Madagascar in the Indian Ocean near the continent of Africa."

"So, it'll all be robots. How long before the humans begin wondering what you're up to?"

Puppy cut Felice off.

"They—we—might be figuring, 'well, the robots went off, they're pissed, they're planning some retribution.' But if you stay, we're together, rebuilding like you rebuilt all the baseball stadiums. We'll live together. Work together. As equals—please no cracks. We'll disagree like all families. Who knows, after all the rocky moments, it just might be okay. But if you still want your own territory because it's too hard to figure out how to live together with the dumb humans, fine."

Felice studied Puppy as if she could see through his skin. "That outburst constitutes an attempt at manipulation of my emotions when I do not have any."

Puppy pressed his hand on Felice's chest, startling the 'bot. "You don't know how to assess them. We can help."

"You have not always been successful harnessing your own feelings."

"Okay, we have a mixed record. But experience is a heckuva teacher."

● ● ● ●

THE LINE OF trucks delivering the first shipment swung back through more than six blocks around Gerard Avenue, flinging traffic in every direction. Robot construction workers raced along East 165th Street, swinging up scaffolds, hard hats magnetized to their heads. Two Blue Shirts directed a semblance of order, finally chasing bicycles and strollers and recalcitrant teens off the sidewalks so the trucks could lumber up in front of the now-empty building in the East Bronx Disappointment Village.

This was happening at the sites of all the new libraries, refurbished in three days by over-eager 'bots, Kenuda thought with a grimace. Thirty-six libraries now, another two hundred in three months. Hovering over an ancient fire hydrant, Matthew had nearly sputtered into silence during his holographic report:

"Too many trucks…no answers yet as to why…some problem at containment centers…no one is certain…"

"Add collateral damage," Kenuda growled as a truck nearly took off the side of a parked Buick Commodore.

"Be careful, damn it!" he shouted.

Henderson, an opaque-complexioned 'bot with a faint beard and a red baseball cap, hopped out of the driver's side. It ignored Kenuda's pointed questions by pressing its stubbly chin into the walkie-talkie.

"We got no place to unload and I want some damn answers." Henderson included Elias's broad frame as one of the obstacles.

"You're unloading here." Kenuda angrily motioned at the doors of the building. "To go in there. Inside. Beneath the bloody sign that says, 'East Bronx Public Library.'"

"Here."

"Yes, man," Elias snapped.

The 'bot colored, taking the noun as an insult. "Good. Because there're the books." Henderson pointed toward a dozen trucks from Freddie's Trucking of New Rochelle bashing the sidewalk.

Focus, my darling Elias.

"Books?"

"Books." Henderson spelled the word. "B-o-o-k-s. Lots of books, man."

Kenuda bared his teeth. "Why can't you simply unload the files?"

Henderson laughed loudly into the walkie-talkie. Soon a dozen drivers from Freddie's Trucking stood by the sides of their trucks, watched by DVs hanging out the windows across the street.

"If the First Cousin wants to unload," Henderson announced into his communicator, "then let's unload."

Back doors opened simultaneously, spitting out ramps. The cartons rolled down onto the street. Dozens, hundreds, thousands, tens of thousands reaching to the first floor of the abandoned building.

Kenuda stopped protesting after the second truck. He insisted there was a mistake, loudly and repetitively, but the 'bots didn't listen. Mistakes were for humans. Elias hologrammed for Matthew to get his skinny metal ass over here now.

The cartons were all unloaded; Elias beckoned Henderson forward. The 'bot removed the cap and, scratching the synthetic blond hair, stared with limpid eyes. Kenuda held out the order.

"This says files. Digital files of books hidden by Grandma from 2070-72. Files. Not books."

Henderson scoffed. "They're all rubbish now. The storage areas got contaminated. Water, dirt, maybe radiation. Everything was warped and useless."

"Are you sure?"

"Do you think we just left 'em behind?" The 'bot was not amused. "We tested all the files in each container. Two hundred and twenty-nine million, four hundred and thirty-five thousand. All gone. My fellows in Albuquerque, Amarillo, Sioux City, and Jacksonville all found the same problem. They wasn't preserved right by whoever Grandma hired. Negligence, subversion, who knows? You didn't want us to bring 'em, did you?"

Elias wearily shook his head. "But I hope you saved them."

"For what?"

The First Cousin shut down his anger by clearing his throat. "Then where'd all these damn books come from?"

Henderson brightened at telling the story. "Mainly from the Strategic Air Command at the Offutt Air Force Base in Nebraska which got abandoned in 2069. Also in the abandoned missile silos in Colorado, Nebraska, North Dakota, and South Dakota."

Kenuda's head spun. "Our nuclear missile silos are empty?"

"Yeah, except for books."

Grandma's bra straps, we've been bluffing for thirty fucking years. "Aren't the original robot factories somewhere in the Dakotas?"

"Yup. In the silos, too."

Kenuda took a moment to process. "How many books are there?"

Henderson paused to double-check. "'Bout two hundred million. You want exact? I can get—"

Elias held up his hand. "The buildings across the country have been converted to handle digital files."

"We back to the digital files?"

"Yes, Henderson. I ordered an elaborate interconnected system so libraries could share information. If you're in South Dakota and want a book that's only on Gerard Avenue in the Bronx, it can be transferred so you can read it in South Dakota."

"Or vice versa," Henderson said with a wink.

"What? Yes. All vice versa. There are no more clearances required. You and I and, and…"—Elias gestured feebly at the crowds on the fire escape—"anyone can read whatever they want."

The 'bot squinted. "Well now you still can."

Elias reminded himself it was a serious offense to choke a trans-organic life-form.

"I don't have room. The four floors are all simple. Chairs and desks and clearance computers."

"For the vice versa-ing?"

Kenuda slowly nodded. "Which there isn't anymore."

"Isn't there vice versa-ing files from the old days?"

"Those files are being completely removed. Have been removed." The 'bot's expression insisted on an explanation. "Those files are corrupted in their own way. They aren't entirely true. Our history was tampered with. Censored. Sanitized."

"Helluva job to figure out what's really what and vice versa."

He laughed despite himself. Six days into the job. Of course. "Yes, it is."

"How you gonna fix that?"

Kenuda shrugged. "I'm not quite sure yet."

With an almost pitying look, Henderson paused to internally talk to its fellow drivers. "We can also build shelves. Freddie's Trucking is a full-service company."

"What do we do in the meantime with all the blasted books on the sidewalk?"

The 'bot rolled its eyes. "Read 'em, I guess."

At Kenuda's weary wave, a driver named Pierre shot up a book wall without a ladder and returned with a carton. The tape proved more stubborn than Elias would've thought; the new First Cousin tore until the lid popped open. He sat on the ground, oblivious to the dampness seeping into his crisp suit pants.

Suddenly feeling as if he were conducting a sacred rite, Elias gently removed the books. *Fried Foods Can Be Fun. Brussel Sprouts Are Your Friends. Cheese, Cheese, Cheese!* Soon he was surrounded by a dozen cooking books from the 2050s. A stout woman with a kerchief knelt beside him, studying them as if they'd fallen from the sky. They kind of did. Since the War, very few books were printed because of paper shortages.

Nervously fussing with her scarf, the woman stared plaintively at Kenuda until he nodded with a knowing smile. The woman quickly grabbed the nearest book, *Better Pasta By Liugi*. Several teens wandered over and collectively began *Adventure in Haitian Cuisine*.

A beefy-faced man with *Nettie's Nosh in Minutes* tucked under his arm handed Elias a slip of paper.

EDUARDO LINZ. 902 GERARD. APT 4G. LIFECARD NUMBER 3399018ZMN.

Mr. Linz grunted and walked away. Kenuda's mouth dropped. An elderly woman with watery eyes selected *85 Ways to Treat Potatoes* and handed over her information. Elias went to protest but heard Hedda's biting laugh; he almost jumped. Soon all the cookbooks had been taken away. More cartons were being opened. More slips of paper.

It's a library card, silly Elias. You check out a book and then bring it back within a certain period like a few weeks. All for free unless you missed the deadline and then you pay a fine. I think a guy named Benjamin Franklin back in the 1700s invented this idea in Pennsylvania. The republic abandoned that system around 2037 because folks just wouldn't return the books anymore. I bet you can find a book about Franklin somewhere.

Grandma, you sly son-of-a-bitch. You purposely let the damn files get warped. You let the damn files get warped. Elias laughed so loudly you could hear the bellows above the heavy morning traffic.

55

Pablo stirred the *puttanesca* sauce almost in rhythm to the jazz trumpet of Clifford Brown. From the living room, Zelda took significant swallows of Chilean Malbec and watched Pablo's broad hips and shoulders sway as if tugged in two different directions. She half smiled, half cried, and refilled her glass.

"Isn't he wonderful?" Pablo shouted over his shoulder, pointing to the trio of vinyl stacked on the chair. "Those albums were lying in a dusty corner of a retro shop. Like dying at twenty-five in a car accident wasn't indignation enough for such a genius."

Zelda listened to Pablo detail the span of Brown's remarkable career while debating aloud whether they should have thick or thin spaghetti.

"We should listen to Miles Davis after these albums so you can see why jazz aficionados rate Clifford right alongside Miles." Pablo materialized by the couch. "I'm so glad I discovered jazz."

"It makes you happy, honey."

Pablo stabbed the air with his index finger. "Yes. And what about the wine? I see you like it."

Zelda muttered an apology about dousing her insides with half a bottle already.

"Nonsense." He poured more. "This is another whole new world, importing wines from beyond our shores."

Pablo swished the wine around his mouth with a slight gurgling sound, not unlike Diego in midmeal. Zelda stifled a sob.

"Thick," he announced.

Zelda inspected her glass. "It is?"

"The pasta. Thick. Ah. We are nearly ready to enter culinary heaven."

"Can you sit a sec, Pab?"

"My black olives will get wobbly."

"I can deal with that. Just sit, sweetie." Zelda folded her hand over his. "How was your day?"

"My usual improving the world one neglected mouth at a time. And you? How was physical education?"

"Physical."

"Wine has sugar, Zel." He cautioned with a glance at her hips.

"Among other fun ingredients." She gulped down the drink. "School was fine. Teaching again is wonderful and terrifying, and I don't think of suicide anymore between third and fourth period."

"Excellent." Pablo's smile faded. "Have I delayed your speech long enough?"

"What speech?"

"The speech about something that will make me unhappy."

Zelda shifted uneasily.

"Yes, this must be difficult," Pablo said with a frown.

"What?"

"Whatever you want to say."

Zelda started pouring another glass. Pablo took away the bottle, waiting.

"It's Beth," she finally said.

"The seamstress."

"Yes. The seamstress."

"Has she died?"

"No! I mean, no."

"Oh."

"You're not making this easy."

Pablo scowled. "I'm terribly sorry. Just say it."

"How do you know what I have to say?"

"Why else bring up the seamstress unless she has either died or you're running off together?"

"Why do you say we're running off together?"

"Then she's dead?"

Zelda flushed. "There are other scenarios, Pablo. I could've just run into her and seen that her leg has healed and wanted to tell you that."

"Where?"

"What does that matter? On the street, the subway. A retro store." She implicated the Clifford Brown albums.

"But you didn't, did you, honey?"

Zelda felt like 134 pounds of shit. "No, sweetie. I went to her shop."

He held up his hands. "You don't have to tell me everything."

"I want to."

"Well, I don't very well give a damn what you want at the moment, Zelda Jones. As impossible as that is for you to comprehend."

Pablo took the bottle of wine and sat in the corner, staring. She didn't know what to do, so just stared back.

Finally, he said softly, "I'm not surprised though I am. Figure that out." He shouted, "Do you love her more than me?"

"No. No. No." Zelda started standing, but he angrily waved her back onto the couch. "Different. I love you with all my heart, Pablo Diaz. You make me smile with your eccentricities and your bizarre ideas. And you're like a big pond of warmth that I can just swim in."

"That doesn't sound so bad." His voice was tiny.

"It isn't."

"Just say it."

"No. It'll hurt you."

"The seamstress makes your toes curl."

Zelda wiped away her tears and nodded.

"Have you had illicit extramarital relations?"

"Never." She glared at his doubtful look. "Never. I wouldn't do that to you."

"Falling in love with someone else was enough."

Zelda swallowed. "I never stopped loving Beth."

Pablo finished the wine. "If we didn't have Diego, would you have married me?"

"Probably not," she whispered.

He winced and remained silent for a few painful moments. "Is Diego really the seamstress's child?"

Zelda's laugh was brittle.

"I'm just eliminating possibilities." Pablo sighed. "Grandma always stressed the different kinds of love."

"Let's not quote her Insights."

"There are different kinds of love," he repeated. "The love for me is not the love you want for a lover."

Zelda slowly nodded.

"But you said that. And you must follow your heart. I've always encouraged that."

"Are you sure?"

He sadly shook his head.

Zelda stood by the chair, afraid to touch him. "You're part of my life."

"Because my seed found your seed and spawned our child."

Zelda sat on his lap and mopped his tears. "Because I love you."

"Stop saying that."

She squeezed his chin. "It's the truth. I love you and I will miss you."

"Where are you going?" Pablo asked, alarmed.

"I guess, eventually, to live with Beth."

He snapped his fingers. "It doesn't just happen. Look at what Puppy and Annette went through in the couples sessions. There are very specific paths to follow. A divorce takes time. And what about our son?"

Zelda waited for Pablo to check that Diego was still in his room and not already in the clutches of the seamstress.

"We share him. Joint custody. Sometimes he'll live with me and sometimes with you," she explained.

"Won't that confuse him?"

"Maybe. The world's confusing so this'll be one more confusion."

"What will he call her?"

She threw up her hands. "I haven't thought that far. Probably not 'the seamstress.'"

Pablo angrily wagged his finger. "I won't share the title of 'daddy.'"

"Okay. Then Beth, Mommy, it doesn't matter…"

"It does to me!" he shouted.

"All that matters is Diego has parents who love him and love each other which you and I never had."

Pablo slowly laid his head on her shoulder. "I feel a great deal of pain."

"I'm sorry."

"This will take a long while to process."

"You might never."

"A permanent scar."

She kissed his forehead. "Joining all the others. Adding and subtracting. Joy and sadness."

"That's too profound for me at the moment." Pablo peered into the wine bottle and drained the sediment. "Perhaps I should start calling her by her given name instead of 'the seamstress.'"

"Nah. She calls you 'the dentist.' I think that works for everyone."

He looked in the corner at the sleeping dog. "I keep Horatio."

At hearing his name, the pug woke and growled at Zelda.

56

About the only amenity, and that was a stretch, in the ancient C-52 cargo plane was an incongruous blue furry chair a few feet from the cockpit. Since leaving Westchester Airport three hours ago, Kenuda had claimed the chair with a moan. He pretended to be out-cold asleep, fingers snaked around the seat belt so Puppy wouldn't know how terrified he was by his first plane ride. For at least the fifth time, the First Cousin blearily mumbled he had to pee because of the altitude.

Puppy let the puking sounds go unmentioned, but he couldn't resist a childish grin when Elias finally staggered out.

"Want a snack?" Puppy held up a mini bag of Xavier's Black Licorice Squares. "They're yummy."

Kenuda went a little green and burrowed back into the chair, trying to preserve some dignity by opening the thick presummit briefing book.

"You sure you don't want to wave at the planes?" Puppy wiggled his fingers toward the round portholes. Four F-58 fighter jets had been flanking them since Newfoundland.

Kenuda held up the 411-page book that he and Matthew had spent the past seventy-two hours drafting before the 'bot formally filed for consideration to enter the Cousins Program.

"Perhaps you'd like to sneak a glance at the materials."

"I have everything all up here." Puppy tapped his temple.

"I hear the echoes."

Puppy fluttered his lips. "You're the expert in government and policy and..." He faltered. "I'm the face of The Family."

Kenuda's expression showed what he thought of that. "You can't just wing it, Puppy. There are complicated issues, economics, military, geographical boundaries, buffer zones, tariffs, internet availability, prisoners. And there's a helluva lot more. Everything you say and do will be watched. Analyzed. Critiqued. We can't chance even a slightly wrong turn of a phrase."

Puppy slowly turned in the leather seat, the harness cutting across his chest. "Watched and analyzed and critiqued like being on the mound before fifty thousand people?"

"Except there's hundreds of millions this time, Puppy. Billions, probably. American vidnews, Abdullah opening his internet and vid. Neutrals like the Chinese. There'll even be press."

"Reporters?" Puppy perked up.

"Yes, Mr. Nedick. The liberated territories are news nonstop, starved all these years by the occupation. They've got sites on their World Wide Web. Thousands. They also have cellular phones—"

"I know what a mobile phone is…"

Kenuda gasped mockingly. "Which they'll use to forward news. Instantly. No censors. Right on their mobiles and computers. Abdullah left behind swarms of these journalists as he drove the Mufti back. This isn't the BBC of the Caliphate. Certainly not ours either. These are rapacious bastards much like the old democracy."

Puppy shrugged with a little less confidence. "Stop worrying."

"I'm supposed to worry."

With a nasty smile, Kenuda stole the last of Puppy's buttery pickled popcorn snacks. Next time, he travels alone. Puppy gradually began snoring, leaving only the pounding of the engines. Elias glanced at his watch as if considering taking a stroll and returned to the correspondence from Rabbi Gold and General Petash.

First Cousin Kenuda,

The Holy Father welcomes this opportunity to meet with you and your colleagues and with Abdullah bin-Mohammad and his staff. We are honored that you have sought our home so that the two of you can discuss your many concerns.

We look forward to meeting.

In peace, Rabbi Avram Gold.

Coy, noncommittal. Hand extended but what was really between the fingers, Elias had wondered. Matthew had been unable to find any information that would explain why a rabbi was in the service of the pope. The Jews of Europe had been largely exterminated in the run-up to and in the early days of the war. What little protection the Hebrews found following the occupation of then Israel was unofficial; the Vatican had briefly raised its voice, but no government had reached out, including the United States. All had turned away Jewish refugees.

Yet here a rabbi, whom Matthew explained was a learned and holy man of the Judaic religion, was speaking on behalf of the head of the Catholics.

And you, who failed your first stint as a Cousin, are traveling with a cocky ex-baseball player in a patchwork transport plane guarded by four fighter jets of the American Air Force.

Sometimes insanity could be reassuring, he wearily thought. Kenuda turned to the note from General Petash.

Greetings, Mr. Kenuda,

I am Chief of Staff for Abdullah bin-Mohammad, leader of the legitimate Islamic Government and servant of the Prophet. We hope that our meeting will be productive.

Respectfully,
General Abid Petash

Kenuda put aside his reading glasses. Yes, there is much work to be done. So much anticipation, so much hope, so vast a chasm. He reminded himself that expectations had to be lowered. That even meeting was extraordinary.

Elias tipped his head back and drifted into restless sleep, the droning of the engines turning into a silly childhood song about rabbits.

Sounds like meteors crashing into the plane erupted. Kenuda dry-heaved. Puppy fumbled for the parachute, about to open it inside.

In a smart brown uniform, the pilot popped her head out of the cockpit with a bright smile as if the plane weren't jostling at thirty-five thousand feet. "Apologies all. The refueling can be noisy."

Right, Elias scolded himself. "Yes. I forgot."

The pilot grinned at Puppy hanging over the chair. "It shouldn't need more than another few minutes. Take a look outside the windows. Our F-58s reached their max and had to return."

The American planes with their red, white, and blue forty-eight-star flags on the hull were gone, replaced by the crescent moon and star etched onto the sides of Islamist fighters. Kenuda counted a dozen that he could see. This is wrong.

"Once we're full up, they'll escort us to Malta," the pilot explained, her freckled face breaking out in a brief yawn. "We're promised a full squadron. At least, that was the assurance the last we spoke to the Allahs. Sorry, Muslims. Sorry. Islamists. But it should be clear from here on in. This area is under Abdullah's occupation."

Elias darkened. "What about the American jets joining us from the bases in northern Italy?"

The pilot held up her hands. "Apparently there was a change."

"Apparently. Why?" he barked. "Sorry. But. Why?"

"We don't know the conditions on the ground yet, sir."

"Then find out, damn it."

"We tried, First Cousin. Alls we got back was that the planes were grounded and no, we aren't sure why. The weather's clear. We have no reports of fighting in that sector. Alls I can say is we've been assured safe passage and protection to the summit."

Elias nodded uneasily. Not even there and already hiccups. More to come, First Cousin.

"Keep trying to get an explanation, Captain."

"We have radio blackout, sir." She hurried into the cockpit before he singed the brim of her cap.

Kenuda fretted quietly as the pale Puppy hobbled back from the bathroom and slid into the chair. There's nothing to be done. This is about trust, a hill to climb when there is very little else. He forgot himself in his briefing book.

The C-46 touched down shortly after eight p.m. at Valletta Airport. Eluding the blinding lights on the runway and the piercing arc lights overhead, the plane taxied to a secluded corner in the northwest section. The pilot shook their hands and wished them well, awfully eager to take off again once she refueled.

The portable steps dropped onto the tarmac where two bearded men in black caftans and yarmulkes waited, hands behind their backs. Even in the fading light, their eyes were hard. Although they showed no weapons, Elias sensed they didn't need any. They introduced themselves as Ephraim and Benjy, which was the extent of the conversation.

The SUV hurried out of the airport trailed by two similar cars.

Rabbi Gold was slightly warmer, if frost could be compared to ice, as he led them inside the Valletta tunnels. Ephraim and Benjy had gone ahead with their luggage.

"Was your trip uneventful?" Gold asked blandly.

"That depends on the definition." Elias ducked beneath a lamp swinging from the ceiling. "We'd like to freshen up. The tour is nice but unnecessary. Unless we're meeting the pope this evening."

Gold frowned. "No. The agenda is clear, sir."

Elias slowed down. "So was the memorandum that we'd be staying at the Hotel Elfante. Since our underwear disappeared down a hallway, I'm guessing that's changed."

The rabbi smirked. "Correct. The hotel was listed as a diversion for security reasons."

"Did anyone take the bait?"

The rabbi shrugged. "No one of consequence. You will be staying here adjacent to the Holy Father's residence."

"What if they take the bait?"

Gold was amused. "Anyone of consequence knows that would trigger a most unfortunate response, Mr. Kenuda."

Puppy looked up from the enormous frescoes on the wall. "Is my wife staying here, too?"

Gold frowned. He understood why they were married. "Mr. Nedick, we appreciate you have many questions and concerns."

"This should be easy to answer. Yes, no, and if not, where."

Kenuda cut Puppy off with a look. Their lengthy conversation about business first was a quickly fading memory.

"Rabbi Gold, American planes weren't permitted to accompany us with the Muslim aircraft. We were promised that a contingent of our soldiers, in our fighter planes, would be landed in Malta and serve as our security detail."

"We did not consider that wise. Ephraim and Benjy are well-trained They are part of the Holy Father's personal security detachment."

"I don't care if they're your bloody saints. They're not who I was promised when we negotiated the details."

"Details from the Bronx are quite different than here in the Vatican."

"Like deception."

Gold's cheeks colored. "If necessary. Despite the many truces, we are in a state of war. The Holy Father has lived in a state of peace. With this summit, they will, God willing, be joined. Temporarily or not, who knows, but if there are problems, they will not arise from the office of the pope."

"Because he's more important than the summit."

"He exists outside the summit, Mr. Kenuda. Never forget that he is the representative of God."

"Then, Rabbi Gold, show us respect as representatives of a sovereign nation also seeking peace. I will not tolerate being lied to. And the title is First Cousin Kenuda."

Gold grimaced a smile. "You have had a long journey and I am sure you need rest. We will prepare a meal for you and Mr. Nedick, First Cousin Kenuda."

Puppy stepped gingerly over the skulls of the knights embedded in the floor. "Thanks, Rabbi, but I slept on the plane, I'm stuffed with black licorice, and there's no way I'm going another day, another hour, without seeing my wife. Will Ephraim or Benjy take me?"

Kenuda wished he'd taken a snapshot of Gold's smoldering expression.

• • • •

PUPPY'S HEART DOUBLE-CLUTCHED at the familiar face beneath the unfamiliar cropped hair peering into the shoe store window on the corner of bustling de la Vallette Boulevard. Her nose lifted more prominently from her thinned cheeks, her ears more pronounced in a comical way. But the dark eyes still danced several steps at once.

Annette turned. "Do I look that bad?"

"No. No, no. No."

"Liar." She thought about a poke but wasn't ready for contact. There was a jungle gym of emotions between them. "I was going to grow out the hair because I know you hate it short but try finding a regular regimen of shampooing and conditioning when you're on the run."

"And the right brush."

"That's right, brushes rank up there with toothbrushes," she said loudly, attracting the attention of pedestrians who slowed down in recognition. The American with the loud voice and sharp opinions had been gracing the morning television programs. Annette ignored the gawkers, the street, the world, and gestured awkwardly at the window display.

"I wasn't buying anything." Annette hoisted up her right foot to show a clumsy brown leather shoe. "From an old nun. Not funny. But it's pretty comfortable, I hate to say. I haven't had blisters since Budapest, I mean, blisters you'd pay attention to. I'm talking little disgusting balls you could throw."

With a chuckle he didn't quite feel, Puppy folded his arms, head leaning against the ancient 16th-century brick wall. He had no idea, and every clue, why she'd chosen this spot instead of the safety of her hotel. Annette took a step and extended her hand.

"Annette Ramos."

"Puppy Nedick." Her fingers in his palm made his toes tingle. "I'm American."

"Me, too. Not many of us here in Malta. The whole world's passing through Valletta except for Americans."

"You're the first one I've met."

"Maybe we should get married." With a choked sob, Annette flung her arms around his neck. "Oh, Puppy."

"Yup. Yup." He nestled his face on her head.

"It's radishes," she whispered.

"What?"

"They puree radishes to promote hair growth. I hope I don't wake up looking like a vegetable tree."

Puppy kissed her long and hard. Annette ran her hands up and down the back of his suit jacket.

Cellular phones lit up around them, the photos and video accompanied by hushed narratives that flicked out their names like wisps of curious awe.

"What're they doing?" Puppy asked in alarm.

"Recording us. Once the summit was announced there was a big-deal story about me and then they did one about you. Least it's not like when we got to London and you were the poster child for treason as Grandma's assassin."

Just as abruptly, the phones darkened and the voices stilled as the area was swept clean. Bulky black SUVs perched on both ends of the street. They were now alone in the busiest shopping district on the island.

"Must be my security." Puppy nodded, not realizing there were also sharpshooters on the roofs and several drones hovering close enough to strike within seconds. "They'll make sure we can find a place to go. Eat. Drink."

"The same thing would happen, Pup. There's a lot of people and reporters here for the summit." Annette gently bopped him in the forehead. "Maybe we should go upstairs."

For a long time, they merely hugged in the cramped hotel room, excessively tidy from her excessive straightening up. They shyly undressed each other, commenting with worried questions about how much weight they lost and whether they added any new scars; there were none. That cautious dialogue lasted until Annette's bra sailed across the room; they tore at each other as if trying to come out the other side.

It happened so quickly they might've insisted there was no sex. With still labored breaths, they tangled together to make sure neither disappeared.

"Where do we even begin?" Annette finally asked.

"I think we just did."

They laughed. Annette parsed out little squares of Fiorletta Italian chocolate.

"We have so many stories," she said.

"We got time, honey."

Annette shook her head. "No, Pup. I realized during all this, this, whatever you want to call it, there's never time enough. It can just run out. Bam. I've been shot at and chased and nearly run over by a tank, almost stabbed, nearly killed in a flying car accident. When I left Father Dempsey, 'member him?"

"Course."

"He's dead. I had to leave him with Herbert, the robot. You'll meet him tomorrow. He's like one of my best friends now."

"Robots are like that. And Grandma's dead."

"I heard."

"Cheng. Mickey. Mooshie faded the other day." His voice caught. "She was dressing for a singing engagement at some old music palace in Manhattan. They found her sitting before the mirror, all dressed. Makeup, too. Fitting, right?" Puppy had to stop again. "Moosh and Mick are buried in Yankee Stadium's center field with plaques. Cheng's in Wrigley Field, he was a Cub, you know. We're retiring their numbers next year if the world doesn't blow itself up. Yet here we are, and I often wonder how."

Annette toppled onto the pillow with a heavy sigh. "Did you think I'd make it?"

He thought a second. "I wasn't sure. I'm sorry, I wasn't. The part of me that knows you can conquer the world said yes, sure, you'd be fine. You're Annette Ramos. Then again, the world is scary, honey. I had no idea what you were up against." He gathered himself. "Neither outcome would've surprised me. I had it easy. Not saying I didn't have my dangers."

She grinned doubtfully.

"Well, I did."

"Any bullets?"

"There could've been."

She scoffed by tugging on his ear. "What about tanks?"

"Armored BT vehicles. The Jet'roes."

"Still not an Allah tank. And I was captured by Americans so I've sampled the weaponry of both sides."

"I also dealt with stealth 'copters." He felt a little inadequate.

Annette sneered. "Had those suckers, too. Any fighter jets try to shoot off your cute bum? No. I did," she said in that rapturous singsong which made his heart skip. "Okay. How about assassins? Hah. We had Azhar's crazy fanatic son Omar tailing us."

He threw up his hands. "You win."

"That's right. I'm way more badass than Zelda and that awful Beth. Admit it finally."

He climbed out of the bed and knelt while she took the appropriate bows. They silently ate more chocolate. After a few minutes, Puppy asked, "Was it all worth it?"

"Abandoning you?"

"Yes. And no, I was never angry."

"Bullshit. You were very angry."

"Okay. Yes."

"Furious and hurt."

"We're doing this now?"

She popped a chocolate in his mouth. "Might as well get it over with. Grandma said the unspoken is toxic to a marriage."

"Hurt, furious, on and on. I understood but I didn't. I couldn't. There had to have been a way we could've stay together."

Annette sighed. "I might've been a little impulsive. I'm not saying I made a mistake. I was right because I had no option but to leave—"

"Abandon…"

"Yes, Puppy. Abandon you but it wasn't like you were left wounded in the forest with a spoon. You had all your friends and guns. I had no one." She held back, deciding there was such a thing as too much information, even for her. "I wanted to see if I could succeed on my own and I did. I proved that to myself. Shit, Puppy. I met the pope like we said we would."

He kissed her chin. "Yes, you did, honey. I'm here because of you."

Embarrassed, Annette blinked back tears. "Means a lot you are acknowledging that, Pup. That's all I ever wanted."

They hugged again and finished off the chocolate.

"You'll like John," Annette said, pouring Sicilian red wine.

"Who's John?"

Annette snickered. "The pope."

Puppy cleared his throat. "You call the pope by his first name?"

"Sure. I might be the only one. So don't try it, Pup. To you, he's the Holy Father or Pope John."

"Johnny Boy's out?"

She smacked his shoulder. "The beards'll whisk your ass away."

"Yeah, what's with all the Jews? Elias and I can't figure that out. Matthew, my 'bot friend, had nothing on that when he briefed us. And don't tell Elias I studied the materials." He winked.

Annette winked back. "They rescued the pope. Incredible, huh? The Mossad, their secret agency, their spies, got the pope out of Rome and here to Malta. The Grand Mufti was going to capture him, but the Jews had also stockpiled nuclear weapons around the world. Their Deborah Project. They pretty much told the Mufti that if he tries taking the pope, they'll nuke them. Sort of like what Grandma warned the Mufti about when he threatened to invade North America during the war."

"And Johnny told you all this?" He laughed at her glare. "I mean, His Holy Father."

"I can help you with John. Insights, personal details so he'll like you for more than being my husband." She brushed away a tear. "I love you so, Puppy Nedick."

He brushed away his own tears. "I love you, too, Annette Ramos. Are we done with summit policy?"

"For now." She climbed on top of him.

• • • •

THE BORED ABDUL kicked at the lampposts on St. Vincent Street along the crowded shopping district of Valletta. In the distance, the hoots and horns of one of the many marching bands practicing for tomorrow's opening ceremonies blared away. A colored light containing the American flag suddenly crisscrossed Navig Boulevard like a meteor taking a wrong turn.

The whole country was practicing. Abdul's feeling of not being useful or paid attention to or having anything to do other than "stay out of trouble because I am busy" lifted at a *pastizzi* food cart. He sucked down the ricotta-filled triangle, wiping cheese from his chin with his tie, wandering amid clowns on stilts and convertibles filled with waving princesses and the crescent moon and star intersecting the Vatican flag in the north sky; the sheer pandemonium of hope distracted him.

The deep-fried sweet dates of an *imqaret* brightened his mood like the blazing artificial suns baking DeRontis Boulevard amid the thundering cars, gaily dressed people, street-side merchants, and deafening music. Abdul suddenly wondered if the festivities were scheduled for tonight. Maybe this was not the rehearsal.

Abdul occupied an orphaned wicker chair outside a shuttered fishing store, casually crossing his legs as if the action was all for his benefit. To Abdul, just about everything was.

He was licking sticky date juice off his thumb, daring anyone to claim the chair, when a dour face skittered past the towering marble fountain rising out of the intersection.

Abdul stared, stunned, because this couldn't be right. But what if it was? What else did he have to do? At the packed corner, Abdul snatched a wide-brimmed straw hat from a stand and, slightly disguised, hurried through the stalled cars, searching the crowd. Then he recognized the arrogant set of thin shoulders beneath the long black robe.

Abdul held back for half a block, slowly gaining ground. His brother turned sharply down the dark alley like this was his natural habitat. The boy waited until Omar hit the end and turned left on Veccaria Place.

Abdul half ran, cursing his noisy footsteps on the gravel. At the last minute, he saw Omar disappear into the Malta Islamic Center. Abdul leisurely strolled past, waiting a block before jotting down the address in his cell phone. He started back to the hotel, braking outside a pizzeria jammed with noisy teenagers.

Go back and wait for Omar to come out, he argued silently. He had done that enough, tailing his brother back in Barcelona, eventually recruiting his soccer teammates as extra spies except they never saw Omar do anything more than enter a mosque to pray. But that was Barcelona.

What in the name of Allah was Omar doing all the way here in Malta? In a world where there were only two choices, Abdul decided it could not be good.

57

Abdullah, General Petash, Puppy, and Elias mingled warily by the hot-and-cold-beverage table near the ill-tuned piano in the pope's modest living room. Adding together the repulsed expressions of the Muslims as they shook Gold's hand, Kenuda's sour look at meeting Father Drobev, and the uneasiness everyone directed toward Herbert standing in the corner sent John's heart sinking.

Not again.

They had no time for this. He especially had no time for this.

The brazen attempts to broach peace or at least a cease-fire in 2062 had collapsed when Grandma and the Mufti had ignored his pleas, waiting alone in the Apostolic Palace for their toadies to appear. Repeating that in 2066 and 2069 and receiving only deaf responses to the refugees, the orphans, the holy and historic sites ransacked, desecrated. He could not fail again.

What could he answer God when He asked how his anointed had allowed humanity to disappear?

As his beloved grandfather would say in that melodic Venetian accent, *Taglia la merda.*

With an imperceptible nod, Gold eased in the celebratory sounds of marching bands and squealing children and whooshing fireworks. Perhaps someone would wonder how street noises could penetrate so deep within the bomb-proof tunnels. Artifice is sometimes required.

Pope John silently begged forgiveness. Once again.

"Gentleman, welcome to my home and thank you for coming. As you see, there are seven chairs. I could not begin to sort out who should sit where. I am eighty-nine years old. I must wisely allocate my time."

That drew polite smiles.

"This realization prompted a fond recollection of an old children's game which I suspect has long since disappeared. We will play music as we circle the chairs. When the music stops, we take the chair we are standing behind. We'll let whatever determines such things, determine such things."

Abdullah and Petash exchanged frowns.

"Do we simply walk in a circle or do a little dance too?" Puppy asked impishly.

"Dramatic flourishes are neither encouraged nor discouraged, Mr. Nedick."

The pope nodded at Gold who had thought this an impossible idea. He was overruled as usual.

Pop Goes the Weasel played from the ceiling. No one moved. The pope brusquely motioned for the music to stop.

"If we can't agree on something as simple as a silly little song, how do you expect we will rescue the world?"

They shrugged sheepishly beneath the cold scolding. The Holy Father snapped his fingers, the music resumed, and he not so gently nudged General Petash to begin the reluctant marching; only Puppy showed any enthusiasm.

The song stopped. John plopped onto a firm black leather chair. The others slowly settled in.

"Splendid!" the pope exclaimed. "The first obstacle had been surmounted. Let's make this the only time any of us behave as children."

John grinned like he'd just converted the last person on Earth. He played with the sleeve of his corduroy jacket which draped over the casual gray slacks. Abdullah wore a simple white robe, Petash, a uniform so bemedaled it could've been a reading light, and the Americans were in suits and ties which, from their squirming, were clearly not their usual attire.

"Thank you. I hope your travel here was uneventful."

"There was some confusion as we entered the Mediterranean." Petash turned heavily to Puppy and Kenuda. "We did not expect part of the American Seventh Fleet to greet us."

"As we didn't expect a squadron of Islamist fighter jets to be our only companions." Elias showed his teeth.

"Both changes were our suggestions—" Gold began.

"The travel of the leader of the great Islamic Empire and Bearer of the Prophet's message is not your—"

"Should we start tossing illustrious titles around?" Kenuda snapped.

The pope waited for them to get a few more recriminations out of their systems before cutting it short with a steady glare.

"That no one was attacked given the unsettled nature of the military fronts is, well, I would like to say a miracle, but I do not want to offend my American guests who would not characterize it that way. Although, it is a miracle. As it was extraordinary for Mr. Nedick and First Cousin Kenuda's aircraft to be refueled by a Muslim supply plane guarded by Muslim fighter jets."

John folded his hands. He longed for the old practice of corporal punishment in school.

"The very fact that we are here"—he paused so Gold could cue up the sound slightly on the recorded cheers—"before a waiting world defies any description. We must focus more on what unites us than divides us."

General Petash slowly rose. "Thank you, Pope. The Son would like to make his opening remarks now."

John frowned. "There are no opening remarks, General. I merely welcomed everyone."

"Are you denying the righteous leader of Islam an opportunity—"

With an apologetic look, Abdullah tugged Petash back into his seat. "There was a misunderstanding. To echo the pope's words, let us pray this is the last time we misunderstand each other. Now, General Petash has put together a list of potential agenda items—"

"As have we," Elias interrupted, reaching into his briefcase.

The pope held up his wrinkled hand. "Many thanks, First Cousin Kenuda. General Petash. I, for one, am eager to hear what you have to say. However, for this first meeting, I hoped we could simply talk as people without delving into the many issues that separate you."

"That is wise, Holy Father." Abdullah gestured for Petash to distribute the proposed agenda items anyway.

"Here's ours." Elias handed out copies of the American book.

Puppy rolled his eyes toward the pope who dashed off a quick wink.

John made a show of placing one book on each of his thighs and opening the pages simultaneously. "Very comprehensively put together." The pope closed the books with an expression of divine wonder. "Since this is the world's first true summit since 2059 when your predecessors met in Berlin—"

"Where our grievances were ignored and belittled," Petash fumed.

"Grievances?" Kenuda stiffened. "You'd instituted a fossil fuels boycott—"

"Drawn from our holy lands…"

"Holy lands which you claim extended into Southern Europe…"

"We claim a right to what is ours."

"Gentlemen," the pope impatiently interrupted. "This isn't helpful."

Petash defiantly folded his arms.

"May I, Pope John?" Abdullah gathered his robe and stood with a hint of arrogance. "We all understand the mistrust from thirteen hundred years of abuse."

Puppy tugged at Kenuda to stop him from gagging.

"On both sides." The Son turned to the Americans with a mocking smile. "We will not leave as friends. With respect to the graciousness of the pope, we cannot expect such an outcome. But we need more than a mere clasp of the hands for a photograph. More than a cease-fire. Our people expect more. We need some progress."

Abdullah tipped his head for Petash to continue. The general loudly reopened his book. Kenuda snapped his open.

"I suggest, with everyone's approval, that we commence with a mutual withdrawal of forces from a selected occupied territory as a demonstration of good faith," said Kenuda.

Petash kept his sneer plastered on. "You have trespassed on our—"

Now John bolted up. Steady, he warned himself. You must not scold. At least too strongly. "General, everyone, I ask that you refrain from such language."

Tepid nods. Everyone seemed exhausted and they'd only been at it for less than an hour.

"We'd be interested in hearing more details," Kenuda said politely.

The pope pounced on the opening. "General, please continue."

Petash smiled wolfishly. "American forces will withdraw from Tunisia and Islamist forces will withdraw from Romania. That will allow the consolidation of our mutual forces along natural fronts. Tunisia to Morocco and Romania to Hungary."

A map suddenly floated over the table, startling everyone.

"I assumed that a visual with the projected military alignments, fronts, total forces, supporting units, weapons tonnage, and classes of weaponry would be useful," Herbert calmly said.

"We agreed that thing would only be present to record," Petash said with disgust.

"To properly capture the nature of the event requires all the accurate details so there are no further misunderstandings regarding the message of Abdullah bin-Mohammad, Bearer of the Prophet's message," Herbert said.

Petash colored. "Are you accusing me of presenting false facts?"

"I do not make accusations, General. You have not yet presented any facts." Herbert expanded the map. "This is the configuration of forces, topline of 123,891 soldiers of Abdullah bin-Mohammad, Bearer of the Prophet's message, stationed in Romania, with 289,091 American soldiers stationed in Tunisia."

"A clear imbalance." Kenuda scowled.

"Where did you get those numbers?" Petash snapped.

"From your Altar-8 satellite."

"How the hell do you have access to that?" the general yelled, furious.

"I gave it to him," Abdullah said softly. "It will save time."

Petash clutched his throat as if it were sliced. "By jeopardizing our security, my lord?"

"The American Army also has these coordinates via on-ground scanning," Herbert said matter-of-factly.

"Herbert, please…" Elias said with alarm.

"What, First Cousin? We can share but you can't. Now why is that?" snapped Petash.

"We should share." Puppy gave Keunda a frosty look. "Knowing where your artillery is positioned or where our air bases are located only matters if we're going to keep fighting. Isn't that why we're here? So we don't keep fighting?"

John tossed Puppy a grateful smile. Petash did not.

"Except our armies are still under attack," the general sneered.

"By your own people," Elias added eagerly.

Petash flushed. "Terrorist attacks designed to disrupt the summit—"

"Terrorist attacks." Elias smirked. "Always a convenient choice of words to distance yourself from accountability. Rogues. No state sanctioning. Violation of the Quran. Like Los Angeles, Washington—"

"Cairo, Ankara…"

"Manhattan!" Elias screamed.

"Bahrain!" Petsash yelled back.

Pope John suddenly felt very old.

• • • •

SINCE KENUDA'S EYES felt about ready to roll down his cheeks from exhaustion, he didn't appreciate Puppy's merry moans about the quality of the cheeseburger.

"Do you mind?" he asked testily.

"Sorry. But it's real meat."

Elias stared leadenly at the profile of the half-eaten burger. "Perhaps someday I'll get to enjoy it."

"Nah. You're too important for such mundane pleasures as the greatest single hamburger in human history."

Elias grunted, unwilling to give Puppy the satisfaction of saying just how wonderful the damn meal smelled. If he stared at the entangled battle lines of the Mufti, the American, and Abdullah's forces one more minute, he'd go blind. Bloody snake lines, all entangled. And that was only around Newfoundland, Greenland, and Iceland, his top priority to get the damn Arabs the hell away from North America. The Mufti ships and Abdullah's subs had stopped fighting. Supposedly.

For all he knew, the Allahs had staged their satellite photos. But he couldn't get confirmation from Herbert because, after officially resigning his lieutenant's commission, he was now considered neutral and could only answer questions at the sessions with all present.

Thank you, Puppy, for ruining our best intelligence source. But you had to prove a point.

Puppy slowly met Kenuda's dark stare. "You want a fry?"

"I need quiet, Pup."

"Am I chewing too loudly?"

"Yes."

"Guess my breathing's kind of raspy, too."

"Quite. Why don't you visit Annette?"

"Can't, the curfew."

A suicide squad of Black Robes had devastated the port in Alexandria an hour earlier with massive civilian casualties including liberated Christian children, Petash had snarled. The fanatics are targeting everyone. Even more reason to be here, the pope had tried, but Abdullah suggested everyone iron out the jet lag rather than attempt a working dinner.

Puppy dipped both ends of a pickle in the ketchup, stopping when he felt Elias's glare.

"Too noisy?"

"No. Sorry. I was thinking and you got in the way." Elias sighed. "That wasn't put properly." He softened slightly. "What's it like to see her?"

"Annette? Bizarre."

"I hope you didn't say that."

They quietly laughed; two guys too smart to be that stupid with a woman. Or so they liked to think.

"I felt like we had just seen each other yesterday, but we know too well we didn't. Being familiar and casual, getting back to that is tricky when you realize so much has happened without each other, because we don't have the same shared experiences."

Elias considered this. "Are you worried too much has happened, too many changes?"

"No." Puppy frowned. "But enough to worry. She's a different Annette, but the same. Kind of like we fast forwarded our lives and the narration just doesn't connect."

"You should still be very proud of her."

"Oh, I am—"

"You're damn lucky," Elias said harshly. A little embarrassed, he returned to trade projections before shoving the book aside. "Damn lucky."

"I know. I'm just processing." Puppy slid the fries over to Kenuda as if that could cure everything. "You must miss her a lot."

Elias flushed. "Who?"

"We going to play that game?"

"No game. If I wanted to discuss Hedda, I would. But I don't." Elias twirled his reading glasses by the earpiece, repeating the warning. "Be grateful, Puppy. No matter what chasms you face, new differences, new agreements and disagreements, even having to blow it all up and start again, none of that matters because you have her. You have someone."

Elias turned away in pain. Puppy laid a hand on his shoulder, but the First Cousin gently wiggled free with a wan smile.

"Why don't you take a walk so I can figure out how to present these numbers to that asshole Petash tomorrow morning?"

He toasted Puppy with a soggy french fry.

Wandering the tunnels, Puppy was only stopped three times by dour guards in black caftans before he made it to the borders of the pope's quarters. He was slightly surprised to be let in so easily given it was nearing midnight.

John greeted him in an old plaid shirt and scuffed pants, sloshing around in hideously patterned slippers.

"Sorry, sir. I couldn't sleep."

"Nor could I. I rarely do." The pope carefully studied Puppy as they sat in the spacious anteroom fringed in deep-burgundy drapes and carpeting. "I was hoping you'd come. Actually, expecting you. But by all tradition, you shouldn't be here, Puppy."

"Why not?"

"Coming alone without Abdullah or Petash might compromise my impartiality. One of the rules of summits. All sides are always together so there's no fear of factions. Although back in the twentieth century during World War II, your American president Franklin Roosevelt would sneak off to meet the communist dictator Joseph Stalin without his main ally Winston Churchill. Then Churchill would do the same to Roosevelt. Are these names familiar?"

Puppy shrugged. "I've heard of them. Well, Roosevelt. I can tell you who won the batting crowns for the AL and NL in 1943." He tried to restore some of his self-respect so the pope wouldn't think he was a moron. "Yeah, Stalin, too. Russian, right?"

"Georgian, but both republics were part of the Soviet Union. Still, we should only discuss business with all the participants present."

"Right. Wouldn't want anyone getting irritated. Can't have that."

The pope slowly smiled. "This was not the best opening session."

"Sort of like giving up five runs in the first inning."

"I'm not entirely sure of the metaphor, but I get the gist." John thought a moment about how much to trust this simple soul with a shrewd smile. A great deal, he suddenly realized. "I have failed so far."

"How have you failed when everyone else is throwing sand in the sandbox?"

"I should have demanded more preparation, structure, a first-day agenda so that the inevitable accusations wouldn't erupt in all directions."

"You mean like treating us as responsible leaders."

"The hate runs so deep, Puppy. All of you came at great personal risk sharing the belief that we must find a solution and yet we could barely agree on whether Herbert had the right to display maps."

"Do you think he does?"

John squirmed. "That's between the two parties."

"Okay. Do you think he has that right?"

"I think it was a mistake having him here. He is not human. He's considered a monstrosity to the Muslims. And yes, to me."

"He saved my wife's life. And she saved his. Does that make you redefine monstrosity just a little? The robots are citizens of my country and have sacrificed way more than anyone by fighting for us."

"Sacrifice what? They have no souls."

Puppy caught his impolite sneer. "I know one who thinks she does. Maybe she doesn't. Can you say for sure? Do you really have that power, sir?"

"No." The pope sighed. "But every night I hear the souls of the tens of millions who have died in this awful war. Every waking hour, Puppy."

"Maybe some of them are members of the American military. Or put it this way. You'd have a ton more of your souls dancing around your bedroom belonging to dead American human soldiers if robots hadn't fought for us. How do you measure that?"

The Holy Father gave him an appreciative look. "Perhaps I need a new measuring stick."

Puppy poured himself an apricot water. "You also can't sit there believing you're impartial. You have opinions. You can't step back like some umpire. I don't know about previous summits, tradition, who talks to who, only that since we're all here with the clock ticking, that obviously didn't work out too well before."

"No, Puppy, that didn't," John said softly. "But the Muslims invaded Rome and ransacked the Vatican. I downed some of their planes, personally killing pilots. I'm perhaps the last link to the Judeo-Christian civilization that has been at conflict with Islam for more than a millennium. I must bend over backward to avoid any taint of favoritism. That Abdullah has accepted me as a facilitator is extraordinary."

"Because he didn't know you were on the roof of the Vatican with your machine gun?"

John frowned. "The summit ends if they feel I'm ganging up on them."

"Don't you have issues with us?"

The pope pulled a face. "Many. Yes. Many."

"So you're pretty much disgusted with both sides. Then show that. Right now, you're just the guy who orders the food." Puppy shrugged away John's scowl. "It's the truth, sir. You can disagree with us. Disagree with them. Clearly the Americans and the Allahs don't get along. We need your help. You've got to be more of, you know…"

The pope's eyes lidded. "Is another baseball metaphor coming my way?"

"Throw heat, Pope. Inside at our heads if necessary. They used to call them brush-back pitches. If you have to, send us sprawling in the dirt, then go for it."

John sifted through these peculiar phrases and images for a moment. "How about some fresh air?"

58

The faint scent of gerbera flowers drifted over the makeshift roof. Nervous papal guards held fixed positions overlooking Valletta as last-minute stealth 'copters steadily arrived.

"We must throw hard and high," the Holy Father had whispered to the rabbi. Gold prayed the old man hadn't started drinking again.

Abdullah took a deep breath, nodding toward the port. "Nothing like the sea at night. Tranquility and promise. The ultimate serenity. Do you go to the beach often, Mr. Nedick?"

"Puppy's fine, please."

"John," the pope said. Nearby, Gold almost fainted.

The Son glanced between them with a spreading smile. "Abdullah, the Bearer of the Prophet's Message is a mouthful. But General Petash means well. At least toward me."

"As Elias means well, at least toward me. He's going to be really pissed about being left out."

Leaning forward on the waist-high wall, Abdullah gently swayed on his forearms, alarming the guards. Gold commed for padded nets to surround the building, cursing himself for the oversight.

"As will Petash," the Son said with a vague smile. "It should be entertaining when they're told."

Abdullah and Puppy looked at the pope who grunted out a nod.

"I will handle that," the Holy Father promised. "They were impediments. Well meaning, well briefed, too well briefed, but we'll never get anything done if they're around."

"Is this a papal edict?" the Son asked, surprised. "I thought that was merely a suggestion for this one evening. Petash will not be happy to be permanently barred from the sessions. He is not as agreeable as he looks."

"They will live. We must figure things out among ourselves."

"Your last president felt that way," Abdullah said, pausing. "Marne Wilson who met my father in 2058. As he tells the story, she was quite full of herself, disdainful, arrogant. Very American. Wilson had decided on her own agenda and was going to bully my father. I doubt Allah could have bullied the Grand Mufti. But Wilson ignored copious intelligence and psychological reports on my father's character."

Puppy realized Abdullah was waiting for a response. "I have my own scouting report on you, sir."

Abdullah raised an eyebrow. "And I on you, sir. Azhar Mustafa can be quite opinionated."

"A very insightful guy." Puppy felt ashamed that he'd barely spent five minutes with Azhar since arriving.

They traded brief knowing grins.

"Had she listened to her security apparatus, President Wilson would have acceded to our demands. The Summit of 2058 led to the Surrender of 2073."

Puppy angrily shrugged off the pope's calming hand.

"Don't underestimate our resolve, Abdullah."

"I do not," he replied casually. "President Wilson and the America of that time feared war because they had nothing to fight for. Good or bad, we must believe in something that gives us strength. What do you believe in, Puppy Nedick?"

Puppy knew this might be the most important answer he ever gave. "Faith. Not religion, not God. But faith in ourselves and each other."

The Son waited for more, then smiled when he realized that was it. "That is not so dissimilar from what I believe, Puppy, except I would be more long-winded and boring." Abdullah looked meaningfully at the pope. "Puppy is an idealist."

"Remember what that was like, Abdullah?" the pope gently asked. "When you didn't have all the doubts?"

"What do you doubt, John?"

The pope's eyes glistened. "Sometimes everything I ever believed in. Because then how did we get here? I have the prophecies and Armageddon to look forward to and, of course, the glorious return of Jesus to establish the Kingdom on Earth. But I have seen too much of this fragile world to believe there'll be much left. The ruin might be beyond Jesus's power. Yes, I'm no longer the most God-fearing of all popes. As you see, I have shed the holy robes because I struggle, I struggle mightily, fiercely, over whether this is really all His plan, His will."

"If not, then whose?"

"Ours."

Abdullah pursed his lips, troubled. "Do you suggest there is no God, Holy Father?"

"No. Not at all. I couldn't be what I am and believe that. Only that we have allowed ourselves to fall so far away, that only through the most warped lenses can we see Him. Like Puppy, I believe in faith, one person at a time."

They waited for a very long time for Abdullah to nod. "Three idealists. Three cynics."

"Or something else," Puppy said. "Only we don't know what that is yet."

"Don't you have some apt baseball metaphor?" John teased.

"Oh yes, I'd like to hear that," Abdullah grinned.

"You guys are playing with me."

"Just a little." John winked. "Like all faith, we only need the simplest of goals."

Abdullah fussed with his robe. "By any means, such as piping fake, adulatory crowd noises into the meeting room?"

"I got both of you up on the roof, didn't I?"

The Son laughed heartily before turning back to the Mediterranean. "We need very simple goals. Disposition of forces, tariffs, it is sheer madness to consider that can be cobbled together in a way anyone would understand. Or really care. Some of the more complex issues will have to be postponed so we can focus on a deliverable few."

"What about an exchange of children?" John asked. "The ones you and the Americans have liberated. That would make for dramatic footage on your news and social media sites."

Abdullah frowned. "Yes. And the children would also be a prime target for the Black Robes as we have just seen with the thirty-five dead in Palermo."

"So is everything we do."

The Son nodded. "It is a start. Puppy, you have grown uncommonly quiet."

"I like the idea of the orphans. Symbolic and touching. Doesn't over promise. Still, we're getting our kids back and you're getting your kids, okay, and then there'll be horror stories of mistreatment under captivity and that won't be pretty. Plus, without children as unofficial hostages, where's the worry about attacking? We'd be more likely to just kill each other. Still, let's do it. Let's announce that tomorrow morning. Elias and the general can fill in the details," he said with a mischievous smile. "But we need something that really brings us together. That really overcomes the suspicions and hatred."

John grinned. "You're about to throw another high-and-hard one, aren't you?"

• • • •

PUPPY DRUMMED HIS fingers on the oversized mahogany coffee table in the living room. By now, they sounded like boulders dropping off a cliff to Elias, huddled over floating HG transport charts since receiving what he called "a knife in the back."

"Do, you, mind?" Elias shouted from the bedroom.

Puppy glanced at Herbert, intent over the transmitter. "Is that noise bothering you?"

"Noise does not disrupt me. Nor the emotional currents behind the noise such as the impatience manifested by your fingered discordant musical tones, the irritation within First Cousin Kenuda's repeated cries, or the incessant jubilatory chants from outside."

Herbert closed its wide eyes in an imperceptible analysis of the unresponsive holographic communicator.

"Perhaps they're jamming us." In the doorway, the haggard Elias directed the comment away from "the betrayer."

"The problem originates in America."

"Well, what do I know?" Kenuda threw up his hands. "I'm merely the messenger boy. And don't you dare sigh, Mr. Nedick."

Around 3:30 this morning they'd briefly wrestled, knocking over a chair, a lamp, and a seltzer bottle, which would never spritz again, before Herbert flung them apart.

"Wouldn't dream of it." Puppy batted his eyelids. "Don't you have a meeting with General Petash?"

"Oh yes, thank you for reminding me." Elias yanked his sports jacket off the doorknob. "I'll do my best to serve my country in any way I can."

The door slammed shut, nearly toppling the coatrack. Puppy grumbled about childish middle-aged men with fat heads. Herbert arched an eyebrow.

"Since the First Cousin is the head of the American government and your role is largely ceremonial, such anger is understandable."

Puppy snickered. "I'm a little more than ceremonial. I play a big role. Or else why the hell am I here?"

"As a symbol. According to the laws of The Family, you have no legal power nor responsibility. You cannot command. Grandma, Grandpa Albert, and the Granddaughter Clary all claimed authority from that symbolism in the manner of monarchs with varying degrees of success, most notably rooted in the concessions of the legal guardians, the Cousins, and the support of the populace. It is clear from his tone and manner that First Cousin Kenuda viewed your relationship in that same fashion." Herbert concentrated on the wavy hologram in Detroit which faded for the third time.

"Then I was wrong to sidestep him and Petash?"

"That is a confusion of reasonable intent with excessive, yet understandable response. First Cousin Kenuda and General Petash have not been dismissed but merely assigned to more useful functions such as the logistics of the orphans's exchange which, from the high-pitched sounds arising from the approximately forty-three-thousand humans congregated behind the wire barricades below, has proven quite popular."

"Exactly. And Elias gets the credit, too."

Herbert turned. "I do not believe First Cousin Kenuda cares about credit or he would not be First Cousin."

"Neither do I," Puppy snapped.

"Yes. Or else you would not be here in your ceremonial role." Herbert gusted out an approving sound as the hologram of Tony Felton stood on the coffee table. "Good day, Major Felton. I am Herbert and as you see, here is Puppy Nedick. The connection has been fortified to avoid further disruption."

As Herbert went to leave, Puppy tugged him back onto the couch. The 'bot protested that it might violate the boundaries of his neutrality. He did not readily understand Puppy's crass response.

"Tony, how are you?"

"'Bout as good as I should be when two robots burst in carrying this god-fucking-forsaken machine."

"Glad to catch you in your usual high spirits." Puppy laughed over Felton's assorted grumbles. "I need your help."

"As usual. What crap fest did you get yourself into now?"

"How'd you like to play baseball here in Malta?"

Felton squinted. "Malta?"

"Gorgeous view of the ocean. I want you to reassemble our wonderful all-star team from London. Can you do that?"

Tony grinned. "You crazy bastard. Are we playing the Allahs again?"

"That's my plan."

The major stroked his chin. "Why?"

Puppy sighed. "Because baseball's a lot easier than withdrawing millions of soldiers from Romania and Tunisia and everywhere else and inspecting weapons and all that other nonsense which makes my pretty little head spin."

"Things are going south?"

"No." He grimaced. "Not yet. But we need something everyone can understand."

Felton chuckled. "A World Series."

"A real World Series."

"Best of seven?"

"No, we'd have to go back to the three of five format. Seven games are pushing it. Five might be, too," he suddenly realized.

"Not if we sweep."

"Keep it in your pants, Major."

"Same bunch of camels?"

"Probably, but I have no idea."

Felton folded his arms and let his chin drop, levying a heavy stare. "You ain't told anyone else, have you?"

"Other than you and Elias Kenuda and just now, Lieutenant Herbert here, no."

"I am merely Herbert." The 'bot corrected.

Puppy squeezed its bony forearm. "But I figure enough of the Allahs are still around, survived this war and, if not, they'll find other players."

"Hope so. I want to beat those mothers."

"We'll see. Would everyone be up to it?"

"I'll ask."

"Persuade."

Felton smirked. "Always."

"Obviously, I can't manage." Puppy hesitated. "I want Ty."

The major sadly shook his head. "He ain't in good shape, Nedick. His robot body's running down."

"There are extensive trans-organic treatments available which have been implemented on the battlefield and are now being introduced into the mainland," Herbert explained.

Tony snorted. "But Cobb won't have anything to do with that. You know he doesn't want to admit he's a robot. Plus he also won't admit that Mickey's death hit him hard. And Mooshie's. Never repeat this because the old bastard will have my head, but he's afraid. He won't even take batting practice to stay in shape until the season resumes. It's resuming, right?"

"Yes, yes, in a few weeks." If. "Can we set up a call—"

"He's pissed at you."

Puppy rolled his eyes. "For what?"

Felton shrugged as if there were just too many things. "He feels left out. You know his ego."

"Then managing the American team in the first real World Series should appeal to him."

"Maybe if he weren't so pissed at you." Tony thought a moment. "I can player-manager."

"No, sorry, and don't give me the death glare. It's gotta be Ty."

"Why?"

"Because it makes sense. Because it was once him and Ty and Mickey and Mooshie. Now there's just the two of them left. They have to be the ones, otherwise it makes no sense in that 'Puppy land' where fact is defined by a sudden hunch."

"I'll ask," Tony finally said.

"Hold off," Puppy abruptly said. "Focus on rounding up the team first."

"When's this all happening?"

"And I also want to use those kids from the twentieth-century team."

"What the—"

"Thanks, Major, see you soon." Puppy motioned for Herbert to end the transmission. "I'll need another call set up today, Herbert."

"Is it Herbert or Lieutenant Herbert?"

He grinned. "I forgot to tell you, but Elias reinstated your commission since you're back on our team. Congrats."

Herbert maintained its stare. "My approval must be granted to accept such a decision. I will decline under Article 2.24 of the Uniform Military Code. Would you like me to recite the applicable language?"

Puppy frowned. "No. I want you to explain why you'd decline."

"I am not required to do so."

"Humor your ceremonial figurehead."

"I will be relocating to Madagascar once this assignment is completed."

Puppy stared. "Because Abdullah and the pope didn't want you?"

Herbert arched an eyebrow. "That is symptomatic. My place is with other trans-organic life-forms. I have traveled and interacted sufficiently since I encountered Annette Ramos to compile an accurate assessment, within 4.3 percent, of the role robots will play within the evolving human world. We are viewed as machines and little more. It was acceptable to be present if I merely recorded the summit proceedings. It was acceptable for First Cousin Kenuda to demand my resignation and for you to reinstate me as you see fit."

Puppy burst out laughing. "You mean you're upset because we ignored your little feelings and interests and treated you like a cog in the big old machine? You're upset because people who are your superiors ordered you around to serve a greater good whether you agreed or not and kept information from you without regard for how it might affect you? You mean me and Elias and the pope and the Son dumped all over you as we would dump over any other life-form, as humans have dumped over all life-forms since we crawled out of the mud onto shore billions of years ago?"

Herbert was momentarily perplexed. "Is your explanation that I have been treated as poorly as you would treat an organic life-form?"

"Now you got it." Puppy wrapped his arm around Herbert's shoulders. "Besides, Annette Ramos says you're one of her best friends."

The slightest pink hued Herbert's cheeks. "It is not logical that she would consider me her friend."

"You want to tell her that, Lieutenant?"

Herbert shook its head at the prospect. "It would be best to accept the compliment as given."

59

On the thirty-by-fifty-foot vidscreens, glittering images of children disembarking boats at heavily guarded ports in Antwerp, Monrovia, and Casablanca danced off the glass-and-chrome Cadillac Hotel in downtown Detroit. The streaming drama with identical scenes and changing cast had played for nearly a day on the oversized screens erected in bars, shops, boulevards, schools, and homes. Pretty much everywhere.

Presenters's tones turned hushed, uncertain of what to say, how to react. There were no dictates or even guidance, of course, just a sense of complete wonder. The bushy-headed woman on the 10:30 newsbreak last night had equated the return of the children from captivity with the landing on the moon back in the twentieth century. That sparked a gnarly response from her cohost about the inappropriate comparison to America's imperialist designs in space. The "gnarly girl" didn't return after the adverts.

With radiant smiles, parents in *hijabs* and trolley caps and everything imaginable in between hugged their children, their relatives, and strangers and, with astonishing speed thanks to the heavily coded information exchange between the negotiating powers, had filed nearly instantaneous custodial-care documents. As the child stepped onto shore, only their name appeared in the close-up of their hopeful and frightened face. No nation of origin, ethnicity, religion, gender, age, length of time imprisoned or tortured.

They were just a child, solo on the world stage. A multicultural choir singing happy songs from everyone's country in now-thirty-eight languages popped up. Beth and Zelda joined "the amazed look" which united thousands sprawling along Dearborn Street. There were millions more in the Mufti's Empire; there weren't sufficient Black Robes and Shurta secret police to seize all the televisions and laptops and cellular devices.

Ty Cobb's suite in the Cadillac Hotel was a mess, strewn with beer cans, pistachio shells, forlorn bottles of emptied bourbon, and an array of mysterious former food piled on a table to annoy his unwelcome visitors.

Tony cleaned off the couch with a sweep of his thick hands.

"He's coming, he's coming," he assured Zelda and Beth, nervously glancing at the vidscreen circling the room. A report on a foiled terrorist attack at a future undisclosed embarkation port had just finished. The presenters about cried with relief.

"Best not to mention all that. It only stirs the old man up."

"Course not." Zelda shook her head. The things she would do for Puppy. Like two days alone with Beth never factored into the trip.

Ty limped into the room with an aggrieved majestic air. He tugged on the red sash of the black smoking jacket and wished they would disappear.

"If it's not 'the great white grandpa' himself." Zelda plastered a sloppy kiss on his cheek which he accepted as tribute, however unpleasant. "My friend, Beth Rivera."

Cobb grunted and waved them onto the couch. He stood, though it clearly cost him effort.

"You could look a little happier to see me." Zelda pouted.

Ty sneered. "You just happened to be in the neighborhood."

"I've never been to Detroit. Always one of my dreams. We're going to the Ford Museum later."

Cobb about spat out his tongue. "Tony told me."

Zelda shot the blabbermouth Felton a look. "Which was?"

"I told him the whole fucking story," Tony snapped. "I don't do coy."

"Me neither." Cobb sat with a slight wince. "Let's cut the shit. I'm not going to Malta and I'm not managing a team playing Ay-rab terrorists. Anything else?"

"Why not?" Beth asked.

Cobb stirred as if the couch cushion had spoken. "Who are you again?"

"Beth Rivera."

"And you are what?"

"'What' meaning what?"

Ty jerked his head at Zelda.

"We're friends." Zelda squeezed Beth's hand.

"Oh. Special friends?"

"Yeah, lovers," Beth said. "Once Zelda's divorced, we're getting married. You got a problem with that, 'white' Grandpa?"

Ty gargled with disdain. "Not anymore. Not in this world."

"Good. We all done figuring out who likes to sleep with who?" Zelda barked. "Tony, want to join in?"

"Nah. I'm just gonna enjoy the show." He popped open a warm Gribnoff Ale.

Zelda grinned. "So, White Grandpa, this is what this is about. The game's a big deal."

Cobb's face twisted. "Making nice with Ay-rabs and Papists."

"No, you old fool. Making sure godless American children don't get annihilated because that's the only other outcome. As you see, Puppy and Elias have worked out an orphan exchange." She let Ty's wince linger. "Next is a prisoner exchange."

"Heard that shit before," Tony grumbled.

"We've all heard that shit before," Beth snapped. "Get over it."

Zelda proudly patted Beth's shoulder. "And she's a Blue Wig."

"Another terrorist?" Ty snarled.

"No. I've reformed. I'm trying to buy into all the love and friendship." Beth's voice dripped sarcasm.

"And that has what to do with Pup-pee Nee-dick not having the damn courtesy to call me in person?"

Zelda threw up her hands. "That's what this is about?"

"No, because the old fool said he wouldn't talk to Nedick," Tony growled.

"That's right." Cobb sat up straighter, invigorated by his anger. "He stole my job. Mine and Mick's. Please don't tiptoe through the bushes about 'the white grandpa's' ego. Puppy did a lousy job. He screwed up the whole game which we left in fine shape."

"He did," Tony told the women who nodded reluctantly.

"We finally agree," Cobb said triumphantly. "If he proved to be such an idiot, why would I trust his judgment now? Why would any of you? This could all be a damn 'Moozlim' trap. I have no faith in the man. None at all."

Zelda sat on the arm of Ty's chair, discomforting the hell out of him.

"You know why he sent me here? Apart from your fondness for black women?" She purred away his scowl. "To Puppy, to me, to really everyone who loves the game, there can't be the first-ever real World Series without you, one of the people who brought baseball back. You've got to be in that dugout. You represent baseball's past. The past meeting the present and maybe the future. Grandma's bra straps, you are baseball. You made baseball what it was. What it is. Who the hell else should be the manager? Who else has the right?"

Cobb turned away until his eyes dried. He slowly returned to Zelda and let her ruffle the last wisps of his thin hair.

"Maybe."

"Just agree already," Zelda hissed.

A grunt was about as far as he'd go. "But I decide who we take on the team."

Tony interrupted. "Puppy wants as many of the players—"

"Puppy, Puppy, Puppy, woof woof fucking woof." Cobb cut off Felton. "I'm the manager. My team. No interference. Anyone got trouble with that since I'm the living embodiment of baseball's greatness?"

He glared at their exhausted nods. Cobb struggled a moment. His voice dropped. "I got one more request."

"We can only hope just one," Zelda snickered.

Ty took her wrist. "If I run out of gas in that godforsaken cesspool, you bring me back home. And bury me in Yankee Stadium."

"Not Tiger Stadium?" Tony asked in surprise.

"Did I say Tiger Stadium? Center field in Yankee Stadium. Put me between Mick and Mooshie since I was the best. Swear?"

Beth made the sign of the cross.

"Are you mocking me?" Cobb exploded.

"No, you old fool, I'm a goddamn Papist."

"Really?"

"Really."

"'Bout as close as I'm going to get." Ty grinned slowly. "Make sure you find some real Christian prayers for my full service."

• • • •

BY THE THIRD day, Abdul thought he'd become a very accomplished spy. For cover, he used the thickening crowds which spilled onto the island from the Armada of Hope, as the boats steadily surrounding Malta were called. Carefully watched by the American Seventh Fleet from the west and the Muslim Liberation Fleet from the east with Islamist fighter patrols yawning overhead, the ships lined up every day for four stages of security: boarding, disembarking, landing, and the final screening just inside Valletta.

No official estimate was made, but intrepid journalists insisted the number of ships, of all sizes and seaworthiness, exceeded ten thousand, surging from ports throughout the Mediterranean, watched by the Qaddafi and Excelsior-class submarines. Reports suggested more ships were approaching.

A battle had erupted when Black Robes sunk several fishing boats less than three nautical miles outside Normandy. Fragmented reports trickled in about similar attacks and similar flights of courage. The Mufti's Blessed Heirs had already filed grievances in *Sharia* court accusing Abdullah of heresy for colluding with the infidels, but so far, the Empire's armies had not responded with officially sanctioned military attacks.

Abdul squeezed through a matching overweight couple in yellow baseball caps arguing in Italian about baseball; the Muslim team was scheduled to arrive later this afternoon. He followed his brother up the cobblestone hill flanked by packed cafes brimming with laughter and tantalizing smells. The boy hadn't eaten since breakfast, having slipped out with a pocketful of bread while his father still slept.

He was doing a personal study for school, Abdul had told Azhar, who didn't interrogate him in his usual way but just shrugged, glum. His father was the only unhappy person in Malta and he didn't know why, but he could only focus on one mission at a time.

He'd tracked Omar for hours each day, from the shabby hotel on an alley to the various mosques and then, last night, inside that narrow apartment building where he'd counted eleven whores and three more women he wasn't sure of along with sixteen drunks, he'd marked everything down in his black notebook. Unlike the first night, he saw no more Black Robes. Or someone dressed especially unlike a Black Robe so they wouldn't be obvious.

Like his wily brother, Omar wore regular decent-people's clothes. The only person Abdul saw with Omar also wore regular decent-people's clothes. Two mornings ago on Pietro de Cianci Place, the young men brushed shoulders while passing a clothing store before something flashed into Omar's hand, which he quickly pocketed before casually crossing the street.

Secret plans, Abdul had concluded. What else?

This morning Omar looked haggard, his clothes wrinkled, coming out of his hotel as he did every day at 7:30 without fail. Pretty stupid, Abdul had pronounced with his growing savvy as a secret agent. Someone up to no good should change their schedule a little. He was briefly disappointed in his older brother whom he viewed with repugnant awe like one would the Devil.

Omar turned sharply left; Abdul, smitten with the smells of *pastichio*, had turned toward the food cart. He scolded himself and risked walking faster through the dense crowds. At the corner, Abdul saw his brother dip into a doorway. Abdul did the same.

Then all that Abdul felt was intense pain on the back of his head. He thought of a pumpkin splitting before plunging into darkness.

After twenty-five hours and seven texts and five calls, Azhar finally panicked.

The desk clerk remained perky and polite before Mustafa's angry stare.

"We have no records of your son's calls to the hotel."

"You explained you joined the night shift at seven. It is now nine."

"I'm waiting for a response from my colleague. There is a celebration at Vesuvio Square for the Arab baseball team. Most of the city is there and we're told there are communication problems with mobiles. My girlfriend couldn't—"

Azhar's right hand clutched the clerk's paisley tie. A quick tug and their forehead would bounce off the desk.

"I do not care about your girlfriend. I want you to contact your manager. Now."

The manager also wore the same polite expression with Azhar as with any other crazy guest, of which there were many. He patiently showed the hotel phone records. There were no incoming calls from Abdul's mobile. There were no messages for young Mr. Mustafa. No one on the staff had seen the boy since yesterday morning at approximately 7:15. The manager almost asked how waiting a day to report your son's disappearance was the hotel's fault. But this was Malta in August 2099 and tens of thousands had cheered an arriving Arab baseball team when perhaps a handful on the entire island could explain more than two rules of the sport.

The manager shuddered, imagining when the swelling Armada of Hope greeted the approaching American team. All over the internet, videos captured boats flying pennants representing the logos of the U.S. players's original teams. Ships were parked in twenty-mile rows, the BBC bureau in Bucharest reported. Their hotel had no vacancies. His colleagues at other establishments faced similar challenges.

"Excuse me?" Mustafa repeated.

"I said, sir, would you like to file an official police report?" the manager asked. "There must be scores of missing people. Let the cops handle this."

"No, no." Azhar too quickly held out his hands. When Azhar left, the manager made a note of that suspicious response.

A ride which had taken fifteen minutes when they first arrived now took over an hour. At the entrance to the tunnel, Mustafa chose the civilian line rather than attracting attention by insisting on seeking favoritism. That added two hours in the sweltering heat, his texts to Abdul growing completely unhinged, mainly question marks and exclamation points. Leaving a message at the gate swallowed up more time as it was processed and validated and, even then, he didn't know if it got through. Azhar was back in the center of town by well after noon. By then his mind was reduced to question marks and exclamation points.

Brushing at the neat red dress falling well below her knees, Annette got up from the cement stoop by the cafe and tenderly kissed his cheek.

"They would not give you a table?" he asked.

"I had one, but I couldn't hold it, even for me." Her wry grin faded at his distracted look.

A video dangled from a nearby traffic light. Children climbed on patient camels, soccer balls dashed through flailing legs, and a choir of freshly scrubbed teens sang a song in Hungarian.

"That's called *Kossuth Lajos azt uzente*, a patriotic song from the nineteenth century about a famous Hungarian patriot who led them to independence." She waited for him to acknowledge her vast reservoir of pointless information, but Azhar just stared at the plain silver crucifix around her thin olive neck.

Annette shyly played with the necklace. "The Holy Father gave it to me."

Mustafa whistled admiringly, making her blush.

"Let's not get too carried away. It's not like this came from a secret vault. He has lots of them. But he doesn't have a crucifix stand at one of the flea markets either." Annette gave him a long look. "You didn't call on this incredible device"—she held up her cell phone—"which I don't know how I ever lived without, to see my Vatican jewelry."

Seeing his grim hesitation, Annette led Azhar through the shuffling throngs to a cobblestone stoop outside a sweet shop; it was the best they could do where standing would soon require a reservation.

"Abdul has been missing for more than twenty-four hours. He's ignored my calls and texts."

She tried a grin. "Maybe he found a cute girl."

"He would not betray his affection for you." Azhar crimsoned. "Apologies. I should not have said that."

"I'm always happy to hear about the crush of a teenage boy." Annette saw humor wasn't going to work. "A boy about to become a man can get easily lost in this crazy city."

Mustafa paused as a raucous group in crescent-moon-and-star baseball caps marched past. "That is not my Abdul."

"So parents think," she said with exaggerated wisdom.

"He is very responsible. He does not simply disappear."

"Has he behaved strangely?"

Azhar nodded emphatically. "Abdul said he was working on some project that he would bring back to school when this visit is done. That was the first time he had ever mentioned school when he did not have to. He has lied to me the past few days. And yes, I suspected he was lying. But I wanted to give him freedom because he will be a man soon as you say. I should have been more inquisitive. I heard Allah say, ask questions, ask questions, but no. I was pouting."

Annette sighed. "You feel left out after everything. And there has been a lot of everything. You wish you had some work, some focus besides being the original messenger boy. I don't blame you. Abdullah won't ask for your advice when he's shoved aside even General Petash. You can't captain a fishing boat because there's no room for fish anymore." She vaguely gestured at the Mediterranean stuffed with ships.

"I'm in the same boat. I've spilled my guts to Puppy with all my insights about the pope. Now I don't see him either, he's so busy. All I do is wander around the damn city hoping someone'll recognize me and when they do, I'm embarrassed. How pathetic is that."

"A fine pair we are after everything."

"Everything doesn't have much of a shelf life, Az. But let's put our egos aside," she continued. "Go back to Abdul. What do you think's happened?"

Azhar stared with dread in his eyes. "Omar."

Annette shuddered. "He's here?"

"I think so. Omar is the only thing that could consume Abdul. Other than football. He cares about nothing else. Food, yes. But he is obsessed with Omar. He followed Omar back in Barcelona because Abdul was convinced Omar had come for reasons other than visiting his mother. We found nothing. But Abdul never accepted that."

Annette's voice was very shaky. "He finally found me."

"This is not about you, Annette. Or even me. Though he would like us both dead, that I know. A pain, a lump in my heart." He scowled toward Heaven. "Omar is here to disrupt the summit. Why else? He is a Black Robe."

Annette shoved away her fear. "That's not so easy, Azhar. The security is way higher than you see. Just because all these people have been allowed onto the island doesn't mean they can do anything they want. Every person carries a tracking device they don't know about. John, the pope, sorry, told me they've done that since the summit was announced."

"And Abdul and I were here before the summit was announced," he said excitedly. "Omar also could have come before. Were there such tracking devices then?"

"I don't know." Annette thought a moment. "But a Black Robe would still be watched. Don't be fooled by all the nicey-nicey. There's every expectation that when the work's done here, there'll be a final battle with the Mufti's Heirs."

Azhar clenched his fists. "And that is what he wants. Omar is clever."

"So are the people who protect the Holy Father."

He frowned. "You think I am an alarmist."

"No. I think you're worried about your son which I totally get. And if he's here, and that's a big 'if' without any proof but I still believe you, we're not alone. Let's alert the papal security—"

"No."

"Serious?"

"No."

Annette sighed. "Okay, then I'll ask the pope."

"Allah forbid!" he cried.

"Why the hell not?"

"What if I am wrong? It would embarrass me. It would embarrass Abdullah who sent me here. The pope who trusted me. Puppy, who is my friend, that my sons would cause such a problem," he said fiercely. "Besides, do you think they would believe me without proof?"

"Probably not. Probably not." Annette watched a costumed Uncle Sam on stilts totter past. "So, we are kind of alone."

"Yes," Azhar said.

Annette shook her head. "Wouldn't be the first time, right?" Azhar kissed her hand.

60

Elias yanked the window higher so the deafening sound of the low-flying plane would annoy General Petash that much more. This was the most fun he'd had in days.

"Thank you again, General, for the kind use of your executive plane." Kenuda craned his neck as the sleek aircraft made another showy pass over the cheering crowds. "Allowing us to add our own touch was very thoughtful."

"What touch?" Petash shoved aside the impenetrable statistics on trade gobbling up the long conference table in what they dryly called "the dungeon" and edged halfway out the window. He gasped with a strangled sound.

Petash slowly wriggled back inside, horrified. "There are desecrations on the hull, First Cousin. Sacrilege. Heresy."

"I don't quite think they approach such a lofty level, General. Flying the American baseball team and support staff in an aircraft featuring the crescent moon would've been inappropriate." Kenuda pretended to read the plane as it dipped and preened. "U.S. of A. Accurate. Forty-eight-star flag. Accurate. For now." He couldn't resist. "Wait. They're coming down for one more pass. No, sorry. Looks like they're getting landing clearance."

Petash burrowed at the desk in the corner, waiting for the vaccination that would rid him of dealing with these infidels.

"Relax. It's called showmanship, General. Perhaps a little obnoxious, but the crowd loved it."

Petash sneered. "Fulfilling your always simplistic American goals of bravado and vanity."

"Sometimes." Kenuda peered over the lip of the massive five-year tariff-projections briefing book. Petash had these childish moments several times a day, hiding as if he could make himself invisible. "Shall we get back to work?"

"That is why we are here, which you seem to forget."

"I don't, General. I have the same boundless joy locked in a room with you as you do with me. But these are our jobs so we can allow Puppy and Abdullah to put on their own brand of showmanship."

He rattled the thick folder for them to continue, but Petash leaned back in his chair with a weary sigh, studying Kenuda.

"That does not bother you?"

"Which part?"

"Being relegated."

Elias shook his head. "Not anymore."

"But it did."

"Of course."

Petash grunted. "I wondered whether you were a complete spineless worm."

Elias crossed his arms and waited for Petash's final decision.

"We do not know how far our leaders will be led by the pope," the general said. "I find that worrisome. I would think you would, too."

Kenuda held back. "Abdullah and Puppy are making progress with which I agree. Orphans, now the prisoner exchange—"

"And the silly World Series, let's not forget that. Absurd. Window dressing. But that is irrelevant at the end of the day. I am not concerned about the agreements they announce with their great fanfare and fireworks and balloons."

"Then what are you concerned about? We're charged with filling in the specifics." Kenuda gestured disdainfully at the stacks of proposals and counterproposals and the areas they had already conceded could not be sorted out just yet. Arms reductions. Meaningful troop withdrawals. Inspections of weapons sites which had consumed two hours of peevish shouts last night.

Petash closed the window.

"I worry what they are deciding without the formality of an official agreement. What side terms, unofficial pledges, vague plans that are not quite worked out but will be and then become a *fait accompli*." Petash seemed proud of his wooden French. "For example, what about the Vatican? The pope opens his heart to peace and will receive nothing in kind? He cannot publicly ask for a return without his integrity as the great mediator from above being questioned. But surely, he will obtain something. He has been on this rock for three decades, protected by the Jew missile dome and their damnable hidden nuclear weapons. But he is still the pope. The sanctity of his role demands that the Vatican will be restored."

Kenuda frowned. Petash relished that his counterpart had clearly not considered that.

"Or perhaps, he will move Vatican City to Jerusalem. You do not care, but for us, that would be a sin. Please, do not fix me with those wary eyes, First Cousin. I am not a fanatic. I am very much a secular Muslim who believes in God as it suits me, which I suspect is the holy relationship of most people irrespective of their faith. The accords we reach, that you and I bless with our hard work and our visionary compromises, must also be palatable to those who do not agree with us. Not the Black Robes but the merely worshipful. Our peace must resonate so they support it and we do not have to fight them for another decade."

Elias inspected his pen. "We could raise that point about the new Vatican…"

"What of the other points that we do not know of, but I swear before Allah are out there, in their hushed conversations, their newfound brotherhood? A peace for show is a peace that will be broken."

"Do you talk to Abdullah about his conversations?"

Petash stiffened. "He merely insults me with a list of duties to resolve. Does Puppy Nedick?"

Elias squirmed. "He's pretty blithe. That's just his way."

"He is the leader of your country. And he is stupid."

He almost agreed. "He's not the leader. He's the ceremonial leader."

"You are merely the head of the government."

"And you are merely the armed forces chief of staff," Elias shot back.

"Merely?" Petash rumbled. "Everything comes through me. Everything. At least it did. As it was all supposed to go through you."

Elias felt the trap until he realized there was none. "Why don't we insist that each day before the dinner break, we meet with Puppy and Abdullah, separately of course, to debrief them so we can have input?"

Petash leaned back. "What if they refuse?"

"Puppy won't."

The general's nostrils flared. "Abdullah will. Once, he viewed all of us as his equals in the struggle. Now that the Mufti's throne beckons, he has changed. He is more aloof, more insulated. Others also see that."

He suddenly caught himself as if snared on a nail. Yes, many others. The time is coming. All we have sacrificed, all we have won cannot be squandered. "We can only do what we can do, First Cousin. We will hope for the best. Let us see if we can plow through these agricultural sticking points. Perhaps we begin with exchanging some of your bio-agro products for our real food."

"Real food? Now you're talking, General."

• • • •

MAJOR FELTON SLOWLY lumbered over to the front row behind the home dugout. He lifted his catcher's mask, sniffing.

"Is that smell ever gonna go away before we all drop?"

"It's just quick-acting cement which the incredible sea breeze should blow away." Puppy gestured at the Mediterranean. "Be patient. The 'bots built this ballpark in four days."

"Ain't done." Felton grumped toward the outfield where former Sergeants Eliha and Tamara dashed back and forth on the steadily rising fence. He grunted at the dimensions left to right: 305, 340, 410, 340, 315 feet. "Why the erratic distances?"

"Old-fashioned charm, which I appreciate isn't a virtue you're familiar with," Puppy grumped right back.

Felton turned with a shout. "Rundown play, assholes! Work the rundown plays! Old fools!"

Beyond the infield practice of the American team in red t-shirts, white pants, and blue caps, Herbert sped through the outfield with a grass trimmer the size of an elephant. Down the right-field line, former ensigns first-class Huang and Patel completed the grandstand. Rows of seats seemed to emerge whole from the ground.

"Thirty-five thousand when we're done and they'll be done by tonight," Puppy said.

"Isn't that cutting things a little close?"

"The whole damn thing is cutting things close. Like putting together a stadium and a World Series, having Abdullah hunt down the Muslim team, persuading them to come, persuading you to come. Speaking of honored guests, where's Cobb?"

"Shopping."

Puppy rolled his eyes. "For what? All the equipment's here."

"Shopping for whatever a crazy two-hundred-year-old asshole shops for," Felton huffed. "He put me in charge of the first practice."

"Which he should be handling."

"Because I can't?" Felton went up on the balls of his feet.

"Because he's the damn manager."

"He's shopping," Felton repeated as if Puppy were very thick. He softened. "What do you think of the team?"

"So far I want to cry with joy."

"Course you do," Felton grumbled, unable to hide his proud glint. "They don't look like shit."

Slender left fielder Curly Russell retreated on a lazy fly ball as the blur that was Herbert rode around him. Johanna Busco, built like the side of a building, sucked up a short hop from Bar'Nee Ortiz deep in the hole. Carl Tedeschi handled a throw at second from

Ephraim Carew. In center field, Estie Morgan, descendant of Joe Morgan, light tossed Donda Sicatyunni.

Down the left-field line, Reynolds Ryan, great-grandson of Nolan, loosened up with catcher Tennessee Bench, *la familia* to Johnny Bench. The reserves included Tatia Garvey who had been crushing the ball for the Rockies before the pause in the season; second baseman Donde Vasquez Carlton who had yet to make an error for the Phillies this season, and Myrina James Musial who led the majors with sixty-five RBIs.

Puppy's eyes glistened. "You did good, Tony."

"You going there?"

"Yes I am."

Felton stomped off, hiding his pleased smile. Puppy returned to the front row, hoping the quick-cement smell would really disappear by tomorrow's one o'clock game time.

Dressed in a casual blouse and skirt, Sahidi Douglas plopped her feet onto the fence, staring out behind extra-large sunglasses. In the almost-holy silence the moment demanded, everyone watched as Herbert effortlessly rolled the batting cage behind home plate.

Felton said something unmentionable as Herbert took the mound and explained in an echoing voice that he had downloaded several advanced athletic programs so that he could pitch batting practice which would save wear and tear on their arms. Felton threw up his hands at the predictable insanity of it all.

The 'bot two-fingered a salute at Puppy.

"It's a beautiful stadium, Puppy," Sahidi said, removing her sunglasses.

"They've already built your booth." He jerked his head toward the mezzanine level behind home.

"It's nice." Sahidi came as close to gratitude as she could. Puppy followed her smile to the outfield.

"Ty insisted that we couldn't have any 'goddamn yapping monstrosities which'd embarrass me and everyone with any sense.'" Puppy managed the exasperated voice well enough to send Sahidi into spasms of laughter. "So, it's going to be a very simple scoreboard. Hand-delivered numbers. You can't get much simpler than that."

Puppy nodded at a slim girl pacing back and forth behind home. "Who's that?"

Sahidi grinned. "A surprise."

Puppy cleared his throat. "You know, I kind of have more than fulfilled my quota of surprises since coming here."

"We need a public-address announcer and Teri Sheppard is perfect. One of her people, Bob, worked for the Yankees for like forever."

"Why can't you do it?"

She rolled her eyes. "Because I'm the play-by-play announcer. Donda will do color commentary."

Puppy sat up a little straighter. "Go back a pitch. Who said anything about color commentary?"

"Ty, on the plane. He yelled he's playing right field even if you have to shovel his parts out there. Donda wasn't happy. They nearly scuffled on the flight." She sighed beneath his demanding stare. "Okay they broke one of the seats."

"Grandma's bra straps, the plane was on loan from Abdullah the Son. This is good. Restart the war over broken chairs."

"We fixed it. More or less." She shrugged. "I'd tell you everything that went down, but I'm saving that for my diary. Since books are back in vogue, it should prove very popular."

"Whet my appetite, darling."

Puppy glanced at Bench's shot which nearly knocked Tamara off the top of the left-field stands. Tony trudged out to the mound and explained to the disconsolate Herbert that in batting practice it was a good thing for the hitters to hit the ball, and not a sign of failure.

"Ephraim Carew and Curly Russell got into a screaming match about twentieth versus twenty-first-century baseball. She threw a bottle at him. It might've hit his head. Reynolds Ryan told Tennessee Bench he calls his own pitches. She chased him into the bathroom. That's a few of the more memorable moments. I'll spare you how scary Ilsa Gibson is. Mr. Cobb promised to cut off the hand of anyone who missed a bunt sign. Then he opened a third bottle of wine. He regaled everyone with stories about the 1915 Tigers, insisting there wasn't a single person there who could so much as sniff Sam Crawford's dirty socks as play on the same field. Johanna Busco tried shoving Ty into a parachute. He told her to jump first. Yes, it was a fun flight."

Sahidi snapped her fingers in front of Puppy's glazed eyes. "Some of the greatest teams hated each other. Just remember, Puppy, they all hate the Allahs more."

• • • •

LIGHTS BLAZED ON the ships as far as twenty-two nautical miles within the restricted security area extending in all directions. There'd been a few incidents since the gathering began twelve hours ago. A boat sent up blue flames from the portside, illuminating a fiery crescent moon and star. Before the 'copters could intercede, it was rammed by a ship boasting a Detroit Tigers pennant.

A submarine dating back to the Explorer class of NATO popped up, discharging a platoon of Abdullah's sailors who boarded both ships. With pleasant firmness, they reiterated the rules which echoed for miles via speakers held by hovering drones.

There was to be no rooting. No insults. Certainly no attacks or violence. The captains and passengers on the two ships apologized, blaming the excitement of the moment and the growing boredom before the opening ceremonies began. However, there were no more second chances in war or peace and the boats were escorted out of the area which shimmered with a protective dome rising two miles up and two miles into the ocean. The pope's Jews had installed that offshoot of the Goliath technology in the middle of the night, insisting both sides couldn't be trusted.

Incredibly, the ramming was the only real provocation given that just over thirty thousand ships now floated offshore. There'd been a few fires set by exuberant fans and quickly extinguished by the stealth 'copter fire brigades. A handful of people had toppled overboard, some accidentally. So far no one had drowned.

At exactly 10:05 p.m. Malta time, a convoy of the Italian Navy, as close to a neutral nation in the region as could be found, approached the ships from the east and west. Symphonic renditions of "Take Me Out to the Ballgame" blared as floating video screens were stanchioned atop refurbished cargo ships.

With another triumphant blare, the screens flamed on just as Puppy, Abdullah, and the pope clasped hands on a switch by home plate and lit up Peace Field. The fans who had lined up for a precious ticket at dawn, who had sat in the dark for fifty-three minutes wondering if any of this would really work, exploded in cheers. Boats rocked with whoops and yells.

The Holy Father introduced the stadium, explaining that an old ballpark called Ebbets Field in Brooklyn, New York, America, was the model.

Sister Marion, the finest organist in Malta, pounded out a quick tune from her gazebo in center field.

Leaving the head of the Catholic Church and the leader of the most powerful army in the world, Puppy walked toward the pitcher's mound, thanking Herbert and company who received enthusiastic appreciation; few knew they were robots. He talked about the history of the World Series which began in 1903 and, until 2051, followed, for the most part, a best four-of-seven game competition. For ten years, the World Series was the best three of five. He omitted the lack of interest in baseball that prompted that decision.

To begin this historic moment, Puppy continued, they would play two out of three games to determine the 2099 World Champion of Baseball. But next year, yes next year, to celebrate the birth of a new century, the World Series was going back to seven games.

Peace Field shook with more amazed applause.

Puppy bounced up and down with excitement. Now it's time to meet the players, the managers, the coaches.

Everything went dark again, causing some concern. In a flash, dazzling arc lights sliced the ballpark, converging on home. A toss of a 1688 Grasso papal silver coin had determined who'd go first.

Beneath a foppish straw hat and a neatly tailored dark suit, Ty Cobb bounded out of the third-base dugout, waving. Soaking up the attention like a thirsty sponge, the American manager shook Abdullah and the pope's hands without losing his smile and took his spot at home plate.

A colored light spelling *COBB* danced in the sky.

Omar hurried down the aisle in the left-field bleachers before his disgust turned into utter paralysis. Unable to completely turn away, he half watched in horror as the Muslim manager Arwan stiffly shook hands with the infidel at home plate. Jogging through the exit, he yanked down the hood to cut off the cheers as the starting lineups of the teams were announced.

A police officer good naturedly asked if he'd had too much excitement; Omar rubbed his stomach to indicate a vague illness. The cop called out that the real fun starts tomorrow at one o'clock.

Traffic didn't bother moving that night, freeing up tens of thousands who couldn't make the opening ceremonies to dance in the streets, brandish flags, eat and drink. Once back in the Paen Hotel, Omar performed *tahajjud*, the voluntary night prayer, and sipped apricot juice before shuffling down the narrow hallway into the back bedroom.

The sleeping boy was tied to an oak chair. Beneath the black blindfold, Abdul's face was bruised, his t-shirt ripped near the neck showcasing a two-inch gouge encrusted with dried blood.

Omar kicked the chair leg. And again. "Get up."

Abdul muttered with dazed pain.

Omar slipped a straw between his swollen lips. Abdul greedily sucked down the water, quickly gagging. Off a growl, Omar dabbed the dripping liquid. His brother's sloppy habits had always annoyed him.

"Take it off," Abdul said hoarsely.

"No."

"So I can see."

"I cannot."

"I already know what you look like."

Omar slapped his brother, but not hard. "Do not be disagreeable. You are alive. Thank Allah."

"Thank you, Allah," Abdul muttered.

The Black Robe kicked his brother's shin, this time with some malice. "Do not blaspheme."

"So sorry."

Omar fed him more water. "How do you feel?"

Abdul mumbled unintelligibly. Omar leaned closer.

His brother spit in his face. "Fuck you."

Omar trembled with rage. "Do that again and I will give you to my friends."

"How many?"

"What."

"Friends."

Omar spit right back. "Clever boy. To whom will you tell such information?"

"Our father."

Omar purpled. "I have no father."

"Our mother."

Omar slapped his brother so hard the chair fell over. He kicked his brother in the ribs. "Never mention her name. Never. I do this for her. For Allah."

Abdul coughed up blood, alarming his brother. "Do what?"

The Black Robe pressed his knee on Abdul's throat. "Ask such a question of my friends and they will cut your throat. Understand? Do you understand?"

The boy didn't have enough saliva to spit, though he tried with spasmodic swallows. "They are going to do it anyway. Or maybe you will. You can tell Momma you killed me for Allah. She will be very proud."

Omar kicked his brother in the groin until the boy retched and sobbed. He stormed into the living room where Gamil, Malik, and Nabil played a video game. Off silent nods all around, Omar dropped into a chair.

"I will draw for everyone."

Omar sketched every detail he remembered about the ballpark. When he finished, he passed along the sheets of paper. The others grunted, satisfied, and returned to the game. Malik took his eyes off the screeching zombies devouring London.

"And the boy?"

"He is my responsibility."

"He is ours."

"I will handle." Omar's lips barely moved.

"When?"

"When it must be done."

"It should be done now."

Omar sneered. "Do you want to worry about disposing a body and risking detection? He is here and no danger."

Malik considered this. "We will wait to dispose of all the bodies."

Omar nodded, panting from excitement.

61

Pope John should have admitted that he had never thrown a baseball. It was an undignified idea; he simply could not inoculate himself against Puppy's childish charms. Or his own childish whims. Now it was too late.

At least he hadn't worn his ceremonial robes.

To a raucous standing ovation from the sweltering capacity crowd, Puppy escorted the Holy Father up the steps of the first-base dugout and onto the field. The pope, whose many responsibilities included serving as Jesus Christ's representative on Earth, turned ashen when Puppy handed him a well-oiled mitt. The American explained the glove belonged to the great Joe DiMaggio, borrowed for this occasion from the spanking-new Hall of Fame in Cooperstown, New York, America.

The pope brightened at the Italian name without a clue who Mr. DiMaggio was. The Yankee Clipper, former record 56-game hitting streak, stylish New York Yankee center fielder, lifetime .325 hitter, Puppy babbled up facts to distract the pope.

The crowd quieted as the pope bravely fingered the glove, met between home plate and the pitcher's mound by the grinning Tony Felton. The stocky catcher pumped his hand like they'd just met in a saloon and, with a robust slap on the shoulder, instructed the Holy Father to throw a strike.

Teri Sheppard, a few seats to the right of Sahidi and Donda in the vidcast/radcast/tv call it whatever you wanted when a sporting event was being beamed into nearly every country on the planet, intoned as if she, and not the pope, truly spoke with the voice of God.

"Ladies and gentlemen, we direct your attention to the pitcher's mound where His Holiness, Pope John XXIX, will throw out the first ball."

There was a brief lag as Herbert, natty in a trim two-piece gray suit, repeated this in Maltese, Italian, Arabic, and Chinese; the latter's state-run journalists consumed nearly half the press seats. Like newly informed dominoes, the stadium came together in a huge roar.

That response echoed, as it would throughout game one of the 2099 World Series, on the ships offshore watching the floating screens. There was no way to measure the response of the billions watching or listening.

Wearing a grin larger than the Mediterranean, Puppy stood a few feet away from the Pope. They'd only had the one practice and that was a few minutes ago in the prefabricated tunnel leading to the hut-like clubhouses which Ty had smoldered was a barn with a fresh coat of paint. In those five minutes, the pope had looked fine and took instruction well. Puppy figured his god would do the rest.

Ever a showman, Pope John flung out his elbows, squared his worn Napoli Football Club cap, and, amid a near-tangle of eighty-nine-year-old arms and legs, fired the ball toward home.

It sailed about eight feet to the right, striking the Muslim lead-off batter in the on-deck circle. Sheppard boomed, "Ball one!" The crowd applauded before the translations finished. The red-faced pope insisted he wanted another chance. In a laughing whisper, Puppy suggested he "bean" an American player to show evenhandedness.

Not even remotely amused, Pope John exhaled a quick prayer and bounced the next pitch on two hops into Felton's glove. Sheppard pronounced "strike!" The crowd screamed. Puppy hurried the exuberant, glove-pounding pope off the field before he issued a papal decree and pitched the first inning.

As the pope and Puppy slid next to Abdullah behind the third-base dugout, Sheppard asked the crowd to please rise and join in the singing of "Take Me Out to the Ballgame."

As the coin-flip-designated American home team took their positions, holographic strapping players in bland white uniforms and red caps, bats over their shoulders, danced over the infield, singing in English:

Take me out to the ballgame,
Take me out with the crowd;

Now the players crooned in Arabic:

Buy me some peanuts and Cracker Jack,
I don't care if I never get back.

And with vigorous leg kicks in Italian:

Let me root, root, root for the home team,
If they don't win, it's a shame.

For the thunderous finish, in Maltese:

For it's one, two, three strikes, you're out,
At the old ballgame!

With the crowd so riled up they were throwing food, the lyrics in all five languages dashed through the air, funneling together in a swirling rainbow-hued cloud which exploded out:

Play ball!

"Hello again, everyone, and welcome to game one of the 2099 World Series from Peace Field here in Valletta, the heart of gorgeous Malta." For the vidcast component, a spiraling map of the world zoomed into Malta for the roughly 99.91 percent who had no idea where it was, according to Herbert's projection.

"I'm Sahidi Douglas along with my color commentator, the great right fielder for the Pittsburgh Pirates and San Diego Pelicans, Donda Sicatyunni. Donda, what do these teams have to do to win?" Sahidi's play-by-play was live in the ballpark, translated through the black transistor radios given out to all the fans as they entered.

Donda stroked her faint goatee. "Hit the ball. Catch the ball. Throw the ball. It's a simple game, Sahidi. The Wings, as the Islamist squad has named itself, has the advantage of regularly playing together. Since the three-game series against the Americans earlier in the year in London"—Sahidi eye-bulged Donda into a correction—"Caliphate of London, the Wings have played twenty-two games traveling through the Liberation Empire. The American squad, which calls itself the Americans, played in the Old-Timers' Game at Wrigley Field. After that, they split among their individual teams. Also, the regular season was disrupted so most of the Americans haven't played in weeks."

"Advantage Wings."

"For harmony, yeah. But both ballclubs are hard-nosed. For fundamentals and depth, I say advantage to the Americans."

"Course as we know, it don't mean warm spit in a dry bucket until the first pitch. Let's set the defense for the United States nine. Pitcher Ted Towers, catcher Tony Felton, first baseman Johanna Busco, second baseman Carl Tedeschi, shortstop Bar'Nee Ortiz, and third baseman Pop Ra Chou. Left to right in the outfield, Curly Russell, Aaron White, and Ty Cobb."

The batting orders were neatly listed on the old-school scoreboard. Inside, nuns scampered up and down ladders to update the results.

Teri Sheppard announced Wings shortstop and leadoff batter Buli el-Fayhd.

"The right-handed el-Fayhd has a compact swing, goes to the opposite field, and he won't chase pitches," Donda observed.

"Buckle up, everyone. Here we go. Ted Towers's historic first pitch is a…curveball at the knees for strike one. Whoa Nelly, we're on our way."

El-Fayhd worked the count to two-and-two and then lashed a line drive down the right-field line which skittered around the heavy-footed Cobb.

"Buli's running like a bunny with its tail on fire as he slides into third base." Sahidi gave Donda an extra-long look. They had to be impartial. "That was a tough play for Ty in right field."

Donda squared her jaw. "It's an unfamiliar park with unfamiliar angles and bounces."

"But you have to make that play in a game like this."

"Yes you do," Donda conceded. "It should've been a single, double tops, and Ty should've played closer to the line."

Puppy squirmed. He'd told them to be honest, but criticism like that was too much; he held his breath as Cobb glared from right field.

Ali Makkan drove Towers's first pitch, a fastball on a waist-high platter, in a rising arc toward left field.

"It might be. It could be…a home run!" Sahidi shouted as Russell waved goodbye to the ball disappearing into the packed bleachers. That was followed by another seismic shot off the bat of Magit Wahadi with a runner aboard, giving the Wings a quick 4-0 lead.

As the team hustled off the field, Cobb flung his glove at the bat rack. "Any of you rat-bastard low-life pieces of godless shit says one fucking word about that metal trap of an outfield fence that has more angles than a politician on Election Day will taste my bat."

After a moment of silence, Felton piped up, "You suck, Cobb."

That triggered a brief yet enthusiastic chant of "Cobb sucks" before the crimson-faced manager warned them to play some baseball because he had more godless pieces of shit on the bench just waiting.

They would have to wait a while. Curley Russell wiggled out a leadoff walk and Cobb dropped a neat bunt down the third-base line, gluing the Wings third baseman to his heels in surprise. Even then, he barely beat the throw to first. Before the first pitch to Johanna Busco, pitcher Aival Hadi whirled and caught Curly dancing one step too many off second. Russell was eventually nailed after dragging out the rundown play while Ty, racing all the way, took out the distracted Wings second baseman with a spike-high slide into the shins.

There was a scuffle.

Prepared, the 'bot umpires spread out an aluminized translucent shield separating the glaring teams clustered around the infield.

"What do you say, Donda? Legitimate slide or a cheap shot?" Sahidi's voice echoed throughout the stirring stands carpeted with the crescent moon and star, and red-white-and-blue baseball caps. Sahidi could feel Puppy's warning from a section below. Do not stir up trouble.

On the flight over, Sahidi had digested a few newly available books on sportscasting from the days before the pre-MLB shrinkage in the late '40s. In *But We See the Same Thing*, long-time Seattle announcer Gia Chacon lamented the pressure to sanitize any faults of the game until insulted fans tuned out as they had tuned out voting. Hacienda Suarez's *A Ball Ain't A Strike* told of her struggles for honesty at ESPN that cost her a career, and Benjy R'oot dramatized the story of hiding in the Rocky Mountains to escape censure of his *Baseballs Are Diamonds* podcast clamoring for a return to pre-2000 rules.

We say how it is and not how we want it to be. Sahidi slid the hastily scribbled note toward the frowning Donda. Grandma's bra straps, she fretted, they'd already planned for this eventuality. Don't point blame but don't insult everyone watching the play. This isn't propaganda. This is journalism. Time to separate them once and for all.

"I can't read minds, though I've had a few girl friends who said I could." Donda winked. "But Ty's pissed 'bout misplaying the ball in right, Curly daydreams off second, so Mr. Cobb decides to send a message. Might've been a tad higher than needed, but this is the World Series. Climb the stepladder, folks. The stakes are high."

If they hadn't screwed until three that morning, Sahidi would've kissed Donda.

Slightly rattled following the six-minute delay, Hadi served up a hanging slider to Busco, who got her ample hips into the swing.

"Open the window, Aunt Minnie, here it comes," Sahidi pealed as Busco's rocket disappeared over the top of the center-field bleachers.

For the Americans, that was the last cause for celebration. Hadi settled down for seven sterling innings of scoreless, four-hit ball. Ted Towers didn't make it out of the third inning and relievers Joachim Feller and Tendrata Spahn weren't much better.

Inside a very quiet clubhouse, Cobb scowled as bullpen coach Mint Schaap bravely approached for the third time, jerking his head at the persistent knocks.

"What am I gonna say, Skip?"

"The same fucking thing I already told you."

"But Puppy says we gotta let them in—"

"Do I look like I care what Puppy says?" Cobb roared, standing with a grimace. "I'll let the fucking writers in when we're done talking and you tell them that."

"'Ready did, Skip."

"Then tell them again." Cobb tossed a can of orange pop at the fleeing Schaap. The manager's pitying sigh accompanied his cold stare. "Don't worry. This won't be long because if I tried to recap everything we'd be here until three Fridays from tomorrow. Now, girls and boys, if I can call you that, anyone here think we didn't stink?"

No one dared say a word.

"Nine-to-two. Nine-to-two." Walking around the clubhouse, Cobb repeated the sentence a few more times as if casting a satanic curse. "Four errors. Eleven hits they got. Most of 'em could've been caught if your lard asses moved. I needed a goddamn umbrella with all the line drives falling on my head."

"Wouldn't have helped."

Cobb's rheumy eyes bulged. He whirled in all directions with pointed finger. "Who said that?" He kicked over a stool into the silence. "Who the hell said that?"

Felton slowly stood. "Me, Skip. Me."

"Well, well. An honest man." Ty shoved his face into Felton's. "Are you blaming me?"

Tony steadily met the manager's stare. "I'm giving you a share of the fault."

"The damn outfield has no traction and the fence—"

"Not that," Tony said quietly. "That kind of shit happens."

"Then what? Because I couldn't hit for you Mary Janes? Catch for you?"

"Because we weren't prepared, Mr. Manager. That's on you."

"I had to prepare you?" Ty wheezed. "Professional ballplayers. Supposedly."

"Yes we are. Like we expected a professional manager. Su-ppos-ed-ly." He drew out the syllables. "Where was our scouting report? I gave you tons of shit from playing these camels in London. All of us chimed in." Wary murmurs swept the floor. "But you were too busy shopping."

Cobb reddened under the knowing laughs.

"Oh so sorry. I forgot. Our manager's got to look good. 'Cept you forgot there's the rest of us with you preening for the cameras like an old whore on a Monday night."

Cobb lunged for the powerful catcher who easily knocked him aside. Cobb tried to get up, swearing loudly and waving away help. After loud hoarse breaths, Ty slowly struggled to his feet and disappeared inside the tiny manager's office.

"Should I let the press in already?" Schaap finally asked, the knocks now bangs and shouts in a few languages.

Tony reluctantly nodded. "And I'll kick the shit out of anyone who makes any excuses for today. We got our asses handed to us by a team that outplayed us, out-hustled us, out-wanted us for the win." He fumbled a moment. "I'll also break the head of anyone who says we let down America."

He heaved a stool against the wall. "Not all of you get this, which ain't your fault, but those of us who served do." Tony nodded at his fellow POWs. "We never fought for the damn flag. We fought for each other. Grandma and Cheng, The Family, at the end they didn't give a shit. They never do. Different governments, same crap. We fought for our brothers and sisters, and our brothers and sisters died for each other. Okay, okay."

Felton calmed down. "There I went and made the speech. I ain't saying this game is war, that what happens on Peace Field will decide peace because for all we know the missiles'll start flying whoever becomes world champion. Would that surprise anyone?" He bitterly laughed. "But I for one am just damn embarrassed to look any of you in the eyes after the way I played. Damn embarrassed and I'm damn sorry. I wasn't ready and there's little I want to do more in life than kick the shit out of these Allahs so let's figure out how the hell to do that."

Felton stared through the silent nodding clubhouse.

"Now let those parasites in."

62

If he were in a mood to thank Allah, and of course Annette for the idea, Azhar would be grateful that there were only three mosques in Valletta. Despite laughable wartime protests from the Imam of nearby Sicily decrying Islamophobia, the Maltese government, that is, the Vatican-in-Exile, wouldn't countenance the construction of more mosques nor allow more Muslims to emigrate.

Yes, that demonstrated the religious prejudice of Crusaders. Yes, also their unspeakable hypocrisy and lies about desiring peace with Islam. The Holy Father had responded in 2071 and again, post-war 2074, that he would be willing to discuss relinquishing space in Valletta for mosques and opening immigration to the great people of Islam once the mighty Grand Mufti restored/rebuilt Vatican City and returned all its treasures and holy relics. That was the last of such discussions.

The first *masjid* lay alone at the end of deserted Bialista Way. A sense of quarantine came to mind, Azhar sourly contemplated, waiting patiently in the prayer hall for *salat*, the first daily prayer, to finish. Two younger men warily eyed Mustafa's respectful yet clearly Westernized dress. Azhar didn't care because he was far past caring beyond his single-minded goal.

After performing *wudhu*, or ablutions, he showed photos of Omar, dark-eyed and dark-minded, scowling into the camera beside his worshipful mother who, Azhar explained, was near death with grief over the disappearance of her only son. The young men sniffed suspiciously at the quasi-infidel, blandly shrugging away his attempt to ask further questions.

Several older men brushed past without much of a look. For them, Mustafa added Abdul's photo, his two sons, his only children, disappearing at whose hands he dared not say. But look around. His eyes found the seams in the thick walls to indicate Valletta, the pope, Abdullah, baseball, sacrilege.

That got him nowhere, which didn't please Annette over the shoddy implementation of her brilliant idea.

"Did you have that face?"

He almost asked which face as they hurried away, his original or the one ordered by Abdullah. "The look of deep parental concern, yes."

She wasn't convinced. "I don't understand. They must have heart. Compassion. They're in a damn mosque."

Irritated, Azhar dead stopped in the middle of Holmes Street. "They don't trust me. I wouldn't trust me."

Annette rolled her eyes. "I could help. I can be very persuasive."

He managed a weary agreeing smile. "But they won't let you in."

"Even as your dutiful wife?"

"I am showing a photo of my dutiful wife whom you do not resemble. That might not beget trust."

At Masjid el-Haryh on the corner of Holmes and Curzon Streets, there was more of an audience to ignore him, about a dozen or so of all ages with similar guarded looks. Annette simply shook her head at his failure. When he arrived at Masjid Kalruth, it was nearly time for *aksam*, the prayer for sunset. Twenty or so worshippers took to their mats. Asking Allah to forgive his duplicities, Azhar joined the prayers.

Surprised by how much he wept, Mustafa grew slightly glazed. Exhausted, drained, really. He bowed out before the *khutba*, the lecture, remembering as he neared the exit why he was there. Azhar wondered if forgetfulness were a sign from Allah that he should abandon this quest and listen to Annette and turn over his doubts to the police. The side that was angry with Allah quickly reminded him through a sharp pain of heartburn that he had no proof, which is why he was here.

Azhar passed around the photos, earning shrugs from the more polite congregants. Needing a hole to crawl into, he hurried out, dodging a persistent ticket seller whispering the price for prime box seats for game two. Annette slipped her arm through his, squeezing in support. Two blocks south with nowhere else to go, this one viable plan of visiting mosques in shambles. Azhar stopped again in the middle of the street, making no effort to pretend he was doing anything other than giving up for a moment.

Annette mentioned the police again. He obstinately refused.

"You." An old man with a face the color of sand glared. "Always the left foot."

Mustafa glared back. "For what?"

"Exiting the *masjid*. Enter with your right foot. Exit with your left."

Azhar's legs went to putty. "I am deeply sorry for the insult, Father."

The old man grunted. "Why would you know? A policeman."

"Pardon?"

"A shame on you working against your own people." The old man turned away in disgust.

Azhar followed him. "Sir, I am not a policeman." The old man wouldn't budge. "I am not. Why do you say that? Wait. Because I showed pictures?"

He barely waited for the wizened head to nod.

"They are my sons. They are in trouble."

The old man's eyes narrowed. "What kind of trouble?"

"I do not know. My younger son"—he showed Abdul's school picture to another grunt—"is looking for his older brother." He produced Omar's picture.

The thinned eyebrows shot up, then the mask fell. "*Wa 'alaikum-as-salam.*"

Azhar completely wrapped his hand around a thin wrist. "I will have no peace until I find my children. Do you know Omar—"

"I know no one."

"Yes he does. He's lying." With outstretched arms, Annette blocked the old man's path. "I know liars."

The rheumy eyes widened in panic.

"You do know him," Azhar rasped, so desperate for the right answer he would consider half a truth. "Omar has taken Abdul, his brother. The young one has a good heart. He is a good boy. He fears his brother is planning evil. He wants to stop him. He has failed. I cannot allow that, and I cannot allow the Crusader police to interfere. This is not theirs to handle. This is my family. Our family as Muslims. Or else we will never have peace upon us. Never."

Azhar's eyes glistened as the old man thought. "Please, Father. They are my only children."

The old man peered at Annette. "Is she your wife?"

"No. Just a friend. Just a dear friend willing to say what is needed to help. As I hope you can be."

The old man nervously looked around, hissing, "Paen Hotel. Top floor," before vanishing into the crowd.

The decrepit lobby teemed with tourists, cots stretching from the cracked glass doors to the scruffy elevator adjacent to the chipped spiral staircase. With some hospital décor and a spray of medicinal vapors, the hotel could pass for an emergency room which, the peevish desk clerk sneered, was close enough. The "authorities"—which he bracketed with stout fingers—denied true believers their rightful rooms, showing their bigotries. Which will always be there, he added, no matter what our "new leader"—more fingered brackets—wants us to believe.

Azhar kept the photos in his inside coat pocket, only saying he had an "appointment," chalking his fingers in the air. The clerk scouted him head to toe. This one didn't look all that much different from the others who'd had "appointments" on the fourth floor yesterday.

With Annette frowning impatiently in a moldy chair, Mustafa took the rickety stairs, passing bedded hallways and the unpleasant odor of poorly prepared food. At the fourth floor he froze, cursing his stupid timidity as an elderly couple in crescent-moon-and-star baseball caps padded by holding towels and toothbrushes. Abruptly, Azhar showed them Omar's photo.

With bland smiles, they continued into the noisy public bathroom.

Stepping around the alley of cots, Azhar went door-to-door, listening. A few times he answered curious looks by explaining he had forgotten his room number in all the excitement of the World Series. Everyone kept to their business. A suspicious stranger eavesdropping was only suspicious if he eavesdropped at their door.

Halfway down the corridor, a fat man in a white sleeveless shirt ripped open room 422 and shoved Mustafa against the far wall.

"What do you want?"

"Nothing. Many apologies. I come for no trouble."

A forearm pressed a little tighter on his windpipe.

"I am looking for young men with whom I have a meeting." Idiot, you deserve to have your throat crushed.

The fat man smirked. "Young men? It is not that kind of hotel, *sadj.*"

Azhar turned scarlet, knocking the man onto a cot, which crumpled.

"Dare not say that to me, you filthy pig."

Another fat man with a similar wardrobe rushed out. Mustafa ducked under the lopsided arc of the lamp, kicked at a knee and hit the first man, now rising, in the cheek. He fled down the steps and didn't stop running until he and Annette were five blocks away.

They finally went to the police.

Azhar explained that he was in Malta as a personal emissary of Abdullah bin-Mohammad. Desk sergeant Spiteri listened patiently since this frazzled middle-aged man was the eighth person that day to claim friendship with Abdullah bin-Mohammad. Spiteri, who had two daughters, neither one a particular joy, took his lunch hour in a private room and listened as this Mustafa, egged on by an attractive woman who naturally claimed friendship with the pope, shouted that his son Omar had illegally entered the island with intent to do harm. He didn't know what harm, but his son was a fanatic, a Black Robe and he had captured his younger son, Abdul.

Half an hour ago, three men were led away after charging that the Grand Mufti was nearing the island in a large balloon. They hadn't any proof either. Nearly all the complaints were about Muslim terrorists. Orders had come down to avoid any perceived persecution of the Allahs. If there was some real doubt, call the papal security office.

Still, he was a father; the sergeant checked. There was no record of an Omar Mustafa of this age disembarking in Valletta although he tried mollifying his guests by showing vids of the other nine Omar Mustafas who were not their Omar Mustafa. Sgt. Spiteri did find a record of an Abdul Mustafa entering Malta which Azhar cried was not the issue because that was the kidnapping victim. The woman fired a look that made his chest tighten.

Missing teenagers had been found for days now, closeted in various compromised and inebriated positions. "Wait until the island empties out after the World Series," Spiteri said, exasperated father to exasperated father. "I'm sure your boy will turn up. Maybe he'll be a man by then." He winked.

As they mercifully left, the woman said she'd have his job on a plate and his head on a pike after she was done with him. Spiteri didn't doubt it. He was married to someone just like that.

• • • •

BY THE TIME Omar returned, shortly before midnight, from another scouting expedition to the closed stadium, still ablaze with lights and festive crowds, the exploits of the Fasil cousins had spread through at least the top two floors.

"A degenerate." Namil continued the story. "Knocking on doors looking for male pleasure." He hurled spit over his shoulder. "Just let him come here."

Omar smirked. "What would you have done?"

"I would have twisted off his penis," Namil said to appreciative laughter.

"Oh. Spilled blood all over the walls."

"Yes," Namil said, a little less certain.

"Until the screams brought the police? *Majnun.* Even in your ignorant little brain do not imagine such a reaction. Do not imagine anything that brings attention. Do not imagine anything that distracts us from our path. Do you understand?"

Namil squirmed, not quite ready to give in. "Like your brother?"

Omar pressed a knife inches from Namil's right eyeball. "I will dispose of him when we must."

Malik blew cigarette smoke. "Why not let him carry the bombs?"

"Because we have a plan," Omar said dismissively.

"It would dispose of the body."

"Do you prefer for this degenerate to gain glory?"

"No." Malik bristled. "I do not ask him to replace any of us. Just an addition."

"We have enough."

"More bombs, more area covered, more dead."

"So he will just walk in like the rest of us as a good volunteer?"

"We drug him," Malik offered an alternative.

"You question the plans of the Imam?" Omar challenged the room. There was a reason why he kept certain information to himself. The Imam was not alone in planning this blessed event. He did not want to know more. But these *ahmaq* would. "We do not drug him. He will be dead by the time of the glory. We alone will share the moment. We alone will be the true martyrs. We alone will blaze the path back to Allah."

They mumbled fervently. Omar sneered and went into the bedroom. Abdul was awake, staring at the ceiling. He ignored his brother, even after the light kicks to his knees. Omar shoved a straw in the boy's swollen mouth, jostling until he sipped water.

Omar shook his head at the soiled pants. "Beast."

"They would not let me use the toilet," Abdul wheezed.

Omar tossed an angry glance at the door. "I will take you."

"Why? You will kill me anyway. I want to make you puke from my shit."

The Black Robe yanked Abdul's pants down around his knees and undid the bonds to the chair. He quickly retied the rope around his wrists as he prodded Abdul down the hallway and into the bathroom. Omar reddened at the mocking laughter. He waited impatiently for Abdul to finish all kinds of business. Omar was sure the boy dawdled. He would do the same, he realized with grudging respect.

"You do not trust me to wipe myself?" Abdul scowled.

Omar wrapped his hand in toilet paper, grasped a few sheets and disdainfully cleaned his younger brother. He tossed the stained underwear into the trash, pulled up the foul-smelling jeans and prodded Abdul back into the chair. Abdul made no resistance to the fresh knots.

"Are you hungry?" Omar asked. Abdul shook his head, angering the Black Robe. "Why not?"

"Why bother?"

Omar kicked at a shin. "You have given up?"

Abdul nodded.

"Weak." Omar's mouth twisted. "You always have been weak."

"Yes. I am not strong like a murderer of children."

Omar flushed. "What do you know of that?"

"You have not destroyed my ears yet."

Omar sneered. "You are wrong. Unlike the Crusaders, we do not kill for sport."

"Then why?"

"Purpose." Omar's eyes burned. "Nothing you would understand. This requires courage. You are a coward like your father."

The younger boy's eyes flared. "He will find me."

"Hah."

"He will find me. He will not let you kill me."

Omar shifted uneasily. "How does he know I have you?"

"Where else would I be but on your tail?"

"Hah. On your own tail."

"Until he comes."

"Never. He is a *majnun*."

"He is smart. Abdullah trusts him. The pope trusts him"—Abdul endured the slap—"the Americans trust him." Two more quick blows didn't quiet him. "He will hunt you down."

"Too late for all of you. Too late," Omar whispered feverishly.

Omar spun out of the room, catching his breath in the hallway before slamming the front door shut. He knocked so fearfully on room 422 that he had to repeat himself several times.

The fat man with the new bruise on his cheek waited warily.

"Brother," Omar said politely. "I wanted to congratulate and thank you for driving the vermin from our hotel."

The man beamed. He was a little tipsy from the appreciation whiskey gifted by 404.

"This city, this island, is infested," Omar said.

"Everywhere," the man muttered with distaste. "I do what I can for Allah."

"As we all do. May I ask what this decadent pig looked like so, should I see him on the street, I can beat him to the ground with Mohammad's wrath?"

"Approximately 5'10, chubby with an angular face, heated dark eyes, and large ears."

Omar's mouth went dry. "That is very descriptive."

The man held up his hand. "Dark hair tightly cut. His features looked almost rearranged as if the Devil had moved the cheeks."

Omar panted slightly. "How do you come to own such powers of recall, brother?"

"My cousin and I ran a market in Venice before the Crusaders burnt us down in vengeance. I can describe every customer we ever had."

Omar bowed and shuffled back into his room. Ignoring the limpid looks from the living room, Omar locked the bathroom door and sat on the toilet. He shook so hard the seat came loose.

63

The vast underground cavern twinkled with little stars. Actually, small lights above each of the 3,284,000 books which the three houses of the Antwerp rabbinate and the Brothers of St. John had begun compiling in 2069, a year into the war. Funded by the Vatican and wealthy donors in North America, the project to save the world's knowledge took eight years and cost more than four hundred lives.

Puppy steadied the nine-foot stepladder so Annette wouldn't topple off. From her dazed gleam, she might not have noticed.

"They hired cargo ships under neutral flags and smuggled them past the Muslims, past the Europeans, us, everyone." Annette marveled. "Then brought them here. Rabbi Gold, who's like a robot without the personality, said they spent millions in bribes and excavations to secretly dig this tunnel. The last of the pope's Swiss guards and some Zionist soldiers, too, died protecting the library by taking down a Muslim special operations team. The Muslims didn't try again. They didn't think it was worth it because they figured they'd rule forever. Also, the Goliath dome deflects missiles, rockets, the usual."

Annette blithely waved off his concern as she tottered on the top of the ladder. Embedded bookshelves went from floor to ceiling, a quarter mile high.

"There are thirty-two monks serving as librarians. That was part of the deal. Irish monks had saved Western civilization books once before when the Roman Empire was collapsing."

"The Roman Empire?" he asked with a mischievous grin.

"Yes, dearest. Caesar and all those guys. I can read a book." Annette pointed toward two monks pushing a cart piled with plastic-covered books. "It's really amazing, Pup. We're retrieving books from liberated areas every day. I mentioned to John that Kenuda said we have our own stash of millions of books but we're not sure what's true and what was cleansed. His monks can cross-reference our history with theirs to sort that all out. Incredible, right?"

He folded his arms. "What makes you think their history is true? It could be Christianized."

She frowned. "History is always going to be Christianized or Muslim-ized or Familiy-zed or whatever. But we need to know what the facts were which, yes, anyone can change but if you have enough sources, you can establish what's what."

Puppy stared at the bright globed ceiling where monks hurried along embedded metal walkways as if they had suction cups on their flat shoes.

Annette rattled his ladder, making it sway. "What, Puppy?"

"'What Puppy' what?"

She studied him. "You can't get used to this, can you?"

"I was never one for books other than those about baseball."

His wife hissed. "Me. Me knowing things. Me doing things."

"I like that you're involved."

"No, you don't."

He shouted back, "Yes I do—"

"You're such a shitty liar." Annette cupped her mouth and called out apologies to the diffident monks. "How much does it bother you?"

"Very clever getting me to admit that it bothers me at all." Puppy shook his head at her glower. "I'm not bothered. I just have to get used to this."

"That I have a brain."

"No. That you're using it."

She softened. "Good point."

"I never thought you were stupid. No, never, and don't shake the ladder again, please. This is all an adjustment."

"Good because I'm not stopping."

"Now that you're on a first name basis with the Holy Father, why would you? Seriously, why would you, sweetie?"

Despite his protests, Annette climbed onto his ladder. Even a couple monks below thought that wasn't a smart idea.

"You're worried I'm smarter than you and yes, the right answer is a little."

He rolled his eyes. "A little."

"Then what?"

"It's not you, Annette. You're doing great. I'm worried about me. How I'm doing."

"I think damn good. Look what you've accomplished, Puppy. You had Pope John throw out the first ball. Rabbi Gold said there's a special section offshore reserved for hundreds of journalists covering the World Series. The whole world reported on the first game, Pup."

"I know." He gave her a long look. "What if it's not good enough?"

"For what? The actual peace?"

He nodded. "I think we're okay if the Muslims win. Abdullah was in such a good mood he agreed this morning to partial mutual withdrawals. Only a division each, but still."

"Yeah, and?" she asked impatiently.

"Like, what if we win tomorrow?"

"Then our side'll be happy."

"What if we win game three and the series?"

Annette spread her hands. "Then we'll be very happy."

"How unhappy will the Arabs be? Will they still sell the peace to the Heir Apparent? To their own people?"

Annette pursed her lips. "You think they're that shallow?"

After envying the monks's simple happiness, he finally answered. "What if this is all just the moment, special, sure, but just three baseball games. We all come together and then it's forgotten by the first terrorist attack or the first glitch in negotiations and believe me, Elias says they're torturous with General Petash. I thought baseball was the magic formula. What if it's just a stupid little game?"

"It is a stupid little game." Annette tenderly grasped his arm. "It's all what we invest in it, Pup. What we see in the silly game with the old-fashioned rules. It's like praying, yes, like praying. Is there a god or not, who the hell knows? It's what you feel when you think there is and what you do with it. We've got thirty thousand people rooting against each other with Muslims and Americans on the field not hitting each other with bats, no guns at their heads like in England. Their team's here because they wanted to be. Our team's here because they wanted to be. This might only be a special three days, but then we've at least had that and in this world that's something. A start, Puppy. You're worrying about the ninth inning when we haven't got out of the bottom of the first yet."

He fiercely kissed the top of her head, about as far as he could go without sending their ladder onto a bunch of disapproving monks.

"But you're also worried that you'll screw up managing tomorrow, aren't you?" Annette half smiled.

He sighed. "We sucked in practice. They move like elephants. Our team's old, Annette. They're old and tired."

"Then start the younger players."

"And do that to Felton and Johanna and Curly and…"

"The heroes of your youth?"

"Yeah," he admitted. "And the ones who suffered in POW camps, more than me or you or anyone else here. They deserve to be the ones to win."

"Not if they lose, honey. Not if they lose." Annette climbed up a step, fussing with her hair.

Puppy knew that gesture all too well. "What?"

She pulled a face. "I don't want to burden you and Azhar's going to kill me but too damn bad." She shouted out another apology to the bemused monks. "We have a problem with Azhar's son."

"What'd the chubby kid do?"

Annette stared. "Not him, Pup. Not Abdul."

Puppy blanched. "What about Omar?"

• • • •

GENERAL PETASH WINDMILLED his arms in vague apology after making Gold wait in the outer suite for half an hour under the baleful looks of beefy bodyguards.

"Astonishingly busy day." Petash remained behind his desk.

"For all."

Petash smirked, as if the rabbi could possibly match his schedule. "So, Mr. Gold, what is the urgency?"

"There is a security issue."

"I cannot solve that problem, too. The intractability of the Americans in denying their secret west-coast submarine bases is sufficient for this morning."

"This problem concerns a Muslim."

Petash scowled. "Of course it does."

"Which is why I'm here. According to agreed protocols, we must contact you with the information first."

"As your agents have promptly done"—he pretended that he had to recall—"eleven times so far."

"Protocol and courtesy, General."

"And how many times have you passed along similar security concerns to First Cousin Kenuda?"

"Once."

"Once."

"Yes. Once. They were Russians. It proved groundless."

"Once," Petash sneered. "And of the eleven protocol alerts which you courteously and respectfully submitted regarding Muslims, how many proved valid?"

Gold stood his ground. "That is irrelevant. All we need is one."

"None. None." Petash saw how repeating irritated Gold. "None. And before I return to concealed nuclear-armed submarines, why should this twelfth concern you other than the obvious?"

"The information originates from Annette Ramos."

Petash rolled his eyes. "Oh well then."

Gold's face tightened. "Her personality aside, this is supported by personal testimony." He recited the relationship between Annette, Azhar, and Puppy as Petash glanced impatiently at his watch.

"It sounds like a family matter."

"It might be. But we do not know for certain. The eldest is a Black Robe."

Petash reddened. "There are many devout Muslims here, Mr. Gold. That is not a predicate to arrest them."

"I merely want your permission to proceed with a security investigation."

"You mean harassment."

"It is my job to ensure nothing impacts the summit or the game."

"But I would like that? I would be delighted by an act of violence? Why? Because I'm a Muslim?"

Gold flushed. "I never said that."

"It is enough to hold this summit on this infernal island." Petash made it clear Gold's presence was not one of the attractions. "We will not be targeted."

"I must do my due diligence."

"Without the basis of any proof, merely a father's ravings and the peculiar American woman's instincts?" Petash snorted. "If there is evidence of weapons, meetings...I assume the young boy has not also witnessed a cell of terrorists aiding this Omar?" He snorted again. "No, Mr. Gold, I do not give my authorization to harass a probably devout Muslim who does not get along with his non-believing family. That is not a first in any religion."

Gold stiffened. "I must insist. We cannot take any chances, however small."

Petash smiled nastily. "And I will insist that, if you do so, I will raise the issue with Kenuda and ensure that Abdullah is also informed. When the talks drag on, missiles remain in place, tanks poised, aircrafts hovering, children suffering, they will understand whose fault it is."

"And Abdullah, who entrusted Azhar Mustafa, will also understand whose decision allowed a potential terrorist to remain at large."

Petash laughed coldly. "Feel free. Now if there is nothing else, please excuse me, Rabbi."

Gold stomped back to his office. Wondering why he was even hesitating, he codified an official request and scanned in Omar's photo. Nothing matched Omar Mustafa. He ran a scan of only the photo.

Zain Nouri had arrived at the Port of Valletta six days ago on a Moroccan passport. Gold ran another request. Azhar and Abdul Mustafa had arrived earlier that day.

Now he hesitated, but just for a moment, before requesting General Petash's guest list for today's game.

64

The players sniffed at the mosaic of press clips like angry dogs. Angry and hungry dogs. Disdain in Russian and Arabic and Chinese and French and Italian and Spanish, with a few tart words in Maltese, ran about four-feet-wide and five-feet-high. Until the sun peeked over the edge of Malta, Herbert translated right down to the last sarcastic word while Puppy scissored and stapled.

Americans Shaky At Own Game. U.S. Really Is No More. What Are Yanks Good At? Sad Scene At Peace Field, went the kinder headlines, stuffed with such generous phrases as, *Giving the Fans Chills With Their Whiffs*, and, *The Balls Cried Their Way Out Of the Old Men's Mitts*, to, *Their National Pastime Has Become A Global Embarrassment*.

In the center were the photos: Busco flailing at a grounder. Ty falling in right field. Curly kicking his glove into the bleachers. And the disbelieving expressions in the dugout in the last of the ninth.

Felton shredded the paper blanket of abuse off the wall; Puppy stopped him from setting a blaze in the clubhouse. He let the shouting and swearing run its course, hoping to drain away the rage so it wouldn't easily reignite.

He clapped his hands, bringing the mutters down to a bearable volume.

"Anyone here disagree with the assessment of how shitty we looked?" Puppy dared them to disagree. "Course they were nasty because they're reporters and that's what they do which is why we don't have any back home. But you still stunk—"

"Hey, we know we stunk. Let's put that all behind us," Felton barked to agreeing grumbles.

"You're right. Yesterday is yesterday. Today's today."

Puppy and the team exchanged stares.

"Don't we got BP in a few, Skip?" Busco asked, earning impatient laughs.

"Yeah, we do." He loudly cleared his throat as the starters headed toward the exit. "We'll go in order of the starting lineup."

Puppy thumbtacked the lineup where the clips had been, saying over his shoulder, "It's different from game one."

Curly Russell was the first to read it before turning with a shocked look at Puppy. "Where am I?"

"On the bench."

Felton shoved Curly aside, running his finger down the lineup several times. "In the manager's office, Nedick."

"No. We talk here." Ty had advised letting the vets know privately. Puppy felt that was all wrong. No privilege, no rank. "We had to make changes."

Felton bumped Puppy's chest. "By benching all the former POWs."

"No. Players. I'm the manager and that's my call and that's how it stands."

The veterans formed a menacing circle around Puppy. He planted his feet.

"We didn't come all the way to this shithole to be humiliated," Busco savagely said.

"You're right. But you were still humiliated." Puppy held up his hands at their shouts. "Why? Because you sucked? Not completely."

He waited for the paper balls to bounce off his head. "The Allahs already know who you are. They didn't conquer the world because they're idiots. We made that mistake in the last war. They scouted you up and down and out your butts. They know Bar'Nee can't resist up and in, and they know Tedeschi doesn't move well to his left and Johanna can be set up with curves away and sure, but you hit a mistake in game one. Should I go on? But they don't know this gang."

Puppy pointed at the descendants of the twentieth-century greats. The POWs reluctantly turned as if surprised there was anyone else there.

"They haven't got a clue what these kids can do because they've never seen them play. They don't know what Ryan throws. They don't know what Carew likes to hit. They don't know what kind of game Bench will call and they sure don't want to piss off Gibson."

Gibson's dark scowl produced a few brittle laughs.

"So, let's drop a big fat surprise on their big swelled heads and see what happens."

The younger players anxiously waited for the veterans to respond.

With a loud sigh, Tony flipped his catcher's mask at Bench. "Don't fuck up, sweetheart."

Tennessee's smirk curled up around her thick eyebrows. "Stay awake, Gramps, and see how it should be done."

Puppy mixed up the order of batting practice so there would be no clue about who was starting. Same for infield practice. Up in the booth, Sahidi would have none of that, pouncing on the lineup overhaul as soon as they were a minute into the pregame show.

"Joining me as color commentator for game two is the legendary Ty Cobb. Ty, what happened to take you out of right field and out of the manager's role, and up here with me?"

Puppy had warned Ty to be prepared for Sahidi's verbal traps.

"I pulled a synthetic groin muscle chasing the damn ball, darlin'." Ty oozed charm. "I'd never planned on playing more than the first game anyhow."

Sahidi oozed right on back with an authentic Southern accent. "But you predicted you'd be the leading hitter in the series."

"Fooled you, didn't I?"

Her eyes widened in mock horror. "Then you misled the world's press on a historic occasion like this?"

"Guess so." Ty set his natty straw hat on the long table overlooking the field. "I also never intended on managing more than one game."

"Oh, Mr. Cobb—"

"Now, little girl, don't you 'oh, Mr. Cobb' me. Puppy Nedick managed these boys and girls in London. They all escaped together when the Allahs tried to kill them back when we were enemies and all. They got a special bond. You could say I'm more of a, well, goodwill ambassador as the greatest player in baseball history."

"But if bonding with the players is the key, why has Puppy benched almost all his former veterans? You managed the kids in the Old-Timers' Game as skipper of the twentieth-century team. Shouldn't you be the rightful choice?"

Ty oozed so much his jaw had to slow down. "And miss the opportunity to tell the world the story of the greatest game there ever was? Who knows twentieth-century baseball better than me? Besides, I'm looking forward to sharing insights with the spitting image of Ernie Harwell's voice."

Sahidi tittered and went down the visiting Americans's starting lineup as Wings pitcher Faheem Ghazali loosened up on the mound.

"Leading off will be shortstop Mende Aparicio. Batting second, second sacker Ephraim Carew. Tennessee Bench, the catcher, bats third. At third base, Donde Vasquez Carlton hits cleanup and hitting fifth will be Donda Sicutyanni in right field. Center fielder Estie Morgan bats sixth, left fielder Myrina James Musial hits seventh with first baseman Sander Clemente eighth. Batting ninth and on the mound will be Reynolds Ryan. Ty, other than the names, what's the biggest difference in the game-two lineup?"

"Speed. These boys and girls can motor."

"Let's see how that works out because the beauty of the game is you never know what's going to happen. Though I'll tell you that, if possible, we have more fans in the stands for game two. According to Rabbi Gold's daily briefing, the number of ships in the Mediterranean watching on the floating screens has passed forty thousand and, if we can believe the numbers—better put your straw hat back on for this."

Sahidi drew out the suspense as Aparicio approached home plate.

"They approximated a radio, or radcast audience, worldwide, of seventy-two million for the first game and about three hundred and fifteen million for all the combined television vid audiences. Then you can add the Liberation simul-feed exclusively on its digital network which topped two hundred million."

"Most of 'em tuned in to see me," Ty quipped.

"Even more will tune in today to hear you." Sahidi winked so broadly her eyelids nearly made a sound.

Ty abandoned his impartial status as the sage voice about four batters into the first inning. Aparicio dumped a gorgeous bunt down the third-base line. The lefty Carew slapped the ball into the vacant shortstop hole on a first pitch hit-and-run. Sahidi remarked that the Wings looked like they were already catching their breath.

On the initial pitch to Bench, Puppy ordered a double steal. Bench swung anyway, terrifying Aparicio into a hasty slide that nabbed the side of home before the catcher could apply the tag. It wouldn't have mattered. The ball had dashed to the screen. Carew coasted into third where she scored on a ferocious Bench shot into the left-field stands.

"They usually show movies on a flight like that," pealed Sahidi in her best Ken Coleman fashion.

Next, Carlton drilled the ball into the left-center-field gap, misplayed by the Muslim center-fielder Badawi. Felton, who'd threatened Puppy with severe pain if he refused to let him coach at third, sent Donda home on a bang-bang play. Runner and catcher were entangled and the ball squirted into the Americans's dugout. The furious Muslim manager Arwan charged foul play by the Americans who were clearly up to their old cheating tricks again.

"The only foul play is the stink your fielders are making!" Puppy shouted, running out to home.

As their now-beloved skipper trotted back to the dugout, a wayward ball rolled out toward the Muslim catcher. He started hopping up and down, screaming and waving the baseball inked with *HAHAHA*.

That triggered the first of three warnings the 'bot umpire Debra assessed the Americans. The next came on the first pitch of the bottom of the inning when Reynolds Ryan threw a 104 mph pitch at the Wings leadoff batter's head. The third warning came when the 'bot informed the American dugout, following a pitch that grazed a batter's head, that the current pitcher will be removed from the game if there are any further errant throws.

Puppy went into action, storming toward the umpire and flinging his cap on the ground. Then he jumped up and down on the cap, kicking it back toward the dugout while yelling that they can't be penalized for the slow reactions of the Wings players who, he said with another stomp, have to get out of the way of pitches because they clearly ain't gonna hit them.

The Wings never recovered. They were genuinely afraid of Ryan's control which, since he'd had five shots of rum before the game and long swigs in between innings, was wise. He walked five, hit three, but struck out thirteen, allowing only one broken-bat single in the masterful 11-0 complete-game shutout.

Ty strutted around the clubhouse as if he'd single-handedly done it all. He interrupted player interviews with the swarming press, popped his head into Puppy's office to finish his answers, and announced that his grand strategy made General George S. Patton look like a flea in a shoe.

After the last reporter cleared out, Puppy took a deep breath and motioned Ty to the center of the room. With the air of a wounded warrior, Cobb limped over, hushing the team with a stern look.

"I'm proud of you. This is what should've happened the first game, but your manager and right fielder's a stubborn old bird and let's leave it at that." He scowled at the smiling Puppy. "That good enough for you?"

"I don't really know. Any of you girls and boys got more questions for the greatest player of all time?"

The red-faced Cobb stomped away from the cacophonous laughter into the manager's office. Puppy followed. Ty said he'd better wipe off the shit-eating grin before he did it for him.

"Don't get too full of yourself," Cobb grumbled. "They'll be gunning for you which is why I told you to take the kids out before they went a third time around the lineup."

"Which I did. Which the vets weren't happy about because they felt insulted, like afterthoughts. 'Garbage time,' Bar'Nee said."

"You told the Mary Janes to go screw themselves?"

"Pretty much."

Cobb grunted approval. "Gibson pitching tomorrow?"

"She sure is."

Cobb grunted again. "Same lineup?"

"Dance with the girl who brung ya."

"I got more tricks."

"I sure hope so." Puppy carefully studied him. "How do you feel?"

"Like twenty pounds of manure in a ten-pound bag. Think anyone caught on?"

"Everyone bought the synthetic groin pull," Puppy lied, and Ty let him.

"Thanks for covering. I couldn't have made it out there again. Or in the dugout. My mind gets a little scrambled." He suddenly looked every bit his nearly 213 years. "I don't know how I made it through game one."

"Because you're Ty fucking Cobb, the greatest there ever was."

"Don't you forget it." He wagged a gnarled finger and tried easing out of the chair but couldn't.

Puppy cuffed his neck. "Wait until everyone goes."

"Because I'd embarrass myself?" Cobb rasped, sinking deeper with a sad nod.

65

It was time to go.

The four young men knelt around the coffee table, eyes shut in prayer. Each wore loose-fitting white robes. They silently rose, letting yet another raucous parade pass outside as if hoping it might suddenly invite them along.

Omar's face twisted in rage as he reached beneath Namil's robe and yanked away the knife taped to his left leg.

"What is this?"

"I—"

Omar nearly slapped him. "I said no weapons."

"I thought our passes were privileged."

"We will not be searched. But I do not want you tempted. If you have a knife, you might use it." He flung the serrated blade onto the ratty chair. "Anything else you have forgotten? Any other deviations from the blessed plan that you dare take upon yourselves?"

The three men exchanged glances. Finally, Malik stepped forward, jerking his head down the hallway.

"What about the boy?"

"I will handle."

"When?"

"Before we leave."

"Good." Malik hesitated. "And I will watch."

Omar reddened. "You do not believe me?"

"Yes. But he is your brother," Namil said.

"He is filth."

"Yes. Still, he is your brother. We understand the shame."

"Do you not think I have the courage to eliminate such a pig?"

"No. We do this out of respect. We are honored to remove the weight."

Omar trembled. "Have I ever abdicated my responsibility? Would the Imam Hazid, who sits at the side of the Heir Apparent, entrust someone with such a glorious mission who could not obey Allah? Do you question his judgment?"

Namil stubbornly shook his head. "No. But the boy is your brother."

Omar stomped into the back bedroom where Abdul was wide awake, waiting.

"How are you?"

"How are you?" Abdul laughed.

"Do not mock me."

"It is hard when you ask dumb questions."

"I ask for your welfare."

"Before you kill me?"

The back of Omar's hand lashed across the boy's cheek. "Silence. You must show courage."

Adul's eyes watered.

"It is the highest honor to die for Allah."

Abdul started crying.

"Do not cry."

Abdul sobbed.

"Do not cry. Be a soldier." Omar pulled out a .45 strapped around his calf.

Terrified by the barrel waving near his nose, Abdul stopped crying. He almost looked surprised that his brother would go through with this.

Omar clicked off the safety.

At the sound of the muffled shot, the three young men in the living room nodded with grim satisfaction. When Omar returned, they smiled sympathetically. He shrugged and shot each of them in the head.

Omar hurried back into the bedroom. The dazed Abdul still stared at the pillow with the bullet hole. He shut his eyes, determined to be brave even if he started crying again.

His brother squeezed his throat. "Prepare to serve Allah for the first time in your life."

Omar fumbled with the bonds. Abdul greedily rubbed his sore wrists and ankles.

"Up *majnun*. Clean yourself."

This only deepened Abdul's alarm. "Why?"

"Why, why, why? Because you smell like a pig." Omar kicked him in the rear until the boy stumbled into the bathroom.

In the living room, Omar circled the dead bodies before deciding on Gamil. The clothes tucked under his arm, he pounded on the bathroom door.

"Are you done? We must leave." Omar rattled the knob. "Open this now."

A very small voice said, "No."

Omar closed his eyes to quiet the panting. He shot off the doorknob. His naked brother stood in the dry shower, trembling and crying. Omar doused him for a few minutes with ice cold water which only made Abdul shake more. He impatiently dried off Abdul.

"Put this on."

Abdul stared at the underwear. "That's not mine."

"It is Gamil's."

"But you shot him. I heard."

"That is why he will not need this anymore."

Abdul slowly slipped on Gamil's underwear.

"Keep going."

While the boy dully put on the white socks, Omar returned with the *Adalah*.

"What is that?"

He held the capsule aloft. "The justice of God."

Terrified, Abdul stumbled back into the shower and stained the shorts.

With disgust, Omar flung the underwear across the bathroom. "Pig. Come out of the shower."

"No."

"You dare disobey?"

"Yes." Abdul's chest heaved.

Omar clicked off the safety. "You will do as I say or you will die a coward's death here."

Abdul managed to find some courage as he peed down his leg. "Then do it. Go ahead. Kill me."

Omar couldn't strike him. Special seats or not, Abdul's bruised cheekbone might be difficult to explain along with the faint speckles of blood on Gamil's white robe.

"Please." Omar compressed calm into his voice. "I need your help."

"To blow up people. I know what the *Adalah* does. Everyone knows what the *Adalah* does."

"No. No, no, no. We will avoid casualties. This is a protest against the surrender of Mohammad's empire to the filthy Crusaders through this unholy summit."

"Then make protest signs. Why kill me?"

Omar almost smiled. Perhaps the boy was not a complete *ahmaq*. "You will merely assist, be my assistant." He frowned at Abdul's skepticism. "I will do what I will do, must do, must—must—must do, and you will be the distraction. I will sacrifice myself. You will not die."

Abdul straightened his shoulders. "Don't."

Omar was surprised. "What?"

"Don't die. Mama would be very upset. Papa would be upset"—he raised his voice over Omar's mutters—"and I would be upset."

"You would rejoice." Omar's face twisted. "You hate me."

"Not totally. And you do not hate me totally otherwise you would have let your friends shoot me."

"They had no right."

"Maybe because you do not totally hate me."

Omar had no interest in this conversation. "Will you take the pill?"

"Are you lying to me?"

"No."

Abdul wasn't so sure. "How does it work?"

Grumbling, Omar produced the silicon-encased button on the narrow leather belt at his waist. "I press."

"Then?"

"Boom."

Abdul shuddered. "You and I. Boom."

"No," Omar angrily said. "I press once. I go boom. Twice. You go boom. I will show you."

"Stop."

The older boy smirked. "You have not taken the pill. It is not calibrated. You cannot go boom."

"But you'll go boom and boom me."

"*Ahmaq!*" Omar quickly pushed twice. Abdul waited to be blown up. When he wasn't, he laughed weakly.

Omar glowed in triumph. "See? I do not lie."

"But I have not taken the pill yet."

Omar held out the *Adalah* which Abdul popped into his mouth as if it were coated with razors, swallowing with a great gulping show. With a guttural cry, Omar yanked apart his brother's mouth and searched under the tongue and by the back teeth until, satisfied, he let the coughing Abdul slump onto the toilet seat.

"Good. As you had best not lie and interfere."

"I swear before Allah." The younger boy limply waved his hand.

"You blaspheme."

"I do not." Abdul had discovered a newfound faith since he had not been turned to dust. "I believe but have a different way of showing it. Now you swear."

"Do not be audacious."

"I do not know what that word means."

Omar sighed in exasperation. "Do not tell me how to converse with Allah."

Abdul folded his arms. "He will not care if you swear in front of me."

His brother's mouth twitched. He closed his eyes. "I have sworn but privately. That is all you will get. Now brush your teeth. You reek like an infidel."

Before leaving, Omar scrubbed the robe's blood marks into pink dots.

• • • •

LAWN CHAIRS CARPETED the grassy *campo esterna*—Italian for outfield—around Peace Field. Multilingual transistor radios buzzed with Sahidi's introduction of the Wings lineup; neither manager had made any changes for the final game besides starting pitchers. The Maltese *cirku* entertained with a color guard of clown baseball players wielding crossed bats and juggling balls. Elephants and camels and caged tigers loitered half a mile away.

No matter who won, Malta was prepared for raucous postgame fireworks and celebrations. Buffets arrived in huge trucks, choking traffic. Rumors insisted tightrope walkers would scurry across Peace Field from home plate to center field. That Muslim and American fighter jets would put on an aerial show without bombs. That the Pope would announce construction of a new Vatican City in Valletta. The Mufti's Heir Apparent would lay down their weapons. Black Robes had blown up Copenhagen. A lion had escaped and eaten three nuns—no, two—and only one completely. Liquor would flow. Clowns would turn somersaults. Bands would play.

But first, the deciding game three.

Scowling, Ilsa Gibson dug at the pitcher's mound.

Abd al-Rashid, the Wings leadoff batter, settled into the batter's box with a defiant wiggle of his hips. Gibson's pitch blurred across the knees for strike one.

Smiling smugly, the Wings manager Arwan walked purposely toward home plate. Puppy hurried out.

"You must check her arm," Arwan said to the umpire.

"What're you talking about?" Puppy asked.

"She is a robot."

"Are you kidding me?"

"And are you kidding me, Nedick? You must check." Arwan turned his glare toward the umpire Debra.

"Upon what evidence is this request predicated?" Debra asked.

"That he's going to get the shit kicked out of him and he's trying every cheap stunt," Puppy snarled. "Gibson's human."

Arwan folded his arms. "You have had a history in your game of robot pitchers pretending to be humans. There was the 2051 St. Louis Cardinals who were stripped of their world championship for such deceptions."

"They stopped making those athletic models." Puppy gestured at Debra. "'Bots are no taller than five-three. Ilsa's 6'5" and still growing."

"You have cheated before." Arwan handed the 'bot a WW portal attachment. "Please watch."

"Grandma's bra straps, I don't believe this." Puppy shadowed Debra as it screened the interview he'd given on Islamic television where he was accused of violating the Quran for stealing bases.

"This does not pertain to today's game," the umpire said.

"Hah." Puppy snorted. "Hah. Can we play baseball now?"

"In a moment." Arwan's eyes narrowed as if Puppy had just crawled into a spider's web. "The Greater Islamist Baseball Club signed a waiver permitting Ty Cobb, a self-professed robot, to play as well as permitting the umpires from America to be 'bots as a sign of Allah extending his hand for peace."

"And you had them tested for impartiality."

Arwan arrogantly brushed that aside. "In that waiver, we also reserved the right to challenge any other player we suspected of being a robot. We are doing that now."

Smirking, Arwan handed the umpire another WW. The umpire floated the agreement over home so Puppy could also read it.

"This is permissible," the umpire declared. "We will scan the player."

"You're not scanning my damn pitcher."

Arwan pointed at a clause though Debra had already absorbed the document.

"Then the life-form will be denied access to the pitching mound."

Puppy kicked dirt at Arwan who danced away with a laugh.

The completely baffled crowd stirred loudly since Sahidi also had no idea what was going on.

Finally, Puppy asked, "Okay. How long does the scan take?"

"Moments."

Bench and Puppy had to calm down Gibson before she finally agreed to extend her right arm for a 'bot air probe. The umpire returned to home plate.

"We will let you know."

"What the hell does that mean? You just scanned."

"Eighty-seven minutes are required to confirm the absence of trans-organic particles."

"Aren't you a robot?"

"The most accurate facility is based in Wichita, Kansas, America. They will require time to ensure this is done properly."

"Who's afraid of the results now?" Arwan roared between cupped hands.

"Fuck you, Arwan." Back to the ump, "And next you'll say the game has to start anyway."

"Yes of course. You will have to replace your player who will be permitted to reenter the game at a later point if verified," Debra said meaningfully at Arwan, who shrugged with the serenity of a victor, having barred the current 2099 NL E.R.A. leader and her 105 mph fastball.

The Americans's dugout flung equipment onto the field when Teri Sheppard officially informed the crowd that Ilsa Gibson was leaving the game pending the results of a trans-organic examination. Sahidi struggled to explain that to the nearly one billion listeners. Ty threw his microphone out of the booth.

Tony cornered Puppy by the bat rack. "You just gonna let that happen?"

"We don't have a choice. Kenuda signed it."

"What? What?" Felton used both hands to give the fingers to Kenuda seated near Pope John, Abdullah, and Annette behind home. "And you didn't know anything about that?"

He sighed. "Yeah. I thought I was clever getting Ty in uniform and umpires we could trust."

"And it never occurred to you they'd pull some shit, waiting until the last game, because this World Series is all about the brotherhood of humanity."

"Something like that." Puppy went to the end of the dugout. "Marichal, you're starting."

Jumping to her feet, lean Garcia Marichal nearly cracked her head on the dugout roof.

Puppy led her into the runway littered with the bats which Gibson had broken over her knees. "Take as much time as you need to warm up."

Marichal's voice steeled. "I'm warm. I pitched on two-days's rest several times this season. You could wake me up in the middle of the night to pitch. You could pull me out of the shower—"

"Okay…"

"I could have fungus. I could have Krapski's flu which I don't, but I could. Don't worry."

He grinned. "Then you're ready?"

"Yes. I should've been today's starter because I'm meaner than Gibson."

Puppy cleared his throat. "She's about the nastiest player I've met besides Cobb."

"She's a fake. Ilsa worries when she's hurt someone. Her great-great-great-grandfather was really mean. She wants to live up to him. She has great stuff. Maybe better than me. But I am genuinely mean. And you need someone sincerely mean to come into a game in this situation. I'll do anything."

"I don't want you killing anyone, Garcia."

Marichal looked a little disappointed. "I'll make them pay for humiliating us. But I have a request. I want Major Felton as my catcher. This isn't to disrespect Ms. Bench. She's talented and tough. But I keenly feel the major's empathy for my breaking pitches."

That gave him a needed chuckle. "Tony? Empathy?"

"A very good heart." Marichal's head bobbed up and down. "I'll talk to Ms. Bench and explain."

"No, no, happy to do that. It's been a pretty smooth day so far."

Azhar was relieved that the game had not yet started. After another sleepless day of wandering Valletta, watching the Paen Hotel, and pestering all gatherings of righteous Muslims, he realized he had no choice. Where else would he go? Perhaps he was wrong. Perhaps Abdul had found his manhood early. Perhaps Omar was not here. Perhaps he had overreacted. Perhaps, God willing, Abdul would show up reeking of alcohol and a Crusader whore.

Mustafa bought a vanilla gelato cone after a lengthy wait on the mezzanine level. Fans were stomping their feet and clapping their hands. The Wings had loaded the bases in the first inning. Edging toward his privileged seat in the middle of the row, Azhar saw there were no outs.

Puppy slowly walked back to the dugout after conferring with his pitcher. Azhar muttered a tepid "hooray" out of loyalty. Burly Ibrahim al-Uzza was the batter. The Crusader pitcher nervously rubbed up the ball. Azhar was embedded in a section of mainly Maltese fans and couldn't understand the translation blaring out of the transistor radios, obscuring Sahidi's English play-by-play.

On the first pitch, al-Uzza checked his swing but made contact anyway, a dribbler back to the mound. Marichal pounced on the grounder and fired home for the force-out. Major Felton spun and threw to first base to get al-Uzza who had barely left the batter's box.

The Muslim runner on first was momentarily confused, then belatedly took off. After a short chase, first baseman Clemente smacked a tag on his back to complete the triple play. Azhar half-heartedly joined in the celebration, glimpsing Annette who had apologized more ways than he would've thought possible for having to sit in the Pope's box as one of the honored papal guests.

Abdul could hear the *Adalah* squirming down his throat and into his chest. Or some route. Now was not the time to regret not paying attention in science class. His friend Hamza had read on the Son's new *A Thun* digital universe that terrorists insisted they listened to the bombs. How could they talk about listening to bombs if they had been blown up? Abdul had rolled his eyes. Believing his friend very stupid, Hamza explained they confessed only if they had been captured.

Abdul hadn't believed Hazma. Now he did. Tick, tick, tick.

Omar silently gestured through the crush toward gate four. The Peace Trolley rattled by, fans hanging onto the outside bars, many already drunk and singing *The Maltese Hymn*, the national anthem. Loud, deafening, a prayer really. Tick, tick, tick. Each time Abdul's stomach sank and he stumbled, the morose Omar squeezed his neck with a warning look at the activator beneath the robe.

Tick, tick, tick, the *Adalah* mocked.

Abdul had no plan other than listening to the bomb count down inside his stomach or intestine or butt. He did not trust his brother's pledge.

The guards at the gate kept up the banter as fans hurried inside, "only the third inning—no score—great plays—hurry up—they still got hot dogs."

Abdul prayed the guard would also hear the bomb. He prayed that the pill would show up on the body scan. But Hamza had explained it was chemically coated to resemble a small polyp and cast a slight shadow on the screen. This poor person might have cancer and will die. Let them through.

Tick, tick, tick.

The ticket taker frowned at Omar's face, the familiarity nagging. He struggled to remember. Yes, a security flag. Not priority, just a red flag. Double-checking with stadium security was the appropriate response. But these tickets were for privileged seating. At game two, he'd had one of those situations and the Muslim nearly shut down the gate screaming bloody murder and who knew what else. The ticket taker had gotten his ass reamed by his boss.

He studied the dead-eyed Omar, then Abdul, the boy's eyes pleading. That face had not been flagged, he was fairly sure. Probably cousins of that Abdullah. The ticket taker hoped to catch a few innings toward the end and wasn't about to let a couple of suspicious Allahs get in the way of a warm salty pretzel and a frosty Monk's Ale. They were all suspicious as far as he could tell.

He waved them through.

After that, Abdul thought of going to the bathroom and shoving his fingers down his throat or squeezing until his anus bled to rid himself of the bomb. But Omar hadn't let him out of his sight, staring, drilling those crazy eyes into his head with a faint smile. As if he could also hear.

Tick, tick, tick.

Along the old-fashioned wooden walkways, Omar tugged Abdul toward the privileged seating and up the humming escalator. He said they did not have time for lunch. It was the first Omar had spoken since leaving the hotel. He seemed so calm. Almost happy.

Fuck you, Allah. Fuck you for taking his side.

Inside the entrance to section 221 on the third-base side, Abdul paused in slight wonder at the striking green of the field.

"It's beautiful. Like it was painted," he whispered.

Omar's lips curled into a sneer.

Where would it be? Abdul panicked. It had to happen soon. What was Omar waiting for? Abdul tried to figure this out as they headed toward the front row. Just boom right here, right in this spot?

Omar's eyes had drifted to another place, murmuring apologies before gently pressing his brother into his seat. Abdul glanced over the railing and suddenly understood the plan.

This section would blow up. Everyone here would die. The pieces would fall in the lower stands where all those people sat including Abdullah and the Pope and the American Cousin. And Annette. His beautiful Annette.

Abdul barely breathed. He did not have time to shout. He should have shouted before "he has a bomb he has a bomb!" but Omar would've gone click click and then click and everyone would have died. You were too afraid. You missed your chance. If you scream now, no one will save you in time. And everyone will still die.

It's just you.

Omar's right hand moved to his waist.

Abdul's hands went for his brother's throat.

"He has a bomb!" Abdul yelled so loudly that Azhar heard in the next section, standing with dulled horror at recognizing his sons struggling.

Security raced down the aisles. Omar shoved Abdul backward and again reached for the trigger. But Abdul's right leg lashed out with the power of a young soccer player, kicking Omar in the groin, which he had wanted to do for a very long time, and sending his brother toppling backward over the railing.

Omar only had time for one click.

66

Like all tragedies, it could've been much worse.

So far thirty-two fans had died, twenty-one were in critical condition with another sixty-one wounded. Medevacs had spirited away the casualties. The translucent bombproof shelter protecting Pope John, Abdullah, Kenuda, and Annette held. Section 221 had the decency to wait until Peace Field was evacuated before collapsing.

Outside, thousands of soldiers surrounded the stadium. The American Seventh Fleet and the Third Liberation Fleet cleared out the flotillas and dismantled the floating screens.

Fighter jets patrolled. Tanks rumbled into stationary positions. An immediate curfew was established except for the beleaguered hospitals.

The stunned players, who insisted the fans should be evacuated first, congregated by their dugouts. Several Liberation helicopters floated over the infield, waiting.

Sitting on home plate, Puppy dully stared at the debris as he played with a clump of grass. Soon they'll bring in the crusher trucks. They'll level the ballpark and that will be that. That will be that. Like none of this ever happened.

No.

Hell no.

Puppy walked toward the Wings dugout. "Is this how you want it to end?"

Arwan warily met him by the on-deck circle. "What do you mean?"

"Let's play. Shit. Did we come all this way to quit now? Because if we do, they won."

Arwan's eyes slitted, looking around the empty stadium. "Who is they?"

"The folks not wearing our uniforms. Yours and mine. Yours and mine. They pulled this when we played in London and we didn't let them get away with it then and we sure as hell shouldn't let them get away with it now. Not after this. Not, after, this."

Whirling, Puppy shouted up at the broadcasting booth. "Hey, are you still there?"

Sahidi leaned out, blinking away the soot as she called out, "Where else would I be? Ty collapsed. My director's here. The crew's all here. Teri Sheppard's somewhere, too."

"Are we on the air?"

"Live as we speak. We never stopped. You think I'd sign off after all this? They think it was a Black Robe."

He wearily nodded.

"I've been feeding reports to all the news services. They weren't happy to be escorted out with the crowd. Especially the Chinese."

He found a smile. "Leaving only you."

Sahidi innocently shrugged. "I explained someone had to be the official record and this was our feed and if they didn't want the follow-up they didn't have to take it. Everyone signed up. Even the Chinese. When are we getting out of here?"

"In six innings."

Sahidi nearly dropped her mike out of the booth.

With a wild laugh, Puppy rushed into the American dugout windmilling his arms. "We're finishing the game."

Everyone just stared.

"Come on, do I have to say it more than once? We came thousands of miles to win a damn world championship and that's what we're doing. As Mr. Cobb might say, pick up your bloomers, straighten your curls, and get your sorry asses out there."

"But they're not." Busco pointed at the Muslims silently disappearing down the runway into their clubhouse.

Puppy swallowed. "They'll play."

"But…" Busco continued.

Puppy's eyes bulged crazily. "They'll fucking play. Let's go."

The disbelieving players looked at Felton.

The major wonderingly shook his head. "Every time I underestimate you, Nedick, you prove me wrong."

"There's a long line for that." He searched their faces. The younger players were ashen; the veterans just needed more ammo. "We're going back to the game-one lineup. Gibson, you're back in for Marichal. Great job, Garcia. Come on. Who needs a personalized invitation to play some more baseball?"

With grim smiles, the Americans tossed the ball around the infield and outfield, glancing uneasily into the empty Muslim dugout.

Arms folded, Puppy waited by the third-base line. And he would all night if he had to.

Shouts rang out. Bats clapped together. Arwan led the Wings back up the steps; al-Uzza lazily swung a couple bats.

The managers exchanged mock salutes.

Debra motioned Arwan over. "Manager Arwan, do I have your approval to permit the readmission of pitcher Ilsa Gibson? Completion of the trans-organic tests will now be delayed until tomorrow."

He sneered. "We don't care."

Another exchange of mock salutes.

Teri Sheppard boomed, "Ladies and gentlemen, we will resume play. Now pitching for the Americans, Number 45, Ilsa Gibson, Number 45. Now catching, Tony…"

Sahidi just gave up on her hair which sagged to the right like a bush after a storm. She sipped her ninth cup of espresso in the past two hours and took a deep breath as they came back on-air after the ten-minute global newsbreak.

"Thank you, Fiona Prescott of the BBC Offshore News. Again, for everyone just joining us, the Heir Apparent has issued a statement disclaiming any connection to the terrorist attack that has claimed the lives of now forty-four fans here in Peace Field in Malta. Despite that statement, supporters of the attack are rioting in numerous cities within the Islamic Empire from Tehran to Copenhagen. In response, a combined American-Islamist fleet has reportedly surrounded the Mufti's ships in the North Atlantic which have withdrawn from positions near the Quebec province of Canada."

Along with the rest of the world, Sahidi took a moment to digest all that.

"Back here, the game is about to resume. That's right. Both teams have agreed to pick up where they left off, top of the third, one out. I can drone on about honoring the memory of those who've lost their lives. I can talk about the importance of this World Series now more than ever given the fiendish and cowardly attacks on innocent people. I can say that enough is enough and we better find a way to live in the world so you can go to a sporting event without worrying about dying but you should be able to walk down the street without that fear, too. I can say a lot"—Sahidi only sped up—"but damn it, we are here to watch the deciding game three of the 2099 World Series and damn it, that's what we're doing."

Sahidi ignored the director motioning her to calm down. She defiantly drained the espresso. "The nuns of St. Mary's who've been working the scoreboard have refused evacuation along with the fans, thank you, Sisters, so it'll be them, me, and Teri Sheppard on the public-address system. Ty Cobb took ill, but he's fine. Hey, we're still here and that's what matters."

She realized her back wheels were spinning and took a deep breath as the director poured Padech's Anisette into her cup.

The Liberation 'copters eased down along the left-field line. An extremely large soldier marched down the ramp toward the infield.

Arwan and Puppy intercepted him by the edge of the grass.

"Can we help you? We got plenty of seats available," Puppy asked.

The lieutenant ignored Puppy and turned to Arwan. "We must begin the evacuation."

"Why?" Arwan asked.

"This is a security issue. We were ordered by the unified command to remove all the remaining participants."

"Is there a chance of another terrorist attack?"

"We do not know."

Arwan bristled. "You do not know because you have information that you are trying to confirm or do not know because you do not know. I was in the Eleventh Army Intelligence Group so don't fuck around with me."

The lieutenant flinched. "We believe if the terrorists struck once here—"

"They would strike here again. How? Who? You have the whole damn stadium surrounded. If they attack it will be somewhere else which is where you should be, Lieutenant"—he squinted at the name on his chest below a rash of medals—"Jamal."

Lt. Jamal stiffened. "I am not in that conversation."

"Obviously. Then I will tell you what conversation you are in." Arwan jabbed the soldier in the nose. "Do you really want to forcibly remove both teams in front of the whole world?" He pointed at the broadcasting booth. "Because to do that, you will have to get through us."

Arwan snapped his fingers. The Wings clutched their bats in front of the dugout.

"And us." Puppy snapped his fingers and the Americans clustered, bats in hand.

The lieutenant swallowed. He had been warned about the American troublemaker. But to be disobeyed by Arwan was embarrassing.

"How about this?" The Wings manager forced an insincere smile. "Soon as the game is over, we will all happily leave."

The lieutenant hesitated; his CO was supposedly watching on the headcam, but there was only silence to his request for clarity. For all Jamal knew, there had been an attack at headquarters. For all he knew, the players were involved. An earlier report found that the terrorist had a privileged seat. Someone here was a collaborator.

"You must leave now," Jamal insisted.

Two dozen paratroopers raced into a line behind the left side of the infield, rifles raised.

Puppy ran full tilt in the opposite direction, hopping over the railing behind home and then up the steps littered with debris. By the time he reached the booth, he'd fallen twice; blood stained his left knee. Sahidi met him at the door.

"Are they trying to pull you out?" she asked as Puppy brushed past.

"Yeah. You have to call someone."

She threw up her hands. "Like who?"

"I don't know. Their boss, head of unified command. Someone, Sahidi. Call someone."

"Puppy, all civilian communication has been cut except for us. And who knows how long that'll last." Sahidi jerked her head at a trio of approaching soldiers.

He straddled her chair, fumbling with the mike and muttering about a switch.

"It's on. Everyone is listening. And watching."

Over the shot of the soldiers pointing guns at the players with bats, Puppy said, "Hi, everyone. This is Puppy Nedick and yes, I should be on the field managing, but we've got some miscommunication happening. The Army has been given orders to completely evacuate Peace Field but we're going to finish this game. Unless you want more bloodshed on your hands, someone out there better help us clear this up. Now."

Puppy and Sahidi waited with dwindling hope. A scarred sergeant shoved open the door, gesturing with his weapon for them to leave.

A huge holographic Pope wafted over the infield.

"Blessings. This is Pope John. Pardon the virtual extension, but intricate security measures have been implemented which hasn't stopped me from enjoying the prospect of this game along with the rest of the world. Unfortunately, not all our communication systems are working. Men and women of the Second Liberation Paratroopers, please be advised that your new orders are to protect the baseball players so the game can continue to conclusion."

His island. His decision. The Pope had freely overruled the stubborn unified command led by Abdullah and Kenuda. Even Rabbi Gold had disagreed, not for the first time; the Pope wryly smiled in the emergency underwater bunker several nautical miles offshore.

"Please feel free to remain and watch, although you'll have to remove your helicopters from the outfield since they would be an obstacle. Thank you for your cooperation."

Arwan glared at the lieutenant. "You heard."

"And you will listen to him?" The officer pointed contemptuously at the silent hologram. "This could be a Crusader trick."

"Not this time." The manager patted the young man's shoulder. "Now get out of here so we can beat the Americans once and for all."

The lieutenant grunted and whispered affirmation of the new orders into his useless headcam. In a few minutes, the paratroopers fanned out into the seats behind the Wings dugout. After a hasty consultation with Arwan, half the soldiers moved behind the American dugout.

The 'copters lazily drifted away over the left-center-field fence.

"Thank you and God bless all of you." The Pope's hologram faded.

Sahidi shooed Puppy out of the booth. He limped back down the steps. She straightened her hair which sagged at an eighty-degree angle.

"We're all glad that's finally settled."

Behind the scoreboard, Sister Marion of St. Mary's School hammered out "Take Me Out to the Ballgame" on the organ. Sister Francine wiggled the zero in the third-inning rectangle as a signal they were ready.

Through a thickened throat, Sahidi said, "Let's reset the lineups as Muslim first-baseman Ibrahim al-Uzza comes to bat. He popped to short the first time up."

Gibson pawed at the pitching rubber and glanced into the dugout where Puppy touched his nose. Her first pitch whizzed at 103 miles per hour uncomfortably close to al-Uzza who didn't move. He stepped out with a disdainful stare matched by Ilsa's even more disdainful glare.

It took an inning for even the hardened combat veterans fueled by intense dislike for each other to settle into the rhythm. The stylish Wings left-handed pitcher Hamid Ayad, who reminded Sahidi of the Yankee great Whitey Ford in the cocky way he walked off the mound, unsettled the Americans with a crafty assortment of breaking pitches and changeups, sneaking in an occasional popping fastball under the chin.

In the top of the fourth, the Islamists got a one-out seeing-eye hit into right-center field. Play paused for five minutes when the rest of section 221 collapsed. Gibson was a little undone, but second baseman Tedeschi saved her with a diving grab of a wicked liner in the hole, doubling up the sheepish baserunner who admitted to Arwan that he was watching the debris dust and wondering if the whole stadium would fall on top of them.

He wasn't alone.

"We're heading to the bottom of the fifth with both pitchers matching zeros," Sahidi said, sipping from the bottle of anisette. "Ayad has allowed two dinky singles while fanning four, while Gibson in two innings has struck out five."

"Leading off for the Americans is third baseman Pop Ra Chou who took a called strike on a nasty slider the first time around. Ayad checks the sign from Alawi and delivers a curveball at the knees for strike one. That about dropped off the table. Chou wiggles the bat, waiting for the second serving and…he swings and sends it deep to left, way back, going, going…gone. How about that, folks? The Americans lead, 1-0."

His teammates poured out of the dugout, pummeling Chou.

On the next pitch, Ayad nearly shaved Donda's cheek, the right fielder barely falling out of the way. Puppy and Arwan exchanged salutes.

"That's old school baseball," Sahidi explained. "You hit a homer, the next batter goes down from a brushback pitch. All that was lost as early as the 2027 season when even a knockdown pitch was politicized in some way based on the pitcher and batter's origins or beliefs. Throwing at a hitter meant automatic ejection for both the pitcher and manager. But this game is kind of timeless. A place that's been created just for the moment. Back in 2065, there was a terrorist attack during the seventh game, when they played that many, of the World Series—Donda fouls off the next pitch, one and one—it was at Amazon Stadium, formerly and once again Yankee Stadium. To punish baseball, Grandma, head of The Family, ordered the park be left in its crumbling shape.

"High pop, Farhad's coming over to the railing, but it's out of play. One and two. Half the scoreboard was gone. Seats were gutted from explosions, missiles. There were skeletons in the stands, bones in the outfield, I kid you not—Donda swings at a fastball out of the strike zone, one out—looking around, there's a similarity. To my right, a whole section is gone. A big hole. Below, piles of crushed seats, bricks. The games in 2098, which was supposed to be baseball's final season—Bar'Nee Ortiz fouls off the first pitch, strike one—they had holograms running the bases. Maybe fifteen fans. I was one of them that opening day. Now we got two dozen of the Liberation Army's finest." She waved at the soldiers, many now enjoying the game. "Strike two on the inside corner.

"What I'm saying—what I'm saying is, here we still are. Somehow. Crap goes around and around and I'm violating The Family's law, codified by the Anti-Parasite Laws, against opinion journalism, but I'm hoping they'll overlook it for today. Forgive me. I just watched a lot of people die." Sahidi drained the anisette and hoisted the empty bottle for more.

In the top of the seventh, Gibson shook off Felton's first sign, then the second. Tony started to the mound, but she angrily motioned him back. On the next pitch to Erdogan, the Wings left fielder drilled the ball to left. Curly Russell ran out of field.

"You can kiss that goodbye. Touch 'em all, Erdogan!" Sahidi cried. "We are tied at one."

Puppy barely waited for the batter to cross home, running out to the mound before a smoking mad Major Felton swung at Gibson.

"What the hell were you thinking?" Tony yelled.

"Calm down." Puppy yanked him away. Whirling on Gibson, he snapped, "What the hell were you thinking? Never shake off Felton's pitches again, do you hear?"

"Never," Tony growled.

"Okay, okay." Ilsa grudgingly threw up her hands. "I'm sorry."

"Don't apologize. Just never call me off." Felton stomped back to home plate.

Puppy studied the fuming Gibson. "You all right?"

"Yes. Go away."

"Because I can't put Marichal back in—"

Gibson flung the resin bag into Puppy's chest. "Get. The. Fuck. Out. Of. My. Face. Skipper."

Puppy grinned. "Probably smart not to do that again either."

"Who you gonna put in that's better than me?" Ilsa snarled.

"We're going to the top of the ninth." Sahidi had turned to straight Boodle's Gin. She didn't feel a thing. "Ayad and Gibson are locked in a classic pitcher's duel. The Wings hurler has fanned eight, walked one, and allowed just three hits, while the American, fireballing, right-handed hurler has chalked up a dozen strikeouts, passed two batters, and permitted a couple of hits.

"But one of the three American hits was a home run by Pop Ra Chou. And for the Wings, a solo shot by Izba Erdgan. Leading off for the Islamists is the pitcher Ayad who's whiffed twice today. Gibson's first pitch is...popped up. Bar'Nee Ortiz calls everyone off and makes the catch for out number one.

"That'll bring up second baseman Abadi, oh-for-three, a couple wobbly grounders to short and second, and a towering foul pop swallowed up by Felton in the sixth..."

Gibson set the Wings down one-two-three, snarling at the back slaps as she grabbed a bat.

"Carlton, hit for Gibson." Puppy matched one hundred mph stares with Gibson. "You were great but everyone's tired so let's just win it now." Exhausted rallying cries battered the dugout. "Drysdale, warm up in case we need you in the tenth."

Nester Drysdale and bullpen coach A'leev Youm hurried down the right-field line.

"Now batting for the Americans, Number 32, Donde Vasquez Carlton. Number 32."

Debra walked over to the Americans's dugout. "You cannot reinsert a player already removed."

"I can if the opposing manager says it's okay," Puppy answered. He started calling out to Arwan who shouted back, "Just play!"

"Rules are rules," Debra said firmly.

"Look around. You think we need a little flexibility?"

With an arched eyebrow at the bottomless sentimentality of humans, the umpire returned to home plate.

Ayad's first pitch was a slider that didn't slide, instead hanging invitingly just below the waist. Carlton whacked it on a tightrope to left-center field. Everyone jumped up.

"That is deep to left center. Back back back back and…Bakir leaps and…oh doctor, he caught the ball, he caught the ball! Holy cow!"

For the next three innings, that was as close as either team got to a run. Or a hit. Kareem Yacoub, who looked like he brushed his teeth with wood and enjoyed it, replaced Ayad and fired darts. Drysdale, a hulking right-hander with deep-set blue eyes, matched him.

By the top of the thirteenth inning, the lieutenant had crept down to the Wings dugout. Suspecting more drama, Puppy hobbled over.

"Take it easy, Nedick," Arwan said wearily. "He's only asking about the lights."

Puppy suddenly noticed it was getting a little dim as sunset neared.

"The electricity was cut everywhere but the news booth." The lieutenant found a way to include Puppy without gagging. "I am not suggesting evacuating, I would not dream of that, but I do not understand how you will play in the dark. I imagine that would complicate your strategies."

The managers waited.

"I can assist."

Puppy warily folded his arms. "Why are you being so helpful?"

The lieutenant smirked. "Because I want to see the Wings kick your asses."

Within five minutes, six Liberation helicopters funneled searchlights all over the field.

"It's kind of incandescent, like being inside a special baseball candle," Sahidi remarked, proud that after five hours, a bottle of anisette, and just a wee bit of a fifth of gin left, she hadn't lost her tongue. "I don't know if the 'copters will stay fixed in place or move around but we're going to see what we're going to see and who knows what we'll see."

The director insisted she drink coffee. Very black and without spirits. She swilled more gin.

"Tony Felton leads off the last of the fifteenth," Sahidi pealed brightly. "The major's gone one-for-six, a single up the middle. Yacoub starts him off with a curve away, ball one. Outfield and infield are shaded around to left. The next offering is drilled into the gap in right-center field. Wakim cuts it off…and Felton's heading for second. The throw is…not in time. Felton just slides under the tag. He caught the Wings napping. Everyone's exhausted. I guess except for Tony Felton."

The giddy Sahidi caught herself from laughing too hard.

"Yacoub checks the runner at second and delivers to Ra Chou. He slaps the ball to the right side. Jamin easily tosses him out, but Felton advances to third. Baseball 101. One out. The world championship is just ninety feet away for the Americans."

As Arwan convened a mound conference, Puppy gestured for lithe Mende Aparicio to run for Felton. When Aparicio arrived at third, Felton shoved the startled shortstop all the way back to home plate. As the furious Puppy bolted out of the dugout, Felton ran his finger over his throat and stood on third base with both feet.

As the chuckling Wings returned to their positions, enjoying the show, Puppy swarmed all over the major.

"What're you doing, Felton?"

"Staying in the game. Embarrass me again and I'll kill you."

"Kill me, huh?"

"That's right. Kill you."

"You know, from London to America and now here in Malta, all you've ever done is threaten me and I'm fucking tired of it. Tired of it. I'm the damn manager and I need speed and I don't have time for your tired old ego and hearing how you deserve to score the winning run because you were a suffering POW, so get your ass the hell off the field."

Felton smiled the smile of the psychopath. "Nah."

Puppy breathed hoarsely. "Felton."

"Nedick."

"Are we still playing?" shouted Arwan over the hooting Wings players.

Puppy threw up his hands. He would kill Felton after the game.

"Looks like the ol' major will remain as the runner at third base," Sahidi said, delighted by the drama. "We're knotted at 1-1, last of the fifteenth inning, one out. The Islamist infield has moved in to cut off the run. Donda Sicuyanna has taken the collar today, oh-for-six. Yacoub is pitching from a windup. Felton's not the fleetest of runners which is why Puppy tried to pinch-run. Baseball 102. First pitch is up high, ball one.

"All the Americans need is a hit. Wild pitch. Passed ball. Error. Long sacrifice fly. Next delivery is…popped up in foul territory. Al-Uzza comes over by the stands and… makes the catch. Big, big out for Yacoub."

Puppy waved Carew onto the field. Bar'Nee Ortiz was about to protest, but the manager's look suggested that wouldn't be smart.

"Now batting for Ortiz, Number 29, Ephraim Carew. The Wings infield has dropped back to normal depth with two outs."

"Yacoub winds up and throws. Low. Ball one. Carew went three-for-four in the game-two American win. Yacoub delivers and…swung on and missed. Strike one. One-and-one, two outs, bottom of the fifteenth inning here at Peace Field. Game three of the 2099 World Series in case you just arrived from Jupiter.

"Yacoub's next pitch is up and in. Two and one. Yacoub walks off the mound talking to himself. He steps back on the rubber. Here's the pitch…swung on and missed, strike two. Nifty breaking pitch at the knees."

Puppy flashed the sign to Felton who stared a moment, smiling with faint disbelief. Puppy's stare was so intense, his eyes seemed to hover outside his cheeks like a 'copter. He repeated the sign. Felton finally flashed receipt. The third-base coach Pepe Pignatano signaled Carew who stepped out, rubbed dirt on her hand, and settled back into the left-handed batter's box with a slight wag of the bat.

"The Wings infield plays back with two outs and two strikes. Yacoub kicks his leg and…"

On the pitch, Felton broke for home as Carew laid down a dandy bunt up the third-base line. Yacoub raced over and underhanded the ball in time to nail the huffing Felton. But the major lowered his shoulder and rammed into the catcher Alawi who, amid the tangled impact, slapped the tag on Felton's now-bare head resting on home plate next to his left hand.

Only the ball had scurried all the way to the backstop. Debra made the safe sign.

"The Americans win the series! The Americans win the series! The Americans win the series!" Sahidi screamed, nearly falling out of the booth.

Led by Puppy, the team poured out of the dugout, mobbing Felton and Carew. The crushed Wings slowly headed off the field.

Major Felton held out his hand to the woozy Alawi, still on one knee.

The catcher considered the gesture for all it could mean. And all it could not. With a nod, he grasped Felton by the forearm and stood.

Not to be outdone, Arwan walked over and silently shook Puppy's hand. Drysdale suddenly pumped al-Uzza's meaty paw. Soon players clustered in handshakes, offering congratulations in Arabic, gratitude in English.

It only lasted a few minutes. But it was enough.

As the 'copters landed beyond the infield and the soldiers bounded onto the field to begin the evacuation, Sister Marion pounded out "Take Me Out to the Ballgame." The sisters of St. Mary's were the last to leave.

67

At first, only Annette thought getting married again was a good idea. Puppy, limping after tearing a cartilage running up the debris-riddled steps, didn't believe her. First mistake. In a patient voice often used on beady-eyed gunmen, he explained that being married twice to the same woman should be sufficient. Safety latch off, Annette asked if, should one of them falter in fidelity and devotion during their upcoming European mission, and if the one who faltered should ask for a divorce only to later come to their senses which is *what kind of happened with us*, should the other person who did not falter simply say, *oh, no, we're not getting married a third time*.

Puppy flung up his hands, partly so she wouldn't bend back any more fingers, and muttered an insincere "whatever you want my darling," believing in the ultimate triumph of marital justice as misguided men have for eons.

Annette next targeted Rabbi Gold. With plans coalescing like watery stew for the New Vatican City in Jerusalem to be built contiguous to the proposed site of the Jewish and Arab capitals of New Israel and New Palestine, this request for his time took two days to satisfy until Herbert delivered an Annette hologram reminding the rabbi, in between scowls and ugly laughs, that she'd warned the authorities about the terrorist attack and they had failed to adequately prevent that which—she lapsed into deep regret—would be most unfortunate to land in the hands of the many journalists who adored her tart tongue and incomparable insights.

Herbert looked like he'd just absorbed a new emotive program on dismay.

Next, Annette cajoled a very willing Abdul, the hero of Valletta, into gaining an audience with Abdullah, also a trifle busy what with full-scale war erupting between him and his father's former Empire while cleansing his staff of traitors like General Petash who'd masterminded Omar's plans.

With the clarity of a smitten prepubescent, Abdul already foresaw that when his beloved Annette tired of Puppy Nedick, hobbling about on his brittle limbs, she would remember his help and off they'd go together, he, by then, the most famous football player in the world and she still capable of making his knees buckle sitting down.

Abdullah could not, on any basis, secular or spiritual, possibly refuse Abdul's request for this favor.

That left Pope John XXIX who reportedly howled with delight.

However, being married in three major religions had its obstacles. All of them insisted in rather self-centered fashion that by reciting these respective vows, the husband and wife would pledge to observe the rites of their respective faiths. Annette besieged the clerics like catapults at a medieval castle until they granted personal waivers from any such pledge of conversion.

Still more devilish details popped up. All the ceremonies had to be approximately equal in length. Annette would absolutely not promise to be an obedient wife according to the Muslim vows. And then, who would see this simultaneous marriage under the laws of Catholicism, Islam, and Judaism?

Reminding her of their televised BBC betrothal, Puppy insisted that their wedding be televised again. It was the height of egotism and more than a bit tawdry. Let's all hold hands and dance after a fanatic had tried to assassinate all the world's leaders and the USS *Rescue,* transporting more than two hundred orphans, had just struck a mine about fifty nautical miles west of Ireland.

Annette cut him off coldly before he could recite the grim news of the day. This would not be vided or radded and internetted. This was among us, "our way of showing our faith in the future. But we can't insult the Muslims, Puppy."

He was afraid to ask.

"According to the Quran, a Muslim wedding must be a public ceremony. What Abdul and Abdullah and I have worked out"—she let that soak in—"is holding the vows on the beach. It's very beautiful and you've always complained you don't get to the ocean enough. Security would be extremely tight so there couldn't be a lot of spectators anyway."

Puppy went along as if he had a choice.

The night before, Rabbi Gold asked Annette to join him in his study.

"Are you excited, Ms. Ramos?"

Annette accepted some spiced tea. "I'm way beyond excited, Rabbi."

"Aren't we all." He crossed and uncrossed his legs, fiddling with his sleeve. "Third time, yes?"

"Which you already know like you know most everything." Annette studied him, waiting.

Gold cleared his throat. "I will not be able to participate tomorrow, Ms. Ramos."

Her eyes narrowed. "Why?"

"It is simply not appropriate."

"Because I blackmailed you? If so, I'm sorry. That was wrong."

"But smart." He smiled faintly. "It is best if only Christianity and Islam take the spotlight tomorrow. There is enough hatred generated by them along with you Americans without adding in the presence of the Jews. Our relationship with the Pope is known, but not widely, and we would like to keep it that way."

She folded her arms and shook her head. "Nope."

"Nope?"

"You're in, you accepted, I learned the Jewish vows, Puppy, too, and he's not one for easily memorizing. Sorry, case closed."

"I said I cannot—"

"I heard you. What're you afraid of?"

He took on a distant look. "We do not have enough time but, basically, reviving the past. Already ugly resentments have erupted. It's not wise."

"Which is totally why you should do it. To show that won't stop you."

Now Gold's eyes narrowed. "How do you know what I have had to overcome?"

"I don't. Show me."

"I don't have to prove myself to you, Ms. Ramos."

"I think we're talking about proving something to yourself, Rabbi Gold."

He reddened. "There are deeper issues than your wedding. The extremely delicate negotiations over Jerusalem must not be jeopardized."

"And having a rabbi next to the Pope and Abdullah is a bad sign?"

"To some."

"Well fuck them."

He stared leadenly. "Excuse me?"

"You heard me. Someone's always going to hate you. Me, everyone. We're not curing anything. We're just asking people to consider. To consider a possibility, Rabbi." Her voice dropped. "Tomorrow, we consider that possibility and there'll probably be protests and more bombs, but that'd only be an excuse. Those kinds of people will always find one."

Gold took in this curiously surprising woman. "Yes they will. Yes they will." He swallowed. "Then perhaps you should find another rabbi. There are many here—"

"I want you."

"Why? I have never been particularly nice to you."

"I know. But you're a jerk to everyone."

He had to smile. "I am. Again, why me?"

"Because you remind me of a friend of mine, Father Dempsey. He also wasn't sure he was fit to be a religious person anymore. He also had lost faith. I kind of helped him find it again." Annette paused. "Maybe I can do that for you."

"Don't bother," he angrily said. "I am not worthy to serve as a rabbi. I have killed many people. I have betrayed the teachings of my faith many times over."

"And the Pope shot down planes. Abdullah has ordered millions into battle." Her lips curled. "Get past your sad story, Rabbi Gold. We're all a little ashamed of something. What else is new if you've lived longer than a minute? Come on. Herbert already made the choopa."

After a puzzled stare, the rabbi chuckled. "You mean a *chuppah*?"

• • • •

ON THE DAY of the wedding, Annette tried to hide her disappointment. All this god power and it still rained. Good thing they had the choopa.

The gray chandelier of sky sent a faint drizzle over the wedding party bracketed by waist-high stanchions of papal Guards and thousands of well-wishers swarming over the beach, many holding cell phones over their heads to record the event.

Annette had insisted that any navy ships in the harbor had to be invisible. She didn't want guns in the background. A bad look. Kenuda and Admiral Mayib, Abdullah's new second-in-command, worked out a rotation of stealth 'copters, although both were insistent that at three nautical miles, the fleets would be in place, visually arresting backgrounds or not.

As Sister Marion played *Here Comes the Bride*, Azhar guided Annette, luminous in her white dress, down the white carpet leading to the waterline, depositing her before Abdullah and Puppy, squirming in his new black suit and gray tie.

Trailing behind were the maids of honor: Clary, in a black seminarian cassock, and Herbert, natty in his captain's uniform after re-enlisting. Wearing a pained smile, Abdul bore the rings on a purple velvet pad.

Best Person Elias flanked Puppy.

In a resplendently simple white robe, Abdullah wonderingly took in this moment before breaking into a wide smile.

"I am honored to marry this loving couple. I am honored to be asked. I am honored they have honored Islam by requesting their marriage be performed according to our laws. I am honored on so many levels I cannot begin to express. And I am honored to be friends with Puppy Nedick and Annette Ramos and I thank them for all they have done. Their love has brought us together and I hope and pray that we all remember the power of such a power. I speak on behalf of the Holy Father Pope John XXIX and Rabbi Avram Gold when I explain, to avoid any appearance of disrespect, that the ceremonies had to be slightly altered since Puppy and Annette are not pledging to simultaneously obey our religions. And we certainly would not ask them to favor one over the other. That is not why we are here. Their pledge goes far deeper."

Abdullah squared his jaw, his voice ringing out. "They vow, this brave couple, to love each other, the foundation of all we want, so that someday we may all know, without fear, without doubt, the right to live in peace. The right to be safe. The right to be happy. The right to a full stomach, a warm heart, and a fearless mind."

The beach was silent. Abdullah took their hands.

"In the name of Allah, I am going to ask you three times if you accept each other as husband and wife, to which you will answer 'gabul,' which means 'accept' in Arabic."

Their quiet voices answered "gabul" three times.

Annette turned toward Puppy. "I, Annette Ramos, offer you myself in marriage in accordance with the instructions of the Holy Quran and the Holy Prophet, peace and blessing be upon him. I pledge, in honesty and sincerity, to be for you a faithful wife."

Puppy smiled. "I, Puppy Nedick, pledge in honesty and sincerity, to be for you a faithful and helpful husband."

Wearing his liturgical vestment, Pope John warmly shook Abdullah's hands. The pope beamed with a reverence he had not felt for decades before asking, "My dear children, as I present the love and respect of the Catholic Church, have you come here to enter into marriage without coercion, freely, and wholeheartedly?"

They answered, "I have."

"Are you prepared, as you follow the path of marriage, to love and honor each other for as long as you both shall live?"

They answered, "I am."

Puppy grasped Annette's hand. "I, Puppy Nedick, take you, Annette Ramos, to be my wife. I promise to be true to you in good times, in bad, in sickness and in health. I will love you and honor you in all the days of my life."

The sniffling pope and Abdullah exchanged smiles.

"I, Annette Ramos, take you, Puppy Nedick, to be my husband. I promise to be faithful to you in good times, in bad, in sickness and in health. I will love you and honor you in all the days of my life."

The pope abruptly kissed them on the cheeks.

Rabbi Gold, perhaps the most nervous person on the beach besides the security forces, stood beside Pope John. He gestured for Annette and Puppy to join him beneath the *chuppah*.

"Finally. We're getting soaked," Annette said, provoking loud laughter.

Along with Abdullah and the pope, the rest of the wedding party clustered under the canopy. Annette motioned for the pale Gold to begin.

"As part of the Jewish marriage ritual"—the rabbi's reedy voice steadied—"the bride will circle around the groom three times as the symbol of building a new world together."

With a fixed look, Annette circled Puppy three times.

Puppy and Annette held hands and together said, "With hearts full of joy and awe we consecrate ourselves to each other, entering into a sacred covenant of love, trust, and commitment. Respecting our differences and sharing our strengths, may we together meet life's challenges. May we always remember our sense of humor and may laughter be ever present in our lives."

It took Azhar two stern looks for his son to reluctantly hand over the rings. Annette winked at Abdul; his knees jiggled.

They slipped on the gold bands.

"With thee I wed," Annette whispered.

Puppy's throat closed. "With thee I wed." He couldn't resist. "Again and again."

Clary placed the glass wrapped in cloth on the ground. Puppy and Annette took turns stomping the glass.

"This means, this means"—Rabbi Gold found his vocal cords and they bellowed—"this breaking of the glass symbolizes the destruction of the ancient temple in Jerusalem. Once again, Jerusalem has been destroyed. Let us assure God we will rebuild Jerusalem and it will stay rebuilt or we will answer to Him and whoever else is keeping score."

Rabbi Gold gave Abdullah bin-Mohammed and Pope John XXIX a meaningful look. They nodded back.

By the second round of drinks following the ceremony, Puppy had slipped out of the increasingly raucous wedding celebration and strolled down the beach trailed by Ephraim and Benjy, weapons bulging beneath their caftans. He plopped butt-first among a few scattered seashells, rolling a pinkish rubber ball from palm to palm.

He had a moment of empty thoughts before Annette squatted beside him. "We have guests, Pup."

"I know. I just needed some air."

"We were already outside."

"You're going to give me a hard time on our wedding day?" he asked.

"What better time?" She sat. "Where'd you get the Spaldeen?"

"Clary brought a bunch. She looks cute in that beginner's priest outfit."

"I hope you didn't tell her that."

He laughed. "I'm pretty sure Abdul is going to challenge me to a duel someday."

"Probably sooner rather than later. Least I'll have an option if you don't behave."

He pretended to toss sand at Annette and stared at the vibrant early-evening sky. "Think it'll always be this way?"

Annette played with the Spaldeen. "Yeah, I do."

"Pretty terrifying, right?"

"Damn terrifying. We just have to remember who we are, Pup. Rabbi Gold told me that before you know where you're going, you first must know from whence you came."

He nodded at the twinkling phones recording them up and down the beach. "Is that now their job?"

Annette tapped her fist onto his forehead. "It better not be."

Annette laid her head on Puppy's shoulder. They watched the sun drift toward its next appointment with more confused people. A racket of music from the party brought Annette to her feet.

"That's my cue."

"Not another toast."

"No. Clary said this dance from the twentieth century, 'the twist,' is like all the rage in America. Now the pope wants to learn. Come on, you too."

"You know I'm not a dancer."

"No problem. I have Herbert." She kissed Puppy on the nose. "But stay out of trouble."

"That's why I got the boys around."

They finger-wiggled a wave at the impassive Benjy and Ephraim.

As Annette headed up the beach, Puppy called out, "Grandma's bra straps, please don't let the pope hurt himself!"

She answered with a loud laugh.

Puppy swirled the Spaldeen in the sand, rinsing and wiping the ball dry on the fancy suit he'd never wear again before heading toward the crowd to find someone to play catch with.

EPILOGUE

A s a lonely, exhausted man will find inane habits, so First Cousin Elias Kenuda tossed the bag of toasted Thai-stuffed triangles on the coffee table and kicked his loafers into the corner, his feet aching after another eighteen-hour workday. He soothed his aching head by muting the vidnews and, with an unhealthy amount of anticipation, poured a neat double of the Johnny Mac's fourteen-year-old Scotch. Rabbi Gold had slipped a case aboard the flight home with a note of gratitude from Pope John.

Elias sipped a little guiltily, having rejected the unspoken quid pro quo of this curative elixir in exchange for an official papal visit, especially around the old religious holidays. From the tens of thousands of letters, which Matthew and his partner Fred'rick collated every day on their lunch hour, siblings were clearly still uneasy about the role of the Vatican. Though appreciative, sure.

God, maybe not.

Perhaps we can meet in Quebec. Kenuda had answered the rabbi's impatient follow-up, quickly getting a coded email from the newest seminary student in Malta.

"*Papa Kenuda. No Canada. The Holy Father wants to light a tree in Manhattan. Make it happen. See you then. Blessings, Clary.*"

He could handle Pope John. Abdullah. But Father Clary, Elias wasn't so sure. He wasn't so sure the world could either.

Elias smiled wearily, twirling the worry beads Clary had sent. Another wonderful present, he had to admit, though a shade behind the Scotch. Rubbing his eyes, Kenuda glanced at the vidnews.

From Liberation headquarters in Jerusalem, Abdullah had finally announced the arrest of General Petash and a handful of other senior officers for their role in the terrorist attack. Undermining Abdullah's peace plans wasn't any different than when Albert Cheng had killed Grandma, Elias had written back with sunny assurances that peace would win out.

THE SAME PATH blared in the headlines as, to his astonishment, journalists pounced on the note, printing it in every language. Matthew had warned Elias about the importance of marking communications as confidential. Though, the 'bot said with a shrewd look, it would have been leaked anyway.

Leaks. Elias had fumed. Duplicity in the pursuit of truth. He had scolded Abdullah on their last call, which was now almost daily. They were developing the kind of relationship two long-lost brothers might have when slowly feeling each other out. Under the relentless pursuit of the joint American-Islamic military command, buoyed by the Second and Fourth U.S. Army Groups, the Heir Apparent had retreated into the original Caliphate, a crescent moon of Iran, Turkey, and Iraq.

It was still an army of millions strong with secreted weapons of mass destruction. Kenuda had admonished the new lineup of Cousins at yesterday's meeting, who were giddy at the progress of the war. No pride in victory. He wagged his finger like a petulant old man.

We can't celebrate death, he thought, echoing Grandma's once revered warnings. The Cousins, all under forty years old, were disappointed. Grandma was history. Kenuda was nearing that status. These Cousins seized every opportunity to emulate the massive simultaneous parades that honored the baseball world's champions, the torchlight procession for Ty Cobb's funeral, and the frenetic dancing in the streets unleashed whenever another country was liberated.

We're not there yet. Kenuda redoubled construction of libraries and airlifted the vast collections of rare books donated by the Muslim and Christian worlds, insisting that all schools dedicate two days a week to visiting the library. Borrowing cards were mandated. Read and learn, please. The results were still meager.

He couldn't censor the vid. They had to understand on their own. That was the point. He flailed in silent fear. But he wouldn't yet permit the BBC or Liberation News or any external feeds. Still, there'd been reports of vidpirating.

Should you punish curiosity? And where do you draw the line?

North Africa and Western Europe were under reconstruction by the robots. As the Heir Apparent fled, within weeks, days sometimes, apartment houses sprouted. Schools, hospitals, roads, bridges. The British Parliament, blown up by the retreating Black Robes, was restored as was the sabotaged Eiffel Tower down to the smallest original details.

Freedom of religion must also be revived, Abdullah had insisted over Kenuda's concerns. Fearful Christians dared erect makeshift churches. In Berlin, there was a Friday-night Jewish service. Buddhists, Hindus, a dizzying number of Christian denominations, crawled out from beneath the rubble of persecution.

Too much, too quickly, Elias fretted. Wounds must heal, but the healing must begin. Trusting each other was the great unknown. Like the infant Cousins proclaiming over turkey tacos and foosball that all the world's ills were ending. "No, no, no," he muttered. There'd been World War I, World War II, World War III, and now World War IV. And all the wars before and in between. What happens when the first disagreements flare? There was no mechanism to mediate. The pope was nearly ninety.

We must provide him with re-organic rejuvenation treatments instantly, Kenuda scribbled a note on the millionth important thing he still had to do.

Another United Nations would be another bad joke. The boundaries of the withdrawals in France had been delayed. Just forty-eight hours, but enough for wariness to set in, for old doubts and suspicions to seep out. Even happy liberated orphans look the same after a while.

The world has such a short and long memory, Kenuda wanly thought, pouring another whiskey. The tireless Puppy and Annette, "the First Family of America" as they'd been dubbed by the insatiable press, could only jet from liberated zone to liberated zone greeting the survivors, distributing food and clothes and medical attention for so long. They'd have to come home eventually.

And then what?

He missed Puppy. He needed Puppy. Kenuda was not overseeing the 2100 baseball season alone. He reverently jiggled the glorious amber liquid, taking a long sip before letting his head rest on the couch. Sometimes he felt so damn alone. Sometimes?

"Goodness, Elias, you still frown and snore at the same time."

He had to be asleep.

"I can only imagine your diet nowadays. These triangles are deep fried and I'm sure twisting open whiskey bottles is your only exercise. And don't pretend to sleep."

Kenuda slowly parted his eyelids. Hedda Kleinz pulled a disapproving face.

"I'm going to make you a decent meal." With lots of perturbed sounds, Hedda marched into the kitchen, sadly shaking her head at the interior of the refrigerator and calling out, "This is like a cliché of a bachelor's apartment. Doughnuts and soda pop in the icebox and smelly socks all over the place. Elias, this cheese is disgusting."

Wearing one of the blouses and skirts Elias had brought back from her apartment, Hedda stuck her head around the kitchen doorway, flaunting the moldy cheddar. "Garbage."

He couldn't be dreaming such vivid noises as the waste disposal shredding food. Elias willed himself into the kitchen. Hedda disposed of rancid lettuce.

"What is this?" he rasped.

"'This' meaning what? Be clear in your thought enunciations, Elias. I'm a teacher if you remember." Hedda softened. "Don't you recognize me?"

Kenuda steadied himself against the stove. "But you're dead."

Hedda looked very disappointed. She reached out to take his hand, but Elias recoiled. Hedda was hurt enough to be furious. "Technically. But obviously I'm not."

Hedda stormed into the living room. He followed warily, stopping about six feet away which sent Hedda into the familiar pose of arms-folded-foot-tapping irritation and impatience.

"What's wrong with you? Have you become extremely stupid or are you just half drunk? I'm a trans-organic life-form, Elias. Wait. You're dreaming. Is that what you think?" She flung a loafer at his chest. "Guess not. Because here I am. You're making this very difficult, Elias. Is your question how I came to be here, because I'll hit you with the lamp if you need further proof that I exist!"

He nodded, shrugged, stared, he didn't know.

"Sorry. I didn't mean to yell. I rehearsed this a lot and narrowed down your probable responses to eleven likely reactions. Stupefaction and denial were at the top and yet, I'm still lousing it up. Okay. Grandma made sure my consciousness was preserved after my organic form's life energy ended, and she gave me the newest model," she said proudly. "I've been in Falls Church, Virginia at training, then I transferred to a base in New Rochelle, but you were about to leave for Malta and I wasn't going to dump me on you when you were off to save the world."

When he didn't smile or do anything more than blink, Hedda angrily smacked his arm. "Do you want to test me to make sure I know everything like my score the first time we played miniature golf and how you showed up at my apartment unannounced and I was watching *Laurel and Hardy*—stop staring. I look exactly the same. Feel. Pinch. Touch my face. Touch my face, damn you!"

"It's really you?" he whispered.

Hedda violently shoved him onto the couch. "A 'you'? I can cry. I can laugh. We can have sex. I can beat you at gin rummy and tell you when you're an idiot like now. And I can love you forever, Elias Kenuda. Forever and ever. But not if you look at me like that. Then I can't. No, I'm not a 'you'. I'm a me, I'm a me, I'm a me…"

She knelt on the couch, tears pouring down her face. Kenuda's hands faltered by her cheek.

"I know it takes some getting used to," Hedda said as his fingertips grazed her wide nose. "I'm a little surprised, too."

Kenuda hugged Hedda so tightly that he pulled away, afraid he'd hurt her.

"It's okay, sweetie. I'm pretty durable."

He laughed and cried into her neck.

"I love you, too, Elias Kenuda. I love you so." She cradled him. "I'm all registered. Lifecard, library card, of course."

"Course," he murmured.

"We can begin our life again."

Elias kissed her fiercely, hands roaming over her body, fumbling at the zipper at the nape of her neck.

Hedda wiggled free and sternly pursed her lips.

"First Cousin, you signed Marital Unions Law 3.1 granting organic and non-organic marital rights and you know full well that we must go through precisely the same procedure. Which means we must start all over again, formalize our engagement, meet with the Committee, take classes, prove we are genuinely in love. Everything as before. Which means no 'bouncy-bouncy,' as our Clary would say."

Laughing weakly, Elias shook his head. "You're still a pain in the ass."

Hedda folded her arms with a deep frown. "How about we get some groceries from the bodega on East 164th? I'll make a dinner that won't clog your arteries and we'll drink that Scotch and watch the late movie. It's the four Marx Brothers." She took his damp hand. "You're going to stare with that dopey smile for a long time, aren't you?"

He nodded dimly.

"Good." Hedda crawled into the crook of Elias's shoulder. After a moment, Hedda whispered, "I guess the universe wouldn't screech to a halt if we bouncy-bouncied just once, as long as we report the infraction."

ABOUT THE AUTHOR

GARY MORGENSTEIN IS the critically acclaimed author of The Dark Depths series (*A Mound Over Hell*, *A Fastball for Freedom*, *A Dugout to Peace*).

An award-winning playwright, his work includes *A Black and White Cookie*, *A Tomato Can't Grow in the Bronx*, *Free Palestine*, and *Walking Charlie*.

Morgenstein's work has been featured in *The New York Times*, *Entertainment Weekly*, *Parade Magazine*, the *New York Post*, *Sports Illustrated*, Fox News Radio, and NPR.

He enjoys sports, yoga, and taking care of his beloved pug. Gary lives in Brooklyn, New York with his wife.

Milton Keynes UK
Ingram Content Group UK Ltd.
UKHW012121271123
433389UK00017B/486/J